Sotheb 655

D1085487

DIVIDED WE STAND

DIVIDED
WE STAND

Britain, the US and the Suez Crisis

W. SCOTT LUCAS

A John Curtis Book
Hodder & Stoughton
LONDON SYDNEY AUCKLAND TORONTO

British Library Cataloguing in Publication Data

Lucas, W. Scott

Divided we stand: Britain, the US and the Suez
crisis.
I. Title
962.05

ISBN 0-340-53666-7

Copyright © W. Scott Lucas 1991

First published in Great Britain 1991

All rights reserved. No part of this publication may be
reproduced or transmitted in any form or by any means,
electronic or mechanical, including photocopying,
recording, or any information storage and retrieval system,
without either prior permission in writing from the
publisher or a licence permitting restricted copying. In the
United Kingdom such licences are issued by the
Copyright Licensing Agency, 90 Tottenham Court Road,
London WIP 9HE. The right of W. Scott Lucas to be
identified as the author of this work has been asserted by
him in accordance with the Copyright, Designs and
Patents Act 1988.

Published by Hodder and Stoughton,
a division of Hodder and Stoughton Ltd,
Mill Road, Dunton Green, Sevenoaks, Kent TN13 2YA
Editorial Office: 47 Bedford Square, London WC1B 3DP

Designed by Behram Kapadia
Photoset by Rowland Phototypesetting Ltd
Bury St Edmunds, Suffolk
Printed in Great Britain by
St Edmundsbury Press Ltd, Bury St Edmunds, Suffolk

To my parents

CONTENTS

CONTENTS

MAPS

Preface

The temptation in evaluating any crisis is to connect it – for the sake of simplicity, narrative, expediency or self-justification – with later events, including those of the present day. For many, the failure to remove the Egyptian President, Gamal Abdel Nasser, from power in 1956 produced later catastrophes like the 1958 Iraqi revolution and the 1967 Six Day War. Anthony Eden, the British Prime Minister in 1956, wrote to Lord Salisbury fourteen years later:

The truth is that some of these militant dictators are unnegotiable. Among them I would put Hitler, Mussolini, [former Indonesian leader] Sukarno, [former Iranian leader] Mussadiq, and Nasser. Attempts to satisfy their appetites only increases them.[1]

In 1990, after the Iraqi occupation of Kuwait, the parallels were between Nasser and Iraqi President Saddam Hussein. Robert Harris, the political editor of the *Sunday Times*, went so far as to claim:

In 1956, two-thirds of Europe's oil came through the canal, giving Nasser, in Eden's words, 'a thumb on our windpipe'. In 1990, two-thirds of the West's oil comes from a region menaced by Saddam. Same windpipe; different thumb. Saddam, like Nasser, is a dictator with aspirations to dominate the Arab world. Like Nasser, he frightens the West because he does not play by the rules. Just as Nasser, days before he seized the canal, promised he would not do it, so Saddam gave similar assurances about Kuwait.[2]

These attempts at comparison are often as misguided as analogies, drawn at the time of Suez, between appeasement of Middle Eastern foes and appeasement of Germany in 1938. Many Britons in 1956 might still have clung to the image of Empire and global power, but the world was far different. The US, once she reluctantly took the stage, assumed the leading role and no rhetoric about the 'special relationship' could assure unconditional American support for British interests. On the contrary, Washington's preoccupation with the Soviet menace often rested uneasily with Britain's traditional concerns outside Europe. More importantly, Asian and African countries, emerging from centuries of foreign domination, were developing policies that had more to do with intra-regional conflict than with relations with the West.

The historian, like the contemporary observer, must beware of looking at Middle Eastern events through a Western prism. The Gulf crisis was initially portrayed by the American and British Governments in terms of the Iraqi threat to Western oil supplies and, later, the Allied coalition's defence of Kuwaiti freedom against Baghdad's aggression and the tyranny of Saddam Hussein. The regional dimension of Iraq's occupation of Kuwait, including the long-running border dispute between the two countries, their dispute over division of oil production, and Baghdad's anger at Kuwaiti insistence upon repayment of loans made during the Iran–Iraq War, was largely overlooked or forgotten.

Most of the literature produced in Britain on the Suez crisis has dwelt upon the dispute in the framework of the Cold War, Anglo-Egyptian relations, or the personal battle between Nasser and Eden. The story has been one of the changing relationship between Washington and London, the Anglo-French-Israeli 'collusion' against Egypt, or the interplay between members of the Eden Government. With the release of government documents, recent biographies of many of the British participants, and the latest historical account, Keith Kyle's *Suez* (published as this book went to press), the events of 1956 have again been under scrutiny. Yet Suez is still seen primarily in a Western, rather than a regional, context. Israeli historians continue to produce many valuable articles, but their focus is upon Tel Aviv's relations with Western powers or tensions between Egypt and Israel. Developments in Arab countries such as Iraq, Jordan, Syria and Saudi Arabia still escape examination.

Originally, this book set out to study how the Anglo-American 'alliance' operated during Suez, but this was impossible while the context was incomplete. How could one explain why the US, while refusing to support Britain's use of force against Egypt, was consulting the British about the overthrow of the Syrian Government? Or why Eden was apparently willing, on the morning of 14 October 1956, to reach a negotiated settlement with Nasser but, six hours later, was ready to collaborate with France and Israel in military operations? London and Washington were not defining events in the Middle East, but reacting to them. One had to recognise patterns within the region – for example, the dynastic rivalry between Saudi Arabia and the monarchies of Iraq and Jordan, Baghdad's vision of federation with Syria, or the recurrent efforts for an Arab-Israeli peace settlement – to understand the evolution of British and American policies.

Yet this, in turn, raised a further problem. It was apparent that American officials, reacting to the complexities of the Middle East, agreed upon general policy in the interdepartmental National Security Council and that this policy was largely implemented by the State

Department and the Central Intelligence Agency. The same could not be said of Britain. No group reconciled the strategies and operations of the Foreign Office, the military and the intelligence services. By 1956, Middle Eastern developments brought at least two differing, even contradictory, policies from London: one implemented by the diplomats, the other by intelligence officers.

Superficial parallels between the Suez crisis and current events often owe more to rhetoric than to reality: enemies and dictators of 1956 are transformed into the villains of 1991, freedom of transit becomes freedom of oil supplies, and removal of Nasser from power is succeeded by the call for the overthrow of Saddam Hussein. The thread of Middle Eastern history does not lend itself to simplistic representation, but comprehension of it is essential to any study of the Anglo-American 'alliance', past and present.

I have benefited from others' advice and guidance during the past six years. Professor Donald Cameron Watt supervised my doctoral research at the London School of Economics. My editor and publisher, John Curtis, helped transform the thesis into this book and Linda Osband's sharp eye removed numerous 'glitches' from the manuscript.

As this project evolved, collaboration with Anthony Gorst on several articles was invaluable. Orna Almog provided me with Israeli documents, while C. J. Morris patiently read the initial drafts. The students in my Suez course at the University of Birmingham kept me on track in the final stages of research. The London School of Economics and the University of London gave financial assistance while the Institute of Contemporary British History allowed me use of its facilities. I would like to thank Araminta Whitley at Peters, Fraser and Dunlop for her diligence in keeping the project moving smoothly.

More than fifty interviewees gave their time and their recollections to help me with this book. I am grateful to the Public Record Office for permission to quote from Crown Copyright material, to the US National Archives and Truman and Eisenhower Presidential Libraries for the use of their documents, and to Princeton University Libraries for citations from the John Foster Dulles Papers. Lady Avon and the Avon Trustees have given approval for access to Lord Avon's private papers at the University of Birmingham, but naturally have no responsibility for any use or interpretation deriving from them. The following publishers have allowed me to cite extracts from their books: Constable, from Anthony Nutting's *No End of a Lesson*; Macmillan, from Alistair Horne's *Macmillan: Volume I*, and Weidenfeld and Nicolson, from Evelyn Shuckburgh's *Descent from Suez*.

Finally, I wish to thank my family and friends for their limitless tolerance. Without them, my 'permanent vacation' in Britain would not have been possible.

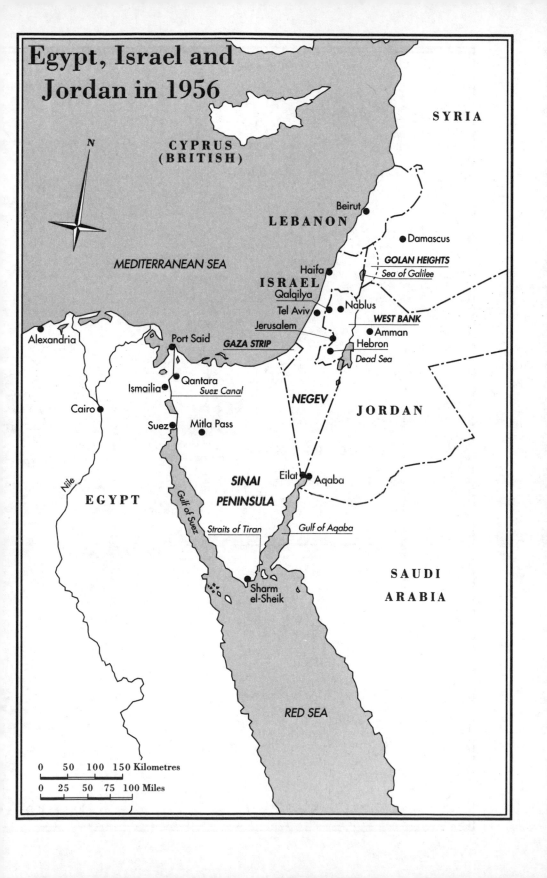

Egypt, Israel and Jordan in 1956

N

SYRIA

CYPRUS
(BRITISH)

● Damascus

LEBANON

● Beirut

MEDITERRANEAN SEA

GOLAN HEIGHTS

● Haifa
Sea of Galilee

ISRAEL

Qalqilya

Tel Aviv ●
● Nablus

Jerusalem
WEST BANK

● Amman

Alexandria
Port Said
GAZA STRIP
Hebron

Dead Sea

Ismailia ● Qantara
Suez Canal

● Cairo
NEGEV

JORDAN

Suez ● ● Mitla Pass

Nile

EGYPT

*SINAI
PENINSULA*

Eilat
● Aqaba

Straits of Tiran
Gulf of Aqaba

SAUDI
ARABIA

Gulf of Suez

Sharm
el-Sheik

RED SEA

0	50	100	150 Kilometres

0	25	50	75	100 Miles

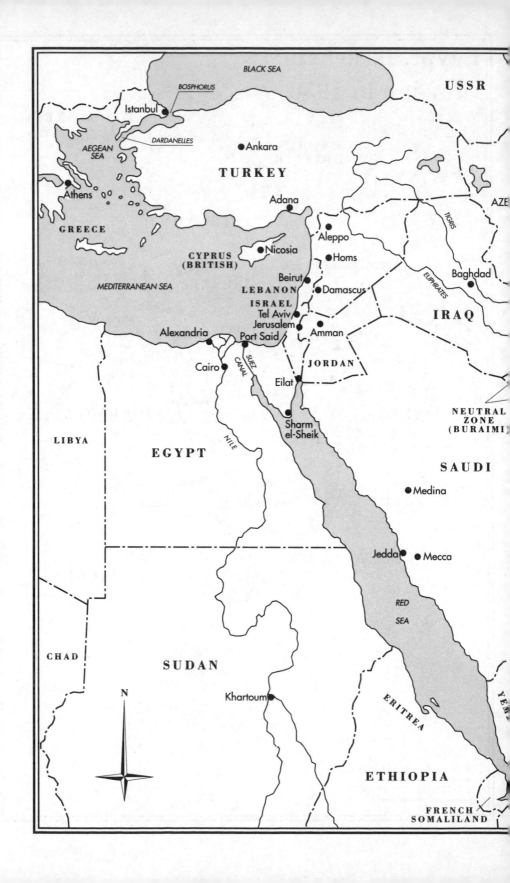

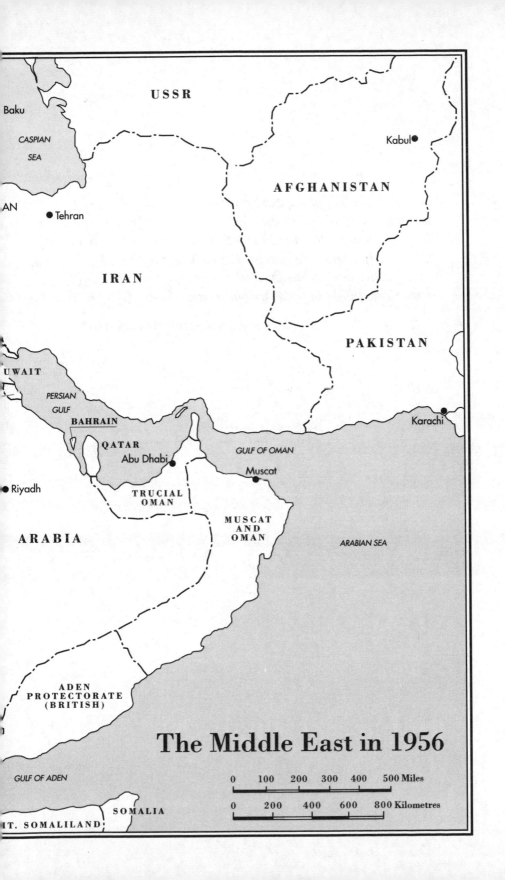

The Middle East in 1956

In the second half of the 20th century, we cannot hope to maintain our position in the Middle East by the methods of the last century. However little we like it, we must face that fact. . . . If we are to maintain our influence in this area, future policy must be designed to harness these [nationalist] movements rather than to struggle against them.

ANTHONY EDEN, 16 February 1953

Introduction

17 November 1956: Walter Reed Hospital in Washington, DC, was an
unusual setting for a meeting to rebuild the Anglo-American 'alliance'.
For more than a week, the British Foreign Secretary, Selwyn Lloyd, on
behalf of the Prime Minister, Anthony Eden, had desperately sought a
meeting with the US President, Dwight Eisenhower, or one of his close
advisers. Finally, the US Secretary of State, John Foster Dulles, suffering from the abdominal cancer that would eventually kill him, agreed to
receive Lloyd in the discreet setting of his hospital room.

In October 1956, the Eden Government, without consulting the
United States, arranged in secret discussions with France and Israel to
attack Egypt and overthrow the Government of Gamal Abdel Nasser.
Since July, when Nasser had nationalised the Suez Canal Company,
London and Paris had prepared for the use of force, but they were unable
to establish the diplomatic pretext for the assault until Israeli troops
invaded the Sinai Peninsula on 29 October. The British and French,
intervening as 'peace-keepers', began bombing Egypt on the 31st. Five
days later, paratroops landed in the Suez Canal Zone, followed by the
main Anglo-French force on 6 November.

Within twenty-four hours of the main landing, the British Government
had been forced to cease fire, largely because of American pressure. The
US had led the United Nations General Assembly in the passage of
resolutions demanding the withdrawal of Israeli forces from Egypt and an
immediate halt to Anglo-French operations. More importantly, the
Eisenhower Administration refused to help London with loans and
supplies of oil from the Western Hemisphere, although the British
economy was on the point of collapse. Even the cease-fire failed to mollify
the resentment of many American officials against the British, and
Eisenhower's advisers continued their 'quarantine' upon private or public
contact with Eden. Only Lloyd's threat that Britain would resume military
operations against Egypt brought the clandestine appointment with
Foster Dulles.

Thus, it came as a surprise when Foster Dulles, near the end of the
conversation, asked Lloyd, 'Selwyn, why did you stop? Why didn't you go
through with it and get Nasser down?' Lloyd later recalled: 'If ever there
was an occasion when one could have been knocked down by the

I

proverbial feather, this was it. Dulles was the man who had led the pact against us . . . and pulled out every stop to defeat us.' The Foreign Secretary merely replied, 'Well, Foster, if you had so much as winked at us, we might have gone on.'[1]

For thirty-five years, those writing about the Suez crisis have shared Lloyd's bewilderment over the apparent contradiction between Foster Dulles's words and American policy. To solve the dilemma, some have adopted Eden's description of Foster Dulles as a hypocrite who betrayed Britain for a misguided vision of American political and religious leadership of the world. Others, however, have portrayed the Prime Minister as a sick, even irrational, man, who destroyed Britain's diplomatic, economic and moral position in the Middle East and the UN as well as the Anglo-American 'alliance'. The biographies and memoirs of British and American participants have generally reflected the positions of their Governments. The most notable exception to this was *No End of a Lesson* by Anthony Nutting, who resigned as Minister of State in the Foreign Office during Suez, but his account was coloured by his personal disagreement with Eden. French participants were more explicit about their 'alliance' with Israel and eventual British involvement, but they knew little about the relationship between London and Washington. Later books, especially *Suez: The Twice-Fought War*, published by *New York Times* journalist Kennett Love in 1970, used interviews with officials in several countries to expand and correct previous accounts, but they still could not get access to unpublished memoranda.

The release of unpublished documents of the British Government in 1987 offered some hope of new explanations of developments during Suez, but most observers were pessimistic that answers could be found. Eden had ordered the destruction of all information about the secret Sèvres meetings between Britain, France and Israel, where the attack upon Egypt was agreed. In the early 1960s, Foreign Secretary R. A. Butler, the most senior Minister in Eden's Cabinet in 1956, asked to see government documents on Suez. Officials showed him a stack of papers, the only Foreign Office files that supposedly remained. Butler was not allowed to see them, nor was he allowed to consult the files of MI6, the British foreign intelligence service. As journalist Peter Hennessy summarised just before the release of the papers in 1987, 'The world's press, who will flock to the Public Record Office at the end for a preview of the papers, are in for a severe disappointment.'[2]

Superficially, this evaluation was correct. No smoking gun remained which confirmed the British motive for 'collusion', nor did any record establish if American pressure forced London to cease fire. Yet this view of Suez is misleading because of its narrowness. The crisis itself did not suddenly arise when Nasser nationalised the Suez Canal Company in July 1956. It was the product of decades of tension between Britain and Egypt and, in a wider sense, London's desperate struggle to maintain its Middle Eastern position. Likewise, the Anglo-American relationship in the region was never a matter-of-fact 'alliance'. American interests might lead Washington to support British policies, either publicly or privately, but at times, notably when the Eisenhower Administration came to power in 1953, the US acted independently of Britain. Co-operation from 1954 to 1956 was based upon a tenuous convergence of aims, for example, the mutual desire for an Arab-Israeli settlement.

Examining Suez in the light of these long-term considerations and the new evidence, a complex explanation of the relationship between Britain and the US begins to emerge. Eden's decision to act with France and Israel, without consulting the US, was motivated in part by the desire to protect Britain's political and military influence in Iraq and Jordan, the cornerstones of her Middle East position. The Eisenhower Administration, as Foster Dulles told Lloyd, desired Nasser's removal from power as much as Britain did, but the military assault upon Egypt endangered American relations with Arab states and undermined covert operations, planned since March 1956 by London and Washington, against Nasser.

Then, as now, British and American policies were not shaped by a single person, acting from a single motive, in a single office. They were the products of officials in numerous agencies, who acted upon assumptions formed by various influences. The task is to move from this simple conclusion to the complex reconstruction of Anglo-American relations in the Middle East in 1956. In the Suez crisis, there were no 'heroes' or 'villains', only men trapped by perceptions of their country's long-term interests, by the strengths and weaknesses of their policy-making systems, and by pressure from the officials of other countries.

The Development of Anglo-American Relations in the Middle East
1945–52

By 1939, Britain's dominant position in the Middle East was firmly established. Seventy years earlier, the Suez Canal had been cut through Egypt to connect the Mediterranean and the Red Sea. It soon became a lifeline to India, as Her Majesty's Government acquired forty-four per cent of the shares of the Paris-based Suez Canal Company. To safeguard its investment, British troops occupied Egypt in 1882. British interests further expanded with the discovery of large oil deposits in the Middle East in the early twentieth century.

With the dissolution of the Ottoman Empire after the First World War, Britain and France divided the Middle East into spheres of influence. Having converted Egypt into a protectorate in 1914, Britain recognised her Arab 'ally', Sharif Hussein of Mecca, as the ruler of the Arabian Peninsula and placed Hussein's sons, Feisal and Abdullah, on the thrones of the British mandates of Iraq and Transjordan. The British also assumed the mandate for Palestine, while France took responsibility for Syria and Lebanon. Only Saudi Arabia, where King Ibn Saud ousted Sharif Hussein in 1926, escaped the 'spheres of influence' settlement.

In the 1930s, Britain confirmed her position with political and economic agreements. Iraq was granted independence in 1930, but the ensuing Anglo-Iraq Treaty guaranteed British rights to military bases until 1957. Egyptian independence was nominally restored in 1922, but British troops occupied the country until the 1936 Anglo-Egyptian Treaty. In exchange for withdrawal from most of Egypt, the British were granted free use of the Suez Canal Base until 1956. Economically, British banks and businesses dominated foreign investment in Egypt, and

London retained its controlling stake in the Anglo-Persian Oil Company and a 37.5 per cent share of the Iraqi Petroleum Company. Politically, King Abdullah of Transjordan was carefully advised by Sir Alec Kirkbride, and Iraqi Prime Minister Nuri Sa'id, more influential than the titular sovereign, was on close terms with British diplomats.

Retention of this position was vital to Britain in the Second World War. The Suez Canal Base, at the pivot of Europe, Asia and Africa, was the largest base in the world, through which supplies and troops were shipped to all theatres of the war. The Anglo-American Middle East Supply Centre in Cairo provided $33 million in aid throughout the area. Although Axis control of the Mediterranean rendered the Suez Canal ineffective, Middle Eastern oil supplies were shipped to Britain around the Cape of Good Hope.

In Iraq, the assumption of power by the pro-German Rashid Ali in 1941 led to a British-sponsored coup and prompted Britain to remove Reza Shah Pahlavi from the throne of neighbouring Iran and to partition the country into British and Soviet spheres of influence. Fearful that the Egyptian Prime Minister, Ali Maher, would welcome a German invasion from Libya, the British Ambassador, Sir Miles Lampson, surrounded the Abdin Palace in early 1942 and forced King Farouk to remove Ali Maher in favour of Nahas Pasha.

If the Second World War highlighted Britain's involvement in the Middle East, it also introduced the US Government into the region. Private American interests, notably religious, philanthropic and educational institutions, had entered the Middle East in the nineteenth century and US oil companies began exploration in Bahrain and Saudi Arabia in the 1930s, but all these efforts were independent of the US Government.

The tradition of non-involvement was gradually overcome by American entry into the war and the growing strain on British resources. US finance was necessary for the Middle East Supply Centre and the Persian Gulf Supply Centre in Iran. When Britain requested that the US take over the annual subsidy to Saudi Arabia's King Ibn Saud, the State Department's Division of Near Eastern Affairs recommended US assumption of responsibility in Egypt as well. After the war, the State Department discontinued the Middle East Supply Centre and introduced a 'free trade' area with equality of opportunity in commerce, transit and trade, and the 'general protection of American citizens [and the] protection and furtherance of legitimate American economic rights, existing or potential'. An interdepartmental committee also recommended $100 million in aid 'for the purpose of furthering the political and strategic interests of the US in the Middle East'.[1]

These plans were undermined by post-war demobilisation, and the

$100 million in aid was not authorised. Only in Saudi Arabia, where American oil companies triumphed in their bid for influence with King Ibn Saud, and in Palestine, which was a special political case, did the US Government retain an interest. In contrast, the British maintained their position in Egypt, Iraq and Transjordan, and they helped Syria and Lebanon achieve independence by evicting Vichy French governments and preventing the Free French from assuming control after the war.

The path to renewed Anglo-American co-operation came from outside the Middle East, specifically Washington's interest in a Greco-Turkish-Iranian 'tier'. In 1946, the US and Britain supported Iran, first against continued Soviet occupation of the north and then against Soviet-backed separatist movements, while resisting Moscow's pressure on Turkey to allow Soviet fortifications in the Bosporus Straits. At the same time, the State Department and the Foreign Office were able to isolate the issue of Palestine, which often divided the American and British Governments, from regional questions. When Britain decided in February 1947 not only to refer the question of their mandate over Palestine to the United Nations but also, for reasons of economy, to withdraw aid from Greece and Turkey, the US responded with the Truman Doctrine. This was noted for its principle of supporting any country threatened by Soviet expansion, but its practical effect was to allocate $400 million in aid for Greece and Turkey and to extend any US commitment to Western Europe to the Greco-Turkish-Iranian 'tier', a possible 'outer ring' defence of the Middle East.

In October 1947, the question of the 'outer ring' was taken up in high-level Anglo-American talks in Washington. For the first time, the US Joint Chiefs of Staff recognised Eastern Mediterranean and Middle Eastern security as 'vital' to American defence. The diplomatic and economic representatives established:

Both Governments should endeavor to prevent either foreign countries, or commercial interests, or any other influence from making capital for themselves by playing Great Britain and the United States off against each other. . . . It should be contrary to their respective policies of either country to make efforts to strengthen itself or to increase its influence at the expense of the other.[2]

In mid-November, the US National Security Council agreed that the US, to protect the Middle East, should defend Italy, Greece, Turkey and Iran. The Council added,

It would be unrealistic for the US to undertake to carry out such a policy unless the British maintain their strong strategic, political, and economic position in the Middle East and Eastern Mediterranean and unless they and ourselves follow parallel policies in that area.[3]

While seeking American assistance to finance economic development and build an 'outer ring' defence, the British hoped to maintain their political and economic interests in the Middle East. The Foreign Office, recognising that resentment among Arab nationalists at British 'domination' and disillusionment with the pashas and monarchs were growing, sought renegotiation of bilateral treaties.

The results were disappointing. Plans to shift the centre of Middle Eastern defence from Egypt to Palestine foundered upon the dispute over a Jewish state. In October 1946, the 1936 Anglo-Egyptian Treaty was tentatively revised, with Britain withdrawing from the Suez Canal Zone to bases in Libya and East Africa, but the agreement collapsed over a dispute about control of the Sudan, jointly governed by Britain and Egypt since 1899. The Portsmouth Treaty, signed by the British and Iraqi Governments in January 1948, was abandoned after violent demonstrations in Baghdad. Only in Transjordan was a treaty successfully revised.

Britain's political difficulties were compounded by economic weakness, as a sterling crisis in 1947 exposed the precarious state of her reserves of foreign exchange. The cost of overseas commitments hastened Britain's departure from the Indian sub-continent, Greece and Palestine, and the Prime Minister, Clement Attlee, even considered withdrawal from the Middle East. In July 1949, the Foreign Office's programme to maintain Middle Eastern influence through economic investment was shelved during the crisis that forced the devaluation of sterling.

With the failure of bilateral co-operation and no money for unilateral initiatives, the British had no alternative to American economic and military support for the Middle East. American and British military staffs developed plans for the presence of American bombers and a marine contingent. Middle Eastern oilfields which could not be defended in the Arabian Peninsula and Iraq would be demolished, while the British held the 'inner ring' of Lebanon, Jordan, Palestine and Egypt. The British agreed to upgrade Abu Sueir airfield in the Suez Canal Zone for the use of American B-29 bombers, and it was informally arranged that American planes would use British bases in Libya.[4]

In November 1949, Assistant Undersecretary Michael Wright, supervising Middle Eastern affairs at the Foreign Office, visited Washington for several meetings with Assistant Secretary George McGhee, the Director of Near Eastern Affairs. McGhee committed the US, in principle, to support of Britain's Middle Eastern position, while noting the obstacles to a co-ordinated Anglo-American policy:

The objectives of the two countries in the area were identical, although there might be a difference of method in seeking to attain them. . . . The difference in methods might arise from the fact that the influence and material interests of the UK and US were not the same in each country. . . . The US Government had no desire to compete with or to hinder the UK in carrying out its policy in the Middle East. The US policy was, however, governed by the limitations imposed by the nature of the US Government, its policy of non-interference, and the difficulty of securing ad hoc treatment.[5]

The US Secretary of State, Dean Acheson, preoccupied with Europe and the Far East, delegated authority on Middle Eastern affairs to McGhee, who told Congressmen in February 1950:

The political loss of the [Middle East] to the Soviet Union would be a major disaster comparable to its loss during the war. . . . The whole area between Greece and India, although constitutionally a relatively stable element, is already threatened by militant communism to the north and would be hard-pressed indeed in its efforts to hold fast to its newly-won independence.[6]

The Arab-Israeli dispute also led the US into a more active role in the Middle East. During the 1948–9 Arab-Israeli war, the US supported the UN embargo on weapons to the region, but Israeli diplomats and pro-Israeli Congressmen pressed for renewed supplies to Tel Aviv. The State Department was also concerned with the effect of the Arab-Israeli dispute upon US aid, almost all of which was being spent to keep Arab refugees alive. Little remained for resettlement or development projects, and irrigation programmes were blocked by disputes between Israel, Transjordan and Syria over division of the Jordan River.[7]

When Britain, recognising the American anxiety, suggested an Anglo-American policy on arms supplies, Acheson responded with the suggestion that the US, France and Britain obtain 'non-aggressive declarations from the Middle Eastern countries' who received Western arms. Issued on 25 May 1950, the Tripartite Declaration not only included Acheson's provision, but also recognised the de facto Middle Eastern frontiers, pending a final Arab-Israeli settlement. Any violation of those frontiers by aggressive action would be opposed by the three powers 'both within or without the United Nations'.[8]

The practical effect of the Tripartite Declaration was limited. The Western powers did not formally guarantee the Middle Eastern frontiers, and any of them could refuse to act against an aggressor. The provision on arms supplies was not enforced until Britain, France and the United States created the Near East Arms Co-ordinating Committee in 1952.

Instead, the Tripartite Declaration had symbolic importance. The US Government had expressed its willingness to intervene in Middle Eastern affairs. Committed to consultations with Britain on regional matters, the Americans hastened exchanges after the outbreak of the Korean War in

June 1950. In September, McGhee and Wright, reviewing the Declaration and Arab-Israeli relations, also discussed Anglo-Egyptian negotiations for a new treaty, oil operations in Iran, and economic aid for the Middle East and South Asia. In October, 'Ambassador-at-Large' Philip Jessup and General Omar Bradley, Chairman of the US Joint Chiefs of Staff, conferred with the British Ambassador to Washington, Sir Oliver Franks, and British military representatives. The British, while favouring the 'inner ring' system based on Lebanon and Jordan, agreed to study protection of Iran against Soviet subversion and defence of the 'outer ring' of Greece, Turkey, Iraq, Iran and Pakistan. After the Truman Administration approved a comprehensive economic and military aid package for the region, McGhee and Franks considered the co-ordination of American aid with British assistance.[9]

The US balked, however, at an unconditional commitment to support Britain. Bradley stated in the October 1950 talks that, 'owing to demands elsewhere', notably Korea, the US could not commit air or ground forces to the Middle East. In wartime, Britain would have to hold the area, without American assistance, for two years.[10] In February 1951, the Istanbul Conference of US diplomatic representatives in the Middle East, while recommending a new security commitment to Greece and Turkey and an American statement of 'its willingness . . . to assist the Near Eastern states to strengthen their capabilities to defend themselves against aggression', rejected a Middle Eastern defence pact. Anglo-American military talks in Malta in early 1951 foundered over the definition of Turkey's role in a regional system.[11]

Britain finally had to use American involvement in Western European defence as a lever for US participation in a Middle Eastern arrangement. In May 1951, the British accepted Turkish membership in NATO *if* the US and Turkey joined a Middle Eastern organisation. In response, the State Department's Policy Planning Staff recommended a Middle East Common Defence Board, led by the US, Britain, France and Turkey, to plan and co-ordinate defence with Middle Eastern countries, Iran and Pakistan. This became the basis of the Middle Eastern Command (MEC), agreed in September between the State Department and the Foreign Office. After France and Turkey joined as sponsors, Egypt was asked to become a founding member on 13 October.[12]

The approach had no chance of success. Talks about revision of the 1936 Anglo-Egyptian Treaty resumed in January 1950, but broke down in mid-1951. On 8 October, the Egyptian Government abrogated the 1936 Treaty.[13] Until June 1953, the MEC and a subsequent proposal, the Middle Eastern Defence Organisation (MEDO), were submitted to Arab countries without reward. The plan depended on the use of the

Suez Canal Base, which could only be guaranteed with an Anglo-Egyptian settlement.

The US never regarded the MEC or the MEDO as military organisations, but as political pacts to link Middle Eastern countries with British defence planning, and many American and British officials subsequently questioned the plan's value.[14] However, just as the Tripartite Declaration brought Anglo-American consultation over the Middle East, discussion of the MEC ensured US involvement in the region. The Americans even considered formal machinery for co-operation with Britain, with joint appreciations by American and British missions in the Middle East followed by meetings at the level of Assistant Secretary. The Foreign Office noted that the US was

clearly ready to play an important part [in the Middle East]. . . . This can only be beneficial to British interests, provided that the somewhat exaggerated respect which they have hitherto tended to display towards Middle Eastern nationalistic movements can be modified by experience.[15]

The initiative was crippled when McGhee left his post in late 1951 to become Ambassador to Turkey and the Foreign Office could not provide extra personnel for formal liaison.[16] Yet overworked officials in the British Embassy in Washington, notably Bernard Burrows and Denis Greenhill, continued informal consultations with the State Department, and an ad hoc body discussed a joint Anglo-American policy on Middle Eastern oil. From October 1950, a British Embassy official liaised with the State Department on 'information policy', an euphemism for covert and overt propaganda operations in the Middle East. Relations between the Pentagon and the British Joint Services Mission remained close.[17] McGhee summarised in March 1952:

Basis of present US-UK cooperation in Middle East, which was initiated by Wright visit to US in 1948 [sic] is understood to be that US will not compete with or seek to displace British responsibilities or interests in Middle East, indeed [we] will seek to strengthen Britain where [we] can; however, US does not recognize any exclusive UK spheres of influence and UK agrees desirability [of the] US making contributions over and above British contributions wherever it is in common interest. Although [the British] show natural cause to protect [their] interests, particularly in Jordan and Iraq, they have not opposed constructive contributions [of] other powers in Middle East.[18]

Washington had given unqualified support to Britain in the Anglo-Egyptian negotiations, and Eden praised the State Department and the US Ambassador in Cairo, Jefferson Caffery. When mobs rioted in Cairo and Alexandria in January 1952, burning British-owned buildings and killing eight Europeans and Canadians, Caffery's representations prevented Egypt from breaking diplomatic relations with Britain.[19]

Yet general Anglo-American agreement on the Middle East could still be subverted by differences in specific cases, especially the Iranian and Egyptian 'crises'. In April 1951, the Iranian Government, led by Mohammed Mossadegh, nationalised the British-owned Anglo-Iranian Oil Company. British officials feared that McGhee, who had made his fortune in the Texas oil business, and other State Department personnel privately welcomed the Iranian action. Several Ministers, including the Foreign Secretary, Herbert Morrison, advocated military force to regain control of the Iranian oilfields and installations, and war was only averted by Attlee's warning that the Americans would not support military intervention. The election of Winston Churchill as Prime Minister in October 1951 did not ease tensions. Acheson cabled McGhee that British intransigence

starts from Churchill with the roar of a wounded lion, becomes more articulate with [Foreign Secretary Anthony] Eden, as he remembers twitting the Laborites for weakness during the campaign, and is fully rationalized by the civil servants. . . . The new ministers are depressingly out of touch with the world of 1951, and they are being advised by the same officials who have allowed the government to follow the AIOC meekly into disaster.[20]

When Churchill visited Washington in January 1952, an argument between Acheson and Eden over Iran wounded Eden's feelings. Conciliatory letters healed any rift and the two sides compromised to make a joint approach to Mossadegh in August 1952, but Acheson's dislike of British policy was unabated.[21] The Secretary of Defense, Robert Lovett, supported by the Joint Chiefs of Staff, wrote:

The risks of continuing our present policy have become unacceptable, and . . . it must be discarded in favor of a policy of action to prevent Iran from falling to communism. Such a policy would involve a willingness, if necessary, to displace British influence and responsibility in Iran as has occurred in Greece, Turkey, and Saudi Arabia. . . . Every effort should be made to obtain British cooperation in this policy, but with or without British cooperation, I believe we must move promptly along these lines before it is too late.[22]

The State Department responded by presenting London with a package for the production and distribution of Iranian oil, warning the British that the US would proceed unilaterally if the proposals were rejected. The Foreign Office gave way.[23]

The threat of high-level Anglo-American conflict was not as apparent in the case of Egypt, yet the seeds for conflict had been planted with the creation of the Central Intelligence Agency (CIA) in 1947. The CIA soon developed plans to support Arab leaders who would co-operate with Washington. Operations in Syria in the late 1940s failed to establish a stable regime, but the CIA soon identified Egypt as the optimal target for intervention. Economic aid, accompanied by social and political reform, could develop the agricultural and industrial potential of the country, as Cairo assumed leadership of the Arab world. To accomplish this, however, the US had to find a new Egyptian regime, as King Farouk was 'no more than a reactionary landowner' and leaders of the ruling party, the Wafd, were more concerned with 'making personal fortunes rather than introducing social reforms'.[24]

The CIA acquired an important ally in 1949 when Caffery, US Ambassador in France since 1946, was transferred to Egypt. Described as vain, suave, aristocratic and aloof by his British and American colleagues, Caffery was a throwback to inter-war diplomats in his manners. On paper, the transfer to Cairo was designed to give him a few years' easy service until his retirement, but the stay proved to be the apogee of Caffery's fame and influence. Supported by McGhee, the Ambassador became formally involved in the Anglo Egyptian negotiations. As Washington expanded the Embassy's staff between 1950 and 1952, Caffery obtained several young, ambitious associates for his 'diplomacy' with the Egyptians and the British.[25]

Egypt's new military training programme in 1950, which planned to send 300 officers to the US, was a boon for the CIA. Promising candidates for American 'support' were identified, and personal contacts were established which could be developed in Cairo. Of the more than fifty officers who studied in the US, at least six were in the Free Officers' movement, the core of the July 1952 coup. Two future members of the Revolutionary Command Council (RCC), Hassan Ibrahim and Abdel Latif Baghdadi, were in the programme, and another member, Gamal Salem, spent several months in the US undergoing medical treatment. Shortly before the revolution, Ali Sabri, the Chief of Air Force Intelligence and a secret supporter of the Free Officers, attended a six-month intelligence course, normally reserved for NATO officers, in Colorado. Sabri hinted later: 'The attendance of many Egyptian officers at US service schools during the past two years had a very definite influence upon the coup d'état in Egypt.'[26]

In late 1951, after a CIA report identified anti-Western nationalism, rather than Communism, as the chief threat to American interests in the Middle East, Acheson convened an interdepartmental committee, chaired by Kermit Roosevelt, one of the CIA's Middle Eastern specialists, to study problems and recommend American action. The committee's report acknowledged, 'Whatever the US can do to bolster both generally and locally the power and prestige of the UK will assist the UK in maintaining stability in the area and will reduce the need for direct action by the US or other Allied powers.' However, the committee also endorsed the CIA's Middle Eastern strategy:

Our principle should be to encourage the emergence of competent leaders, relatively well-disposed toward the West, through programs designed for this purpose, including, where possible, a conscious, though perhaps covert, effort to cultivate and aid such potential leaders, even when they are not in power.[27]

The committee's identification of Egypt as the primary target for operations coincided with Acheson's increased concern after the riots in Cairo in January 1952. He observed, 'The [British] "splutter of musketry" apparently does not stop things as we had been told from time to time that it would.' If the British position could not be held by force, a negotiated settlement was imperative. On Caffery's advice, the State Department asked the British to recognise King Farouk of Egypt as King of the Sudan, but Churchill, supported by backbench Conservative opinion, insisted that Britain's Middle Eastern role depended on the maintenance of her position in Egypt. The Foreign Office claimed that recognition of Farouk betrayed the Sudanese, who had been promised self-determination and self-government.[28]

In February, Roosevelt had launched the operation to change the Egyptian Government. The primary objective was a 'peaceful revolution', hopefully led by Farouk, to defuse extremist opinion and encourage economic and social development; however, when Farouk refused to co-operate, Roosevelt looked for 'other possibilities'.[29]

He soon found the Free Officers plotting a coup. In October 1951, Ahmed Hussein, later Egyptian Ambassador to Washington, had put Roosevelt in contact with the group, and the CIA operative now used this link to meet Free Officers' spokesmen in Cyprus. The contacts were carefully chosen. Sabri was trusted by Farouk, Abdel Moneim Naggar was related to Queen Narriman, and Colonel Abdel Moneim Amin was a wealthy member of the court. The meetings with Roosevelt eventually produced a discussion with the future Egyptian leader, Colonel Gamal Abdel Nasser. They also fostered important contacts between the Officers and the US Embassy, notably the Assistant Air Attaché, Lieutenant-Colonel David Evans, and the Political Secretary, William Lakeland.[30] In May, Roosevelt, after consulting Caffery, concluded to Acheson that the 'popular revolution' favoured by the State Department was not feasible, and that only the army could cope with Egypt's problems.[31]

In July 1952, disagreement between American and British representatives nearly turned into public division when King Farouk threatened to replace the Prime Minister, Hilali Pasha, whom the British considered fair and honest, with the allegedly corrupt Hussein Sirry Pasha. Eden wished to tell Farouk that the change would 'lead to disaster for him and Egypt', but Acheson, acting on Caffery's advice that 'any carrying out of British proposals . . . would be the beginning of the final evacuation of the British from the Middle East and of the eventual evacuation of our own interests', withheld his support, as the State Department did 'not believe that the US should involve itself in Egyptian domestic political crisis'.[32] State Department officials noted on 21 July: 'It is becoming more and more difficult to give support to the British in the measure they desire since we are less and less convinced of the correctness of this position.'[33]

The 'hands-off' policy worked. For the Free Officers, the choice of the discredited Hussein Sirry to replace Hilali symbolised the corruption of King Farouk and his advisers. After Evans was told on 13 July that the rebels would act within the next few days, Caffery issued a statement discreetly condoning the forthcoming revolution: 'The policy of the US is not to interfere in the domestic politics of another country and this policy has been strictly adhered to in this embassy.'[34] On the 23rd, a group of army and air force officers seized power, forcing Farouk's abdication three days later. General Mohammed Neguib was installed as the leader of the ruling junta, the RCC, which included Nasser.

The coup had averted immediate Anglo-American conflict, but it now posed a more complex issue: the ability of American representatives in Cairo to establish American independence of Britain in the Middle East, regardless of exchanges between the State Department and the Foreign Office. The 'old guard', on whom the British relied for information and influence, had been swept away by the Free Officers, with whom Britain had few links. Conservative MP Julian Amery learned from a British instructor of the Egyptian General Staff that a group of officers was ready to seize power. He passed that information to Eden, but the Foreign Secretary replied that he 'had been assured by the Department concerned that the Army was loyal to the King'.[35] The first assessment of the British Embassy in Cairo, that 'a young Air Force officer . . . generally considered to have . . . sympathies' with the Wafd party, which had been in power until January 1952, was wildly inaccurate, and Eden later admitted, 'The coup happened so quickly that no one was aware as late as the morning before.'[36]

Significantly, the first assurances by the Free Officers during the coup were not given to the British but by Sabri to the Americans. Evans had to arrange a meeting between a spokesman of the RCC and a British

Embassy official, while the State Department warned London that 'foreign intervention', including a British military operation, 'would be disastrous'.[37]

Between July and October, Evans was consulted almost daily by Sabri or Naggar. Lakeland established a channel to Nasser through Mohammed Heikal, a journalist for the newspaper *Akhbar el-Yom*, owned by Mustafa Amin, another CIA agent. The Agency also 'communicated' with the RCC through General Hassan Touhami. When the Air Attaché, Colonel Greco, 'order[ed] Evans not to approach contacts in the Egyptian military', he was removed from Cairo and replaced by Evans, and a new Army Attaché, Colonel H. R. Greenlee, was appointed to work with the RCC. Through Evans, the Egyptians offered 'an unofficial committee to fight Communist activities and propaganda', composed of Egyptian military representatives and the American, British and French Military Attachés. The RCC also proposed that a US expert 'maintain contacts with civilian authorities' on matters such as land reform. The State Department accepted both proposals.[38]

The CIA was now the leading Western influence upon the Egyptians. The station in Cairo was soon reinforced with a new head of station, James Eichelberger, and Miles Copeland, an energetic operative who had served in Syria. The station operated from houses in the suburbs of Cairo and a flat rented in the name of a correspondent for the American broadcasting station, CBS. When President Truman's successor, Dwight Eisenhower, asked Kermit Roosevelt 'if he had the right to make decisions on subjects that should properly be in the [Anglo-Egyptian] treaty', Roosevelt 'replied, rather annoyed, "Why yes – eh, yes."'[39]

By September 1952, differences between Britain and the US had resurfaced. The Americans encouraged the RCC's programme for land reform despite the doubts of the civilian Prime Minister, Ali Maher, about the plan. When the RCC forced Maher to resign on 7 September, the State Department, on Caffery's advice and without consulting the British, issued a supportive statement: 'The Department sees no basic alteration of policies in this development, since the program of the Egyptian Government remains based on principles rather than personalities.' The Foreign Office was enraged. Eden asked the State Department to reconsider its 'encouragement [of the] more extreme elements in Egypt' and minuted privately: 'Caffery could not be worse. Ought we not to tell the Americans what we think of him?' The immediate crisis passed with the mediation of the British Ambassador to Egypt, Ralph Stevenson, and Caffery finally persuaded the RCC to establish contact with the Foreign Office through the British Embassy.[40]

The independence of the US Embassy in Cairo was illustrated by an incident in January 1953. Since October, the American Minister, Robert McClintock, had conferred with RCC members about Anglo-Egyptian negotiations, Middle Eastern defence and the supply of American arms to Egypt. At one meeting, probably on 12 January 1953, McClintock, under British surveillance, gave the Egyptians details of top-secret discussions between the US Assistant Secretary of State, Henry Byroade, and the Foreign Office. London demanded McClintock's immediate recall, and the Minister returned to Washington in March despite Egyptian protests. A British officer in Cairo wrote:

I am struck by the damage the Americans have done here, in their attempts to woo the Egyptians, by communicating to them details of what we had hoped to achieve in our negotiations. . . . If we fail to get an efficient base, it is at least arguable that it would be largely the Americans' fault.[41]

Was there a working Anglo-American 'alliance' in the Middle East? To the extent that American policy was directed from Washington, the Truman Administration moved towards co-operation with the British. Britain's lead in the Middle East relieved the US of the financial and military burden of defending the region, and Acheson was eager for British support at the height of the Korean War and the Cold War against the Soviet Union.

Yet American policy was not the product of a single source. CIA and State Department representatives in the Middle East saw no reason to use the same methods as their British counterparts. While the latter paid lip service to economic and social reforms as they supported existing leaders in the region, the Americans, doubting that pashas and monarchs would adopt policies for economic development and political stability, encouraged nationalist movements and cultivated leaders who would work with the US. The National Security Council, composed of Truman and his chief advisers, finally yielded to these views and concluded that it would use aid and propaganda to 'support or develop those leadership groups in the area which offered the greatest prospect of establishing political stability oriented toward the free world'.[42] Foremost among those leaders was General Neguib and a reserved but influential lieutenant-colonel named Nasser.

2

Division and Reconciliation
1953–4

President Truman declined to run for re-election in 1952, and the Democratic Party's nominee, Illinois Governor Adlai Stevenson, was soundly defeated by a newcomer to American politics, General Dwight D. Eisenhower. Supreme Commander of the Allied Expeditionary Force in North Africa and Europe in the Second World War and the first commander of NATO forces, Eisenhower had been drafted by the 'internationalist' wing of the Republican Party to prevent the Party's return to isolationism and to regain the Presidency, held by the Democrats since 1933.

Despite its internationalism, the accession of the Eisenhower Administration to power on 20 January 1953 meant that co-ordination of Middle Eastern policy with Britain was no longer standard practice. Like its predecessor, the Administration was fervently anti-Soviet and committed to the NATO 'partnership', but it did not equate the Atlantic alliance with unconditional co-operation outside Europe. 'Alliance' in these areas would be evaluated on a case-by-case basis, undertaken only when it fulfilled specific American objectives.

Eisenhower had a great respect and admiration for the legend of Churchill, writing, '[Churchill] comes nearest to fulfilling the requirements of greatness in any individual I have met in my lifetime,' but the Churchill of legend was not the Prime Minister who returned to power in 1951. When Churchill visited Washington in January 1953, emphasising 'that he would like to re-establish with General Eisenhower the sort of relationship which existed between President Roosevelt and Mr Churchill', Eisenhower replied, 'Of course he wished to have the closest possible relationship with Mr Churchill but . . . the making of decisions must go through regular channels.' The President wrote in his diary:

[Churchill] most earnestly hopes and intends that those countries shall enjoy a relationship which will recognize the special place of partnership they occupied with us during World War II. . . . In the present international complexities, any hope of establishing such a relationship is completely fatuous. . . . The two strongest Western powers must not appear before the world as a combination of forces to compel adherence to the status quo.[1]

American 'independence' of Britain was expressed in the 'anti-colonialist' rhetoric, increasingly pointed at Britain, of Eisenhower's officials. Writing in mid-1954, after France's defeat in Vietnam, the President asserted: 'The British always think their colonialism is different and better. Actually, what they want us to do is go along to help keep their empire.' Told by an American publisher that Nasser had said that 'he did not see how America – which was founded after a war with England – could support the colonial ambitions of either England or France', Eisenhower replied that he 'couldn't agree more with Nasser'. He informed Churchill that 'colonialism [was] on the way out as a relationship among peoples' and suggested a speech that would 'deal with the need for education and announce the co-operative purpose of great nations in the Western world to bring educational opportunities to all peoples we are able to reach', so that they 'achieved political, cultural and economic standards to attain their goals' within the next twenty-five years. Churchill's reply was dismissive:

The sentiments and ideas which your letter expresses are in full accord with the policy now being pursued in all the Colonies of the British Empire. In this I must admit I am a laggard. I am a bit sceptical about universal suffrage for the Hottentots even if refined by proportional representation.[2]

As early as May 1953, Eisenhower's advisers tried to convert rhetoric into policy. Preparing for a summit in Bermuda between Eisenhower, Churchill and the French Premier, Joseph Laniel, Eisenhower's 'special assistant', C. D. Jackson, advised:

[Britain] must be persuaded, through a solemn conference called for that purpose alone, that if they are to have any hope of preserving their commercial advantage through their crumbling world, they must allow us occasionally to take a front position. . . . Out of Bermuda must emerge tripartite unity, but at the apex of the triangle there must be the US, in the person of President Eisenhower. This role should not be sacrificed because of a very human feeling of decency and generosity towards an opinionated old gentleman [Churchill] who is still sufficiently sharp and selfish to grab every advantage with bland assurances of unwavering esteem.[3]

The CIA suggested:

Bermuda might show concern about a general issue like colonialism and invite someone like [Indian leader Jawaharlal] Nehru or Neguib to come to Bermuda or submit his views by wire. The appearance of other statesmen in Bermuda, or Bermuda exchanges of view with them, would turn Bermuda into a world forum, instead of a Big Three Western Atlantic club.[4]

State Department officials asked that the conference communiqué avoid reference to the Near East, Africa or South Asia: 'The US is trying to use its influence to further a solution of the various disputes of the area. To be successful, the US must secure an independent position, in order to give confidence in its efforts.'[5]

British Governments soon found a *bête noire* in the US Secretary of State, John Foster Dulles. The son of a Methodist minister and grandson of Secretary of State John Foster, Foster Dulles was an imposing man, well over six feet tall and largely built. Although he was mild-mannered, his steely gaze and grave demeanour gave him an appearance of tenacity, and his call for a spiritual basis to foreign policy bordered on evangelism.

Before his appointment as Secretary of State, Foster Dulles was often inconsistent in the application of his Christian values in international affairs. As a young lawyer, he was closely involved with Europe, working with the American delegation at the 1919 Paris Peace Conference and with the Dawes Committee on German reparations, and he favoured American co-operation with Germany in the 1930s. By 1939, he had adopted isolationism, only to propose internationalism and a world organisation three years later. In 1945, that same internationalism rejected the leadership of the United Nations for that of a strong United States.

Forced as Secretary of State to develop a consistent framework for the implementation of foreign policy, Foster Dulles built it upon two inflexible principles. The first was that the spread of Soviet Communism had to be reversed or at least checked. He had praised the Yalta conference of February 1945 as an example of collaboration among the great powers, but within twelve months he was arguing that the Soviet Union sought social revolution throughout the world and compared Stalin's *Problems of Leninism* with Hitler's *Mein Kampf.* He was instrumental in the Republican Party's support for the Truman Doctrine, the Marshall Plan, NATO and American entry into the Korean War.[6] Bipartisan agreement crumbled with the approach of the 1952 Presidential elections, and Foster Dulles unveiled the strategy of an American 'counter-offensive' against Communism:

There is one solution and only one [to the problem of international Communism]; that is for the free world to develop the will and organize the means to retaliate instantly against open aggression by Red Armies, so that if it occurred anywhere, we could and would strike back where it hurts, by means of our choosing.[7]

The second overriding principle for Foster Dulles was his idea of 1945 that peace and the security of the Free World could only be guaranteed by American leadership. In a series of articles in 1946, he recommended that American military power deter the Soviets while the US 'competed with the Soviet Union for the minds of men', spreading American ideals, based on religion, throughout Asia, Africa and the Middle East. In these areas, influenced by Britain, France and other European powers throughout the twentieth century, the example set by the US would lead emerging countries to independence and association with the Free World.[8]

The tension caused by Foster Dulles's emphasis upon American pre-eminence was compounded by his manner. In private conversations with foreign leaders or in public statement, he unwittingly appeared two-faced and deceitful. Robert Bowie, the head of the State Department's Policy Planning Staff, described Foster Dulles's negotiating style:

In presenting something to different people, he would describe it to each in the way which seemed most persuasive to him. . . . It was as if a man had been lighting a topographical map from several directions. You would see a very different set of phenomena and when these two people maybe got together and compared notes, they sometimes would feel, 'Well he has given us two different descriptions, two different proposals.'[9]

Foster Dulles's deputy, Walter Bedell Smith, told by Eden, then Foreign Secretary, that it was 'so difficult to understand what [Foster Dulles's] real policy was', supposedly replied 'with many oaths', 'Do you think we did?'[10] Eden concluded in his memoirs: 'My difficulty in working with Mister Dulles was to determine what he really meant and, in consequence, the significance to be attached to his words and actions.'[11]

Tedious and long-winded in his exposition, sometimes lecturing upon legal points, sometimes upon 'moral' behaviour, Foster Dulles found it difficult to adapt his position in the course of debate and rarely sought compromise. Trying to win public acceptance of his argument, he often lacked discretion away from the conference table. During his service with American delegations to meetings in the late 1940s, he was suspected of leaking information to the press to influence negotiations, and the British were still wary during his tenure as Secretary of State.

Most significantly, Foster Dulles, explaining his complex legalistic thoughts to others, was prone to oversimplification. The result, at press conferences, appearances before Congress and private talks, was the disastrous impression that he was driven by ideology to a black-and-white view of the world.[12] A member of the Policy Planning Staff summarised, in exaggerated but indicative fashion, one of Foster Dulles's expositions to a Congressional committee:

I was absolutely amazed. . . . I struck out whole parts of it and rewrote whole parts of it. The things he'd said! He goes around the world and starts with Canada. He takes a few slams at Canada – their inferiority complex, their ambivalent attitude to the United States – but points out that it's a very important piece of real estate and should be humored along. Then he jumps to the United Kingdom. They have all their good days behind them and they don't really amount to much any more, and they're ultra-sensitive, but they're important real estate, and should be kept sweet.

He said France was the place where they have all those mistresses and dirty postcards, but it's a damned important piece of real estate because it's got all those canals and highways leading directly to Germany. Then he's in Germany, and how those people have cut the throat of the world twice in a generation, but they're a really vital piece of real estate. Then he turns to the Scandinavians and how, through every important crisis, they got a free ride on other people's backs. The Italians: they've been an asset to their enemies in every war they've fought. The Middle East: full of Arabs, but also full of oil and air communications.[13]

Despite these defects, Foster Dulles, working with his brother Allen, the director of the CIA, was the man who implemented American foreign policy. The guidelines for policy were approved by the National Security Council under Eisenhower's supervision, but operations were outside the Council's immediate purview. The National Security Adviser, Dillon Anderson, explained that the Council was 'never conceived by the President to be a command post'. The President was not an initiator of action, preferring to 'pass on ideas, stimulate ideas', by his department heads and special assistants. Moreover, Eisenhower 'did not feel that he wanted to know the specifics of . . . covert activities'. This was especially true of policy towards the Middle East, as Eisenhower had little knowledge of the area.[14]

The President and Foster Dulles soon formed a close partnership. As John Hanes, Foster Dulles's personal assistant, recalled:

The President respected the Secretary for his technical knowledge of history and foreign policy. The Secretary was convinced that the President's instinct as to what the probable reaction of people would be to any course of events was virtually unerring, whether it be the American people or a foreign government or something of this sort.[15]

Eisenhower enthused:

There is probably no one in the world who has the technical competence of
Foster Dulles in the diplomatic field. He has spent his life in this work in one
form or another and is a man of great intellectual capacity and moral courage. . . .
All of the work that Foster does is in my name, since I am constitutionally charged
with the conduct of foreign relations. Foster himself has been glad that he might
do this because it was his conviction that no man of our times has had the standing
throughout the world that seems to be mine.[16]

Foster Dulles carefully maintained his position. Secretary of Defense
Charles Wilson and the Joint Chiefs of Staff usually supported the State
Department; when they differed with Foster Dulles, they almost always
deferred to the State Department–CIA axis. Eisenhower's National
Security Advisers, in contrast to later Administrations, rarely intervened
in the implementation of foreign policy. Only the Secretary of the
Treasury, George Humphrey, using his oversight of foreign aid and other
State Department expenditure, checked Foster Dulles's actions, but,
once a programme was authorised, he did not interfere with the Dulles
brothers.[17] Special assistants appointed to advise Eisenhower on foreign
policy were rejected by Foster Dulles, who cut off their access to the
President and screened them from the formation of policy.[18]

Inevitably, Foster Dulles's style clashed with that of his British
counterpart, Eden. To many, Eden, with his aristocratic manner and
impeccable sense of dress, was still the 'golden boy' of international
diplomacy. Becoming Foreign Secretary in 1935 at the age of thirty-eight,
his resignation in February 1938 over Anglo-Italian negotiations soon
linked him to opponents of appeasement, notably Churchill. When
Churchill replaced Neville Chamberlain as Prime Minister in 1940, Eden
soon became his Foreign Secretary and heir-apparent.

Eden and Foster Dulles first met in 1942, when the latter visited
London as chairman of a religious commission. Eden wrote after the
encounter: '[Americans] know very little of Europe, and it would be
unfortunate for the future of the world if US uninstructed views were
to decide the future of the European continent.' In May 1952, Eden
discussed Foster Dulles's possible appointment as Secretary of State with
Eisenhower, then a candidate for the Republican Presidential nomi-
nation. Eden may not have asked Eisenhower not to choose Foster
Dulles, but he at least warned the future President that Foster Dulles was
not popular in Britain.[19]

Foster Dulles was unaware of Eden's approach to Eisenhower, but
the Secretary's advisers quickly labelled the Foreign Secretary as vain,
pompous and effeminate. To them, he represented the delusion of a

Britain that did not realise that she was no longer a great power. Herbert Hoover Jr, Foster Dulles's deputy from 1954 to 1956, 'could not abide' Eden, and another official said that he 'had never met a dumber man'. John Hanes concluded:

Every time I saw Eden I always felt an overwhelming sense of personal vanity, and Dulles was just the opposite. Dulles may have had intellectual vanity but not personal vanity at all. Just personality-wise, they were destined not to work together; you know, [Eden's] homburg and all the rest, and his rather languid manner – a calculated English aristocracy. It wasn't Dulles' dish of tea.[20]

The British Ambassador in Washington, Roger Makins, added:

Dulles was a lawyer and an intellectual so he developed his thought at some length. Eden was an intuitive man and so he got bored listening to this long exposition and did not take it in. At the end he would make one or two intuitive remarks to give his position which Dulles did not take in.[21]

The rituals of diplomacy and common Anglo-American interests in Europe prevented a public clash between Eden and Foster Dulles until 1954, but Eisenhower's inauguration brought an immediate review by the State Department of co-operation with Britain in the Middle East and Iran. Ironically, the reconsideration brought US agreement with Britain on the need for stronger action against the Mossadegh Government and its nationalisation of the Anglo-Iranian Oil Company. In November 1952, London had asked the Truman Administration to join covert operations to overthrow Mossadegh, but no action was authorised. In contrast, the National Security Council in January 1953 accepted the estimate of the US Ambassador in Iran, Loy Henderson, that an Anglo-Iranian settlement was no longer possible and that Mossadegh would eventually be replaced by the Tudeh, the Communist Party of Iran.

By February 1953, British officials from MI6 were visiting Washington to discuss details of a coup. Patrick Dean, the Chairman of the Joint Intelligence Committee and the head of the Foreign Office's Permanent Undersecretary's Department, also attended the talks. After Eden's visit to Washington in March, the National Security Council approved Operation AJAX, a coup to be planned, funded and supported by the CIA and MI6. In August 1953, Mossadegh was overthrown and the Shah of Iran was restored to power.[22]

The American review reached far different conclusions on Egypt. In early January 1953, Assistant Secretary of State Byroade and the Foreign Office had agreed upon the joint presentation to President Neguib of proposals on the Suez Canal Base, Middle Eastern defence, and American economic and military aid for Egypt. In essence, the Americans were actively supporting the British.[23]

Eisenhower and Dulles retreated from the agreement. They feared that the Revolutionary Command Council, dissatisfied with the slow progress of the Anglo-Egyptian discussions, would turn against Britain. The President told Eden, when he visited Washington, that American involvement now depended upon Egyptian willingness to receive an Anglo-American presentation. When the RCC rejected the initial approach by the British and American Ambassadors, Caffery and Stevenson, Eisenhower, to Churchill's horror, refused further American participation:

If the US walks into a conference with [Britain], against the wishes of the Egyptian Government, then the only obvious interpretation would be that our two governments, together, are there to announce an ultimatum. An uninvited guest cannot possibly come into your house, be asked to leave, and then expect cordial and courteous treatment if he insists upon staying.[24]

The US Embassy in Cairo, supported by the State Department, now argued that the points of the package agreed in January between Byroade and British officials were not interdependent. The US might push Britain into a settlement on the Suez Canal Base without ensuring Egypt's commitment to the Middle Eastern Defence Organisation.[25]

Foster Dulles's Middle Eastern tour in May 1953, in which he visited six Arab countries, Israel, Turkey and Pakistan, was the catalyst for the change in general American policy. He was especially shaken by his stop in Cairo, where, over two days, he met Neguib, Nasser and other RCC members. Nasser told him that American proposals for Middle Eastern defence were the 'perpetuation of occupation' and added:

I can't see myself waking up one morning to find that the Soviet Union is our enemy. . . . I would become the laughing-stock of my people if I told them they now had an entirely new enemy, thousands of miles away, and that they must forget about the British enemy occupying their territory.[26]

Foster Dulles cabled the State Department:

From talks with the Egyptians, I believe that, while they realize chaos and destruction of their regime would inevitably be an aftermath of open hostilities, they will choose that rather than make concessions to the British, which they consider would publicly be looked upon as infringing Egyptian sovereignty. Their emotions are so great they would rather go down as martyrs than concede.

The RCC was sponsoring guerrilla operations against British troops in the Canal Zone; the British were planning the reoccupation of Cairo and Alexandria. Thus, the US 'must abandon [her] preconceived ideas of making Egypt the key country in building the foundations for a military defence of the Middle East'.[27]

Foster Dulles was also depressed by other regional problems. After discussions with Arab leaders and the Israeli Prime Minister, David Ben-Gurion, he was convinced that a formal Arab-Israeli settlement was not possible. The US would 'have to move step by step upon segments of [the] problem that [would] reduce tension', including the question of Palestinian refugees, the status of Jerusalem, assurances against Israeli aggression and distribution of American aid. Syria offered 'some promise' as an emerging Arab country under the firm control of General Adib Shishakli, but she was 'very unpopular with [her] neighbours' and 'no adequate substitute for a stable Egypt'. Even the US relationship with Saudi Arabia was insecure:

Given the temperament and age of King Ibn Saud, it was quite possible that he would decide to throw away his alliance with US, conclude the oil concession and the [US rights to the Dhahran] air base, and throw in his lot with some other nation which he might feel was a more faithful ally.

In the short term, Foster Dulles recommended that the US reaffirm the Tripartite Declaration of 1950, reassuring Arabs that Israeli aggression would not be tolerated, and improve relations with Syria and Saudi Arabia. Britain would be urged to enter discussions to end the Anglo-Saudi dispute over boundaries on the Arabian Peninsula, especially the Buraimi oasis.

In the long term, the US would assert her independence of British policy through two measures. Firstly, the US would end unqualified support of Britain in the Anglo-Egyptian discussions and ask the British to compromise over the status of the Suez Canal Base. Secondly, Western plans for the Middle Eastern Defence Organisation would be abandoned, as Egypt's instability made the pact 'a future rather than an immediate possibility'. Instead, Foster Dulles proposed the 'Northern Tier' defence system of Turkey, Iraq, Pakistan and Iran. Turkey was securely in NATO; Iraq, with a 'forward-looking' government, was the Arab country 'most plainly concerned with the Soviet threat'; Pakistan, with her 'martial and religious characteristics, . . . could be made a loyal point' for the US; even Iran could be an asset if the US could 'concentrate on changing the situation there'.[28]

If British actions jeopardised American interests, then the Administration would form its own policy. Foster Dulles concluded:

British position rapidly deteriorating, probably to the point of non-repair. Generally in the area . . . we find an intense distrust and dislike for the British. The days when the Middle East used to relax under the presence of British protection are gone. Such British troops as are left in the area are more a factor of instability rather than stability.[29]

He announced on television that the peoples of the Near East and South Asia were

suspicious of the colonial powers. The US, too, is suspect because, it is reasoned, our NATO alliance with France and Britain requires us to try to preserve or restore the old colonial interests of our allies. . . . The day is past when [nationalist] aspirations can be ignored.[30]

In the summer of 1953, the tripartite summit in Bermuda was postponed when Churchill suffered a stroke and Eden temporarily left office because of gall bladder problems. The subsequent visit of the Acting Foreign Minister, Lord Salisbury, to Washington only produced a series of acrimonious talks with Foster Dulles. Churchill had been angered that Foster Dulles, on his Middle Eastern tour, had presented General Neguib with an American revolver from President Eisenhower, and the symbolic differences over the handling of Egypt soon led to practical difficulties. The Americans insisted that British rigidity over provisions for their base in the Suez Canal Zone doomed the Anglo-Egyptian negotiations, while Salisbury and his officials were annoyed that the US Embassy in Cairo conferred with the Egyptians without consulting their British counterparts.

Only after several days of bargaining did Salisbury and the British military representative, General Brian Robertson, regain some optimism. Although the US refused to underwrite new British proposals for operation of the Base, she agreed to their 'underlying principle', and Eisenhower, using a draft written by Foster Dulles in consultation with the British, wrote to Neguib, urging him to consider the new British offer carefully.[31]

Salisbury and the British Cabinet did not know that the Americans were already mediating the Anglo-Egyptian dispute. The 'Egyptian' proposals presented to the British in early July were based upon a State Department draft passed to Cairo, and American 'support' for Salisbury's reply was only given after British assurances that the only outstanding issues were the availability of the Base in wartime, the agreement's duration and a reference to free transit of the Suez Canal. Without revealing the source of the 'Egyptian' proposals, Foster Dulles told Salisbury that they were favourable on the first two of these points. When Caffery reported Robertson's belief that the Washington talks had revived US support for the British position, Foster Dulles snapped:

Robertson's statement reflects wishful thinking. We are not 'backing' either Britain or Egypt. In certain respects we share the British position, in other respects we share the Egyptian position, and in many respects we strongly backed the Egyptian viewpoint in our talks here with the British.[32]

The Americans also refused to accept British policy on other Middle Eastern issues. Salisbury proposed that the Buraimi oasis be placed under international supervision pending arbitration between Saudi Arabia and the British-supported Trucial Sheikhdoms of Abu Dhabi and Muscat and Oman (the present-day United Arab Emirates). The US, recognising that even an 'international' presence in Buraimi would be a loss of face for King Ibn Saud, declined. On Foreign Office advice that it was 'inexpedient to join issue with the Americans on this question at a time when we were seeking to reach agreement with them on matters of much greater moment', the British Cabinet agreed not to press the point.[33]

Meanwhile, the US announced that she would forge a Northern Tier defence grouping, with or without Britain's help. Foster Dulles summarised: 'If military assistance were given to Pakistan and if Persia, Iraq, Turkey, and perhaps Syria all came in together, a bulwark of strength would be built along the northern area of the Middle East.' He informed US missions on 30 July that $50 million for military aid was available as a lever for the co-operation of the Northern Tier states.[34]

Anglo-American relations deteriorated over Egypt. An agreement was imminent in late September, with the Egyptians compromising on a clause for freedom of transit through the Suez Canal and the agreement's duration, when talks stalled over Britain's insistence that technicians remaining at the Canal Zone Base be allowed to wear military uniform. The State Department suspected that the British introduced the uniform issue to sabotage the talks, and Foster Dulles warned Eden, who had returned to the Foreign Office, that the US might break publicly with Britain.[35]

Eden was in a near-impossible position. A negotiated settlement with Egypt was unacceptable to many backbench Conservative MPs, especially after the Suez Group was formed by Colonel Charles Waterhouse and Julian Amery in 1953 to unite the opposition. No Ministers joined the Group, but Churchill was privately sympathetic.[36] The Prime Minister and Eden had quarrelled about the Anglo-Egyptian negotiations periodically from April 1952, and Eden's agreement with the Egyptians in early 1953 on the future status of the Anglo-Egyptian Sudan was greeted by Churchill's complaint that he never realised 'that Munich was situated on the Nile'.[37] More than once Amery passed the Prime Minister in the House of Commons to be urged by Churchill, 'Keep up the good work.'[38]

The Cabinet refused to concede the demand that British technicians wear military dress, and a frustrated Foreign Office found a scapegoat in Ambassador Caffery. They accused him of saying, privately but widely, 'that the British have bungled negotiations from the start' and refusing to affirm that British proposals on availability of the Base had US support.

The Permanent Undersecretary, Sir William Strang, protested to the US Embassy in London, and Eden, speaking to General Alfred Gruenther, the commander of NATO forces, 'made several rather uncompromising remarks about Caffery's attitude'. Foster Dulles put the onus on Britain over the issue: he would only consider the recall of Caffery after a formal British request.[39]

In fact, Foster Dulles had no intention of transferring Caffery, the 'mediator', while the Anglo-Egyptian discussions were in progress,[40] and the dispute over the Ambassador was superseded by the question of US aid to Egypt. In autumn 1952, Kermit Roosevelt informed the new regime that the US was considering the provision of military equipment, and the Assistant Secretary of Defense, William Foster, visited Cairo to consider an Egyptian 'shopping list'. He was sufficiently encouraged to suggest a military mission, led by Ali Sabri, to the US, but the outgoing Truman Administration was unwilling to commit itself to the supply of arms.[41]

In January and May 1953, the new Administration approved the delivery of $11 million of military equipment, but vehement British protests postponed the shipments. On 14 November, Foster Dulles warned Eden:

This settlement has dragged out to a point where we cannot continue much longer without very grave effect upon all our Arab relationships. If you felt that it was likely there would soon be new moves in the Suez matter which might produce agreement, we could still hold up briefly but our time is fast running out.

At the tripartite summit in Bermuda, rescheduled for December, Foster Dulles gave Eden an ultimatum. Either the British put the points agreed with the Egyptians into writing, ensuring that new arguments would not be introduced into the talks, as had occurred with the question of military uniform for technicians, or the US would proceed with economic aid to Egypt.[42]

Eden was concerned that Foster Dulles's request for a written document might lead the Egyptians to reintroduce issues that had already been settled. A 'transatlantic essay contest', with four messages between Churchill and Eisenhower and one from Eden to Dulles, followed, as the Prime Minister threatened to 'go it alone' in Egypt and withdraw support for the US policy on Communist China.[43] Finally, the British retreated and consented to a draft Heads of Agreement, setting forth points of agreement and differences in the Anglo-Egyptian talks.[44]

The Foreign Secretary barely survived the crisis. Twelve members of the Suez Group wrote to Churchill that Britain had to retain full control of Base facilities and that 'British combatant units [must be] strong enough to make effective our right to reinforce the Base in case of

necessity', and they tabled a motion in the House of Commons condemning the negotiations with Egypt. Churchill, while critical of the Foreign
Office in private, supported Eden before the 1922 Committee of Conservative backbenchers and the Commons to ensure the motion's defeat;
however, the Prime Minister told the Cabinet at the end of December that
the negotiations should be abandoned if agreement was not reached in the
near future.[45]

While the British were distracted by the Egyptian problem, the US
proceeded with military aid to the Middle East and the formation of the
Northern Tier defence. In September 1953, the State and Defense
Departments agreed in principle to $30 million in military grants for Iraq,
Syria, Saudi Arabia, Israel, Jordan and Lebanon, with $50 million to be
set aside for Egypt and Pakistan. After visits to Washington by Pakistani
leaders in November, Eisenhower approved the provision of military aid,
and the Joint Chiefs of Staff concluded:

The time might be propitious for encouraging Turkey, Pakistan, Iran, and
possibly Iraq or a combination thereof to form a defense association of indigenous forces under an indigenous command advantageously located with
relation to the current threat.[46]

Unable to provide sufficient aid to meet Pakistani demands, the
Foreign Office agreed that if the 'Americans [decided] to make the offer,
we would not wish to stand in the way'. Only in December did Eden have
second thoughts:

We are not at all clear what it is the Americans are proposing, and I think our
main objective should be to find out what they have in mind. If it is a question of
American bases in Pakistan, then I think we should warn them that this might
seem provocative to the Russians. . . . There would also be no harm in telling
them about the message we have had from Nehru [objecting to the plan].[47]

Eden voiced his fears to Foster Dulles at Bermuda, but the Foreign
Office did not press its argument and the State Department acted with
unexpected speed. On 28 December, the Turks agreed to the American
suggestion of a Turkish-Pakistani pact. The US Ambassador in Karachi
consulted the Pakistanis the next day, and Eisenhower formally authorised military aid for Pakistan a week later. When Foster Dulles told Eden
at the Berlin Conference of Foreign Ministers that he and Eisenhower
had decided that 'they must go ahead' despite Indian objections, the
Foreign Secretary merely expressed his hope for a British role in the
Northern Tier through Iraqi participation.[48]

Eden's acceptance was much more than deference to American
pressure. It reflected a significant change of policy: Britain would no

longer base her Middle Eastern position upon Cairo, but upon Baghdad and Amman. Caught between American pressure for concessions in the Anglo-Egyptian negotiations and right-wing pressure to stand firm, the Foreign Office and Chiefs of Staff concluded that the only alternatives to an agreement with the Egyptians were complete withdrawal from the Canal Zone or indefinite occupation of the Base despite Egyptian opposition and 'terrorist' activities. Eden considered a coup against the Neguib Government, but Ambassador Stevenson replied, 'There is no [political] alternative for Egypt: assassination of Neguib would lead to one of Neguib's lieutenants, presumably Nasser [assuming power].'[49]

The Foreign Office also sought a strategy to block further US intrusion upon Britain's Middle Eastern position. In autumn 1953, the Iraqi Government, requesting the re-equipment of two army divisions and the creation of a third, approached the US as well as Britain, the traditional supplier of its military needs. The State Department drafted a 'memorandum of understanding' with the British Embassy in Washington to permit a 'readily identifiable' US contribution to Iraq while maintaining the British position. The British Embassy in Baghdad did not trust its American counterparts, however, and some Foreign Office officials shared its sentiments.[50]

The solution to both these problems lay in the idea of an Iraqi-Jordanian axis. In March 1953, Eden approved British military plans, stemming from a 1952 review of global strategy, to base Middle Eastern defence upon Iraq and Jordan. The Foreign Secretary was content for plans to evolve slowly until the American initiative in Iraq and the collapse of the Anglo-Egyptian talks. Simultaneously, Jordan requested the build-up of British forces with the stationing of an armoured squadron in Ma'an in the southern part of the country.[51]

On 12 January 1954, Eden defined the new policy:

[We] should make it plain that our positions in Iraq and Jordan were clearly related. . . . If we are to have any position in the Middle East, our authority must be based on close relations with Jordan and Iraq. . . . The chances of Egyptians becoming our friends are slight. Israel cannot fulfil our purpose. Iraq and Jordan are friendly and could be made more so.[52]

The Chiefs of Staff redeployed forces from Egypt to British bases in Libya (which signed a twenty-year treaty with Britain in 1953), Jordan, Iraq, Cyprus and Aden. British troops, supported by air cover, would push out from the 'inner ring' defence line around Jordan and Lebanon to defend Iraq. After the Cabinet agreed, the RAF base at Amman was reopened, with a fighter squadron permanently stationed there, and an armoured squadron was sent to Aqaba on Jordan's southern coast.[53]

Once the new defence policy was established, the Foreign Office agreed to operate the Suez Canal Base with civilian technicians. Pressed by the Americans, Nasser, who had ousted Neguib as Prime Minister in March 1954, accepted British re-entry into the Base in the event of war or the threat of war against an Arab state or Turkey, and the US promised aid to Egypt *after* a settlement was reached. Churchill was still doubtful, but the persistence of the Foreign Office and Chiefs of Staff, American pressure, and the advent of the hydrogen bomb forced him to reconsider the value of 'digging in'. Heads of Agreement for an Anglo-Egyptian Treaty were initialled on 27 July 1954 and the Treaty was signed on 19 October.[54]

Meanwhile, the Turks and Pakistanis, prompted by the US, announced their intention to form a pact on 19 February and confirmed the agreement on 2 April. The US signed military aid agreements with Iraq on 21 April and Pakistan on 19 May. While British representatives in the Middle East still believed that US resources would overwhelm any British plans, the Foreign Office reiterated that American military and economic aid to the Northern Tier was established and that Britain's task was to regain political leadership of the area through revision of the 1932 Anglo-Iraqi Treaty.[55]

The Americans' next objective was resolution of the Arab-Israeli conflict. Believing that the Truman Administration's favouritism towards Israel had prevented successful American mediation, the Eisenhower Administration had implemented a policy of 'impartiality'. When Israel attempted in September 1953 to divert water, claimed by Syria, from the Jordan River, economic aid to Tel Aviv was suspended until the Israelis ceased diversion. Eisenhower then appointed a special emissary, Eric Johnston, to negotiate an amicable division of the waters. When this was achieved, issues such as the status of Jerusalem, the settlement of Arab refugees and the elimination of trade boycotts could be addressed. On 17 November, Johnston reported that the Arabs had warmly received his mission. He recommended a second visit in early 1954 to pursue the initiative.[56]

The second Johnston mission was overshadowed by killings on the Arab-Israeli borders and an attempt by Byroade, overseeing Near Eastern affairs, to check Israeli 'expansionism'. Byroade believed that 'Israel's unpredictable and uncontrollable dynamism [was] the major present source of danger in the Near East'. He asked Foster Dulles to warn the Israeli Ambassador that 'persistence by Israel in her present policies will result in damage to Israel-US relations and may force us into a position of open opposition to Israel'. The Secretary agreed 'that the Israelis have embarked on a deliberate policy of making things worse in the hope that, by so doing, they may force us to make peace on the Arabs', but he added, 'Until we are in a position of offering [the Israelis] some better alternative . . . I do not think that merely to upbraid them is going to be very productive.' When Byroade persisted in his argument in two public speeches, Foster Dulles, under pressure from American Jewish groups as well as the Israeli Government, prepared for the transfer of his Assistant Secretary: 'Byroade should be moved out for many reasons, including his own morale. Unless you adopt an all-out Zionist policy, it is [a] hard road.'[57]

In contrast, the third Johnston mission in June 1954 renewed hope for a settlement. Plans for international supervision of the Jordan River's waters were supported by the Arab League. Johnston was 'much encouraged at the prospect of obtaining Arab co-operation', especially from Egypt, and the chairman of the Arab committee claimed, 'Apart from a few technical points, agreement is complete between Johnston and us.'[58]

In July 1954, the National Security Council reviewed the progress of its Middle Eastern policy. With the Anglo-Egyptian problem resolved, the Council linked the progress of a Northern Tier pact to an Arab-Israeli solution. Failing this, the US could not openly join Turkey, Pakistan, Iran and Iraq. Congress, with its large pro-Israeli lobby, would demand an American guarantee of Israeli borders in exchange for accession to a pact with Arab membership, but a guarantee of Israel in advance of an Arab-Israeli settlement would indicate American favouritism towards the Israelis.

To reduce border tensions and improve chances for a wide-ranging settlement, the Council acted to deter an attack by Israel or the Arab states. Economic aid would be cut off, and trade sanctions would be imposed to force an 'attacking state to relinquish any territory seized'. The establishment of a naval blockade and additional military steps would be considered. Other countries would be urged to take similar measures, and UN support would be sought.[59]

As in 1950 with the Tripartite Declaration, the Arab-Israeli issue forced the Council to recognise the need for Anglo-American co-operation. While 'independent' action had brought results, especially in the Northern Tier, the US could not advance towards an Arab-Israeli settlement without the help of Britain, who still retained the diplomatic lead in Iraq and political and military dominance in Jordan. Moreover, the Anglo-Egyptian agreement might renew British prestige in Cairo. The Council acknowledged that, as British support for the Northern Tier was an 'important factor' in determining its success, 'efforts should be made to overcome the doubts now held by the UK, particularly regarding the inclusion of Iran', and the initiative for an Arab-Israeli settlement should be defined 'in collaboration with the UK'.[60]

The Council could rely upon military co-operation, which had continued since 1953 through Anglo-American staff conferences in Washington. Meetings in December 1953 considered the stationing of Allied air forces in Cyprus, Libya, the Persian Gulf and Jordan, and pre-stocking of equipment in southern Turkey to supply the Middle Eastern theatre in wartime.[61] Six months later, the US Joint Chiefs of Staff unexpectedly requested detailed planning studies on the Middle East. Discussions between Britain, the US and Turkey would be followed by Anglo-American discussions to establish the concept of operations for Middle Eastern defence and to draft plans to secure lines of communication between Egypt, the Persian Gulf and one major oil-production complex. The Joint Chiefs of Staff subsequently agreed to consider provision of American-controlled nuclear weapons for Middle Eastern defence.[62]

With the Americans offering renewed diplomatic co-operation, the Foreign Office hastened to unite London and Washington on the Arab-Israeli question. On 2 October, Eden broached the idea to Foster Dulles of a joint *démarche* to the Arab states and Israel, followed by negotiations in which one side and then the other would be consulted by Anglo-American mediators. CIA officials sounded out the Egyptians and Israelis about the idea, arranging a meeting between Nasser and the former Israeli Chief of Staff, Yigael Yadin.[63] On 17 November, the State Department accepted the British suggestion, and Foster Dulles and Eden agreed that Assistant Undersecretary Evelyn Shuckburgh, supervising Middle Eastern affairs at the Foreign Office, would visit Washington in January 1955 to meet Foster Dulles's special representative, Francis Russell. The project was codenamed ALPHA.[64]

The reconciliation in policy between the two Governments occurred despite a worsening in personal relations between Foster Dulles and Eden. The first hints of conflict came at the Berlin Conference of Foreign Ministers between Britain, the US, France and the Soviet Union in February 1954. Foster Dulles, for reasons of ideology and domestic politics, was hesitant to include China in a peace conference on Korea and the French conflict with Vietnam, despite Eden's pressure for concessions. The US Assistant Secretary of State, Livingston Merchant, observed:

Eden was always to be counted on, but it had to be very clearly a true crunch. Anything short of that, he was always willing to give away . . . a little bit of the US position. . . . I often felt that he was too diligent in his search for the compromise of the uncompromisable.[65]

The French position in Indochina deteriorated in April with the large garrison at Dien Bien Phu under siege. The US considered intervention with her air forces and nuclear weapons, and Foster Dulles travelled to London to get British support. The initial meetings with Eden were promising. Foster Dulles settled for a statement that committed Britain and the US to consult with other countries about collective defence for South-East Asia.

Unfortunately, Foster Dulles understood that the consultations would occur before the Geneva Conference on Korea and Vietnam, while Eden implied to the House of Commons that he would pursue the discussions *after* the Conference.[66] Thus, when Foster Dulles called a nine-power meeting of ambassadors in Washington for 20 April, Eden instructed Ambassador Makins to decline the invitation:

Americans may think the time past when they need consider feelings or difficulties of their allies. It is the conviction that this tendency becomes more pronounced every week that is creating mounting difficulties for anyone in this country who wants to maintain close Anglo-American relations. We at least have certainly to bear in mind all our Commonwealth partners, even if [the] US doesn't like some of them.

Told of Eden's rejection, Foster Dulles exclaimed, 'Eden has double-crossed me! He lied to me!'[67]

When the Geneva Conference opened, relations went from bad to worse. Foster Dulles walked out on a meeting with the British and complained to Eisenhower:

The US was eager to beat the Communists at their own game and to sponsor nationalism with the independent colonial areas, which was in accordance with our historic traditions, but . . . we were restrained from doing so by a desire to cooperate with Britain and France in Asia, in North Africa, and in the Near and Middle East. This, however, did not seem to be paying any dividends because, when the chips were down, there was no cohesion between us.

Eden, 'fed up with Dulles', retorted after another dinner with the Secretary and his assistants in which the Americans 'all went for him, saying United Kingdom had let US down, etc.': 'All the Americans want to do is to replace France and run Indochina themselves. They want to replace us in Egypt too. They want to run the world.'[68]

Foster Dulles's departure from the Conference eased the situation, and Eden was instrumental in arranging the final agreement on Indochina, which was acknowledged, but not signed, by the American delegation. The damage had been done, however. Foster Dulles allegedly told journalists:

The US had weakened her leadership and her mission in the world by supporting or appearing to support British and French policies in the Middle East and North Africa, thus incurring the charge of being an imperialist power. Egypt and Saudi Arabia were given as examples. Some way must be found of reestablishing the American moral position on the issue of colonialism and taking the initiative rather than remaining on the defensive.

Makins reported to Eden:

Foster Dulles is a vain fellow, and his *amour propre* was deeply wounded when, on his return from Geneva, the American press cheerfully recorded that he had suffered the worst defeat in American diplomatic history, at the same time as they were reporting the bouquets being showered on your splendid efforts in the cause of peace and in bringing the two sides together at Geneva. This is galling to a man whose ambition is to go down in history as one of the great American Secretaries of State.[69]

Problems arose in the Americans' 'backyard' in Guatemala, where the US, through economic measures, diplomatic pressure and covert support for guerrillas, was trying to topple the Government. When the British and the French supported Guatemala's appeal to the UN Security Council, Eisenhower joined Foster Dulles in the attack upon the British:

[We should] use the veto [in the Security Council] and show the British that they have no right to stick their nose into matters which concern this hemisphere entirely. The British expect us to give them a free ride and side with them on Cypress [*sic*] and yet they won't even support us on Guatemala. Let's give them a lesson.

Foster Dulles told the US representative to the UN, Henry Cabot Lodge, to

let the British know that if they took an independent line backing the Guatemalan move in this matter, it would mean we would feel entirely free without regard to their position in relation to any such matters as any of their colonial problems in Egypt, Cypress [*sic*], etc.[70]

The next day, 26 June, Churchill and Eden arrived in Washington for meetings with Eisenhower and Foster Dulles. Churchill accepted Eisenhower's request to withdraw British support of Guatemala in the Security Council and then asserted, 'Dulles has said a couple of things to Eden that need not have been said.' Eisenhower responded by telling Foster Dulles:

Eden feels the Secretary has been so correct at times in conversation that he (Eden) does not quite gather what the Secretary is driving at. He (Eden) thinks the Secretary avoids telling him things as he thinks Eden is dumb and [Dulles] doesn't give Eden the chance to say he (Eden) is not as dumb as he looks. He (Eden) seemed to plead for close ties. . . . If the Secretary lets him feel close, it may pay off.

The following day, Eden and Foster Dulles had a productive discussion about Indochina and the Anglo-Egyptian discussions, and agreed to consider Anglo-American machinery to prevent further differences. Eisenhower concluded in a letter to Churchill: 'I think one of the major advantages we may have gained from [the meetings in Washington] is what seems to me an obvious drawing together of Anthony and Foster in their thinking and relationships.'[71]

To some extent, this easing of tension between Foster Dulles and Eden continued until Eden's accession as Prime Minister in April 1955. The two eventually co-operated on the formation of Western European Union for European defence, and the crisis over Indochina receded. The Geneva Conference had a lasting impact, however. Eden later wrote:

My difficulty in working with Mr Dulles was to determine what he really meant and, in consequence, the significance to be attached to his words and actions. I know that I was not alone in this, but the consequences were unfortunate for Britain, the weaker partner.

According to his assistants, Foster Dulles had concluded:

The British throughout the world were a rapidly declining power. He was convinced they no longer had any basic will to meet international responsibilities, that they were attempting to duck out all over the world, that they were trying to put as good a face on it as possible, but that you simply could not count on the British to carry on in any responsible way or, indeed, form an effective bulwark with us against anything. . . . He had absolutely no regard for them internationally. He felt that they were clumsy and inept, as opposed to their carefully nurtured reputation of being the opposite, and he . . . had no admiration for them.[72]

Foster Dulles once exclaimed to Eisenhower that 'the happiest day in his life [would] be when we don't have to modify our policies etc. to keep up a façade of unity'.[73]

However, the policy-making systems in Washington and London not only prevented the clash of personality between Eden and Foster Dulles from dictating Anglo-American relations in the Middle East, but also limited differences between American and British representatives in the field. The CIA station in Syria was in close contact with the dictator, General Adib Shishakli, but his fall in February 1954 and the return of instability renewed Anglo-American interest in preventing the loss of Western influence in Damascus. The Trucial Sheikhdoms of Abu Dhabi and Muscat and Oman continued to vie with Saudi Arabia for control of the Buraimi oasis, but Britain, after repeated requests from the Eisenhower Administration, submitted the question of Buraimi's status to a five-member tribunal.[74]

With the British agreement to leave the Suez Canal Base, American aid might have usurped Britain's traditional position in Cairo. On 28 July 1954, the day after Britain and Egypt initialled the Heads of Agreement, Foster Dulles authorised Ambassador Caffery to discuss economic and military assistance with the Egyptians, and $40 million in economic aid was set aside. Covertly, the CIA developed Egypt's military intelligence and internal security forces, and Egyptian security officers attended courses in the US on anti-Communist measures. CIA Director Allen Dulles, through the former head of military intelligence for Nazi Germany, Reinhard Gehlen, hired the famous commando Otto Skorzeny to find 100 German advisers, paid by the CIA, to train the Egyptians.[75]

The possibility of American dominance in Egypt through aid never arose, however. Under the Military Defence Assistance Act (MDAA), any recipient of aid had to accept a US military mission, but Nasser insisted that he could not accept foreign troops on Egyptian soil so soon after the agreement to end the British 'occupation'. The Dulles brothers tried to circumvent the MDAA. Of the $40 million in economic aid, $5 million would be diverted to arms purchases, and an additional $3 million from Eisenhower's 'executive' budget would be offered for 'certain morale-building items of military equipment such as uniforms and staff transportation'. The CIA's Kermit Roosevelt and Defense Department officials presented the package to Nasser and gave an Egyptian intermediary the $3 million 'sweetener' in a suitcase, but the Egyptian President refused to divert any money from the package of economic aid. Considering the $3 million a bribe, Nasser used it to build a monument to the CIA: an ostentatious tower in Cairo, now opposite the Hilton Hotel, known locally as 'Roosevelt's Erection'.[76]

The long-term threat to renewed Anglo-American co-operation came, outside the 'alliance', from action by Middle Eastern leaders, notably efforts by the Iraqi Prime Minister, Nuri Sa'id, to establish leadership of the Arab world through Iraq's position in the Northern Tier and Middle Eastern defence pacts. In September 1954, after a failed attempt at rapprochement with Egypt, Nuri suggested replacement of the Anglo-Iraqi Treaty of 1930, due to expire in 1957, with a multilateral system and British use of bases in Iraq. Eden and Shuckburgh were hesitant, since Nuri had tabled vague schemes in the past without results, and they suspected that his real motive was Iraq's long-standing wish for union with Syria. If Nuri was serious, however, and his plan led to the revision of the Anglo-Iraqi Treaty, the proposal could be 'an ingenious one'.[77] London's 'wait-and-see' attitude seemed to be vindicated by Iraqi talks with Turkey in mid-October. Nuri's ideas were still imprecise, and it was merely agreed that the Turkish Prime Minister, Adnan Menderes, would visit Baghdad in January 1955.[78]

The initial Turkish-Iraqi talks did not threaten Anglo-American co-operation. A new US Ambassador, Waldemar Gallman, was sent to Baghdad in September to encourage the Iraqis, and Washington urged Turkey to bring Iraq into the Turkish-Pakistani Pact.[79] However, Britain and the US supported the Northern Tier for different reasons. The Americans sought a combination of countries oriented against the Soviet Union, the British an 'umbrella' for their Middle Eastern treaty commitments. With events developing quickly and haphazardly, the Foreign Office never perceived the American emphasis on an 'indigenous' grouping free of overt Western participation, while the State Department never appreciated the British priority of revision of the Anglo-Iraqi Treaty.

The uncertain position of Egypt also hindered Anglo-American relations. The 1954 Anglo-Egyptian Treaty ended open hostility between London and Cairo, but it did not bring the 'new era of co-operation and mutual understanding' sought by the British. When Anthony Nutting, Minister of State in the Foreign Office, asked about Egypt's participation in Middle Eastern defence, Nasser was evasive. Nutting reported optimistically: '[The Egyptians are] reluctant to take any overt steps in this direction at present, although they expressed hope of being able to do so in [the] not too distant future,' but Ambassador Caffery was more perceptive:

The greatest mistake the British (or we) could make at this moment would be to attempt to force the Egyptian pace towards participation in area security arrangements including the Western powers. I am convinced that this will come to pass, but the Egyptians, and only the Egyptians, must decide when the time is ripe.[80]

Both Britain and Egypt were soon diverted from the matter, Britain by Nuri's proposals for regional defence, Nasser by an assassination attempt upon him by the Moslem Brotherhood and his subsequent removal of General Neguib, long a discredited figurehead, from the Presidency. Most importantly, Nasser established that an Arab-Israeli settlement was a precondition for Egyptian military co-operation with the West. The Foreign Office's Evelyn Shuckburgh minuted in early December: 'I am not at present convinced that we want to press the Egyptians over defence arrangements. It would be more useful if they would help us over Israel.' Eden endorsed the statement.[81]

3

Seeds of Conflict
February–September 1955

On 20 February 1955, Eden, visiting Cairo, met President Nasser for the first and only time in his life. The ostensible reason for the encounter was an exchange of congratulations over the new Anglo-Egyptian Treaty, but Eden's primary objective was Egyptian co-operation with Britain in a Middle Eastern defence system. Within nine days, that vision was shattered. Egypt refused military ties with the West, and the Anglo-Egyptian rapprochement was replaced by distrust. The Arab world was polarised between Cairo and Baghdad, and secret Egyptian-Israeli negotiations for peace were replaced by preparations for long-term conflict. The chain of events leading to the Suez crisis had been established.

The contrast between Eden and Nasser at their dinner at the British Embassy could not have been more striking, the Foreign Secretary in full evening dress, the Egyptian President in his lieutenant-colonel's field uniform. Eden, who had studied Arabic and Persian at Oxford, surprised Nasser by greeting him in classical Arabic and embarking upon a discussion, sprinkled with Arab proverbs, on Islamic civilisation. Nasser later commented, 'What elegance! It was made to look as if we were beggars and they were princes!' His officers suspected that Eden was trying to upstage them and impress his wife Clarissa, who was present at the dinner. Anthony Nutting later wrote: 'After dinner . . . [Eden] sat back on the sofa, when Nasser was speaking, with his eyes slightly averted and a look on his face which suggested that he was saying to himself, "What can this young officer tell me about international politics?"'[1]

Yet the meeting was far from acrimonious. Nasser, though baffled by

Eden's aristocratic manner, respected his knowledge and diplomatic skill. The Foreign Secretary reported to Churchill: 'I was impressed by Nasser, who seemed forthright and friendly although not open to conviction on the Turkish-Iraqi [Pact]. No doubt jealousy plays a part in this, and a frustrated desire to lead the Arab world.' It was Clarissa Eden who found Nasser's informal dress and casual manner rude and insulting, an impression of increasing importance in the following months.[2]

Discussion centred upon Egyptian-Iraqi relations and the Turkish-Iraqi Pact, which had been initialled on 12 January. Eden argued that a united defence as far north as possible was in Egypt's interest, reinforcing the point with a fifteen-minute presentation by General Sir John Harding, the Chief of the Imperial General Staff. Nasser agreed that Middle Eastern defence against the Soviet Union should link Iraq with countries to the west and south, but he argued that this should be under a unified Arab command free of foreign 'influence'. He reminded Eden that Israel, not the Soviet Union, was the main concern of the Arab states. Eden said that Nasser 'should not treat this pact as a crime'. Laughing, Nasser replied, 'No, but it is one.' Unmoved, Eden refused to oppose the final signature of the Turkish-Iraqi Pact. He predicted to Foster Dulles, 'Nasser would denounce [the] treaty at time of signature and . . . there would be Egyptian efforts in Iraq to bring about the downfall of Nuri [Sa'id].'[3]

The two men parted amicably, but their relationship was now the hostage of events outside Britain and Egypt. The announcement by Turkey and Iraq that they intended to conclude a defence pact had surprised the Foreign Office. On 11 January, the British Chargé d'Affaires in Baghdad, Robin Hooper, reported that Nuri Sa'id was not seeking a formal agreement. At most, Turkey and Iraq would arrange for staff conversations and free transit for military equipment through their countries. American officials in Baghdad agreed with the assessment. Shuckburgh summarised: 'I am doubtful whether this is really a problem which cannot very well wait.'[4]

Thus, when the Turkish-Iraqi agreement was initialled, the Foreign Office was forced into a hasty decision. Egyptian support of the Northern Tier was the optimal solution, but, failing that, Britain had to choose between a defence strategy centred upon Cairo and one centred upon Baghdad. The redeployment of British forces in the Middle East, begun in 1953, and Nasser's refusal to allow foreign troops in Egypt in peacetime, precluded the former option. Without a satisfactory revision of the 1932 Anglo-Iraqi Treaty, due to expire in 1957, the latter would be lost as well.[5]

On 14 January, Eden wrote to Nuri that he was 'much encouraged' by the Turkish-Iraqi announcement and implied that an Anglo-Iraqi arrangement should follow. Advised by Michael Wright, the British Ambassador in Baghdad, that an Anglo-Iraqi treaty under cover of the Turkish-Iraqi Pact was 'as solid a basis [of agreement] as it is possible to secure', the Foreign Office, without waiting for Cabinet authority, advised Iraq and Turkey on 10 February that Britain was prepared to accede to the Pact. Anglo-Iraqi military talks on British requirements in Iraq concluded successfully on the 22nd, two days before the final signature of the Turkish-Iraqi Pact.[6]

Meanwhile, a period of calm on the Egyptian-Israeli border was suddenly dashed by changes in the Israeli Government and its security policy. Between 1952 and February 1955, Egyptian and Israeli leaders, including Nasser and Moshe Sharett, Foreign Minister and then Prime Minister of Israel, secretly sought a peace settlement. In August 1952, Israeli and Egyptian diplomats met in Paris, and discussions between the Israeli and Egyptian Foreign Ministries began in early 1953. Israeli officials even met Nasser in July 1954 to 'reassure him of Israel's understanding of his aspirations and its keen interest in negotiating a peaceful settlement with him'. The talks were 'intimate and intense', although they 'did not yield significant political results'. After the Knesset, the Israeli Parliament, endorsed negotiations with Egypt in September, Israeli officials met special envoys from Cairo to discuss the resolution of specific issues, including Israeli transit through the Suez Canal. The Egyptian and Israeli Governments were also contacted by third parties, including British M Ps Maurice Orbach, Richard Crossman and Colonel Cyril Banks; the Pakistani Foreign Minister, Zafrullah Khan; Ralph Bunche, the former head of the United Nations Commission for Palestine; the President of the American Jewish Congress, Jacob Blaustein; the Maltese Prime Minister, Dom Mintoff; the Canadian Foreign Minister, Lester Pearson; the American Jewish leader, Ira Hirshman; and Elmore Jackson, a prominent American Quaker.[7]

Sharett, however, faced continuous opposition within the Israeli Government to any concessions to the Egyptians until Cairo promised a peace settlement. Although Sharett's predecessor, David Ben-Gurion, 'retired' in 1953, he appointed those who shared his belief in strong measures against the Arabs, notably the Defence Minister, Pinhas Lavon, and the Chief of Staff, General Moshe Dayan, and maintained contact with them after his retirement. Ben-Gurion had always advocated a policy of 'reprisals' against the Arab states – from November 1951 to November 1952, while thirty-nine Israelis were killed in border incidents, 394 Arabs were slain in Israeli raids – and the policy continued during his 'retirement'. Just before Ben-Gurion left office, Dayan became Chief of Staff, and Force 101, a special commando unit, was established for reprisals. In October 1953, over the objections of Foreign Minister Sharett, Force 101 attacked Qibya in Jordan, killing fifty-three people. Nine major raids and numerous 'minor' ones were carried out during 1954, often without the approval of the Prime Minister's Defence Committee.[8]

Israeli policy was complicated in June 1954 when Israeli military intelligence, without Sharett's knowledge, activated a spy ring in Cairo. Attempting to poison relations between Egypt and the West and ruin Anglo-Egyptian negotiations, the ring set off explosions in British- and American-owned buildings. The saboteurs were arrested by the Egyptians in the summer of 1954. Two were executed in January and another committed suicide. The crisis provoked in Israel by the episode led to the resignations of Colonel Benjamin Gibli, the head of military intelligence, and Lavon in February 1955.[9]

Sharett won a victory with the removal of Lavon, but he lost the battle when Ben-Gurion succeeded as Defence Minister and wrecked the Egyptian-Israeli contacts. He immediately sent a letter to Sharett demanding that the Prime Minister, who also served as Foreign Minister, not interfere with the Defence Ministry: 'A consultation with the Prime Minister is also a consultation with the Foreign Minister, but consultation with the Foreign Minister is one thing and constant intervention by the Foreign Minister and his subordinates is quite different.'

Although the situation in the Gaza Strip had been peaceful, Ben-Gurion and Dayan demanded a strike against Egypt. Teddy Kollek, the Director-General of Sharett's office, met Ben-Gurion three times and Dayan once. He repeatedly warned the Israeli Foreign Ministry that the Israel Defence Forces were 'bound and determined to get revenge' for the execution of the 'Lavon' spies, the suicide of another, and the Egyptian seizure of the *Bat Galim*, an Israeli ship which defied the Egyptian blockade of the Suez Canal, but the Foreign Ministry paid little attention. Reluctantly, Sharett approved a modest raid into Gaza, which Ben-Gurion and Dayan turned into a large-scale attack on a military camp on 28 February. Two Israeli platoons blew up pumping installations and bombarded army camp buildings with light mortars while Egyptian reinforcements were ambushed with Molotov cocktails. Thirty-eight Egyptians were killed.[10]

Sharett was misled by Dayan, who estimated that ten Egyptians would be killed, and he confronted Ben-Gurion at a Cabinet meeting about reprisals. In reply, Ben-Gurion defined a new Israeli policy. Regardless of Arab attitudes, the raids were necessary to display Israel's military superiority over the Arabs and to bolster the confidence of the Israeli public and army. He dismissed the opposition of the United Nations and

Western countries to the reprisals, since Arab oil would always prevent others from supporting Israel's case.[11]

Gaza was a turning-point in Arab-Israeli relations. In March, Sharett narrowly prevented the adoption of Ben-Gurion's proposals for the occupation of the Gaza Strip and the abrogation of the Egyptian-Israeli Armistice Agreement, but after Mapai, the dominant party in the Government coalition, lost seats in the July elections, Ben-Gurion was asked to form a government. Sharett remained as Foreign Minister, but only for the sake of Western opinion towards Israel and the unity of Mapai. Meanwhile, Nasser abandoned a policy of restraint on the border and agreed to the organisation of *fedayeen* (commando units) to carry out raids into Israel. He renewed efforts to acquire arms from the US and Britain, and discontented Egyptian army officers demanded approaches to other sources, notably the Soviet bloc.[12]

Gaza also spurred the development of a Franco-Israeli 'alliance'. Evicted from Syria and Lebanon during the Second World War, and excluded from Anglo-American discussions on the Middle East between 1950 and 1955, the French sought an outlet for a Middle Eastern role. Israel, anxious for arms and refused large deliveries by London and Washington, provided the opportunity.

The appointments of French Ambassador Pierre-Eugène Gilbert to Israel and Israeli Ambassador Jacob Tsur to Paris in 1953 improved cultural and diplomatic contacts, and military talks led to a visit to France by Dayan and Shimon Peres, the Director-General of the Israeli Ministry of Defence, in June 1954. After further talks in August between Peres and the French Secretary of Air, Jacques Catroux, the French agreed to sell 155-millimetre guns, AMX-13 tanks and thirty fighters, including six Mystère II jets, to Israel. In January 1955, Catroux informed Tel Aviv of France's willingness to supply the Mystère IV, one of the most advanced jet fighters in the world. The Israeli secret service provided intelligence on nationalist movements in North Africa to the French, and France supplied information on nuclear research and development to Israel.[13]

Finally, Gaza sounded the death knell for Egyptian accommodation with the Turkish-Iraqi Pact, which was directed against the Soviet Union rather than Israel. If Syria, Jordan and Lebanon joined the Pact, the Egyptians might be isolated against the Israelis. To prevent this, Nasser sought an Arab defence pact linking Egypt and Syria, with support from Saudi Arabia and later accessions by Jordan and Lebanon. He told the British Ambassador, Stevenson, on 5 March that the Turkish-Iraqi Pact was an 'established fact', but new inter-Arab agreements, led by Egypt, would be an 'equally accomplished fact'. The next day, Egypt, Syria and Saudi Arabia signed an agreement for military co-operation.[14]

From this point, Anglo-Egyptian compromise was almost impossible. Military co-operation had been tentatively discussed by Lord Mountbatten, the First Sea Lord, and Nasser in December 1954, but it was abandoned in February when General Sir Charles Keightley, the Commander-in-Chief of Britain's Middle Eastern forces, discovered that the Egyptian Chief of the General Staff, General Abdel Hakim Amer, was no longer interested. Nasser had suggested to Stevenson that Britain serve as the 'co-ordinating factor' with inter-Arab pacts led by Egypt, but the British Ambassador to Jordan, Charles Duke, argued that British acquiescence would be a 'letdown of Jordan' and suggested that Britain disrupt the Egyptian-Saudi-Syrian agreement by inviting the Jordanians to join the Turkish-Iraqi Pact. Nutting wrote: 'I think this is right. We cannot reverse or appear to reverse our fears now.' Eden minuted: 'Excellent.'[15]

On 15 March, the Cabinet approved, in principle, negotiation of a new Anglo-Iraqi Treaty and accession to the Turkish-Iraqi Pact. The only recorded objection came from the Chancellor of the Exchequer, R. A. Butler, who was concerned about the expense of British arms supplies to Iraq and states who subsequently joined the Pact. Britain's formal accession turned the Turkish-Iraqi Pact into the Baghdad Pact on 5 April. The following day, Eden succeeded Churchill as Prime Minister.[16]

The speed of events temporarily separated London and Washington in their Middle Eastern policies. Ironically, before the Turkish-Iraqi statement of 12 January, the Americans worried about British hesitancy over the Northern Tier. A US Embassy official told Shuckburgh that, even if Nuri's actions

should result in a break-up of the Arab League, . . . the Northern Tier would provide an alternate centre of attraction around which the Arab States might group themselves and this would not, in their opinion, be a bad thing.

Shuckburgh commented after the meeting: 'If the American policy succeeds, it may be a great success, but I think it is risky and may well fail. We must avoid blame for its failure.[17]

On 27 January, Shuckburgh informed the State Department of the Foreign Office's change of heart: the Turkish-Iraqi Pact should be welcomed as a step 'towards an arrangement which we hoped would maintain for us our basic defence requirements'. The State Department responded: 'Mr Dulles' preliminary reaction was that he would favour eventual US association with the Pact provided . . . the US would only be involved in the event of aggression from outside the area.' On certain questions, notably Iranian accession, the US was still more eager than Britain for rapid development of the Pact.[18]

After Nuri's proposal of 27 January, endorsed by the Turks, that the US and Britain be invited to join the Pact, the State Department reversed its position. The Foreign Office was informed that, while quick con- clusion of the Turkish-Iraqi Pact was essential, American accession was problematic because of the opposition of pro-Israeli groups in Washington. US Embassies in Baghdad and Ankara were not to imply that the US was willing to join. Eden informed the Cabinet on 15 March that the 'US are unlikely to accede [to the Pact] in the immediate future', but that they 'might . . . consider acceding to it at an appropriate time'.[19]

In late March, the State Department put the question of accession to rest. Problems with Congress were anticipated because of a draft pro- vision in the Pact that disputes between signatories were to be settled within the framework of the UN Charter. According to pro-Israeli lobbyists, the provision implied that a dispute between a signatory of the Pact and a non-member, e.g. between Iraq and Israel, did not have to be resolved within the Charter's framework. The Foreign Office noted that the legal point was 'extremely poor', but missed the political point. Israeli opposition, inside and outside Congress, was an insuperable obstacle to US accession.[20]

The division between Britain and the US was mitigated by their co- operation over Operation ALPHA, the top-secret effort for an Arab- Israeli settlement. Shuckburgh travelled to Washington in January to establish the method of approach to Egypt and Israel and the guidelines for the settlement, which were based on State Department proposals. The American negotiator, Francis Russell, established that Israel would cede small areas of territory to unify Syrian and Jordanian villages with their farmlands. More importantly, Egypt and Jordan would be connected through a wedge of territory, with its base on the Egyptian border and the point on the Jordanian frontier, north of the Israeli port of Eilat. Using a bridge over the main road, both Arab and Israeli traffic would cross the junction point on the Jordanian border.

Shuckburgh argued that the Israeli concessions were inadequate and that 'there was barely enough in the plan for the Arabs to make it worthwhile going ahead', but he gave way to the Americans. Visits by Russell to London in March and April confirmed the arrangements. In addition to the territorial settlement, Egyptian-Israeli agreement would be sought on the American plan for division of the Jordan River. With an international loan, Israel would compensate Palestinian refugees dis- placed from their homes by the 1948–9 Arab-Israeli War. The US, besides contributing $200 million towards the international loan, would provide $395 million in economic and military aid for the Arabs. When the settlement was reached, Britain and the US would guarantee Arab-Israeli borders.[21]

Shuckburgh hoped to use the Eden visit to Cairo to broach ALPHA, informing the Foreign Secretary:

You believe that you can speak frankly to Nasser because you know he has the realism to recognise that Israel has come to stay, and you believe that he has the courage to lead the Egyptians and other Arab peoples away from their sterile recriminations towards a settlement that will release their energies and strengthen their self-confidence.

The issue was overshadowed, however, by the discussion of the Baghdad Pact, Nasser saying only that a 'corridor' to Jordan was unacceptable.[22]

On 5 April, US Ambassador Byroade finally tested Nasser's reaction to Anglo-American mediation between Egypt and Israel. Nasser agreed that the issue should be considered after the forthcoming Afro-Asian conference at Bandung, Indonesia, but he claimed that he could not take the initiative until the Arab world had 'calmed' after the Turkish-Iraqi Pact and Gaza. Shuckburgh and Russell continued to work on the details of the settlement, finally agreeing that territorial adjustments should be based on the cession by the Israelis of two 'triangles' of land, the points of which would meet in the Negev desert.[23]

If Nasser had co-operated on the Arab-Israeli question, Anglo-American organisation of Middle Eastern defence might have proceeded smoothly, but the spectres of Gaza and the Baghdad Pact haunted the Egyptian President. Rumours arose at the Bandung Conference of an Anglo-American attempt to isolate Egypt in the Middle East. Nasser complained to Stevenson about reports that the British Embassy was spreading anti-Egyptian propaganda, including allegations that Stevenson urged other ambassadors not to meet Nasser at Cairo airport upon his return from Bandung. According to Nasser, US personnel in Egypt and Arab states were spreading rumours about the Revolutionary Command Council's instability, the American representative in the Sudan was conspiring against Egypt, the Eisenhower Administration was sabotaging foreign support for the High Aswan Dam and undermining the Egyptian economy through its cotton policy, and the Americans were intending to pressure Egypt into making peace with Israel.[24]

Taken aback, the State Department had second thoughts about the approach to Nasser and considered alternative initiatives with Jordan and Lebanon, but, under Foreign Office pressure, it authorised Byroade to speak to Nasser on 9 June.[25] ALPHA, however, had been eclipsed by the question of arms supplies to Egypt. The increase in military aid promised for Egyptian signature of the 1954 Anglo-Egyptian Treaty never materialised. After his trip to Cairo and the Gaza raid, Eden, anxious 'about the effect of military and political defeats upon Nasser's regime', suggested the release of sixty-four Centurion Mark III tanks, on order since 1949, and immediate supply of six of thirty fighters purchased by Egypt in 1951, but the Minister of State, Anthony Nutting, objected that this might cause a 'dangerous explosion in Israel'. Shuckburgh's compromise of the release of thirty-two tanks and immediate supply of six fighters was finally accepted, but Britain refused to offer new equipment, such as the Centurion Mark VII tank, to Egypt.[26]

While the British dithered, Nasser learned of France's arms agreements with Israel. Pressed by his army to prevent further Israeli 'aggressions', he approached Chou En-lai, the Chinese Premier, at the Bandung Conference with a request for arms. Chou replied that China was dependent on Soviet supplies, but promised to pass Nasser's inquiry to Moscow. On 19 May, the Soviet Ambassador to Egypt, Daniel Solod, told Nasser that the Soviet Union would supply Egypt with arms in exchange for later payment in cotton and rice.[27]

Before Byroade could present ALPHA to Nasser on 9 June, the Egyptian President expressed 'his feeling of personal guilt at the death of his soldiers in Gaza'. He warned: 'I beg you to understand that this is the last time I shall ask for arms from the US. If I do not get them from you, I know where I can and [I] will ask the Soviets for them.' The Foreign Office tried to intimidate Egypt, instructing Stevenson to tell Nasser that acceptance of arms from the Soviets would 'be considered a very serious act'. The Egyptian President bluntly replied:

I have tried my utmost to obtain from you the arms required for the defence of my country, but I have not been successful. I cannot stand with folded arms in the face of Israel. I consider what you have just said as a threat which I am not prepared to accept. You are free to do whatever you like and I am free to do as I please.

On 16 June, he repeated to Byroade that he was

still aware of long-range disadvantages of Soviet arms aid. However, partly for morale effect in army and partly for security of Egypt, he still felt a desperate need to obtain additional supplies of military equipment which would continue in time of trouble.[28]

Some Foreign Office officials, including Shuckburgh, recommended an offer to an Egyptian arms mission, still lingering in London,[29] but Eden, now Prime Minister, had turned against Nasser. Incensed by Egyptian propaganda, which supported Saudi Arabia's claim to the

Buraimi oasis, Eden scribbled in bright red ink across telegrams from the British Embassy in Cairo. On one he wrote: 'If these representations [for the cessation of Egyptian propaganda] have no effect, what do we do next? Anything in our powers to hurt Egypt without hurting ourselves?'; on another: 'This is gross impertinence by [the Egyptians] who are likely to be attacked and destroyed by Israel before long. I hope we give them no help.'[30]

The Foreign Secretary, Harold Macmillan, wrote to the Prime Minister: 'We may well have to consider such measures [to hurt Egypt] . . . but I do not want it to come to this if I can possibly help it.' Eden, undeterred, continued to treat minor incidents as a challenge to the British position. When the Egyptians passed a routine report on Buraimi to the Secretary-General of the Arab League, he wrote: 'This kind of thing is really intolerable. Egyptians get steadily worse. . . . They should surely be told firmly no more arms deliveries while this goes on, or at least warned that we will take this position publicly unless they stop.' Macmillan found a new method of coping with Eden, writing, 'I don't think we need answer Prime Minister's minute at all,' while Shuckburgh made the case for co-operation with Cairo:

The plain fact is that, however disappointed we may be in the attitude of Colonel Nasser and his colleagues, we can see no alternative Egyptian Government in sight which would be any better. . . . We have an interest therefore in giving him such support as is necessary to maintain him in power which includes providing a certain amount of toys for his armed forces.

The Foreign Secretary, however, had neither the time nor the motivation to press his point in Cabinet against the opposition of other ministers, notably Minister of Defence Selwyn Lloyd.[31]

On 30 June, the Egyptians sent a list of equipment, valued at $27 million, to Washington. Eisenhower, labelling the request as 'peanuts', authorised a first instalment of $11 million, but the deal foundered over the method of payment. Short of dollars, Nasser had to obtain the arms on credit or trade Egyptian cotton for them. Egypt's refusal to accept a US military mission precluded the former, and the US, because of domestic cotton surpluses, had no wish to pursue the latter.[32] When he received no reply from the Americans, Nasser accepted the request of Dmitri Shepilov, the editor of *Pravda*, to visit Cairo on 22 July to discuss arms supplies from the Eastern bloc to Egypt.[33]

Only after the State Department learned of a possible Egyptian-Soviet deal from the CIA station in Cairo and Israeli sources did Foster Dulles tell Eisenhower that he 'planned to notify Nasser that we would sell certain military equipment to Egypt as desired by him'. However, the

Secretary, pursuing 'impartiality', added the proviso that the US 'would have to be in a position to sell to Israel also'. Eisenhower suggested telling the Israelis of American plans, and Foster Dulles retreated from an immediate commitment: 'This might be useful but it had better be deferred until we discovered whether in fact the Egyptians would buy [American arms].'[34]

The ALPHA negotiations had diverted Foster Dulles from the immediate crisis with Egypt. As early as February, the Israeli Ambassador to Britain, Eliahu Elath, surmised that Britain and the US were planning an Arab-Israeli settlement with territorial concessions by Israel,[35] and Foster Dulles had unwisely hinted to Prime Minister Sharett, 'We are making good progress in formulating the possibilities of appropriate and effective steps which the US might take.'[36] In late May, the Israeli Ambassadors to Britain, the US and France were called to Tel Aviv 'in light of information that US and UK [were] giving serious consideration [to a] possible settlement [of] Israel-Arab issues'. The State Department feared an Israeli public statement that 'would of course seriously damage the ability [of] US and UK [to] influence Arabs [to] move toward settlement as we would appear [to] be acting on Israeli Government initiative'.[37] Foster Dulles, spending a weekend in South Carolina, devised the idea of an American statement to pre-empt the Israelis.[38]

After initial opposition,[39] the Foreign Office agreed that an American statement was necessary, but the British explicitly linked ALPHA to the Baghdad Pact and Middle Eastern defence. In exchange for British support of Foster Dulles's statement, the Americans would promise to join the Baghdad Pact as soon as an Arab-Israeli settlement was completed. Meanwhile, the US would finance the supply of British Centurion tanks to Iraq and give military support to Britain if fighting erupted in the Middle East after Foster Dulles's speech.[40]

By mid-August, the Americans agreed that they would pay for ten Centurions to Iraq if the British paid for two, and more tanks would be shipped in 1956. Foster Dulles would make a very general statement, identifying the problems of Arab-Israeli borders, Palestinian refugees and division of the Jordan waters, without mentioning ALPHA and Anglo-American consultations. Twenty-four hours later, Macmillan would issue a supporting statement.[41]

All was not settled, however. By 19 August, the State Department and the CIA had evidence of a Soviet arms offer to Egypt. Fearing that exposure of Moscow's support for Cairo would force the US to abandon 'impartiality' and back Israel, Foster Dulles moved his speech from 8 September to 26 August. Eden wrote: 'The Americans are behaving disgracefully. This is their third change of plan over this operation. . . .

We should hold the Americans responsible for any flare-up which may occur in the area.' As late as 25 August, the Prime Minister threatened to ask Eisenhower to cancel the speech, but was checked by Macmillan.[42]

Foster Dulles's statement, given before the Council of Foreign Relations in New York, was an anti-climax. Stripped of any reference to ALPHA, it issued general platitudes about the need for a comprehensive settlement that would solve 'the tragic plight of the 900,000 [Palestinian] refugees', the 'pall of fear' over Israeli expansion and Arab aggression, and 'the lack of permanent fixed boundaries'. There was no tangible element that either the Arabs or the Israelis could seize upon to endorse the speech. The Israeli Government was 'restrained and sympathetic', but warned against any concessions of territory. Nasser complained about the lack of specific proposals, and Iraq, Lebanon, Syria and Jordan withheld reaction until the Arab states could discuss the matter. Meanwhile, the Johnston mission for division of the Jordan River, eclipsed by Foster Dulles's statement, foundered because Jordan wavered over the terms and the unstable Syrian Government could not accept an agreement with Israel.[43]

Neither the British nor the Americans comprehended that Foster Dulles's statement had been superseded by other events. On 22 August, three weeks after Ben-Gurion agreed to lead a new government, Israeli patrols crossed the Egyptian border and occupied positions in the Gaza Strip. Desperate intervention by the US Embassy prevented Egypt from launching a large-scale attack, but Nasser authorised *fedayeen* raids into Israel. In turn, Ben-Gurion requested an assault upon Egyptian positions at Khan Yunis on 31 August. Sharett opposed the raid, but gave way when Ben-Gurion and Dayan threatened to resign. Thirty-six Egyptians were killed.[44]

Foster Dulles had received an assurance from Sharett, through the US Ambassador, Edward Lawson, of Israel's peaceful intentions, provided Egypt withdrew the *fedayeen*, but Assistant Secretary George Allen, supervising the Near East, surprised the Secretary with the news of the attack upon Khan Yunis. Foster Dulles asked 'how [Sharett] could reconcile what happened last night with what he says about no action [by Israeli troops]'. Allen replied glumly, '[He] can't reconcile it.'[45]

Before the attack on Khan Yunis, Nasser told American contacts that he would accept a cease-fire if Israel withdrew from the Gaza Strip, but he now faced further Israeli 'retaliations'. France was reportedly offering Mystère IV fighters to Israel while suspending arms deliveries to Egypt, and the State Department, preoccupied with Foster Dulles's speech, continued to ignore the Egyptian arms request of 30 June. Until late August, Allen mistakenly thought a reply had been made to Nasser.[46]

The State Department was also confused because it could not verify the *completion* of the Egyptian-Soviet arms deal. Nasser had told Byroade on 8 August 'that the Army . . . was particularly suspicious of the US and made it clear that he was in no position to advocate the adoption by his supporters of a pro-American line in the absence of some concrete moves by the US'.[47] A week later, the Egyptian Ambassador in Washington, Ahmed Hussein, visiting Cairo, told Byroade and the CIA station chief, James Eichelberger, that the Soviets had offered Egypt 100 MIG fighters, 200 tanks and jet bombers, but he added that Nasser had not made a definite reply. Foster Dulles told his brother Allen that 'he did not know how seriously we should take the Russian proposals about Egypt'. Only on 29 August did the CIA meet Foster Dulles's request 'to work up information on some of the things these people might be doing about offering arms to the Arabs, etc.'[48]

Nasser probably decided to complete the deal after the renewed conflict on the border with Israel. The CIA concluded:

Prime Minister Nasser is impressed with the weakness of his position and feels strongly that he must secure arms and economic help at the earliest possible date. Whether he would, if unable to secure this type of aid elsewhere, accept Soviet military and economic assistance is not at the moment entirely clear, but there is a serious risk that, for internal political reasons, he might feel himself driven to this.[49]

Despite the report, the State Department refused on 15 September to meet Egypt's arms requests, citing the 'severe practical difficulties' of financing the purchases and insisting, 'Positive steps by [Nasser] such as a start in exploring Secretary's statement [of 26 August] would bolster greatly case for accommodating Egypt on financing'. Byroade protested, but the State Department repeated its position on the 20th.[50] On 19 September, the CIA station in Cairo passed information from a highly placed Egyptian source to Washington: 'GOE acceptance Soviet arms offers likely. . . . Soviet offer said to be almost embarrassing in size.'[51] Two days later, Nasser confirmed to Byroade that Egypt would receive approximately $80 million in arms from the Soviet bloc, with submarines, 100 tanks and 200 planes, including MIG-15 fighters and Il-28 bombers. Soviet technicians would be in Cairo for three months to set up the equipment and to train Egyptian forces in its use.[52]

Developments in Egypt coincided with difficulties in Anglo-American discussions over the Middle East. Undersecretary of State Herbert Hoover Jr insisted to Ambassador Makins that 'the US Government continued to regard the Baghdad Pact as the best foundation on which to build the defence of the area', but he offered no further evidence of

American support. Eden resented Foster Dulles's lead on ALPHA and minuted on 29 August: 'Our long-standing credit in the area is not receiving the credit it deserves.' Two days later, he added: 'Mr Dulles started all this, and if he has got himself into trouble [with Arab or Israeli reaction], it is not for us to help him out.'[53]

After a few months in 10 Downing Street, Eden was increasingly temperamental and erratic. Despite his image as a suave, unflappable diplomat, he had always been highly strung, quick to anger with Foreign Office personnel and just as quick to be conciliatory. One official summarised the difference between Ernest Bevin, Foreign Secretary from 1945 to 1951, and Eden: 'Bevin wouldn't throw a book at your head.' Eden's knowledge of international affairs only added to this shortness of temper. Shuckburgh, Eden's Private Secretary at the Foreign Office from 1952 to 1954, wrote:

Eden knew all about the Office and he seemed to me to know all about international affairs. On his arrival, my role as Private Secretary suddenly took on a different aspect; instead of being concerned to explain and justify the Foreign Secretary to the Office, I found myself justifying the Office to the Secretary of State and defending startled officers from his all-too-experienced and well-documented strictures.[54]

Conservative MPs in 1952 spoke of a 'nervy' Eden 'always losing his temper in Cabinet, Foreign Office, and elsewhere'. Small incidents continued to unsettle him. For example, in 1955, the new Prime Minister noted that a policeman at Hyde Park Corner had not saluted his car. He asked his Press Secretary, William Clark, 'Why didn't he salute? Are they all Communists now?'[55]

Three influences exacerbated Eden's temperamental nature. Firstly, his second marriage to Churchill's niece, Clarissa, in 1952 reinforced his ambition. The union, in contrast to Eden's first marriage, was a happy one. To many observers, Clarissa was attractive, intelligent and devoted to her husband's happiness. She was also very protective of his reputation, treating criticism of him as a personal attack, and her sense of dignity was easily offended. In an incident seized upon by the press in January 1956, she requested that a tenant on the grounds of Chequers, the Prime Minister's country mansion, move a line of washing where it could not be seen by the public.[56]

Clarissa's effect upon her husband also intruded upon Government business. She resented praise of R. A. Butler, the Chancellor of the Exchequer from 1951 to 1955, whom she considered her husband's rival for the succession to Churchill, and regarded other politicians with suspicion. She was also affected by her cousin, Randolph Churchill. As leader writer for the *Evening Standard*, he was a vehement critic of the Prime Minister, and he often called Clarissa to tease her to 'the verge of hysteria, tears and fury'. Philip de Zulueta, Eden's Private Secretary at 10 Downing Street, summarised that her influence on Eden was 'disastrous', as she was 'always stirring up Anthony when he didn't need it, and did not calm him'.[57]

Even after Eden's accession to the Premiership, many diplomats perceived Clarissa as a significant catalyst for her husband's behaviour. At the Geneva Summit of 1955, one of Foster Dulles's aides, Roderick O'Connor, complained:

Mr Eden . . . was quite interested in keeping this impression of glamour, as much to [Clarissa] as to the public. He was obviously taking sunbaths or a sunlamp every day, because throughout the entire conference he had a blooming, vigorous tan. He was quite chagrined, I think, because he didn't come out of the conference as the outstanding diplomat.[58]

Secondly, Churchill's delay in the transfer of power to Eden was a continual irritant. When Churchill was elected in October 1951, he spoke of handing over to Eden within a year, but the Prime Minister's love of power and the role of international statesman postponed his departure until April 1955. Eden chafed under the wait. As the months passed, he developed a 'constant anxiety about the Premiership [and] impatience with the Prime Minister for staying on, for fear [that] some other aspirant might overtake him in the race for the succession'.[59]

Relations between Eden and Churchill were also tested by the latter's attention to foreign affairs. Differences between them over the conduct of the Anglo-Egyptian negotiations and the Prime Minister's desire to mediate a Soviet-American rapprochement led to lengthy and heated arguments which depressed Eden for days afterwards. The Foreign Secretary often talked of retirement or a transfer to another Ministry.[60]

Finally, Eden was perpetually affected by his health. Throughout his career, he suffered from a number of ailments, aggravated by stress and overwork, but he nearly lost his life in 1953, when, during an operation to remove gallstones, a surgeon cut the biliary duct. Two more operations, one in America, removed the immediate danger, but the duct could not be repaired completely. The bile seeping into Eden's bloodstream acted as a steady poison, keeping him in constant pain. Periodically, inflammation of the bile duct would trigger a high fever. Although the fever only lasted for twenty-four to seventy-two hours, Eden would be languid for days after the attack.

From 1953, Eden relied on painkillers, notably Pethidin, commonly used for women during childbirth. Shuckburgh wrote that Eden was always accompanied on his travels by an assortment of analgesics, ranging from aspirin to morphine. The claim of William Clark that Eden, after his bouts of fever, used amphetamines to break his lassitude cannot be confirmed, although a senior Whitehall official said that Eden admitted 'practically living on Benzedrine'.[61]

Yet it was only after Eden's accession as Prime Minister that these influences adversely affected his performance. Andrew Stark, Eden's Private Secretary in 1954, recalled:

Although his health had periods of fitfulness, Eden liked the excitement of the job and loved particularly the tensions of it. He was succeeding in his efforts, which makes all the difference. He was achieving. He liked the excitement as long as it was working.[62]

At 10 Downing Street, increased responsibility brought an increased workload and, with it, increased stress. As one Foreign Office official noted: 'If Eden had been run over by a bus in 1955, he would have gone down in history as a great Foreign Secretary.'[63] Eden, the specialist in international affairs, struggled to cope with domestic issues. Never a sociable man in Whitehall and the Commons, he had few friends among his peers. Moreover, his relations with key Cabinet members, notably Butler and Macmillan, were strained.[64] Some Conservative back-benchers noted in April 1955: 'Eden, Butler and Macmillan are "not a triumvirate, but a trinity". . . . The others will be watching Eden and . . . he may well be pole-axed in 18 months' time.' Butler remarked: 'Anthony's father was a mad baronet and his mother a very beautiful woman. That's Anthony – half mad baronet, half beautiful woman.'[65]

Tensions were exacerbated by Eden's persistent interventions, by phone and memoranda, in the affairs of his Ministers. Eden later described this as his adherence to former Prime Minister Stanley Baldwin's 'method of frequent consultation alone with each of his principal colleagues', but it soon provoked resentment, especially from Macmillan. The Foreign Secretary wrote: 'It was quite clear that Eden wanted to get rid of me; he kept on sending me little notes, sometimes 20 a day, ringing up all the time. He really should have been both Prime Minister and Foreign Secretary.' After one clash with the Prime Minister in August 1955 over ALPHA, Macmillan opined, 'I might as well give up and let him run the shop.'[66]

The Prime Minister's relationship with the press was also tenuous. As Foreign Secretary, Eden, persistently worried about his image, was obsessed by the media:

A facet of Eden's worry about his succession was his intense preoccupation with what was said about him – or not said about him – in the press. . . . Neither of the

Edens could wholly rid themselves of the idea that Foreign Office influence with the press, such as it was, should be used to support the Secretary of State's personal ambitions in the Government.[67]

By October 1955, he was commenting that leaders in the *Daily Telegraph* were 'worse than anything the Nazis had ever done' and summoning the editor of the *Daily Mail* to reprimand him.[68]

Eden's social contacts with newspaper owners and editors were far from relaxed. As the US Embassy assessed, 'Lady Eden appears to have created rivals and even enemies in London society whose influence unfortunately extends beyond the drawing room.' Michael and Pamela Berry, the owners of the *Daily Telegraph* and traditional supporters of the Conservative Party, disliked the Edens, possibly because of Eden's avoidance of social functions organised by Lady Berry. She once asked the Labour Party leader, 'Tell me, Mr Gaitskell, is it possible to get rid of a Prime Minister in peacetime?' Neither the *Telegraph*'s editor, Sir Colin Coote, nor the assistant editor, Donald McLachlan, had a high opinion of the Prime Minister. The publications of Lord Beaverbrook, a friend of Churchill, had considered Eden too 'soft' since his pursuit of the Anglo-Egyptian negotiations. Eden's Press Secretary, Clark, had been a journalist at the *Observer*, and he maintained excellent contacts with the press; however, he was overburdened with the projection of the Government's policies, let alone the Prime Minister's personal campaigns. The anti-Eden press was bolstered by Conservative dissidents, including the Suez Group, and, possibly, Cabinet members. The Berrys, Coote and the colourful Conservative MP, Robert Boothby, all supported Macmillan to succeed Eden.[69]

While Eden produced diplomatic successes, there was no need to worry about press coverage. His accession as Churchill's 'heir', a general election in May 1955 which increased the Government's majority in the Commons, and the Geneva Summit in July, the first meeting between the British, American, and Soviet heads of government since 1945, maintained Eden's image as a great statesman. Within months, however, the Prime Minister was in trouble. A tax-cutting budget, issued just before the general election in the spring, eventually fuelled inflation and worsened trade deficits, threatening the stability of the pound. By the autumn, journalists reported increasing dissatisfaction, especially among businessmen, with Eden's delays in reorganising the Government and tackling inflation. The *Spectator*, a right-wing journal, commented:

There is a terrifying lack of authority at the top. It becomes more and more clear that, contrary to what many Conservatives said, Sir Winston Churchill was far more important as a directing, energizing force than even his colleagues realized.[70]

 Amidst the economic and political problems of the Eden Government, the Middle East held a low priority. The Anglo-Egyptian Treaty, signed despite the efforts of the Suez Group, and the Baghdad Pact had been secured. ALPHA's top-secret status kept the Arab-Israeli issue off the public agenda. While Egyptian propaganda was an irritant, especially for Eden, it was of little concern to the British public.

All this changed when Colonel Gamal Abdel Nasser, with some help from the Soviets and the CIA, made a speech in September 1955.

4

The Search for an Egyptian Policy
September–October 1955

T he Americans' immediate objective, upon confirmation of the
Egyptian-Soviet arms deal, was to block its announcement.
However, the CIA, for unknown reasons, had little confidence
in Ambassador Byroade, and the State Department suspected that
Byroade was too close to Nasser to be objective. On 20 September, the
Ambassador cabled Washington with bitterness:

I find it impossible to understand why I have not been informed of Department's
reasoning in turning down repeated and increasingly urgent recommendations
[for the sale of arms to Egypt]. . . . By our unwillingness to manipulate a few
million dollars, we are permitting the situation to deteriorate to a point where a
chain reaction of nature that will constitute a major defeat for US policy in the
Middle East, as contrasted to that of the Soviet bloc, is highly probable.

Byroade had also upset Nasser by talking to his British counterpart about
the arms deals, and the Egyptian President had turned to the CIA station
to keep Washington informed. Undersecretary of State Hoover told
Foster Dulles the same day:

Apparently there are misunderstandings and difficulties with respect to our man
[Byroade] who is there, and [I] would not feel satisfied we had done everything in
our power unless [the CIA's] Kim [Roosevelt] could go himself and talk with
[Nasser]. That would probably raise an explosion on the part of our man
[Byroade] there . . . but enough is involved, if it is true, that we should not let it
stand in our way.[1]

Foster Dulles agreed. The CIA station chief in Cairo, James
Eichelberger, contacted Nasser's confidant, Mohammed Heikal, to ask
the Egyptian President to 'keep his pants on' until Roosevelt, ac-

companied by Miles Copeland, who served in Cairo from 1953 to 1955, met Nasser on 23 September. Roosevelt, realising that the arms deal was a fait accompli, surprised Nasser by suggesting that the Egyptian leader, who wanted to keep the deal secret, make a speech containing a gesture of peace towards the Israelis. Nasser assented, and an American-Egyptian working party began drafting the statement.[2]

Foster Dulles reported to Eisenhower, who was at the 'Western White House' in Denver, Colorado: 'It seems to be authentic that [the Soviets] are giving a massive lot of arms to the Egyptians, theoretically to be paid for by cotton – it is $100 million worth.' Foster Dulles considered a propaganda offensive against the deal, but dismissed the idea: 'The Army will overthrow him [Nasser] if he refuses to take it. [I don't] think he is happy about it but he is held in power by the Army.' He did not mention the Roosevelt mission to the President.[3]

The following morning, Eisenhower suffered a major heart attack. He was cut off from all business for two weeks and only received a general account of events until his return to Washington in early November. Foster Dulles was left in command of American policy. CIA Director Allen Dulles confirmed to his operatives in Cairo, 'Nasser remains our best hope and we believe State Department will within limits of overall policy cooperate to mitigate long-term effects of arms deal if Nasser in turn cooperates.'[4]

The British, who were not told about the Roosevelt mission and relied on the Americans for their limited information about the impending Egyptian-Soviet deal,[5] were in disarray. Shuckburgh recommended a 'vigorous effort' to persuade Egypt to abandon the deal, but could only suggest an approach by Byroade and the British Ambassador, Humphrey Trevelyan, to Nasser. Francis Russell, in London to discuss ALPHA with Shuckburgh, suggested American accession to the Baghdad Pact and guarantee of Israel's frontiers, but Shuckburgh rejected the guarantee as 'fatal to the Western position' with the Arabs. He continued, 'We must somehow keep Egypt on our side even to the extent of paying a very heavy price which may well include having to abandon Israel.'[6]

Deputy Undersecretary Harold Caccia, reviewing the Shuckburgh–Russell talks, had another idea: 'We may have to get rid of Nasser, especially if he becomes publicly committed to the contract.' Macmillan's only immediate response was to berate the new Egyptian Ambassador, but the Foreign Secretary privately seethed: 'We really cannot allow this man, who has neither the authority of a throne nor of a Parliament, to destroy our base and threaten our rear.'[7]

The Foreign Office did not realise that the matter was in the hands of the CIA, who had no desire to be rid of Nasser. On 26 September,

Roosevelt, Copeland and Nasser spent three and a half hours discussing the draft announcement of the arms deal, including the passage offering an Egyptian-Israeli détente. Nasser 'drew [the] line at outright conciliation gesture towards immediate future ("deaths [of] Egyptian soldiers too fresh in memories our people")', but agreed to a statement 'asserting peaceful intentions and stating desire [to] discuss directly with Secretary Dulles concrete steps to reduce Arab-Israeli tensions'.[8]

A duty officer interrupted to say that the British Ambassador had requested a meeting with Nasser. Through the window, the Egyptian President and the Americans watched Trevelyan's car travel from the British Embassy across the Nile River to Nasser's apartment. Roosevelt advised Nasser to tell Trevelyan that the arms were being supplied not by the Soviet Union but by Czechoslovakia, then he and Copeland went upstairs.[9]

The meeting with Trevelyan was brief. The Ambassador issued Macmillan's warning that the deal could 'not be allowed to go on', but Nasser calmly replied that the deal was done. It had been completed '10 or 12 days ago' after he had 'waited for months and got nothing' from the West. His only consolation for Trevelyan was that, as 'the British had dominated Egypt for 70 years, . . . he had no intention of substituting Russian for British domination'. Meanwhile, 'it was all very cheerful [upstairs]', according to Copeland, with 'jokes about what would have been the look on the British Ambassador's face had Kim or I interrupted his meeting with Nasser to ask, "Excuse me, Gamal, but we're out of soda."'[10]

After Trevelyan left, Nasser and the Americans drove to the residence of a relative of Ahmed Hussein, the Egyptian Ambassador to the US, meeting Byroade, Eric Johnston and Eichelberger. The meeting was congenial until a 'tired and emotional' Byroade complained about the beating of the US Embassy's Labour Attaché by Egyptian workers in the Suez Canal Zone. Nasser, who had previously complained about the Attaché's activities, replied that the Attaché 'was spying and provoked some of the workers'. Byroade, losing all sense of diplomacy, criticised the 'Egyptian police state' and described the Revolutionary Command Council as 'a lot of juvenile delinquents'. When he added, 'One of my men is badly beaten and you try to make excuses for those who did it. I don't understand it,' Nasser replied, 'All right. If you don't understand it, we had better leave until you do.'[11]

Byroade and Nasser were used to speaking 'frankly' with each other, and the Egyptian President soon dismissed the incident. The argument, however, worsened the tenuous relations between the CIA and Byroade, and Roosevelt and Johnston asked Washington to recall the Ambassador because of his 'extraordinary behaviour'. Learning of the cable the morning after his outburst, Byroade telephoned the CIA man at a 'safe house' and demanded to see the message. When Roosevelt hesitated, the Ambassador warned, 'If you don't bring that Goddamn cable here, I'm coming over with my Marine guard and taking it.' Roosevelt gave in. An embittered Byroade cabled the State Department:

Neither I nor any member of the embassy staff under my control have taken any part in encouraging Nasser to make a statement. . . . Neither were messages which apparently have been available to you from Cairo on this subject shown to me or my staff.[12]

The situation was further complicated when Foster Dulles and Macmillan, in New York for the opening of the UN General Assembly, 'got more and more worked up' as they discussed Egypt. Shuckburgh recorded:

The thought of Soviet technicians sitting on the airfields which we built, and to which we have to return in case of an emergency under the [Anglo-Egyptian] Treaty, was too much for HM [Macmillan], and Dulles could not bear the ingratitude for the money US has spent on [Egypt].[13]

Macmillan asserted, 'We could even make life impossible for Nasser and ultimately bring about his fall by various pressures.'[14]

The next day, Foster Dulles told Hoover of the meeting's conclusions:

We have a lot of cards to play with Nasser although they are mostly negative. The waters of the Upper Nile – we can strangle him if we want to. We can develop the Baghdad group and ruin the cotton market. We can switch this year's economic aid from Egypt to Iraq.[15]

In a personal letter, Foster Dulles threatened Nasser with the consequences of his actions: 'It is possible that you may not have realized fully the seriousness with which such a transaction will be viewed in the US and the consequent difficulty of preventing it from marring the existing good relations between our two peoples.' Noting that the US had assisted Egypt in the Anglo-Egyptian negotiations, provided economic and military aid, and revised her cotton policy to prevent damage to the Egyptian economy, Foster Dulles implied that American policy could be reversed at any time.[16]

Foster Dulles's choice of confrontation undermined the CIA's accommodation with Nasser. He informed the US Embassy in Cairo:

We do not believe that any statement by Nasser about Egypt's peaceful intent in making arms pact with Soviet [Union] will serve to mitigate in any substantial degree inevitable public reaction in US and elsewhere and he should not be encouraged to believe that it would.

Coincidentally, the Foreign Office leaked information of the arms deal to British newspapers, who published the story on 27 September. Outraged, Nasser removed Copeland's paragraph on détente with Israel, replaced it with an anti-American passage, and reserved radio time for his speech. An emergency meeting with Roosevelt softened Nasser's rhetoric, but it did not restore Copeland's paragraph.[17]

Not only had the Roosevelt mission failed to ease the blow of the arms deal, but it had also disrupted the work of the US Embassy in Cairo. On 28 September, Foster Dulles told Hoover that Byroade should be recalled for consultations. Hoover agreed, but noted that Byroade was supposed to deliver Foster Dulles's warning letter to Nasser. He pondered, 'Johnston and Kim [Roosevelt] cannot do it. On the other hand, we might send [George] Allen there.' Foster Dulles agreed. Allen would also 'find out *re* the relationship between Byroade and Nasser. . . . It [was] impossible to have a crisis and no recourse to the head of government.'[18]

The plan backfired. Nasser perceived that Foster Dulles was circumventing Roosevelt, just as the CIA had circumvented Byroade, because the policy of confrontation had triumphed in Washington. He warned Roosevelt: 'I will throw [Allen] out' if he delivered an ultimatum. Roosevelt appealed to Washington for 'no leaks to press of message Allen is bringing in'.[19]

When Allen arrived at Cairo airport on 30 September, Byroade boarded the plane and warned him, 'If you say anything about an ultimatum, your ass is out of here right now.' General Hassan Touhami, an associate of Nasser and a CIA contact, followed Byroade with a similar message from Roosevelt and Johnston. Allen told waiting reporters that his trip was a routine visit to a Middle Eastern country. Few believed him, but the veneer of goodwill was intact.[20]

Nasser finally received Allen the next day after allowing him to linger in the waiting-room for one and a half hours. To soften the tone of Foster Dulles's letter, Allen did not show it to Nasser, but read the text, changing 'I' to 'we' throughout and covering Foster Dulles's signature. Nasser simply noted 'the change in the Israeli situation last February' and reminded Allen that the US had not replied to numerous Egyptian arms requests. He concluded: 'I have been through a nightmare since [Gaza] which your Secretary of State may not be able to realize.' Allen was given no chance to expand on the contents of Foster Dulles's message. A second meeting on 3 October was equally futile.[21]

Meanwhile, the Foreign Office and State Department reviewed long-term policy towards Egypt. British officials considered Caccia's idea of removing Nasser from power. Even Shuckburgh, who advocated conciliation because of ALPHA, wrote: 'We must first try to frighten Nasser, then to bribe him, and, if neither works, get rid of him.' T. E. Bromley of the African Department, who had advocated arms shipments to Egypt throughout 1955, now concluded that Britain 'might in the last resort have . . . to try to overthrow Nasser . . . to stop the rot, since once Russian technicians are in Egypt, there is no knowing how far the damage may extend'. It was left to A. J. Wilton, the desk officer for Egypt, to point out the flaw in the policy: 'No outstanding military figure or group . . . [can] consolidate the loyalty of the armed forces. . . . A Syrian-pattern situation would most probably develop with rival military figures rising and falling rapidly.' The Wafd party might try to reorganise itself or ally with a military group, but this would be difficult because the Wafd did 'not command any particular emotional loyalty'.[22]

Shuckburgh, visiting Washington, was asked by Allen Dulles 'whether [the British] thought [former Egyptian President] Neguib would be a possible alternative'. The idea was dismissed because Neguib, under house arrest since his removal from the Presidency in October 1954, had faded from public view and commanded little support within the Egyptian armed forces. Instead, the State Department 'had various suggestions for "squeezing" Egypt by cutting off economic aid, etc., and . . . mentioned again the alternative policy of joining the Northern Tier and trying to get other Arab States in'. Other possible measures included a refusal to help Egypt in the international cotton market and pressure on the World Bank to withhold funding for the Aswan High Dam.[23]

Following the State Department's lead, the Foreign Office concluded that a far-reaching regional policy, rather than direct action against Nasser, was the best option. Ivone Kirkpatrick, the Permanent Under-secretary, might have persisted with plans to overthrow Nasser, as he was convinced that the Egyptian leader was controlled by the Soviets, but he was on vacation. Caccia cabled Macmillan on 30 September: '[The] main object should not be to oust Nasser or, far less, to damage Egypt.' Instead, Britain should stop or limit the arms deal and demonstrate to other Arab countries that Egypt's policy would not benefit her in the long run. The US should be brought into the Baghdad Pact, military aid should be increased to Iraq, and the Sudan should be pressed to announce her independence, precluding any possibility of Egyptian control of her affairs.

Caccia argued that a comprehensive programme against Egypt 'might even discredit Nasser to the point where he was removed by Egyptian processes alone. . . . If this came about, it would have happened without our direct interference in Egyptian politics.' He concluded:

We should prefer to see the effects of the positive acts . . . before a decision is taken that we, i.e. the Americans and ourselves, must try to oust Nasser. It may come to that later. Even then we should be careful not to damage our best candidate by too obvious or too early sales-promotion.[24]

The 'best candidate' was the septuagenarian Ali Maher, the former Prime Minister who had been dismissed by the Revolutionary Command Council in September 1952, and who had been agitating against the regime throughout 1955. In April he told an American contact, 'The RCC is diabolically clever: it is using Soviet intelligence methods, German police and propaganda methods, and British bribery to keep itself in office.' He claimed that there were between 10,000 and 30,000 political prisoners, including 8,000 students, in Egypt and argued that assassination was the only option for a change of government. He also sent an emissary to see Ambassador Stevenson. He was a questionable choice to succeed Nasser, lacking both the support of the armed forces and the political machinery of the Wafd, but there was no foreseeable alternative.[25]

Yet another shift in American policy precluded consideration of this long-term programme. At dinner on 2 October, according to Macmillan, Foster Dulles

took the gravest and most pessimistic view. . . . The Egyptian deal was not an isolated event. The Russians were corrupting also Syria, Saudi Arabia, and trying Libya. They would soon start on Iraq. . . . Dulles asked if we had enough troops to reoccupy Egypt.[26]

However, the CIA station in Cairo and State Department officials, trying to convince Foster Dulles 'that Nasser did not want to go over to the Communist side' but hoped to play a neutralist role in the Middle East, were recommending less drastic long-term measures. By 30 September, Shuckburgh reported to Macmillan that the State Department had agreed 'on the need to distinguish between discrediting Nasser and hurting Egyptians', using the economic measures mentioned to Shuckburgh in Washington.[27]

Conferring with Macmillan on 3 October, Raymond Hare, Foster Dulles's unofficial adviser on the Middle East, explained:

Consideration could . . . be given to the application of progressive pressure but, in so doing, we should bear in mind the complications which could arise if Nasser were forced out with no better candidate in sight; difficulty in taking any constructive regional steps if Egypt were forced into a hostile position; the ominous prospect of promoting a real split in the Arab world with the West backing one group and the Communists the other.

Foster Dulles added, 'We should not take any threatening or drastic step at this time. . . . Unpleasant events which we might instigate should have the appearance of happening naturally.' It was 'not a very attractive policy but . . . [there was a] lack of a better alternative'. Macmillan agreed: 'We must accept this diplomatic defeat and try to narrow and limit it. . . . We should now talk to Nasser more in sorrow than in anger and tell him that he must endeavour to reduce his commitment with the Soviet bloc.'[28]

Reverting to his initial reaction to the arms deal, Foster Dulles told his brother Allen that it was 'difficult to be critical of countries which, feeling themselves endangered, seek the arms which they sincerely need for defense'. On 22 September, the Israelis had occupied the demilitarised zone of El Auja, only withdrawing after UN protests. In a speech on 2 October, Nasser displayed French documents indicating that 120 aircraft, 115 tanks and 100 armoured cars had been supplied to Israel, and a British intelligence report of May 1955 stating that 'there was every reason to believe that Egypt had no aggressive intentions of any kind'. Both documents were later verified as authentic by British officials.[29]

Moreover, Eden, despite his anger at Egyptian propaganda, offered no opposition to Soviet arms shipments to Cairo, as he was occupied with his possible leadership of East–West co-operation. Apart from asking Macmillan for 'an estimate from our Ambassador in Cairo as to Nasser's present position, the extent of his support, and the chances of any rival, e.g. AM [Ali Maher],'[30] he left the question of dealing with Nasser to the Foreign Office and concentrated on an accommodation with the Soviet Union. To achieve this goal, he was willing to accept the arms deal.

Trevelyan had concluded on 26 September:

I see no reason that [Nasser] would not have preferred to get arms from the West and [he] only decided to accept the Soviet offer when he felt he could wait no longer in the face of increased tension on the Gaza frontier and internal pressure. . . . A thorough reversal of our policy of friendship to Egypt could hurt her to a certain extent but would extensively damage our own interests here and endanger our interests elsewhere.

Eden commented: 'I am much impressed by [Trevelyan's] force and cogency. We must not cut off our noses.' As for the Soviets, Britain had 'nothing to hide and it [was] surely better that the four Powers should discuss the situation than we should embark on arms competition'. By 29 September, Eden was anxious to send a personal message to the Soviet Premier, Nikolai Bulganin.[31]

The State Department was concerned that Eden's initiative would set the precedent of consulting the Soviets on Middle Eastern matters. Macmillan agreed with the Americans, and in several days of debate with Eden via cable requested a delay in the despatch of the message to Bulganin.[32] The Prime Minister commented: 'If we'd waited on the

Americans, I'd never have gone round Europe after EDC [the European Defence Community] was smashed, we'd never have had a Geneva Conference. They're always unprepared to act.'[33] Eden wanted to ignore Macmillan, but finally decided to obtain Cabinet approval on 4 October. To pursue his initiative, he was willing to sacrifice Anglo-American co-operation:

Our interests in the Middle East were greater than those of the US because of our dependence on Middle Eastern oil and our experience in the area was greater than theirs. We should not, therefore, allow ourselves to be restricted overmuch by reluctance to act without full American concurrence and support. We should form our own policy in the light of our interests in the area and get the Americans to support it to the extent we could induce them to do so.

While the message to Bulganin did not propose a four-power conference, it asked the Soviet Union to consider the 'special responsibilities' of the Great Powers.[34]

Eden's personal venture did not override long-term Foreign Office policy, however. The Cabinet of 4 October noted that it was 'inadvisable to subject the Nasser regime to overwhelming pressure. It was doubtful whether such pressure could be made effective and a rebuff would be bad for our prestige in the Middle East.' Instead, Egypt should be isolated in the Arab world through increased arms supplies by Britain to her Arab allies. Macmillan also received Cabinet agreement to offer arms to Iran to bring her into the Baghdad Pact and to offer the Sudan immediate independence.[35]

The immediate task was to co-ordinate British and American policies. Foster Dulles and Macmillan had established a close working relationship, but British Ministers wanted strong and decisive action, even if this conflicted with American interests. Ambassador Makins summarised:

We have advanced ahead of the Americans on three fronts, the Russian, the Persian, and the Iraqi. . . . While I fancy that [Foster] Dulles has taken this in good part, there is a risk (perhaps not too great) that they may not come up to us, or go off at a tangent, and that we may find ourselves out on one of these various limbs.[36]

The first point of contention was Iranian accession to the Baghdad Pact. British qualms about the cost of strengthening Iranian forces, strongly expressed by Eden and shared by Macmillan,[37] were removed by the Egyptian-Soviet arms deal. The Foreign Secretary informed Foster Dulles on 26 September of his changed position and cabled Eden: 'One of the cards we may want to play in offsetting the Egyptians' arms deal with Czechoslovakia may be general strengthening of the Baghdad Pact.'

At a Ministerial meeting on 5 October, the Chiefs of Staff cited the strategic advantages of Iranian accession. Eden, noting Iraqi support of the measure, agreed.[38]

Foster Dulles was hesitant, telling Allen Dulles, 'Russia might regard it as a reprisal against Egypt and any hopes of quietening the situation would disappear and it would lead to a step against us and things would be worse.' To fend off the Joint Chiefs of Staff, who favoured Iranian accession as a riposte to the Soviets, Foster Dulles complained to Secretary of Defense Wilson about the cost of rearming the Iranians.[39] In the end, however, Foster Dulles decided that he would not risk breaking American ties with Iran. On 11 October, when the Iranians announced their intention to join the Baghdad Pact, the State Department followed the Foreign Office's lead in publicly welcoming the news.[40]

With the possible crisis over Iran averted, both the Americans and the British reviewed long-term Middle Eastern policy. The National Security Council restated its commitments, made in July 1954, to act against any aggressor, Arab or Israeli, and its intention to collaborate and develop plans 'with the UK, and to the extent desirable and feasible, with France and Turkey'. Specific economic and military actions, including suspension of aid, a trade embargo and naval blockade, would be considered with the British. Foster Dulles would inform the Arabs and Israelis privately that the US would 'seek to prevent resort to armed aggression by either Israel or the Arab States and, if it should occur, seek to stop it quickly'.[41]

The British reappraisal was spurred by a report by the Foreign Office's Robert Belgrave, which noted that Britain spent, apart from her obligations under the Anglo-Jordanian Treaty and to the United Nations Relief and Works Administration, less than £2.25 million per year in the Middle East, although most of the 300 per cent increase in British consumption and production of oil over the next twenty years would come from the region. The Cabinet approved the principle 'that our position in the Middle East is vital to the economy of the UK and that Her Majesty's Government should be prepared to spend in the area on a scale more closely related to our essential interests there'. A working party was established to draft recommendations for expenditure.

Macmillan reiterated the Foreign Office's formula to counter the Soviet Union's 'deliberate policy of opening up another front in the Cold War':

We should adapt a policy of moderation in our dealing with Egypt and we should endeavour to persuade the Americans to do the same. We should concentrate on helping other Arab States who behaved loyally, while at the same time demonstrating that there were limits to the extent to which we could be provoked.

Eden agreed, but, like Foster Dulles, considered the possibility of wooing Cairo back to the West. In particular, funding for the Aswan High Dam 'could be a trump card'. The Cabinet agreed.[42]

The first Aswan Dam across the Nile was built in 1902 and heightened in 1912 and 1933, but its extension could not provide an adequate supply of water for the rapidly growing Egyptian population. In 1947, a Greek engineer presented the Egyptians with a plan for a new dam, 100 metres high, 800 metres long and 1,000 metres wide at the base. The proposal was considered, but shelved until the military took power.[43]

In spring 1953, the Egyptians appointed consulting engineers from Britain, Sweden, Italy and the US, and Eugene Black, the President of the World Bank, endorsed the Dam's construction. Byroade, then Assistant Secretary of State, and Eisenhower also recommended the initiative, but financial constraints forced Foster Dulles to reject American assistance for the project in July.[44]

The Egyptians continued to negotiate with a private Anglo-German consortium, but plans were in the preliminary stages when the Soviets offered to finance the Dam in October 1955. This prompted Eden to set aside his call for 'independence' of the Americans in the Middle East, and on 21 October he asked the US Embassy to raise the issue of the Dam with the State Department.[45]

On 26 October, Macmillan and Foster Dulles met to reconcile the developing policies amidst reports that Egypt would sign a defence pact with Syria and Saudi Arabia the following day. Although Shuckburgh wrote that there was 'little unanimity and few ideas of what to do', Macmillan was optimistic. Foster Dulles was ready 'to try to get the Aswan Dam for a Western group', and the Americans agreed to send political and military observers to the first meeting of the Baghdad Pact Council in November. Foster Dulles also hinted at accommodation with the British policy on Jordan and Syria. According to Macmillan, 'Mr Dulles asked me whether we could not bring pressure upon Jordan to join the Baghdad Pact. He thought it would be a fine thing if they did.' Foster Dulles was 'ready for counteraction in Syria', believing that it 'was the nearest thing in the Middle East to a Soviet satellite'. While the Secretary noted, 'It would be hard for [the US] to be benevolent about an Iraqi attack upon Syria,' Macmillan maintained that Foster Dulles 'was moving in the direction of being less averse to, if not wholly favouring, a coup d'état by the Iraqis'.[46]

By promoting discussions between Foster Dulles and Macmillan, the Egyptian-Soviet arms deal had taken the Anglo-American 'alliance' in the Middle East beyond ALPHA and military discussions. The CIA, although it could help persuade Foster Dulles that confrontation with

Egypt was unwise, no longer had the freedom to act independently of Britain, while those State Department officials who were suspicious of the British had no choice but to defer to the Secretary. Macmillan could not curb Eden's whims, but by advising caution and appealing to the Cabinet, he could stall the Prime Minister while warning the State Department of any forthcoming initiative.

Removal of Nasser from power was not a viable option because of the need for his co-operation in ALPHA and the lack of an alternative government, but a two-phase policy to protect the Western position could be developed. The provision of funds for the Aswan High Dam should persuade Nasser to co-operate with Britain and the US. If, however, the Egyptians continued to flirt with the Soviets, Cairo could be isolated by the development of the Baghdad Pact, support of Iraq and destabilisation of pro-Nasser governments such as the Syrian regime. The State Department and CIA concluded:

We should have one more good go-around with [Nasser] in an endeavor to reach an understanding. If we fail, then we can reassess our position and determine what to do next with considerably more flexibility than we feel free to do at present.[47]

No amount of informal planning, however, could substitute for a formal Anglo-American 'alliance' in the Middle East, and two significant problems remained. Firstly, Macmillan, who spent as much time abroad as he did in London, could not be a full-time minder to the Prime Minister, and Eden could suddenly circumvent the Cabinet to launch one of his projects. Secondly, although Foster Dulles and Macmillan were moving towards a general accord on the Middle East, differences remained. British Ministers and Foreign Office officials desired an 'activist' policy to counter any threat to British interests, but the Americans, whose position in Saudi Arabia was unchallenged, preferred a more cautious approach in their long-term effort to contain the Soviet Union. Even Macmillan believed that, in the end, Britain's position in the Arabian Peninsula and the Baghdad Pact could not wait for US acquiescence.

5

An Uneasy Partnership
October–December 1955

S ince the 1930s, ownership of the Buraimi oasis, lying between
Saudi Arabia and the Trucial Sheikhdoms of Abu Dhabi and
Muscat and Oman on the eastern coast of the Arabian Peninsula,
had been disputed. As American and British oil companies vied for the
rights to exploit Middle Eastern resources, they sought additional territory for exploration, and local rulers were eager to expand their kingdoms.
In 1933, King Ibn Saud of Saudi Arabia granted the concession for oil
exploration to a subsidiary of Standard Oil of California, later reorganised
as the Arabian-American Oil Company (ARAMCO). Meanwhile, the
British, cherishing not only the oil of the Sheikhdoms but also their
strategic position on the Persian Gulf and the Arabian Sea, secured the
thrones of the Sultans and encouraged them to set their borders as far
inland as possible. Immediate conflict was averted in 1935, when the
British Government promulgated the 'Red Line Agreement' defining the
boundary between Saudi Arabia and the Sheikhdoms, but the Saudis
never recognised the border.

Exploration indicated that the oasis's oil resources were negligible, but
the Saudis desired it as a bridge for access to the sea, while the British
sought Buraimi 'to consolidate the southeastern corner of the Arabian
Peninsula into a single political entity'.[1] The truce over Buraimi collapsed
in August 1952, when, after an Anglo-Saudi conference failed to reach
agreement, a Saudi envoy with forty horsemen established a base in one of
the oasis's eight villages. The British refused negotiations until the Saudis
left and tried to impose a blockade upon the occupied area, a measure
which angered the Eisenhower Administration and led to accusations of
'colonialism' during Lord Salisbury's visit to Washington in July 1953.

The blockade failed to dislodge the Saudis, and the British, as part of the reconciliation with the US in late 1954, agreed to arbitration by an international tribunal with one Briton, one Saudi and three 'neutral' representatives.

The proceedings soon degenerated, with each side accusing the other of bribing local tribes and maintaining military forces in the oasis. The British, who had suspected that American oil companies, allied with US Government officials, had used the nationalisation of the Anglo-Iranian Oil Company in 1951 to break the British monopoly and obtain a share of production, now believed that ARAMCO, collaborating with some State Department and CIA representatives, was assisting the Saudis. It was alleged that ARAMCO lorries were transporting Saudi troops into Buraimi and that CIA operatives were giving gold Cadillacs to village chiefs. The Foreign Office instructed its lawyer, Sir Hartley Shawcross, to emphasise 'the multitudes who have sold their tongues' to Saudi Arabia, but to exercise caution because '[British] witnesses have received quite large sums from us'.²

In September, the Foreign Office learned of the Tribunal's draft decision, which did not attribute bribery to either side: 'Incidents of subversion by either party have not been legally proved before the Tribunal but such incidents may have occurred. . . . The Tribunal requests both parties to prevent such incidents in accordance with the arbitration agreement.' More importantly, the Tribunal recommended, over British opposition, a central commission to oversee the oasis. No unilateral measures against the Saudis were adopted. Shuckburgh ordered the British representative on the tribunal, Sir Reader Bullard, to leave the proceedings.³

On 18 October, the Cabinet approved the abandonment of arbitration and the seizure of Buraimi. Eight days later, as Foster Dulles discussed Middle Eastern policy with Macmillan in Geneva, troops of the Trucial Sheikhdoms, led by British 'advisers', occupied the oasis. They allegedly discovered documents indicating that Saudi Arabia and ARAMCO were plotting to seize the territory.⁴

Foster Dulles expressed disdain for the British occupation to Macmillan on 26 October, noting, 'The King of Saudi Arabia had told us that he expects us to support him in his efforts against the British in the south,' but he was not 'unduly concerned' or 'unpleasant'.⁵ Other State Department officials were not as accommodating. Foster Dulles's deputy was Herbert Hoover Jr, the son of an American President whose relations with the British had been based on mutual suspicion. Hoover Jr had surveyed the Saudi oil reserves during the Second World War, as American and British diplomatic representatives competed for influence with King Ibn Saud. In 1954, after the overthrow of the Mossadegh Government, Hoover led the American delegation that negotiated with the British and the Iranians over the reorganisation of the Anglo-Iranian Oil Company. Short-tempered and hard of hearing, Hoover was far from the ideal diplomat, and he was convinced that the British were trying to sustain a Middle Eastern position that was doomed.

The day after the occupation, Hoover told Makins that 'he had been taken aback by [the British] action. . . . He hoped that, in the future, we would not think it necessary to "do that kind of business with one another" and that we would be able "to play it together from now on".'[6] Foster Dulles commented to Macmillan: 'Our people in Washington had been annoyed about the suddenness of the British action in Buraimi and the absence of any prior information about it.' An American intelligence report of 1 November assessed: 'The UK action [in Buraimi] may drive the Saudis and Egyptians together in the Gulf area.'[7]

Faced with the British fait accompli, the Americans did not press their objections, but the issue was far from resolved. Instead, it was overtaken by renewed Egyptian-Israeli conflict. An American intelligence report of 31 October warned that the atmosphere on the Egyptian-Israeli border was 'extremely tense, with an outbreak of fighting likely at any time. [US] Embassy Tel Aviv sees the possibility of wider hostilities.' Israel was expected to purchase $50 million of arms 'with heavy concentration on French jet planes and tanks'. The fears were soon justified. On 2 November, Ben-Gurion, formally taking office as Prime Minister, told the Knesset that he would meet Arab leaders to discuss a settlement. That evening an Israeli military force drove UN military observers out of the demilitarised zone and attacked the Egyptian village of El Auja, killing at least fifty people and taking forty prisoners.[8]

The State Department responded by warning the Israeli and Egyptian Ambassadors that it would support UN action against any aggressor in the area. The Israeli Chief of Staff, General Dayan, was undeterred. He called for 'an early confrontation with the Egyptian regime, which is striving toward a war for the destruction of Israel, in order to bring about a change of regime or a change in its policy', and presented Ben-Gurion with a plan to capture the Straits of Tiran, which controlled access to the Red Sea. Ben-Gurion requested postponement of the plan, but only because Foreign Minister Sharett was in the US seeking economic and military aid.[9]

The renewed fighting gave Eden, whose note to Soviet Premier Bulganin about the Egyptian-Soviet arms deal had produced no results, his opportunity to save the Middle East. Shuckburgh commented: 'It has occurred to [Eden] that with Eisenhower sick, [West German Chancellor

Konrad] Adenauer sick, Macmillan and Dulles engaged with Molotov in Geneva, there is only one great man left in the world capable of giving a lead and that is himself.'[10] The Prime Minister, with Kirkpatrick's help, had drafted a long message to Nasser 'to ask Egypt where she stands', but the Foreign Office rejected the initiatives as too risky. There were few inducements for Egyptian co-operation that Britain could offer uni-laterally, and Nasser might publicise Eden's approach, embarrassing the British.[11]

Eden then thought of inviting Egyptian and Israeli representatives to Cyprus, but internal disturbances on the island precluded this. However, G. G. Arthur of the Foreign Office had just examined new approaches to the Arab-Israeli problem and concluded:

I can only see one possibility: that we should move towards some acknowledge-ment of the validity of the [1947] UN resolution on Palestine. . . . [This] would be a blow to the Israelis, but we must face the fact that, if we are ever to bring about a Palestine settlement, we shall have to be nasty to the Israelis at some stage.

Eden incorporated the idea into his speech at the Lord Mayor's Dinner at the Guildhall on 9 November, suggesting a settlement on the basis of 'the 1947 and other United Nations resolutions'.[12]

Although Eden mentioned 'other United Nations resolutions', his reference to the 1947 resolution commanded attention. In the 1948–9 Arab-Israeli War, Israel gained territory beyond the 1947 boundaries. Occupying the Negev desert, she prevented any land link between Egypt and Jordan. Nasser called the speech the 'first constructive declaration since the Palestine War', but Ben-Gurion insisted that it had 'no legal, moral, or logical basis' and that it was likely to increase Arab aggression and lead to Israel's dismemberment. He told the US Ambassador, 'It is an attempt to eliminate Israel – not by [the] people of Great Britain but by [the] present government which considers Israel [a] nuisance and feels it could make [a] deal with Arab states if Israel no longer exists.'[13]

Undermining ALPHA, Eden's venture dealt another blow to the Anglo-American 'alliance'. Foster Dulles was not notified of the Prime Minister's initiative until a few hours before the speech.[14] He later told the National Security Council:

Eden had tried to drag him into supporting this speech at the very last moment, but . . . [he] had bucked at full endorsement. . . . It was plain enough that the UK was trying very hard to swing support over to the side of the Arabs and to regain the lost British position with the Arab States.[15]

The Americans were preoccupied with Sharett's visit to the US. Fearing that he would appeal to the American public for money and support, forcing the Administration to bow to public pressure and assist the Israelis, the White House issued a statement on 9 November:

While we continue willing to consider requests for arms needed for legitimate self-defense, we do not intend to contribute to an arms competition in the Near East because we do not think such a race would be in the true interest of any of the participants. . . . True security must be based upon a just and reasonable settlement [i.e. Foster Dulles's speech of 26 August].[16]

Antagonising the Israelis, the Guildhall speech made the Americans' task more difficult. By 11 November, Eden, worried about press reaction to his speech, abandoned his independent stance and sought American support. He wrote to Foster Dulles: 'I am sure that we must persevere and that we have the essentials of an agreement here,' but the long-term damage was done. The Israelis, who knew of secret Anglo-American discussions since the spring, always linked Guildhall with ALPHA. To them, Eden's speech meant that Britain's desire to return the Negev to the Arabs, possibly to establish British bases there, had triumphed over the general call for negotiations in Foster Dulles's statement. Eden's protests that the speech was not a commitment to the 1947 borders were dismissed by the Israelis, and the Prime Minister and Shuckburgh added to the furor, telling Israeli Ambassador Elath that 'if Israel would not accept Eden's proposals, she would damage herself'. Hoover wrote to Eisenhower: 'Eden's speech appears . . . to have undermined the British position in Israeli-Arab matters, leaving the US as the only arbiter in whom the Israelis still retain some confidence.'[17]

Yet Buraimi and Guildhall were overshadowed by Britain's attempt in December 1955 to obtain Jordanian accession to the Baghdad Pact, which defied American warnings that the project was ill-timed. On this occasion, the project could not be dismissed as Eden's whim, as it was a mission sanctioned by the Foreign Office, the British military and the Cabinet.

The genesis of the mission was a forthcoming visit to Amman by the Turkish President, Celal Bayar, to request Jordanian accession to the Pact. Eden minuted to Macmillan on 14 October that the idea was 'worth considering' as Britain 'must tie to [her] Treaty all Arab States we now can', but the Foreign Office was hesitant. Makins told Hoover that Britain did not believe that Jordan could be persuaded to join the Pact, 'but they did not want to discourage the Turkish Government'.[18]

Foster Dulles had suggested to Macmillan on 26 October that Britain encourage Jordanian accession, but the Secretary was soon influenced by officials who opposed an approach to Jordan. The result was a harmful ambivalence in American policy. On 1 November, a US Embassy official, acting on State Department and CIA instructions, told the Foreign Office that the US Ambassadors in Lebanon and Jordan would tell those Governments that accession to the Pact was undesirable at the moment. Two days later, Makins warned London that Foster Dulles's apparent support of Jordanian accession depended upon ALPHA's success. As late as 8 November, however, Francis Russell, the American envoy for ALPHA, informed Shuckburgh that the US had no objection to Jordan's accession 'if the Turks could persuade her to do so'.[19]

Amidst the uncertainty, the Foreign Office told the British Embassy in Amman that Turkey's efforts should be endorsed, and King Hussein told British Ambassador Duke on 9 November that Jordan was ready to join the Pact 'given the necessary backing'.[20] The same day Foster Dulles finally decided against Jordanian accession. Nasser confirmed to Byroade that he was 'ready to discuss Palestine on a confidential basis . . . if nothing new happened, meaning if neither the US nor any other Arab States should join [the Baghdad Pact]'. Foster Dulles told Macmillan:

The introduction into the Pact of Israel's neighbours presented a new problem and would make it more difficult for the US to support the Pact. Unless Lebanon, Syria, and Jordan were ready to make peace with Israel (which he doubted), he rather wondered whether it was wise to bring them in.[21]

The decision to proceed rested with Macmillan. Eden, concerned with the Guildhall speech, 'was beginning to wonder whether it was wise to press Jordan hard to join the Pact. This might rile the Egyptians, who were showing signs of being reasonable.' He also worried that, as 'Israel might be contemplating a preventive war in Jordan', Jordanian accession might pull Britain into a conflict with Tel Aviv. However, Macmillan, supported by Duke and General Sir John Glubb, the commander of Jordan's army, the Arab Legion, concluded that the need to strengthen the Baghdad Pact and support King Hussein outweighed the risk of upsetting Nasser, especially after the completion of the Egyptian-Saudi-Syrian Defence Pact in late October. On 19 November, Macmillan instructed Duke to tell Hussein that Britain welcomed 'early' Jordanian adherence to the Pact. The British would provide ten Vampire fighters as a 'gift' and would consider further supplies of equipment when 'Jordan had . . . taken her place in a Middle Eastern defence organisation'.[22]

Macmillan's opinion was reinforced at the Baghdad Pact Council by the Turks, who argued that Jordanian and Lebanese accession would be 'giving a positive example to all the countries of the Middle East'. Duke suggested that Britain double her annual subsidy of £10 million, providing an extra army division, if Amman joined the Pact. Shuckburgh, after conferring with Macmillan and General Sir Gerald Templer, the Chief of the Imperial General Staff, recommended an offer of tanks and guns, reaffirmation of the British guarantee under the Anglo-Jordanian Treaty, and more RAF fighters at Amman and Mafraq.[23]

Upon his return from the Baghdad Pact Council, Macmillan wrote to Eden:

> I very much fear that, if we do not get Jordan into the Baghdad Pact now, she will drift out of our control. . . . We should . . . present this to [the Jordanians] and more or less compel them to come in. In the final result, we may have to say that we cannot continue our financial and military support for a country which will not stay on our side in grave issues and then the Israelis will get them.

Shuckburgh noted on 25 November: 'Prime Minister is understood to have agreed with the policy considered.' Five days later, Macmillan approved Shuckburgh's idea that Templer should visit Jordan to arrange the accession.[24]

The Templer mission, which lasted from 7 to 14 December, was a diplomatic disaster. Although the King supported accession, the British overestimated the commitment of the Jordanian Government to the Pact. Four Palestinian Ministers from the West Bank blocked the Cabinet's approval of accession, and their resignations on 13 December toppled the Government. The formation of a new Cabinet under the pro-Pact Hazza Majali lifted Foreign Office hopes, at least for a Jordanian statement of intent to accede, but public demonstrations continued. As Duke left a meeting with the Jordanian Minister of the Interior, his car was stoned, one of the rocks breaking the fountain pen in his coat pocket. On 19 December, Hussein told Duke that Government officials were participating in the disturbances and some Cabinet Ministers were threatening to resign unless Prime Minister Majali issued a statement against the Pact. Reluctantly, Hussein, who relied not only upon the British subsidy but also on Saudi and CIA money to maintain his tenuous position, dissolved the Jordanian Parliament to try to restore order.[25]

Foster Dulles warned Macmillan on 6 December that, because of ALPHA, the US would not support the Templer mission: 'We need to keep in mind our present plans to make another try through Egypt towards an Arab-Israeli settlement. An immediate move to expand the Baghdad Pact would probably deny us Nasser's co-operation.' Templer's failure particularly upset Eisenhower, who wrote: 'The British never had any sense in the Middle East. . . . [I am] a little "afraid" of the results of the Baghdad Pact.'[26]

If the crisis over the Templer mission, added to the conflicts over Buraimi and Guildhall, had occurred during 1953–4, as the US was pursuing an 'independent' policy in the Middle East, it might have produced open conflict between Washington and London. By the end of 1955, however, British acceptance of American 'independence' and the American recognition of British influence were embodied in working relationships. Foster Dulles and Macmillan respected and admired each other, while Shuckburgh and Russell, who had become close friends, used ALPHA as the foundation for a regional plan.

On the day of the Guildhall speech, Shuckburgh and Russell drafted a paper defining Anglo-American co-operation. The two countries would 'not write off Egypt' for the moment, but 'if . . . Egypt [was] clearly lost to Western influence, [they] should have to consider policies which would minimise the harm which she could do to Western interests'. The US would 'maintain liaison with the Baghdad Pact Council and . . . give material support to its members', including the participation of American diplomatic and military observers in the Baghdad Pact Council's first meeting.[27]

The Shuckburgh–Russell discussions eased the turbulence caused by Guildhall, and the Egyptian reaction to Eden's speech was more positive than Washington expected. The Egyptian Foreign Minister, Mahmoud Fawzi, indicated that Egypt would start negotiations with Israel on border changes to provide an Egyptian-Jordanian frontier, some repatriation of Palestinian refugees to their homes in Israel with full compensation for the rest, and free transit through the Suez Canal. Nasser confirmed this on 27 November.[28]

Foster Dulles, still upset with Sharett's visit to the US, decided to confront him. He told the Foreign Secretary on 21 November that a settlement was essential for Israel's survival. The settlement might involve territorial adjustments by Israel, including part of the Negev, but its value to Israel was 'incomparably greater' than the cost of the concessions. Foster Dulles warned Sharett that Israeli refusal to compromise would 'put us all in great peril' and 'would be forcing us to make a very grave choice'.[29]

The State Department was anxious to arrange Egyptian-Israeli talks before the first Soviet arms shipment reached Cairo, forcing the US to consider increased aid to Israel. A special peace mission was first suggested in late October, with Arthur Dean, a friend of Foster Dulles, Dean Rusk, a future Secretary of State, and Milton Eisenhower, the President's brother, suggested as emissaries. On 28 November, Hoover proposed to Eisenhower that a mediator visit Cairo, and a further exchange with Sharett convinced Foster Dulles that, despite the Foreign

Minister's outward intransigence, Israel would accept a mediator and consider some territorial changes.[30]

Covert discussions between Nasser and CIA officials, and talks with Nasser's military liaison, Major Hassan Touhami, in Washington, established that Nasser would welcome American mediation.[31] The Americans also concluded that time was running short for a settlement. In September, the Egyptians had closed the Gulf of Aqaba to Israeli shipping, preventing Israel's access to the Red Sea, and the Israeli military and the Government predicted that Egyptian troops would be trained in the use of Soviet equipment and ready to attack in the summer. With the Johnston plan for division of the Jordan waters dormant, the Israelis were preparing to resume diversion of the river, even at the risk of war with Syria. Certain officials in Tel Aviv, notably Sharett, told American contacts that Nasser 'must be destroyed'. The US Embassy concluded:

Israelis have been hoping internal forces in Egypt, possibly aided and abetted by US, would bring about Nasser's downfall, particularly if Nasser was to receive setbacks as a result of localized military activities. This has not come about and Israelis are bit non-plussed by failure USG to adopt more vigorous policy towards Egypt since conclusion [of] latter's Soviet arms deal.[32]

On 8 December, Eisenhower endorsed a mission to Cairo and Tel Aviv. The State Department and the CIA approved Robert Anderson, a Texas oil man, close confidant of Eisenhower and former Secretary of the Navy, as the envoy. The Foreign Office was hesitant about the 'telescoping' of ALPHA through the use of a special representative, but deferred to the American lead, as Shuckburgh and Russell continued to confer over the settlement's details. On 5 January, Foster Dulles confirmed to Makins that Anderson would soon travel to the Middle East 'in the framework of our agreed policy'. The mission was codenamed BETA.[33]

The continuation of ALPHA implied that Britain and the US would still seek Nasser's co-operation. Their principal incentive was funding of the Aswan High Dam. In late October, Foster Dulles, under the influence of Hoover and Secretary of the Treasury Humphrey, wavered in his support for the project, but proceeded when Macmillan suggested 'telling Nasser we are prepared to undertake it if he meets two conditions: (1) not buying unnecessary arms; (2) settling with Israel'.[34] Eden, fretting that the Soviets might usurp the Western position, wrote to Eisenhower on 26 November: 'If the Russians were to succeed in this [aid to Egypt], they would, of course, be ruthless with the Sudan and abuse their control of the Nile waters. The outlook for Africa would be grim indeed.'[35]

Eisenhower asked Foster Dulles if there was 'any reason not to go out for the Dam in Egypt'. Foster Dulles wondered if 'Nasser [was] trying to get a bid and then let the Russians better the terms', but concluded: 'It is a risk we are taking but [I] think we have to.'[36]

When the National Security Council debated the issue on 1 December, Foster Dulles argued:

If the Egyptians accepted [aid for the Dam], it would certainly be impractical for Egypt to switch to a Soviet satellite status, at least while the project was in the course of construction. Moreover, the presence of so many engineers, technicians, and other people from the Free World in Egypt would constitute a strong influence in keeping Egypt on the side of the Free World.

Humphrey vigorously opposed the extension of foreign aid, but Eisenhower intervened to support Foster Dulles and dismiss Humphrey's fears of 'creeping socialism' and increased Egyptian cotton production competing with US output. The National Security Council agreed that the US would provide eighty per cent and Britain twenty per cent of the West's $200 million contribution to the project, matching the $200 million loaned by the World Bank. Egypt formally accepted the offer on 17 December, and the World Bank, Britain and the US agreed to send *aides-mémoire* to Egypt explaining the detailed conditions for provision of the assistance.[37]

Anglo-American co-operation now reached the highest level. Eisenhower was amenable to Eden's request, in his message of 26 November, for a summit in Washington on Middle Eastern questions. Foster Dulles worried that the summit would 'give a crisis atmosphere; [the British] will talk about the Baghdad Pact and making it into a second NATO', but Eisenhower declared, 'It might show after all we are people others like to come see. It is possible that by letting them come now, it will show a position of influence [for the US].' The next day, Eisenhower and Foster Dulles scheduled the meeting for late January.[38]

With agreement reached over ALPHA and policy towards Egypt, the outstanding problem for Foster Dulles and Macmillan was the reconciliation of American interests in Saudi Arabia with British opposition to Saudi activities. On 25 October, Foster Dulles told Macmillan of CIA information that the Egyptians were supplying arms to Saudi Arabia, who paid with royalties from ARAMCO.[39] At the Baghdad Pact Council meeting in November, the Iraqi Prime Minister, Nuri Sa'id, suggested that the US withhold Saudi royalties for six months to prevent Saudi funding of 'anti-Western' and 'anti-Iraqi' forces in Syria and Egypt.[40] Macmillan cabled Eden: 'It may be a question of Anglo/US action to upset King Saud [who had succeeded his father, King Ibn Saud, in late 1953] and remove this canker.'[41]

However, when Macmillan suggested a joint study of possible measures by American and British Governments and oil companies, Foster Dulles cautiously replied, 'I believe it would be useful for us to exchange information regarding Saudi activities but it will be difficult for us to reduce or control Saudi Arabia's income.'[42] On 15 December, at the NATO Council in Paris, Russell told Shuckburgh that 'some [State Department officials] were doubtful about the policy of giving way to the Saudis, but . . . all had the feeling that [Britain] tended to act without due consideration for American interests'. It was agreed that Shuckburgh would visit Washington in January 1956 to discuss the issue.[43]

Macmillan even tried to convince Foster Dulles that British retreat from Buraimi would provoke the Trucial Sheikhdoms to turn to the Soviets for protection. Unconvinced, Foster Dulles stalled, proposing a joint study during Shuckburgh's visit to Washington. The outlook was not favourable. The Foreign Office's Permanent Undersecretary, Ivone Kirkpatrick, cabled Shuckburgh: 'I made a fairly savage attack on the American Minister this morning [about Buraimi and the Arabian Peninsula], emphasizing that the Americans were playing the Russian game and violating justice!'[44]

Once again, it was Eden, reacting to political pressure, who jeopardised a joint resolution of the problem. The pound, recently made 'convertible' against the dollar, was under severe strain, and the autumn 'pots and pans' budget of the Chancellor, Butler, which raised taxes on all goods, including household items that had previously been exempted, but did not take far-reaching steps to check inflation and government spending, was extremely unpopular. This in turn provoked dissension within the Cabinet. Butler criticised Eden for the lenient spring budget, which had been electorally popular but fuelled inflation, while the Prime Minister castigated the Chancellor for opposing increases in corporate taxes.

Eden, labelled as indecisive and dithering by the press, responded by reshuffling his Cabinet in December. As early as August, he had resolved that Macmillan would have to leave the Foreign Office. Eden wanted to direct foreign policy, but Macmillan was an independent and strong-willed Foreign Secretary. Pestered by the Prime Minister's messages and phone calls, Macmillan ignored the minutes unless the Prime Minister repeatedly pressed his point. Eden wrote in his diary that he 'thought Harold too woolly generally', considering 'too many things at once'. He complained: '[Harold] follows Dulles around like an admiring poodle and that is bad for Foster and worse for British interests in the Middle East.'[45]

Realising that the dismissal or even demotion of Macmillan, a senior Minister with widespread support in the Conservative Party, was not possible, Eden seized upon an alternative to solve the problems with his Chancellor as well. Butler would become Lord Privy Seal and Leader of the House of Commons, and Macmillan would take over the Exchequer. The changes were delayed by the Geneva Conference of Foreign Ministers and then by the autumn budget, but, on 21 December, Eden appointed Selwyn Lloyd as Foreign Secretary. Lloyd was Minister of State in the Foreign Office under Eden from 1952 to 1954 and Minister of Defence in the first Eden Cabinet. He was far from docile, having clashed with Eden over the Anglo-Egyptian negotiations in 1954; however, he spoke no foreign languages and rarely travelled abroad.[46] Lacking confidence in his grasp of foreign affairs, he was more amenable than Macmillan to the Prime Minister's 'consultations'.[47] Harold Beeley, Assistant Undersecretary in charge of Middle Eastern affairs in 1956, summarised: 'Selwyn Lloyd was a modest man. . . . Eden, of course, had a great reputation as an expert in foreign policy and I think Selwyn felt that he ought not to challenge Eden's judgement.'[48]

The Macmillan–Foster Dulles relationship, which had sustained the 'alliance' despite interference from Eden, had been disrupted. In 1953, Macmillan had referred to Foster Dulles as 'the most dunder-headed man alive', who moved 'from blunder to blunder'. In contrast, as Macmillan left the Foreign Office, Foster Dulles wrote:

I am terribly disappointed to learn that the Cabinet shift which you mentioned to me as a possibility has actually occurred. . . . I have come to have great trust and reliance in you and because of this I have looked toward the future with greater confidence.

Macmillan replied, 'Just as this country's connexion with America is the most important thing in its foreign relations, so our own personal connexion was at all times in the front of my thinking. I think our work together was useful and good.'[49]

The question was whether Shuckburgh and other Foreign Office personnel could win over Lloyd before Eden embarked on plans that jeopardised their links with the Americans. Within days of the Cabinet change, however, that issue was a secondary consideration. The legacy of the Templer mission to Jordan suddenly threatened to destroy any British position in the Middle East.

6

Towards a Summit
January–March 1956

W hen King Hussein assumed the Jordanian throne in 1953, he was eighteen years old. His grandfather Abdullah, the first King of Jordan, had been assassinated in 1951, and his father Talal had been forced to abdicate because of mental instability. He was to rule over a country split between native Bedouin and a large minority of Palestinians. Most of the latter lived on the Jordan River's West Bank, annexed in 1950 by Jordan, or had resettled in Jordan after being displaced from their homes during the 1948–9 Arab-Israeli War. It was uncertain whether their first loyalty was to King Hussein or to the restoration of Palestine.

Jordan's relations with her neighbours were even more uncertain. To the west lay Israel, ready to occupy the West Bank; to the east was Saudi Arabia, traditional rival of the Hashemite kingdoms of Jordan and Iraq. Even the bonds with Iraq could be a hindrance: while Baghdad's financial and military support was welcome, the Iraqi monarchy might seek to unify the two countries, eclipsing Hussein in the process. Finally, Jordan was now caught between Britain's designs for an Iraqi-Jordanian axis and Egypt's opposition to Western direction of Arab defence.

The Arab Legion, led by General Glubb and other British officers, and the British subsidy had helped safeguard Hussein's throne, but the King's dissolution of the Jordanian Parliament in late 1955 failed to quell 'nationalist' disturbances supported by money and propaganda from Egypt and Saudi Arabia. On 7 January, Glubb anxiously asked the Foreign Office for British and Iraqi reinforcements. Four days later, the British Cabinet approved the despatch of two paratroop battalion. to Cyprus, with another battalion on forty-eight-hours' notice in Brit iin.

One wing of RAF aircraft was redeployed from Habbaniya in Iraq to Amman, and the British armoured regiment, stationed near Aqaba in southern Jordan, prepared to travel north. British forces were authorised to take retaliatory air action against Saudi troops, who had massed on the border with Jordan.[1]

The immediate threat to Hussein was short-lived. By 12 January, the British Embassy reported that the situation had stabilised. Nasser assured Ambassador Trevelyan that Egypt would stop inciting Jordanian demonstrations if there was no further attempt for Jordanian accession to the Baghdad Pact. Saudi troops did not cross the border, and the British battalions remained in Cyprus.[2]

Suddenly, crisis turned into an opportunity for Britain to revive the Iraqi-Jordanian axis without expanding the Baghdad Pact. Proposals, first made in early 1954, for the defence of Jordan against Israel were revived by the British Defence Co-ordinating Committee for the Middle East (BDCC). The BDCC argued that Israel would quickly overwhelm Jordanian forces in an Arab-Israeli conflict. Jordan could only be defended if Britain airlifted two brigades into the country and, using fighter squadrons in Jordan and fighters and bombers from Cyprus, neutralised the Israeli air force within seventy-two hours. In January−February 1956, the Chiefs of Staff refined and approved the plan, codenamed CORDAGE.[3]

Paradoxically, the disastrous Templer mission increased Iraq's role in Anglo-Jordanian relations. Britain had linked her effort with direct Iraqi-Jordanian co-operation, encouraging Baghdad's proposals for economic agreements with Amman and persuading Iraq to promote her diplomatic mission in Amman to Embassy status.[4] Hussein's need for support during the riots in Amman expanded Iraq's economic interest in Jordan into diplomatic and military initiatives. On 29 December, Nuri Sa'id wrote to the King to encourage him to stand firm. In reply, Hussein requested a meeting in Baghdad and, at the height of the demonstrations on 9 January, asked that an Iraqi division prepare to enter Jordan. Although the subsidence of the emergency rendered immediate Iraqi intervention unnecessary, Hussein's talks with Nuri in mid-January led to military staff discussions on the long-term deployment of Iraqi troops in Jordan. Hussein also rejected an Egyptian-Saudi-Syrian offer to replace the British subsidy to the Jordanian economy and the Arab Legion.[5]

Iraqi and British interests coincided: a strong Iraq controlling Syria and sharing the economic, political and military supervision of Jordan with Britain. This would indirectly link Syria and Jordan with the Baghdad Pact and isolate Egypt and Saudi Arabia if they did not co-operate with the British. To expand her influence in Syria, Iraq considered an increase in 'subsidies' for pro-Iraqi newspapers and politicians, visits by Syrian dignitaries and students to Iraq, and a new radio station transmitting from Baghdad throughout the region. The British Ambassador to Syria, John Gardener, met Iraqi officials in Baghdad to suggest similar activities in Jordan and Lebanon.[6]

It remained for Britain to include the Americans in the plans. In early January, Shuckburgh was visiting Washington to prepare for the Eden–Eisenhower summit. A brief for Shuckburgh argued that Britain obtained no direct advantage from her presence in Jordan, but her departure would prompt Israel to annex the West Bank of the Jordan River, leaving the Saudis, Syrians and Iraqis to fight for eastern Jordan. Any reduction in the British presence 'would have a serious, and perhaps decisive, effect on [Britain's] position in Iraq'. Eden went further, suggesting that Britain openly endorse Iraqi union with Syria and/or Jordan.[7]

Appealing to Eisenhower on 16 January, the Prime Minister linked the Iraqi-Jordanian question not only to Britain's campaign against Egyptian and Saudi intrigue, but also to the American struggle with the Soviet Union. Eden asserted that Saudi money was bribing officials, buying newspapers in Syria, Lebanon and Jordan, and threatening to replace the British subsidy to Amman:

It [is] increasingly clear that the Saudis, the Russians, the Egyptians, and the Syrians are working altogether, and . . . if we don't want to see the whole Middle East fall into Communist hands, we must back our friends in Jordan and in Iraq. If the Saudis have their way, there will be nothing left for anybody but the Bear [the Soviet Union].[8]

The plans were undone by the spectre of Buraimi. The situation had worsened in December 1955, when Britain supported an offensive by the Sultan of Muscat against a rival, the Imam of Oman. The short-tempered Ivone Kirkpatrick told the US Minister in London, Walworth Barbour, that 'US efforts to restrain local Sheikhs resisting Saudi pressures and subversion are playing into Soviet hands' and 'asked bluntly whether [the US] desired the Saudis to achieve complete hegemony over [the Arabian] Peninsula'. The State Department was undeterred, as Hoover maintained that the Saudis were a headstrong people and 'you had to work with them and could do no good by frightening them'. He presented Shuckburgh with a memorandum warning, 'It is . . . difficult to see how the US could oppose a [UN Security Council] resolution incorporating the principles of peaceful settlement through some form of arbitration or negotiation.'[9]

Shuckburgh's hands were tied by Lloyd, who reiterated, in a Cabinet Paper of 9 January, 'We must firmly resist any pressure to induce us to return to arbitration' or to negotiate directly with the Saudis, as 'the irretrievable distortion of the views of the local tribespeople by Saudi actions . . . make it almost inevitable that we should lose'. Frustrated, the State Department asserted that Saudi opposition to the Iraqi-Jordanian axis arose from their fear of strong Hashemite regimes in Iraq and Jordan. Shuckburgh 'found [himself] having to clear [Britain] of the imputation of "imperialism"'.[10] The American threat was obvious: either the British compromised on Buraimi, or the US would not support the general British strategy. Shuckburgh allegedly snapped, 'America might wake up and realize that Iraq represents the solution of the West in the Middle East.'[11] Only the intervention of Francis Russell saved the talks, as he reminded Shuckburgh that Foster Dulles was more receptive than Hoover to British views and suggested a message from Lloyd to the Secretary of State.

With discussion of Buraimi adjourned, Anglo-American co-operation was renewed. The State Department acknowledged the vital importance of Middle Eastern oil and transport routes, the Soviet threat to the region, and the necessity of Anglo-American defence of the area.[12] Specifically, both sides concluded that Egypt's co-operation was still necessary for the success of ALPHA and the Middle Eastern mission of Robert Anderson, Eisenhower's special envoy. As Shuckburgh's deputy, G. G. Arthur, drawing upon the conclusions of a conference of Britain's Middle Eastern ambassadors, summarised:

Nasser is more likely to be able to help us get a settlement than any alternative government in Egypt. We should not therefore undermine Nasser until we are convinced that he will not help when it is reasonable for him to do so.[13]

The US agreed to act under the Tripartite Declaration against Arab or Israeli aggression and to give all support to the Baghdad Pact short of accession. Closer links between Iraq, Syria and Jordan would be promoted, as long as they did not alienate Egypt. In return, Shuckburgh retreated from an aggressive policy for Iraqi-Syrian union.[14]

The successful conclusion of Shuckburgh's talks was soon overshadowed by Eden's petulance and pessimism. On 3 January, Donald McLachlan of the *Daily Telegraph* launched a vitriolic press campaign against the Prime Minister:

Why are Conservatives around the country restive, and Ministers and backbenchers unenraptured with their leader? There is a favourite gesture of the Prime Minister's which is sometimes recalled to illustrate this sense of disappointment. To emphasise a point, he will clench one fist to smack the open palm of the other hand – but the smack is seldom heard. Most Conservatives, and almost certainly some of the wiser trade union leaders, are waiting to feel the smack of firm Government.[15]

Anthony Nutting recalled when the Prime Minister read McLachlan's words: 'I have never seen Eden so stricken. He was positively writhing in the agony of this barbed shaft which, unlike some of the blunter and cruder assaults of the Opposition, had struck him at his weakest point.'[16] Eden's Press Secretary, William Clark, complained: 'AE had too much vulnerability to press attack and . . . Clarissa [Eden] aided it.' After the Prime Minister's wife noted, 'Of course, RAB [R. A. Butler] is criticised more, but that criticism is justified and the criticism of Anthony isn't,' Eden petulantly told Clark, 'Of course, I don't care about this at all. If [Conservatives] want, they can get rid of me and go back to Winston.'[17]

The *Daily Mirror*, which supported the Labour Party, used quotes from the Conservative press for its leader of 5 January: 'Eden is a FLOP. . . . Even the TORIES are saying it now.' The Prime Minister, through Clark, asked journalists to curb their criticism, but the *People* reported on 8 January that Eden was 'now all set to retire' and would 'be succeeded by Mr Butler', forcing 10 Downing Street to issue a denial. Eden counter-attacked in a speech at Bradford on 18 January:

I do not have to advise this great Yorkshire audience not to believe everything they read in certain London newspapers. I know that one or two of these cantankerous newspapers claimed that they were reflecting public feeling. They were doing nothing of the sort. What they were doing was to try to make you think and feel what they wanted you to. I am sure you will always be on your guard against such methods. That way lies the denial of democracy.[18]

Beset with fears of a worsening economy, Eden was embarrassed not only by the near disaster in Jordan, but also by the Labour Party's exposure of a shipment to Belgium of 'demilitarised' tanks which were armed and re-exported to Egypt. Speaking to US Ambassador Aldrich about Buraimi, Eden 'lost his temper and flared up bitterly about the US wanting always to have Britain abandon its interests and give away its rights'. He then informed Shuckburgh that Nasser's 'object was to be a Caesar from the Gulf to the Atlantic and to kick us out of it all'.[19]

The trip on the *Queen Mary* to the summit with Eisenhower did not improve the Prime Minister's spirits. Shuckburgh wrote that Eden was 'very suspicious of American intentions and absolutely distrusts Nasser. He seemed thin, nervy, and, in a curious way, frivolous.' The Prime Minister complained at the limited time allocated for meetings with Eisenhower, a condition imposed by the President's doctors because of Eisenhower's recent heart attack, and told Lloyd:

I am not going to be treated like this. I will take the next boat home. . . . It is no use talking to Dulles and the State Department, though you will do it very well, Selwyn dear; they cannot treat the British Prime Minister like this.[20]

Fortunately for the Foreign Office, the combination of Eden's temper and conflict over Saudi Arabia was eclipsed by a sudden shift in Foster Dulles's attitude towards Egypt. In mid-January, Robert Anderson, accompanied by the CIA's Kermit Roosevelt, began Operation BETA with a trip to Cairo. After his first meeting with Nasser, which lasted for four hours, Anderson cabled optimistically to Washington:

I have the impression that [Nasser] is confident of his ability to dispose of a settlement between Egypt and Israel and still maintain a strong position in the Arab world if he is positively and in the right way [supported] by the Western powers and their allies and if he is not impeded either by adverse propaganda or by aggressive arrangements.[21]

According to Roosevelt, Anderson was even more enthusiastic at first, believing that Nasser had accepted American ideas on territorial adjust- ments and resettlement of Palestinian refugees, and would eventually agree to direct talks with Israeli officials. Unfortunately, there was a problem of communication. Roosevelt recalled that, during Anderson's initial twenty-five-minute presentation, 'In his amiable way, Nasser was nodding at everything Anderson said and Anderson thought he was making historic advances . . . [but his] Texas drawl was so thick that Nasser couldn't understand a thing he said.' Roosevelt acted as inter- preter, but could not clear up any ambiguities in the conversation. He later claimed that, when he explained to Nasser that Anderson sought direct Egyptian-Israeli negotiations, Nasser interjected: 'I could never do that. I'd be assassinated. Go stop him. Don't let him send that cable!' A few days later, Roosevelt reported:

[Nasser had] been disturbed at the possibility that he may not really have understood Anderson's proposal nor had we understood his reply to it. . . . There were very few foreigners that he could talk to with any confidence that they were understanding him and he was understanding them.[22]

Anderson's mission was already in trouble. Foster Dulles had cabled the envoy:

It is imperative for us to know soon whether or not settlement can probably be concluded. We would have great difficulty in getting Israel to sit by waiting for six months while Egypt absorbs arms. . . . Furthermore, by summer, political competition [in the US Presidential election] will be at level which would greatly militate against our then taking effective part in [a] settlement.[23]

However, Nasser emphasised that he could not satisfy Foster Dulles's wishes, given the time-consuming process of agreeing upon the elements of an Egyptian-Israeli settlement, consulting other Arab nations and arranging direct negotiations with Tel Aviv. He complained to CIA officials: 'This problem is seven years old and many people have tried to solve it. Mr Anderson seems to think that only three days after his arrival, he can get us to agree and arrange an immediate meeting with Ben-Gurion.'[24]

Travelling to Israel on 23 January, Anderson made no progress with Ben-Gurion, who refused to discuss specific proposals in advance of direct Egyptian-Israeli negotiations. The Americans concluded that the only hope was to establish the Egyptian position on eight to ten issues, apart from Nasser's demand for Israeli cession of the Negev desert to establish an Egyptian-Jordanian land link. The proposals would be presented to Ben-Gurion, who might then consider some compromise over the Negev. After Anderson's return to Cairo on 26 January, Nasser endorsed the establishment of a secret working party, composed of the Egyptian Minister of the Interior, Zacharia Mohieddin, and CIA officials, to discuss the 'package'.[25]

For Foster Dulles, however, the initial misunderstanding between Nasser and Anderson was an indication that the Egyptians were refusing genuine negotiations. At the first summit meeting with Eden on 30 January, Foster Dulles complained that 'the Egyptians were dragging their feet'. This allowed Eden to comment, without fear of rejection, that he 'did not know how long we can go along with Nasser. [He is an] awful fellow.' When Eisenhower joined the talks, Foster Dulles commented that 'little could be done until we knew more about what might be expected of Nasser in Egypt'. Eden noted: 'It was difficult to know whether Nasser could be dealt with. If so, our course of action in the Middle East could go one way; if not, it should go another.'

The President repeated the view of an American businessman that 'Nasser was not one who would cut off his nose to spite his face', but Foster Dulles rebutted: 'Nasser talked intelligently and made a fine impression. However, he made violent anti-Israeli statements on the one hand, while on the other saying privately that a settlement is possible.' Eisenhower then turned to the British and asked 'if they had lost confidence in him [Nasser]'. Eden carefully answered, 'It was difficult to evaluate Nasser, who was a man of limitless ambition,' only for Foster Dulles to interject: '[He] did not mind ambition, which was a healthy thing that could be played upon. However, Nasser might have become a tool of the Russians.'[26]

Despite his anger, Foster Dulles realistically assessed that, unless

BETA was abandoned, accommodation with Nasser must continue. Eden and Lloyd agreed: 'It is the policy of the United Kingdom Government, in so far as it is compatible with their main objectives, to retain the friendship of the Egyptian Government.' However, an important precedent had been established. If the Anderson mission failed, then the US would seek Britain's co-operation in a programme to undermine Nasser's authority. This in turn encouraged the Americans to accept Britain's defence of her Middle Eastern position.

The British had come to Washington hoping 'to put teeth in the Tripartite Declaration' of 1950. Not only would this confirm Western interest in an Arab-Israeli settlement, but, by reassuring 'friendly' Arab states that Britain and the US would defend them against Israeli aggression, it would check the spread of Soviet influence and anti-Western sentiment. Foster Dulles was hesitant about a public statement of intent to enforce the Tripartite Declaration, as US military action required a Congressional resolution, but he accepted Eden's suggestion of Anglo-American military studies. Eisenhower agreed to Foster Dulles's proposal that Britain and the US

make clearly evident our resolution to react to an outbreak of hostilities in order to forestall such an outbreak. . . . We should consider a possible UN resolution and other steps in the UN to establish a basis for action if it should be required.

The next day, Admiral Radford, the Chairman of the US Joint Chiefs of Staff, concluded his talks with General William Whiteley, the head of the British Joint Staff Mission. Radford confirmed: 'Our naval forces alone could establish an effective maritime blockade of Israel, and with a few reinforcements in the Persian Gulf and Red Sea, we could blockade Egypt also.' Eisenhower endorsed immediate steps that did not require Congressional consent, notably stationing of warships in the Eastern Mediterranean with visits by cruisers and destroyers to Middle Eastern ports.[27]

Eden again sought a formal commitment by the Americans to the Baghdad Pact. He bitterly recalled in his memoirs:

Having played a leading part to inspire the project, the US held back while Britain joined it. . . . The repeated hesitation perplexed and harassed our friends in Turkey and Iraq, Iran and Pakistan. They strengthened Russian and Egyptian will to destroy the Pact and overthrow the Governments which supported it.[28]

The recollection is misleading. Shuckburgh had accepted that American accession was not forthcoming, and Lloyd merely asked Foster Dulles for increased American aid for countries in the organisation. Eden added, 'He understood US difficulties which prevented its adherence. He hoped, however, [that] the communiqué following the current talks would give some support for the Pact.'[29] The final communiqué accordingly noted that the Baghdad Pact had 'an important part to play in the economic and political development of member countries' and served 'the interests of the area as a whole'. The State Department agreed to seek more Centurion tanks for Iraq in 1956 and additional economic aid for Iran.[30]

The two sides even moved towards compromise on Buraimi. Foster Dulles and Eisenhower, deferring to British insistence that they could not return to arbitration, suggested that a high-ranking British representative meet King Saud. Although Britain refused any concessions on the status of the oasis, Foster Dulles and Eisenhower left the issue for direct Anglo-Saudi talks.[31]

Lloyd and Eden were only rebuffed when they asked the Americans to block oil royalties to the Saudis. Hoover argued that the royalties were a private transaction between Saudi Arabia and the Arabian-American Oil Company, and a cut-off risked Saudi retaliation against American oil concessions and use of the Dhahran air force base. Instead, the State Department suggested that King Saud be persuaded to devote revenues to social projects instead of 'expensive toys' like arms and 'air-conditioned Cadillacs by the gross'. Shuckburgh concluded: 'We thought all this not at all bad.'[32]

The Iraqi-Jordanian axis, as well as action against Syria, could now be linked to forthcoming action against Nasser. Foster Dulles noted that 'various plans had been put forward by the Turks and Iraqis to effect a change in Syria', but added that none of those plans 'seemed sufficient to warrant our support'. Lloyd assented, 'Before taking any action in Syria, it would be wise first to strengthen relations between Iraq and Jordan and to stabilize the situation in those countries,' and Eden confirmed, 'We must decide later, not during this trip, where we should go in relation to Egypt, and what our attitude toward Nasser should be.'[33]

The summit laid the foundations for an unprecedented Anglo-American concord on Middle Eastern policy. Eden cabled Butler: 'My personal conviction is that this is the best meeting in Washington we have ever had.'[34] While British and American military staffs continued discussions, the US and Britain conducted patrols of two destroyers off the Israeli coast, two off the Mediterranean coast of Egypt, and two in the Red Sea. On 22 February, the US Joint Chiefs of Staff agreed to Anglo-American military plans to enforce the Tripartite Declaration. The State Department and Foreign Office examined economic sanctions to be levied against the aggressor in a Middle Eastern conflict and discussed measures to safeguard the supply of Middle Eastern oil.[35]

Meanwhile, the British proceeded with the development of Iraqi-Jordanian links. On 15 February, Jordan requested a British assurance of support in case of an Israeli attack upon an Arab state, and British intelligence reports indicated that the Israelis would take 'provocative action on or about 1st March'. The Chiefs of Staff refused to inform Amman of CORDAGE, the plan for the defence of Jordan, but they agreed to talks between the British Defence Co-ordinating Committee for the Middle East and British officers of the Arab Legion. On 28 February, the Cabinet approved a formal reply to Jordan: while Britain was not obliged under the Anglo-Jordanian Treaty to aid Jordan if Israel attacked another Arab state, the Tripartite Declaration would bring Britain 'side-by-side with Jordan' to resist Israeli aggression, provided Jordan did not take precipitate action against Israel.[36]

The persistent question was whether Eden would be patient enough to accept the Foreign Office's development of Middle Eastern policy. Within days of the summit, the Prime Minister was writing angrily on telegrams from Cairo suggesting an Iraqi-Egyptian rapprochement. Exclaiming that Nasser never kept his bargains, Eden concluded: 'I fear that [British Ambassador] Trevelyan is very gullible. I hope you will not take his advice. Better bad terms between Nuri and Nasr [sic] than weaken Nuri which this might do.'[37]

Domestically, although the press campaign against the Prime Minister had eased, he now had a formidable rival within the Cabinet in the Chancellor of the Exchequer, Macmillan. The animosity between Eden and Macmillan, for which no specific cause has been found, dated from the Second World War. Eden's Private Secretary, Oliver Harvey, recorded in 1943 that Macmillan, the British representative in the Mediterranean, was

anxious to maintain a sort of *droit de regard* over all our French and Italian relations. . . . AE does not wish to encourage this and part of the idea of the appointment of Duff [Cooper] and [Noel] Charles to the French and Italian [governments in exile] is to cut [Macmillan] out of the picture. I can't think why [Eden] dislikes Macmillan (though he certainly is a bore) and is even jealous of him.

Eden's Principal Private Secretary, Pierson Dixon, noted that Eden, resenting Macmillan's reporting directly to the Prime Minister, Winston Churchill, said, 'We already have two Foreign Secretaries [himself and Churchill]; I am not going to have a third.' Meanwhile, Macmillan thought that Eden was overburdened, commenting:

[Eden] seemed so far away when he saw him. . . . Obviously he was taking nothing in. . . . Anthony had too much for any one man to do, should give up the

Foreign Office where he was handicapped by Winston's constant interference. . . . There ought to be a change. I think I could get on with the 'old boy'
[Churchill] better than most people.

The crisis between the two men culminated in August 1944, when
Eden sent Dixon to Italy to abolish Macmillan's post of Resident Minister
in the Mediterranean. Macmillan wrote: 'I resent being got out by the
back door. . . . I shall now fight my position to the bitter end.' He
eventually received Churchill's support to keep the post.[38]

With Eden concentrating on foreign affairs and Macmillan on housing
and defence, they rarely clashed during the Churchill Government of
1951–5, although Macmillan made no secret of his ambition to become
Foreign Secretary and complained about collaboration with a 'queer man
like Eden'. Eden's attempt to control the Foreign Office while Macmillan
was Foreign Secretary renewed hostilities, however, and Macmillan
shrewdly accepted the Exchequer in December 1955 on certain conditions, including assurances that he could bring in outside advisers and
reorganise the Bank of England and that he, not Butler, would be the
Minister in charge of domestic affairs. He soon criticised Eden's
speeches on domestic issues: '[I] think you would not be wise to attempt
an essay on economics. There are too many experts.'[39]

In February, Macmillan forced a showdown with Eden in the Cabinet,
when he insisted upon cuts in bread and milk subsidies. Eden, fearing that
the resulting price rises would fuel inflation, was firmly opposed, but the
Chancellor threatened to resign if the measures were not adopted. After
seven Cabinet meetings and negotiations through intermediaries, Eden
conceded most of Macmillan's demands. The subsidy on milk ended in
July, while the bread subsidy was reduced immediately with abolition to
follow in the near future. The US Embassy assessed: 'If the economic
outlook improves dramatically, but foreign affairs, which are regarded as
Eden's particular province, do not improve, the chances for Macmillan [to
succeed Eden] would be still brighter.'[40]

Under pressure, the Prime Minister plagued Lloyd with phone calls,
tore up the Foreign Secretary's draft messages to Foster Dulles on
Buraimi, launched verbal tirades against Nasser, and vetoed the despatch
of telegrams to Jordan or Saudi Arabia without his personal approval.
Kirkpatrick noted: 'Selwyn's only ambition is not to get into trouble.[41]
Lloyd had to make a gesture to Eden or risk dismissal from his post. On 22
February, he told Ministers of his forthcoming Middle Eastern tour and
proposed 'a firm line on Egyptian propaganda. . . . [Our] objective would
be to make it clear that Egypt could not expect further help from us unless
she changed her policy towards us.' The Cabinet agreed. Anglo-Egyptian
relations were at breaking-point.[42]

7

The Turning-point: London March 1956

On 1 March, the Jordanian Prime Minister, Samir Rifai, acting on orders from King Hussein, summoned General Glubb, the commander of the Arab Legion, and asked him to leave the country within two hours. Eden's urgent appeal to Hussein was refused, although the deadline for Glubb's expulsion was extended to twenty-four hours.[1] Britain's Middle Eastern position, which had survived the Templer mission, was in jeopardy once more.

Although Glubb's dismissal occurred without warning, his relationship with the young King had been far from carefree. In May 1955, Hussein complained to General Gerald Templer, the Chief of the Imperial General Staff, and General Charles Keightley, Britain's commander of Middle Eastern forces, that Glubb tried to control Jordan's internal affairs, would not co-operate with the Jordanian Defence Ministry and supported 'his own favourites'. Matters worsened when Glubb insisted that Wing Commander Jock Dalgleish, the head of the Royal Jordanian Air Force since June 1953 and a good friend of Hussein's, should be replaced in February 1956.[2]

On 28 February, Rifai, fearing British opposition, refused Hussein's request to transfer control of the Jordanian police from Glubb to the Ministry of the Interior. The following day, Glubb recommended the dismissal of eleven Jordanian officers and the transfer of thirty-four others to police or civilian departments. At an acrimonious meeting, Hussein refused to endorse the General's proposals for the reinstatement of certain officers, the dismissal of the 'troublesome' ones and the delay of 'Arabisation' of the Arab Legion until 1985. After the encounter, Hussein, who had a penchant for fast cars, relaxed in an adviser's blue Cadillac. It was then that he decided to dismiss Glubb.[3]

Within days, Lloyd concluded that the 'King's action had been taken on the advice of a group of young officers'. The Foreign Office told the US Embassy that it had no evidence of Egyptian or Saudi intervention in Jordanian affairs, and the Foreign Secretary later confirmed that the 'principal reason for Glubb dismissal was King's resentment at taking guidance and advice from a man so many years his senior'. Even Eden, in his memoirs, admitted that the problem was Hussein's 'personal dislike which had grown to something of a phobia' about Glubb's control of Jordanian defence. The influence of Major Abu Ali Nuwar, recalled from the Jordanian Embassy in France to become Hussein's *aide-de-camp* over Glubb's objections, may also have been significant. Journalist Joseph Alsop claimed that Nuwar 'paint[ed] his beautiful burning eyes' and owed his later appointment as Chief of the General Staff 'to a highly equivocal relationship with the young king'.[4]

On 1 March, however, Eden and his Ministers were convinced that Nasser had prompted or forced Hussein to remove Glubb. Since January, Eden and the Foreign Office had collected reports of an Egyptian propaganda campaign against the General. The 'Voice of the Arabs' radio station, assumed to be the mouthpiece of Nasser's Government, announced that the Jordanian people were 'capable of purging the Jordanian army of Glubb and his followers'. It was alleged that Glubb, having halted the advance of Iraqi and Jordanian armies towards Tel Aviv in 1948, 'directed with his own hand the poisonous dagger with which the imperialists stabbed Palestine'.[5]

By an unfortunate coincidence, Lloyd arrived in Cairo on the day of Glubb's dismissal. At dinner, during a three-hour discussion, Nasser, 'fatter and more self-confident than when [Lloyd] last saw him in 1953', proposed a 'truce' in Anglo-Egyptian sparring. If Britain would 'freeze the membership of the Baghdad Pact, with no more recruitment of Arab states', Nasser would halt anti-British and anti-Pact propaganda and revive, with Iraq, the Arab Collective Security Pact, which might eventually be linked to the Baghdad Pact. Lloyd did not reject the proposal, but stated that he must consult other Baghdad Pact members and the British Cabinet.[6]

Near the end of the dinner, a British Embassy official passed a note about Glubb's dismissal to Ambassador Trevelyan, who informed Lloyd upon their return to the Embassy. When Lloyd visited Nasser the next day, he believed that the Egyptian President, at worst, had engineered Glubb's removal and, at best, had withheld the information from him. Nasser, however, did not learn of the news from Jordan until late evening on 1 March or early the next morning. Unaware of Hussein's motives, he believed that the British had asked Glubb to resign.

The result was farce. Lloyd asked Nasser, 'You are aware, Mr President, of what has happened in Jordan?' Nasser replied, 'Yes, it's good, isn't it?', to which Lloyd rebutted, 'What's good about it?' Nasser explained his assumption that Britain approved the change because it 'would improve the position in Jordan and strengthen [Hussein's] regime'. Lloyd, incensed at 'this pretence' of Nasser's, charged that Egypt had been responsible, through propaganda or direct action, for Glubb's removal and warned of the bad effect on Anglo-Egyptian relations. Proposals for an Anglo-Egyptian 'truce' fell by the wayside.[7]

The situation worsened when Lloyd left Cairo and arrived in Bahrain on the Arabian Peninsula. En route from the airport to the British Residency, Lloyd's motorcade encountered demonstrators protesting about the lack of social reform and the control of the country's policies by Sir Charles Belgrave, the British adviser to the Bahraini ruler. Sand and pebbles were thrown at the procession, some cars were jostled, and one of their windows was broken. Lloyd cabled: 'I did not have as exciting a time in Bahrain as is described here,' but his conclusion that, 'Although the Glubb incident was a bodyline ball in the middle of the innings, . . . an accommodation with [Nasser] is not impossible to start on a tentative basis,' was immediately dismissed.[8]

The news of Glubb's removal convulsed Eden with fury. Anthony Nutting was with the Prime Minister until 5 a.m. trying to calm him: '[Eden] put all the blame on Nasser and brushed aside every argument that mere personal considerations had in fact influenced Hussein's arbitrary decision. . . . He decided that the world was not big enough to hold both him and Nasser.' Nutting wrote that he pressed the need for deliberation:

[Eden] called me nothing but a Foreign Office clerk and said I didn't understand anything about politics and the implications of this dismissal for Britain and her Prime Minister. At one point he said, 'You won't accept any arguments against Nasser, you are in love with Nasser.'[9]

About midnight, Eden called Shuckburgh at his home in Henley after the day's work at the Foreign Office, snapped, 'Are you in the country? I thought you would be looking after your business,' and summoned him back to London.[10]

Hussein publicly confirmed Jordan's friendship with Britain and respect for the Anglo-Jordanian Treaty, but the Prime Minister was not pacified. Shuckburgh wrote that Eden, intervening constantly with phone calls and messages, was 'now violently anti-Nasser, whom he compares with Mussolini'. He ordered Shuckburgh to consider reoccupation of the Canal Zone Base by British troops.[11]

With Lloyd absent and Eden in an aggressive mood, an Anglo-Egyptian showdown seemed inevitable. On the evening of 4 March, Eden convened a meeting at Chequers, attended by the Lord President, Lord Salisbury; the Minister of Defence, Walter Monckton; Templer; the Chief of the Air Staff, Air Marshal Dermot Boyle; Kirkpatrick; Nutting; and Shuckburgh. The Prime Minister insisted upon a tough line, and Kirkpatrick lent support, calling for withdrawal of the British subsidy and denunciation of the Anglo-Jordanian Treaty. All present agreed that British officers of the Arab Legion should leave Jordan. The only sign of moderation was an attempt, probably led by Shuckburgh, to soften the tone of a statement to be made by Eden to the House of Commons the next day.[12]

This was the high-water mark of Eden's policy of reprisal, as Foreign Office officials finally mobilised support for a conciliatory line. Glubb, meeting Eden, Nutting, Shuckburgh and other officials, 'made a most noble impression – no harsh words against the King of Jordan and a real understanding of the boy's desire to get rid of him'. He warned: 'It would not be right to come down on Jordan like a ton of bricks. . . . Do not pull out, do not cut the subsidy. Stop sending telegrams and let the dust settle down.'[13]

The British Ambassador to Jordan, Charles Duke, rejected withdrawal of the subsidy and denunciation of the Anglo-Jordanian Treaty, since 'action against General Glubb might have been directed only against him personally and . . . the manner of his dismissal might have been due to the awe in which he had come to be held in Jordan'. The Cabinet agreed that a wide-ranging statement should be considered further, and Eden's address to the Commons asked only for the relief of British officers from their commands in the Arab Legion.[14]

Shuckburgh and Nutting, trying to save the long-term Foreign Office strategy, argued that Jordan would repair her relations with Britain 'if we could find a way of letting them back through the Iraqis'. Telegrams from Baghdad indicated that Prime Minister Nuri Sa'id and the monarchy were 'waking up a little to the facts of life' and considering a meeting with Hussein. Shuckburgh and Nutting recommended that Britain suggest Iraqi assistance, through military forces and partial takeover of the British subsidy, to Amman.[15]

When Ministers met late on the evening of 5 March to decide upon British policy, Shuckburgh and Nutting found a sponsor in Macmillan. Over the dissent of Salisbury and Butler, who wanted to jettison the Anglo-Jordanian Treaty, the Chancellor obtained agreement to the policy of an Iraqi-Jordanian axis. He told Shuckburgh after the meeting, 'I have gained you a day or two to rescue the work of forty years.' Apparently, Macmillan convinced Eden that the Iraqi-Jordanian front would block Nasser's hopes in the Middle East.[16]

The next day the Cabinet approved the decisions of the Ministerial meeting, although Eden still spoke of Egypt as 'the main threat to [British] interests' in Iraq and the Persian Gulf[17] and cabled Lloyd that Nasser's hopes of an Anglo-Egyptian 'truce' over the Baghdad Pact were misplaced:

I am absolutely sure that we must do nothing to lead the members of the Baghdad Pact to think that we are considering limiting the membership. It could be fatal even to explore this with them at the present time.[18]

Eden was about to paint himself into a corner with his tough posturing. On the one hand, he assured the public that Britain would react firmly to Glubb's dismissal. He showed his resolve over the crisis in the British colony of Cyprus, where the guerrilla movement E O K A was demanding union with Greece, by ordering the jamming of Greek broadcasts to the island and the deportation of Archbishop Makarios, the leader of the Greek Orthodox community, to the Seychelles. On the other hand, the Cabinet had approved the Foreign Office's conciliatory approach towards Jordan, and Eden had been warned that public denunciation of Amman might inflame anti-British nationalists and topple King Hussein.[19]

The Opposition trapped the Prime Minister in a Commons debate on Jordan on 7 March. In his memoirs, Eden claimed that he had inadequate time to prepare his winding-up speech, but Foreign Office staff, including Shuckburgh, spent all of 7 March drafting the statement, which was a concise summary of Britain's need to work with, rather than against, Jordan as part of a long-term strategy in the Middle East.[20] However, when the Opposition dared him to give an immediate sign of British strength, Eden strayed from his script to produce the image of Britain vigorously defending her interests against foreign threats. Unable to support the rhetoric with an aggressive policy, he tried to shout down his hecklers. He failed miserably, leaving the chamber 'pretty broken' and saying only, 'Noisy, noisy.' The *Economist* claimed: 'Sir Anthony was bowled middle stump by Mr Gaitskell.' Drew Middleton of the *New York Times* wrote that Eden was 'subjected to a storm of vituperation and abuse beyond anything heard in the Commons since the last days of Neville Chamberlain's Prime Ministership', and a British columnist added:

Sir Anthony suffered a blow to his prestige that was clearly reflected in the silent, devastated ranks on the Conservative benches behind him. . . . If the year goes on as it has begun, it will not be Sir Anthony but Mr Harold Macmillan who reigns in Downing Street in 1957.[21]

Despite Eden's woeful performance, the Government had a majority of sixty, a typical figure, in the division, but it refuelled the public campaign against Nasser. Malcolm Muggeridge had described Eden in *Punch* as a 'general whose instinct is always to retreat and whose words of command have about as much dynamism as a [BBC] Third Programme talk on the place of the potato in English folklore'.[22] Humiliated by the Opposition, the Prime Minister now sought to bury this image with total victory over Egypt.

The choice lay between Eden's wish for quick, decisive action and the Foreign Office's strategy of long-term 'isolation' of Nasser. On 10 March, Shuckburgh, learning of ALPHA's death, defined the situation:

The Tripartite Declaration [was] a mere stop-gap; its sole justification was that it held the ring while [an Arab-Israeli] settlement was sought. This is a situation of grave national emergency. If the Jews attack, then perhaps we can find means of saving ourselves by falling upon them [but] unless the Israelis commit an aggression, we are daily becoming more committed to go to war against a Soviet-armed Arab world as soon as they feel strong enough or fanatical enough to attack Israel.[23]

Stressing the need for consensus within the Commons and with the Americans, Shuckburgh posed six questions, answering the first two himself. There was no alternative to Egypt as the route to an Arab-Israeli setttlement because of the weakness of Jordan, Syria and Lebanon. Nor could Britain impose a settlement upon the Arabs and Israel because of Israeli refusal to cede territory and American preoccupation with the Presidential election. Since an immediate settlement was impossible, Shuckburgh pondered: 'If we have despaired of Nasser, ought we to seek to overthrow him and if so, how? We must have full American co-operation in any such effort.' Britain had to decide how Nuri and the Baghdad Pact could be sustained, how King Saud of Saudi Arabia could be detached from Nasser, and whether the United Nations, and thus the Soviet Union, should become more involved in the area.[24]

Nutting answered Shuckburgh's questions on 12 March. To isolate Nasser, Britain should bring the US into a strengthened Baghdad Pact, forge the Iraqi-Jordanian axis, detach Saudi Arabia from Egypt and install a pro-Western government in Syria. Meanwhile, military and economic aid, including funding for the Aswan High Dam, would be withheld from Egypt.[25]

Eden quickly replied. He called Nutting, who was having dinner at the Savoy, and snapped: 'It's me. What's all this poppycock you've sent me? I don't agree with a single word of it.' When Nutting explained that he was trying to establish Britain's long-term position in the Middle East, Eden responded:

But what's all this nonsense about isolating Nasser or 'neutralising' him, as you call it? I want him destroyed, can't you understand? I want him removed, and if you and the Foreign Office don't agree, then you'd better come to the Cabinet and explain why.[26]

Nutting explained the need to find another leader for Egypt, but Eden persisted: 'I don't want an alternative and I don't give a damn if there's anarchy and chaos in Egypt.'[27]

Fortunately for the Foreign Office, two issues distracted Eden. The first was progress towards reconciliation with Jordan. Sir Alec Kirkbride, adviser for more than thirty years to King Hussein's grandfather, King Abdullah, reported to the Cabinet after a visit to Amman:

The King's dismissal of General Glubb . . . was essentially an act directed against General Glubb personally; it was not designed to disrupt Jordan's relations with the UK; and both the King and the Prime Minister of Jordan were now most seriously disturbed at the possibility that a lasting breach might thereby be created in the relations between the two countries.

He added, 'What was immediately required was an assurance that the UK Government were not proposing to withdraw their support from Jordan and an offer to discuss the terms on which British officers might serve with the Arab Legion in the future.' While Eden was 'clearly put out by what Kirkbride had to say', the Cabinet expressed 'general agreement . . . that it would be inexpedient' to assume that Anglo-Jordanian relations could not be restored.[28]

On 10 March, Britain's need to maintain good relations with Jordan increased when Egypt, Syria and Saudi Arabia renewed their offer, first made in January, to replace the British subsidy to Jordan. The Foreign Office confirmed three days later:

It is most important that we should bring the Iraqis and Jordanians much closer together. . . . It would be better to proceed through closer bilateral arrangements between Jordan and Iraq in the first place, leading possibly to some trilateral arrangements to include us.[29]

The opportunity to develop the Iraqi-Jordanian axis came on 14 March, when Hussein met King Feisal II of Iraq, Crown Prince Abdul-Illah and Nuri Sa'id at H-3, a pumping station on an Iraqi oil pipeline. Hussein told Ambassador Duke that the talks were 'most satisfactory', as Iraq and Jordan would establish a joint defence council similar to the

Anglo-Jordanian Defence Board. The British Chiefs of Staff confirmed on 22 March:

[While] existing facilities and the stationing of forces in Jordan are not militarily essential to UK strategy, . . . overriding political considerations demand the retention of UK influence and interests in Jordan. . . . Support for Jordan should include the continuation of a subsidy, the setting up of a Military Mission to advise the Arab Legion and the Royal Jordanian Air Force, and assurance of UK intention to stand by the Anglo-Jordanian Treaty.[30]

Secondly, Eden's attention turned from Egypt to Bahrain and the Persian Gulf states. As early as 3 March, Eden was writing minutes to the Minister of Defence, Monckton, ringing Foreign Office staff and demanding emergency meetings. When Eden drafted a telegram authorising British military action in Bahrain, Nutting reminded the Prime Minister that progress was being made towards an accommodation between the ruler and his reformist opponents. Shuckburgh added that it would be a 'fatal error to make use of British forces except in a moment of extreme emergency'.[31]

Rebuffed by the Foreign Office, Eden pressed Monckton:

We cannot allow the oil to be endangered. Therefore, a plan must be worked out without delay as to what reinforcements are necessary and where they can be put. . . . Both the political and military difficulties have got to be overcome.[32]

Eden's interventions were so persistent that the Cabinet Secretary, Norman Brook, asked Shuckburgh to reassure the Prime Minister. Shuckburgh complained:

Nutting, Kirkpatrick, and I feel that we, alternately, are rejected by the PM as no good, not on the job, unhelpful. . . . [Eden] seems to want to march troops in and arrest the [reformist] 'Higher Executive Committee' with whom Bernard [Burrows] is now negotiating. . . . We have now got to a state where each telegram that comes in causes Ministers to meet, telephone one another, draft replies, and curse everybody.[33]

Bahrain had become an official's nightmare, but Eden's obsession gave the Foreign Office a clear field on wider issues. Nutting's minute was finally considered at a meeting on 16 March at 10 Downing Street.[34] On the 21st, Lloyd returned from his tour to present the Cabinet with a modified version of Nutting's minute of the 12th. The Foreign Secretary warned:

It was evident that [Nasser] was aiming at leadership of the Arab world; that, in order to secure it, he was willing to accept the help of the Russians; and that he was not prepared to work for a settlement of the Arab dispute with Israel. . . . It was now clear that we could not establish a basis for friendly relations with Egypt.

However, as Nutting suggested, a direct confrontation with Egypt was rejected in favour of a long-term policy of 'isolation':

We should seek increased support for the Baghdad Pact and its members. We should make a further effort to persuade the US to join the Pact. We should seek to draw Iraq and Jordan more closer together. We should try to detach Saudi Arabia from Egypt by making plain to King Saud the nature of Nasser's ambitions. We should seek further support for Libya, in order to prevent the extension of Egyptian or Communist influence there. We should seek to establish in Syria a Government more friendly to the West. We should counter Egyptian subversion in the Sudan and the Persian Gulf. There were also possibilities of action aimed more directly at Egypt – e.g., the withholding of military supplies, the withdrawal of financial support for the Aswan Dam, the reduction of US economic aid, and the blocking of sterling balances.

In all this we should need the support of the US Government. The first task would be to seek Anglo-American agreement on a general realignment of policy towards Egypt.

Despite his earlier castigation of Nutting, Eden had no alternative to present to the Cabinet. He asserted that 'he was in full agreement' with the Foreign Office approach and authorised Lloyd to present the package to Foster Dulles.[35]

The Foreign Office had apparently won the policy-making battle, but Eden's concession was incomplete. Without Ministerial consent or the knowledge of Foreign Office officials, Eden apparently authorised a separate policy for dealing with Nasser. Officers of MI6 and unofficial representatives contacted Egyptian military personnel and politicians who were prepared to form a government if Nasser was overthrown.[36]

In early 1956, a group of rebel officers formed 'The Supporters of Justice'. Julian Amery, the backbench Conservative MP, member of the Suez Group and Macmillan's son-in-law, had been a British intelligence officer in Egypt in the Second World War and had maintained excellent contacts in the country since then. Unlike the British Government, he knew about the Free Officers' movement in Egypt and their plans for the 1952 coup months before it happened. In 1956, Amery discussed the replacement of the Egyptian leader with a 'shadow government' of the rebels. The dissidents said that they would assume power after Britain had toppled Nasser by covert or overt means. Amery passed selected portions of the talks to 'certain friends' in the intelligence services. The CIA and MI6 subsequently exchanged lists of dissident Egyptian officers.[37]

How could Eden have authorised planning against Nasser which not only bypassed the Foreign Office but was incompatible with the Cabinet's policy? The answer lay in the Prime Minister's temper, MI6's desire to topple 'anti-British' governments, and direct liaison between Eden and the intelligence services through the Permanent Under-secretary's Department of the Foreign Office (PUSD).

Formed in 1948, the PUSD contained a planning section, the Permanent Undersecretary's Committee, which was supposed to be a co-ordinating body for long-term planning by the Foreign Office, the military and service departments, and the intelligence services. By 1956, the planning section had little influence upon policy-making; instead, the PUSD primarily functioned as an adjunct to MI6 and other depart-ments in operational matters.

Formally, the PUSD was supervised by Kirkpatrick and Lloyd. The Foreign Secretary, however, was occupied with the burdens of his post, and Kirkpatrick, familiar with covert operations and a strong proponent of action against Egypt and the Soviet bloc, did not interfere with MI6's plans. The result was that Eden gave MI6 carte blanche, despite the possible impact of the intelligence service's plans upon the Foreign Office's more cautious approach.*

The Crabb incident in April 1956 illustrated the problems of this 'system'. When Soviet leaders Nikolai Bulganin and Nikita Khrushchev visited Britain, MI6 wanted to discover why the cruiser on which they travelled, the *Ordjonikidze*, was faster than British warships. When the cruiser docked in Portsmouth Harbour, the service hired a frogman, Commander Lionel 'Buster' Crabb, RNVR (retired), to inspect its hull. His first mission was successful, but he never surfaced from the second. His decapitated body was washed ashore in the summer.[38]

Eden knew nothing of the mission until a Soviet note, two weeks after Crabb's disappearance, asked for an explanation of a frogman floating near the *Ordjonikidze*. He told Ministers that, asked by the Admiralty about the mission a few weeks before the Soviet visit, he had written 'a clear and precise minute, expressly forbidding anything of the kind'. An inquiry by Sir Edward Bridges, the former Cabinet Secretary, cleared Ministers and senior MI6 officials of responsibility for the event, claiming that the operation had been planned and implemented by junior personnel of MI6. In December 1956, Eden approved Bridges's recom-mendation that Dean, 'in his personal capacity, undertake an inquiry into

---

*In an interview with the author, Sir Patrick Dean, the Assistant Undersecretary supervising the department in 1956, stated that the PUSD 'was a liaison department and was consulted on specific issues, defence matters and that sort of thing'. He also confirmed that he was Chairman of the Joint Intelligence Committee, 'which met every week and produced a report on current world developments'. Dean denies that he was in any way a link or channel between Eden and MI6 (author's interview with Sir Patrick Dean).

the question of balance between military intelligence on the one hand, and civilian intelligence and political risks on the other'.[39]

The fiasco arose because Eden had given MI6 the authority to gather information on the Soviets without ensuring that he knew of all operations. John Henry, a MI6 technical officer who knew of the Crabb operation, commented: 'You know what Eden is like. One minute he says you can do something, the next minute not. We thought it was an acceptable risk to take.' MI6 referred the Crabb mission to the then Foreign Officer Adviser, Michael Williams, for approval, but Williams had just learned of the death of his father. Confronted with the proposal at the end of the day, he approved it without referring it to higher authority.[40]

The same system encouraged MI6, without consulting Foreign Office officials outside the PUSD, to plot Nasser's downfall. A new head of MI6, Sir Dick White, was appointed to prevent a repetition of the Crabb fiasco, but his career had been spent in MI5, the British domestic intelligence service, and he needed time to adjust to MI6 procedures. Williams, after taking a leave of absence, was replaced as Foreign Office Adviser in July 1956 by Geoffrey Macdermott. As the US Embassy noted, 'The reshuffle of the chain-of-command of certain intelligence units after the embarrassing episode of Commander Crabbe [sic] . . . brought increased authority to Dean.'[41] The result was two British foreign policies, one developed and implemented by Foreign Office officials, the other by Eden and MI6. George Young, MI6's Deputy Director in charge of Middle Eastern operations, later wrote:

As happened with Major General John Sinclair [the Director of MI6 from 1953 to 1956] . . . the outsider was totally lost. His orders bore no relation to reality so that they were ignored on the working level; sometimes with successful outcome as in setting the stage for the overthrow of [Iranian leader] Mossadegh, and sometimes disastrously as with frogman Crabbe [sic].[42]

8

The Turning-point: Washington
March 1956

The Eisenhower Administration was also reviewing the Middle
Eastern situation. Throughout February, the President's envoy
for Operation BETA, Robert Anderson, had pressed the
Egyptians for proposals to put to Israel. CIA officials, working with the
Minister of the Interior, Mohieddin, and Ali Sabri, another member of
Nasser's inner circle, drafted a letter from the Egyptian leader to
Eisenhower. Nasser asked for 'the establishment of Arab sovereignty over
a satisfactory substantial territory connecting Egypt and Jordan', the offer
to Palestinian refugees of repatriation to Israel or compensation for their
land, the negotiation of a solution on Jerusalem's status 'acceptable to the
world community', termination of the state of belligerency, followed by
the removal of the Arab economic boycott of Israel and restrictions on the
passage of Israeli shipping through the Suez Canal and the Gulf of Aqaba,
and agreement on the Jordan waters' plan. As late as 21 February, Nasser
confirmed to a CIA representative, probably Roosevelt, that he was
committed to the outcome of the CIA's talks with Mohieddin and
Sabri and that he was ready to resume discussions with Anderson. The
CIA official estimated that there was even a twenty per cent chance
that Nasser would soon agree to a direct, high-level meeting with the
Israelis.[1]

The Administration, however, was under pressure from American
politicians and Israeli diplomats to increase arms shipments to Tel Aviv,
especially after public controversy over the shipment of eighteen light
tanks to Saudi Arabia. On 23 February, Foster Dulles informed Ambassador Makins that time for finding an Arab-Israeli settlement was
short and that it was 'doubtful that the US Government could hold off on

arms to Israel'.[2] The next day, the Secretary told the Senate Foreign Relations Committee:

It would seem that Israel's security could be better assured, in the long run, through measures other than the acquisition of additional arms in circumstances which might exacerbate the situation. . . . The US does not exclude the possibility of arms sales to Israel at a time when it will preserve the peace.[3]

The Israelis were far from reassured. The US Ambassador, Edward Lawson, said that he 'had never seen Ben-Gurion so emphatic, so forceful, or so emotionally upset and, on several occasions, so near to tears'. Ben-Gurion pleaded: 'If the answer [on arms] is to be no, please let it be said now. It [is] a question of life or death. We are in mortal danger.'[4] The Israeli Director and Deputy Director of Military Intelligence told American contacts that the entire Egyptian army was in the Sinai, and the Israel Defence Forces were urging Ben-Gurion to attack 'before it was too late'.[5]

Foster Dulles was caught in a dilemma. If he maintained his faith in BETA, he risked a showdown with the pro-Israeli lobby in an election year. If he increased US arms to Israel, he would doom the efforts of Anderson, who had obtained Eisenhower's approval of a last effort with Nasser. The Egyptian leader would be asked to promote the agreement upon the Johnston plan for the division of the Jordan waters 'on condition that the US and UK would not attempt to expand the membership of the Baghdad Pact'.[6] The Secretary responded with a dual approach. Publicly, the US would support the enforcement of the Tripartite Declaration and the UN's efforts to conclude an Arab-Israeli settlement. Privately, the State Department would endorse arms supplies to Israel through third countries and, if Anderson's last efforts failed with Egypt, review its position towards Nasser.[7]

The British immediately tried to exploit Foster Dulles's changing position. Makins advised London: 'The Americans are groping too for a policy, and need our help and advice. Moreover, they are evidently bracing up to the necessity of accepting additional responsibility in the Middle East.' Eden wrote to Eisenhower on 5 March:

There is no doubt that the Russians are resolved to liquidate the Baghdad Pact. In this undertaking Nasser is supporting them and I suspect that his relations with the Soviets are much closer than he admits to us. Recent events in Jordan are part of this pattern.

Asking for American accession to the Pact and more Centurion tanks to Iraq, the Prime Minister concluded: 'Certainly we should accept, I think, that a policy of appeasement will bring us nothing in Egypt. Our best chance is to show that it pays to be our friends.'[8]

Lloyd, in Karachi for a Ministerial meeting of the South-East Asian Treaty Organisation, conferred with Foster Dulles the next day, but the request for American accession to the Baghdad Pact was premature. Foster Dulles had not forgotten the failure of the Templer mission to Jordan, and Anderson's faint hopes in Egypt rested upon a moratorium on Pact membership: 'There was still a sufficient chance to salvage something from our relations with Nasser.' Moreover, 'a political crisis over US relations with Israel', provoked by Congressional debate over accession, 'would be the one thing that might rob President Eisenhower of victory [in the Presidential election]'. Nutting commented to Eden, 'It does not seem that the Americans have yet hoisted in that appeasement of Nasser simply does not pay and that whatever "bargain" you make with him he will break.'[9]

Within the next twenty-four hours, however, Foster Dulles reached that conclusion. On 5–6 March, Anderson held his third set of meetings with Nasser. The Egyptian leader firmly refused to meet an American Jewish leader, let alone an Israeli. He then introduced the 'completely new and discouraging element' that Egypt would 'not put the proposal forward as its own idea', but would 'have to discuss the appropriate outside source to make the proposals'. Nasser, who was meeting Anderson during a summit with King Saud and the Syrian President, Shukri Quwwatli, apparently had learned that he could 'not lead the other Arab States or [he] would end up leading [himself] alone'. He might even share the fate of Jordan's King Abdullah, assassinated in 1951 after secret talks between Jordanian and Israeli officials.[10] Foster Dulles told Lloyd:

Unless Nasser did something definite soon, we would have to 'ditch' him. By something definite, he meant an immediate cessation of propaganda against the Baghdad Pact and the West, acceptance of the Johnston plan, and definite steps toward a settlement of the Arab-Israeli dispute.[11]

Shuckburgh, talking to American officials in London, wrote: 'Today both we and the Americans really gave up hope of Nasser and began to look around for means of destroying him.'

On 8 March, Foster Dulles sent Eisenhower the results of a 'speculative exercise' on a programme against Egypt. Possible measures included US adherence to the Baghdad Pact; a settlement of the dispute between Britain and Saudi Arabia over Buraimi; a Congressional resolution authorising Eisenhower to act with the UN to ensure Arab and Israeli compliance with armistice lines; 'substantial military support' to Saudi Arabia and Iraq and accelerated programmes for Iran and Pakistan; and defensive arms to Israel.[12] The President adopted Foster Dulles's position:

We have reached the point where it looks as if Egypt, under Nasser, is going to make no move whatsoever to meet the Israelis in an effort to settle outstanding differences. Moreover, the Arabs, absorbing major consignments of arms from the Soviets, are daily growing more arrogant and disregarding the interests of Western Europe and the US in the Middle Eastern region. It would begin to appear that our efforts should be directed towards separating the Saudi Arabians from the Egyptians and concentrating, for the moment at least, in making the former see that their best interests lie with us, and not with the Egyptians and with the Russians.[13]

Approval of an Anglo-American campaign against Nasser awaited the return of Anderson and Foster Dulles to Washington. On 9 March, Eisenhower replied to Eden's letter of the 5th: 'It may be that we shall be driven to conclude that it is impossible to do business with Nasser. However, I do not think that we should close the door yet on the possibility of working with him.' The President agreed to forty Centurion tanks for Iraq and increased aid to Iran and Pakistan, but 'questioned whether adherance [sic] by the US to the Baghdad Pact now is the right answer'.[14]

Three days later, Anderson briefed Eisenhower and Undersecretary of State Hoover. Unable to arrange direct Egyptian-Israeli negotiations, he could only suggest letters from Eisenhower to Ben-Gurion and Nasser expressing the President's disappointment. The meeting concluded that 'a suitable tripartite resolution [on the Arab-Israeli issue] should be introduced in the Security Council at an early opportunity' and that 'we should make every attempt to try to effect a split between Saudi Arabia and Egypt'.[15]

ALPHA had been doomed from its inception. Nasser would only accept a settlement that provided a common Egyptian-Jordanian border, rather than transit rights or a 'corridor' across the Negev desert. The Israeli Government would not consider cession of the Negev. The two positions were irreconcilable, regardless of the inducements offered for a settlement. Nasser, presented with the plan for a flyover and an underpass allowing Egyptian and Israeli transit across the two triangles of territory ceded to the Arabs, asked: 'Supposing one of our soldiers wanted to piss and did so from the overpass on to some Israeli in the underpass – wouldn't that start a war?' Anderson allegedly retreated to the suggestion that the Egyptians and Jordanians could use the overpass for six hours while the Israelis halted their traffic and vice versa.[16]

Yet American plans for Middle Eastern defence against the Soviet Union depended upon ALPHA's success. Unless the Administration admitted defeat, it had to 'find' another government in Israel or Egypt that would consider compromise. Even if Nasser had not antagonised the

West with the arms deal with the Soviets, even if he had not disagreed with British plans, American politics dictated Foster Dulles's inevitable decision. With a campaign for re-election imminent, Eisenhower could ill-afford to be perceived as 'anti-Israeli'. When ALPHA was launched, Foster Dulles told Shuckburgh:

The Arabs must be made to comprehend the continued power of American Jewry and the fact that, if Arab attitudes continued to be unreasonable, the balance of focus may shift from their side. . . . After 1955, the Arab-Israeli problem would be in US domestic politics and, if the Republicans failed to offer measures acceptable to American Jewry, the Democrats would surely promise to make a reasonable settlement possible.[17]

Briefing Anderson before his departure in January, Foster Dulles outlined the 'bargaining positions' the US could use to extract concessions from Egypt and Israel, but it was soon obvious that American pressure could only be applied against Cairo. The Secretary noted: 'Nasser would be willing to pay a considerable price to get the support of the US in limiting the Baghdad Pact to its present Arab membership . . . with Egypt maintaining its hegemony of the Arab countries.' Economically, 'in relation to cotton . . . [the US] could either destroy or help Egypt's market' and withhold finance for the Aswan High Dam. Finally, the US could construct a canal, financed by oil companies, outside Egypt.

Israel was immune from these threats, as the pro-Israeli lobby in Congress precluded any withdrawal of American aid. Foster Dulles's only suggestion was to warn Tel Aviv:

There was . . . a growing realization that backing Israel might be very costly to vital US national interests. Israel from now on would have to play the part of a good neighbor to the Arabs and not seek to maintain itself by its own force and foreign backing. Unless the Israelis realized this, they were doomed.[18]

Eisenhower recorded the significance of Anderson's failure in his diary. While both Israel and Egypt had refused to make concessions, the President rationalised: 'Nasser proved to be a complete stumbling block. He is apparently seeking to be acknowledged as the political leader of the Arab world.' In contrast, Israel was 'a tiny nation, surrounded by enemies. . . . [It had] a very strong position in the heart and emotions of the Western world because of the tragic suffering of the Jews throughout 2,500 years of history.' Eisenhower concluded:

I think we can hold Libya to our side through a reasonable amount of help to that impoverished nation, and we have an excellent chance of winning Saudi Arabia to our side if we can get Britain to go along with us. Britain would, of course, have to make certain territorial concessions, and this she might object to violently. If Saudi Arabia and Libya were our staunch friends, Egypt could scarcely continue intimate associations with the Soviets, and a certain Egyptian would no longer be regarded as a leader of the Arab world.[19]

British pressure upon the US now paid dividends. Eden wrote to Eisenhower on 15 March:

I send you herewith a most secret note of Egyptian intentions of whose authenticity we are entirely confident. . . . It adds nothing startlingly new to what we both suspected. It does, however, confirm the wide range of Egyptian ambitions against the Saudis, as well as Iraq and Jordan.[20]

The note claimed 'absolutely reliable information' that a conference of Egyptian Ambassadors and Ministers in January had agreed that Egypt's 'ultimate aim was to form United Arab States' of republics 'with no Customs, a common educational and economic system and an Arab Currency Bank which would control the financial affairs'. This would be established by:

 (i) the unseating of Nuri el Sa'id, the Iraqi Prime Minister, and the frustration of the Baghdad Pact;
 (ii) the overthrow of Hashemite families in Iraq and Jordan;
 (iii) the overthrow of the monarchy in Libya and the establishment of purely Arab republics in Tunisia, Algeria, and Morocco . . . ;
 (iv) whilst Saudi Arabia would be encouraged to partake in Egyptian moves against Iraq and Jordan, the long-term policy was first to isolate Saudi Arabia as the only remaining Monarchy in the Eastern Arabian States and then to remove King Saud . . . ;
 (v) in order to implement this policy, Egypt was despatching educational missions to all the Arab States. Several of the personnel of each mission had been trained as intelligence agents before their departure.[21]

MI6 was busily compiling reports from LUCKY BREAK, an operative in Cairo who controlled an agent that was allegedly within Nasser's 'inner circle'. On 8 March, Ambassador Trevelyan wrote to Shuckburgh of 'information from a generally well-informed source' that 'Nasser has already decided to engage in hostilities with Israel and has even decided that June would be the best time (our troops will then be out of the Canal Zone)'.[22] The report was passed to the US Embassy in London on the 21st. Meanwhile, British military representatives in Washington were informed that Anglo-American discussions must consider 'the probability that Egypt is more likely to be the aggressor'.[23] The information was suspect, and Nasser assured US Ambassador Byroade that he did 'not want to gamble so foolishly with the future of my own country',[24] but Eisenhower's developing antagonism towards Nasser had been reinforced. He replied to Eden: 'Assuming that the information therein contained is completely authentic, it seems to me to give a clue of how we – your Government and ours – might operate with the greatest chance of frustrating Soviet designs in the region.'[25]

Members of Eisenhower's Administration were also advising the President to take a firmer line. Since January, the US Information Service had prepared for a campaign against Egypt with 'steps to cut back on materials that enhanced the prestige of Nasser' and 'production and use of materials in support of moderate Arab elements'. A typical measure was the removal of film in a USIS newsreel of Nasser reviewing troops.[26] Admiral Radford, the Chairman of the Joint Chiefs of Staff, warned Eisenhower: 'If the US does not join the Baghdad Pact, there are signs the Pact may disintegrate. . . . The time may be coming when we will have to serve some notice on certain of the Middle Eastern countries.' Admiral Arleigh Burke, the Chief of Naval Operations, added, 'By dumping cotton, great pressure could be exerted [on Egypt]. Similarly, by curtailing oil output in some areas, the flow of money [to anti-Western activists] might be curtailed.'[27] Hoover, telling Eisenhower about an Israeli request for twenty-four F-86 fighters and anti-tank weapons, remarked, 'It might . . . seem desirable for us to give them a very few items, more in the nature of radar equipment than airplanes and anti-tank weapons, and at the same time fulfill some of the requests which we have from Saudi Arabia.' He concluded: 'Nasser appeared to be becoming a progressively increasing menace. We were therefore giving added attention to methods of splitting the Saudis away from the Egyptians and to obtain closer relations with Libyans.'[28]

On 23 March, the Joint Chiefs of Staff formally recommended US adherence to the Baghdad Pact. Most importantly, an ad hoc Middle Eastern planning group, established in late February to consider American policy if an Arab-Israeli settlement could not be achieved, drafted a summary on 14 March of measures against Nasser.[29]

After a British *aide-mémoire* informed the Americans of the Cabinet's adoption of a long-term programme against Nasser, Foster Dulles received a request from CIA Director Allen Dulles for a meeting 'on something urgent . . . about the Middle East'. On 24 March, at Foster Dulles's home, the two brothers were joined by James Angleton, Director of the CIA's Counter-intelligence Staff and the chief CIA contact with Mossad, Israel's foreign intelligence service; Kermit Roosevelt; Hoover; Assistant Secretary George Allen; William Rountree, Allen's deputy for Near Eastern affairs; Francis Russell; and Herman Phleger, the State Department's chief legal officer. The meeting considered the memorandum of 14 March and the following questions:

1) Can Nasser rally Arab world behind him and precipitate war with Israel?

2) Can we at the same time win the Saudis away from alliance with Nasser and bolster Iraq?

3) What is oil situation and what losses can Western Europe and NATO tolerate?

4) What are vulnerabilities re loss of [oil] production and loss of transport?

5) Can Iraq be built up as a rival to Egypt having regard to a) our Israeli policy and b) our Saudi Arabian policy?

6) [Deleted]

7) Can Communist atheism be explored?[30]

The revision of the memorandum became Operation OMEGA, the cornerstone of Anglo-American co-operation against Nasser. Foster Dulles informed Eisenhower on 28 March:

In view of the negative outcome of our efforts to bring Colonel Nasser to adopt a policy of conciliation toward Israel, we should, I believe, now adjust certain of our Near Eastern policies, as indicated below.

The primary purpose would be to let Colonel Nasser realize that he cannot cooperate as he is doing with the Soviet Union and at the same time enjoy most-favored-nation treatment from the United States. We would want for the time being to avoid any open break which would throw Nasser irrevocably into a Soviet satellite status and we would want to leave Nasser a bridge back to good relations with the West if he so desires.

The policies indicated below would in the main be coordinated with the United Kingdom.

I. As regards Egypt:

1. Export licenses covering arms shipments to Egypt, whether from Governmental or commercial sources, will continue to be denied by the US and the UK.

2. The US and the UK will continue to delay the conclusion of current negotiations on the High Aswan Dam.

3. The US will continue to delay action on pending Egyptian requests for grains and oil. . . .

4. The US will hold in abeyance any decision on a *CARE* program [of economic aid] for Egypt for 1956 . . . or, alternatively, approve an $8 million program for the first quarter, leaving until later a decision on the balance [of $100 million] for the year.

5. Expanded radio facilities will be offered to Iraq to counter Egyptian broadcasts.

II. As regards other countries:

1. The US and UK will commence negotiations with the Sudan with a view to developing – [deleted] – a situation of influence in that country which would minimize Egyptian influence and its control of the head waters of the Nile.

2. Intensify present efforts to stabilize the situation in Libya.

3. Encourage the UK to maintain present treaty relationships with Jordan and help it to prevent a situation in which a pro-Egyptian coup d'état would succeed . . . [deleted]

4. Give increased support to the Baghdad Pact, without actually adhering to the Pact or announcing our intention of doing so. In addition to accelerated aid to the Pact countries, this support will consist of amending the nature of our participation in the Military Committee of the Pact, such as by assigning high-level officers who could join more actively in military discussions than our observers have in the past. We will also display an increased interest in the economic aspects of the Pact by endeavoring to coordinate our aid programs with the Pact organization, wherever feasible, and by sending high-level officers to represent the United States in economic meetings related to the treaty organization.

5. We will undertake an intensified program in Ethiopia to enhance the Western position in that country.

6. We will continue to take all practicable steps to counter Egyptian and Soviet influence in Yemen and the other Arabian principalities. King Saud's assistance will be solicited.

7. The US will seek to dissuade the Israelis from undertaking work at Banat Ya'qub [to divert the waters of the Jordan River], or from taking other precipitate steps which might bring about hostilities and thus endanger the whole Western position in the Near East to the direct advantage of the Soviets.

8. For a further indefinite period the US will continue to deny export licenses for any major military items to Israel and the adjoining Arab States (this excepts Saudi Arabia and Iraq). We would, however, be sympathetic if other Western countries wished to sell limited quantities of defensive arms to Israel.

9. We will continue to press for effective UN action to reduce area tensions.

10. We will endeavor to strengthen pro-Western elements in Lebanon by immediately offering economic aid in the form of grants or loans for projects designed to create the most favorable impact on public opinion. (The French might sell limited quantities of military equipment.)

11. It is extremely important that the American position in Saudi Arabia be strengthened. We must find ways, in connection with the negotiation of a new [Dhahran] air base agreement . . . of assuring King Saud that some of his military needs will immediately be met and others provided for subsequently. We will press the British to undertake a generous agreement on the Buraimi issue. . . .

III. In addition to the foregoing course of action, planning should be undertaken at once with a view to possibly more drastic action in the event that the above courses of action do not have the desired effect. This plan should cover: [paragraph deleted]

Foster Dulles's long-hand notes offer clues to 'more drastic' action. Pressure would be placed upon the price of Egyptian cotton through dumping of American supplies on the international market; Egyptian radio transmissions would be jammed; an Export-Import Bank loan for Israel would be arranged; and the US would 'study Syrian assets' for a possible coup if Damascus continued to follow Nasser.[31]

That afternoon, Eisenhower considered the memorandum at a meeting with Foster Dulles, Hoover, Allen, Rountree, Reuben Robertson of the Department of Defense, Secretary of Defense Wilson, and Radford. Eisenhower emphasised, 'We should make sure we concert the overall plan with the British – i.e., with Eden and Lloyd.' At the same time, the plan to build up King Saud to offset Nasser 'would probably require a settlement of the Buraimi issue, for which we would ask as a *quid pro quo* a better attitude on the part of the Saudis toward Iraq'. Apart from the precondition of an Anglo-Saudi agreement over Buraimi, Foster Dulles was given a free hand to implement OMEGA.[32] Eisenhower wrote in his diary:

I have authorized the State Department to start work on all of the attached points [in the OMEGA memorandum]. A fundamental factor in the problem is the growing ambition of Nasser, the sense of power he has gained out of his associations with the Soviets, his belief that he can emerge as a true leader of the entire Arab world – and because of these beliefs, his rejection of every proposition advanced as a measure of conciliation between the Arabs and Israel. . . .

[I hope] that we begin to build up some other individual as a prospective leader of the Arab world. . . . My own choice of such a rival is King Saud. . . . Arabia is a country that contains the holy places of the Moslem world, and the Saudi Arabians are considered to be the most deeply religious of all the Arab groups. Consequently, the King could be built up, possibly as a spiritual leader. Once this was accomplished, we might begin to urge his right to political leadership.[33]

The Middle Eastern Policy Planning Group, originally set up to oversee ALPHA, was directed to supervise OMEGA, with Raymond Hare, a former Ambassador to Saudi Arabia, taking charge.[34]

Two measures were immediately significant in the battle against Nasser. The first was the decision to let negotiations on the funding of the Aswan High Dam 'languish'. In February, both the Foreign Office and the State Department intervened to prevent a breakdown of discussions between Egypt and the World Bank, not only to save the Dam, but to prevent the breakdown of the Anderson mission for an Egyptian-Israeli accord. The Bank agreed to provide its $200 million, and the Egyptians suggested amendments to the British and American conditions for their $200 million contribution to the project.[35] Nasser wanted the two countries to commit aid for both stages of the project, rather than the initial stage alone, because he feared that Britain and the US might subsequently withhold the 'second-stage' funding, suspending construction of the Dam. As late as 8 March, Eisenhower told a Republican governor, 'We want Egypt to build that dam. [The] problem is to get Congress to deal sensibly.'[36]

Then the Americans, for domestic reasons, began to have doubts about the Dam. The pro-Israeli lobby opposed any assistance to Egypt. Fiscal conservatives thought the Dam a wasteful foreign-aid project, and Congressmen from Southern states feared that the increased output of Egyptian cotton would depress the price for cotton from their states. By 24 March, Secretary of the Treasury Humphrey and Undersecretary of State Hoover, both of whom opposed the negotiations with Egypt in December, were swinging Administration sentiment against the Dam.[37]

Secondly, OMEGA confirmed the pivotal position of Syria in Middle Eastern affairs.[38] Throughout 1955, British and American representatives in Syria sought a pro-Western coalition of right-wing parties that could restore 'stability', but a suitable leader could not be found. In August, Shukri Quwwatli, financed by the Saudis and supported by the Egyptians, won the Presidential election.[39] With an internal solution unlikely, London and Washington considered Iraq's desire for union with Syria. In the summer of 1955, the Iraqis conferred with Adib Shishakli, who held power in Syria from 1951 to 1954, and an Iraqi envoy asked British and American officials if they would 'recognise a Syrian Government which came into power by a coup d'état'. On 4 October, Iraqi Prime Minister Nuri Sa'id told the British and American Ambassadors:

[Syria] was in the grip of an evilly-disposed minority. . . . Iraq could not allow the situation to deteriorate much further. [I] would like at this stage to 'speak gently' with the Syrians and urge them to improve their regime and get rid of subversive elements and those unfriendly to Iraq. If this failed to achieve its object, [I] would want to intervene in Syria, if necessary by force.[40]

Michel Ilyan, a leading Syrian politician since the 1940s, told the British that the only way 'to save Syria from the Communists was to invite the Iraqis in'. He also informed the US Ambassador to Syria, James Moose, that he was planning to go to Baghdad, 'where he had many good friends; however, time for his trip was not ripe'.[41]

The Foreign Office opposed 'overt Iraqi action', but G. G. Arthur proposed a long-term programme, co-ordinated with the Americans and Iraqis, for Iraqi-Syrian union:

(a) bribery within Syria, by or on behalf of Iraq. The Syrian Army should be the main target;
(b) the rapid build-up of the Iraqi forces . . .;

(c) propaganda in Syria in favour of Iraq, designed especially to bring home to Syrians the economic advantages to be derived from friendship with the Iraqis;

(d) . . . efforts to subordinate the Syrian economy to Iraq's, e.g., by an Iraqi loan to Syria;

(e) measures, overt and covert, to counter Saudi influence in Syria;

(f) propaganda designed to bring home to the Iraqi public the importance to them of a stable and friendly Syria.[42]

Shuckburgh and Macmillan seized upon this as a 'Machiavellian scheme' for Iraqi-Syrian union. The British Ambassador to Syria, John Gardener, reported that Britain could 'bring about the merger of Syria with Iraq any time we like if given enough money'.[43]

Despite Foster Dulles's complaints to Macmillan about Syrian behaviour, the State Department rejected sponsorship of Iraqi-Syrian union, primarily because of Saudi Arabian opposition to a 'Greater Iraq' and Israeli suspicion of Iraqi forces on her border.[44] James Moose reported a request by the banned Partie Populaire Syrienne, possibly in co-operation with Shishakli, for American support for a coup, but the CIA was 'very leery' about the plan and Foster Dulles 'did not want to start anything unless it would succeed'. Instead, the Americans thought immediate action 'needed to be directed towards bringing the right-wing groups [in Syria] together'.[45] By the time of the Eden–Eisenhower summit, Britain and the US had neared agreement on a programme similar to Arthur's memorandum and linked it to the Iraqi-Jordanian axis and further action against Egypt. Nuri reiterated to Lloyd on 10 March that, 'provided that the Turks and Israelis had been squared beforehand and that the Americans would acquiesce, he was confident that he could mount the operation in Syria at short notice'.[46]

On one level, the events of March 1956 drew the British and Americans into a 'conditional' alliance against Nasser. While the interests of the two countries still differed, each recognised a long-term threat to its objectives and believed that co-ordination of policy was preferable to unilateral action. In another sense, however, there was no Anglo-American 'alliance' because there was no single British policy. The Foreign Office had secured Cabinet support for a programme, but that policy was a long-term one. Meanwhile, Britain's intelligence services, under the general mandate given to them by Eden, prepared a 'shadow' Egyptian government for power without consulting the Foreign Office and considered political changes in other Middle Eastern countries. Eventually, such action would conflict with American interests and the methods of OMEGA.

9

The OMEGA Discussions
April 1956

O n 31 March and 1 April, Wilbur Eveland, a Middle Eastern
specialist seconded by the CIA from the Department of
Defense, and James Eichelberger, the CIA station chief in
Cairo, held a series of meetings with George Young, the Deputy Director
of MI6 responsible for Middle Eastern operations, Nigel Clive, MI6's
Political Officer, and other British officials. After Eveland and
Eichelberger prepared an 'intelligence appreciation' with MI6 and heard
British proposals for OMEGA's implementation, Allen Dulles and
Kermit Roosevelt would confer with MI6.

MI6 had convinced Eden of Nasser's evil intentions, and Young and
Clive set out to do the same for the Americans:

Nasser's aims are total destruction of Israel; Egyptian domination of all Arab
governments and elimination of all Western positions in the Arab area; material
extension of Egyptian influence in North Africa, particularly Libya. In order to
realize his ambitions, Nasser has accepted full-scale collaboration with the
Soviets, and is prepared to allow the Soviets whatever role in area they desire in
order to assure himself of their support. Nasser is now taking the initiative for
extension of Soviet influence in Syria, Libya, and French North Africa. Egypt
must therefore be regarded as an out and out Soviet instrument.

MI6 was counting on the twenty-five reports sent by the operative
LUCKY BREAK from Cairo since November 1955. LUCKY
BREAK allegedly controlled an agent in the highest ranks of the
Egyptian Government. Whether the source was passing information he
believed to be genuine or creating false reports to turn London against
Nasser, the intelligence caused a furor within the British Government. As
early as 29 November, Eden's Press Secretary, William Clark, wrote: 'It

is clear that Nasser has gone further than I'd ever supposed towards a tie-up with the Communists. It is impossible to believe that we can go on supporting him in the long-run.' Macmillan, then Foreign Secretary, wrote to Ambassador Makins in Washington: 'We are afraid that Nasser, whether innocently or deliberately, is dangerously committed to the Communists. Consequently, we believe that it would be advantageous, in any event, to overthrow him if possible.'

The British evaluation provoked immediate conflict with Eveland and Eichelberger. The CIA, with excellent contacts within the Egyptian military and Nasser's 'inner circle' of advisers, was suspicious of MI6's appraisal. Young snapped that, since the Agency was 'apparently not yet prepared for categorical acceptance of [the British] reappraisal of Nasser, [the CIA's] intelligence coverage in Egypt must be regarded as poor', and CIA reports passed to MI6 in recent months were 'rubbish'.

Not content with an intelligence appreciation, Young and Clive presented a three-phase plan of operations, embellishing it with comments like 'Britain [is] now prepared to fight its last battle' and 'no matter what the cost we will win'. The first phase was a 'complete change in Government of Syria', to be achieved within a month. The British could achieve this alone, 'but, if necessary', they would consider 'joint action with Iraq, Turkey, and possibly Israel'. Turkey would create incidents on the Syrian border, Iraq would agitate the tribes on the Iraqi-Syrian frontier and the pro-Iraqi Partie Populaire Syrienne would infiltrate Syria from Lebanon. Syria would not be annexed by Iraq, but 'a firm pro-Iraqi government' would emerge in an 'extension of Hashemite influence'.

In the second phase, the British would 'undertake efforts to exploit splits in [Saudi] Royal Family and possibly utilize their position [in the] Trucial States to hasten fall of [King] Saud'. If the CIA was unwilling or unable to assist, the British would consider 'joint action with Iraqis or action behind Iraqi front'. Finally, Britain would prepare action against Nasser 'in anticipation of violent Egyptian reaction to phases 1 and 2'. Possible measures ranged from sanctions

to use of force (both British and Israeli) to tumble the Egyptian Government. . . . Extreme possibilties would involve special operations by Israelis against Egyptian supply dumps and newly acquired aircraft and tanks, as well as outright Israeli attack [upon] Gaza or other border areas.[1]

The Americans were taken aback. Collaboration with Israel would turn the Arab world against the West, but Young had advocated operations with the 'snipcocks'. The attempted overthrow of King Saud risked the American oil concession and use of the Dhahran air base. Eveland had joked to Eichelberger that Britain would ask the US to do away with

Nasser. Eichelberger responded seriously: 'If our British cousins [MI6] had their way, that would be just the plan.' Eichelberger was so disturbed that he allegedly told Egyptian contacts about MI6's eagerness to remove Nasser from power. Foster Dulles told Henry Cabot Lodge, the US Ambassador to the United Nations, after the follow-up meetings between Allen Dulles, Roosevelt and MI6: 'The British are making more drastic plans than we are.' He explained to a Congressional delegation:

Unless and until we can bring the UK around to our view, it would be a mistake to identify ourselves too closely with them in the Near East. . . . The British have made a number of mistakes in the area. They are in a state of undeclared war with Saudi Arabia. The UK broke off arbitration on the Buraimi matter and then took over the area by armed force. They act in this way without consulting with the US. . . . In Jordan the British went ahead, against our advice, in attempting to force Jordan's adherence to the Baghdad Pact. . . . In Egypt the British have very bad relations with Nasser.[2]

Some of the damage caused by MI6 was repaired in Anglo-American diplomatic and military discussions. Makins met Foster Dulles on Easter Monday, 1 April, to consider the various elements of the OMEGA programme.[3] Air Chief Marshal Sir William Dickson, the Chairman of the British Chiefs of Staff, met Eisenhower, and they agreed upon the 'large hazards in an Arab "bloc" extending from Pakistan to Dakar, with weak and unstable governments and institutions, and resulting vulnerability to Soviet penetration'. The President stressed 'the importance of [British and American] information, propaganda, and political warfare activities in the area' and the need to develop OMEGA:

We have very considerable assets in the area, if we would just make use of them. . . . We should try to build up a 'design' for our actions in the Middle East. . . . Actions should be under the direction of selected, very astute individuals.[4]

Dickson assured the Americans:

When he had left London, the British had been in a bit of a flap about the situation in the Middle East and felt the current was running against them. More recent messages . . . seemed to indicate that, while there was serious concern, London was not in a state of flap.[5]

Ambassador Aldrich confirmed from London that the 'recurring panic in the highest quarters here was allayed, at least for the time being'.[6]

The Foreign Office's caution was evident as it tried to prevent Nasser from learning of the Anglo-American plans. Foster Dulles had warned the British: 'We did not believe it would be productive for us to cooperate publicly on a joint basis, as it would perhaps carry the implication of ganging up.'[7] The Foreign Office had prematurely antagonised Nasser after the Egyptian leader gave interviews to the *Sunday Times* and the *Observer* in late March to indicate his desire for conciliation with Britain. The next day, a Foreign Office statement not only remarked that Nasser's deeds did not match his words, but also rejected any moratorium on new Arab membership of the Baghdad Pact. According to Trevelyan, Nasser took this as a 'declaration of war' by London.[8]

Trevelyan was instructed to avoid any reference to Egypt's blindness to the Communist threat, since this might indicate how seriously Britain viewed Nasser's collaboration with the Soviet bloc. When the British press, probably after Eden's 'leak' to Joseph Alsop, published headlines of 'British plans to hit back at Nasser',[9] the Foreign Office stated publicly that the speculation was groundless. Lloyd assured the State Department:

I have given no indication publicly or off the record that any new policy towards Nasser has been decided upon. I regard the whole matter as still under confidential discussion with the US Government, and when decisions are taken, their public handling will require careful consideration between us.[10]

After the Treasury's representative in Egypt returned from a visit to London, Trevelyan wrote to Shuckburgh: 'High officials in the Treasury particularly seem to have been very free with their proposals on what to do with Nasser, which include the most extreme solutions.' Shuckburgh commented, 'We have played the hand in exactly the opposite way from what we pretend to wish.' A. J. Wilton, supervising the Egyptian desk, added, 'British public feeling has seriously reduced the chances of our being able to temporise successfully', as Nasser told US Ambassador Byroade that Britain was 'now treating him publicly as an enemy'.[11]

Eden, however, persisted in his vitriolic denunciations of Nasser, and *The Times* publicised his attitude with virulent anti-Nasser leaders, arguing on 14 April:

The attempt to stabilise the Middle East in co-operation with Egypt is now over. Egypt has shown no desire to help. Britain must turn increasingly towards Iraq . . . and must make it clear to Egypt that non-co-operation does not pay. . . . If, while [Iraqi Prime Minister] Nuri Pasha tries to improve relations with friendly elements in Syria, Lebanon, and Jordan, [then] Britain and the United States can combine to reduce the Egyptian nuisance and check Saudi Arabian bribery, more difficult situations – and more difficult remedies – may be avoided.[12]

The Prime Minister was also complaining to journalists of American inaction, forcing Shuckburgh to apologise to Aldrich about the 'leaks from highest sources'.[13] The articles that followed prompted Eisenhower to speak to Foster Dulles 'about constant references in the press to the effect that the British Government is getting awfully sore with you and me and saying we are vacillating around about the Middle East'. Foster Dulles replied that he did 'not think it wise unless we are in agreement to take on the liability of the British situation. . . . They are so panicky – they need us publicly and it is all right if they are willing to pay the price.'[14]

The Americans were more successful in disguising their change of policy towards Egypt. Part of the 'cover-up' was a sustained effort to give Nasser a copy of his favourite film, *It's a Wonderful Life*, starring Jimmy Stewart. After unsuccessfully trying to buy a print from the director, Frank Capra, Nasser asked for Byroade's assistance in November 1955. The State Department fulfilled the request, and Byroade presented Nasser with the film, with English dialogue and French and Arabic subtitles, in May 1956.[15]

Eventually, the Foreign Office was able to overcome the belligerent rhetoric of other British agencies and resolved outstanding problems of Anglo-American co-operation. On 24 March, the Saudis proposed high-level discussions on Buraimi in New York. Foster Dulles repeatedly told Makins:

The key to any constructive program in the area involved the winning away of the Saudi Arabians from their present alignment with Egypt. . . . He strongly believed the situation was so serious that the UK might have to pay a price to split the Saudis from the Egyptians.

Lloyd finally authorised a mission, headed by the Parliamentary Under-secretary of State, Douglas Dodds-Parker, to visit Saudi Arabia by the end of April.[16]

Although the American military was unable to persuade Foster Dulles and Eisenhower to join the Baghdad Pact, American membership of the Economic and Counter-subversion Committees and the military liaison group were approved by Eisenhower on 19 April.[17] Britain and the US agreed to encourage the supply of arms to Israel through third countries, notably France and Canada, and approved the immediate sale by France of twelve Mystère IV fighters to Tel Aviv. Eden wrote that Britain had 'to continue [her] trickle' of arms to Israel and authorised delivery of six fighters and heavy artillery.[18] Discussions of possible sanctions against Egypt continued,[19] and the US Joint Chiefs of Staff agreed to further planning talks with the British.[20]

At the highest level, Anglo-American co-operation was fostered by the visit in April of Soviet leaders Bulganin and Khrushchev to London. Eisenhower wrote to Eden:

At the back of our minds must be the very grave threat in the Middle East. . . . I fully agree with you that we should not be acquiescent in any measure which would give the Bear's claws a grip on the production or transport of oil which is so vital to the defence and economy of the world.[21]

Foster Dulles confirmed to Makins:

If fighting came about, after every effort had been exhausted to find a peaceful solution of the Middle Eastern problem which would not deprive Britain and Western Europe of the oil of the area, . . . we would find, in one way or another, a way to be with you.[22]

Although little was decided at meetings with the Soviets, Eden wrote optimistically to Eisenhower:

In the Middle Eastern talk, I made plain to them that we had to have our oil and that we were prepared to fight for it. They accepted this and, though they continued to inveigh against the Baghdad Pact, I think they may have begun to understand that it is a protective pad for our vital interests and not a dagger pointing at their guts.[23]

MI6's threat to OMEGA had been negated, but other tests awaited. France, trying to quell rebellion by Algerian nationalists supported by Egypt and fearing British domination of the Middle East through the Baghdad Pact and treaties with Iraq and Jordan, had turned co-operation with Israel into an 'alliance'. In October 1955, the French Ministry of Defence agreed to the supply of seventy-two Mystère IV fighters, AMX tanks and other equipment to the Israelis. Completion of the deal was delayed, first by American objections to the deliveries and then by protests from the French Foreign Ministry. However, a change of government in France in early 1956 strengthened ties with Israel, as the Socialists, the dominant party in the French coalition, were philosophically close to the Mapai party of Prime Minister Ben-Gurion.[24]

In mid-March 1956, the French Government made a last effort at rapprochement with Egypt with a visit to Cairo by the Foreign Minister, Christian Pineau. Like Eden in 1955, Pineau was charmed by the Egyptian President. He later wrote:

The first impression was, contrary to expectations, almost always good. . . . Nasser did not have anything in common with Hitler, in his physique or in his behaviour. . . . One sensed him hesitant when he spoke of the future, as if that depended not on him but on God alone.

Pineau told the Prime Minister, Guy Mollet, 'I think sincerely that Nasser is not a second Hitler. . . . I am sure that he will never be the dictator of the Middle East.'[25]

Apparently, Pineau promised that France would show no interest in the Baghdad Pact in exchange for an Egyptian moratorium on training and aid to the Algerian rebels. Nasser refused to halt arms supplies, but gave his 'soldier's word of honour' that no rebels would be trained in Egypt. Encouraged, Pineau persuaded Mollet to allow French representatives to meet emissaries of the Algerian rebels, but the effort was abandoned when the plan leaked to the French press.[26]

The thaw in Franco-Egyptian relations was over. The number of French troops in Algeria was increased from 230,000 to 330,000. The Mollet Government decided to authorise deliveries of military equipment to Israel, without informing Britain and the US, and to arm Arab countries outside Egypt to foster 'the hopes of many of them to remain independent in the face of the imperialism, the economic colonialism, of the two "powers", the US and the Soviet Union'.[27]

The French support reinforced the hardline policy of Ben-Gurion and General Dayan. In November and December 1955, they proposed that Israel seize Sharm el-Sheikh at the southern tip of the Sinai Peninsula, guaranteeing Israeli control of the Straits of Tiran and the Gulf of Aqaba and access to the Red Sea. Moderates in the Israeli Cabinet narrowly rejected the proposal, but Israeli 'reprisals' continued. Without consulting his Cabinet, Ben-Gurion authorised an attack upon the Syrians at Kinneret on 11 December, killing more than fifty soldiers. The operation undermined the attempts of Foreign Minister Sharett to obtain American arms, but Ben-Gurion was unrepentant. He argued that, with the developing relationship with France, Israel would not need weapons from the US.[28]

The Anderson mission delayed further Israeli discussion of measures against Egypt, but fighting erupted on the Egyptian-Israeli border in April. Israeli forces bombarded the town of Gaza, killing more than sixty people and injuring more than a hundred. Nasser responded by sending more *fedayeen* into Israel. Fourteen Israelis and ten *fedayeen* were killed in the following five days.[29]

Initially, the Americans showed little concern,[30] but the continued killings convinced Foster Dulles that American action was necessary to prevent war. A White House press release defined three principles that guided American policy. Firstly, the US 'supported in fullest measure' the mission of the United Nations Secretary-General, Dag Hammarskjøld, to restore peace in the area. Secondly, the US, in accord with the UN Charter, would 'observe her commitments, within constitutional means, to oppose any aggression in the area'. Thirdly, the US was 'determined to support and assist any nation which might be subjected to such aggression'.[31]

Eden, partly to deter fighting, partly to quell criticism in Parliament, asked the Americans to state publicly that Britain and the US had 'both made plans for intervention if necessary', but Foster Dulles refused, since the secret Anglo-American discussions on enforcement of the Tripartite Declaration were unknown to Congress. Instead, the Secretary sought preparations by the American military. The CIA agreed to consider the possibility that the Soviets would send 'volunteers' to support Arab forces, and Admiral Radford agreed to move the Sixth Fleet into the Eastern Mediterranean.[32] Plans were drafted for Operation STOCKPILE, in which arms would be held on an American ship in the Mediterranean, to be supplied to the victim of aggression, and twenty-four F-86 fighters would be stationed in Cyprus and turned over to Israeli pilots if the Arab states attacked Tel Aviv.[33] Meanwhile, Eisenhower sent personal messages to Ben-Gurion and Nasser asking both sides, 'even under extreme provocation, [to] avoid retaliatory action which could have the gravest consequences'. Nasser promised Byroade that he would halt the commando raids, and the danger passed as the remaining *fedayeen* left Israel.[34]

The Arab-Israeli situation had been calmed, but OMEGA now encountered problems within the Anglo-American 'alliance'. The programme depended upon effective economic measures against Egypt, but the British did not have the financial and economic strength to enforce sanctions against Egypt. In January 1951, a Foreign Office study concluded that economic measures and counter-measures would 'cripple the Egyptian economy', but 'do very severe damage to our own' as well. In December 1951, the Cabinet again considered economic sanctions, but accepted the Foreign Office's conclusion that restrictions would endanger the lives of British nationals in Cairo and Alexandria.[35]

The Foreign Office finally told the State Department in April 1956 that measures against the oil-producing states or even Egypt alone 'were fraught with danger for Britain', including sabotage of the Iraqi and Saudi oil pipelines to the Mediterranean and blockage of the Suez Canal by Egypt. When the Americans pressed their request for a planning paper on sanctions, Shuckburgh reluctantly conceded, 'I suppose it can do no harm as long as we don't lead anyone to think that "sanctions" can be applied by the Western Powers to the Arabs.'[36]

Not surprisingly, Eden, who had been temporarily restrained by the Foreign Office, soon plagued the Anglo-American partnership. He complained to Churchill:

Although [the Americans] are willing to work closely with us in discussing common policies for the Middle East, it is difficult for them to admit publicly that they are doing so – especially in an election year. . . . Their unwillingness to let it be known that we are at one on this important issue diminishes the influence which each of us could exercise in the area.[37]

The Prime Minister inconveniently chose the Buraimi issue to make his challenge. He told Lloyd that, with recent Saudi attempts to subvert Britain's position in the Gulf, negotiations would be a sign of British weakness. Lloyd was forced to suspend the mission and ask the State Department about 'the precise means by which King Saud would be detached from Nasser'.[38] William Rountree re-emphasised that American friendship with Saudi Arabia was a vital part of OMEGA, and Foreign Office officials admitted that 'even half-hearted American support is better than none'. On 19 April, Lloyd authorised the despatch of the Dodds-Parker mission to Saudi Arabia.[39]

Eden then considered Britain's position in the smaller Arabian states, claiming that there was a 'serious possibility that British forces might be needed to protect oil interests in Kuwait and the Persian Gulf'. Lloyd was sceptical, commenting that the 'feudal' attitudes of the Bahraini ruler and his British adviser, Sir Charles Belgrave, regarded 'even reasonable constitutional demands as tantamount to rebellion'. Cabinet Secretary Norman Brook cited a 1953 Cabinet Paper, endorsed by Eden, which argued that nationalism precluded the stationing of Western forces in Middle Eastern and Persian Gulf states. Brook concluded, 'If we believe that, in some of these countries, the nationalist movement will come uppermost, we ought to take steps to ensure that we are not found, at a crucial moment, to be backing the wrong horse.'[40]

Eden's Private Secretary, Frederick Bishop, wrote to Brook:

I wish I could say that the Prime Minister received your views with delight or even appreciation, but you will not be surprised to know that, having disagreed with the views expressed by the Foreign Secretary, he did not feel that the general principle you suggested could easily or safely be applied in Bahrain.

Pressed by Eden, Minister of Defence Monckton supported the despatch of another company to the Persian Gulf and possible reinforcements from Libya or Cyprus.[41] Even this did not satisfy the Prime Minister, who insisted on immediate placement of a reserve battalion in Kenya and a full battalion in Aden, at the southern tip of the Arabian Peninsula, to support British troops in Bahrain. The Cabinet agreed in May that Belgrave should eventually be replaced, but the debate over troop deployment continued until Nasser's nationalisation of the Suez Canal Company in July 1956.[42]

By the end of April, the Foreign Office and State Department had made substantial progress on OMEGA despite the interference of other agencies. As Adam Watson, the head of the Foreign Office's African Department, noted, 'We must push on with the various lines of action . . . to which the State Department have now in general agreed.'[43] Yet the programme, which required long-term political, economic and psychological measures, could not replace Nasser overnight. Pressed for a quick solution to Britain's problems in the Middle East, Eden impatiently commented, 'We seem to have to do all the giving to please the Americans. Hardly satisfactory.' Reviewing a letter from Eisenhower to Churchill, he wrote:

Although [the Americans] are willing to work closely with us in discussing common policies for the Middle East, it is difficult for them to admit publicly that they are doing so, especially in an election year. There has been an unhappy revival of that phrase 'no ganging up', and we have strongly protested against it. Their unwillingness to let it be known that we are at one on this important issue diminishes the influence which each of us could exercise in the area. It also puts a considerable strain on our relations.[44]

Time for OMEGA was already running short.

10

OMEGA – The First Steps
May–July 1956

On 3 May, Foster Dulles and Lloyd, attending the NATO Foreign Ministers' meeting in Paris, reviewed OMEGA. When the two men last met in Karachi in March, they had disagreed on measures such as American accession to the Baghdad Pact. Now they were ready to proceed with a co-ordinated programme. Although the initial talks were disappointing for some participants,[1] a policy was agreed on the Aswan High Dam. When Foster Dulles suggested that Britain and the US 'drag our feet but not . . . let the project drop', Lloyd agreed: 'We should let the project languish, but without giving Nasser any excuse for saying that it was our fault.'[2]

The two sides also reconsidered the troublesome issue of Saudi Arabia. The British, believing that they had satisfied American conditions with the Dodds-Parker mission, wanted to define the plan to detach King Saud from Nasser. The Americans wanted results from the Anglo-Saudi talks before proceeding. When Lloyd asked about the status of US proposals, Foster Dulles admitted that little progress had been made and commented that he attached great importance to improved Anglo-Saudi relations from the Dodds-Parker discussions. Lloyd finally showed his hand, saying that, to deter Saudi Arabia from her evil ways, the 'soft-pedalling' of the Saudis must be stopped.[3] Rountree and Shuckburgh had heated but inconclusive exchanges, with Shuckburgh finally complaining:

It was surprising to us that the Americans seemed to have one idea only for dealing with King Saud and that was to persuade his opponents and victims to appease him. We often had the impression . . . that the Saudis enjoyed a remarkable degree of sympathy in Washington and that there is, in effect, a kind of blind spot towards their misdeeds.

No progress was made in the Anglo-Saudi talks before Nasser's nationalisation of the Suez Canal Company in July.[4]

Co-operation between the State Department and the Foreign Office was now so established, however, that the dispute over Saudi Arabia did not halt Anglo-American planning. Besides the decision on the Aswan High Dam, general agreement was reached on two measures. Firstly, Foster Dulles and Lloyd formally approved the supply of more jets from third countries to Israel. Pineau formally told his counterparts that, besides the first twelve Mystère IVs delivered to Israel in April, France was also sending twelve Mystère IV and twelve Mystère II fighters. Foster Dulles repeated his request, made in March, to the Canadian Foreign Minister, Lester Pearson, to supply F-86 fighters.[5]

Secondly, Foster Dulles and Lloyd discussed STRAGGLE, the operation to intervene in elections or sponsor a coup in Syria, and agreed that 'the country was already practically in Communist control'. Upon his return from Paris, Foster Dulles authorised CIA and State Department evaluation of Syrian contacts who could put a pro-Western government in power. A week later, Lloyd called a Foreign Office meeting to consider the Middle Eastern situation. Discussion on Syria was devoted to STRAGGLE.[6]

Lloyd also informed Foster Dulles that the Jordanian Government could not maintain control without Western assistance. Serious problems had hindered the development of the Iraqi-Jordanian axis, as Jordan was dissatisfied with the level of Iraqi economic aid and the stagnation of Iraqi-Jordanian staff talks. When Colonel Abu Ali Nuwar, the Jordanian Deputy Chief of Staff, travelled to Beirut, Damascus and Cairo in April for military discussions, Iraq suspended aid and recalled her Ambassador from Amman.[7]

Anglo-American plans were tested when Egypt, to protect her supply of weapons, recognised Communist China on 16 May. During his visit to Britain in April, Khrushchev indicated that Moscow would join any UN embargo on arms to the Middle East, and the Egyptians received reports of the agreement between Foster Dulles, Lloyd and Pineau to supply arms to Tel Aviv. Nasser concluded that, under an arms embargo, Egypt would be militarily inferior to a rearmed Israel. His solution was to establish an alternative source of supply through links with Communist China, who had been barred by the US from entering the United Nations.[8]

Foster Dulles's immediate reaction was to tell the Egyptian Ambassador to the US, Ahmed Hussein, 'Every time I appear before Congress, the matter of the Dam is thrown at me. The situation in the Congress is boiling over the combination of arms for Saudi Arabia, no arms to Israel, [and] Egyptian recognition of Communist China.'[9] After his anger subsided, however, Foster Dulles refrained from overtly punishing Cairo. He informed an official from the US Treasury, 'Israel and others had recognized Red China. We don't act on [the] basis of any one single fact. The whole situation has to be evaluated.' Foster Dulles admitted to C. D. Jackson, a former special assistant to Eisenhower, 'I think recognition of Communist China by Nasser was some indication that the Egyptians do not feel confident that they can get arms indefinitely from the Russians.'[10]

As Foster Dulles told Hussein, the real effect of recognition was upon Congress. On 1 June, the US Minister in London, Walworth Barbour, told Kirkpatrick, 'The Administration now thought that, in the altered climate of opinion, there was no chance whatever of inducing Congress to stump up money for the Aswan Dam.' This posed a dilemma for the State Department: 'If Nasser turned to Russia and the Dam was built by a crowd of Russian technicians, that would be regarded as a diplomatic victory for Russia and a diplomatic defeat for Mr Dulles.' The solution was to sustain Nasser's hope of aid for the Dam while privately carrying out the Foster Dulles–Lloyd agreement to let the project languish.[11] The British considered the same problem and concluded, 'We should not be in a hurry to go back to the Egyptians . . . however . . . we must keep Nasser in play for the time being.'[12]

The flaw in the Anglo-American strategy was that the Soviets could offer to finance the Dam at any moment. The British and Americans would then have to reverse policy and proceed with funding of the Dam or withdraw their offer and accept the Soviet deal with Cairo. When the Soviet Foreign Minister, Dmitri Shepilov, announced in mid-June that he would visit Egypt, the US Embassy in Cairo speculated that he would offer Soviet financing of the Dam to Nasser.[13]

Neither side was prepared to meet the Soviet challenge. The State Department tentatively proposed a riparian conference of states with interest in the Nile waters, including Sudan and Ethiopia, but the British were hesitant and Undersecretary of State Hoover admitted to Ambassador Makins that the Americans had no definite strategy. The alternatives were to resume negotiations with Nasser, persist with the proposal of a riparian conference, or withdraw, using the 'best possible formula'; for example, the suggestion that the Dam's cost would cause undue interference with Egypt's economy and internal affairs.[14]

Further delay by Britain and the US increased misunderstanding with the World Bank and the ill-will of the Egyptians. Visiting Cairo on 20–21 June, Eugene Black, the President of the Bank, asked Nasser why he could not reach agreement with Britain and the US when the Bank was ready to proceed. Nasser answered that London and Washington had not replied to Egypt's amendments, proposed in February, to the Western *aides-mémoire* on the details of funding. The Foreign Office and State Department disregarded Black's advice to make a definite statement in reply to the Egyptian amendments, and the Bank was never told of the Foster Dulles–Lloyd decision to let funding 'languish'.[15]

Between 11 and 13 July, Foster Dulles finally shifted from the 'wait-and-see' attitude towards withdrawal of the Western offer. Shepilov offered Nasser a $400 million interest-free loan for the Dam, but Nasser declined because he feared long-term economic dependence upon Moscow.[16] Foster Dulles could now risk rebuffing the Egyptians, and he had already recalled the embattled Byroade from Egypt despite the Ambassador's close relationship with Nasser.[17] The Americans also knew that Nasser was ready to drop the Egyptian amendments to the British and American conditions for funding of the Dam. Egypt would not insist upon an immediate Western commitment to fund construction in the long term, as well as the first stage, and would promise not to use any materials or technicians from the Communist bloc. Ambassador Hussein would return from Cairo in mid-July to tell Foster Dulles of the new position.[18]

On the morning of 13 July, Foster Dulles visited Eisenhower at the President's farm in Gettysburg, Pennsylvania. Foster Dulles said:

Instead of [Shepilov's visit] leading to a Russian proposal to build the dam as many had anticipated, the Egyptians were now back saying they would take our proposal on the original terms and withdraw their own counterproposals. . . . We were not in a position now to deal with this matter because we did not know of the legislative situation. Also our views on the merits of the matter had somewhat altered. . . . We were considering this carefully and would consult with the President next week.[19]

The State Department was in control of American policy. Between December 1955 and July 1956, there is only one recorded instance of Eisenhower expressing an opinion, let alone making a decision, about the Dam. On that occasion, his thoughts were superfluous because of the development of OMEGA. Furthermore, the President was effectively removed from office on 8 June with a severe attack of ileitis that required surgery, and he did not return to the White House until 15 July. During that period, his only recorded consideration of foreign policy matters was the authorisation of missions by the U-2 reconnaissance plane.[20]

Foster Dulles returned to Washington to tell Makins that 'he had mentioned the matter to the President at Gettysburg this morning and would be discussing it with him early next week'. He added that 'his opinion was hard against proceeding' for several reasons, notably Congress's attitude, Egyptian discontent at the economic austerity and reduced military spending that would be required to finance the Dam, and the 'serious inflationary effect' of the project. He concluded, 'Assuming that we decided to take this course, it might be better to tell the Egyptians what the situation was, while holding out hope that they would recover economic aid in some other form.'[21]

While the Aswan High Dam dominated discussion of OMEGA, other elements of the plan were implemented between May and July. The threat to the Western position in Syria was highlighted when the Government of Sa'id Ghazzi resigned on 2 June over student protests about Syria's economic links with France and French policy in Algeria. For two weeks, a series of Syrian politicians failed or refused to form a Cabinet, as right-wing parties failed to reconcile their differences; then Sabri Asali, who served as Prime Minister in 1954 and 1955, formed a Cabinet with two Ministers of the Ba'ath (Socialist) Party, including Minister of Foreign Affairs Salah Bitar. The British Ambassador, John Gardener, cabled London: 'Situation here is serious; if the pro-Iraqi elements now succumb, it will be some time before they can re-emerge.'[22] Several sources indicated that Asali and the Ba'ath leader, Akram Haurani, had agreed on a statement of government policy, including the proclamation of an Egyptian-Syrian union 'open to all Arabs who have no defence treaties with Foreign Powers'. Left-wing army officers, led by Colonel Mustafa Hamdun and Captain Abdel Hamid Sarraj, threatened a coup if the statement was not issued.[23]

Gardener's hopes rested with a group of officers who formed the anti-leftist Arab Liberation Party. If that group co-operated with political figures, notably Michel Ilyan, the Ba'ath and the left-wing army officers might be checked. Gardener asked the Foreign Office: 'Would it be possible when discussing the situation with Nuri to urge that Lian [Ilyan] and Co. should be encouraged financially to continue their struggle? Also Jallal ul Sayid [an agent for Britain working inside the Ba'ath Party]?'[24]

The CIA had the same idea. On 1 July, Kermit and Archie Roosevelt met Ilyan, who requested aid to offset spending by the Egyptians, Saudis and Soviets. To defeat left-wing elements, Ilyan sought control of Damascus and Aleppo with the help of a few senior army officers and newspapers bought from Egypt and Saudi influence with Western money.[25]

British and American efforts soon yielded dividends. Support was obtained from tribes on the Iraqi-Syrian border and from the Moslem Brotherhood. With Iraqi assistance, former President Hashim Atassi returned from Rome to build a right-wing coalition, and Colonel Nafuri of the Arab Liberation Party was introduced to Ilyan by the Iraqi Minister in Damascus. The Syrian Chief of Staff, General Shawkat Shuqayr, resigned on 7 July after a row with the Minister of Defence and right-wing officers. Gardener was 'reliably' informed that Ilyan and Adnan Atassi, the son of the former President, had decided to 'eliminate' leading left-wing army officers and to form a right-wing government without Asali, the Ba'ath and the military. Ilyan and his collaborators 'fled' to Lebanon on 13 July, possibly because of a left-wing backlash against their efforts, possibly to meet American, British or Iraqi representatives in Beirut. Wilbur Eveland, working for the CIA, wrote to an American journalist about his travels to Damascus: '[I] might even see Brother Sarraj [the head of Syria's domestic intelligence service] at the airport – going the other way. . . . Things are looking up.'[26]

At the same time, the Foreign Office fought off a challenge within its ranks to the Iraqi-Jordanian policy. The Permanent Undersecretary, Kirkpatrick, thought Britain's annual subsidy of £12 million to Jordan was being wasted. He instructed Ambassador Wright in Baghdad to consult Prime Minister Nuri Sa'id, only to be rebuffed by the Ambassador:

[This] would suggest we are prepared to abandon Jordan to Egypt and Syria before Jordan has crossed the Rubicon by her own action; it would not do much to explain our motives in terms of the situation as a whole; and I would expect the effect on [Nuri] to be extremely depressing, with possible consequences on his conduct of policy.

Eden wrote to Lloyd: 'Clearly we must do all we can to hold on to Jordan until better arrangements are possible elsewhere.' British officials considered a £2,000 'subsidy' to General Nuwar, who was about to become Chief of Staff of the Arab Legion.[27] Meanwhile, the US agreed to Nuri's request for $8 million in economic aid for Jordan.[28]

Iraqi-Jordanian discussions after the meeting of Kings Hussein and Feisal II in March had been disappointing, with Hussein despairing about 'the helpless attitude of the Iraqi authorities in the face of Egyptian activity', but on 17 June, General Nuwar and the Iraqis agreed upon an Iraqi-Jordanian Defence Committee and the despatch of an Iraqi division to Jordan if Israel attacked the Jordanians. The immediate barrier to further progress was Nuwar's request for small arms, ammunition and equipment worth £800,000. Nuri, contending that Iraq was short of funds, asked if Britain could finance the purchases. In reply, the British offered to strengthen the Royal Jordanian Air Force with twelve Venom fighters in 1957 and twenty-four Gnat fighters in 1958–9.[29]

Once again, British plans were affected by Arab-Israeli tension. In early July, General E. M. Burns, the commander of the UN Truce Supervision Organisation, concluded from talks with Ben-Gurion and the new Israeli Foreign Minister, Golda Meir, that 'the Israelis [were] now likely [to] take unilateral action with Jordan in event border incidents continued'. King Hussein repeated this to the British Ambassador and the US Chargé d'Affaires, as Jordanian troops mobilised and the Arab Legion requested £1 million of ammunition from British stocks.[30]

Burns's initial reports were exaggerated, and an Israeli source, probably the Director-General of Ben-Gurion's office, Teddy Kollek, said that the Israelis had decided upon no further reprisals. The source added, however, 'In case of future serious . . . incidents originating from Jordan, Ben-Gurion was authorized to take the necessary action without further Cabinet consideration.' The State Department agreed with Makins that Israel had established, for the record, that all peaceful processes were exhausted.[31]

The Israeli threat hastened Britain's re-evaluation of her position in Jordan. Although the Chiefs had concluded in late June that the Anglo-Jordanian Treaty was 'now an embarrassment and . . . of little further value', and that 'the stationing of British forces in the country was not strategically necessary', they added that a British presence was desirable if it satisfied Britain's political aims. The Foreign Office confirmed that political objectives outweighed the cost of the subsidy and the commitment of British troops. At the Anglo-Jordanian Defence Board in mid-July, British representatives told Nuwar that Britain would defend Jordan with air and naval forces if Israel attacked.[32]

Britain also accelerated her psychological campaign against Nasser. In March, Sydney Hebblethwaite of the Foreign Office's Information Research Department, responsible for covert propaganda, urged British information officers in the Middle East to use 'their best endeavours to cultivate the appropriate key personalities of the small broadcast stations in their countries so as to ensure that through such friendly contacts, anti-British criticism is reduced and a little more space is given to objective news about Britain'. Hebblethwaite subsequently asked the Regional Information Officer in Beirut to remind information officers to 'report two or three times a year on the success of their attempts to penetrate local broadcast stations'.[33] Newer and more powerful transmitters were considered for British stations in Libya, Aden and Kuwait, and the Iraqis, after extensive efforts by the Foreign Office, erected a transmitter in September 1956 which was more powerful than any Egyptian station.[34] John Rennie, the head of the Information Research Department, and his deputy, Norman Reddaway, told Press Secretary Clark of their desire for more 'black' propaganda from British radio stations.[35] Lloyd even pressed Ian Jacob, the Director-General of the BBC, to help: 'The BBC was too respectable. In most instances, it was good, but in others it might be more aggressive, although certain aspects of offensive broadcasting had better be done through other agencies.'[36]

In June, Douglas Dodds-Parker chaired an ad hoc committee directed to study non-military measures to maintain Britain's Middle Eastern position. The Middle East (Official) Committee had recommended a one-off allocation of £50,000 to build VHF radio stations and supply receivers 'to counter Egyptian propaganda in the Middle East'. The Dodds-Parker Committee expanded this to propose an increase of £568,000 in annual spending and £330,000 in capital expenditure for broadcasting. Besides the second short-wave transmitter in Aden and two transmitters in Libya, the Committee endorsed a medium-wave relay station in Cyprus for the BBC, and a system of VHF broadcasting for the Persian Gulf.[37]

After the early stumbles in the planning of OMEGA, the Foreign Office had linked its plans for the Iraqi-Jordanian axis and the isolation of Nasser in the Middle East without provoking open Anglo-Egyptian conflict. Shuckburgh wrote to British diplomats in the Middle East:

Both we and the Americans feel that it is most important not to show Nasser our hand too early. Although he is bound to realise to some extent what we are doing, we are anxious to keep him in doubt and to avoid a break with him for as long as possible.[38]

Lloyd told the Egyptian newspaper *Al-Akhbar* on 18 June, as the last British troops left the Suez Canal Base: 'There are no actual disputes or conflicts between Great Britain and Egypt which justify the present lack of confidences between the two countries.' A week later, the *Daily Herald* printed Nasser's reply:

Now that the Egyptian people have won their independence and that there are no longer any foreign troops on Egyptian soil, a completely new chapter opens and we want that chapter to be one of real friendship and of friendly co-operation.[39]

The rapprochement was an illusion. A Cabinet Paper, drafted by the Foreign Office, considered whether Britain 'should move over to a more overtly hostile line towards [Nasser]'. The Paper noted:

[Our] policy, as agreed with the Americans, has been not to adopt an attitude of open hostility to Nasser but rather to keep him guessing about our ultimate intentions, while doing what we can to weaken his influence in Egypt and other Arab states by covert methods. . . . The time for a change may come after we have dealt with the Aswan Dam, but there is no alternative regime in sight in Egypt and such a change will push him [Nasser] more firmly in the hands of the Russians and covert reprisals against our economic interests.

The memorandum concluded, however, that once Nasser was weakened by the measures in OMEGA, 'we shall be able to indulge in activities which he will see are directed against him by us. It is in preparation for that phase that we must have our machinery ticking over.'[40]

On the eve of his departure from Cairo, Byroade appealed to the State Department to repair relations with Egypt. He was sharply rebuked:

From beginning, present Administration has based its Near Eastern policy in large part on cooperation with Egypt often at considerable political cost, both domestic and foreign, relying upon repeated assurances [that] Egypt intended [to] work with [the] West. US took numerous concrete steps showing its support while Egypt made vague promises contradicted by actions. By summer 1955, Egyptian intentions had become apparent. Nevertheless US made further effort by offering sell arms and offer on Aswan Dam. These in turn rebuffed by Soviet bloc arms deal, recognition Communist China, and strongly anti-US and anti-West propaganda and activities in Egypt and abroad. US relied to outer bounds of prudence upon Egypt's promise. In face of record, Department would be negligent if it continued [to] proceed on faith while Egypt follows course detrimental to [the] US.[41]

II

Western Attack, Egyptian Counter-attack
19–26 July 1956

At 4 p.m. on 19 July, Ahmed Hussein walked into Foster Dulles's office. When Hussein left the office an hour later, American support for the Aswan High Dam had been withdrawn.

In later years, American officials, to blame Egypt for the events leading to the Suez crisis, perpetuated the myth that Foster Dulles was forced into the withdrawal. Hussein allegedly entered the office, demanded 'a huge commitment over a period of years' from the US and threatened that the Egyptians had a Soviet offer 'in their pocket'. Foster Dulles replied that, in that case, Egypt would not need American help.[1]

In fact, Hussein's behaviour had nothing to do with the withdrawal, which had been planned by Foster Dulles over the past six days and confirmed at a State Department meeting on 19 July.[2] At 3.40 p.m., Foster Dulles told his brother Allen, 'If [I do] nothing, Congress will chop [funding for the Dam] off tomorrow and [I] would rather do it. . . . If [the Soviets] do make this offer, we can make a lot of use of it in propaganda with the satellite bloc. [We will say that] you don't get bread because you are being squeezed to build a dam.' When asked how the decision would be justified, Foster Dulles replied that 'he would put it on the ground that since the offer was made, the situation has changed and so on. On the whole, it is too big an affair to swing today.'[3]

As Hussein entered the office, Foster Dulles threw an 'artificial tantrum':

We believe that anybody who builds the High Dam will earn the hatred of the Egyptian people because the burden will be crushing. . . . We don't want to be hated in Egypt; we are leaving this pleasure to the Soviet Union if they really want to do it!

Foster Dulles added, 'We doubted that we could obtain funds from Congress to carry out the work. . . . No single project in the Mutual Security Program was as unpopular today as the Aswan Dam.' Only then did Hussein reply:

Although he himself still thought it would be a mistake for Egypt to accept the Russian offer, he feared it would be extremely difficult for his Government to do so. The Egyptian people had been told that they need arms and the High Aswan Dam, and it would not be easy to explain to them that they could not have the latter if the Russians were willing to provide it.

The Egyptian Ambassador left the office to face reporters. The State Department had already released a statement asserting that 'developments' meant 'the ability of Egypt to devote adequate resources to assure the project's success has become more uncertain than at the time the offer was made'.[4]

The concern over Egyptian economic capacity was a charade. As early as 6 June, William Rountree suggested a public statement

couched in such a manner that it would be embarrassing for the Egyptians to seek assistance from the US. . . . We might indicate that the magnitude of the project was such that Egyptian independence for action would be endangered if Egypt was beholden to any foreign country for consideration of the Dam.[5]

In fact, Foster Dulles's hand had been forced by Congress. On 16 July, the Senate Appropriations Committee, reviewing the foreign aid bill for the fiscal year 1957, insisted upon an amendment prohibiting finance for the Dam without the authorisation of the Committee.

The Eisenhower Administration had faced repeated Congressional attempts to limit executive control of foreign policy. In 1954, it narrowly defeated the Bricker Amendment, which required Congressional approval of any executive agreement with a foreign country. If Congress now approved the Appropriations Committee's amendment, any allocation of foreign aid might be subject to Congressional veto. William Knowland, the Republican leader in the Senate, warned Foster Dulles on 17 July that the Administration would 'proceed at its peril' if it tried to fund the Dam. The Secretary then hinted, 'We have just about made up our minds to tell the Egyptians we will not do it.' When Knowland indicated that 'the committee won't be taking [the amendment] until Friday [20 July]', Foster Dulles assured him that 'it might well be taken care of by then and action on the bill won't be necessary'.[6]

Just as it was convenient for the Americans to blame the Egyptians for withdrawal of finance for the Dam, British politicians later criticised Foster Dulles for triggering the Suez crisis with his unilateral and abrupt actions.[7] Eden, however, knew of Ambassador Makins's conversation of

13 July with Foster Dulles and agreed with the Secretary's intention to cut off funding. Lloyd told the Cabinet on 17 July of American plans and added:

It would probably be best to indicate to the Egyptians that, in view of their commitments for expenditure on armaments and military installations, the two Governments had been forced to the conclusion that the financing of the Dam, even with the assistance which had been proposed, would be beyond Egypt's resources.[8]

After the State Department confirmed its plans to Makins the following day, the Foreign Office informed the Ambassador, 'It will suit us very well if Mr Dulles speaks as you foresee.'[9]

On the morning of 19 July, Foster Dulles told Makins of his final decision. Makins responded that the British 'point of view on the substance of the problem seemed to [him] much in line with the US view [although Britain] would prefer to play it very much longer and not give a definite refusal'. Foster Dulles said he preferred this, 'but, after consultation with [the] President, he had come to the conclusion that Congressional circumstances simply did not allow this. . . . He was not prepared to let the control of foreign policy pass to the Congress.'[10]

Foster Dulles then informed Eisenhower, who was about to leave for Panama, of the cut-off and showed the President the State Department's proposed statement. Eisenhower made no changes. The meeting lasted twelve minutes.[11]

The British were not agitated about Foster Dulles's action. Eden allegedly commented, 'Oh good, oh good for Foster. I didn't really think he had it in him,' although he paused and added, 'I wish he hadn't done it quite so abruptly.' Lloyd merely told the Cabinet on 20 July that it was 'clear that the UK Government should similarly withdraw'. The Cabinet authorised an announcement at noon that would 'emphasize the economic considerations which led us to this decision and would give the Egyptian Government no ground for assuming that it had been taken for political reasons'.[12]

Nasser was returning with the Indian Prime Minister, Nehru, from a summit with the Yugoslav ruler, Tito, when he heard the news of the withdrawal. He said later, 'I was sure that Mr Dulles would not help us by financing the Aswan Dam. . . . I was surprised by the insulting attitude with which the refusal was declared, not by the refusal itself.'[13] Nasser was especially incensed at the implication in the State Department's statement that Egypt had neither the resources nor the management skills to construct the Dam, operate the economy and expand military forces. He told Ambassador Byroade:

This action of Mr Dulles is an action against me by a great power, and no great power can take action against me without taking into account the necessary consequences of it. . . . The necessary consequences are that you fellows are out to kill me, and all I can do is protect myself. I tell you this. I am not going to be killed.[14]

After Nehru left Cairo, Nasser considered Egyptian reaction to the withdrawal. One option was nationalisation of the Suez Canal Company, a symbol of Western involvement in Egyptian affairs. More than eighty per cent of its stock was held by French and British shareholders, and its concession to oversee shipping through the Suez Canal expired in 1968. Since 1954, the Egyptians had considered their eventual takeover of its activities.[15] In early July, when Nasser told Hussein to accept the American conditions on funding for the Dam, he added, 'Ahmed, do you know Egyptian history? Do you know about the Suez Canal? Before you go back to Washington, go to a bookshop in Cairo and buy a book about the Canal.' Hussein began to raise objections, but Nasser interjected, 'Keep your nerves and it will turn out all right.'[16]

Nasser completed an 'appreciation' of the situation on 23 July. He received information from Cyprus, where guerrillas fighting for union with Greece provided photographs of British military installations and radio stations, and from Malta, where the labour movement provided reports. Nasser recognised that Britain's immediate impulse would be to reverse the nationalisation, but he realised weeks of preparation would be needed to assemble the equipment and the troops necessary to occupy the Canal Zone. As time passed, the pressure of public opinion would dissuade Britain from action and push her into negotiations with Egypt. By the end of September, Nasser estimated, the danger of war would be twenty per cent. While France might join Britain in military action, despite Anglo-French conflicts in the Middle East, and the US would give 'their blessing under the table', Eden could not act quickly and would not accept Israeli participation.[17]

The main deterrent to nationalisation was the economic risk for Egypt. The country had little foreign exchange to compensate the Suez Canal Company's shareholders, and it did not have the technical expertise to build the Aswan High Dam alone. Moscow could not be relied upon to provide aid for the Dam: on 21 July, Shepilov said that the Soviet Union was 'not interested in financing it [as] Egypt was in need of general economic development'. Nasser apparently gambled that Egypt could keep the Canal open and earn enough revenue to keep her economy afloat. He later told a British reporter that the Egyptians had £60 million in reserves which, with an additional £10 million of Egyptian holdings that the British were due to release in January 1957, would compensate the

Company. The net profits from supervision of Canal transit, which had been £19 million in 1955, would then support the economy. Egyptian assets would be set against the £61 million in gold held by the Company in Cairo to meet any problems of foreign exchange.[18]

In a speech on 24 July, Nasser responded to the withdrawal of funding for the Dam:

Our reply today is that we will not allow the domination of force and the dollar. I will tell you on Thursday, God willing, how Egypt has acted so that all its projects – such as [the Dam] – may be projects of sovereignty, dignity, and not those of humiliation, slavery, domination, rule, and exploitation.[19]

Thursday was 26 July, the culmination of celebrations of the anniversary of the 1952 revolution. The centrepiece was Nasser's speech, to be broadcast by the 'Voice of the Arabs', in Menshiyeh Square in Alexandria before 250,000 people. A reference in the speech to 'de Lesseps', the industrialist who supervised the Suez Canal's construction, was the signal for three groups of men to seize Suez Canal Company offices in Cairo and at both ends of the Canal.

'By turns sarcastic, condescending, and occasionally facetious', speaking in a heavily colloquial dialect, a relaxed Nasser began the two-and-a-half-hour speech with a long review of 'imperialistic efforts to thwart Egyptian independence'. He then recounted the story of the Aswan High Dam from its inception to the American withdrawal. During the story, Nasser compared Eugene Black, the President of the World Bank, to 'de Lesseps'. Fearful that his collaborators would not hear the signal, Nasser repeated the name thirteen times in his address. He then announced the nationalisation, setting off a ten-minute ovation. The US Consul, N. S. Lakas, summarised:

In the space of a half-hour, Nasser succeeded for the first time in capturing the imagination of the rank and file and converting them into active supporters. . . . Among normally pro-Westerners, there is grudging admiration for the man who in one week managed to recover from a major setback on the High Dam to administer a stinging blow to Western powers.[20]

Nasser's departure from the Square was impeded several times by the crowd, dancing and chanting, 'Long live Nasser, Lord and Saviour of Egypt and of the Arabs.' Lakas recorded: 'Attempts to kiss the President's feet, hands, and face were numerous and in one instance the Minister of the Interior . . . was forced to shield Nasser from the adulations of devotees who persisted in climbing into [his] automobile.' All that was left after the celebrations was a float of 'the Sphinx swallowing a British soldier with the British flag sewn on his derrière'.[21]

The nationalisation surprised the West. While the Suez Canal Company's financial operations had sparked conflict with the Egyptian Government, the dispute had been defused in June 1956 with an agreement that the Company would be exempt from Egypt's Exchange Control Law. In return, the Company would finance $60 million in bonds issued by the Government. The State Department's deliberations over the Egyptian response to withdrawal of funding for the Dam never considered action against the Company. The Division of Near Eastern and African Affairs surmised that the Egyptians would step up anti-Western activities in Saudi Arabia and Libya, and the US Embassy in Cairo predicted that Nasser would terminate the operations of the US-backed International Co-operation Administration. The Americans even prepared a press release if Nasser announced Egypt's rejection of technical aid from the US. Only the French Ambassador to the US, Maurice Couve de Murville, warned of nationalisation.[22]

Nasser's action immediately affected OMEGA. After the CIA's 'probing operation' in Syria, the Dulles brothers did not endorse collaboration with Ilyan, but they agreed that CIA funds should subsidise bids by American oil companies, competing against the Czechoslovakian Government, for the construction of the refinery at Homs. Other steps included the 'buying' of support for the West in Jordan, the forging of pro-Western links between Iraq, Jordan, Libya, Saudi Arabia and Syria, and pressure upon King Saud to renew American rights to use the Dhahran air base and to break his 'alliance' with Nasser.[23]

MI6 thought that the Americans were too cautious. George Young warned Wilbur Eveland that Britain and Iraq would proceed with plans for a coup in Syria and complained about Washington's 'foot-dragging' in accepting British operations. However, when Eveland asked if a coup had been planned against Nasser, Archie Roosevelt, supervising American operations against Syria, replied, 'Certainly not yet. We'll watch [Nasser] carefully and concentrate on creating a friendly bloc of Iraq, Syria, Saudi Arabia, and Jordan.'[24]

Nasser's nationalisation of the Suez Canal Company changed all plans. The CIA decided that the electoral process would take too long in Syria and that Operation STRAGGLE, the plan for a coup, must be implemented. Ilyan asked Eveland and Archie Roosevelt for a 'half-million and at least thirty days' to install a new regime. The target date was the end of August.[25]

Most importantly, the nationalisation of the Suez Canal Company threatened Foreign Office control of a long-term programme against Nasser. After 26 July, British policy was defined by a number of committees. At the top, Eden and a select group of Ministers supervised action through the Egypt Committee, while the Egypt Official Committee, composed of senior civil servants and chaired by Cabinet Secretary Norman Brook, established the political aims of a military operation to overthrow the Egyptian Government. The Defence Transition Committee of middle-level officials considered administration of Egypt by a British military government. A select group of military planners, most of whom had served on the Suez Canal Zone Base, drafted operations to meet the instructions of the Egypt and Egypt Official Committees.

Middle Eastern planning remained under the Foreign Office's supervision, but the ad hoc system of committees disrupted its efforts. In the confusion, MI6 was encouraged to implement its own policy. While the Foreign Office and the military co-ordinated OMEGA with the Americans, MI6, after the talks with the CIA in April, only discussed general objectives with the US and the Foreign Office. It remained to be seen whether the Foreign Office and the State Department could again pull the Eden Government back from direct confrontation with Egypt.

12

Britain's Quest to 'Hit, Hit Now, and Hit Hard' 26–31 July 1956

E den was dining with King Feisal II, Crown Prince Abdul-Illah and Prime Minister Nuri Sa'id of Iraq when news came of Nasser's nationalisation of the Suez Canal Company. Nuri allegedly told Eden, 'You have only one course of action open and that is to hit, hit now, and hit hard. Otherwise it will be too late. If [Nasser] is left alone, he will finish all of us.'[1] As the Iraqi party departed, they passed a bust of Benjamin Disraeli, the Prime Minister who obtained Britain's forty-four per cent stake in the Suez Canal Company in 1875. 'That's the old Jew who got you into all this trouble,' Nuri remarked to Eden. The Prime Minister's reaction is not recorded.

Eden immediately summoned the Chiefs of Staff, the French Ambassador, Jean Chauvel, and the American Chargé d'Affaires, Andrew Foster, to 10 Downing Street. Lloyd, the Lord President, Lord Salisbury, the Lord Chancellor, Lord Kilmuir, and the Commonwealth Secretary, Alec Douglas-Home, joined the discussion, which started at 11 p.m. and lasted two hours. Eden's Press Secretary, William Clark, recorded: 'Eden made it absolutely clear that military action would have to be taken and that Nasser would have to go. Nasser could not be allowed, in Eden's phrase, "to have his hand on our windpipe".'[2] Foster cabled Washington: '[British] Cabinet takes an extremely grave view of situation and very strong feelings were expressed, especially by Eden, to the effect that Nasser must not be allowed to get away with it.'[3]

The Prime Minister was frustrated, however, when the military was unable to carry out his wishes. Clark recalled:

The question that Eden put perfectly clearly was when we can take military action to topple Nasser, free the Canal. . . . The answers that he got, which were slightly horrifying, were that we could not do this. . . . Britain had the capacity to deal with Mau Mau [insurgency in Kenya] or with the Doomsday, with an atomic war, [but] we did not have plans for a little local episode in the Eastern Mediterranean.[4]

Fulfilling the Anglo-Egyptian Treaty of 1954, British troops completed their evacuation from the Suez Canal Zone in June 1956, and the Chiefs of Staff concluded in March that a landing of three to four divisions was necessary to reoccupy the Zone and keep the Canal open. On 3 July, the Chiefs assessed, as did the civilian Dodds-Parker Committee and Eden: 'We can no longer rely solely on the threat of military force to attain political stability, and we must therefore devote much more of our non-military resources to this end.' Britain should not retain rights to the Canal Zone Base after the expiry of the Anglo-Egyptian Treaty in 1961, since 'the relatively small functions which [the Base] fulfil in the Cold War could be met by other arrangements'.[5]

The Chief of the Imperial General Staff, General Sir Gerald Templer, opposed landing a lightly armed force in Egypt, while General Hugh Stockwell noted that paratroops were out of training and landing-craft were out of commission. British troops in Cyprus were occupied with the guerrilla movement EOKA, and pilots were untrained. Furthermore, British forces had serious problems with equipment. Hunter fighters suffered from jammed guns and engines that surged unexpectedly. Valiant bombers had no bomb sights, and Canberra bombers were not cleared for high-altitude flights. Troops only had old breech-loading rifles from the Second World War, compared to the semi-automatic Czech rifles available to the Egyptians, and no airborne anti-tank guns.[6]

Lord Mountbatten, the First Sea Lord, advised Eden that the British fleet could sail from Malta within a few hours, collecting Royal Marine Commandos at Cyprus and landing them at Port Said, at the northern end of the Suez Canal, in three to four days, but he continued:

Though the 1200 Marines could seize the Causeway, they would have great difficulty maintaining themselves there in the face of Egyptian opposition. I recommend that unilateral action by the Royal Navy and the Royal Marines should not be taken.[7]

The three Chiefs of Staff closed the discussion by threatening to resign if immediate operations were pursued. They formally agreed the next day that it was essential that the operation have 'overwhelming force from the outset'.[8] Lieutenant-Colonel Kenneth Hunt, who drafted the subsequent plan against Egypt, recalled:

What . . . became crystal clear was that the idea of dispersing the Egyptians with only light forces, which people like myself favoured, wouldn't be accepted. The

Air Force were only prepared to use any aircraft in large numbers and only if they did something to neutralise the Egyptian Air Force beforehand. . . . [And] you can't do a paratroop drop in the face of [Egyptian] MiG-15s [Soviet-made jet fighters] without solid air cover.[9]

British Ministers could only sit helplessly while the military weaknesses were detailed in front of the American and French diplomats. Clark observed 'one of the Private Secretaries passing notes in larger and larger type to the Prime Minister saying: "Please do remember not all [present are] Privy Councillors." '[10]

With Britain unable to act alone, 'the question confronting [British] Cabinet tonight', Andrew Foster recorded, 'was, of course, extent to which US would go in supporting and participating in firm position vis-à-vis Nasser in terms of economic sanctions and, beyond that if necessary, military action'. With no authority to give an answer, Foster could only agree to meet Lloyd and Eden the following afternoon.[11]

The next morning, the Cabinet authorised Eden to ask Eisenhower to send a representative for consultations with Britain and France. It then considered the legal position. Contrary to the Government's claims during the crisis, Ministers recognised that Britain was 'on weak ground in basing our resistance on the narrow ground that Colonel Nasser had acted illegally. . . . From a narrow legal point of view, his action amounted to no more than a decision to buy out the shareholders.' Unable to use existing law to justify military action, the Cabinet constructed a new legal principle 'on wider international grounds':

The Canal was a vital link between the East and the West, and its importance as an international waterway, recognised in the [Constantinople] Convention signed in 1888, had increased with the development of the oil industry and the dependence of the world on oil supplies. It was not a piece of Egyptian property but an international asset of the highest importance, and it should be managed as an international trust.

Having concocted a formula for the use of force, the Ministers reviewed Britain's military options. The Chiefs of Staff estimated that the three divisions necessary to defeat the Egyptians 'could be made available . . . but, as a great quantity of vehicles and other heavy armoured equipment would have to be transported to the area by sea, the necessary preparations for mounting the operation would take several weeks'. They also warned, 'It was important that the operations should be so planned as to reduce to the minimum the risk [that] the other Arab States would be drawn into supporting Egypt.'

Led by Eden, the Cabinet dismissed the military's caution:

Failure to hold the Suez Canal would lead inevitably to the loss, one by one, of all our interests in the Middle East, and even if we had to act alone, we could not stop short of using force to protect our position if all other means of protecting it proved unavailable.

The Chiefs would prepare a military plan, while Mountbatten requisitioned necessary shipping and strengthened the naval presence in the Eastern Mediterranean and the Red Sea. The Board of Trade would prepare for the restriction of Middle Eastern oil deliveries to Britain and ensure an adequate supply of shipping for trade and the military operation. With France, the Treasury would block Egyptian currency balances in London and Paris. Most significantly, the Egypt Committee, consisting of Eden, Salisbury, Lloyd, Home, Monckton and Macmillan, was appointed to oversee British policy. Butler, the Lord Privy Seal and a possible opponent of the use of force, was ill with a virus and excluded from the Committee. Eden's goal was clear: plans would be made for

the worst case, that is, the British having to 'go it alone' without the allies and it was made pretty clear that the French are almost certain to join in. . . . The Prime Minister stated that his object was to get rid of Colonel Nasser personally and his regime, whom he regarded as the principal enemies.[12]

In Washington, the timing of Nasser's nationalisation forced Eisenhower, who had little to do with American policy in the Middle East, into action. Foster Dulles was visiting Peru, and the President decided that the crisis was not serious enough for the Secretary's immediate recall. Significantly, Eisenhower refused to condemn the nationalisation as illegal and distinguished the Suez crisis from the case of Iran in 1953, when the CIA and MI6 sponsored the overthrow of the Government that nationalised the Anglo-Iranian Oil Company. The nationalisation of the Suez Canal Company was 'not the same as nationalising oil wells', since the latter exhausted natural resources while use of the Canal built them up. The logic was spurious, but it established that Eisenhower would not sponsor force against Nasser just to regain control of transit through the Canal.[13]

Like the British Cabinet, the President considered whether action against Egypt could be supported on 'wider international grounds'. Undersecretary of State Hoover noted that Nasser had prematurely ended the ninety-nine-year concession granted to the Suez Canal Company in 1869 and added that Egyptian interference with the Canal's operations would break the 1888 Constantinople Convention guaranteeing freedom of transit to all nations. Eisenhower showed some sympathy for British feelings, noting, 'No nation is likely to allow its nationals to be held in what amounts to slavery, operations of the Canal may suffer, and we and many other countries have a concern over its operations,' but he took no action other than a public statement emphasising that the US regarded the situation 'with utmost seriousness and [was] consulting with others affected'.[14] Hoover concluded, in a cable to Foster Dulles in Peru, 'that, while strong position should be taken to preserve Western status in Middle East', he and Eisenhower 'did not believe confiscation of company was in itself sufficient reason for military invasion. Some other overt act would be [needed to be] justified in adopting such measures.'[15]

The State Department informed Foster in London, 'Nasser's action in expropriating an international utility was in a very different category to the expropriation of, e.g., an oil company', and suggested taking the case to the UN. When Foster presented these views, Lloyd countered:

[We] must, from the outset, be prepared to take military measures, if necessary. Political and economic measures were not enough. Nasser would laugh at them. We must first establish between our three Governments that we are prepared to go to the limit.

A tripartite note to Egypt should reject nationalisation and demand that an international body control the Canal:

If the Egyptians refused, we should have to take strong action. This might mean denouncing the 1954 [Anglo-Egyptian] Agreement and reoccupying the Canal Zone (with the support of other Governments). Among other possibilities it might mean the use of naval escorts to ensure free passage through the Canal.[16]

Eden wrote to Eisenhower on 27 July: 'If we do nothing, our influence and yours throughout the Middle East will, we are convinced, be finally destroyed.' He then presented the Cabinet's legal justification for action:

We should not allow ourselves to become involved in legal quibbles about the rights of the Egyptian Government to nationalise what is technically an Egyptian company or in financial arguments about their capacity to pay the compensation which they have offered. I feel sure that we should take issue with Nasser on the broader international grounds.

Most significantly, Eden rejected OMEGA in favour of overt measures: 'We are unlikely to attain our objective by economic pressures alone. . . . My colleagues and I are convinced that we must be ready, in the last resort, to use force to bring Nasser to his senses.'[17]

Eden's message finally convinced the Americans that 'unless [the US could] introduce an element of restraint, Eden and Pineau [would] tend to move much too rapidly and without really adequate cause for armed intervention'. Eisenhower and Hoover agreed that the Deputy Under-secretary of State, Robert Murphy, should immediately go to London. However, they did not absolutely reject support for the use of force:

If the British or the French were to pull out their pilots, insurance companies would not then cover ships in passage through the Canal; the result would be a halt in operations. If they [the Egyptians] tried to seize or hold the pilots, the UK would undoubtedly use force and would undoubtedly be justified in the eyes of the world.

Hoover added that 'his feeling, in which Secretary [of the Treasury] Humphrey agrees, is that we must move strongly in the Middle East – otherwise the whole Middle East position will be quickly challenged'.[18] The Joint Chiefs of Staff had concluded that nationalisation was 'militarily detrimental' to US control of military bases and NATO:

[Action was required] which can reasonably be expected to result in placing the Suez Canal under a friendly and responsible authority at the earliest practicable date. . . . If action short of the use of military force cannot reasonably be expected to achieve this result, the US should consider the desirability of taking military action in support of the UK, France, and others as appropriate.[19]

The Americans simply wanted time to obtain support, both inside and outside the US, for the use of force if it was necessary. Eisenhower replied to Eden:

While we agree with much that you have to say, we rather think there are one or two additional thoughts that you and we might profitably consider. . . . We are of the earnest opinion that the minimum number of maritime nations affected by the Nasser action should be consulted quickly in the hope of obtaining an agreed basis of understanding.[20]

On 27 and 28 July, the Egypt Committee drafted a plan of action. To limit Egypt's room for financial manoeuvre, Macmillan was authorised to secure control of the Suez Canal Company's assets and £130 million in Egyptian sterling balances in London. The Committee ordered the deployment of a second carrier to the Mediterranean, the preparation of two ships to transport army and RAF personnel and equipment, and four-day notice for a cruiser and three destroyers of the Home Fleet to sail to the Middle East.

The Chiefs of Staff now raised the subject of co-operation with Israel:

Militarily, it would be to our advantage if the Egyptian armoured division now astride the Canal could be induced to move east of the Canal. A demonstration by Israel might achieve this, but such a move would tend to range the other Arab States on the side of Egypt, and it was an essential aim of our policy to isolate Egypt from the other Arab countries.[21]

The Foreign Office agreed. On 19 June, the British Embassy in Israel had been advised 'not to take the Israelis into our confidence. . . . It might easily damage us or our Baghdad Pact allies with Arab opinion if there were the least suggestion that we had agreed with the Israelis on a policy of "cutting Nasser down to size".'[22] The Israeli Ambassador, Eliahu Elath, was 'unofficially' told on 28 July that British preparations were to Israel's advantage, but 'it was essential that Israel should keep out and that Ben-Gurion should keep quiet'. Lloyd warned the French against sending Mystère jet fighters to Tel Aviv 'to keep Israel out of the situation, as much in Israel's interest as anyone'.[23]

Finally, the Committee tackled the problem of co-operation with the US. Since Eisenhower had refused to sanction force without diplomatic preparation, such as an appeal to the United Nations, pursuit of the military option risked division with Washington. The Committee brusquely decided to test the Americans:

It was not . . . thought wise to hold such a conference immediately; it would be preferable to delay until military preparations were sufficiently advanced to enable forceful action (should this be necessary) to follow hard upon the presentation to the Egyptian Government of any plan approved by maritime countries.[24]

The gamble was ill-advised. Eisenhower had told Murphy and Hoover that 'if any sweeping action . . . [was] taken, [it] should involve all the maritime powers'. Hoover then told Ambassador Makins that the US sought international administration for the Canal, but 'at present, that is to say in default of some further overt act by Egypt (riotous action against foreigners, imprisonment of pilots), military action could not be justified'.[25]

With the US reluctant to join military operations, Britain turned to France, her traditional rival in the Middle East. In March 1956, talks between Mollet and Eden foundered upon differences over the Baghdad Pact,[26] but any conflict was now subordinated to the goal of overthrowing Nasser. The day after the nationalisation, Pineau warned the US Ambassador, Douglas Dillon:

French Government takes most serious view of the affair and likens it to seizure of Rhineland by Hitler. . . . Inevitable result [of failing to oppose Nasser] would be that all of Middle Eastern pipelines would be seized and nationalized within the next three months and Europe would find itself totally dependent on the goodwill of the Arab powers.[27]

Mollet added that 'Nasser's deal with the Soviets for arms [was] the parallel to the Hitler–Stalin Pact of 1939', and that his *Philosophy of the Revolution* was the 'perfect parallel to *Mein Kampf*'.[28]

In London, the French Chief of Naval Staff, Admiral Nomy, allegedly said, '[Anglo-French action] would teach those damned Arabs the lesson they long needed'. Lloyd reported, after discussion with Ambassador Chauvel:

The French were ready to go all the way with us. They would be prepared to put French forces under British command if this was necessary, and they contemplated making land and air forces available as well as naval forces.

Eden, without consulting the US, instructed the Chiefs of Staff to talk informally with Nomy.[29]

Murphy arrived in London on 29 July for the discussions with Pineau and Lloyd. Before the first meeting, he cabled Washington to define US policy on collaboration with Britain and France. The telegram, endorsed by the State Department, if not by Eisenhower personally, became the cornerstone of the American position:

We do not believe that our action should relate principally to the question of the legal right of Egypt to effect a nationalization of this company. The American interest relates rather to the right freely to use an essential international waterway, the free access to which is guaranteed by the Constantinople Convention of 1888. . . .

We believe that whatever action is decided should be taken only after an estimate of the facts and that the decision should take fully into account the effect of such action on world public opinion. We desire to have the closest affiliation possible with the UK and France, but we believe that whatever action is taken should, if possible, have a broader basis than the interests, however important, of those three powers. The interest of other nations, especially maritime and trading nations, is important and their association and support, it seems to us, is essential. . . .

The question of eventual military intervention does not seem to arise. It would depend on developments. For the present we believe it should be delegated to the background. We feel equally strongly that the Arab-Israeli question should be segregated from the present issue.[30]

Pineau immediately showed his distaste for American policy. He told Lloyd, 'The question for [France] was not only of the Middle East but also of Algeria. . . . One successful battle in Egypt would be worth ten in North Africa.' Lloyd agreed with Pineau, but carefully described the position to Murphy:

The whole Western position in the Middle East would be jeopardized if Nasser gets away with this action. NATO, Western Europe, and other parts of the world [would] be at mercy of a man who has shown himself irresponsible and faithless. . . .

Political and economic pressure was unlikely to have any effect on Nasser unless he knew that there were military sanctions in the background. It was therefore necessary to proceed with military preparations as far as possible, in case it was necessary to take military action.

In contrast, Pineau was blunt to the point of being offensive: '[I do] not agree with the US approach to this whole question. . . . [Nationalisation] was a direct result of the decision made by the US Government not to finance the Aswan Dam.' Lloyd's assurance that 'it was not intended to make any military ultimatum to Nasser at the present stage' saved the talks, but he re-emphasised that 'HMG had decided to be ready to use force if necessary'.[31]

The next day, Eden confronted the American position, inviting Murphy to 10 Downing Street for lunch. The Prime Minister accepted the American desire to avoid force, but requested, in the event of Anglo-French action, that the US 'keep a watchful eye on the Soviet Union and . . . restrain Israel'.[32] Eden had not retreated from military operations. Instead, he was ready to use an international conference as diplomatic cover for military preparations. He told Lloyd and Pineau, 'Action against Egypt if it were necessary would . . . in any case, take time to prepare. If the Conference could achieve this end without prejudicing the eventual action that might be necessary, it might be admirable.' The Prime Minister's policy was accepted by the Egypt Committee later in the day.[33]

Eden thought that he had accommodated the Americans. In fact, he and other British Ministers horrified Murphy. Hosting a dinner for Murphy on 30 July, Macmillan asserted that three British divisions could defeat Egypt within the next six weeks at a cost of £400–500 million, 'which [Britain] couldn't afford but would pay'. He concluded, 'If [Britain] had to go down now, the Government and . . . British people would rather do so on this issue than become perhaps another Netherlands.'[34]

Lloyd later argued that Macmillan's comments to Murphy 'led to a misunderstanding of [the British] position, particularly by Eisenhower', since, 'up to then, Murphy had no reason to think that we were contemplating hasty action'. Macmillan wrote in his diary: 'It seems that we have succeeded in thoroughly alarming Murphy. He must have reported in the sense which we wanted, and Foster Dulles is now coming over post-haste.' Yet, while Macmillan's comments were delivered with a lack of diplomatic subtlety, they differed little in essence from those by Lloyd and Eden, who merely added the proviso 'in the last resort' regarding force.[35]

Foster Dulles, who had returned from Peru, had been encouraged by the agreement of Deputy Undersecretary Harold Caccia with Murphy that 'consideration of [military] intervention should be relegated to the background', but he had told Eisenhower, after Murphy's first meeting with Lloyd and Pineau, 'It looks as though the impression we got from Murphy at noontime that they were more moderate has given way to a stronger line they want to take.' Murphy now reported:

[Eden and Lloyd] said British Government has decided to drive Nasser out of Egypt. . . . They expressed simple conviction [that] military action is necessary and inevitable. . . . Each said in substance [that] they ardently hoped US would be with them in this determination, but if we could not, they would understand and our friendship would be unimpaired.[36]

Foster Dulles immediately obtained the President's agreement that Murphy insist upon the international conference and avoidance of force. The Secretary told Makins, 'The US Government would not be in sympathy with any attempt to make the Egyptian Government rescind their nationalisation decrees, or to regard them as inoperative, under the threat of force.' His only concession was that, 'if the Egyptians refused to attend the conference or if, when there, they refused to consider reasonable proposals for the international supervision of the canal and of the provisions of the Suez Canal Convention, then the situation would be created which might call for a different approach'.[37]

The comments of Macmillan, who had worked closely with the Americans in 1955 on Middle Eastern policy, merely hastened Foster Dulles's departure for London. In a White House meeting on 31 July, Foster Dulles noted: 'The British had taken a firm, considered decision to "break Nasser" and to initiate hostilities at an early date for this purpose.' The meeting almost unanimously condemned the British. Eisenhower asserted, 'The British were out of date in thinking of this as a mode of action in the present circumstances,' and the Secretary of the Treasury, George Humphrey, added, 'It looked as though [the British] were simply trying to reverse the trend away from colonialism and turn the clock back 50 years.' Only the Chief Naval Officer, Admiral Arleigh Burke, defended the use of force:

Nasser must be broken. . . . This should be accomplished with economic and political means. If, however, these are tried and prove insufficient, the UK should then use armed force, and we should declare ourselves in support of their action.

Eisenhower responded, 'We must consider what the end [of force] could be. It might well be to array the world from Dakar to the Philippine Islands against us.' He acknowledged, and Foster Dulles agreed, that the US had to 'make Nasser disgorge what he has seized', but they never hinted that military action was the correct method. The Secretary concluded, 'There [was] just a chance that he [could] dissuade [the British], perhaps a bit at a time, gradually deflecting their course of action.'[38]

After the meeting, Eisenhower drafted a letter to Eden, to be hand-delivered by Foster Dulles:

I received the message, communicated to me through Murphy from you and Harold Macmillan, telling me on a most secret basis of your decision to employ force without delay or attempting any intermediate and less drastic steps. . . . I cannot overemphasize the strength of my conviction that some such method [of negotiation] must be attempted before action such as you contemplate should be undertaken. . . . Public opinion here, and I am convinced, in most of the world, would be outraged should there be a failure to make such efforts. Moreover, initial military successes might be easy, but the eventual price might become far too heavy. . . .

Foster Dulles added a covering note that the US was not consenting 'to the going through the motions of having an intermediate conference but to the use of intermediate steps as a generous and sincere effort to settle the problem and avoid the use of force'.[39]

On 31 July, the Egypt Committee refused the American request that any new international body controlling the Canal act under the auspices of the United Nations; condemned the three-power communiqué drafted by the US, because it mentioned Soviet participation in an international conference; and suggested that Britain and France act without the US in convening a conference. Lloyd noted: 'There might be advantage in going ahead together and leaving the USA and USSR on the sidelines. The Americans often followed where others took action.'[40]

Within a week, the Anglo-American 'alliance' had been suspended. Eden had conceded the need for a conference, but the fundamental British and American positions were incompatible. Unless Nasser renounced the nationalisation of the Suez Canal Company, the Egypt Committee was committed to the use of force. The Americans were committed to international consensus before recourse to the military option. Ironically, the responsibility for reconciling the differences now fell upon Eden's antagonist, Foster Dulles.

13

The Dance of Diplomacy
1–14 August 1956

D espite his clumsy diplomatic manner, Foster Dulles had an acute sense of other countries' policies and objectives. Thus, when he arrived in London on 1 August, he immediately tried to ease British fears. He told Harold Caccia of the Foreign Office that 'the Americans were entirely at one with [the British] in considering it to be intolerable that the future management of the Canal should be in the sole hands of Colonel Nasser'. However, he repeated, 'Steps should be taken which showed a genuine desire to reach an acceptable international solution for the control of the Canal by means other than the use or the threat of the use of force.'[1]

In contrast, Lloyd adopted Macmillan's tone when he met Foster Dulles: 'If Nasser were to get away with his action, we should lose the pipelines and our oil supplies. Our economy would then be slowly strangled. . . . Nasser was a paranoiac and had the same type of mind as Hitler.' Foster Dulles did not waver, but he tried to present the American rejection of force and preference for OMEGA in terms acceptable to the British:

Egypt was under the dictatorship of a man who had avowed that the use of the Canal was not for the benefit of the nations of the world but for the satisfaction of his own national ambitions. A way had to be found to make Nasser disgorge what he was attempting to swallow.

Foster Dulles then clearly defined American policy:

The US Government did not exclude the use of force if all other methods failed. However, the use of force, if not backed by world opinion, would have disastrous results. It would involve the loss of Western influence in all the Moslem countries, unless it were intended to take the whole of the Middle East by force. Such action would be highly dangerous, and even if the Soviets did not openly intervene, they would activate resistance, send 'volunteers', and supply weapons. . . . He doubted if the US Government would be able to associate themselves with an operation involving force, which had not been preceded by genuine efforts to reach a satisfactory solution by negotiation. In such a case it would not be possible to get the necessary legislation through Congress.[2]

Lloyd understood the American position, later writing, 'At this stage . . . I had no complaints at all about Dulles' own reaction to Nasser's conduct.'[3] However, Foster Dulles made the mistake of using the same approach with Eden, who was ready to seize on any pretext to justify military action. When Foster Dulles spoke of making Nasser 'disgorge the Canal', the Prime Minister, ignoring the rest of Foster Dulles's statement, assumed that the Secretary had been won over by British firmness. Foster Dulles's proviso of 'force if all other methods failed' was interpreted by Eden as a request to go through the ritual of an international conference before invading Egypt. The Prime Minister subsequently told British newspaper editors:

He had frankly expected Dulles to be rather negative but Dulles began and continued very well. . . . Dulles freely committed himself to the stand that the canal should not be left in the sole control of Egypt and should be brought under an international authority.[4]

Foster Dulles and Eden met twice: at lunch on 1 August, with Lloyd, Salisbury, Murphy, Aldrich and advisers, and on the morning of 2 August on their own. American observers at the first meeting were struck by the uneasiness between Foster Dulles and Eden and were critical of British intransigence. Roderick O'Connor, Foster Dulles's personal assistant, recalled that Eden opened the meeting by alleging that Nasser's action breached the 1888 Constantinople Convention on transit through the Canal. O'Connor continued:

Dulles asked to see the treaty. Mr Eden was taken very much by surprise and ordered his private secretary to find the treaty. It was half an hour before they got hold of a copy of it and it was soon obvious, in the context, that neither Eden nor any of his staff had really read the darned thing.[5]

Eden repeated his words to Murphy: 'If [the US] could keep Russia out of open intervention, by the assurance that if Russia came in [the US] would be in, [Britain] and the French could and would take care of the rest.' Similarly, Foster Dulles, while again stating that 'the question was how [Nasser's] course should be reversed and he could be brought to "disgorge"', objected to military action. US public opinion would not support a venture 'which, at this stage, could be plausibly portrayed as motivated by imperialist and colonialist ambitions in the general area'. Not only would Britain and France face sturdy Egyptian opposition, assisted by the Soviet Union, but 'all the Arab and part of the Moslem world would be arrayed against the UK and France', and Britain 'would be in trouble in the United Nations'. Eden conceded that he would 'give a try to the conference method, if it could be pushed ahead quickly'.[6]

The meeting on 2 August later aroused controversy. In his memoirs, Eden faithfully recorded Foster Dulles's opinion that 'a way had to be found to make Nasser disgorge what he was attempting to swallow'. Eden also noted that Foster Dulles believed:

It should be possible to create a world opinion so adverse to Nasser that he would be isolated. Then if a military operation had to be undertaken, it would be more apt to succeed and have less grave repercussions than if it had been taken precipitately.

These comments did not differ from those made to Lloyd, but Eden also asserted that Foster Dulles assured him that, 'in the event of an Anglo-French military operation against Egypt', Britain 'could always count on the moral support and sympathy of the United States'. The Prime Minister's claim is unsupported by any account, even Lloyd's. Furthermore, Eden told Iverach MacDonald of *The Times* on 3 August that, while Foster Dulles had 'freely committed himself to an international authority', he had not promised American support for force if the conference failed: 'Nothing had been decided [except] that each of the three powers would then have full liberty of action to do whatever seemed necessary.'[7]

Foster Dulles had not given Eden a blank cheque for military action. He had merely restated the American position that preferred covert methods to the overt use of force. However, by stressing that he shared Eden's determination to topple Nasser, he fostered the illusion that the US would not oppose unilateral British measures. Robert Bowie, the head of the State Department's Policy Planning Staff, summarised:

It was a sort of cat and mouse game, in which Dulles was constantly trying to manoeuvre the situation so that force wouldn't have to be used and that still a satisfactory solution could have been gotten. Eden was trying to manoeuvre the situation in such a way that the use of force would be legitimately justified.[8]

In contrast, Lloyd reached agreement with Foster Dulles over the international conference. Foster Dulles accepted that the tripartite communiqué 'should contain a strong condemnation of Egypt's action and an affirmation of the need to place the Canal under international control'. He also conceded that the United Nations should not supervise an international authority. In return, Lloyd agreed that Britain, France and the US should invite twenty-four countries, Egypt and the Soviet Union among them, to the conference. Eden was dissatisfied, but the Cabinet agreed that, 'if this was the price of US co-operation, it must reluctantly be accepted'.[9]

The bargaining continued the following day. After two long meetings with Lloyd and Pineau, Foster Dulles agreed to the conference starting on 16 August and accepted that the three powers 'would not consider ourselves bound by an adverse majority [at the conference]' and that 'it should not last more than one week'. To protect the American position on military action, he stated formally: 'The US joins in the program . . . on the assumption that it represents, and will be implemented as, a genuine effort to enable relevant free world opinion to express itself on the subject of international operation of the Suez Canal.' He cabled Eisenhower: 'I think we have introduced a valuable stopgap into a dangerous situation and, while the danger is still there, we have perhaps made it more remote and more manageable.' The Middle East Policy Planning Group, over-seeing OMEGA, restated its commitment 'to take action to reduce Nasser's power . . . in agreement with the UK'. The recommended measures were similar to those first proposed by Foster Dulles in March.[10]

The façade of Anglo-American agreement could not solve the funda-mental division over force, however. Inviting Foster Dulles to dinner, Macmillan emphasised

Britain's determination not to let [Nasser] get away with it. . . . If the Canal result was to be the destruction of Great Britain as [a] first-class power and its reduction similar to that of Holland, the danger should be met now. . . . If we should be destroyed by Russian bombs now that would be better than to be reduced to impotence by the disintegration of its entire position abroad. No one wanted to see another Munich.[11]

If conflict with Egypt was 'manageable', the Egypt Committee did not consider it 'remote'. The Cabinet had approved the call-up of 20,000 reservists, with the Queen signing the order on the rear end of a horse at Goodwood racecourse, and the Committee accepted joint planning with the French in principle. Admiral Nomy, accompanied by high-ranking officers from the French army and air force, returned to London on 2 August for discussions.[12]

Other opinion offset American opposition to a firm British line. The British Embassy in Paris reported 'the remarkable unanimity of French parliamentary and public opinion' for a showdown with Nasser. The National Assembly approved, by a vote of 422-150, a motion which expressed indignation at the nationalisation and demanded the 'most energetic measures' to reverse it.[13] While the Indians sought a negotiated settlement and the Canadians were concerned about the use of force, New Zealand's Prime Minister, Stuart Holland, supported Eden and Australia's Prime Minister, Robert Menzies, who initially advised that military action 'would split the Western world', soon endorsed 'the prompt and firm reaction of the UK Government'.[14] In Iraq, Nuri suggested that Western ships not pay dues to Egypt, since Nasser would halt traffic, giving 'the maritime powers a good case for military action'.[15] The British Ambassador to Moscow, William Hayter, and his French and American colleagues believed Soviet intervention against Britain was unlikely.[16]

The British press, with the exception of the *Manchester Guardian*, the *Observer* and the *New Statesman*, urged an immediate show of British strength. *The Times* set the tone on 2 August:

If Nasser is allowed to get away with his coup, all the British and other Western interests in the Middle East will crumble. Quibbling over whether or not [Nasser] was 'legally entitled' to make the grab will delight the finicky and comfort the faint-hearted but entirely misses the issues.[17]

Most importantly, the Government received all-party support in the House of Commons debate on 2 August, the last day before the summer recess. Hugh Gaitskell, the leader of the Labour Party, who was present at Eden's dinner for King Feisal II of Iraq on 26 July, wrote in his diary:

I said that I thought they [the Government] ought to act quickly, whatever they did, and that as far as Great Britain was concerned, public opinion would almost certainly be behind them, but I also added that they must get America into line.

The next day, Gaitskell told the Commons, 'We deeply deplore this high-handed and totally unjustifiable step by the Egyptian Government.' After a meeting of the Shadow Cabinet on 30 July, Gaitskell told Eden that 'force would be appropriate in self-defence or, at any rate, in circumstances which could be properly justified before the United Nations'. He also suggested that Britain and the West increase arms shipments to Israel.[18]

In the debate of 2 August, Gaitskell vehemently denounced Nasser, asserting:

This episode must be recognised as part of the struggle for the mastery of the Middle East. . . . It is all very familiar. It is exactly the same that we encountered from Mussolini and Hitler in those years before the war.[19]

Yet Gaitskell did not offer unconditional support for the Government, as Eden later claimed. Labour MPs John Hynd and Douglas Jay, who had learned from W. N. Ewer of the *Daily Herald* of the Government's military preparations, persuaded Gaitskell to mention Britain's obligations to the UN: 'We must not . . . allow ourselves to get into a position where we might be denounced in the Security Council as aggressors or where the majority of the Assembly were against us.' Any dispute over the legality of Nasser's action should be taken to the International Court of Justice.[20]

Gaitskell's position was similar to the American policy, but his belli-cose comments about Nasser were seized upon by the press, the Commons and the Government. If Britain resorted to force without UN support in the immediate future, Gaitskell could either accept the invasion or support the hated Nasser against Britain. Following the debate, Jay told Gaitskell of Ewer's information that the Foreign Office was 'contemplating war'. After reading the press of 3 August, Gaitskell tried to protect his position, writing to Eden:

While one or two members of our Party indicated in the debate that they would support force now, this is, I am pretty sure, not the general view. . . . If Nasser were to do something which led to his condemnation by the United Nations as an aggressor, then there is no doubt, I am sure, that we would be entirely in favour of forceful resistance, but I must repeat, [as] I said in my speech yesterday, that, up to the present, I cannot see that [Nasser] has done anything which would justify this.

Eden gave no specific assurances about the use of force, and the Egypt Committee proceeded with military planning.[21]

British Ministers even considered MI6's idea of collaboration with Israel. As early as December 1955, Lloyd asked Ambassador Elath if Israeli forces could invade Egypt and reach the Suez Canal within five days. When Elath replied that this was possible, Lloyd asked if '[Israel] would return to [her] borders' after the invasion. Elath confirmed, 'We would have no intention to occupy an Arab territory.'[22]

It was Macmillan, however, who seized upon the concept as part of a British military operation. At the Egypt Committee on 2 August, he commented, 'It would be helpful if Egypt were faced with the possibility of a war on two fronts.' He wrote to Eden:

If I were in [Israel's] position I should certainly intervene and get all the advantage I could. All history shows that statesmen of any character will seize a chance like this and the Jews have character. They are bound to do something.

Surely what matters is that what they should do is to help us and not hinder us. We don't want them to go off and attack Jordan.[23]

The following day, the Chancellor chaired a special meeting with Lord Salisbury, Leslie Rowan of the Treasury, the British Ambassador to France, Gladwyn Jebb, and Foreign Office officials. After the meeting agreed that Britain's 'primary object should be the early establishment of an acquiescent Government in Cairo', the idea of Israeli co-operation was accepted:

The disadvantages of Israeli participation did not outweigh the disadvantages of failing in the military enterprise, but the meeting was of the opinion that Israeli assistance should, if possible, stop short of active intervention. Israel's presence alone should tie down considerable Egyptian forces. The meeting recognised that it would probably be difficult, perhaps impossible, to restrain the Israelis, who could in any case be expected to try to extract a price for meeting our wishes.[24]

Macmillan then presented his proposal to the Egypt Committee. Lloyd, fearing association with the Israelis would ruin Britain's position in the Arab world, opposed the Chancellor. Eden was furious with Macmillan for intervening, commenting that it was 'none of his business anyway', and the Committee agreed that the Israelis should not act before the maritime conference. Lloyd subsequently told Elath

in no uncertain terms how important it was to Israel's interests, not only to keep right out of the Suez Canal question, for the time being, but to exercise the greatest possible restraint during this time to keep the situation on the frontiers with her Arab neighbours quiet.[25]

The French were not as hesitant. After the Egyptian-Israeli border fighting in April, Shimon Peres, the Director-General of the Israeli Ministry of Defence, travelled to Paris and said that Israel was resigned to a 'preventive war' against Egypt. In June, Ben-Gurion removed the greatest obstacle to collaboration with France against Egypt when he forced the resignation of Foreign Minister Sharett, who favoured Israeli co-operation with Washington rather than Paris, and replaced him with Golda Meir. Within days, Peres agreed with the French Minister of Defence, Maurice Bourges-Maunoury, upon Franco-Israeli operations against Egypt. Bourges-Maunoury authorised the delivery of seventy-two Mystère IV fighters to Israel, including the twenty-four already cleared with Britain and the US and forty-eight to be supplied without their knowledge. On 22 June, Peres, the Israeli Chief of Staff, General Dayan, and the Chief of Army Intelligence, General Yehoshafat Harkabi, met representatives from the French Ministry of Defence and intelligence services to confirm the arrangements.[26]

The day after Nasser's nationalisation, the French Chief of the General Staff, General Paul Ely, the Chief of the Air Staff, General

Maurice Challe, and Colonel Louis Mangin, an 'aide' to Bourges-Maunoury who also worked for the French foreign intelligence service, SDECE, asked Peres for information on the strength and location of Egyptian troops. Ben-Gurion agreed to meet the request, and Dayan proposed three alternative plans: the seizure of the Sinai Peninsula, the capture of Sharm el-Sheikh at the entrance to the Gulf of Aqaba, closed by Egypt to Israeli shipping, or the annexation of the Gaza Strip. Ben-Gurion, fearing Egypt's Soviet-made bombers and fighters, said that Israel was not equipped for war and should await her opportunity to take advantage of the Suez crisis.[27]

The Israeli military swiftly acted to correct its deficiencies. On 7 August, Peres met Bourges-Maunoury; General Ely; Bourges-Maunoury's chief aide, Abel Thomas; and Admiral Pierre Barjot, later the Deputy Commander-in-Chief of the Anglo-French military operation against Egypt. Bourges-Maunoury asked Peres how long Israeli forces needed to reach the Suez Canal. Peres replied, 'Five to seven days.' Asked if Israel would work with France, Peres immediately assented. France launched a complicated plan to provide forty-eight Mystère IV fighters to the Israelis. The planes, labelled with identification numbers matching those of Mystères already delivered to Israel, flew from France to Brindisi, Italy, under the pretence that they were returning from Tel Aviv to Paris for repairs. The planes would then refuel and depart from Brindisi for Israel.[28]

Despite their inability to plan with the Israelis, the hawks in the British Cabinet maintained pressure for immediate operations. Eden wrote to Eisenhower on 5 August, combining acceptance of diplomatic steps with a resolution to stand firm:

We have . . . gone to the very limits of the concessions which we can make. . . . I have never thought Nasser a Hitler, he has no warlike people behind him, but the parallel with Mussolini is close. . . . The removal of Nasser and installation in Egypt of a regime less hostile to the West must therefore also rank high among our objectives.[29]

The Chiefs of Staff, assuming that they were to achieve Britain's public objective, the seizure of the Suez Canal Zone, had recommended an assault upon Port Said at the northern end of the Canal, but Macmillan, committed to the unstated goal of overthrowing Nasser, favoured a direct assault upon Alexandria, Egypt's second-largest city, and Cairo.[30] Conferring with Churchill on 5 August, he asserted, 'Surely if we landed, we must seek out the Egyptian force, destroy them, and bring down Nasser's government.' The two men pored over maps, and Churchill 'got quite excited for a time'. The next day, the former Prime Minister met Eden and stated, in words echoing Macmillan:

I was very glad to hear that there would be no weakening about [the invasion of Egypt from] Libya. . . . On the other side a *volte face* should certainly free our hands about Israel. We should want them to menace and hold the Egyptians and not be drawn off against Jordan.[31]

Eden, piqued at the collaboration between Macmillan and Churchill, initially refused to distribute Macmillan's paper proposing an attack upon Alexandria from Libya, but he finally permitted discussion in the Egypt Committee on 7 August. Supporters noted that British commanders had doubts about a landing in the Canal Zone and preferred striking Alexandria if French troops were available. Critics pointed to the difficulties of eventual operations against Cairo and asserted that an attack on Port Said was needed to sustain Britain's public claim that her only goal was international control of the Canal. Lloyd interjected that an attack from the west upon Alexandria 'would precipitate serious political trouble in Libya' and might lead to abrogation of the Anglo-Libyan Treaty.[32]

While the Chiefs were directed to review their military plans, the Committee formally linked diplomatic and military processes:

Some diplomatic exchanges with the Egyptian Government would have to be carried through after the end of the Conference. . . . On the other hand, a military operation, once it was mounted, could not easily be delayed for more than a few days, and, if force was to be applied with sufficient speed after a final Egyptian rejection of our reasonable demands, the preparatory movements must begin at a relatively early stage – some of them, indeed, before the end of the international conference.

The dilemma for Britain was how to force Nasser's downfall while retaining the favour of world opinion. The solution became the cornerstone of British policy:

Any military action against Egypt should be launched in retaliation against some aggressive or provocative act by the Egyptians. . . . The Government might be compelled to take advantage of any provocative act by Egypt, even though it came at a time when the preparations for military operations were less well-advanced than might have been desired.[33]

On 10 August, the Chiefs of Staff presented the new concept of operations to the Egypt Committee. Accepting the private goal of overthrowing Nasser, the Chiefs now endorsed an assault against Alexandria, albeit from the sea rather than from Libya. The revised plan also had military advantages. An attack on Port Said would overcome light Egyptian defences to take immediate control of the Canal, but it was a poor starting-point for an advance into Egypt. Beaches were shallow and muddy, and the port facilities were close to the town and limited in their capacity for the unloading of troops. The march along the Canal on a narrow causeway was hazardous and would delay an assault on Cairo. Alexandria had excellent harbours and good beaches. Although Egyptian defences were heavier there than at Port Said, they could be 'taken out without difficulty', and the airfield could be quickly occupied. Alexandria was also 200 miles closer than Port Said to Malta, the main launching-point for operations.[34] The Egypt Committee approved the plan, and General Sir Charles Keightley was appointed supreme commander. The operation was initially codenamed 'Hamilcar', but the British discovered, after painting large Hs to identify equipment, that the French translation was spelt 'Amilcar'. The plan was renamed MUSKETEER.[35]

The Committee's only problem with MUSKETEER was discussion of the plan with French military authorities because 'French security was notoriously bad'. Ironically, the fear was not that the French would pass the information to the Israelis, but to the Egyptians through the French Embassy in Cairo. Minutes before the first meeting with French planners on 8 August, General Hugh Stockwell, the future commander of land forces for MUSKETEER, told his Chief of Staff that the proposed change of plan for an attack upon Alexandria could not be revealed. The Chief of Staff recalled:

The best I could do when the joint meeting started was to pass round a note, surreptitiously saying no surprise was to be shown at whatever General Stockwell said. . . . General Stockwell then gave a brilliant exposition which left the impression that our plans were to land at Port Said rather than Alexandria.

Ministers finally agreed that the use of French troops could be discussed, provided their destination was not revealed. It is not recorded whether the Chiefs of Staff thought this policy was realistic.[36]

As the British established their policy of military plans supported by a diplomatic pretext for action, the Americans tried to convert that pretext into genuine negotiations between Britain and Egypt. On 30 July, Nasser told US Ambassador Byroade that, while he 'knew he was fighting with his back to the wall', he was anxious not to provide a pretext for military action. Egypt would compensate the Suez Canal Company's shareholders and maintain efficient operation of the Canal.[37] Four days later, Nasser bluntly informed Byroade that acceptance of international control for the Canal 'would mean a return of colonialism'. He could not attend the maritime conference, as 'it was clear that not only was the agenda fixed but the decisions were already made'. Instead, he would sign a new agreement guaranteeing international use of the Canal.[38]

Establishing the link with Byroade, Nasser not only made his views known in Washington, but received information of Anglo-French plans from the State Department, the US Embassy and the CIA station in Cairo. Foster Dulles allegedly passed a message to Nasser through the Ambassadors of Baghdad Pact countries that 'Eden would stop at nothing in order to harm Nasser' and that Egypt would be wise to compromise over the Canal. He told the Canadian Ambassador:

In the recent past, the United Kingdom's actions in the international field had seemed to have an emotional basis, [such as] the Buraimi offer, the deportation of Makarios, and the efforts to bring Jordan into the Baghdad Pact. It seemed to him that the British had been quite 'jittery' and had taken impulsive and drastic actions in an effort to remain strong.[39]

Only the Joint Chiefs of Staff continued to argue for support of Anglo-French military action, but, on 8 August, Eisenhower blocked further initiatives by the US military. He informed Foster Dulles, 'In the [National Security] Council, he welcomes anybody, but in the main he looks to [Foster Dulles] for judgement in political matters and to the military for various consequences.' Eisenhower wrote in his diary that force under extreme circumstances might be necessary, but,

if Nasser were to prove (1) that Egypt could operate the Canal and (2) would indicate an intention to abide by the Treaty of 1888, then it would be nearly impossible for the US ever to find real justification, legally or morally, for use of force.

Working with Foster Dulles, he ensured that the Joint Chiefs of Staff's views were not adopted by the National Security Council.[40]

Ambassador Makins suggested co-operation on non-military measures with the US to block Nasser's control of the Canal. For example, he met Arthur Flemming, the Director of the Office of Defense Mobilisation, to consider the supply of American oil to Britain in an emergency. Letters were despatched to US oil companies enlisting their co-operation, and a meeting was set for 15 August.[41] Makins optimistically reported that Eisenhower's decision to summon Congressional leaders to Washington, possibly to consider a special Congressional session, was 'a convincing demonstration of the gravity with which the Administration view the situation'. Foster Dulles confirmed to certain journalists, off-the-record, that the US was prepared to provide oil to Europe and might finance part of the cost. After Makins told Eisenhower of British concern at a remark by Secretary of Defense Wilson that Suez was a 'relatively small incident', the President emphasised the seriousness of the situation at a press conference, although he then stressed:

I can't conceive of military force being a good solution, certainly under considerations as we know them now, and in view of our hopes that things are going to be settled peacefully. . . . Here is something that is so important to the whole world that I think a little sober second thinking is going to prevail in a good many quarters.[42]

The Ambassador's assessment was astute. Eisenhower, in an election year, and Foster Dulles, fearing renewed attempts to curb executive control of foreign policy, were unable and unwilling to act without Congressional authority.[43] The Administration was also concerned that the status of the Panama Canal, controlled by the US under a treaty with the Panamanian Government, might be questioned if international control was sought for the Suez Canal. Using the 1888 Constantinople Convention as the basis for an international conference, Foster Dulles hoped to distinguish Suez from Panama, since the latter had never been regulated by international agreement.[44]

Eden, however, was in no mood to be patient, and he scheduled a broadcast on television and radio on 8 August to define the British case against Nasser. Conditions for the transmission were not optimal. Because of a shortage of space, Eden made the speech from a temporary studio, which was cramped, heavily curtained and without air-conditioning. The glare of the studio lights made reading difficult and Eden was forced to wear his reading glasses. Press Secretary Clark later said that Eden 'was convinced that those Communists of the BBC were shining the lights into his eyes'. Clarissa Eden, who had long been convinced that the BBC and newly established Independent Broadcasting Authority were involved in 'a conspiracy against her husband', wrote an angry memorandum to Clark about the arrangements, complaining that her husband's eyes 'were made up like an early Charlie Chaplin'. She concluded, 'I consider it a scandal that the Prime Minister, wanting to give an important message to the nation, should be so hampered by a handful of inefficient and conceited amateurs.'[45]

The conditions only heightened Eden's anger, and he directly challenged Nasser:

We cannot agree that an act of plunder which threatens the livelihood of many nations shall be allowed to succeed, and we must make sure that the life of the great trading nations of the world cannot, in the future, be strangled at any moment by some interruption to the free passage of the Canal. . . . Our quarrel is not with Egypt, still less with the Arab world; it is with Colonel Nasser.[46]

Makins reported that the speech was 'thought to have clarified the issues very well and to have hit just about the right note'. Ambassador Jebb wrote from Paris: 'Everybody thought it first-class.' In a British Gallup poll of 10

August, seventy-four per cent of respondents favoured the freezing of Egyptian assets in Britain, and sixty-five per cent approved of the military preparations.[47]

Any British optimism was misguided, however. Makins overlooked the American press, which highlighted the Eisenhower Administration's role as peace-maker. In a veiled attack on Eden, the *Washington Post* praised Eisenhower's press conference of 8 August as a 'calm expression of hope . . . in marked contrast to some of the exhibitions of muscle-flexing abroad'. At home, Gaitskell wrote to the Prime Minister that nationalisation was 'only a threat not, in my opinion, justifying retaliation by war' and emphasised this in public statements, while Labour MPs Douglas Jay and Denis Healey issued a clear warning to Eden in a letter of 7 August to *The Times*:

If the Government seriously mean to use military force over Suez other than in self-defence, or in pursuance of our international obligations and the UN Charter, they will do so in defiance of very large sections of opinion in this country.

Although most British people polled by Gallup favoured steps short of force, only thirty-three per cent endorsed military action.[48]

Most importantly, Eden's challenge to Nasser exposed the charade of British efforts at a diplomatic settlement. Nasser had privately informed Byroade and the Indian Ambassador that Egypt would call her own international meeting, but, after Eden's speech, the Egyptian President could publicly blame Britain for his unwillingness to attend the conference in London:

[He] had been inclined to accept the invitation to the London Conference because he was sure of Egypt's rights but to accept the invitation would now be against Egypt's dignity owing to the military threats and the Prime Minister's announcement that he did not trust Nasser.[49]

The most significant advantage of the Prime Minister's strident rhetoric was its strengthening of Anglo-French ties. The British finally agreed that French commanders could be given full details of military plans, provided that Mollet and Bourges-Maunoury were the only French politicians to receive the information.[50] After three days of talks between Jebb and French officials in Paris, it was agreed that military operations would seek free passage through the Canal and a 'democratic, non-militarist Government' in Egypt. France agreed to discourage Israel 'by all possible means from attacking its neighbours and to accept the Baghdad Pact', although 'very great prudence should be exercised in seeking to extend its membership', a reference to Syria and Lebanon.[51]

All that remained was confirmation of the military arrangements. Eden did not raise the issue in Cabinet on 14 August. Some Ministers, searching for alternatives, introduced OMEGA and Ambassador Makins's idea of non-military measures:

The effect of any economic sanctions would . . . be greatly increased if the United States were prepared to co-operate. The main objective should be to ensure that it was made apparent to the Egyptian people that Colonel Nasser's action had failed to fulfil his promises of improving their standard of living. If Colonel Nasser could be discredited in this way in the eyes of his own and other Arab peoples, a reaction might quickly set in.

The Prime Minister, without going into details, continued to emphasise the military option:

Agreement to pay all [Canal] dues to a blocked account . . . should quickly cause Colonel Nasser to lose prestige. If he were to retaliate by stopping shipping from using the Canal or by taking action against the employees of the Suez Canal Company, a new situation would have arisen which would warrant use of force against Egypt.[52]

Only at the Egypt Committee in the afternoon did Eden present a timetable for military action. Cabinet Secretary Norman Brook assumed the completion of the London Conference by 23 August, rejection of the Conference proposals by Egypt on 5 September, sailing of the assault force from the United Kingdom on 7 September, and the landing in Egypt on 20 September. Acutely aware of the need for a pretext for the invasion, Eden suggested postponing the military timetable for five to six days to ensure that all necessary diplomatic steps had been taken.[53]

The strain was beginning to affect the Prime Minister, who was taking pethidine and various placebos to dull the pain from his bungled gall bladder operation of 1953. Press Secretary Clark added that Eden's wife, Clarissa, was doing 'her best to set him off at every turn'. Eden exploded at headlines in the tabloids and berated Foreign Office officials for statements such as 'we believe in peace'.[54] Frederick Bishop, Eden's Private Secretary, returned from Chequers to tell Clark 'of terrible tantrums over the weekend [of 11 August] with him [Bishop] slamming the door and PM bouncing out of bed to shout at him'. Richard Powell, the Permanent Undersecretary at the Ministry of Defence, later recalled:

[Eden] was very jumpy, very nervous, very wrought up. . . . He regarded almost the destiny of the world as resting on his shoulders. . . . I had to have a scrambler telephone installed in my flat so that he could ring me up and talk about these things.

William Dickson, the Chairman of the Chiefs of Staff, said that he 'had never been spoken to in his life in the way the PM several times spoke to him'. Commonwealth Secretary Home later admitted:

We were under extreme pressure, and the pressure wasn't of course lessened because the Prime Minister was not undoubtedly well. The meetings were probably not methodically conducted as they would have been in times of lesser stress.[55]

The tension spilled over into conflict with the BBC. The day before Nasser's nationalisation of the Suez Canal Company, Ministers in the Policy Review Committee concluded:

Overseas broadcasts . . . were paid for by the Government and it was reasonable that they should reflect Government policy. Too much importance was at present being attached to the argument that the reputation of the BBC for impartiality and trustworthiness should be maintained.

Lloyd was instructed to 'consider by what means the Government could best secure a larger measure of control over the content of broadcasts to the Middle East and East Asia', including the appointment of a Foreign Office official to oversee Britain's propaganda campaigns.[56]

By early August, Eden was furious at the BBC Home Service's attempt to 'balance' its coverage, for example, by reporting Nasser's statements. He wondered if members of the BBC were 'enemies or just socialists'. His anger increased when the BBC refused a broadcast by the Australian Prime Minister, Menzies, as this would mean three pro-Government broadcasts without Opposition reply. The Corporation relented after a call from Clark warning that Eden might 'take some drastic action which would be permanently harmful to the BBC'. Eden asked Clark to stop transmission of a programme on 15 August featuring Salah Salem, the Egyptian Minister of National Guidance, but the Press Secretary replied that this was impossible.[57]

In fact, the BBC, on its Home, Arabic and Overseas Services, was far from pro-Egyptian, emphasising the common ground between the Government and the Opposition in the Commons debate of 2 August, the 'futility of Nasser's economic plans', including Egyptian operation of the Canal, and the threat posed by Nasser's nationalisation to Asian as well as Western interests. This was overlooked by Eden, who wrote to Sir Alexander Cadogan, Chairman of the BBC Board of Governors and former Permanent Undersecretary of the Foreign Office, on 16 August:

Of course, the Government have no intention of interfering with the freedom of the BBC to try and reflect, as well as educate, public opinion in this country, but I hope that the Governors will bear in mind the very heavy responsibility which rests on the BBC at this crucial time.

Clark recorded: 'Other ministers, including the Chancellor and the Colonial Secretary [Alan Lennox-Boyd], are even fiercer [than Eden] and are looking up the rules to see how they could control broadcasting.' The immediate crisis passed with a meeting between Eden and Ian Jacob, the Director-General of the BBC, on 17 August, but Kirkpatrick warned Jacob that Ministers were considering 'governmental control in the Overseas Services and . . . the curtailment of the £5 million grant in aid of the BBC and its expenditure in other propaganda enterprises'.[58]

Three weeks after Nasser's nationalisation, Britain was no closer to an effective riposte. Immediate military action could not be carried out, and effective punishment of Egypt required American support. Ministers recognised that Foster Dulles's vision of Egypt 'disgorging' the Canal relied upon diplomatic procedures and the formation of an international coalition, but 'hawks' like Eden and Macmillan were unwilling to set aside the military option. The more Eden insisted to Eisenhower that military measures were necessary, the more the President sought a compromise to prevent bloodshed. By 14 August, the President, drawing upon the ideas of Robert Bowie of the State Department's Policy Planning Staff, was suggesting a 'supervisory board of five persons designated by such countries as Egypt, France, India, and Sweden, who would have a voice in the selection of a general manager who would be in charge of Canal operations'. Foster Dulles replied that the idea was 'in line with my thinking. . . . It might even be necessary to minimise the role of Britain and France, assuming dependable alternatives could be found.'[59]

14

Washington's Leash upon London
15 August–3 September 1956

The plan drafted by Foster Dulles, Lloyd and Pineau for the first London Conference was simple. Of the twenty-four countries invited to gather at Lancaster House on 16 August, only Egypt, rejecting any challenge to her sovereignty over the Suez Canal, and Greece, disputing the status of Cyprus with Britain, refused to discuss the nationalisation of the Suez Canal Company. Led by Britain, the US and France, a majority of the remaining twenty-two nations would agree to the establishment of an international authority to control transit through the Canal. A delegation would then present the plan to Nasser. If he accepted it, the Suez crisis was over. If he refused it, the countries supporting international control would consider further measures against Egypt. The American requirement for diplomatic consultations to establish an international consensus would be satisfied, and Britain would be free to launch military operations.

The threat to this scenario was an American shift from the demand for 'international control' to a call for 'international supervision' of canal traffic, which was compatible with Egyptian control of the waterway. Yet Foster Dulles again assuaged British sensibilities. He dismissed press reports that he and Eisenhower told Congressional leaders that the US would accept an international body with 'advisory' powers and expressed concern 'at the suggestions in some US papers that there was a difference between the UK and US positions'. After lunch with the Secretary, Eden wrote in his diary: 'Foster seemed quite as firm as before and ready to table the [tripartite] resolution himself. He also seemed not to exclude possibility of joint use of force.'[1]

Foster Dulles's sympathy allowed Eden to cling to the hope that the

US would accept the military option. The Prime Minister reported to the Egypt Committee on 16 August that Foster Dulles 'had implied that [the US] recognised the possibility that force might be used in the last resort, since he had asked whether we will be ready to justify such action before the United Nations'. Military preparations would not be postponed, despite indications that Nasser would not give the necessary pretext for the use of force.[2]

Meanwhile, Lloyd's co-operation and Eden's complacency led Foster Dulles to conclude that the American view was prevailing with Britain. He cabled Eisenhower:

There is, I think, a growing realization of magnitude of the task of military intervention and of the inadequacy of their military establishments to take on a real fighting job of this size. . . . I do not mean to imply that they may not take the plunge if things go badly here, but they are much less apt to do so than two weeks ago.[3]

This atmosphere of Anglo-American agreement, based upon mutual misunderstanding, continued as the Conference opened. Introducing the resolution for international control, Foster Dulles contended that Egypt's nationalisation violated the 1888 Constantinople Convention, which guaranteed freedom of transit, because it denied the international character of the waterway. He proposed that a new Convention establish an international body, with Egyptian representation, to replace the Suez Canal Company. Egypt's sovereign rights would be recognised, and she would be guaranteed a 'fair' percentage of Canal revenues.[4]

Inevitably, the fundamental difference between Britain and the US soon resurfaced. Foster Dulles never committed himself on the question of force, but British Ministers assumed that this would follow the Conference. At dinner with Foster Dulles on 18 August, Macmillan stated:

There are only three choices: (1) Nasser voluntarily takes a proposal along lines of US paper or (2) we compel Egypt to take it; (3) we accept Nasser's refusal. In the last event, Britain is finished, and, so far as I am concerned, I will have no part in it and will resign.[5]

Eden warned Foster Dulles the next evening that 'he had suspended military preparations during . . . the Conference but further action could not long be delayed'.[6] Macmillan claimed that the Secretary 'really agreed with our position', but Foster Dulles commented to the State Department, 'Support [in Britain] for a strong line has dwindled to a point where if Nasser rejects, the Macmillan policy can scarcely be carried through and . . . some form of a governmental crisis may result.'[7]

Eisenhower, recognising that insistence upon international control would bring a breakdown in negotiations with Egypt and Anglo-French use of force, was prepared to split from Britain over the issue. Possibly acting upon covert American discussions with Ali Sabri of the Revolutionary Command Council, he again proposed a body with supervisory capacity. Nasser could appoint the operations manager of the Canal, who would be approved by an international board of directors. In effect, the President was supporting a plan presented by the Indian delegation to the Conference as an alternative to the Anglo-American-French proposals.[8] Foster Dulles replied that it would be 'very difficult and perhaps impossible' to get Britain and France to abandon the concept of an 'international operating authority'. Eisenhower finally conceded the argument, writing that he 'merely hoped that negotiations would not collapse over detail of operating arrangements'.[9]

The tripartite proposal for international control of the Canal was accepted by eighteen of the twenty-two delegations on 23 August, and it was agreed that a five-member committee would present the plan to Nasser. India, Ceylon, Indonesia and the Soviet Union dissented, but Foster Dulles thought that the support of eighteen countries was 'a more impressive result than we anticipated'. He concluded:

If Nasser refuses to let his government even deal with this committee, then there will be a serious crisis. If meetings and exchanges of views take place, then the chance of a peaceful settlement will, I think, be considerable.[10]

Foster Dulles was asked by Eden, Lloyd and Macmillan to chair the committee, but declined, as it might put the US in the conspicuous position of confronting Nasser. The Australian Prime Minister, Menzies, agreed to lead the mission to Cairo.[11]

The British left the Conference with mixed feelings. Eden, certain of American support on 16 August, was unsure after his dinner with Foster Dulles on the 18th. He told the Egypt Committee that Foster Dulles 'was not in favour of provoking Colonel Nasser into taking further action which would justify the use of military force', nor would US troops join an operation because 'the US Government could not justify going to war over oil in the Middle East'. The Prime Minister was forced to misconstrue Foster Dulles's words to sustain the illusion of American backing for force:

Mr Dulles had warned the Soviet Foreign Minister that the US Government would not stand by if the UK and France were involved in a war, which suggested that, in the event of hostilities, the US would at last materially help.

In fact, Foster Dulles had merely reminded Foreign Minister Shepilov that the US would intervene if the Soviets attacked Britain and France in defence of Egypt. Moreover, he insisted, despite Eden's objections, 'that he had encountered a general feeling that the British public would not support the use of force'.[12]

International control of the Canal might be imposed upon Egypt through non-military measures, but this raised further problems with the Americans. The Egypt Committee, noting the conclusions of a Treasury working party, acknowledged that Britain could not administer unilateral sanctions against Egypt, as the Egyptians could retaliate by closing the Suez Canal and Arab countries could interfere with oil pipelines. However, Foster Dulles told Macmillan that the US Government would not advise American-owned ships to withhold dues from the Egyptian Canal Authority, and the State Department had no authority over US ships operating under the flags of other countries, notably Liberia and Panama. The Secretary confirmed to Eden on 18 August, '[There was] little more that the US Government could do in the way of exerting economic pressure.'[13]

Foster Dulles's hesitancy stemmed from division within the Eisenhower Administration. Secretary of the Treasury Humphrey, opposing measures which interfered with American markets, initially refused to 'freeze' Egyptian funds in the United States. He only relented when Foster Dulles argued that the funds might be needed to offset the claims of American shipowners forced to pay the Egyptian Canal Authority. If the shipowners, following the British plan, no longer paid the Authority, Humphrey would argue that the freezing of Egyptian assets was no longer justified.

Eden presented his dilemma to the Cabinet on 21 August:

Care would have to be taken to avoid giving the impression that the Committee [taking the eighteen-power plan to Cairo] were prepared to negotiate with the Egyptian Government. . . . They would . . . have the function of bringing pressure to bear on the Egyptians to accept the declaration of principle as a basis for the subsequent negotiation of a treaty.

This depended upon American enforcement of the plan, however, and Foster Dulles 'seemed at present to be reluctant to contemplate any further financial or economic pressures on Egypt'. When Lloyd asked that evening what should be done if Nasser rejected international control, Foster Dulles requested discussions 'without commitment' because 'the economic problems that would be raised were of a very complicated nature'.[14]

After the Conference, Lloyd tried again, telling Foster Dulles, 'Colonel Nasser . . . would look like a fool if he could not lay his hands on any dues. The result would probably be that he would stop ships going

through the Canal.' The manoeuvre backfired. Foster Dulles immediately objected that, because ships denied passage through the Canal
would have to go around the Cape of Good Hope at the southern tip of
Africa,

this would result in a serious loss of revenue, Western Europe would be deprived
of oil, and the price would go up. . . . [The Administration] were prepared to use
their influence with the oil companies to send tankers around the Cape . . . [but]
it would be impossible to take any of these measures without preparing public
opinion in the US.[15]

With no alternative except to concede defeat to Nasser, some Ministers
began to consider the unthinkable: acting without the US. A paper by the
Egypt Official Committee, charged to define the political goals of military
operations, listed the first objective as a new Egyptian government. While
'some difficulty [might] be experienced in finding competent Ministers', a
large number 'of formerly prominent and able figures, not necessarily of
marked party affiliation', were dissatisfied with Nasser. Press Secretary
Clark commented: '[I] read [the paper] with some cold shivers. . . . I still
find it quite impossible to believe that we really shall do all this.'[16]

The Information Research Department, technically in the Foreign
Office but working closely with the intelligence services, was already
emphasising the use of radio to destabilise Nasser's regime. While
Britain's network of Middle Eastern radio stations openly provided
'information' supporting the British case over Suez, British and French
'black' stations began broadcasting 'disinformation' into Egypt on 28 July.
A 'Free Egyptian' station, transmitting from France, operated on a
frequency close to that of the 'Voice of the Arabs', while the British
conducted operations from Libya, Cyprus and Aden. The Israelis detected a mobile station, with an Iraqi announcer, calling for the assassination of Nasser and transmitting coded messages. The call sign was V for
'Victory' over the opening bars of Beethoven's Fifth Symphony, a reminder of covert broadcasts by the Allied Resistance in the Second World
War. The British Foreign Office confirmed that the station had been
heard in Britain, although it would not verify if it was British-operated.[17]
At home, the Information Research Department supplied the BBC with
material on Nasser.[18]

The 'disinformation' campaign was not limited to the airwaves. In
another British operation, a forged pamphlet was attributed to the 'Government of Egypt Information Department' and sent to oil companies in
Egypt. The document implied that Nasser would establish an Egyptian-
dominated Arab committee to exploit Middle Eastern oil, denying the
resources to Egypt's 'enemies' and supplying them to her 'friends'.[19]

All that remained was a pretext for military action. Lord Salisbury told Macmillan, 'It must, I feel, now be for the Foreign Office to produce one [provocation] which is likely to exasperate Nasser to such an extent that he does something to give us an excuse for marching in.' A group of Ministers suggested removing munitions from the Suez Canal Base, which was still overseen by British 'technicians', but six weeks were needed to move the supplies, since the Egyptians were responsible for the transportation. On 22 August, the Egypt Committee delayed the target date for military action by four days to 19 September.[20]

For the first time, the decision to pursue the military option aroused disquiet within the British Cabinet. Macmillan's avid leadership of the 'hawks' was already raising suspicion. Clark wrote of the Chancellor leaving his residence at 11 Downing Street, travelling briefly to the Foreign Office and returning for a meeting with Eden, acknowledging cheers all the while. Macmillan was 'clearly cutting himself a big swathe at the moment, in the expectation that he just might succeed Eden'. The Chancellor proposed a 'master plan' with the fall of Nasser, the 'disappearance' of Jordan, Iraq's annexation of Syria and possibly Lebanon, and a final Arab-Israeli settlement. He concluded, 'We must not be like Louis 18th [of France], returning in 1815 to a dull restoration, but rather like Napoleon breaking through the Alps towards the unification of Italy.'[21]

Clark also recorded that Commonwealth Secretary Home was firm about the need for force, but

regretted (and [I] think [Cabinet Secretary Norman] Brook does too) the hurry with which the PM pushed that vital decision through Cabinet without time for a proper discussion. In fact, I gathered the whole Cabinet is a bit weak and searching almost desperately for a moral basis for action. In particular RAB [Lord Privy Seal Butler] is discouraged by the whole outlook and has come back from holiday a very damp influence. The worst part is the thought of bombing which may really revolt the conscience of the nation but which is, he [Home] says, necessary to control [Egypt].[22]

While Home wrote to Eden of Butler's concern 'that we have got ourselves into a position where we should press the button before we have a moral basis for action which will carry conviction in the country, the Free World and the Conservative Party', the Prime Minister wrote to the Minister of Housing, Duncan Sandys, who questioned the Cabinet's exclusion from discussion of military operations:

Knowledge of these details must, for obvious reasons of security, be confined within the narrowest possible circle. Such political guidance as the military authorities may need in the preparation of their plans must continue to be given by me, in consultations with a small number of my most senior Cabinet colleagues and, as necessary, such Departmental Ministers as may be concerned.[23]

If doubts had been limited to Ministers outside the Egypt Committee, Eden could have continued to circumvent the Cabinet, but on 24 August the Committee's unity was shattered by the Minister of Defence, Walter Monckton. The argument occurred over the diplomatic and military timetable, as Lloyd noted that deliberations in the United Nations could only begin about 4–5 September after Nasser rejected the eighteen-power plan. The Minister of War, Antony Head, explained the consequences: since the Security Council's conclusions might not be known until 11 September, the seventeen-day interval between the decision for military action and the beginning of the attack meant another delay in military operations from 19 September to 28 September.[24]

A few days earlier, Eden had been uncertain of the American attitude, but Foster Dulles had inadvertently given the Prime Minister new hope. An hour before the Egypt Committee met, the Secretary saw Eden to warn him against the use of force. Learning from Lloyd that 'there would be a button pushed early in September and after that everything would happen automatically and be irrevocable', Foster Dulles reiterated to Eden on 24 August that Eisenhower's letter of 31 July 'was as relevant today as then in its reference to the dangers of military action'. Yet the Secretary left a loophole for the Prime Minister to exploit. To delay any recourse to force, he suggested a British appeal to the United Nations: 'If possible a situation [should be] created so that if force had to be used, the primary responsibility could be put upon Egypt through their perhaps using force to prevent transit through the Canal.'[25]

Far from being deterred by Foster Dulles, Eden believed that the Americans were indicating that they would not oppose military action if it could be established as a response to Egyptian intransigence. He and Macmillan now asked the Egypt Committee for a commitment that Nasser's rejection of the eighteen-power plan and the Security Council's support of international control of the Canal would be sufficient for the use of force. Moreover, they requested the authority to order military operations before the Security Council's decision was announced, reducing the gap between action in the United Nations and D-day.[26] Monckton was aghast that the 'PM and Chancellor were trying to rush things through. . . . He could not agree to press the button now, which made war inevitable.' Eden, 'strongly supported' by Macmillan, Salisbury and Home, 'took the view that [Britain] had no alternative. We must secure the defeat of Nasser, by one method or another.' The 'hawks' triumphed.

Although the Committee did not commit itself to the invasion of Egypt after the UN discussions, it asked Monckton to work with Head and the Chiefs of Staff to deploy forces in the Mediterranean, decreasing the seventeen-day interval between political decision and military action.[27]

Monckton was isolated in the Committee. Clark concluded that Eden and Macmillan had 'made [Monckton] feel very low, no longer essential, and he will have to go when the crisis is over'. Colonial Secretary Lennox-Boyd wrote to Eden:

I remain firmly convinced that if Nasser wins, or even appears to win, we might as well as a government (and indeed as a Country) go out of business. . . . I was horrified by the doubts expressed by the Minister of Defence.[28]

Members of the Committee urged Eden to obtain formal support from the Cabinet, since Monckton's alliance with Butler, the senior Minister outside the Committee, and discontented junior Ministers could produce a rebellion. Home wrote to the Prime Minister:

Even before Walter's outburst at our Committee this morning, I had thought that I had better warn you that I see a definite wavering in the attitude of some of our colleagues towards the use of force. . . . [Minister of Agriculture] Derry Amory, for instance, who is one of the most stable of our colleagues, feels the deepest anxieties, but I think would be ready to face up to it if all the processes of UNO had been exhausted. . . . The anxiety of some, Rab for instance, might be removed if we didn't have to go on thinking in terms of button-pushing and dates and had plenty of time for diplomatic manoeuvre.[29]

Salisbury, the leading proponent of a token appeal to the United Nations followed by military action, advised the Prime Minister:

Both you and I knew that [Monckton] had, for some time, had doubts about a firm policy over Suez, but I suspect that there will be a measure of support for his views when the Cabinet meets on Tuesday [28 August]. Rab is clearly not happy, and I gather . . . that he has been making enquiries and finds there are quite a number of others, especially among the younger members of the Cabinet, who have not yet made up their minds.[30]

Brook gave Eden an 'intelligence report':

The Cabinet are . . . agreed that we must stop [Nasser's] action at all costs and that, in the last resort, if all other methods fail, we must be able to show that we have made an honest effort to reach settlement by peaceful means and have exhausted all the other methods.

The division lay between Ministers who favoured postponement of force until genuine negotiations were exhausted and those who wished to use the diplomatic process to establish a pretext for invasion. Among the former were:

W.M. [Monckton], RAB, Selkirk, Chief Whip [Edward Heath] . . . Kilmuir (?), [Minister of Labour Ian] MacLeod, Amory (?). The unknown quantities might be J.S. [James Stuart, Secretary of State for Scotland], B-H [Minister of Works Patrick Buchan-Hepburn], and D.E. [Minister of Education David Eccles]. The rest I would expect to be pretty solid.

While suspect in places – Kilmuir was actually a firm supporter of force – the analysis was generally correct.[31]

The issue was complicated when a split occurred among Ministers seeking a pretext for military measures. Lloyd, increasingly concerned with the need for American support 'at the highest level', insisted upon the approach to the UN. If Britain delayed, the Soviet Union would probably ask the Council to prevent Anglo-French use of force, and moderate opinion at home and abroad required the security of UN endorsement of operations. Eden, fearing that opponents of Anglo-French action would protract the discussions, suggested presentation of the issue to NATO, a safe audience for Britain. The Egypt Committee finally authorised Lloyd to confer with the US and France about the UN approach, as Eden deferred to Salisbury's insistence upon linking the Security Council and military action.[32]

The decision was a tactical success. Eden used it to seize the initiative in the Cabinet on 28 August, obtaining agreement that Britain would approach the Security Council 'if the support of the US and others was assured'. Lloyd then asked that the Government not advise pilots to leave the Egyptian Canal Authority, despite the Suez Canal Company's wishes for a stoppage on 7 September.

With these conciliatory moves, the 'hawks' won one tactical victory. They earned a second by introducing military action as a *defensive* move against Egypt. Macmillan presented a Treasury paper, which concluded that the costs of military preparations (£12 million through September 1956 and £25 million each subsequent year) and military action (up to £100 million) were small compared to the cost of a cut-off of British oil through the Suez Canal and Middle Eastern pipelines.

Monckton, using arguments similar to those of the Americans, counter-attacked:

If, together with the French, we took military measures against Egypt, our action would be condemned by a substantial body of public opinion in countries overseas, including several of the independent countries of the Commonwealth. Within the United Kingdom, opinion would be divided. Our vital interests in other parts of the Middle East would also be affected; we must, in particular, expect sabotage against oil installations in other Arab countries. Moreover, once we had sent military forces into Egypt, it would not be easy to extract them; we might find ourselves saddled with a costly commitment.

Salisbury, however, used the decision to appeal to the UN to steer a course between Macmillan and Monckton:

[If] we were satisfied that the success of Colonel Nasser's policy would undermine our national economy and destroy our influence as [a] world Power, we should be resolved to take whatever action was necessary to defeat that policy. . . . Before any military measures were taken, we should have recourse to the procedures of the United Nations, but if the United Nations failed to secure international justice, it would have failed to fulfil its purpose.

Butler, who might have led a movement against force, was cautious, saying only that '[the Egypt Committee] should be able to show that, before resorting to force, they had taken all practicable steps to secure a satisfactory settlement by peaceful means'.

Eden had obtained Cabinet deference to the Egypt Committee. He summarised:

It was evident that the Cabinet was united in the view that the frustration of Colonel Nasser's policy was a vital British interest which must be secured, in the last resort, by the use of force. He fully recognised that, before recourse was had to force, every practicable attempt should be made to secure a satisfactory settlement by peaceful means, and it must be made clear to the public, both here and overseas, that no effort to this end had been spared. At the same time, we could not afford to allow these efforts to impose an undue delay.[33]

The Egypt Committee later agreed to a new D-day of 26 September.[34]

The 'hawks', however, had avoided the question of how Britain would proceed without the Americans. The US was negotiating to renew her right to use the Dhahran air base in Saudi Arabia. Fearing that Anglo-French use of force would undermine the talks and oil concessions, the Americans pursued a solution through King Saud, who was reportedly 'extremely unhappy about Nasser but was hesitant to oppose him openly at this time'.[35]

On 23 August, Robert Anderson, undertaking a new mission for Eisenhower, met King Saud and the Saudi Foreign Minister, Prince Feisal, in a series of meetings in Riyadh. Anderson asked the Saudis to urge Nasser's acceptance of international control of the Canal and supported the request with a threat: if Egypt's nationalisation was unchallenged, Saudi Arabian oil would be worthless, as the US would help Europe develop nuclear energy as an alternative. To reinforce Anderson's claim, the CIA planned Operation RAINBOW, in which a huge dummy facility, designed to appear as an experimental high-technology power plant, would be built at a secluded site in the West and the 'information' leaked to Soviet intelligence.[36]

The ploy failed. Feisal dismissed the idea as impossible and warned that the Saudis would not tolerate Anglo-French action with Israel against Egypt. Moreover, he contended that Egypt had the right to nationalise the Suez Canal Company and that there was no reason why nationalisation should affect transit through the Canal.[37] Nevertheless, the Americans continued to encourage Saudi mediation, with Eisenhower and Saud exchanging messages throughout September and October and the King sending his close adviser, Yusuf Yassin, to Cairo to meet Nasser.[38]

Trying to win American support for British plans, Eden now played the Communist card. He wrote to Eisenhower on 27 August:

I have no doubt that the Bear is using Nasser, with or without his knowledge, to further his immediate aims . . . first to dislodge the West from the Middle East and second to get a foothold in Africa so as to dominate that Continent in turn. . . . This policy is clearly aimed at Wheelus Field [US air base in Libya] and Habbaniya [Iraqi air base used by Britain] as well as at our oil supplies.

All this makes me more than ever sure that Nasser must not be allowed to get away with it this time. We have many friends in the Middle East and in Africa and others who are shrewd enough to know where the plans of a Nasser or a Mossadegh would lead them but will not be strong enough to stand against the power of the mobs if Nasser wins again.[39]

Eden's rhetoric no longer affected the Administration. On 30 August, Foster Dulles used the Communist threat to justify American *opposition* to force:

Regrettable as it might be to see Nasser's prestige enhanced even temporarily, I did not believe the situation was one which should be resolved by force. . . . [Britain and France] would make bitter enemies of the entire population of the Middle East and much of Africa. Everywhere they would be compelled to maintain themselves by force, and in the end their own economy would be weakened virtually beyond repair and the influence of the West in the Middle East and most of Africa lost for a generation, if not a century. The Soviet Union would reap the benefit of a greatly weakened Western Europe and would move into a position of predominant influence in the Middle East and Africa.

The President, Foster Dulles recorded, 'entirely agreed with me in this basic analysis. . . . This was not the issue upon which to try to downgrade Nasser.'[40] At the National Security Council, Admiral Radford made one last attempt at American support for Anglo-French military action, but Eisenhower concluded: 'The limit of what we can consider doing now is to take the necessary steps to prevent the enlargement of the war if it immediately breaks out.' Significantly, he decided that the recall of Congress in special session was unnecessary.[41]

Replying to Eden's letter, Eisenhower, using Foster Dulles's draft, agreed 'that the underlying purpose of [Soviet] policy in this problem is to undermine the Western position in the Near East and Africa and to weaken the Western nations at home', but added:

I am afraid, Anthony, that from this point onward our views on the situation diverge. . . . Even now military preparations and civilian evacuation exposed to public view seem to be solidifying support for Nasser which had been shaken in many important quarters. . . . I must tell you frankly that American public opinion flatly rejects the thought of using force, particularly when it does not seem that every possible peaceful means of protecting our vital interests has been exhausted without result.[42]

Eden had no reason to misinterpret this unambiguous warning, described by Macmillan as 'a very hesitating and defeatist message, urging caution and appeasement', but he continued to delude himself. 'Racing back, almost in despair', from his vacation home in Broadchalke to London, he insisted that 'US was in favour of our continued moves. . . . Foster advocated going on.' While the President might not be amenable to military action, Foster Dulles was the driving force behind American policy: 'The only thing that's true to Eisenhower in that [letter] is his signature and that's illegible.' Told that the Committee presenting the eighteen-power plan to Nasser was not leaving for Cairo on 31 August, a twenty-four-hour delay in the British diplomatic and military timetable, the Prime Minister 'expressed horror'. He clasped his head and groaned, 'Oh these delays. They are working against us. Every day's postponement is to Nasser's gain and our loss.'[43]

The Americans were not the only irritant for Eden. Oliver Poole, the Chairman of the Conservative Party, informed Eden that 'an increasing number of people became less prepared to support armed intervention' as time went on. Poole concluded:

The fact is that the majority of people in this country want the best of both worlds. They want negotiations with Nasser to end in a diplomatic victory for this country with as much loss of face to Nasser as possible and with a solution to the control of the Suez Canal which will be acceptable to Great Britain and France, and at the same time, they are unwilling to take the final step of military intervention, particularly if this is to be done by Great Britain on her own.

Although fifty-nine per cent of the respondents in a Gallup poll of 31 August approved of the Government's handling of the situation, the poll did not determine if the approval was of military steps or negotiations.[44]

Moreover, the Commonwealth was far from united behind Britain. Canada was 'unlikely to move significantly in advance of the US', South Africa would avoid any commitment unless a large number of countries were involved, and Pakistan, even if sympathetic to the use of force, could not support it with words or action. India, supported by Ceylon, would 'actively oppose' an attack 'by all diplomatic means'. The Australian Prime Minister, Menzies, was Britain's staunchest friend, 'but with every year that passes, Australia [was] becoming more determined not to get out of step with the US on major issues'. New Zealand was the 'most likely' Commonwealth country to support force, 'but even she [might] hesitate if the US and Australia [hung] back'.[45]

Yet Eden, over the past five weeks, had supervised the development of a British system which was dedicated to the overthrow of Nasser, sealing his accomplishment with the Cabinet decision of 28 August. His 'ally' in the Middle East, Iraqi Prime Minister Nuri Sa'id, urged the British to

see the matter through, using force if necessary, but in such a way that Nasser would be obliged either to give in or to fire the first shot. . . . It was life or death for the West as well as Nasser.

After Nuri's statements were repeated by Crown Prince Abdul-Illah, Eden circulated copies of the comments to Cabinet members, adding, 'All this points to our having little time in hand.'[46]

MI6 persisted with plans to overthrow the Egyptian Government. After Allen Dulles reported his talks with MI6 officers, Foster Dulles told Frank Wisner, the CIA's Deputy Director of Operations, that his brother 'hadn't put his point across. . . . "They" were more determined than ever to proceed along a certain line.' Wisner replied, 'It was clear to [the CIA] that [Britain and France] were still pulling the throttle open, undoubtedly connecting it with other matters.'[47]

Moreover, the Foreign Office, which could have checked the rush towards the use of force, had been emasculated by the ad hoc system of committees and by the deference of its Permanent Undersecretary, Ivone Kirkpatrick, to Ministerial demands. When Assistant Undersecretary Harold Beeley tried to intervene, writing 'that the gravest consequences would follow from a failure [of the use of force] to deprive Colonel Nasser of control over the Canal', Kirkpatrick challenged:

It seems to me easy to enunciate these views – which are sound and, I think, generally accepted here, but it is more difficult to draw up a programme which will achieve the end, 'Defeating Nasser without resort to force'. . . . I shall be grateful for ideas.[48]

Kirkpatrick had no qualms about the American attitude. He commented on Eisenhower's letter of 3 September: 'We might bulldoze [the Americans] into suitable economic and psychological measures simply by threatening that, if they do not agree, we shall have no alternative but to have recourse to force.'[49] He later explained his motives to Ambassador Makins in Washington:

If we sit back whilst Nasser consolidates his position and gradually acquires control of the oil-bearing countries, he can and is, according to our information, resolved to wreck us. If Middle Eastern oil is denied us for a year or two, our gold reserves will disappear. If our gold reserves disappear, the sterling area disintegrates. If the sterling area disintegrates and we have no reserves, we shall not be able to maintain a force in Germany or, indeed, anywhere else.[50]

Kirkpatrick immediately drafted a message, which Eden amended and sent to Eisenhower on 6 September. Using his experience at the British Embassy in Berlin in the 1930s, Kirkpatrick justified the maintenance by force of Britain's Middle Eastern position. It remains the clearest exposition of the case put by the 'hawks':

In the 1930s Hitler established his position by [a] series of carefully planned movements. . . .
    In more recent years Russia has attempted similar tactics. . . . The seizure of the Suez Canal is, we are convinced, the opening gambit in a planned campaign designed by Nasser to expel all Western influence and interests from Arab countries. He believes that, if he can get away with this and if he can successfully defy 18 nations, his prestige in Arabia will be so great that he will be able to mount revolutions of young officers in Saudi Arabia, Jordan, Syria, and Iraq. (We know from our joint sources that he is already preparing a revolution in Iraq, which is the most stable and progressive.) These new Governments will in effect be Egyptian satellites if not Russian ones. They will have to place their united oil resources under the control of a united Arabia led by Egypt and under Russian influence. When that moment comes, Nasser can deny oil to Western Europe and we shall all be at his mercy. . . .
    I agree with you that prolonged military operations as well as the denial of Middle Eastern oil would place an immense strain on the economy of Western Europe. I can assure you that we are conscious of the burdens and perils attending military intervention. But if our assessment is correct and if the only alternative is to allow Nasser's plans quietly to develop until this country and all Western Europe are held to ransom by Egypt acting at Russia's behest, it seems to us that duty is plain. We have many times led Europe and the fight for freedom. It would be an ignoble end to our long history if we tamely accepted to perish by degrees.[51]

Kirkpatrick reinforced the point to US Minister Walworth Barbour:

If the Americans came to the conclusion that they could not join us in applying economic pressure, there was no alternative but to use force. . . . We were not prepared to perish gracefully in order to give satisfaction to some of our friends.[52]

Kirkpatrick, with little first-hand knowledge of the US and no love lost for Americans, was misguided in his attempts to frighten the Eisenhower Administration. The US never accepted the contention that Egypt was 'acting at Russia's behest' in nationalising the Suez Canal Company, and Britain's repeated allegations of Nasser's intentions were unsupported by further evidence. In the Middle East, the only leaders who called for Nasser's overthrow by force were those in Iraq, Egypt's rival for leadership of the Arab world, and even Nuri argued that 'the pressure of opinion of many countries' was preferable to the use of force.[53] The Shah of Iran 'gave getting rid of Nasser a very high priority', but did 'not believe that this [would] be achieved by the use of force . . . because it would require the total occupation of Egypt, making Nasser a martyr, and arouse the whole Arab world'.[54] The Libyan Ambassador in London may have said 'that wise men must see the danger of Nasser succeeding', but his Government would not allow British troops to march from Tripoli into Egypt.[55] The British claim that Saud had said to Prince Za'id of Iraq 'that it would be bad if Nasser emerged triumphant, for . . . if he succeeded the regimes in Iraq and Saudi Arabia would be swept away' did not impress the Americans, who had a more accurate view of the Saudis from the Anderson mission.[56]

The only evidence in British records of Nasser's 'subversion' before the Suez War is an MI6 report, 'from rather a direct source', of the development of an Egyptian organisation in Libya 'to sabotage British equipment and attack British troops and communications'. The British decided to warn King Idris 'and obtain his co-operation', while exposing the plot and 'pointing the moral to King Saud and others'. British officials in Libya clearly indicated, however, that the Egyptian actions were not designed to overthrow the Libyan Government or to kill Idris, but to prevent British forces invading Egypt from Libya.[57] Only in late November did the Americans conclude that 'Egyptian officials and groups under them have been responsible for certain terroristic acts and sabotage', with Libya expelling the Egyptian Military Attaché, the Lebanese claiming that the Egyptian Military Attaché and Commercial Counsellor were 'unmistakably implicated' in the dynamiting of buildings, and evidence of an 'autonomous paramilitary organisation' under the Egyptian Military Attaché in Syria.[58]

Foster Dulles told the President that 'he did not think the [Kirkpatrick] note was very well thought out. . . . [He] did not think you could go to war to preserve influence.' Eisenhower agreed that 'the British had gotten themselves into a box in the Middle East. They have been choosing the wrong issue in which to get tough', as they had with the Anglo-Saudi dispute over Buraimi. To halt the transatlantic exchanges, the President personally drafted the reply to Eden, noting, 'The only usefulness it might have is in its attempt to destroy Anthony's apparent fixation that delay or long, drawn-out negotiations might result in catastrophe for Great Britain and the West.'[59]

The note to Eden, revised by Foster Dulles, emphasised OMEGA and Foster Dulles's recent idea of the Suez Canal Users' Association (SCUA) as methods to curb Nasser:

The result that you and I both want can best be assured by slower and less dramatic processes than military force. . . . We can, for example, promote a semi-permanent organisation of the user governments to take over the greatest practical amount of the technical problems of the Canal, such as pilotage, the organisation of the traffic pattern, and the collection of dues to cover actual expenses. . . .

There are economic pressures which, if continued, will cause distress in Egypt.

There are Arab rivalries to be exploited and which can be exploited if we do not make Nasser an Arab hero.

There are alternatives to the present dependence upon the Canal and pipelines which should be developed, perhaps by more tankers, a possible new pipeline to Turkey, and some possible rerouting of oil, including perhaps more from this hemisphere. . . .

Gradually it seems to me we could isolate Nasser and gain a victory which would not only be bloodless but would be more far-reaching in its ultimate consequences than could be anything brought about by force of arms. In addition, it would be less costly both now and in the future.[60]

While Britain and France were mobilising their forces at home and in the Mediterranean, they could accept the American insistence upon conference-making, but the fleets were now deployed, the fighters and bombers stationed in Libya, Malta and Cyprus, and the paratroopers, marine commandos and army divisions equipped for the landing in Egypt. When Nasser rejected the eighteen-power plan and the Security Council called for international control of the Canal, the diplomatic pretext for invasion would be in place. At that point, Eden either had to go to war without the Americans or admit that he marched thousands of men to the Middle East only to march them back again. Once more, the Prime Minister was rescued from his predicament by Foster Dulles, who had devised a new proposal for Anglo-American co-operation against Egypt.

15

Force Revised
4–11 September 1956

On 3 September, the Menzies Committee, representing the eighteen powers who agreed upon international control of the Suez Canal at the London Conference, met Nasser to seek his 'agreement' to their plan. Despite the outward show of courtesy, the meeting was a diplomatic charade. On 13 August, Menzies declared in a televised speech in Britain, 'We cannot accept either the legality or the morality of what Nasser has done.' Outspoken to the point of abruptness, he had destroyed any credibility that he might have had as a negotiator. An Egyptian journalist commented: 'Blunt, hostile, and arrogant, Menzies was like a bull in a china shop. He offended even England's best friends among the correspondents. We began to refer to him as the Australian mule.'[1] Even if Menzies was in a conciliatory mood, he had been instructed by Eden to refuse all negotiations over the eighteen-power plan, while Nasser had publicly stated on 12 August that he would never accept international control of the Suez Canal.

The initial conversation between the Committee and Nasser was amiable, with Menzies, who had become familiar with Nasser through BBC newsreels, imitating Winston Churchill and quoting from George Bernard Shaw's *Major Barbara* to entertain the Egyptian President. The discussion was not as good-natured when Menzies saw Nasser alone and warned:

I have good reason to know that the UK and French Governments take a most serious view of Egypt's actions. You would be most unwise to assume that the use of force is ruled out in the absence of a satisfactory settlement by agreement.

Menzies cabled the British Foreign Office: 'We, for our part, have gone to some lengths to create an atmosphere in which reasoned discussion can occur, avoiding any implication that the Committee is bearing an ultimatum.' Nasser had a different impression, complaining to Loy Henderson, the American member of the Committee, 'I want to reach an Agreement; instead you send this Australian mule to threaten me.'[2]

The next evening, Menzies, after explaining the details of the eighteen-power plan, repeated the threats: 'If there is an agreement [by the eighteen powers] to create a users' committee, you say there will be trouble, but if there is no such agreement, I can assure you that there will be trouble.' Nasser replied, 'If Menzies was trying to convey the idea that rejection of these proposals would lead to trouble, he was quite prepared to let it come at once.' The other members of the Committee intervened to explain that they were not making any threats. Only then did Menzies retreat:

Nasser had misunderstood his meaning; we certainly did not intend to make direct or implied threats; he was trying to point out that the international tension would continue to exist until satisfactory arrangements for the future of the canal could be concluded.[3]

On the evening of 5 September, after another forty-minute presentation by Menzies, Nasser rejected the eighteen-power plan as a 'restoration of collective colonialism' and a form of 'domination or seizure', although he expressed his willingness to consult with user nations over rates and freedom of transit.[4] Menzies later claimed that his position was undermined by Eisenhower's press conference that morning, in which the President said, 'We are determined to exhaust every feasible method of peaceful settlement. . . . [The US position] is not to give up, even if we do run into other obstacles.'[5] Menzies wrote:

Whatever sketchy chances we ever had were, I think, fatally injured by the astonishing intervention of President Eisenhower, whose statements during our conference were received with glee by the Egyptians and were undoubtedly treated by Nasser as indicating that he could safely reject our proposals.[6]

Eisenhower's statement might have removed the threat of force carried by Menzies to Cairo, but it did not prevent a possible settlement. Given the seven-hour time difference between Cairo and Washington, Nasser probably had not learned of Eisenhower's statement before the meeting with the Committee. Even if Nasser knew, British Ambassador Trevelyan noted: '[The statement] was not crucial at this point. Nasser would not have given way in any case.' Henderson informed Washington on 4 September that the Committee could not get Egyptian agreement and

Menzies wanted to break off talks; only the efforts of Henderson and the Iranian and Swedish members persuaded him to continue. Neither his report nor that of Menzies to the Foreign Office mentioned Eisenhower's speech as an influence upon Nasser.[7]

The Egyptian counter-proposal for a new convention fixing tolls for Canal passage divided the Committee. Menzies said that the mission could only discuss the eighteen-power plan, but Henderson, backed by the Iranian and Swedish representatives, insisted on a further meeting to discuss Nasser's views. Menzies, instructed by the British that Nasser's rejection of international control had to be publicised by 8 September so that Britain could appeal to the Security Council, stemmed dissent by giving an *aide-mémoire* of the Committee's position to the Egyptians on 7 September.[8] Nasser replied at length two days later. Both documents were 'memoranda for the record' rather than efforts at negotiation. All Menzies had to show for his efforts was a case of dysentery, which left him bed-ridden for two days.[9]

Menzies, writing to Eden, launched a vitriolic diatribe against Nasser:

Egypt is not only a dictatorship, but it has all the earmarks of a Police state. The tapping of telephone lines, the installation of microphones, the creation of a vast body of security police – all these things are accepted as commonplace.

In his memoirs, Menzies recorded:

Nasser was a man of imposing physique and presence; obviously the master of his Government, of much intelligence, but with some marks of immaturity and inevitable lack of experience. But he was impressive and clearly courageous.

However, he wrote to Eden at the time: 'So far from being charming, [Nasser] is rather gauche, with some irritating mannerisms, such as rolling his eyes up to the ceiling when he is talking to you and producing a quick, quite evanescent grin when he can think of nothing else to do.' Menzies also failed to mention the Egyptian offer to consult with user nations on tolls and freedom of transit, giving Eden the false impression that Nasser had not put counter-proposals to the Committee.[10]

The British now wanted perfunctory discussions at the UN followed by military action, but Foster and Allen Dulles recalled 'that if the 18-power proposals were rejected, then military intervention by the British should be regarded as a very serious possibility', and the US Embassies in London and Paris reported British and French eagerness to invade Egypt. Foster Dulles concluded to Eisenhower that his talks with Eden, Macmillan, Salisbury and Lloyd indicated that 'the British were determined to move militarily unless there was clear acceptance of the 18-Power plan by Nasser by around the 10th of September'.[11]

Foster Dulles held out against a British appeal to the Security Council, but he realised that he could not hold the position indefinitely. Spending Labor Day weekend at his vacation home in Canada, he 'reflect[ed] in semi-retirement'. Since 'probably 98 per cent of the traffic would voluntarily follow non-Egyptian guidance', Britain, France and other user nations could supply pilots for ships, and any problems could be handled 'through the Naval craft authorized to be stationed at each end of the Canal'. If Egypt did not keep the Canal clear of obstructions, the user nations had a right to keep the Canal 'free' under the 1888 Constantinople Convention. Foster Dulles thought the plan would

'deflate' Nasser and be a better alternative than force. . . . It rests squarely on the 1888 Treaty and, if Nasser uses force to obstruct this program, he would be violating the [UN] Charter and its 'renunciation of force' Covenant.[12]

On 4 September, the Secretary told John Coulson, the British Chargé d'Affaires, 'The users would run the Canal themselves. . . . Nasser would thus see the dollars slip out of his hands. He was much more likely to be deflated by the loss of these revenues than by the threat of force.' Eden welcomed the 'promising suggestion', provided that the US employed the pilots of the user nations to guide ships through the Canal and paid transit dues to a users' account. Lloyd, cabling Foster Dulles on 6 September that it was 'most urgent' to co-ordinate the move to the UN, added that a users' association could be included in the presentation of the eighteen-power plan to the Security Council.[13]

The introduction of Foster Dulles's plan coincided with a British review of MUSKETEER. The military operation had every chance of success until 26 September, but, because of deteriorating weather in the Mediterranean, it could not be launched after 6 October until the spring. The seventeen-day interval between the decision to launch operations and the invasion meant that the Egypt Committee had to act by 19 September. With Nasser's reply to the Menzies mission coming on the 9th, there was insufficient time to complete discussions in the Security Council and convene a special Parliamentary session to endorse an attack against Egypt. Moreover, the high level of Egyptian casualties in the British assault upon Alexandria and Cairo worried military leaders and politicians. When the First Sea Lord, Mountbatten, complained to the new First Lord of the Admiralty, Lord Hailsham, that the Navy was to be used 'to shoot up and butcher women and children', Hailsham allegedly replied, 'Oh God, oh God, what can I do? I'd no idea we were in this awful position.'[14]

General Keightley, the Commander-in-Chief of MUSKETEER, was also concerned about the political effects of the operation:

It is . . . of the greatest importance that this invasion of Egypt is launched with our moral case unassailable and the start of the war clearly and definitely Nasser's responsibility and no one else's. . . . The problem is whether it appears likely that this moral case can be achieved within the next few weeks and, if not, whether some other plan which can be launched at a much later date is required.

Keightley devised a new plan, MUSKETEER REVISE, which could be operational until the end of October and required only eight days between decision and implementation. The assault upon Alexandria, followed by an advance upon Cairo, was abandoned. Instead, aerial and naval action, supported by psychological warfare, would break down 'Egyptian resistance to Western operation of the Suez Canal and enable Allied forces to secure the Canal Zone'. In Phase I, Allied bombing would destroy the Egyptian air force to prevent counter-attacks against British and French forces on Cyprus. When this was accomplished, Phase II, an air offensive upon key military and economic targets accompanied by propaganda from 'black' radio stations, leaflets and announcements from 'voice' aircraft, would turn the Egyptian population against Nasser, forcing his resignation or a coup d'état. After Nasser's fall, British and French troops would land at Port Said in Phase III, taking control of the Canal Zone before occupying Cairo and establishing a military government.[15]

Eden's immediate reaction to REVISE was consternation, since the plan had no provision for a quick occupation of Alexandria and Cairo. He disputed the estimate of 'unpredictable' autumn weather in the Mediterranean, the assumption of an eighteen-day lead time for MUS-KETEER, and the claim that MUSKETEER could not be main-tained beyond 6 October. According to Mountbatten, when Keightley repeated his doubts about MUSKETEER,

[He] got an imperial rocket. He was told to mind his own business and carry out his orders and not question what was going on in the future; he wasn't there to argue with the Prime Minister; he was there to do what he was told, and he was kicked out.[16]

On the morning of 7 September, Eden confronted the Chiefs of Staff, claiming that the devastation and loss of life caused by REVISE's extensive air assault would be greater than that caused by MUS-KETEER, since Egypt would not resist a landing at Alexandria. General Templer replied that the advance from Alexandria to Cairo would take twenty-three days if the Egyptians opposed the invasion. Eden retorted that the Egyptians were cowards, an assertion challenged by Mountbatten and Keightley.[17]

However, because of his inability to establish a diplomatic pretext to launch MUSKETEER in the near future, Eden finally had to give way, recording in his diary: 'I was not at first much enamoured of [the plan], but in discussion, and as Chiefs of Staff amplified it, became more reconciled.' He told the Egypt Committee that the new plan had advantages, given 'a reasonable certainty that it would be effective'. The Committee agreed to resume its discussion of REVISE in three days' time.[18]

To prepare a pretext for REVISE, the Committee decided 'that no further advice should be given' to Suez Canal Company employees to remain at their posts. The Foreign Office informed the French, and the stoppage of work was scheduled for 15 September.[19] The Minister of Transport, Harold Watkinson, linked the employees' withdrawal not only to military action, but also to Foster Dulles's plans. Britain and France, followed by the US and other maritime nations, would instruct their ships to withhold transit dues from Nasser and join Foster Dulles's association of Canal users. Meanwhile, Operation PILEUP would congest the Canal with enough ships to bring complaints from shipowners and the maritime nations. 'All offers [by Egypt] of compromise methods of transit [would] be refused as unsafe', and Operation CONVOY would station pilots, employed by SCUA, on warships at each end of the Canal. If Nasser refused passage to ships with these pilots, the warships would lead a convoy through the Canal. Further resistance by Egypt would bring war, while acceptance of the convoy by Nasser would render Egyptian control of the Canal worthless.[20]

Unfortunately for the Committee, the Americans, spurred by Eden's strident letters, had anticipated the British review and acted quickly to block military action. Eisenhower was still pursuing alternatives to international control, asking Foster Dulles:

Why wouldn't it be possible for the big nations to buy up all the stock of the Suez Canal and give 49 per cent to Egypt and say that is our solution? . . . In this way the Egyptians would get [the] Aswan Dam, which is what Nasser wants.[21]

The Secretary vetoed the idea while maintaining his objection to an immediate British appeal to the Security Council to establish the pretext for the use of force. Told that the Foreign Office could not delay announcing its appeal to the Council for more than twenty-four hours, Foster Dulles told John Coulson, 'What [Britain was] proposing was in effect to enlist support to force upon Egypt the conclusion of [a] treaty bestowing new rights on the users of the Canal.'[22] He refused to co-sponsor a draft resolution with Britain and France and would not promise opposition to any amendment prohibiting the use of force against Cairo.[23] Lloyd cabled Makins that Britain and the US were further apart than at any time since July 26. I cannot accept the present US thinking that the two problems of settling the Canal issue and deflating Nasser can be separated . . . and there appears to be little common ground between us at the moment as to how to achieve either of those objectives.[24]

Once again, Foster Dulles reassured Makins about American intentions:

Of course, Nasser could not be allowed to win in this contest. . . . The President did not exclude the use of force in the last resort. Between us we could get Nasser down, and the US Administration were quite determined that this should happen.

The Secretary reminded the Ambassador that '[the US] saw no end to the consequences of military intervention. . . . She did not believe the methods and the tempo which [Britain and France] were advocating were the right ones.'[25]

Britain's hope for American co-operation lay in strong economic sanctions. To make the Users' Association attractive to London, Foster Dulles offered help with the plans for emergency oil shipments. More significantly, he indicated that he would reconsider the American position on payment of dues to the Egyptians. He told Makins:

We were in a position to bring great pressure on Nasser short of armed force. Nasser could be forced to accept cooperation with the West or else take the onus of the consequences of his action. . . . His proposal was therefore three-pronged: the Users' Association, the oil operation, and other economic pressures.[26]

Kirkpatrick told Walworth Barbour that the combination of Eisenhower's message of 9 September to Eden, which had emphasised 'alternative measures' to topple Nasser, and Foster Dulles's presentation to Makins 'encouraged' the Foreign Office to believe that 'there [was] a large measure of identification of views between' Britain and the US. Lloyd, pessimistic about Anglo-American co-operation a few days earlier, enthused to Aldrich, 'the UK Government is particularly pleased with the Secretary's plan for an association of canal users because it constitutes a "slap in the face" for Nasser, and . . . it will be popular in Parliament for that very reason'.[27]

Suddenly, British Ministers had an option besides war without the US or abandonment of force. REVISE gave them an extra month for manoeuvre, while the Users' Association could be the instrument for Anglo-American co-operation, establishing a pretext for force if Nasser impeded the plan. On 10 September, the Egypt Committee confirmed that the approach to the Security Council would be postponed to explore

Foster Dulles's 'ingenious' proposals. REVISE was approved and Watkinson was authorised to proceed with Operations PICKUP and CONVOY to hinder Egyptian supervision of Canal transit.[28]

By adopting REVISE, Ministers had shelved an 'orthodox' military plan, relying on an amphibious assault supported by aerial power, for an operation whose success was dependent upon effective psychological warfare and covert operations. At the outset of the Suez crisis, the Chiefs of Staff 'strongly supported' General Templer's plan for psychological warfare as an element in MUSKETEER, and the Egypt Committee authorised its development.[29] Nigel Birch, the Secretary of State for Air, wrote to Lloyd:

I should have thought that a well-conducted campaign might have paid dividends. For example, rumours started in Egypt that, if we met prolonged resistance, Cairo and Alexandria would be atom-bombed, might have some startling results if the balloon went up.

An interdepartmental working party established the Information Co-ordination Executive of civil servants, who oversaw the work of a psychological warfare unit, commanded by a lieutenant-colonel in London with a forward element in Cyprus. By early September, a special eighteen-man unit was formed at Aldershot from 23 Signals Regiment.[30]

These arrangements became a central part of REVISE. In Phase II, 'all necessary resources' would be mobilised 'for carrying out an intensive campaign of propaganda which will have the object of inducing the Egyptian Government, people, and armed forces to cease resistance, of raising popular pressure on the Government, and of intensifying the effects on Egyptian morale of [Anglo-French] air attacks'.[31] Brigadier Bernard Fergusson, with previous experience of covert operations in Palestine and Malaya, was appointed to lead the operation.

In preparation for the assault, the number of stories 'planted' with British newspapers, the 'independent' BBC and the London Press Service increased. The Arab News Agency, a 'private' organisation which had MI6 operatives among its directors, produced stories which the BBC's Arabic Service station at Sharq-al-Adna, Cyprus, was instructed to broadcast. The Regional Information Officer in Beirut provided material to 'one or two of the newspapers in the Middle East to which [Britain had] access'. Code phrases like 'the beacon is flashing for the third time' were issued on Britain's covert radio stations by 'freedom groups', who claimed: 'Brothers! Nasser must be made to stop gambling with Egypt's future at our expense, or he must make way for a more experienced statesman. Our whole future demands it!' A BBC relay station in Cyprus, broadcasting in medium-wave through the Middle East, was completed in October.[32]

The psychological warfare was based upon extensive collection of intelligence and development of covert operations against Nasser. Since the spring of 1956, the Egyptian Embassy in London was a priority target for code-breaking by Britain's domestic intelligence service, MI5. By June, the British were showing the State Department copies of telegrams from the Egyptian Embassy in Moscow.[33] Specially modified Washington aircraft of 192 Squadron carried out electronic surveillance of Egypt and other Middle Eastern countries and sent the results to the Government Communications Headquarters (GCHQ) at Cheltenham. On 20 September, Lloyd congratulated E. M. Jones, the Director of GCHQ: 'Since the tension in the Middle East began to grow and particularly since Nasser's seizure of the Suez Canal, I have observed the volume of material which has been produced by GCHQ relating to all the countries in the Middle East area.'[34]

MI6 drafted plans for Nasser's assassination, notably a scheme to inject nerve gas into the Egyptian leader's office, which was allegedly approved by Eden before he suspended it in favour of military operations. Similarly, the former CIA operative, Miles Copeland, claimed that Eden suggested shooting Nasser or putting poison in his coffee. Copeland, visiting Cairo during the Suez crisis, joked with Nasser, 'Turn your head, Gamal, and let me see if I can put this poison into your coffee. Why wouldn't it work?' The Egyptian leader, pointing to his bodyguards, replied, 'There are two reasons right behind you.'[35]

In the end, intelligence from its agents in Egypt and from GCHQ convinced MI6 that assassination would probably make Nasser a martyr and reinforce anti-British opinion in Egypt. Instead, REVISE would be the catalyst for Nasser's overthrow. Anglo-French bombing of Egypt, combined with psychological warfare, would arouse so much public discontent that dissident Egyptian politicians and military officers could seize power.

MI6 suffered a blow in late August when the Egyptians broke up the service's operations in Cairo, arresting thirty people, including three British and one Maltese agent, and expelling two officials of the British Embassy.[36] The arrests, however, did not affect the contacts between dissident Egyptian officers, 'The Supporters of Justice', and MI6 outside Egypt. On 27 August, Conservative MP Julian Amery and two MI6 officers met conspirators in France. The dissident officers then conferred with civilians about the assassination of Nasser and his Ministers and the installation of a government headed by Saleh ed-Din, the Egyptian Foreign Minister from 1950 to 1952. General Mohammed

Neguib would emerge from house arrest to take the Presidency.[37] Amery summarised:

Their plan was not to overthrow [Nasser] because they did not think that this was on but they thought that [Nasser] would have gone and then they would have taken over and come out and said, 'Don't come to Cairo, we'll have an international conference: you are in charge of the Canal at the moment, but we will make a new plan.'[38]

In another plot, the British worked with Squadron Leader Mohammed Khalil, the Chief of Intelligence for the Egyptian air force, after representatives of Mustafa Maraghi, a former Minister of the Interior, and Husayn Khayri and Prince Namouk, relatives of King Farouk, contacted Khalil about the assassination of Nasser. Meetings between MI6 operatives, notably John Farmer and David Crichton, and the dissidents occurred in Beirut, Rome, Geneva and Munich, with Khalil, who was actually working for Nasser, being paid £162,500 by the British. Both conspiracies were subsequently broken up by Egyptian security forces in 1957 and the main Egyptian plotters arrested. MI6's involvement was revealed in the subsequent trials, although no Britons were prosecuted.[39]

The Foreign Office had always recoiled from the overthrow of Nasser because of the lack of an alternative regime. A. D. M. Ross, the Assistant Undersecretary supervising the Middle East, had noted on 28 July:

Nasser's grip is strong. There is no alternative in sight; the man who expelled foreign troops from Egypt, the spokesman of Arab nationalism and the champion of Arab military strength has a powerful hold over the people.[40]

Ambassador Trevelyan reported from Cairo that he had 'no serious evidence [of dissent] in the armed forces or police' and that the public was 'largely apathetic'. Military commanders cautioned, 'It would be unwise to assume that an Egyptian Government would quickly be forthcoming which would be willing to cooperate with us. . . . [We] would have to maintain forces in Egypt for years.'[41]

Yet MI6 did not believe a specific replacement for Nasser was a prerequisite for implementation of REVISE, for the operation would create the conditions for an alternative government to emerge. Four days after Amery and the two MI6 officers met the Egyptian dissidents in France, a military intelligence report assessed the situation. It admitted, 'One of the main strengths of the present regime is the absence of any coherent opposition in the country and the at-least outward unity of the Army', but added that there was 'a considerable element of the population which, if not disillusioned by the unfulfilled promise of EUTOPIA [sic], are at least critical of the regime'. Furthermore, the unity of the armed forces might 'well be only skin deep even in the Army. . . . Rifts have outwardly been healed but it is considered likely that little would be needed to reopen them.' Two days later, another report concluded:

The materialistically-minded Egyptian civilian is unlikely long to sustain the rigours of wartime economy or the actual experience of battle and remain faithful to the Regime. . . . It seems less likely to be a question of 'if there is a collapse of public morale and support for the Regime' as of 'how quickly that will take place'.[42]

The Egypt Official Committee, responsible for the political directive for operations, also hinted at MI6's confidence:

There were good reasons to believe that, given the defeat of the Egyptian Army and the collapse of the Nasser regime, a successor Government could be formed which are able to maintain law and order. . . . This prospect would be enhanced if the functioning headquarters, in or near Cairo, of such Nasser agencies as Army Intelligence, the Liberation Rally, and the National Guard could be eliminated at an early stage by Allied military action.[43]

The Foreign Office was told little, if anything, about MI6's plotting with the dissidents. In September 1956, the British Embassy in Cairo was asked for 'names, addresses, telephone numbers, and background of any people who should be borne in mind' as successors to Nasser. The Oriental Counsellor, Trefor Evans, visited London to give an oral appreciation of the situation, but the only candidate to lead Egypt, as in 1955, was Ali Maher, the former Prime Minister. According to J. B. Flux, expelled from Egypt after the round-up of the British spy ring, Maher said that he was ready to form a government and had names of Cabinet members 'in his pocket'.[44]

REVISE's flaw was that, without full knowledge of MI6's operations, civil servants and military planners could only assume, on the strength of MI6's assurances or on blind faith, that an alternative to Nasser would emerge after the launch of Anglo-French air operations and psychological warfare. The ad hoc committees established in July 1956 were no solution, as their brief was administrative, defining political control of Egypt after the landing of British troops and the installation of a new Egyptian government. Technically, the Egypt Committee oversaw REVISE and MI6's activities, but it had neither the time nor the expertise to concentrate on operational details.

Within the Foreign Office, only Kirkpatrick, Patrick Dean, the Superintending Undersecretary of the Permanent Undersecretary's Department, and Geoffrey Macdermott, Dean's deputy and the Foreign Office Adviser to MI6, received intelligence and information of British plans against Egypt, and Macdermott was rarely informed about intelligence operations. Kirkpatrick expressed concern at Eden's wish to kill Nasser, but he never tried to check MI6's plans. Furthermore, from September, Eden increasingly circumvented Kirkpatrick, as Dean, promoted from Assistant Undersecretary (Grade 4) to Deputy Undersecretary (Grade 2) in August, became the Prime Minister's channel for ad hoc action.[45] According to Assistant Undersecretary Ross:

As things began to hot up, [Eden] did take Dean over as his Foreign Office man. . . . As the crisis developed and decisions became more and more crucial, it was not so much the Foreign Office submitting advice as Eden using a member of the Foreign Office to do what he thought had to be done.[46]*

The adoption of REVISE also brought a significant change in the system of military planning. MUSKETEER had been drafted by a group of planners, most of whom had served in the Suez Canal Base, and co-ordinated by a committee of about fifty officers. REVISE, however, was developed by a small team, probably led by air force personnel, who were not part of the 'ordinary' machinery for planning. Those officers who had drafted MUSKETEER were sceptical about the aero-psychological campaign in REVISE. Kenneth Hunt noted: 'We didn't quite see how it was going to happen. . . . Nasser was too much what the Egyptians needed. The last thing we were going to be able to do was overthrow Nasser.'[47] This group, however, was effectively excluded not only from planning, but also from the intelligence assessments of the Egyptian situation.

Thus, despite Keightley's recognition that MUSKETEER had to be replaced because of diplomatic considerations, his military commanders were dissatisfied. The land commander, General Hugh Stockwell, 'discouraged and on edge', expressed 'considerable apprehension' about the change in plans. The air commander, Air Marshal Denis Barnett, explained:

With the first plan against Alexandria, one could perceive what would be the likely political aim underlying it, but with MUSKETEER REVISE and an assault on Port Said and just going down the Canal, it was extremely difficult to detect exactly what the political aim would be and how it would contribute to toppling Nasser. . . . In this area of psychological type of operation, my feeling is that [it] will only succeed if it is with overwhelming force.

*Dean denies that he was used by Eden in this way except on one occasion. On 24 October, when the Prime Minister wanted a Foreign Office official to participate in negotiations with the French and Israelis, Eden summoned Dean, who found his unexpected instructions so surprising and out of line with his normal role that he went straight to Kirkpatrick for confirmation that he should obey them (author's interview with Sir Patrick Dean and Dean letter to author, 26 April 1991).

British planners noted that REVISE

required considerable resolution from HMG in authorising the necessary programme of air bombing in the face of adverse world opinion. . . . We again voiced our anxiety lest HMG might find this pressure irresistible at some stage before Phase II had achieved its aim.[48]

The arguments were in vain. The intelligence services and the advocates of psychological warfare had convinced Keightley that REVISE was feasible.

The French still had to be convinced of the merits of the new British strategy. Meeting Eden and Lloyd on 11 September, Mollet and Pineau were cynical about the Users' Association, the latter saying,

This is just another Dulles bluff. . . . Trying to unravel this latest scheme will get us all so involved that by the time we find the whole affair is impracticable, everyone will be bored to death by our threats.[49]

To prevent the British from moving too closely towards Washington, Mollet revived Churchill's 1940 proposal for Anglo-French union:

The two Governments declare that France and Britain will no longer be two nations but a single Anglo-French Union. The constitution of the Union will consist of common bodies for defence, foreign policy, finance, and economic affairs. All French citizens will immediately become citizens of Great Britain; every British citizen will become a citizen of France.[50]

The British feared the effect of the Union on the Commonwealth, and the plan was eventually killed off by a Ministerial committee.[51]

The French Ministers, over the objections of their military commanders, finally accepted the Users' Association and REVISE.[52] Meanwhile, the new British strategy was presented to the Cabinet. Lloyd contended that the Users' Association would 'directly involve the US' with Anglo-French planning and deprive Egypt of eighty per cent of transit dues, and Macmillan reluctantly saw the organisation 'as a step towards the ultimate use of force'. Dismissing fears that the Treasury could not afford a military operation, he turned the economic argument against opponents of force: 'A quick solution to the crisis would restore confidence in the pound', but delay would 'undermine our financial position'.

Monckton again opposed the military option, but, as in the 28 August debate, Lords Kilmuir and Salisbury supported the use of force. Even Butler conceded that Tory MPs would support military action 'if they were satisfied that all practicable steps had been taken, without success, to secure a settlement by peaceful means'. Eden summarised, 'If [peaceful means] should fail, we should be justified in [the] last resort in using force to restore the situation.'[53]

Unwittingly, Foster Dulles's ploy to prevent Britain's resort to force had given the 'hawks' renewed hope. In accordance with the earlier timetable for MUSKETEER, Parliament had been recalled in special session for a two-day debate on Suez on 12–13 September. Eden would now unveil the Users' Association, having accepted Foster Dulles's request that it be presented as a British idea. He would explain that the Association would exercise its rights under the 1888 Constantinople Convention, that it would provide pilots for all ships transitting the Canal, and

that all dues payable by the users' ships would forthwith be paid to the new organisation. . . . If the Egyptian Government sought to interfere with the operations of the organisation or refused to extend the necessary cooperation on land, then the Egyptian Government would be regarded as being in breach of the Convention of 1888, and users could take such steps assumed fit to them to enforce their rights.[54]

After Parliamentary sanction was obtained, the Government would await Nasser's inevitable rejection of the international organisation. Then the 'hawks' would have their war.

16

Impaled on a SCUA
12–18 September 1956

Hoping for the best, the British had built their strategy around the Users' Association, but the Egypt Committee had recognised on 10 September that Foster Dulles's 'ingenious' proposals might be 'more in the nature of delaying tactics to provide time for further reflection and negotiation in an election year'. Within twenty-four hours, even before Eden's presentation of the plan to the House of Commons, the Committee's fears were confirmed. Foster Dulles admitted to Eisenhower that his immediate motive was appeasement of British opinion rather than punishment of Nasser:

We had to keep the initiative and to keep probing along various lines, particularly since there was no chance of getting the British and the French not to use force unless they had some alternatives that seemed to have in them some strength of purpose.[1]

Presented with Eden's draft announcement, Foster Dulles backed away from any hint of commitment to the use of force. He commented that the US could not commit herself to the provision: 'Users could take such steps as seemed fit to them to enforce their rights', although users might *individually* exercise their rights. He also repeated his assumption that Britain was prepared for the cost of sending ships around the Cape of Good Hope. The Foreign Office informed Makins that Britain was prepared to face 'economic consequences', but with the long-term approach, rather than a 'short, sharp struggle' against Egypt, Britain must rely upon American assistance for payments for oil. Kirkpatrick wrote to the Ambassador: 'If Middle Eastern oil is denied to us for a year or two, our gold reserves will disappear; if our gold reserves disappear, the sterling area disintegrates.'[2]

Foster Dulles had committed himself to an economic plan that he could not fulfil. Secretary of the Treasury Humphrey opposed 'hand-outs' to the British and any provision of aid might require Congressional approval. Foster Dulles tried to escape by arguing that Nasser would not obstruct navigation by ships of the Users' Association if he was aware of diversion around the Cape as an alternative, rather than an obligatory step, for the users. However, he then sabotaged his plan by reiterating that 'the US Government would only be able to ensure that US flagships paid [dues] to the new organisation and . . . the application of this requirement to [US-owned] ships under the Panamanian and Liberian flags would require further consultations'. Since ninety to ninety-five per cent of US-owned ships sailed under other countries' flags, Foster Dulles effectively allowed them to pay dues to Egypt.[3]

Despite Foster Dulles's wavering, Makins reassured the Foreign Office:

Perhaps I misheard you, but I did not follow your apparent doubts about American participation, bona fides, and so on. They have all worked like Trojans . . . and with great energy on the political and economic aspects of their proposals but, of course, much still depends on our skill in leading them along.[4]

US Ambassador Aldrich verified that Lloyd still expected that, 'if . . . Nasser should refuse the proposed plan, the UK and France would be on as firm ground as possible in taking whatever measures then seem to be desirable'.[5]

Eisenhower now made his first important intervention since July. While Foster Dulles apparently did not exclude the possibility of force if Nasser blocked Canal traffic, provided the US did not have to join the action, the President believed, 'We are sitting on a keg of dynamite.' Asked at a press conference if Anglo-French military action would be justified if pilots walked out and traffic through the Canal broke down, Eisenhower replied:

Justified, probably, in taking steps and conferring with Nasser. . . . That doesn't mean that they are justified at that moment in using force. . . . We established the United Nations to abolish aggression, and I am not going to be a party to aggression if it is humanly possible.[6]

By allowing that Britain and France 'would be free to take steps to assure their rights', a concession Eisenhower did not accept, while avoiding the employment of the Users' Association as an economic instrument against Nasser, Foster Dulles made promises he could not fulfil. The Egypt Committee recognised the apparent contradiction in American policy, but believed withdrawal of pilots and the success of Operation PILEUP would halt traffic through the Canal, forcing the US to support Anglo-French restoration of order. On the morning of 12 September, the Committee agreed that Lloyd should arrange consultations to establish the Users' Association. The Chancellor of the Exchequer, Macmillan, accepted that a loan from the Export-Import Bank, the only aid that Humphrey would allow, would not help Britain, since the loan would have to be repaid in dollars, but 'with Congress not in session and the Presidential election pending, the US Government could scarcely be expected to volunteer any wider undertaking'.[7]

Eden's statement in the Commons ruined the strategy. Neglecting to inform Gaitskell about SCUA, Eden failed to ensure Opposition agreement. He then highlighted the threat of force:

THE PRIME MINISTER: I must make it clear that if the Egyptian Government should seek to interfere –
HAROLD DAVIES [Lab., Leek]: Deliberate provocation.
THE PRIME MINISTER:– with the operations of the Association, or refuse to extend to it the essential minimum of co-operation, then that Government will once again be in breach of the 1888 Convention. (Hon. Members: Resign!) I must remind the House that what I am saying (An Hon. Member: What a peacemaker!) is the result of exchanges of views between three Governments. In that event HMG and others concerned will be free to take such further steps –
MR S. O. DAVIES: [Lab., Merthyr Tydfil]: What do you mean by that?
THE PRIME MINISTER: – as seem to be required –
MR S. O. DAVIES: You are talking about war.
THE PRIME MINISTER: – either through the United Nations or by other means, for the assertion of their rights. (Hon. Members: Oh!)

Eden concluded his speech with a clear warning to Nasser:

In these last weeks I have had constantly in mind the closeness of the parallel of these events with those of the years before the war. Once again we are faced with what is, in fact, an act of force which, if it is not resisted, if it is not checked, will lead to others. . . . We must help reproduce, step by step, the history of the thirties. We have to prove ourselves wiser this time and to check aggression by the pressure of international opinion, if possible, but, if not, by other means before it has grown to monstrous proportions.[8]

Eden 'did not see how anyone could have done better' with the speech, but his Press Secretary, William Clark, wrote:

The Prime Minister's introduction to the users' club could not have been more belligerent, which will make it a difficult article to sell; Gaitskell's advocacy of the UN could not have been more pacifist, which also adds to the trouble.

Gaitskell told the US Embassy that Eden's statement confirmed his 'worst suspicions that certain elements in Her Majesty's Government were determined to get rid of Nasser by force'.[9]

Foster Dulles was furious. He had approved a British statement without the threat of force, assuming that 'the general tone of the PM's remarks [would] be reasonably conciliatory or at least not particularly bellicose', but he now faced a call to war. He told a colleague:

[I am] embarrassed because Eden kind of knocked this whole plan down. . . . Eden went a little out-of-bounds. . . . He wants to show [the Canal] is a lifeline and it can't be cut – and so justify war. That is where our policy splits.[10]

The Secretary soon retaliated. He had agreed to a press conference on 13 September to support Eden's 'idea' of SCUA, but he deviated from his prepared text. Asked if users' ships would travel around the Cape rather than force their way through the Canal, he replied, 'It is not our purpose to try to bring about a concerted boycotting of the Canal. I think, under those conditions, each country would have to decide for itself what it wanted its vessels to do.' He was even more devastating when asked if rerouting of ships was, in effect, a boycott, answering:

It is not a boycott of the Canal as far as I know to refrain from using force to get through the Canal. If force is interposed by Egypt, then I do not call it a boycott to avoid using force to shoot your way through. We do not intend to shoot our way through.

Asked whether SCUA would guarantee the passage of Israeli ships, Foster Dulles completed the demolition of his plan, responding, 'Well, I am afraid that the Users' Association is not going to be in the position to guarantee anything to anybody; we can't even guarantee anything to our own ships.'[11]

Technically, Foster Dulles did not retract his promise to allow other powers to protect their rights, since he only said that the US would not use force. Journalists, however, knew that Foster Dulles, not Eden, had created SCUA and assumed that he was speaking for all members. To them, Foster Dulles had publicly withdrawn the 'last resort' of force as a bargaining lever against Egypt. Eden later complained:

[Foster Dulles's] words were an advertisement to Nasser that he could reject the project with impunity. . . . Such cynicism towards allies destroys true partnership. It leaves only the choice of parting, or a master and vassal relationship in foreign policy.[12]

The effect was immediately felt in Parliament. Gaitskell asked, 'Is [the Prime Minister] prepared to say on behalf of HMG that they will not shoot their way through the Canal?' Deprived of American support for force, Eden fell back upon recourse to the Security Council:

Would HMG give a pledge not to use force except after reference to the Security Council? . . . It would certainly be our intention, if circumstances allowed, or in other words, except in an emergency, to refer a matter of that kind to the Security Council. Beyond that, I do not think that any Government can possibly go.[13]

Eden had intended, in response to public opinion and the wishes of some Tory MPs, to announce Britain's appeal to the Security Council. The Chief Whip, Edward Heath, whispered to the Prime Minister upon his arrival for the debate, 'There will be no division if you announce that you are going immediately to the UN.' During the debate, a meeting of 150–200 Tory backbenchers was convened with Eden and Lloyd present. A majority of sixty recommended that the Prime Minister reassure the House of Commons that the government would not use force 'outside the UN'. To try to save the Government's position, a former Attorney-General, Lionel Heald, was persuaded to assure the Commons that Britain would comply with her international obligations.[14]

The plan was upset when Gaitskell's badgering forced Eden to alter his speech and reveal his intentions prematurely. The impression was given that recourse to the UN was a desperate response to Foster Dulles's abandonment of SCUA. Eden's previous commitment to the use of force seemed hollow, and the press widely labelled his statement a 'climbdown'.[15]

The public outbursts of Eden and Foster Dulles ruined six weeks of Anglo-American negotiations. After Eden's speech of 12 September, Foster Dulles decided that the effectiveness of the Users' Association as an economic sanction against Nasser was no longer an issue. Only a peaceful settlement mattered. He told Humphrey after his press conference of 13 September, 'We are not at war yet. [I] feel better today than for some time. . . . We never expected the plan to work anyway.' Foster Dulles then informed Eisenhower that he would attend the second London Conference to establish SCUA, as 'all [my] associates feel very strongly the British and French will mess it up and no one of less stature than [me] can handle Eden, Lloyd and Pineau'.[16]

In contrast, Eden saw no possibility of a peaceful settlement that would punish Egypt, as 'American torpedoing of their own plan on the first day of launching it left no alternative but to use force or acquiesce in Nasser's triumph'. Pineau complained about the 'lack of definite policy in Washington. . . . The US inability to agree on sanctions is bringing about the very result it seeks to avoid, namely, the use of military force.'[17]

Anglo-French plans now depended upon the walk-out of the 165 non-

Egyptian pilots of the Egyptian Canal Authority. Only forty Egyptian pilots remained, and Lloyd's of London raised the cost of war-risk insurance by 250 per cent to ships using the Canal. However, against all expectations, the Authority maintained the flow of traffic with the Egyptian pilots, supplemented by thirty Egyptian and eleven Greek recruits, by organising convoys and allowing some captains to pilot their vessels through the Canal. On 16 September, forty ships, an above-average figure, passed through the canal, 254 transited during the next week, and a record fifty-seven ships passed through the canal on 7 October. Lloyd's reduced its premiums and shippers withdrew the fifteen per cent surcharge placed on cargoes. By 18 September, Watkinson told the Egypt Committee and shipowners that PILEUP had failed.[18]

In desperation, Ministers returned to the idea of collaboration with Israel. Lloyd, despite his opposition to the idea, asked the Canadian Foreign Minister, Lester Pearson, 'whether, if things dragged on, Israel might not take advantage of the situation by some aggressive move against Egypt. . . . This might help Britain out of some of her more immediate difficulties.' Lloyd eventually agreed with Pearson

that the long-range results and, indeed, even the short-range results of such action would be deplorable and dangerous; that such action by Israel would certainly consolidate Arab opinion behind Egypt; that even Arab leaders who might now be worrying about Nasser's moves would have to rally behind him.[19]

The Egypt Official Committee, drafting the political directive for military operations, confirmed:

It is politically most important that there should be no association or appearance of association between [British] forces and Israeli forces. HMG will declare an appropriate area of Sinai and Egypt west of the Canal and of the waters off the Egyptian coast to be a combat area and issue a warning that any land, sea, or air forces found in that area not belonging to the forces under your command will be enemy forces.[20]

Yet a private, high-level initiative allowed at least one British Minister to establish contact with the Israelis. In early September, Colonel Robert Henriques, MBE, writer, soldier and member of a prominent Anglo-Jewish family, consulted Monckton about a forthcoming trip to Israel. On Monckton's advice, Henriques spoke to General Oliver, the Vice-Chief of the Imperial General Staff, and General Charles Haydon, chief of intelligence in the Middle East, before lunching with Minister of War Head, who had served at Combined Headquarters with Henriques in the Second World War.

Head cautioned that Henriques's trip 'could do untold harm in Israel just at this moment', but when Henriques asked if he could do any good, Head asked him to tell Ben-Gurion:

At all costs, Israel must avoid war with Jordan, but if, when Britain went into Suez, Israel were to attack simultaneously, it would be very convenient for all concerned. Britain would denounce Israel's aggression in the strongest possible terms, but at the peace negotiations afterwards, Britain would help Israel to get the best possible treaty.

Henriques transmitted the message about 20 September. Ben-Gurion smiled and said, 'We have heard such promises before.'[21]

Whether from remorse, false hope or concern about the British position, Foster Dulles had second thoughts about his burial of the Users' Association, telling Eisenhower, 'Despite the fact that the Users' Association proposal had gotten off to a bad start through Eden's presentation, it was now being better understood and . . . might be widely acceptable.'[22] For the third time since 26 July, the Secretary was going to try to salvage American influence upon the Eden Government.

17

Sliding towards a Settlement
19 September–4 October 1956

On 19 September, representatives of the eighteen nations who sanctioned the proposals of the first London Conference reconvened at Lancaster House to hear the report of the Menzies mission and to consider their next steps. The previous day, Foster Dulles, after talks with Lloyd and Pineau in the afternoon and Macmillan and Salisbury in the evening, described his role as mediator to Eisenhower:

My general impression is that the British and the French have quite isolated themselves, even from what are naturally their closest friends. . . . The United States is the only bridge between the British and the French and the rest of the countries here.[1]

Yet twenty-four hours later, the British thought that they had won over Foster Dulles. In his opening speech to the Conference, the Secretary simply introduced the Users' Association, but he became worried in the afternoon about 'a series of very weak speeches which put all the emphasis upon the necessity for peace and no emphasis at all upon the need for what the United Nations Charter calls a settlement "in accordance with the principle of justice and international law"'. He interjected:

I do not care how many words are written into the Charter of the United Nations about not using force; if in fact there is not a substitute for force, and some way of getting just solutions of some of these problems, inevitably the world will fall back again into anarchy and chaos.[2]

Foster Dulles had not sanctioned the use of force; however, because he was conscious of Anglo-French anger after his press conference of 13 September, he used a tone which implied that a 'just solution' would be imposed upon Nasser, if necessary. At the least, this indicated that the

US would use SCUA as an economic sanction. The British inferred that Foster Dulles had reverted to the statement originally agreed on the Users' Association, allowing each power to take necessary action to preserve its rights. Eden even outlined REVISE to the Secretary, explaining, '[We] had now altered [our] military plan so that instead of having a fixed date, [we] were able to hold the military threat in status quo without any prohibitive expense.'[3]

In the long run, the speech was disastrous. Having raised British expectations, Foster Dulles had no economic or military measures to satisfy them. Macmillan warned the Secretary 'that he would rather pawn the pictures in the National Gallery than accept humiliation at Nasser's hands', but Foster Dulles admitted to American journalists that there was 'no desire . . . to use the Users' Association to establish a boycott of the Canal' and that 'the Users' Association [was] not a device for denying Egypt any income at all with respect to the Canal'.[4]

On 20 September, William Clark recorded 'a day of deepening depression'. When the Conference concluded the next day, depression turned into near panic. Foster Dulles's speech had raised other countries' fears that they might become involved in an economic or military war with Nasser, trapping the US between Anglo-French determination and the caution of most of the eighteen nations. Even the name for the Association was a cause for dispute. The American suggestion of CASU (Co-operative Association of Suez Canal Users) was highly obscene in Portuguese and, as Lloyd recalled, 'Various other combinations were tried. Almost all of them meant something revolting, usually in Turkish.' Finally, it was discovered that SCUA offended no one.[5]

A more substantial problem was Pakistan's insistence that SCUA's sole purpose was negotiations with Nasser. The Scandinavian countries were sceptical about the plan, and Spain was close to rejection. When Japanese delegates pressed Foster Dulles to clarify details, British hopes for the 'just solution' faded. The Secretary admitted that 'de facto operating cooperation at the local level' would be necessary. For example, if Egyptian law allowed only Egyptian pilots to transit the Canal, the provision of foreign pilots for SCUA would collapse. The section on dues gave no indication of pressure, saying only that 'any user of the Canal *may* pay to SCUA'.[6]

Clark wrote on 21 September, after Foster Dulles again refused any commitment to force American shipowners to pay dues to SCUA instead of Egypt:

A ghastly day with all the worst expectations turning up. Dulles pulled rug after rug from under us and watered down the Canal Users' Association until it was meaningless. . . . Pineau came in and seemed almost on the edge of dissolving the [Western] alliance.

The French were allegedly pacified by the announcement that Eden and Lloyd would visit Paris the following week and by a private agreement that the Queen would tour France in 1957.[7] Eden, who had informed Churchill on 10 September that 'the Americans seem very firmly lined up with us on internationalism', now wrote to him: 'I am not very happy at the way things are developing here. . . . Foster assures me that US is as determined to deal with Nasser as we are – but I fear he has a mental caveat about November 6th [Presidential election day].'[8]

Disillusioned with SCUA, the British reverted to UN discussions as the pretext for military action. Eden, Lloyd and Foster Dulles discussed the topic on 20 September, Lloyd arguing for a meeting as early as possible and Foster Dulles asking for a delayed approach.[9] Eden then confirmed to Lloyd, 'I agree with you that it [the Security Council] must be called together early next week, even if only for a preliminary meeting.' Informed of this by Lloyd after the Conference, Foster Dulles requested ten days for the eighteen powers to join SCUA.[10]

In essence, Britain had finally decided to pursue the military option at the expense of Anglo-American agreement. Because of weather conditions and troop morale, REVISE could not be implemented after the end of October. The decision to launch the operation was required by the 20th. If Britain heeded Foster Dulles's wishes, the Security Council's endorsement of the British position and Parliamentary sanction for military action might not be arranged by then.

On 22 September, on Eden's instructions, the Foreign Office informed the British Embassy in Washington that the decision to appeal to the Security Council would be announced at 9 p.m. (4 p.m. in Washington). Makins replied frantically that Foster Dulles could not be informed, as he was not landing in Washington before 4 p.m. Fifteen minutes before the announcement, the British, 'from courtesy', postponed the press release until 3 p.m. on the 23rd.[11]

At the airport, Foster Dulles told John Coulson that the British action was 'sound', but said that he thought Eden had agreed to wait for progress on SCUA. Fearing that hasty recourse to the Security Council might dissuade Iran, Pakistan, Ethiopia and perhaps Sweden and Denmark from joining the Association, he asked for a further twenty-four-hour delay in the announcement. Eden refused, and the press release was issued.[12] Foster Dulles said on American television that he thought 'very well' of the British petition to the UN. Privately, he was livid, telling the Australian Ambassador, '[The British] moved awfully fast without quite knowing what they were doing. . . . There was no decision when he left [London] and he was told when he got off the plane.'[13]

Now that Britain was considering 'going it alone' with the French, the old problem was revived: could Britain and France proceed without Tel Aviv? During July and August, the French limited co-operation with Israel to general discussions and deliveries of equipment, but, frustrated by delays in the Anglo-French timetable, France approached the Israelis in early September about military planning against Egypt. The Israeli Chief of Staff, General Dayan, alerted his forces: 'Our political circumstances obliged us to be capable of going into action and operating all our aircraft . . . and not to be caught in a position in which we would have to pass up favourable political opportunities to strike at Egypt.' Dayan's Chief of Operations, Major-General Meir Amit, was questioned by Admiral Pierre Barjot, MUSKETEER's Deputy Commander-in-Chief, in Paris about Israeli intervention 'if appropriate political conditions arose in the immediate future'.[14]

When it became apparent that SCUA was not a vehicle for force, the French decided upon a Franco-Israeli attack against Egypt. The Director-General of the Israeli Ministry of Defence, Peres, discussed 'the objectives and methods of REVISE' with the French Minister of Defence, Bourges-Maunoury, on 19 September. Dayan set three conditions for Israeli participation: first, France would treat Israel as 'an ally with equal rights'; second, Israel would not be brought into conflict with Britain; third, Israel would 'rectify its border with the Sinai', acquiring Sharm el-Sheikh, at the southern tip of the Peninsula, and control of the Gulf of Aqaba. After the second London Conference, Bourges-Maunoury sent a birthday card to Ben-Gurion confirming that France would meet Israel's conditions. On 25 September, the Israeli Cabinet instructed Dayan, Peres and Foreign Minister Meir to travel to Paris. Ben-Gurion hinted to the Central Committee of his party, Mapai, 'There are some grounds to hope that before long Israel will have a true ally.'[15]

About 23 September, Pineau broached the possibility of Anglo-French co-operation with Israel to Lloyd and Eden. Pineau allegedly claimed: 'Eden showed a good deal of interest; Lloyd a great deal of reticence. . . . Nevertheless I was able to persuade them to give me a kind of carte blanche to undertake further negotiations with the Israelis.'[16] Pineau later disclaimed this account, but Bourges-Maunoury confirmed to Peres:

When Pineau left London disappointed . . . he was able to throw this at Eden: 'It seems that we have no choice but to work hand in hand with the Israelis. . . .' The British Prime Minister . . . reacted in a flaccid tone: 'On condition that they do not hurt the Jordanians. . . .' From this, [I conclude] the English will not attempt to interfere with the operation.

Dayan added that Pineau said,

The feeling in French Ministry of Defence circles is that military operations against Egypt are essential and that France should launch them – even if she has to act alone. If she does, they believe that Britain, in the end, will join in the campaign.

In essence, Eden refrained from supporting a Franco-Israeli operation, but indicated that London would not oppose the initiative.[17]

Macmillan now had a unique opportunity. Not only had he advocated co-operation with France and Israel, but he was visiting the US in late September. If the Chancellor could persuade Eisenhower, with whom he had served in the Second World War, to accept British military action against Nasser, an Anglo-French or even an Anglo-French-Israeli attack upon Egypt could be contemplated.

Furthermore, while Macmillan was the most fervent 'hawk' in the Cabinet, 'going it alone' with France posed problems, since his political future depended upon American financial assistance. On 8 August, Sir Edward Bridges, the Permanent Secretary at the Treasury, warned that the Suez crisis placed Britain's balance of payments and foreign reserves under considerable pressure, and he reiterated on 7 September 'the vital necessity from the point of view of our currency and our economy of ensuring that we do not go it alone and that we have the maximum US support'. Treasury official Leslie Rowan warned Macmillan on 21 September that £250–£300 million of foreign reserves had been lost in the last two months, bringing Britain near the Treasury 'floor' of $2 billion (£700 million) in dollar balances. Confidence in sterling

would not survive a war followed by protracted negotiations, resulting even in the fall of Nasser and the corresponding restoration of our prestige in the Middle East. It is unlikely that . . . the US would be ready to join in any far-reaching actions in the Middle East prior to the Elections.

Macmillan minuted: 'This is gloomy, but very likely correct.' On the same day, a Treasury paper estimated that Britain would lose £164 million ($466 million) in foreign reserves if supplies of Middle Eastern oil were halted.[18]

After a visit to his mother's home state of Indiana, Macmillan travelled to Washington for a thirty-five-minute meeting with Eisenhower on 25 September. The Chancellor cabled Eden that 'nothing very specific had emerged'. He added, 'The President understands our problems about Nasser, but he is, of course, in the same position now as we were in May

1955, with an impending general election.' In his diary, Macmillan also claimed:

On Suez, [Eisenhower] was sure that we must get Nasser down. The only thing was how to do it. I made it quite clear that we could not play it long, without aid on a very large scale – that is, if playing it long involved buying dollar oil.[19]

In contrast, Eisenhower's version of events never referred to Nasser's overthrow. He merely told Foster Dulles of a 'nice chat' about the British appeal to the Security Council and Macmillan's opinion that 'the Users' Association [was] a good thing'. Subsequently he recalled that 'Harold said that, if it came to the worst, they'd go down with the bands playing, the guns firing, and the flags flying', but he could not understand what Macmillan was implying. Ambassador Makins, the only witness to the meeting, recalled, 'I was expecting Harold to make a statement, say something important on Suez – but in fact he said nothing. . . . Nor did Eisenhower say anything. I was amazed.'[20]

Macmillan's day ended with a tense meeting with Foster Dulles. After castigating Britain's appeal to the UN, in a manner suggesting that 'he was warning [Britain] against entering a bawdy-house', Foster Dulles indicated that he would order US-flagged ships to avoid paying dues to Egypt if Britain and France faced the consequences, including blockage of the Canal; however, he still insisted that he had no authority over US-owned ships under other countries' flags. Moreover, Britain would have to pay, in dollars, for the diversion of oil from the Western Hemisphere if the Canal were blocked, a cost estimated at $500,000–$700,000 per year. Cornered, Macmillan admitted, 'The detour [of ships around the Cape of Good Hope] was really not a practicable possibility for any length of time. The UK could not afford to borrow more dollars.'

Foster Dulles evaded the request and asked for a return to OMEGA: 'The US Government was prepared to do everything it could to bring Nasser down, but . . . the most effective way of doing so was to let the present situation in the Canal continue and use other means of pressure which would shortly be discussed between us.' The Chancellor simply replied, 'The present military situation was such that [Britain] could, without undue expense, hold action in abeyance.'[21]

Macmillan had been clearly warned about the limits of American action, but the Chancellor put events in a positive light to the Foreign Office. Noting Foster Dulles's readiness to force US-flagged ships to pay dues to SCUA, Macmillan thought, inexplicably, that the Americans would press US-owned ships, short of legislation, to withhold dues. As for Foster Dulles's warning that Britain must finance the diversion of oil, Macmillan only said that Foster Dulles believed that the economic dangers of Nasser's reaction to withdrawal of dues 'might be very serious'.[22]

Macmillan went even further in 'unofficial' reports to Eden, hinting at a US 'blind eye' towards, if not support for, force. He noted Eisenhower's anxiety about the Presidential election, but informed Eden that the President was 'really determined, somehow or another, to bring Nasser down' and understood that Britain 'must win or the whole structure of our economy would collapse'. Macmillan also alleged that, after he said that he did 'not think [Britain] could stand for six months' waiting for OMEGA's success, Foster Dulles conceded, '[He] quite realised that we might have to act by force. . . . Our threat of force was vital, whether we used it or not, to keep Nasser worried.' Macmillan then presented Eden with an important, but misleading, interpretation of American policy. He noted that Foster Dulles had asked, as he and Eisenhower had helped the Prime Minister during the May 1955 British general election by agreeing to the Geneva summit with the Soviets, if Britain 'could not do something in return and hold things off until after November 6th'. Macmillan's implication was clear: because of the Presidential election, the Americans could not intervene *against* military action.[23]

In fact, Foster Dulles, indicating that the US would proceed with OMEGA after 6 November, was warning Macmillan that the Americans could not condone a showdown with Nasser before then. Makins had already cautioned the Foreign Office, 'Although the President and Dulles have been careful not to exclude the possibility that force may have to be used, there is in my judgement no prospect . . . that the US will themselves participate in military action before November 6.'[24] On 29 September, Deputy Undersecretary Robert Murphy reiterated the message to Macmillan. If Britain refrained from acting before election day, OMEGA could then be implemented: 'The position would be quite different. . . . Between us, we should be able to encompass [Nasser's] downfall within a few months. It was high time that Nasser's pretensions and those of the other Arab states were deflated.' Significantly, Makins recorded that nothing Murphy said was inconsistent with the views of Eisenhower or Foster Dulles. The Ambassador later assessed that there was 'no basis at all for Harold's optimism'.[25]

Given Macmillan's political experience, it is unlikely that he misinterpreted the American sentiment against force. Instead, the Chancellor was trying to bolster Eden with the impression that Eisenhower and Foster Dulles would not risk public division with two NATO allies and oppose Anglo-French action. Press Secretary Clark recalled that, upon Macmillan's return,

HM casually remarked to Eden, 'I had a few words with Eisenhower. Of course he's an ill man but as brave as ever. . . . Of course, you saw the President too, didn't you, Selwyn [Lloyd]?' This was very much a putdown of Selwyn for whom HM had total contempt, as being then 'Deputy Foreign Secretary to the Prime Minister'. Selwyn, blushing, replied, 'No,' thus HM was very much one-up. . . . Then HM came on strong – 'I don't think there is going to be any trouble from Ike – he and I understand each other – he's not going to make any real trouble if we have to do something drastic.'[26]

For Macmillan, Britain had to proceed with her military plans and hope that the US would accept the action. If nothing was done, the Government would drift into negotiations with Egypt, with disastrous political and economic consequences. As Kirkpatrick complained:

In two years' time, Nasser will have deprived us of our oil, the sterling area fallen apart, no European defence possibly, unemployment and unrest in the United Kingdom, and our standard of living reduced to that of the Yugoslavs or Egyptians.[27]

Yet Macmillan, for all his efforts, returned from the US to find the Egypt Committee considering a genuine attempt for a peaceful settlement. Some Ministers were having second thoughts about the abrupt decision to act without the US, and Macmillan's absence removed an influential voice from the Committee. Foreign Office officials, almost all of whom except Kirkpatrick were wary of force, had been excluded from policy-making, but they seized the opportunity of the approach to the UN, and Lloyd, increasingly concerned with the American attitude and world opinion, was ready to support them. He explained to the Canadian Foreign Minister, Pearson, that he was 'as ready to bash the Egyptians as anybody', but 'he had to ask himself where his country and the Commonwealth would stand after the job of bashing had been done'.[28]

Lloyd told the Egypt Committee on 25 September that it was impossible to reject all proposals for negotiations and introduced a plan, drafted by the Indian Foreign Minister, Krishna Menon, for a 'system of guarantees, controlled by arbitrators', between the Egyptian Canal Authority and SCUA for the development of the Canal and transit dues. The Committee noted that arrangements for international consultation were 'probably more satisfactory than any proposal that could be agreed with Egypt after the expiration of the original concession [to the Suez Canal Company] in 1968'. Although 'such a scheme would . . . need some effective sanctions', Lloyd was authorised to speak with Menon.[29] Even Eden was considering negotiations, telling the Cabinet that he hoped to persuade the French 'that it would not be possible to reject at the Security Council all suggestions for further negotiations between the parties to the dispute', although Ministers finally concluded, 'If it became clear that the United Nations were powerless to enforce respect for international obligations, we should not be content to stand aside and see them flouted.'[30]

The British hesitancy led to a 'very difficult' meeting of more than two hours with Mollet and Pineau on 26 September in Paris. Eden recorded that the French 'did not like [UN negotiations] at all. . . . They [stood] by the 18-Power proposals and [were] not prepared for any modification of them.' Eden concluded:

My own feeling is that the French, particularly M. Pineau, are in the mood to blame everyone, including us, if military action is not taken before the end of October. M. Mollet . . . would like to get a settlement on reasonable terms if he could. I doubt whether M. Pineau wants a settlement at all.[31]

The US Ambassador to France, Douglas Dillon, was informed that the Prime Minister was 'very satisfied' because the French 'push for more drastic action' had been checked by the 'good sense of Mollet'.[32]

Privately, Eden admired the French determination. Norman Brook wrote to Churchill:

The PM was deeply impressed by the youth and vigour of M. Mollet's Government. . . . They are by far the best French Government he has seen since the war. Over Suez they are tough and uncompromising. He believes that we may be at the beginning of something like a renaissance of strength in France.[33]

However, without a pretext for military action, Eden could not reverse the trend towards British acceptance of negotiations. Lloyd told the Egypt Committee that, although he would stand by the eighteen-power proposals, 'this need not mean that the Western Powers should refuse to consider any counter-proposals put forward by Egypt'. The Committee noted that the Menon plan 'would at least provide for international supervision' and could be developed to allow international control of the Canal.[34]

MI6, which had been feeding information to the 'hawks', still pressed Eden to reject negotiations. Ambassador Aldrich reported to Washington:

[The British] still believe that various Governments friendly to the West in the area are imminently threatened by Egyptian- and Soviet-instigated subversion. They fear violence or even assassination. This feeling is periodically fanned by intelligence reports to which they give credence.[35]

Eden decided, before embarking upon negotiations, to test Eisenhower with another personal appeal:

You can be sure that we are fully alive to the wider dangers of the Middle Eastern situation. They can be summed up in one word – Russia. . . .

There is no doubt in our minds that Nasser, whether he likes it or not, is now effectively in Russian hands, just as Mussolini was in Hitler's. It would be as ineffective to show weakness to Nasser now in order to placate him as it was to show weakness to Mussolini. . . .

The Prime Minister pleaded for US-owned ships to pay transit dues to SCUA as a sign of American intentions.[36]

Meanwhile, France, 'abandoned' by the British, sought final agreement on action with Israel. On 30 September, Golda Meir, Peres and Dayan met Pineau, Bourges-Maunoury and General Maurice Challe, the Chief of the Air Staff, in Paris. Pineau suggested that, if Israel attacked Egypt, Britain and France could 'intervene' as peace-keepers and control the Suez Canal. He insisted that the invasion of Egypt must occur before 6 November:

[The Americans] would not take the responsibility of deliberately breaking the Atlantic alliance before the elections. . . . They could not alienate . . . the great number of pro-Israeli voters in the US by taking a position against Israel.

On the other hand, if Eisenhower is elected, Dulles will no longer hesitate to make an agreement with the Russians, at our expense, to protect the interests of the oil lobby in the US. He will no longer hesitate to impose sanctions against Israel in the event of her intervention [in Egypt].[37]

Meir wanted to consult the US, but Pineau refused:

We must not put [the Americans] in a position of having to say yes or no since they could only say no because of the oil lobby. That would get us into a much more difficult situation than if we hadn't consulted them.

He asked for Franco-Israeli planning, with or without British participation. Dayan and Meir agreed, although the latter requested a guarantee that Britain would not attack Israel if Israeli-Jordanian fighting followed action against Egypt. French Chief of Staff Ely, in discussions with Dayan, agreed to the supply of additional equipment, notably 100 Sherman tanks and 300 half-tracks, to Israel, although he declined to commit French forces in a simultaneous attack. A date of 20 October was set for the military operation.[38]

Foster Dulles, excluded from the discussions in London, Paris and Tel Aviv, was in an unfamiliar and uncomfortable position. He complained to Henry Cabot Lodge, the US Ambassador at the UN, 'We don't know what they are after. The French are eager to get into a fighting war. . . . The British Cabinet is divided; I don't know where the balance of power lies.'[39]

The Secretary responded hastily at a press conference on 2 October. Firstly, he rejected economic pressure upon Egypt, within or without the Users' Association. Asked about collapsing the price for Egyptian cotton through the 'dumping' of American cotton surpluses, he replied, 'It may be that ways can be found if they are sought . . . which would be somewhat disturbing to Egypt's cotton market, but we are not now engaging in any economic war against Egypt.' Secondly, he repeated that 'there were never "teeth" in [SCUA], if that means the use of force'. Finally, he attacked Britain and France:

The US cannot be expected to identify itself 100 per cent either with the colonial powers or the powers uniquely concerned with the problem of getting independence as rapidly and as fully as possible. . . . I hope that we shall always stand together in treaty relations covering the North Atlantic, [but] any areas encroaching in some form or manner on the problem of so-called colonialism find the US playing a somewhat independent role.[40]

Foster Dulles's outburst resulted from pique rather than policy, but it was a catastrophic failure of judgment. As Nasser asserted that his struggle against Britain was a fight against colonialism, Foster Dulles's remark implied American support for Cairo. The following day, Foster Dulles told Makins that 'he had been drawn into a line of discussion which was in itself undesirable' and 'his remarks had been given a connexion which he did not intend'. Moreover, the typescript of his answers was released to the press before he saw it.[41]

Despite Foster Dulles's repentance, American and British journalists speculated that he was privately pursuing an American 'middle course' between Egypt and the Anglo-French position. *The Times* commented, after a private briefing by Press Secretary Clark:

Mr Dulles's wavering course over the Suez issue has been watched in Britain with patient understanding because of the realisation that the US is on the eve of a presidential election and whatever he does or says has to pass the test of that scrutiny, but some of his words at yesterday's press conference can hardly claim the indulgence of that understanding any longer.[42]

When Eden received news of Foster Dulles's statement, he flung the report at Nutting and snapped, 'Now what have you to say for your American friends?' He protested to Washington: 'It would be . . . dishonest to pretend that the press conference did not give a severe shock to public opinion here. . . . Anything which could be said by Mr Dulles to redress that balance will buttress peace.'[43]

It was too late to 'redress the balance'. At the National Security Council, Foster Dulles complained that 'never before in recent years' had the US been in an international crisis with no idea of British and French intentions. Eisenhower, who was receiving reports of top-secret talks between CIA officials and Ali Sabri, reaffirmed, 'The US would be dead wrong to join in any resort to force. We should instead hold out for honest negotiations with the Egyptians.'[44] Eden complained to Iveragh MacDonald of *The Times*, 'We have leaned over backwards to go along with [Foster Dulles] and now look. How on earth can you work with people like that? It leaves us in a quite impossible position. We can't go on like this.'[45]

On 3 October, the remaining 'hawks' in the British Cabinet desperately tried to renew the commitment to force, using Foster Dulles's 'betrayal' and the Franco-Israeli links. They protested:

Our objectives would not be fully attained if we accepted a settlement of the Suez Canal dispute which left Colonel Nasser's influence undiminished throughout the Middle East. . . . There was evidence that he was already seeking to foment discontent with the existing regimes in other Arab countries. Disturbing reports had been received of dissident movements in Libya, Saudi Arabia and Iraq.

The solution to the problem came from Pineau, who had told Eden that Israel had 'made up her mind to attack within three weeks' and asked, 'What should the Western allies do about it?' Two Cabinet Ministers later recalled that it was mentioned that 'the Jews had come up with an offer' to attack Egypt. The effort was in vain, however, as the Foreign Office prohibition on overt co-operation with Israel and Lloyd's insistence on negotiations with Egypt were upheld. Eden rationalised, 'If [the Egyptians] continued to be obdurate, world opinion might be ready to support a recourse to forceful measures.'[46]

After two weeks of tension, Foster Dulles's 'colonialism' statement and the British reaction apparently signalled the breakdown of Anglo-American relations, but the two sides had continued to discuss the implementation of OMEGA. On 20 September, Eden and Foster Dulles discussed 'setting up a very secret working party . . . in London to consider continued economic and political means of weakening and lessening the prestige of the regime of Colonel Nasser'. The next day, Foster Dulles and Lloyd agreed to 'take the matter up immediately'.[47]

Informed by Foster Dulles of the discussions, Eisenhower 'felt that [the US] should have nothing to do with any project for a covert operation against Nasser personally', and when Undersecretary of State Hoover said that 'one of our agencies' had a plan 'on how to topple Nasser' quickly, the President replied:

An action of this kind could not be taken when there is as much active hostility as at present for a thing like this. . . . A time free from heated stress holding the world's attention as at present would have to be chosen.[48]

Nevertheless, in early October, Foreign Office and MI6 personnel, including Patrick Dean, discussed OMEGA with State Department and CIA officials, including the Roosevelts, in Washington. It was agreed that the coup against the Syrian Government through Operation STRAGGLE would be implemented by the end of October, and the CIA passed $165,000 to its contact, Michel Ilyan, to implement the coup.[49]

Unfortunately, this co-operation was undermined by MI6's independent activities. During the summer of 1956, the intelligence service worked with the Iraqis, the banned Syrian group Partie Populaire Syrienne (PPS) and Syrian military conspirators. While the Americans cleared their operation with British officials, MI6 withheld information from the Americans. MI6 probably consulted the Iraqis in summer 1956 about the return to power of the former dictator Adib Shishakli before the Americans, who doubted Shishakli had widespread support within Syria and worried about his heavy drinking, forced his departure from Lebanon.[50]

By October, the British Military Attaché in Beirut and General Daghestani, the Iraqi Deputy Chief of Staff, were discussing the details of a new plan. A PPS paramilitary force would seize Homs, and Salah Shishakli, the former dictator's brother, would lead his men against Hama. Other PPS troops would occupy key positions in Damascus and assassinate left-wing army officers. Tribes, such as the Druze in the south and the Alawites in the west, supplied with Iraqi arms, would simultaneously rebel. Politicians involved in the plot included Adnan Atassi, a former Ambassador to France; his cousin Faydi Atassi, a former Minister of Foreign Affairs; former Minister of Justice Mounir Ajlani; and former Minister of State Hassan Atrash, a Druze leader. It is not clear if Ilyan, the chief American contact for STRAGGLE and well-known to the Iraqis and the British, played a role in the Anglo-Iraqi planning.[51]

For the moment, the Anglo-American 'alliance' had survived. Despite the manoeuvres of MI6 and the outbursts of Foster Dulles, the State Department, the CIA and the Foreign Office maintained contacts over OMEGA and relations between military staffs were close. More importantly, the Egypt Committee, having taken the decision in late September to proceed without the US, had played into the hands of British officials who sought a negotiated settlement, since the appeal to the Security Council was not overseen by ad hoc committees but by the regular Foreign Office machinery. Ministers who had been following Macmillan's call for war now had second thoughts about fighting without an attempt to resolve the dispute through the UN. Lloyd, accused by some of being 'Eden's poodle', had become the most important figure in British policy-making.

18

Force Dismissed
5–14 October 1956

Upset with Eden, misinterpreted by Macmillan and ignored by the Egypt Committee, Foster Dulles had one last card to play. If he could personally influence Lloyd, he could tilt the balance in London against force. Before the Security Council considered Suez, he warned Lloyd and Pineau:

There must be some international participation in the operation of the Canal. [The US] also believed, however, that every possible effort must be made to secure this objective by peaceful means and that the use of force would be a desperate remedy.

Lloyd stood firm, using words reminiscent of Kirkpatrick and Eden:

We knew the Egyptians were planning a coup in Libya; they had arms ready there for use and there was a plot to kill the King. King Saud was also threatened. In Iraq Nuri was now in control but there was dissatisfaction amongst some of the younger officers and this was likely to grow if we continued to do nothing. Jordan was already penetrated and Syria was virtually under Egyptian control.

Pineau added, 'Nothing less than the existence of NATO was at stake.'

Foster Dulles insisted that, 'If force were used, we could write off Pakistan, Iran, and Ethiopia. The position in Africa would be worse and not better.' Once again, however, he left an ambiguity which could be exploited by Britain and France. According to the American record, Foster Dulles said:

Sometimes one must use [force] without the prospect of a satisfactory outcome, but force is not a measure which will improve our prospects in Asia and Africa; and it is a great illusion to think that it would. . . . The use of force in violation of the Charter would destroy the UN.

The British record, however, suggested that Foster Dulles would allow force in the last resort:

The *potential* use of force must be kept in existence. . . . We must make it clear in the Security Council that if a real effort to get a peaceful settlement . . . failed, it would then be permissible to consider force as an alternative.[1]

Eden was temporarily absent from British policy-making. In October, his wife Clarissa entered University College Hospital, ostensibly for a dental operation.[2] Visiting her, the Prime Minister was struck by a high fever, a recurrent effect of his 1953 gall bladder operation, and admitted for the weekend. On 7 October, when his temperature returned to normal, he cabled Lloyd with renewed vigour:

In the last resort, action will be necessary. It is therefore very important that, while appearing reasonable, we shall not be inveigled away in negotiaton from the fundamentals to which we have held all along and that we should not be parted from the French.[3]

Unfortunately for Eden, Foster Dulles, despite his token acknowledgment of force as a last resort, was giving Lloyd no opportunity to reject negotiations. When the Foreign Secretary urged him to 'give [SCUA] a few vitamins' through the endorsement of economic sanctions, Foster Dulles demanded that American ships withhold dues from Egypt and pay them to SCUA *after* British and French ships had done so. If the US acted first, her ships might be denied passage through the Canal while the vessels of Britain, France and other countries freely transitted. The Secretary's position amounted to a delaying tactic, since British and French vessels could not begin paying dues to SCUA until it was organised and compensation arranged for the Suez Canal Company.[4]

Representatives of fourteen countries had met the previous week to implement plans to divert more than ninety per cent of Canal revenues from Nasser, but the Americans refused to finance the diversion of shipping around the Cape of Good Hope. The French warning, '*il faut coloniser le canal ou canaliser le colonel*', was unheeded. Pineau complained that the Association was 'for drowning fish', while the *Daily Telegraph* commented, 'SCUA has become as harmless to [Nasser] as a jester's bladder'.[5]

Eden's absence and Foster Dulles's pressure on Lloyd reopened divisions within the Egypt Committee. The Foreign Secretary, supported by the Foreign Office, was ready to talk to the Egyptians, but in London, Macmillan, regaining his former influence, steered the Egypt Committee towards a firmer position. Under his leadership, the Egypt Committee instructed Lloyd to stand firmly upon the eighteen-power plan in the Security Council and insist that the US pay dues to SCUA.[6]

The position of Macmillan, who allegedly threatened to resign if a compromise was struck with Egypt, was expected. More intriguing was the emergence of Anthony Nutting, the Minister of State at the Foreign Office, as a 'hawk'. Nutting was one of the rising stars of the Conservative Party. Still in his thirties, he was well-liked in the Commons and had quickly risen to the second-highest post in the Foreign Office. With his eloquent speech and refined manner, he was considered by many as a protégé, if not a younger copy, of Eden. In December 1954, Henry Cabot Lodge wrote to Eisenhower: 'If you could invite him down to lunch and give him a little of your time, it would be a fine thing for the USA because I feel sure he will be Prime Minister someday.'[7]

Although personal problems and New York society gossip hindered Nutting while he was attending the UN disarmament talks in late 1955, almost prompting his recall to London and transfer from the Foreign Office, he soon returned to prominence. Because of Lloyd's frequent trips abroad, Nutting often served as a de facto Foreign Secretary in the shaping of British foreign policy. Working with Shuckburgh, he had been instrumental in the adoption of the Foreign Office's long-term programme against Nasser in March 1956. While his relationship with Eden could be tempestuous, he was friendly enough with the Prime Minister to serve as a personal adviser on occasion.[8]

On 8 October, Nutting met Menon, who was promoting his plan for international co-operation in the Canal's administration. Although India would not propose military sanctions, Menon suggested binding arbitration, possibly enforced by economic sanctions, in a dispute between Egypt and the Canal users. Nutting minuted, "There might even be some slight improvement for us' in the package, but warned, 'At present . . . [it is] unwise to treat the plan as other than a piece of Indian private enterprise.'[9] The next morning, Nutting persuaded Eden to reject the Menon proposals. He argued that co-operation between SCUA and the Egyptian Canal Authority should not extend beyond advice offered at joint sessions and rejected any reference of disputes to the International Court of Justice or the UN.[10]

Lloyd, however, was already discussing variants of the Menon plan with Pineau and the Egyptian Foreign Minister, Mahmoud Fawzi, and the Security Council adjourned on 9 October to allow the three to confer under the auspices of UN Secretary-General Dag Hammarskjøld. Fawzi said that the Egyptians would accept the 1888 Constantinople Convention or a new agreement concerning the Canal. They would designate a percentage of revenues for the Canal's development and fix the level of tolls through negotiation. They would endorse an arbitration tribunal, with one Egyptian member, one member from SCUA and an impartial chairman. Finally, they would welcome Britain's ideas on enforcement of the tribunal's decisions.[11]

Eden had to accept the negotiations, since halting the talks would put Britain in the wrong before world opinion and ruin any pretext for force. Instead, he suggested to the Egypt Committee that Lloyd ask Fawzi for details of Egyptian proposals to 'spin out' the talks. Meanwhile, Foster Dulles would be pressed to agree that dues could be withheld from the Egyptians if they violated any agreement reached with SCUA. Just in case the Egyptians were conciliatory, Eden added the proviso that Egypt should abandon her blockade of Israeli shipping through the Canal, an almost impossible condition for Cairo to accept.[12]

Lloyd, however, quickly obtained further concessions from Fawzi, who agreed, without qualification, that the Canal should be insulated from Egyptian politics. Lloyd warned the French that negotiations with Egypt meant 'any resort to force would be ruled out in the immediate future' and cabled Eden: 'I doubt whether Pineau really believes that a peaceful settlement is possible and I am not entirely convinced that he wants one.'[13]

The Foreign Secretary's message was clear. Unless Britain halted negotiations immediately, incurring the disapproval of international opinion and ruining any diplomatic pretext for the use of force, REVISE would have to be suspended. The reply to Lloyd was considered by Eden, Monckton, Watkinson, Brook, Kirkpatrick and Ross of the Foreign Office. Finally, the 'hawks' were defeated. Macmillan was absent, Watkinson was disillusioned by the failure of Operation PILEUP, and Monckton's aversion to force was unabated. The meeting conceded:

The present proposals would at least provide a system of international co-operation with a considerable measure of financial control. Moreover, the consortium of the Users' Association and the Egyptian Board to some extent satisfied the requirements for an international authority postulated in the 18-Power proposals.

The only reference to force was agreement upon a clause, to be linked to the UN Charter, that any Egyptian hindrance of free navigation would 'constitute an act of aggression which justified the injured country in taking action to protect its interests'.

The Egypt Committee had intended to end the UN talks by 12 October to allow the 'consultation' of Parliament about the launching of REVISE, but it accepted Eden's recommendation:

Provided the present pressure was maintained on Egyptian representatives in these negotiations, [the Foreign Secretary] should not feel himself bound to terminate the discussions by the end of this week [12 October] if at the time it appeared that a satisfactory agreement would shortly be obtained.

Eden cabled Lloyd that he was 'delighted to see that [you] fought so hard' in the negotiations and concluded, 'I know you will do your best to keep the French in line.'[14]

Lloyd's antagonist was no longer Fawzi but Pineau. He cabled Eden on 11 October:

Pineau's heavy cold has now translated itself into a fever and his influence upon our discussions is almost entirely negative. . . . I am doing my best to keep him in line, but he seems determined (a) to prevent any agreement, (b) to present our negotiations in the worst possible light, (c) to end up with an expression of opinion by the Security Council which would tie our hands.

Late in the evening, however, the talks produced 'Fawzi's quite definite statement that Egypt would leave the Users to organise themselves as they wished. Egypt would recognise the association and would accept the dues paid through it.'[15]

The following afternoon, Lloyd and Fawzi accepted 'Six Principles' for operation of the Canal:

1. There should be free and open transit through the Canal without discrimination, overt or covert;
2. There should be respect for Egyptian sovereignty;
3. The operation of the Canal should be insulated from the politics of any country;
4. The level of dues should be fixed by agreement between users and owners;
5. A fair proportion of the dues should be allotted to development [of the Canal];
6. Affairs between the Suez Canal Company and the Egyptian Government should be settled by arbitration, with suitable terms of reference and suitable provision for the payment of the sums found to be due.[16]

All eleven members of the Security Council, including the Soviet Union, supported the Principles. The issue, Lloyd wrote, was 'how were these principles to be implemented?'[17] Pineau insisted that he could not stay in New York beyond 14 October, and Lloyd realised that a detailed agreement could not be reached in forty-eight hours. Therefore, he and Pineau introduced the eighteen-power plan as the 'most appropriate' means to implement the Six Principles. Lloyd recognised that the Soviet Union would veto this, but hoped that a substantial majority for the plan would bolster Britain's negotiating position. Significantly, Fawzi offered to continue talks with Lloyd and Pineau anywhere in Europe except Paris and possibly London.[18]

The Americans were now optimistic about the prospect of a peaceful settlement. Foster Dulles told the National Security Council that Britain appeared 'to favor a compromise settlement but are deeply concerned on how they can square such a compromise with the strong positions which they have taken publicly'. To reinforce British 'moderates', Foster Dulles finally conceded that, once SCUA was established, US-flagged ships would be mandated to pay Canal dues to the Association and US-owned ships would be encouraged to do likewise.[19]

In his relief, Eisenhower spoke too freely, telling a press conference:

It looks like here is a very great crisis that is behind us. I do not mean to say that we are completely out of the woods, but I talked to the Secretary of State just before I came over here tonight and I will tell you [that] in both his heart and mine there is a very great prayer of thanksgiving.[20]

He enthused to Foster Dulles:

Perhaps it is just as well that when we are together our talk must be of Suez or Morocco or South Vietnam. Because I assure you that I am even more tongue-tied than you (and sometimes I blame my inadequacy on my Germanic origin) in trying to tell *you* the rewards I have received from our association.[21]

Lloyd was not as impressed. Incensed that the President spoke before the Security Council vote on the eighteen-power plan, he told Foster Dulles that he 'was disgusted by the way in which our hand is weakened at every stage of this business by what is said over here'.[22]

Despite the Foreign Secretary's concern, nine countries supported the eighteen-power plan in the Council, with only Yugoslavia and the Soviet Union, using the veto, opposed. Lloyd informed Eden that 'the suspicion that we were treating the United Nations simply as a formality has been dissipated'. The option of military action was still open, since Britain emerged 'without any result enjoining us against force or to set up a negotiating committee. . . . With the changed atmosphere here, we can count on a more understanding reaction if we have to take extreme measures.' This could only be undertaken, however, if Egypt refused to continue discussions. Lloyd concluded, 'We are now committed to further interchanges with Egypt without a time limit.'[23]

On the morning of 14 October, Eden and Nutting read Lloyd's final report. The Prime Minister could have overruled Lloyd's call for genuine negotiations. He told the Conservative Party Conference the previous day, 'We have refused to say that in no circumstances would we ever use force. No responsible government could ever give such a pledge.' To rapturous applause, Eden repeated that Britain would not accept Egyptian control of the Canal. Two days earlier, Nutting delivered a similar statement with the same results.[24]

Privately, however, Eden's resolve for military action had disappeared. A cable to Lloyd, drafted by Nutting and approved by Eden, suggested further negotiations:

Should not we and the French now approach the Egyptians and ask them whether they are prepared to meet and discuss in confidence with us on the basis of the second half of the resolution which the Russians vetoed? If they say yes, then it is for consideration whether we and the French meet them somewhere, e.g. Geneva. If they say no, then they will be in defiance of the view of nine members of the Security Council and a new situation will arise.[25]

This cable, the most significant of the Suez crisis to that point, was soon lost among government documents, and British accounts of Suez have conveniently neglected to mention it. In his memoirs, Eden, portraying himself as the antagonist of the 'evil' Nasser, ridiculed the UN talks:

The notion gained currency that the Security Council had prepared the terms for a peaceful and just settlement of the dispute. . . . Perhaps the most disturbing feature of all these discussions was the utter indifference shown by the UN to the international aspects of the crisis.

He did not refer to his suggestion of further negotiations with Egypt, claiming instead that he rejected Hammarskjøld's idea of a meeting in Geneva as of 'no real value'.[26]

Nutting's account, which criticised the Prime Minister for his obsession with a showdown with Egypt, also ignored the key telegram. The Minister of State claimed that, at lunch on 14 October, he tried to steer the conversation to Lloyd's good work in New York, but Eden only talked about the praise he received at the Conservative Party Conference. Lloyd's memoirs recorded his final report to Eden, but did not mention the Prime Minister's reply.[27]

Ultimately, Eden and Nutting were forced into their decision by a lack of options. British and French commanders faced the approach of winter weather and declining morale. On 1 October, twenty-four reservists were arrested after protesting about operations. REVISE's command in London delicately noted: 'Reports of recent incidents show that certain soldiers appear to have forgotten the correct method of ventilating complaints and are adopting methods which are protected in civil life but are forbidden in the Army.'[28]

On 12 October, the British Chiefs of Staff authorised the replacement of REVISE in a week by the 'Winter Plan'. While the Plan, like REVISE, used an aerial assault and psychological warfare in Phases I and II, the bombing of Egypt 'might occupy 10 to 14 days or even longer' because of adverse weather conditions, shorter daylight hours, and selective targeting to ensure few civilian casualties. More importantly, because of the release of reservists and shipping from duty, no landing of troops on open beaches could be attempted until spring 1957.[29]

For the moment, the Suez crisis was over. The Americans were not directly responsible, but, in the end, the sustained pressure by Washington against force delayed British action long enough for other influences, such as Foreign Office opinion and the restrictions on the military timetable, to take effect. For the 'hawks', the 'alliance' may have operated to Britain's disadvantage, but it had worked none the less.

19

Force Resurrected
14 October 1956

At 1.30 p.m. on 14 October, Eden's telegram proposing negotiations with the Egyptians in Geneva was despatched to Lloyd in New York. Ninety minutes later, two French envoys, Acting Foreign Minister Albert Gazier and General Maurice Challe, brought a proposal from Prime Minister Mollet. By 4 p.m., the Anglo-French military option had been revived.

Gazier introduced the French initiative by asking what action Britain would take if Israel attacked Egypt. Puzzled, Eden noted that Britain, France and the US had agreed in the 1950 Tripartite Declaration to oppose any aggression across Arab-Israeli frontiers, but Gazier persisted, inquiring if Britain would act under the Declaration when Israel invaded Egypt. The Prime Minister, finally recognising the French plan, asked Nutting, 'Didn't your agreement [the 1954 Anglo-Egyptian Treaty] say something about our *not* being obliged to send troops if Egypt was attacked by Israel?' Nutting correctly answered that the Treaty had nothing to do with the Egyptian-Israeli question and did not nullify British obligations under the Tripartite Declaration. Eden was crestfallen, but 'could scarcely contain his glee' when Gazier noted that Nasser recently stated that the Declaration did not apply to Egypt.

Nutting, desperate to protect the Foreign Office's policy prohibiting co-operation with Israel against Egypt, asked Gazier how the French knew of a possible Israeli attack upon Egypt. Gazier hesitated, and Eden instructed his Private Secretary, Frederick Bishop, to stop taking notes. Challe then revealed the French plan. Hours after Israel invaded the Sinai Peninsula, Britain and France would order the Egyptians and Israelis to withdraw their forces either side of the Suez Canal, and an

Anglo-French force would occupy the Canal Zone. Challe indicated that France had already made 'preliminary soundings' with Israel and had been encouraged enough to approach the British. Eden, attempting to conceal his excitement, said that he would answer the proposal by 16 October, but revealed his thoughts when he dismissed Nutting's request to question the French about the secret delivery of more than sixty Mystère IV fighters to Israel.[1]

Eden was far from pro-Israeli. He had studied Arabic at Oxford and, as Foreign Secretary in the 1930s, had worked for closer British ties with Arab states, including negotiation of the 1936 Anglo-Egyptian Treaty. During the Second World War, he had proposed the formation of the Arab League and rejected Cabinet proposals for the creation of a Jewish state. Israeli sentiment was far from appeased by Eden's renegotiation of the Anglo-Egyptian Treaty in 1954, the formation of the Baghdad Pact and the Guildhall speech. Since July, Eden had supported Lloyd's rejection of any connection with Israel in the Suez crisis, and he had turned down Pineau's proposal in later September for collaboration with Tel Aviv. Why then did the French make yet another approach to Eden and why did the Prime Minister now endorse tripartite co-operation?

The answers lie in three aspects of Middle Eastern affairs, apparently unrelated and unconnected to the Suez crisis: the Franco-Israeli 'alliance', tension on the Israeli-Jordanian border and British sponsorship of the Iraqi-Jordanian axis. To alter the British position, some cause had to be found, and the French discovered it in the Israeli-Jordanian conflict. Gazier and Challe only had to convince Eden that, if he rejected their approach, Israeli-Jordanian troubles would lead to an Anglo-Israeli war and the dissolution of the Iraqi-Jordanian 'axis'.

Killings on the Israeli-Jordanian border, which had threatened war in July, resumed on 10 September, when seven Israeli soldiers were slain in Jerusalem, allegedly by Jordanian attackers. Israel's 202 Brigade, the mobile force for reprisals, demolished a police post near Hebron the next evening, killing nineteen. After three Israeli watchmen were killed on 12 September, ten Jordanians died in an Israeli attack upon the police post at Gharandal.[2]

Jordan's King Hussein was desperate. Hoping for Egyptian assistance, he supported Nasser's nationalisation of the Suez Canal Company, but Egypt was preoccupied with Anglo-French military preparations.[3] General Nuwar, the Jordanian Chief of Staff, asked Saudi Arabia for £12 million in military equipment, but King Saud only agreed to £2–3 million, spread among Arab states, 'mostly in ships and dates'. Syrian forces were inadequate and her Government unstable. So Hussein, despite dissatisfaction at earlier Iraqi-Jordanian staff talks and lack of Iraqi aid, met King

Feisal II, Crown Prince Abdul-Illah, Prime Minister Nuri Sa'id and the Iraqi Chief of Staff on 14 September to request that the Iraqis send a division to Jordan immediately. Unwilling to put troops under Nuwar's command, the Iraqis refused, but they offered to send two or three brigades if Jordan accepted a 'proper plan with command structure and defined roles'. According to Nuri, Hussein, in 'a very nervous, agitated state', was calmed 'somewhat' by the meeting.[4]

Hussein's approach gave Britain a new opportunity to forge an Iraqi-Jordanian defence system. Lloyd wrote that the despatch of an Iraqi division into Jordan 'would have the advantage that, were Jordan to disintegrate, a substantial portion of Jordan would remain under Iraqi control'. The Chiefs of Staff suggested 'approaching the Iraqis with a view to informing the Jordanian Government that, in the event that [Iraq] put forces into Jordan, [Jordan] could expect to have air support from the RAF stationed there'.[5]

Tension rose as the Iraqi-Jordanian staff talks stalled over the question of command and the Israelis stepped up reprisals. After an attack upon Israeli archaeologists by a Jordanian soldier, Israeli troops overwhelmed another police post near Jerusalem in the 'biggest actual military operation since the 1948 armistice', killing more than thirty. On 27 September, Nuri invited the British Ambassador, Michael Wright, to join discussions with the Jordanian Foreign Minister.[6]

The Foreign Office had a difficult decision. Wright's attendance would indicate British approval of the Iraqi deployment, but Teddy Kollek, Ben-Gurion's chief aide, told US Ambassador Edward Lawson that Israel would occupy Jordanian territory if 'a single Iraqi soldier moved into Jordan'. On the other hand, Iraq and Jordan would interpret refusal to uphold the Anglo-Jordanian Treaty as British abandonment of her Arab allies. The Baghdad Pact would be undermined and Jordan might join the Egyptian-Saudi-Syrian bloc.[7]

The Foreign Office stood by the Iraqi-Jordanian axis. If Israel attacked Jordan, Britain would provide air and naval support to Amman, and Nuwar's forces could draw upon £7 million of British stocks. Israel would be told that Britain would honour the Anglo-Jordanian Treaty, and US support would be sought for the Iraqi deployment. Wright presented the decision to Nuri and the Jordanian Foreign Minister on 29 September.[8]

Two days later, the Egypt Committee endorsed the measures, although the Defence Committee, unwilling to risk Israeli opposition without American backing, modified the instructions from 'all available air and naval support' to 'air and naval support . . . to the greatest extent possible in the circumstances obtaining at the time'. The Foreign Office's hand was strengthened, however, when Ben-Gurion told Lawson that

Israel would not object to the Iraqi deployment if she had advance notice, no heavy equipment was moved into Jordan, no 'unreasonably large number' of Iraqi troops were moved, and no Iraqi troops were deployed on the West Bank. Reassured, Foster Dulles urged Britain to 'clinch the matter immediately', as it 'might undermine Nasser's position in Jordan, Syria, and Lebanon and cause the Jordanians and other Arabs to turn more to Iraq'.[9]

On 6 October, after Ben-Gurion asked for further information on the size of the Iraqi force and an assurance that it would be far from the Israeli-Jordanian border, Lawson warned the State Department that Israeli assurances were based on information that the Iraqi deployment was a token force of several hundred troops. The US Counsellor added, 'In the back of his mind, Mr Ben-Gurion does not view with any happiness the prospect of a large force in Jordan.' The Foreign Office dismissed Lawson's concern, however, since Iraq now planned to deploy only one battalion, far from the Israeli border.[10]

Diplomatic confusion now caused an important delay. The State Department, believing the Iraqi deployment was imminent, told Lawson to wait before approaching Israeli officials, but the despatch of the battalion was delayed by the Iraqi-Jordanian dispute over command. The British Chargé d'Affaires in Tel Aviv, Peter Westlake, finally asked the Foreign Office on 9 October if Lawson could give Ben-Gurion details of the deployment.[11]

Meanwhile, Israel seized the diplomatic and military initiative. Foreign Minister Meir had always feared an Iraqi presence on Israel's border, telling Lawson in July:

Iraq as a neighbor might be worse but at most no better than Jordan despite [the] latter's uncertain, precarious state. Iraq had attacked Israel with great force in 1948. She had refused to sign [the General Armistice] and is technically still in a state of war with Israel.[12]

She now told Lawson that conditional agreement to the Iraqi deployment was withdrawn because of Nuri's statement, printed in *The Times* of 7 October, that Israel should accept a frontier settlement based on the 1947 borders, ceding territory to the Arabs. She warned, 'Israel will not sit by while these events develop. We will not make it so comfortable for them. We are not going to be destroyed without a struggle.'[13]

At 11.55 p.m. on 10 October, 'very heavy Israeli artillery and mortar fire' began on a twelve-mile front from Qalqilya to Tul Karra in Jordan. An Israeli division was involved, one brigade crossing the border and two waiting in reserve. Tanks shelled the Jordanians across the border, and light aircraft carried out reconnaissance. The police station in Qalqilya was destroyed by mortar fire and, by 1.47 a.m., some Israeli troops were five miles inside Jordan. More than seventy Jordanians were killed and more than forty wounded before the attack ended, and the Israel Defence Forces lost eighteen men, an unusually high total for a 'reprisal' operation.

Most of the Israeli casualties occurred when a company of more than fifty men, blocking the approach of Jordan's army, the Arab Legion, to Qalqilya, was ambushed by a Jordanian battalion which Israeli intelligence had overlooked. The Israelis scrambled two Harvard and two Mustang fighters to 'give the impression of a large-scale attack being carried out by a mobile column with air support'. Two tank squadrons, one infantry battalion and other fighters were readied to go into battle at first light.[14]

The Israelis officially claimed the raid was a 'hastily planned, organised and carried out' reprisal for the murder of two Israeli farm labourers on 9 October. They also asserted that four *fedayeen*, who killed three Israeli Druze on 12 September, were released by Hussein and subsequently murdered five Israelis, a claim denied by the Jordanian Chief of Staff, General Nuwar. On 8 October, the Israelis allegedly transmitted the names of the four *fedayeen* to Jordan, but received no response.[15]

The official Israeli explanations are belied by the nature of the raid. An entire Israeli division had never been used for a 'reprisal', and the operation required days of advance preparation. As Duke, the British Ambassador to Jordan, noted: 'The types and numbers of weapons employed in the . . . incident were not justified by the opposition to be expected.' Abel Thomas, Bourges-Maunoury's chief aide and a participant in secret Franco-Israeli discussions, summarised, 'Under the pretext that Iraqi troops had expressed their intention to invade Jordan and had made some incursions there, . . . Israel had created the *casus belli*' for an Israeli-Jordanian war.[16]

One purpose of Qalqilya was to warn Britain and Jordan to halt the Iraqi deployment. The day after the raid, the Israeli Government publicly stated:

Iraq's entry into Jordan . . . would mean that she was again sending military forces into the territory of a State adjacent to Israel – and this after deliberately refusing to conclude an armistice agreement with Israel. [Iraqi] action would be a direct threat to the security of Israel and to the validity of the Israeli-Jordanian armistice agreement.[17]

On 12 October, an 'anxious and indecisive' Meir requested that Westlake provide information within forty-eight hours on the size of the Iraqi deployment, its destination and the type of equipment involved. When

Westlake repeated that Britain would honour her obligation to defend Jordan, Meir replied that this 'amounted to an ultimatum . . . creating a radical change in the situation'.[18]

Two days later, a public statement by Meir claimed, 'The movement into Jordan of Iraqi troops would be part of a scheme designed to serve the territorial ambitions of Iraq and to bring about a radical change in the status quo in the area.' A further Cabinet statement expressed 'concern and astonishment' at 'the threat of the British Foreign Office that Britain will implement the Anglo-Jordanian Treaty against Israel'. Peres, the Director-General of the Israeli Ministry of Defence, told his senior officials:

I don't know whether we'll be able to wait until the Iraqi thing begins and reaches us before we fight. . . . I am convinced that the French sincerely wanted, and still want, to fight Nasser, [but] I am very suspicious of British machinations.[19]

The Israelis underlined their determination to stop the Iraqi deployment by threatening to seize the West Bank of the Jordan River. The *Jerusalem Post*, recognised as the voice of the Israeli Government, had hinted on 7 October, 'If Jordan crumbles, Israel could not sit with folded hands and Egypt would not inherit [her].' The following week, the *Post* argued, 'From the British point of view, the bringing of Iraqi troops into Jordan is an insurance that the rapidly disintegrating puppet state she had set up will not fall to the Egyptians when its inevitable end comes about but to a member of the British [camp].' 'Reliable' informants told the British Consulate in Jerusalem and Embassy in Tel Aviv that the Israeli Cabinet, upset by the information from Westlake 'about the number of Iraqi troops and their length of stay in Jordan, . . . intended to take part of the West Bank from Ramallah to Nablus and the North', as it thought both the US and France would remain neutral. On 15 October, the Israeli Ambassador to the US, Abba Eban, told Foster Dulles, '[We] think Jordan is breaking up and it is a question of grabbing the pieces.' Although Foster Dulles discouraged Israeli action, a high-level meeting, with Eisenhower present, assumed that Jordan might be partitioned between Israel and Iraq, and the US 'must be ready to deal with the situation in which the people and territory of the country would be absorbed by others'.[20]

Israel had assumed a great risk with Qalqilya. CORDAGE, the British military plan to neutralise the Israeli air force and blockade the Israeli coast if Israel attacked Jordan, was operational despite the Suez crisis. On 9 October, the Chairman of the Chiefs of Staff, Air Chief Marshal Sir William Dickson, said that he was 'very concerned about the potential air threat to Cyprus from some of the neighbouring countries in the Middle East, who possessed modern aircraft which were capable of penetrating our existing air defence of the island'. The Chiefs decided to reinforce the air defences of Cyprus, not only against Egypt, but also against Israel. The next day, they concluded, '[We] should bring home very forcibly to Ministers that we could either go to the aid of Jordan against Israel with sea and air power, or we could launch MUS-KETEER [REVISE]; we could not do both.'[21]

Ben-Gurion had recognised the risk, telling the Knesset on 19 June, '[War with Jordan] would bring Israel into conflict with the British army and . . . I will never send Israeli defence forces to fight any European, American, British, Russian or French army.' He also knew that a large-scale Israeli attack upon Jordan might prevent Britain joining a Franco-Israeli attack upon Egypt, writing on 6 October: 'In my opinion, France will not act without Britain, so we must not give the British any pretext just now to slip out of the affair.'[22]

If the only motive for Qalqilya was the prevention of the Iraqi deployment, then the raid might have been delayed. However, for French and Israeli military planners, there was another, more important motive for the attack, for Qalqilya was an essential part of the preparations for a war against Egypt.

When Dayan returned on 2 October from the Franco-Israeli military talks in Paris, he issued the warning order for an attack on the 20th. Israel would strike into the Sinai Peninsula while French forces destroyed the Egyptian air force and occupied the Canal Zone. For the plan to succeed, the Israelis had to prevent a build-up of Egyptian air and land forces in the Sinai, which would impede their advance, but the mobilisation of Israeli forces would alert Cairo to the impending assault.

To solve the problem, a special unit, codenamed the 'Esau' team, was established to disguise the purpose of Israeli military preparations. The mobilisation would appear to be directed against Jordan, rather than Egypt. This would be accomplished with a three-phase operation. In the first phase, during the planning of the Franco-Israeli invasion of Egypt, Israel would emphasise her lack of military preparedness and the threat to her from the Iraqi deployment into Jordan. In the second phase, as Israel mobilised her forces in the Southern Command, she would also concentrate her troops in the Northern and Central Commands and embark upon 'initiation of activity along the Jordanian border'. This phase would start ten days before the Franco-Israeli attack on 20 October. In the third phase, as Israeli units gathered in assembly areas for the invasion, Egypt's attention would be diverted from the main assault upon the centre of the Sinai by activity in the Gaza Strip in the northern Sinai and continued deception operations against Jordan.[23]

As the French and Israeli military staffs devised the assault upon Egypt, the Northern and Central Commands were ordered to increase their readiness and plan offensive missions into Jordan under the codename 'Babel', the traditional Jewish name for Iraq. Only four men in each Command knew of the deception operations, and the commanding officers of the Commands were excluded by Dayan from planning conferences. Military intelligence officers collecting information about Egypt and Jordan were informed that the latter was Israel's real target. On 3 October, Israel withdrew from the Israeli-Jordanian Mutual Armistice Commission and, two days later, she forbade UN observers from investigating 'border incidents' in Israeli territory.[24]

Qalqilya and the ensuing Israeli threats to seize the West Bank were a vital part of the second phase of 'Esau', which began on 10 October after Phase 1 had been completed. Admiral Barjot, the Deputy Commander of REVISE, had issued a 'Secret and Personal Instruction' with '*Hypothese* 1 [for Israel]', which assumed 'benevolent neutrality on the part of Great Britain', including permission for France to use airfields in Cyprus. Despite Ben-Gurion's refusal to proceed without the British, Dayan discussed the details of the Israeli attack, Operation KADESH, with his Orders Group on 8 October. In Paris, Peres and Abel Thomas signed an agreement on the political and military aims of operations.[25]

Thus, Dayan's military objectives regarding Jordan coincided with the political objectives of Foreign Minister Meir, who was determined to halt the Iraqi deployment. It is an intriguing and, to this point, unanswerable question whether Dayan informed the Israeli Cabinet, or even Ben-Gurion alone, of the operational details of 'Esau'. The Prime Minister was finally persuaded of the need for a raid into Jordan in a seven-and-a-half-hour Cabinet meeting on 7 October, but it cannot be determined if Dayan revealed the Israeli military plans to support Meir's political arguments.[26]

Moreover, it is possible that Qalqilya had a wider military purpose: to scare the British into a tripartite assault upon Egypt. As soon as Dayan returned from Paris with the order for an attack on 20 October, he encountered unexpected and almost insuperable opposition from Ben-Gurion. The Prime Minister, who had been in London during the Blitz of the Second World War, feared Egyptian bombing of Israeli cities. With only a limited number of Mystère IV fighters ready for operations, the Israelis could not ensure that Egypt's Soviet-made Il-28 bombers could be prevented from attacking successfully. A pre-emptive strike by French or British bombers upon the Egyptian air force was essential. Ben-Gurion stated, 'My conclusions [on the Franco-Israeli plan] are unfavourable . . . stemming from the assumption that the English will not take part and will not permit the French to operate from Cyprus.' Dayan persuaded Ben-Gurion not to reveal his objections to General Challe, but the Prime Minister, after extensive questioning of Challe and Colonel Louis Mangin, the representative of the French intelligence services, only allowed further planning if the French agreed that Britain must approve the operation. According to Dayan, Ben-Gurion believed that there was only a twenty per cent chance of London's endorsement.[27]

Salvation for Dayan may have come from an idea of Pineau's, broached at the Franco-Israeli discussions on 30 September. A week earlier, Eden, referring to the Israeli-Jordanian tension, allegedly exclaimed to Pineau, 'What a pity that these incidents were not taking place on the Egyptian border!' Pineau deduced that the British Cabinet would co-operate with Israel against Egypt to avoid an Israeli-Jordanian war. At Ben-Gurion's discussion of 3 October with Challe and Mangin, Dayan noted cryptically: 'If the thing [the Franco-Israeli operation] is postponed at present, it might be that something will be cooked up in France and Jordan.'[28]

It is possible, though impossible to determine, that Dayan then conferred with Challe or Mangin on the use of the deception operations against Jordan as a lever for British co-operation. General André Beaufre, the commander of French land forces for MUSKETEER, later wrote: 'It seems that the [French] Colonial Office tried some complicated manoeuvre in Jordan to incite Nasser to attack Israel and so provide justification for our operations.' On 13 October, Eden asked Nutting if France had put the Israelis up to attack Jordan. Nutting replied that Foreign Office experts thought this was possible. The French Ambassador to Israel, Pierre-Eugène Gilbert, who knew of the talks between Dayan and the French planners, told his British counterpart, John Nicholls, that France had not encouraged recent Israeli reprisals, but 'some Ministers might well have taken the line that a good display of aggressiveness on any of Israel's frontiers would be helpful to the West in the context of the Suez situation'.[29]

The secretive nature of Franco-Israeli consultations led to the erratic behaviour of French officials in early October. Pineau knew of Ben-Gurion's initial agreement to the Iraqi deployment into Jordan, but never informed officials of the French Foreign Ministry.[30] Therefore, Pineau's officials, citing Israeli opposition, repeatedly warned Britain against the Iraqi deployment and representatives of the French Embassy in Tel Aviv told the Israelis that 'they fear[ed] that the English want to conquer Jordan [and] Syria with the help of the Iraqis'. At the same time, the French Embassy in Washington told the State Department that Pineau did not object to the Iraqi deployment. A British Foreign Office official noted the conflict in French thought and came close to the truth: 'One cannot help suspecting that the French and Israel are in collusion over all this.'[31]

Challe had become an instrumental figure in Franco-Israeli planning. Leaving Israel about the time of the Cabinet meeting of 7 October, he travelled to Paris and New York to inform Mollet and Pineau of developments. Pineau, who had obstructed negotiations with Fawzi and Lloyd, embraced the talks after Challe's visit, a mission from General Yehoshafat Harkabi, the Israeli Chief of Military Intelligence, and the raid on Qalqilya. Apparently, Challe's task, given Ben-Gurion's insistence that the British consent to Franco-Israeli military operations, was to ensure that Pineau spun out negotiations while Ben-Gurion's wishes were met. Challe then returned to Paris to be despatched with Gazier to Britain.[32]

When Gazier and Challe met Eden on 14 October, they did not begin with a discussion of the Suez crisis, but of Jordan. Gazier appealed to Eden to stop the Iraqi deployment, asking the Prime Minister whether Britain wanted to provoke Israel further. Nutting replied that it was Britain's idea to move the troops, but Eden cut him short and said that he would ask the Iraqis to suspend the deployment temporarily. Only then did Gazier ask about the British reaction to an Israeli attack upon Egypt.[33]

The Suez War was not the product of a Franco-Israeli 'conspiracy'. The complex conditions that fostered it involved not only Arab-Israeli tension but also the development of British and French policies in the Middle East and North Africa. Qalqilya may have been only a deception operation rather than a plan to provoke Britain into co-operation with Israel. Yet, intentionally or accidentally, the Israeli raid into Jordan, rather than Eden's 'irrationality' or an act by the Egyptians, was the catalyst for the tripartite attack on Egypt. It gave the French the opportunity to renew their pressure upon the British and Eden, forced to suspend military operations for several months, the excuse to embark upon a new effort for the overthrow of Nasser.

20

Collusion
15–24 October 1956

E den's immediate priority was to prevent British intervention for
Jordan against Israel. When Nutting, supporting Ambassador
Duke in Amman, suggested on 13 October that Britain defend
Jordan, Eden allegedly replied, 'I will not allow you to plunge this country
into war merely to satisfy the anti-Jewish spleen of you people in the
Foreign Office.' After the Gazier–Challe visit, he directed Nutting to
instruct Duke:

It is manifestly not in our interest nor in Jordan's interest to treat raids as an act of
war and intervene. . . . [The Jordanians] seem to be nurturing the idea that they
can safely destroy the military value of the Arab Legion, dispense with British
land assistance, and rely on the RAF to win the land battle, but that is a lethal
illusion.[1]

Suspending the Iraqi deployment, Eden asked Nutting, 'Do you want
Israel to attack Jordan?' The Minister of State replied acidly, 'I thought our
policy was to prevent Israel attacking anything,' but his protests were futile.
The Foreign Office instructed Ambassador Wright, on 15 October:

There are reasons which cannot be divulged but which make it essential that [the]
move should not take place for 48 hours. . . . You may tell Nuri for his own
information that the Prime Minister personally attaches great importance to this.

The British Embassy in Amman was informed: 'It is clear that if we treat a
raid as war and deploy our air force against Israel . . . the consequence
would be not only Israeli air attacks on our airfields in Cyprus and Jordan
. . . but war against Jordan and the occupation of the country.' Four days
later, Eden instructed Kirkpatrick: 'No Iraqi troops or stores into Jordan
at present.'[2]

Eden's sudden decision to work with France and Israel threw British policy into disarray. After Qalqilya, the Foreign Office and Air Ministry only agreed to 'demonstration' flights of Hunter fighters from Cyprus to Jordan and supply of 25-pound ammunition to the Arab Legion, but CORDAGE, the British military plan to defend Jordan, was still in effect. Half of Britain's Middle Eastern air force was placed on six-hour readiness with the remainder on twelve-hour alert. Although General Templer had warned the Chiefs of Staff on 2 October, 'If we went to war with Israel, the effect required to neutralise the Israeli Air Force would make it impossible to mount MUSKETEER at the same time,' General Sir Charles Keightley assured the Chiefs, 'With forces now available, [we] were in a strong position to overcome any Israeli opposition in a few days.'[3]

The British Defence Co-ordinating Committee for the Middle East was not as confident. Because of the recent supply of French jets to Israel, the Committee argued, 'Too little margin of superiority over the Israeli Air Force is allowed in our current plans for CORDAGE.' It suggested immediate readiness of the RAF squadrons earmarked for REVISE, transfer of Venom fighters from Germany to Cyprus, and assignment of bombers at Malta 'for offensive action against Israel as well as Egypt'. The Carrier Task Group in the Eastern Mediterranean would be placed on twenty-four-hour alert, while the British land force at Aqaba in southern Jordan prepared to seize the Israeli port of Eilat.[4]

The situation neared the level of farce. Eden allowed Nutting to inform two Foreign Office colleagues of events, but objected to the briefing of the Foreign Office Legal Adviser, Sir Gerald Fitzmaurice: 'That's the last person I want consulted. The lawyers are always against our doing anything. For God's sake, keep them out of it. This is a political affair.' Nutting consulted Kirkpatrick and Ross. Despite Kirkpatrick's advocacy of force against Egypt, he and Ross objected vehemently to the French plan. Lloyd's work in New York would be undone, the Tripartite Declaration of 1950 would be ignored, the US would oppose the plan and the UN would condemn it, the Commonwealth would be divided, the stability of pro-Western regimes in the Middle East would be jeopardised, and the security of British and French oil installations would be endangered.[5]

Eden rejected the brief out of hand and presented the Challe–Gazier plan at an 'informal' meeting on 16 October with Secretary of State for War Head, Minister of Defence Monckton, the President of the Board of Trade, Peter Thorneycroft, Lord Chancellor Kilmuir, and possibly Macmillan. Nutting summarised his objections and Monckton mildly protested, but the other Ministers agreed with Eden.[6]

Lloyd, ordered by Eden to return from New York, arrived at 10 Downing Street as the meeting was in progress. Nutting greeted him with the news that negotiations with Egypt were suspended. Lloyd allegedly said, 'We must have nothing to do with the French plan.' In the meeting, however, Lloyd held his objections, merely requesting that he and Eden travel to Paris that afternoon rather than the next day. Afterwards, Nutting tried to change his Minister's mind, but Lloyd, resigned to following Eden's wishes, rationalised that negotiations with Egypt were useless because Nasser would not honour any commitment.[7]

Eden and Lloyd's discussions with Mollet and Pineau lasted until 1.30 a.m. All officials, even the British Ambassador to France, Gladwyn Jebb, were excluded from the meetings. Lloyd made a final attempt to save negotiations with Egypt, arguing that, while Britain and France could not obtain the eighteen-power plan, they might arrange some form of 'international control', with strict regulations on the level of tolls and percentage of revenues devoted to the Canal's development. Differences would be referred to an independent body, whose decisions would be enforced through appropriate sanctions. Mollet, supported by Pineau, said that this was 'quite unsatisfactory'.

Pineau then played the French hand, indicating that Israel would act before the Arabs received more Soviet arms. Eden repeated, 'If Israel attacked Jordan, we were bound to go to Jordan's help,' but added, 'We did not regard ourselves as under any obligation towards Egypt under the Tripartite Declaration.' Eden and the French agreed that the United Nations was not a serious impediment, as 'it was not thought likely that the Security Council would reach agreement on any action to be taken'. More significantly, Eden argued, 'The US Government would be no more anxious than the French or British Government to take action under the Tripartite Declaration' to punish Israel for her aggression. It was agreed 'that if Israel were to act before the end of the American election campaign, it was most improbable that Congress could be resummoned or, if resummoned, would give this authority [for the intervention of US forces]'. Non-military action by the US, notably economic sanctions against an aggressor, was not discussed.

Finally, Mollet established Eden's position: 'If Israel attacked Egypt, would UK feel bound to intervene under the Tripartite Declaration?' Eden 'thought the answer to that would be "no" but he would confirm that to M. Mollet after he got back to London'. Mollet asked, 'In the event of the likelihood of hostilities in the vicinity of the Canal, would the UK Government intervene to stop them?' Eden 'thought the answer to that question would be "yes"'. He left two notes with the French to be delivered to the Israelis:

(1) In the event of any threat of hostilities in the neighbourhood of the Canal, the French and British Governments would call the belligerents to halt and withdraw from the immediate vicinity of the Canal. If both agreed, no action would follow. If one or both refused, Anglo-French forces would intervene to ensure the free passage of the Canal.

(2) In the event of hostilities developing between Egypt and Israel, HMG would not come to the assistance of Egypt because Egypt was in breach of a Security Council resolution [on the passage of Israeli shipping through the Suez Canal] and had moreover repudiated Western aid under the Tripartite Declaration.[8]

Disheartened, Lloyd told Nutting the next morning that 'he hoped that [Britain] would not have to be directly associated with these [Franco-Israeli] talks, at any rate at the political level'. Nutting 'had seldom seen a man more confused and unhappy', but he only added to Lloyd's worries when he threatened to resign if Britain colluded with France and Israel. The Foreign Secretary gave a nervous laugh and remarked, 'There's only one worse thing than having a yes-man on one's team, and that's having a no-man like you.'[9]

A more enthusiastic Eden told Iveragh MacDonald of *The Times* of the Gazier–Challe approach and the meeting in Paris,[10] but he withheld the details from the Egypt Committee, merely telling them that Iraqi troops were to be held at the Jordanian frontier 'at the suggestion of Jordan. . . . Meanwhile, the French Government were urging the Israelis to refrain from any precipitate action.' Regarding Suez, Lloyd reported that Egypt had proposed further negotiations and 'it would be inexpedient to reject such a suggestion'.[11]

Like Gazier, Eden cited Jordan as the reason for a new policy:

The political situation in Jordan was unstable, and there were signs that Israel might be preparing to make some military move. . . . [We] had our obligations under the Anglo-Jordanian Treaty, but it would be contrary to our interests to act, at this time and alone, in support of Jordan against Israel.

He then presented the Gazier–Challe formula:

If [Israel] contemplated any military operations against the Arabs, it would be far better from our point of view that they should attack Egypt. . . . He had therefore thought it right to make it known to the Israelis, through the French, that in the event of hostilities between Egypt and Israel, the UK Government would not come to the assistance of Egypt.

According to Lloyd and Butler, the Prime Minister also asked that 'Britain and France should go in to safeguard the Canal and the shipping in it' when Israel attacked Egypt. Butler vaguely suggested 'an agreement with the French and the Israelis designed to free the Canal and eventually to internationalise it', and Lloyd expressed his anxiety over the effect upon Arab opinion of Anglo-French operations with Israel. Neither was willing, however, to oppose Eden.[12]

The Cabinet endorsement of Eden's action ensured Britain's estrangement from the US. On 13 October, Foster Dulles had indicated that SCUA would eventually transfer up to ninety per cent of the revenues it received to the Egyptian Government. Anxious that any agreement with Egypt should contain effective sanctions, Lloyd appealed to Foster Dulles to modify his position, but Foster Dulles had already informed the Foreign Office:

I gather that it is now your view that SCUA should serve as a means of exerting pressure on the Egyptian Government by withholding dues. Our idea, made clear from the beginning, is that it was to be a means of practical working cooperation with the Egyptian authorities which would seek to establish de facto international participation in the operation of the Canal.[13]

Foster Dulles's original intention of using SCUA as a device to force Egyptian acceptance of international control of the Canal had been forgotten. He reiterated to Lloyd in a letter of 19 October. 'I cannot feel that the primary purpose of SCUA to cooperate with Egypt has changed.'[14]

The Americans knew from U-2 reconnaissance flights about Israel's acquisition of seventy-two Mystères, but they expected the Israelis to attack Jordan. When Foster Dulles complained to Allen Dulles, 'I do not think that we have really any clear picture as to what the British and French are up to there,' he was reassured that the CIA was 'fairly well' aware of developments in Egypt.[15] In fact, the CIA missed the first public hint of Israeli co-operation with Britain and France. Addressing the Knesset on 15 October, Ben-Gurion read a poem about Israel's strength, a disguised reference to arms shipments from France, and commented, 'I am as confident, as every one of our commanders, that any conflict with the Egyptians or the rest of the Arab armies will end in victory.'[16]

Privately, Ben-Gurion remained pessimistic about co-operation with Britain. The day after the Challe–Gazier meeting with Eden, Joseph Nachmias, the Israeli Military Attaché in Paris, transmitted the French plan, but, to persuade Ben-Gurion of Britain's desire to work with Israel, implied that the proposal came from Eden. The Prime Minister was dissatisfied, since the British and French would not attack Egypt simultaneously with Israel, but would occupy the Suez Canal Zone *after* the invasion of the Sinai. He saw 'the height of British hypocrisy' in the plan and wrote: 'The British plot, I imagine, is to get us involved with Nasser and bring about the occupation of Jordan by Iraq.' Despite these fears, Ben-Gurion's priority was to ensure that Britain and France did not act without the Israelis. He cabled Nachmias:

In connection with the arrival of the representatives of England to Paris, you should contact the French immediately and ask them whether the meeting can be made tripartite. The representatives of Israel are ready to come immediately in utmost secrecy.[17]

Meanwhile, Eden prepared for implementation of the Gazier–Challe plan. When the British representative to the UN, Pierson Dixon, suggested that Jordan was entitled to defend herself against Israeli attacks, the Prime Minister replied that 'it would be very dangerous for us to attack Israel in the Security Council'. He wrote to Lloyd:

I am much concerned by the line taken by Sir Pierson Dixon over the Jordan complaint. The blame is not entirely on one side, but he makes it appear that it is, and aligns himself with the Russians. . . . I am really concerned about the effect of this on Israel. The French warned us how suspicious of us the Israelis are.[18]

Eden told his military enough to halt REVISE's replacement by the 'Winter Plan', but not enough to stand down the British alert against Israel. The Chiefs of Staff vetoed the British Defence Co-ordinating Committee's plan to capture the Israeli port city of Eilat, but they agreed to 'A) air operations at maximum intensity to neutralise the Israeli Air Force, B) blockade and naval bombardment as soon as the air situation permits, and C) such operations as are necessary to secure Aqaba [in Jordan]'. The British fleet in the Mediterranean was put on twenty-four-hours' notice and prepared to sail to the Eastern Mediterranean, as Mountbatten cabled naval commanders:

The real danger time is between now and the date of the American election. . . . The Jews may well think that now is their last chance to square matters up with the Arabs and that they will confront everybody with a fait accompli before they are geared to do anything effective.[19]

Six squadrons of bombers were sent to Cyprus and one and a half to Malta. Hunter fighters were reinforced on Cyprus by Venoms from Germany. The operational headquarters for CORDAGE moved from Malta to Cyprus on 21 October and took precedence over REVISE's command structure.[20]

The Foreign Office's Levant Department knew of the measures on 16 October, but the Permanent Undersecretary's Department, the liaison with Eden for covert action and planning, was not informed of CORDAGE's development until the 18th.[21] The PUSD's action is in a file that is missing from the Public Record Office, but Eden finally intervened on 22 October when he received a request to retain the New Zealand cruiser, *Royalist*, for the operation. He wrote to Lord Hailsham, the First Lord of the Admiralty: 'I trust that there is no likelihood of our fighting Israel on behalf of Jordan and we have done all we can to discourage Israel from follies in this direction.'[22]

As Eden wrote to Hailsham, British, French and Israeli representatives were meeting at Sèvres outside Paris. On 21 October, General Challe and Colonel Mangin arrived in Jerusalem to 'escort' the Israeli delegation in a DC-4 given by President Truman to General de Gaulle. Ben-Gurion threatened to turn back if the French still favoured a unilateral Israeli invasion followed by Anglo-French intervention and warned the envoys, 'If you intend to present the British proposal to us, the only benefit of my journey to France [will be] that I will make the acquaintance of your premier.'[23]

The first formal Franco-Israeli meeting occurred over lunch on 22 October, with Mollet, Pineau and Bourges-Manoury leading the French delegation. Ben-Gurion tested support for his 'master plan' for the Middle East, which he had harboured for years. This involved, 'before all else, naturally, the elimination of Nasser', the partition of Jordan between Iraq and Israel, the division of Lebanon, with portions to Israel and Syria and the remainder as a Christian state, the installation of a pro-Western government in Syria, and international status for the Canal.[24]

When the French offered no reaction, Ben-Gurion challenged them by arguing that operations against Egypt should not be undertaken immediately. The Soviets might intervene, and Eisenhower would 'feel freer after the elections' to adopt a position of benevolent neutrality towards the invasion and to warn off Moscow. Mollet protested:

Perhaps, in the end, we would convince the US in favour of a common programme . . . but we would lose valuable time, and possibly even the chance to act. . . . As for British participation, any delay is likely to be fatal. I know Eden personally, and I am absolutely convinced that he is an enthusiastic supporter of common action . . . but his domestic situation is deteriorating.

Pineau added that the Soviets were busy with uprisings in Hungary and that the US was preoccupied with the Presidential election. Bourges-Maunoury argued that, if the operation was not launched within a few days, 'France would have to withdraw. . . . The beginning of November is the final date.' He then made the commitment essential to Ben-Gurion: French planes and pilots would operate from Israeli bases and support the Israeli land advance while French ships patrolled the Israeli coast and bombarded Egyptian ports. Ben-Gurion's 'objections' to an operation led by an Israeli advance suddenly disappeared. Dayan proposed an Israeli paratroop drop in the Sinai, followed by a French ultimatum to Egypt to cease resistance and the bombing of Egyptian airfields. Ben-Gurion concluded that the invasion could start 'tomorrow' if Britain co-operated.[25]

Meanwhile, Eden, spending the weekend at Chequers, consulted an inner circle of Ministers, including Lloyd, Macmillan, Butler, Head, Kilmuir and Home. Cabinet Secretary Brook and the Permanent Under-secretary of the Ministry of Defence, Richard Powell, were also present. Eden suggested that Powell might go to Sèvres, but Powell responded that it might be better to send an envoy with diplomatic experience. The Prime Minister then suggested Patrick Dean, but Ministers finally decided that Lloyd, using the excuse of a cold, should cancel his appointments and travel to France.[26]

Lloyd, still unhappy about co-operation with Israel, was further shaken when his automobile, en route from Villacoublay airfield to Sèvres, was nearly hit by a speeding car, and according to French officials the serious tone of the occasion was further undermined by the false moustache that he had donned.* After he spoke with the French about Israeli intentions, the three sides convened. Ben-Gurion's secretary, Mordechai Bar-On, wrote:

[Lloyd's] voice was shrill and started with an unpleasant tone of cynicism and a humour dry as a clay shard. His face gave the impression of something stinking hanging permanently under his nose. The snobbish air of his entire personality, prevents him from opening himself up to his fellow negotiators and sheds on the entire conversation a cold and formal atmosphere.

Lloyd's impression 'was of a roomful of utterly exhausted people, mostly asleep. One young man was snoring loudly in an armchair. Ben-Gurion himself looked far from well.'[27]

Ben-Gurion again tried the gambit of a Middle Eastern 'master plan'. Lloyd ignored the scheme, but, unlike the French, seized the initiative, arguing that 'it was possible to reach agreement with Egypt over the Suez Canal within seven days'. Lloyd restated the 'British' plan: if Israel would attack Egypt *alone*, Britain and France would subsequently intervene to safeguard the Suez Canal and stop the fighting. He refused the proposal of Ben-Gurion and Dayan for a limited Israeli paratroop drop since Britain needed a 'real act of war' to justify Anglo-French intervention as 'peace-keepers'.

The meeting was at breaking-point. Lloyd recalled:

Ben-Gurion himself seemed to be in a rather aggressive mood, indicating or implying that the Israelis had no reason to believe in anything that a British Minister might say. He said in his book that I treated him like a subordinate.

While Ben-Gurion, restraining his anger, scraped his chair back and forth on the floor, Bourges-Maunoury unveiled his idea of French air

*British officials have derided this French assertion as 'ridiculous' (private information).

cover for Israeli operations, but Lloyd objected that this would prove Anglo-French 'collusion' with Israel. When Ben-Gurion asked if Britain had considered the damage that Israel might suffer from Egyptian bombing, Lloyd replied that he was negotiating on the basis of the Challe–Gazier formula and that the Israeli plan for direct Anglo-French support had surprised him. In essence, the French had agreed one scheme with the British and another with Israel.[28]

The Anglo-Israeli dispute centred upon the interval between a large-scale Israeli invasion of Sinai and Anglo-French bombing of Egypt. Ben-Gurion wanted twelve hours; Lloyd offered no less than forty-eight. A compromise suggestion that France intervene twelve hours and Britain forty-eight hours after the Israeli attack was unacceptable because the French did not have the bombers to neutralise the Egyptian air force. Ben-Gurion proposed a loan of British bombers to the French on the lines of the 'Destroyers for Bases' deal between the US and Britain in the Second World War, but Lloyd snapped that the American destroyers had not been worth anything.[29]

Discussions continued past midnight without compromise, and Lloyd returned to Britain, thinking that the 'collusion' had been aborted. Eden told the Cabinet on 23 October:

From secret conversations which had been held in Paris with representatives of the Israeli Government, it now seemed unlikely that the Israelis would launch a full-scale attack against Egypt. The UK and French Governments were thus confronted with the choice between an early military operation or a relatively prolonged negotiation [with Egypt].

However, Eden still thought a British concession, such as French use of facilities on Cyprus, could be made. Lloyd loyally supported the Prime Minister and insisted that there would be no settlement with Egypt because 'he saw no prospect' that it 'would diminish Colonel Nasser's influence throughout the Middle East'. Lloyd's Private Secretary, Donald Logan, was sent to Paris to tell Pineau that the Cabinet had not reached a conclusion.[30]

Lloyd had given up the Foreign Office's effort to control policy. He told Nutting, 'You, my dear Anthony, will no doubt be delighted to hear that it doesn't look as if the French plan will come off,' but, asked what he would do, said:

I am so confused and exhausted that I honestly have no advice to offer any more. It would really be better to leave it to a group of the colleagues, such as [Minister of Agriculture] Derry Heathcoat-Amory or [Minister of Works] Patrick Buchan-Hepburn, to decide.

The comment verged on the nonsensical, since junior Ministers like

Heathcoat-Amory or Buchan-Hepburn could not lead a Cabinet revolt.[31]

At Sèvres, the French and Israelis searched for compromise. Ben-Gurion rejected Challe's idea that Israel bomb one of her cities, Beersheba, and blame it on Egypt to justify Anglo-French intervention. Peres proposed that the Israelis send a ship through the Suez Canal, forcing an Egyptian response that would justify war. Most importantly, Dayan modified his original plan. Israeli paratroopers would launch a surprise attack on the Mitla Pass, seventy miles inside Egypt and thirty miles from the Suez Canal, while armoured columns crossed into Sinai. Britain and France would intervene thirty-six hours later.[32]

Pineau could now take Dayan's plan to London in the evening. Lloyd, with Eden absent, refused to abandon hope of a peaceful settlement and described the advantages of the solution sought at the UN, but he gave way when the Prime Minister joined the meeting. Eden and Pineau decided that they 'might serve notice on the parties to stop and withdraw a certain distance from the Canal and threaten them with military intervention by France and Britain if that was not done'. Consultation with the US was rejected 'owing to their preoccupation with the election campaign and the generally unsatisfactory nature of our exchanges with Mr Dulles about US action of any character'.[33]

The British Cabinet was informed the following morning that 'France had just recognised the urgent need to bring [the Security Council] issue to a head', especially after their capture of the *Athos*, a ship allegedly loaded with Egyptian arms for Algerian rebels; however, 'they were unwilling to use the gun-running incident as a ground for taking military action against Egypt; they preferred that such action should be based on grounds which concerned the UK as well as France'. It was hinted:

It could . . . be assumed that if [an Anglo-French operation] were launched, Israel would make a full-scale attack against Egypt, and this might have the effect of reducing the period of preliminary [aerial] bombardment. The second objective of the operation would be to secure the downfall of Colonel Nasser's regime in Egypt.

The Foreign Secretary was defeated once and for all, as the idea that Britain could agree to negotiations in Geneva if Egypt produced suitable proposals was now rejected:

If such a demand were made, the Egyptians were likely to comply with it – by producing within the specified time proposals which, though unsatisfactory, would appear to afford a basis for discussion. In that event a breaking [of talks] could only be reached after several days of discussion. . . . [Britain] could frame [her] demands in such a way as to make it impossible for the Egyptians to accept them – being resolved, on an Egyptian refusal, to take military action designed to overthrow Colonel Nasser's regime.[34]

With Lloyd scheduled to make a speech in the Commons that afternoon, Eden instructed Dean to return to Sèvres with Donald Logan.[35]

At the same time, Ben-Gurion finally accepted Dayan's plans. While paratroopers dropped into the Mitla Pass, armoured columns would attack towards Rafah on the northern coast of the Sinai, Abu al-Agheila in the centre, and Sharm el-Sheikh at the southern tip. The assault would begin on the afternoon of 29 October with Anglo-French bombing of Egypt at first light on the 31st and the airdrop of two French paratroop brigades into the Canal Zone two days later. To disguise the Mitla Pass operation as a 'raid', decreasing the chance of Egyptian aerial counter-attack, Israeli armoured columns would not seize the towns of Rafah and Gaza until the Egyptians realised that the paratroop drop was part of a co-ordinated invasion.[36]

The second set of talks in Sèvres were an anti-climax. Dean's instructions were simply to ensure that Israeli action against Egypt was significant enough to justify Anglo-French intervention, as Pineau had indicated to Eden the previous evening. Indeed, Pineau told the Israelis thirty minutes before Logan and Dean arrived that Eden had already agreed to strike Egypt thirty-six hours after Israel crossed into the Sinai. After 'a somewhat desultory recapitulation' of issues, the Israelis refused to give details of their operational plans, but Dean and Logan judged that they had extracted enough to satisfy Eden, and the French and Israeli delegations concluded that, while the British officials were not empowered to take further decisions, enough had been done to secure an agreement.

Towards the end of the meeting, Dean and Logan overheard a typewriter in the next room. A three-page document, in French on plain paper, was soon produced. The 'Sèvres Protocol' recorded that Israel would launch 'a full-scale attack' on the afternoon of 29 October. The next day, the British and French Governments would demand that Egypt and Israel cease fire and withdraw ten miles either side of the Suez Canal, while Anglo-French forces established a 'temporary occupation of the key positions on the Canal'. The inevitable Egyptian refusal of the ultimatum would bring an Anglo-French attack 'early on October 31st'. An annex, signed by France and Israel and withheld from the British, stated that French fighters and pilots would be based on Israeli airfields and French ships would protect the Israeli coast. After signature of the Protocol, which called for the endorsement of 'the three governments', one copy was provided for each delegation.[37]

Secretly, without the knowledge of their Parliaments, their publics and most of their civil servants, and, in Britain's case, her military commanders, Britain, France and Israel had declared war upon Egypt.

21

Preparing for 'Peace-keeping'
24–29 October 1956

P atrick Dean arrived at 10 Downing Street at 11 p.m. to brief Eden, Butler, Macmillan, Mountbatten and Head, who became Minister of Defence when Monckton formally resigned on 18 October. The Ministers were satisfied with the Protocol, but Eden, dismayed that the collusion had been recorded, instructed Dean and Logan to return to Paris in the morning to destroy all copies of the agreement. Pineau, fearing that the return of Dean and Logan might arouse suspicion, did not receive them with open arms. They were left in a locked room for hours, without food or drink, while Pineau phoned the Israelis. Ben-Gurion, still sceptical that Britain would abide by the Protocol, refused Eden's request.[1]

Eden told the Cabinet on 25 October:

The Israelis were, after all, advancing their military preparations with a view to making an attack on Egypt. . . . The French Government were strongly of the view that intervention would be justified in order to limit the hostilities and that for this purpose it would be right to launch the military operation against Egypt which had already been mounted.

If Israel attacked Egypt, Britain and France would issue their ultimata, and the Anglo-French force would act against any country refusing the terms. Eden admitted 'the risk that we should be accused of collusion with Israel', but gave a confused justification:

If an Anglo-French operation were undertaken against Egypt, we should be unable to prevent the Israelis from launching a parallel attack themselves; and it was preferable that we should be seen to be holding the balance between Israel and Egypt rather than appear to be accepting Israeli cooperation in an attack on Egypt alone.

Ministers supporting Eden alleged that the British action was 'defensible in international law, for we should be intervening to prevent interference with the free flow of traffic through the Canal', a flimsy excuse since the Egyptians, despite British and French efforts, had ensured passage through the Canal. Others rationalised:

A crisis in the Middle East could not now be long delayed. If . . . force might ultimately have to be used, would it not be used more effectively and with more limited damage if we acted promptly now when an Anglo-French operation was already mounted?

The Cabinet was not unanimous, however, and dissenters produced a range of arguments. An ultimatum to Egypt and Israel to hold their forces at least ten miles from the Suez Canal would 'not appear to be holding the balance between Israel and Egypt', since it would allow Israel to establish a line ninety miles inside Egypt. The UN might object to Britain and France usurping its peace-keeping function. Most significantly, the dissenters foresaw that 'our action would cause offence to the US Government and might do lasting damage to Anglo-American relations. There was no prospect of securing the support or approval of the US Government.' Eden, bolstered by Macmillan's assessment that the Americans would not oppose British action, remained firm, and the Cabinet accepted the Prime Minister's statement.[2]

While Eden indicated to the Cabinet that Britain knew of an impending Israeli attack, that is different from revealing British collusion in an Israeli invasion. The Prime Minister, to maintain security and minimise the possibility of division within the Cabinet, probably limited the details of Sèvres to an inner circle of Ministers. Despite this, Eden's 'official' biographer criticised dissidents, especially Monckton and Heathcoat-Amory, for not pressing their objections, although the former Minister of Defence had continually reminded Eden of his opposition to the use of force except as a last resort. Given the agreement between senior Ministers to proceed, Monckton and junior Ministers could not upset Eden's strategy. A dissenter could have resigned, at the cost of his career, but, as of 25 October, he had no cause to present to the Commons or to the public. An Israeli attack was anticipated, but it had not yet occurred.[3]

Those who knew of Sèvres never challenged Eden, although Lloyd recorded that there were four Ministerial meetings on 25–26 October.[4] As one Minister recalled, 'We were offered the poisoned chalice, we had the choice of draining it to the bitter dregs or dashing it from our lips.'[5] Macmillan remained a fervent 'hawk', and Home and Head fully supported the decision to act with Israel against Nasser. Butler had doubts, but would not vote against the Prime Minister. Instead, he told Hugh

Massingham, the political editor of the *Observer*, that his fellow Ministers were 'mad' without elaborating further.[6]

Moreover, no senior Minister heeded possible UN and US opposition to Anglo-French intervention. Eden had been repeatedly warned by the Americans *not* to use military force and *not* to act before the Presidential election, but he later wrote that he

thought that [the US] would be indignant with us and lecture us and the Israeli Government and Egyptian Government for having seized the Canal and that they would then 'watch the Bear'. Convinced as I was that the Soviet Government would take no action, I thought that the US Government would then seize this unique opportunity and put forward their own proposals for the future of the Suez Canal . . . and also put forward proposals for an Arab-Israeli settlement.[7]

Macmillan admitted that, while it was 'absolutely vital to humiliate Nasser . . . , we must (if we possibly can) keep the Americans with us, or we shall have no chance of getting out of our financial ruin'. Unlike France, Britain had not withdrawn reserves from the International Monetary Fund, for fear of triggering a run against the pound. Yet the Chancellor took no action to ensure that military operations were not upset by economic weakness and refused to keep his Treasury staff informed of developments. Makins, the former British Ambassador to the US, arrived on 15 October to take up his duties as Permanent Secretary to the Treasury. He discovered that 'Selwyn didn't want to see me – Anthony didn't want to see me – even Harold. . . . I knew absolutely nothing, was told absolutely nothing, but I realised that something very big was in the wind.'[8] Makins discovered the plans, but he was not informed by Macmillan of the imminent Israeli attack upon Egypt until 28 October. When Makins responded, 'We've got to make preparations,' Macmillan insisted, 'You can't tell anyone about this.' It was finally agreed that Makins could speak to Cabinet Secretary Brook.[9]

Macmillan apparently expected the US to take no action *against* the British, even if the Americans were not supportive. In his memoirs, he admitted 'a heavy responsibility' for the mistake and said in 1971, 'My judgement was wrong. . . . [My] instinct [was] that the Americans didn't wish to be informed when we took the final action . . . because that would embarrass them . . . but would support us when action was taken.'[10]

This explanation rested upon Macmillan's claims *after* Suez. The Chancellor, a prolific diarist, left no entries between October 1956 and February 1957. He subsequently claimed that the pressure of time forced the suspension of the entries, a curious statement for a man who was able to read numerous books, including essays on Machiavelli, during the crisis. Years later, he changed his story and said that he had destroyed some entries and then discontinued them at Eden's request. With no written evidence available, Macmillan maintained that Anglo-American division would not have occurred if he had been Foreign Secretary: 'I would have persuaded Eisenhower, or Foster, to back us – or say to the Cabinet, "We can't move."' Since Macmillan, as Chancellor, had that opportunity after his visit to Washington, his claim was whimsy, if not outright deception.[11]

Likewise, Macmillan tried to absolve himself of blame for the collusion by insisting:

I can't honestly say I liked it. . . . I was in a difficult position; I took no part in the details (looking back on it, they weren't very clever) and therefore didn't wish to criticise. . . . I think if I'd perhaps had more experience, I would have taken a stronger position in insisting on knowing just exactly how they were going to bring it about; and what were the chances of its success and what were the dangers.

As Macmillan was the foremost proponent of British co-operation with Israel and approved the collusion when he was informed of it by Eden, the excuse is somewhat misleading.[12]

Still, it is puzzling that Macmillan misinterpreted Eisenhower's and Foster Dulles's emphasis on OMEGA and aversion to the use of force. Eden's Private Secretaries allegedly speculated that Macmillan 'was planning to overthrow Eden', but it is more likely that the Chancellor decided that Britain had to risk attacking Egypt, even without assurances of American support. As Chancellor, Macmillan was obsessed with a secure supply of oil for Britain, writing after the failure of the Templer mission in December 1955: 'The game is not over yet; and we have got to win. . . . For if we lose out in the Middle East, we lose the oil. If we lose the oil, we cannot live.'[13] In his last surviving diary entry for 1956, dated 4 October, Macmillan wrote:

We must, by one means or another, win this struggle. Nasser may well try to preach Holy War in the Middle East and (even to their own loss) the mob and the demagogues may create a ruinous position for us. Without oil, and without the profits from oil, neither UK nor Western Europe can survive.[14]

Whatever Britain's economic situation, Macmillan wanted war. On 26 October, he told the Cabinet that Britain would lose up to £300 million in foreign reserves in November and said sterling's role as an international currency could only be saved if the pound was devalued and all of Britain's financial resources were mobilised. Yet the Chancellor never mentioned the impending attack upon Egypt.[15]

British commanders of REVISE were unable to object to Sèvres, as they were given misleading information about collusion. On 25 October, a planning paper for the Chiefs of Staff noted: 'In the event of the Israelis attempting to take advantage of this situation to extend their frontiers, we would have to demonstrate to the Arab world our determination to uphold the existing armistice lines.' After the signature of the Protocol, Generals Keightley and Stockwell were informed that REVISE might be implemented at less than the ten days' notice required in the plan, but they were not told that the operation was authorised until 26 October. An unsigned memorandum for Eden merely argued that Keightley 'should . . . be directed to go ahead' with preparations for an assault against Egypt under the cover of Operation BOATHOOK, a communications exercise between Cyprus and warships in the Mediterranean.[16]

Keightley was not told that plans had been co-ordinated with Israel. When he expressed his anxiety about military operations, 'Eden gave him a severe dressing down and told him that these were questions with which military commanders should not concern themselves'. The General was probably told only that British intelligence knew of an imminent Israeli attack, which would provide the excuse for Anglo-French seizure of the Suez Canal. For unknown reasons, Mountbatten did not give details of Sèvres to Keightley. He simply informed Admiral Guy Grantham, the Commander-in-Chief of Britain's naval forces in the Mediterranean:

We have definite reports that Israel is mobilising and requisitioning civilian transports. Our estimate is that they are likely to be ready for war about Monday [29 October] or possibly Tuesday, but no overt step may be taken by us at present.[17]

Stockwell, who left London for Malta on 26 October, was the first British commander to learn of the new plans. During a stopover outside Paris, he was informed by his French subordinate, General André Beaufre, of the 'Israeli plan and timings', although Beaufre probably did not tell Stockwell that this was co-ordinated between British, French and Israeli politicians.[18] Stockwell's Chief of Staff later recalled:

There were two or three rather dilapidated wartime huts. . . . There were one or two odd gendarmes standing about, sucking their teeth. . . . Meanwhile I and the other officers of General Stockwell's staff sort of hung about kicking our heels. Eventually [Stockwell] came out of the hut and took me to one side and told me what he had learnt from General Beaufre, which was in a nutshell that it was likely that the Israelis were going to attack Egypt and that we would undoubtedly get involved.[19]

Upon arrival in Malta, Stockwell passed the news to Grantham and Vice-Admiral L. F. Dunford-Slater, REVISE's naval commander. The trio acted without instructions from London, redeploying carrier groups from Malta to Cyprus, loading the amphibious assault force and sailing

HMS *Tyne*, the headquarters ship for the British commanders, to Cyprus under the cover of Operation BOATHOOK.[20]

REVISE's air commander, Air Marshal Denis Barnett, was in Cyprus supervising the shift of the Air Task Force Headquarters from Malta for Operation CORDAGE against Israel. Told nothing of developments, he asked on 25 October that his forces be stood down from the six-hour alert for CORDAGE and that, with the reduction in tension, formal responsibility for REVISE and CORDAGE be given to the Air Officer Commanding Levant, the peacetime British commander. The Assistant Chief of Air Staff for Plans flew to Cyprus to 'clarify the situation', but Barnett only learned of plans for Anglo-French intervention when Keightley arrived in Cyprus. As Barnett entered the Commander-in-Chief's office, a paper blew on to the floor: 'Hooknoses D-Day 29 Oct.'[21]

There was now little co-ordination between British political and military planning. Still believing that REVISE was suspended, the War Office turned its attention to other exercises and release of reservists over Christmas. The Ministry of Works even tried to remove REVISE's planners from their 'bunker' in Montagu House Annex. Stockwell noted the unsolvable problem. To make the Anglo-French ultimatum appear genuine, Eden insisted that there should be no alert before 30 October. Yet the landing in Egypt in Phase III of REVISE, planned for twenty days after the announcement of an alert, was now scheduled for 8 November. Only ad hoc preparations by Stockwell, Grantham and Dunford-Slater could narrow the gap between REVISE's timetable and the Prime Minister's demand for a quick occupation of the Canal Zone.[22]

In contrast, the mobilisation of Israeli troops began on 25 October, and French assault troops left Toulon and Marseilles on the 27th. Three French fighters supplied high-octane jet fuel to Lydda airfield in Israel, and large deliveries of French arms were off-loaded on the Israeli coast.[23] 'Extremist' parties, notably the anti-Western National Socialists, had gained seats in Jordanian elections on 21 October, and Jordan joined the Egyptian-Syrian military command three days later. Dayan's mobilisation no longer appeared to be directed against an Iraqi-Jordanian axis, but an Egyptian-Jordanian-Syrian grouping.[24]

For the Americans, the first indication that something was amiss came when the US Embassy in London could not provide an account of the Anglo-French meeting of 16 October to the State Department. Concern increased when French Cabinet Minister Jacques Chaban-Delmas told US Ambassador Dillon that Britain and France were collaborating with Israel to attack Egypt on or about 10 November. Foster Dulles told Eisenhower on 21 October that he was 'baffled to know the real purposes of the British and the French'. Although Britain and the US were working on 'long-term economic projects', i.e. OMEGA, the British were considering 'alternatives', such as 'an inspired attempt against Nasser' to provoke anti-Western demonstrations justifying British military action to 'defend' foreigners, reoccupation of the Suez Canal Base, or the cut-off of Canal tolls to Egypt. Drawing upon his conversation with Macmillan, Foster Dulles could only be 'confident that the British and the French would not resort to any of these measures before [the Presidential] election. . . . [He] was more fearful as to what might happen after the election.'[25]

The signs were increasingly ominous. U-2 flights photographed the Israeli mobilisation and the sailing of British and French ships to the Eastern Mediterranean, although the US Air Attaché in Tel Aviv, out of sympathy for Israel, apparently withheld news of Franco-Israeli preparations.[26] The French, after the capture of the *Athos*, hijacked a plane carrying five leaders of the Algerian nationalists. Monckton told Ambassador Aldrich that he had resigned as Minister of Defence because he believed the use of force against Egypt would be a 'great blunder'.[27] Most significantly, American signals intelligence detected an increase in traffic between Tel Aviv and Paris, although they could not decode the messages for immediate evaluation.

The Watch Tower Committee of representatives from the State Department, the CIA and the military was convened after the US Military Attaché in Israel reported that his driver, a reservist with one arm and one leg and blind in one eye, was called up for service. The Committee noted that British intelligence had 'crawled into a shell' and that Dayan was reportedly in France. Robert Amory, the CIA's Deputy Director for Intelligence, reported that Eden was so mad at Nasser that he would 'team up with anyone' to overthrow the Egyptian leader. Only James Angleton, the head of the CIA's counter-espionage, with close contacts with Mossad, dismissed the chances of an Israeli attack.[28] On 27 October, a White House meeting drafted a message from Eisenhower to Ben-Gurion requesting 'no forceful initiative on the part of your Government which would endanger the peace and the growing friendship between our two countries'.[29]

However, the Americans continued to see 'Jordan as the most probable direction' for an Israeli attack. Eden and Lloyd had told General Al Gruenther, the outgoing Supreme Commander of NATO forces, that the Israeli-Jordanian situation and Egyptian involvement in Jordan was 'of more fundamental importance' than the Suez crisis. Ambassador Eban, summoned by Foster Dulles, found the Secretary studying an 'enormous map of Israel and Jordan'. Foster Dulles 'strongly expressed concern and the difficulty [the US] had in interpreting Israeli mobiliz-ation as purely defensive', but Eban maintained that Israel had no aggressive intentions.[30]

When Aldrich saw Lloyd on 28 October, the Foreign Secretary blatantly lied to cover up the collusion. Aldrich reported to Washington:

[Lloyd] said with feeling and . . . evident conviction that a major Israeli attack either on Jordan or Egypt at this time would put Britain in an impossible situation. . . . He was unwilling to believe the Israelis would launch a full-scale attack upon Egypt despite the temptation to do so in the present circumstances. He also said categorically that his recent conversations with the French gave him no reason to think the French were stimulating such an Israeli venture.

Lloyd predicted that negotiations with Egypt would resume within a few days and assured Aldrich that the Cabinet was 'prepared to give him a reasonable period in which to seek a negotiated solution'. He even carried out the charade of agreeing to 'a five-step programme' with Aldrich for SCUA and collection of Canal dues.[31] In contrast, Patrick Dean, spending the afternoon of the 28th with Chester Cooper, the CIA liaison with British intelligence, hinted, 'You and I are in much trouble, and it isn't because of [the uprising in] Hungary.'[32]

Eisenhower sent a second message to Ben-Gurion, requesting that Middle Eastern countries 'refrain from any action which can lead to hostilities', and issued a statement publicising the communication. Foster Dulles was informed by John McCloy, a director of Chase Manhattan Bank, that there had not been 'a significant transfer of funds from Israeli bank accounts': McCloy did not realise that Israel had withdrawn most of her balances weeks earlier.[33] Only on the late evening of 28 October did the Watch Tower Committee conclude that Egypt was the Israeli target, and the Joint Chiefs of Staff informed US military posts:

Past Egyptian provocations, the key role of Egypt in the Arab threat [to Israel], and UK involvement with Jordan indicate the attack will be launched against Egypt in the near-future, under the pretext of retaliation and exceeding past raids in strength.[34]

The next morning, Eisenhower felt that the Israeli situation was 'a little better' and Foster Dulles added, 'We have gained 24 hours.'[35] At 5 p.m. Cairo time, as President Nasser was at a children's party for his son's birthday, Eden was preparing for a dinner for the Prime Minister of Norway, and Eisenhower was campaigning in Florida, four low-flying Israeli Mustangs cut Egyptian telephone lines in the Sinai and 395 Israeli paratroopers dropped into the Mitla Pass. Eban was explaining to Rountree that Israeli mobilisation was a 'security measure', unconnected to the Anglo-French conflict with Egypt, when news of the attack reached the State Department. Rountree commented drily, 'We have obviously been having an academic discussion. . . . I am certain, Mr Ambassador, that you will wish to get back to your embassy to find out exactly what is happening in your country.'[36]

Foster Dulles did not react until 3.40 p.m. (10.40 p.m. in Egypt), as an advance Israeli land force linked up with paratroopers at the Mitla Pass. He phoned Lodge, the US Ambassador to the UN:

The Israelis have moved into Egyptian territory. We don't know yet in what force or whether it is [a position] from which they will retire. . . . The British and French are coming in and we will see if they will act in the UN calling upon the Israelis to withdraw. Partly it is to smoke them out to see where they stand.[37]

The Anglo-American 'alliance' in the Middle East, reconstructed in the previous two years, was about to undergo its sternest test.

22

Alliance Endangered
29–31 October 1956

The 'hawks' finally had their war with Nasser, but Britain's diplomatic, economic and military forces were unprepared for the conflict. Ambassador Nicholls, on the instructions of Levant Department officials who were unaware of collusion, had approached Ben-Gurion to say that Britain 'hoped no further action is contemplated against Jordan'. Ben-Gurion replied, 'I think you will find your government knows more about this than you do.' Because of this reference to Sèvres, which Nicholls did not appreciate, his telegram to London was classified 'Top Secret' and the uncensored copy circulated only to Kirkpatrick and Dean. It was subsequently given general circulation with Ben-Gurion's remark excised, but the 'Top Secret' label was not removed. For some officials, this was the first clue that the British Government was circumventing the Foreign Office.[1]

The Levant Department, still concerned about Israeli mobilisation, asked Nicholls to communicate Britain's 'grave concern at recent moves and [the] hope that no action will be taken to endanger the peace'. Eden halted the despatch of the instructions, but Nicholls took the initiative and asked Golda Meir on the morning of 29 October for an assurance that Israel would not attack Jordan. She said drily, 'I think I can give you that assurance.'[2]

Roger Makins had returned to London in early October and his replacement as British Ambassador to Washington, Harold Caccia, did not leave for the US until 1 November. The British Chargé d'Affaires, John Coulson, was not sent instructions by Eden and Lloyd until 6.10 p.m., more than two hours after the Israeli attack. Britain welcomed tripartite consultations, but the Tripartite Declaration was not applicable, since Nasser had stated that the Declaration did not give Britain and the US the right to intervene in Middle Eastern affairs. Eden and Lloyd speculated that Israel had acted because of Egyptian mobilisation, Nasser's public assertion that Israel should be liquidated and Jordan's accession to the Egyptian-Syrian military command.[3]

Meeting Coulson and the French Ambassador, Herve Alphand, on the afternoon of 29 October, Foster Dulles said that the US was ready to request in the Security Council that Israel withdraw while UN members suspended aid to Tel Aviv. The Secretary agreed with Coulson that military intervention under the Tripartite Declaration was inappropriate, but suggested financial and economic sanctions. Coulson innocently replied that he thought London would favour this procedure.[4]

Foster Dulles was not so trusting, telling William Knowland, the Republican leader in the Senate, '[Our] guess is it [the Israeli attack] has been worked out with the French at least and possibly with the British. . . . He had an inkling but it was a quick operation – we thought [Israel] would attack Jordan.'[5] He arranged a meeting at the White House with Eisenhower, Undersecretary of State Hoover, Secretary of Defense Wilson, Admiral Radford, Allen Dulles and Eisenhower's staff. Allen Dulles still thought that the Israeli attack was a 'probing action', but Foster Dulles noted the French supply of Mystères to Israel and 'a very large number of messages between Paris and Israel', which the CIA had not been able to decode, on 28 October. He speculated, 'The French and British may think that – whatever we may think of what they have done – we have to go along with them.'

The French assumption that Eisenhower would not intervene because of the Presidential election was immediately shattered. The President 'did not really think the American people would throw him out in the midst of a situation like this, but if they did, so be it'. He favoured an immediate approach to the UN while notifying Britain, 'We recognise that much is on their side in the dispute with the Egyptians but . . . nothing justifies double-crossing us.' Wilson held out against support of Egypt, but Hoover, worried that Arab states would ally themselves with the Soviets if the US backed Britain and France, and Radford agreed with the President. Foster Dulles also favoured pressure on the British, although he thought there was 'still a bare chance to "unhook" the British from the French'.[6]

After the meeting, Eisenhower told Coulson that the US 'planned to get [to the Security Council] first thing in the morning – when the doors open – before the USSR gets there' and asked the British to do likewise. Coulson, still without instructions from London, reasserted that Britain would approach the Council 'if only because, otherwise, the belief would spread throughout the Arab world that we were behind the Israeli move'.[7]

The first sign of trouble came when UN Secretary-General Hammarskjöld asked for an immediate Council session. The British representative, Pierson Dixon, agreed that the Council should 'at least call on Israel to withdraw her forces', but he said that he had no instructions from London. US delegate Lodge, normally on good terms with Dixon, reported, 'It was as though a mask had fallen off, [Dixon] was ugly and not smiling.' Dixon allegedly chastised Lodge, 'Don't be so damn high-minded,' and described the Tripartite Declaration as 'ancient history and without current validity'.[8]

Although the British Cabinet approved the draft ultimata to Egypt and Israel to withdraw ten miles either side of the Suez Canal, to be issued by Eden in the Commons on the afternoon of 30 October, Ministers realised that the American attitude could not be ignored. Before the meeting, Lloyd protested to Aldrich about the American resolution condemning Israel, since the Israeli action was 'a clear case of self-defence'. Aldrich warned that, if the US and Britain took opposing positions in the Security Council, the impression would be given that 'the Israeli action had been contrived with the United Kingdom and France as a move to get rid of Nasser'.

Aldrich later claimed that Lloyd promised that 'HMG would immediately cite Israel . . . as an aggressor against Egypt', but Lloyd denied this, insisting that he emphasised 'the assurances which we received that Israel did not contemplate any attack on Jordan'. The American record of the conversation indicated that Aldrich misunderstood Lloyd's firm resolve to prevent an Israeli attack against *Jordan* as determination to prevent an attack against *Egypt*. All the same, Lloyd was clearly playing for time.[9]

The Foreign Secretary asked the Cabinet, in the light of Aldrich's position, to consider whether Britain 'should attempt to persuade [the US] to support the action which we and the French were proposing'. The bombing of Egypt could be deferred for twenty-four hours while an approach was made to Washington. Supporting Lloyd, Macmillan belatedly admitted that, in a protracted war, American financial help might be needed. Ministers did not postpone military action, but they approved an immediate approach to the Americans:

Even though it was unlikely that the US Government would respond to such an appeal, we should do our utmost to reduce the offence to American public opinion which was liable to be caused by our notes to Egypt and Israel. Our reserves of gold and dollars were still in need of assistance, and we could not afford to alienate the US Government more than was absolutely necessary.[10]

Eden cabled Eisenhower that 'Egypt has to a large extent brought this attack on herself by insisting that the state of war [with Israel] persists, by defying the Security Council [over Egypt's ban on Israeli shipping through the Suez Canal], and by declaring her intention to marshal the Arab States for the destruction of Israel'. The last line of the letter, however, held out the possibility of Anglo-American co-operation: 'We feel that decisive action should be taken at once to stop hostilities. We have agreed to go with you to the Security Council and instructions are being sent this moment [to Dixon].'[11]

The Prime Minister's cable crossed Eisenhower's request for 'help in clearing up my understanding as to what exactly is happening between us and our European allies – especially between us, the French, and yourselves'. Citing the French sale of weapons to Israel, increased radio traffic between Paris and Tel Aviv, and Dixon's 'completely unsympathetic' behaviour, Eisenhower concluded:

It seems to me of first importance that the UK and the US quickly and clearly lay out their present views and intentions before each other . . . so that we may not, in any real crisis, be powerless, to act in concert because of misunderstanding of each other.[12]

The letter concealed the fury of Eisenhower, who was being restrained by Foster Dulles. At a White House meeting on the morning of 30 October, the President complained:

He wondered if the hand of Churchill might not be behind this, inasmuch as this action is in the mid-Victorian style. . . . He did not see much value in an unworthy and unreliable ally and . . . the necessity to support them might not be as great as they believed.

Eisenhower only sought Anglo-American agreement because of Foster Dulles's assessment that 'the US could not sit by and let [Britain] go under economically'. The Secretary told Lodge, 'We are anxious to carry the Br[itish] – it is basic and goes to the heart of our relations all over the world and we have to give them a reasonable time.'[13]

Any possibility of Anglo-American reconciliation was soon dispelled. On the afternoon of 30 October, Kirkpatrick finally cabled the Government position to diplomatic posts. He explained, 'The Israeli attack on Egypt [seemed] undoubtedly to be an act of aggression. On the other hand, Egypt [had] called this on herself' through her refusal to reach a peace settlement with Tel Aviv and her defiance of Security Council resolutions on the closure of the Suez Canal to Israeli shipping. British policy was 'to take the most decisive steps open to them to bring hostilities to an end'.[14]

Britain's quandary was that she could not allow a Security Council resolution which condemned the Israeli invasion. Dixon, 'white-faced and hostile', refused to endorse an American letter to the Security Council that stated Israel had 'penetrated deeply into Egyptian territory' and spoke of 'steps for the immediate cessation of the military action of Israel against Egypt'. Lodge, again 'shocked by [Dixon's] attitude and tone', told Foster Dulles that Britain would only support the US resolution if references to Israeli action were removed. Foster Dulles, after speaking with Eisenhower, told Lodge to proceed, simply modifying the reference to 'the military action of Israel *against* Egypt' to 'the military action of Israel *in* Egypt'.[15]

Eisenhower and Foster Dulles now knew that Britain, to some degree, had accepted or encouraged the Israeli attack. The President was especially bitter:

We will not help [Britain and France]. [I do] not think we should call a special session of our people to get dollars to help them out. . . . They are our friends and allies and suddenly they put us in a hole and expect us to rescue them.

He concluded, '[I] want [Eden] to know that we are a Government of honor and stick by what we say.'[16]

At 4.30 p.m. on 30 October, Eden informed the House of Commons of the Anglo-French demand that Egypt and Israel cease fire, withdraw their forces ten miles from the Suez Canal within twelve hours, and allow an Anglo-French force to occupy the Canal Zone. Refusal by either side would subject it to Anglo-French military action. The 'impartial' ultimatum was blatantly transparent. At the time of Eden's announcement, the main Israeli force was between fifty and one hundred miles from the Canal, so Israel could advance forty to ninety miles and still comply with British demands.[17] When Gershon Avner, the Counsellor of the Israeli Embassy in London, received the ultimatum from Kirkpatrick, he 'thought that some secretary must have omitted one or two zeros after the figure [for Israeli withdrawal east of the Canal]. Mr Pineau and Mr Kirkpatrick . . . smiled as he revealed his surprise.'[18] William Hayter, the British Ambassador to the Soviet Union, had attended a Kremlin reception where Soviet Foreign Minister Molotov told Ambassadors that Britain and France were behind the Israeli invasion. Hayter assured the Ambassadors that Molotov was wrong and that Britain would vote for UN measures to halt the Israeli aggression. He returned from the reception to find the ultimatum: 'I could not believe my eyes. I even began to wonder if I had drunk too much at the Kremlin.'[19]

The damage of Eden's announcement was compounded by a lack of diplomacy. Gaitskell and his colleagues had been increasingly convinced, after the furor of early August, that the Government would only use force after genuine negotiations with Egypt collapsed. Given only fifteen minutes' notice of the ultimatum, Gaitskell told Douglas Jay, 'I shall never believe anything that Eden says to me in public or in private.'[20] In the Commons, the Labour leader criticised Eden's refusal to ask the Security Council for prompt Israeli withdrawal from Egypt and stressed the Government's failure to consult the US and the Commonwealth.[21] Aldrich called at the Foreign Office at 1.30 p.m. for Lloyd's answer about an approach to the Security Council, but Lloyd's Private Secretary asked Aldrich to return later in the afternoon. Aldrich did so and was told that Lloyd was in the Commons. Only when Eden was speaking did Kirkpatrick present Aldrich with the British ultimatum. The Ambassador commented 'sadly that he was afraid there would be hell to pay'.[22]

Eden's telegram to Eisenhower justifying the ultimatum was not despatched to Washington until 5.45 p.m. He disingenuously cabled that his 'first instinct would have been to ask you to associate yourself and your country with the declaration, but I know the constitutional and other difficulties in which you are placed'. Instead, he appealed for American 'support [for] what we have done, at least in general terms'. The message did not reach Eisenhower's desk until 8.30 p.m., London time.[23] The Prime Minister claimed that 'cyphering delays' had occurred, but the Americans suspected that he presented them with a fait accompli. Foster Dulles complained to Senator Knowland, 'The evidence is that the Israelis were used as a decoy [for Britain and France]. . . . He had solemn assurances they would not – though they were private.' An hour later, he told Eisenhower that the ultimatum was 'about as crude and brutal as anything he has ever seen'. The President agreed 'that it was pretty rough'.[24] Foster Dulles then summoned the beleaguered Coulson to talk about the 'pretty brutal affair' of the ultimatum and to complain:

We were facing one of the greatest tragedies, not only for our trust in each other but also for the world situation. Just when the Soviet orbit was crumbling and we could point to a contrast between the Western world and the Soviet, it now looked as though the West was producing a similar situation.

The British Minister could only say, 'It was extremely difficult for him to believe the UK had had any part in urging the Israelis to attack Egypt.'[25]

Adding insult to injury, Britain and France requested suspension of the Security Council session, scheduled for 3 p.m. in New York, so that Eden's speech could be studied. Foster Dulles was in no mood to consent. Nor was Eisenhower: 'All right with him that [the US delegation] go ahead – after all [Britain and France] haven't consulted with us on anything.' Another message to Eden and Mollet, intended for publication, emphasised Eisenhower's 'deep concern at the prospect of this drastic action'.[26] A Foreign Office official quipped, 'It's rather fun to be at Number 10 the night we smashed the Anglo-American alliance.'[27]

William Clark even alleged that an agitated Eisenhower phoned Eden but was connected to the Press Secretary by mistake. The President launched into a string of expletives and said, 'Anthony, you must have gone out of your mind,' before realising that he was not speaking to Eden. No other source has confirmed the story, although Clark did receive a call from Aldrich giving the text of Eisenhower's published message to Eden.[28]

Britain's position at the UN had been sabotaged. Dixon obtained an adjournment of the Security Council's morning session of 30 October, but, 'obviously shaken', had to read the ultimatum at the afternoon meeting. Lodge refused Dixon's plea for another delay and tabled the US resolution, which not only called for Israeli withdrawal but, in a clause directed at Britain and France, for all UN members to refrain from the threat or use of force. Dixon publicly asked Lodge not to press for a vote, but when the US delegate demanded an immediate decision, Dixon and the French representative, Henri Cornut-Gentille, vetoed the measure. The Soviet representative cleverly resubmitted the American resolution without the requirement that UN members refrain from force. Britain and France again cast vetoes, indicating support of the Israeli invasion.[29] Dixon reported to London that 'the Anglo-French action [has] been greeted by our friends with shocked surprise' and desperately hoped for Anglo-American reconciliation: 'Mr Lodge did his best, but was clearly under firm instructions to oppose us at every point.'[30]

Dixon received no assistance. Nasser, 'completely relaxed and at his ease', told Ambassador Trevelyan that Egypt would defend her rights against aggression. British commanders, fearing effective Egyptian use of anti-aircraft fire and fighter aircraft at dawn on 31 October, delayed the bombing of Egyptian airfields for twelve hours, but Eden told the Cabinet that air operations would begin at dusk.[31]

Even before the implementation of REVISE, Britain was in trouble. Countries were lining up in the UN to condemn any further aggression upon the Egyptians, and Eden's ultimatum was a charade, alienating the Labour Party, splitting the British public and confusing his own diplomats. The Americans realised that both France and Israel had been planning an assault upon Egypt, so Eisenhower's wrath was reserved for the British, the 'allies' who had betrayed his trust. Foster Dulles's main concern was to safeguard American 'moral' leadership of the world, condemning British and French 'colonialism', if necessary:

Two things are important from the standpoint of history. It is the beginning of the collapse of the Soviet Empire [because of the Hungarian uprising]. The second is the idea is out that we can be dragged along at the heels of British and French policies that are obsolete. This is a declaration of independence for the first time that they cannot count upon us to engage in policies of this sort.[32]

23

Britain's Last Chance
31 October–1 November 1956

After the immediate shock of the Israeli attack, Eden's ultimatum, and the public dispute between Ambassadors Dixon and Lodge in the UN, the decision for Foster Dulles was whether to invoke the United for Peace Resolution in the Security Council. Under the Resolution, established during the Korean War, an issue before the Council, in this case the demand for Israeli withdrawal and the threat of action against any country supporting the Israelis, could be referred to the General Assembly if at least seven of the Council's eleven members agreed. When Senator Knowland asked on 31 October if an Assembly meeting was scheduled, Foster Dulles hesitated and 'doubted we can have one before the regular one in two weeks'. The Secretary was soon forced to reconsider: Britain and France had begun bombing Egypt, and an American journalist told him that collusion with Israel

started with the French and the British were not in on it until a few days ago and . . . wanted to be sure there was no danger of war between Israel and Jordan. . . . When they got the assurance that would not be the case, they got in.[1]

Britain's only possible salvation was delaying the passage of an Assembly resolution long enough to take control of the Suez Canal Zone, possibly provoking the Egyptians to overthrow Nasser. Even Eisenhower was prepared to accept a fait accompli if intervention was quick and successful. After reading the British ultimatum to Egypt, he had drafted a message for Eden:

It is hard for me to see any good final result emerging from a scheme that seems certain to antagonise the entire Moslem world. . . . I assume, however, that you have gone too far to reconsider so I must further assume that your plan is so worked out that you foresee no dreary and unending prospect stretching out ahead.

I think I faintly understand and certainly I deeply sympathise with you in the problem you have to solve. Now we must pray that everything comes out both justly and reasonably peacefully.

Foster Dulles thought 'the last part is a bit too much, assuming it is all going to happen'. Eisenhower agreed to hold the letter until the morning of 31 October, but then postponed its despatch indefinitely.[2]

Dixon valiantly defended the British position. Asking Lodge on 31 October for 'a cooling-off period of only twenty-four hours', he finally obtained the US delegate's agreement to delay action by the Security Council. Lodge informed Foster Dulles that an issue could also be referred to the Assembly through a petition by a majority of the Assembly's members. Britain and France favoured this because 'it takes longer and both have hope of being able to work something out'. The Secretary gave way: 'Get it [the Council session for 3 p.m.] called off and say we would sign and do it by petition.' He told State Department officials:

The matter should be kept active in the Security Council, at least today, until it can be shown that the Security Council has really exhausted all courses available to it; this would amount to a stalling operation short of stultifying the sound position of moral principle which we have so far held.[3]

Dixon was finally undone by the Soviets. At 5.13 p.m., Lodge told Foster Dulles that the Soviet Union would only refrain from introducing a Council resolution condemning Britain, France and Israel if the matter was referred to the Assembly. Foster Dulles instructed Lodge, 'Go ahead and vote for [reference to the Assembly]', but added, '[I] would not have the [Assembly] meeting before Friday [2 November].'[4]

Foster Dulles's ambivalence was apparent throughout the US Government. When the RAF first bombed Egypt, U-2 reconnaissance flights from the American base at Adana, Turkey, were passing over the area. The Americans gave the photographs to the British, who replied, 'Warm thanks for pictures. It's the quickest bomb damage assessment we've ever had.'[5] The Chief Naval Officer, Admiral Arleigh Burke, suggested loaning amphibious craft to the British, but he soon found himself preparing for confrontation. Asked by Foster Dulles if the Sixth Fleet could prevent the Anglo-French carrier force from reaching Egypt, Burke answered:

We can stop them, but we will have to blast hell out of them. . . . The British, the French, and the Egyptians and the Israelis, the whole Goddamn works of them we can knock off, if you want, but that's the only way we can do it.

Burke ordered the Commander of the Sixth Fleet 'to have his bomb[er]s up, to be checked out, so as to be able to fight either another naval force or against land targets, and to make sure of all his targeting data'. When the Commander asked, 'Who's the enemy?', Burke instructed, 'Don't take any guff from anybody.'[6]

At this point, Eisenhower, uninvolved in discussions of UN strategy, was a catalyst for American public opinion rather than an actor in policy-making. While moderate in tone, his national broadcast of 31 October concentrated on the faults of the invasion of Egypt. The US, 'not consulted in any way' by Britain, France or Israel, retained her right to oppose the attack, and the matter would be pressed in the UN. The President concluded with a subtle warning to Britain and France: 'The peace we seek . . . means the acceptance of law, and the fostering of justice, in all the world.'[7]

American criticism was not the only source of pressure upon the Eden Government. On 31 October, Nutting decided to resign as Minister of State in the Foreign Office, agreeing to Eden's request not to make a public statement, at least for a few days. The Prime Minister allegedly concluded, '*Tout casse sauf l'amitié*. I hope, in spite of all this, that we shall see something of each other in the future.' Nutting, once Eden's close friend and protégé, never saw him again.[8] Eden's Private Secretary, Philip de Zulueta, allegedly passed on the request of the Chief Whip, Edward Heath, that Press Secretary Clark 'hint to the Press that Nutting was terribly under the influence of his American mistress and anyway was not quite himself now-a-days'.[9]

Assistant Undersecretary Ross, who also knew about the collusion, recommended adoption of the UN resolution for Israeli withdrawal:

We appear to be pitching into the Egyptians but do nothing about the Israelis. We can and should say that we would deal with the Israelis as soon as our hands are free but it would be better if the Assembly would make this their business.[10]

The First Sea Lord, Mountbatten, had worried throughout the crisis about British relations with Arab countries and had asked Eden to sign a statement that the military carried no political responsibility for its actions. He now submitted his resignation to the Prime Minister, but it was not accepted.[11]

In the Commons on 31 October, Gaitskell, 'in brilliant form', queried if the US was consulted about the ultimatum and accused the Government of 'violating' its relations with Washington, the Commonwealth and the UN. In response, Eden 'spoke haltingly with frequent interruptions, failing to win command of the House and, in general, making a poor impression'. He did not deny his 'blackout' of the US, but argued that, while the Canal was necessary to British survival, it was only a secondary concern for the Americans: 'I do not think that we must in all circumstances secure agreement from our American ally before we can act ourselves in what we know to be our vital interests.'[12]

That evening, Lloyd tried to avoid the charge of collusion:

It is quite wrong to state that Israel was incited to this action by Her Majesty's Government. There was no prior agreement between us about it. It is, of course, true that the Israeli mobilisation gave some advance warning, and we urged restraint upon the Israeli Government and, in particular, drew attention to the serious consequences of any attack upon Jordan.[13]

In his memoirs, Lloyd claimed that the Sèvres talks did not meet the *Oxford English Dictionary* definition of 'collusion' as a '*fraudulent* secret understanding', but this argument carefully avoided the relevant points. The Sèvres Protocol constituted a prior agreement, withheld from Parliament, between Britain and Israel to invade and bomb Egypt. To cover himself, Lloyd had written to Pineau, for the record, after Sèvres:

It must be clear, in view of what we said yesterday, that the UK has not asked the Israeli Government to undertake any action whatever. We merely asked ourselves what our reaction would be in the event that certain events transpire.[14]

Protecting the façade of the Anglo-French ultimatum, Lloyd lied, not only to the Commons but to the world. He later admitted:

If I thought it would save British lives, protect British property, and serve British interests to conceal part of the facts from Parliament, I would not hesitate for a moment to do so, particularly when active hostilities were taking place or there was an inflammatory situation.[15]

The Americans were never fooled. Although CIA and State Department officials did not know of Sèvres, they summarised, after the Suez War:

The British accepted a situation in which the Israelis were to play the part of *deus ex machina* in the plot. They became accessories both before and after the fact. This amounted to constructive collusion on the British part. . . . Eden and Lloyd knew what they were getting themselves into, although they have not fully admitted it.[16]

At home, the Conservative majority in the Commons allowed the Government to maintain the ruse, but Britain's Arab friends could not be as accommodating. The Iraqi Prime Minister, Nuri Sa'id, warned:

If immediately, or within a day or two at most, action by HMG to compel Israel [*sic*] forces to withdraw from Egyptian territory could be achieved, position would be altered very much and perhaps decisively for the better. But, failing this, he doubted whether Iraqi regime and government could hold the position much longer. A week was the very outside.

Kirkpatrick weakly replied to Ambassador Wright that Britain's action was 'merely an emergency and temporary fire brigade operation to prevent Israel inflicting a crushing defeat on Egypt'. Wright, after further meetings with Nuri and the Iraqi monarchy, responded:

My own appreciation is that, unless very early action is taken . . . , the Government and public security may be in danger. . . . It is now literally imperative that something should be said or done to correct the false impression, which events are creating, that HMG are attacking Egypt in collusion with Israel.[17]

Even the Commonwealth offered little support for British action. The Indians were bitterly opposed, and the Government of Ceylon expressed 'shock and perturbation'. The Pakistani Government was under public pressure to leave the Commonwealth and evict Britain from the Baghdad Pact. The Canadians, who consistently refused to endorse military action, were infuriated that they learned of the ultimatum from the press. New Zealand's Prime Minister, Stuart Holland, publicly defended Britain, but wrote to Eden of his concern at Anglo-American conflict and the lack of British consultation with the Commonwealth. Australia's Prime Minister, Menzies, remained Eden's firmest supporter, but he asked Eden to 'make it [his] personal business to do everything possible to secure some broad basis of agreement with the US'.[18]

Yet Britain could have overcome these difficulties if military operations had quickly brought the collapse of the Egyptian Government or even control of the Suez Canal. Foster Dulles and his officials had threatened the Israelis with limited economic sanctions, including the suspension of economic aid, unless Israel withdrew from Egypt, but they had not decided upon any measures against Britain and France.[19] The British Minister in Washington, Coulson, noted: 'Most people (including Mr Murphy, the Deputy Undersecretary of State . . .) stress the need for a speedy outcome of our operation.'[20] In a draft letter of 1 November, written *after* the Security Council referred Suez to the General Assembly, Eisenhower advised Eden:

The very second you attain your minimum objectives. . . . I think you could probably ease tension greatly by doing the following. One, instantly call for a cease-fire in the area; two, clearly state your reasons for entering the Canal Zone; three, announce your intention to resume negotiations on the basis of the Six Principles agreed by the UN; four, state your intention to evacuate as quickly as the Israelis return to their own national territory and Egypt has announced her readiness to negotiate in good faith on the basis of the Six Principles.[21]

Eisenhower confirmed in a 1964 interview:

We assumed that, if the three nations did attack, they would all move at one time, and it would be over in almost twenty-four hours. . . . Had they done it quickly, we would have accepted it. . . . They could have taken over and then got out of there. There'd have been no great crisis in the world.[22]

Eisenhower's Staff Secretary, Andrew Goodpaster, concluded, 'We were waiting and waiting and nothing happened.'[23] The Dulles brothers agreed on 1 November that 'Nasser may be toppling because of the demolition of his Air Force and the defeat of his forces in the Sinai'. Allen Dulles thought Nasser's fall 'would benefit the US position if the President called for a cease-fire and offered mediation'.[24]

The Americans assumed that Britain, having risked the 'alliance' and condemnation by international opinion, was prepared to overwhelm Egypt quickly with the conventional use of ground troops. When Foster Dulles told Eisenhower of the ultimatum, the Secretary estimated that British and French troops would be in Egypt by 1 November. The President replied, 'Aren't they partially in now?' That evening, with no landing imminent, Eisenhower allegedly commented, 'I've just never seen Great Powers make such a complete mess and *botch* of things.'[25] An American military intelligence summary on 1 November, based on information from French military and intelligence sources, concluded:

Landing of French and UK troops in Canal Zone expected any moment. UK and France, with forces currently available, have capability of seizing key points Canal Area, including Port Said, Ismailia, and Suez, within 36 hours. They have capability securing control Canal Area, including establishing strong points east and west of Canal, within seven to ten days.[26]

As late as 2 November, the US Army Attaché in Cairo cabled: 'Troop landing in Egypt appears imminent, but timing and place unpredictable.'[27]

In fact, under REVISE, no troops were to be landed until Egyptian resistance was ended through bombing and psychological warfare, a process estimated to require ten days. The prerequisite for this, the neutralisation of the Egyptian air force, was quickly achieved despite technical problems that made RAF planes 'look almost Victorian' compared to their French counterparts. Within hours of the bombing on 31 October, most Egyptian planes on the ground were destroyed or forced to distant bases. REVISE's Air Force Headquarters reported: 'It appears likely that Phase II [the bombing of economic and military targets and psychological warfare] . . . can start sometime tomorrow [2 November].'[28]

Even Phase 1 was beset with political problems, however. Bombers despatched to attack Cairo West airfield were diverted, as American civilians were being evacuated along roads adjacent to the airfield. The attack against Cairo Radio was postponed because of fear of civilian casualties – the military thought that the main transmitter, Abu Zabal, located fifteen miles from Cairo, was in the centre of the city.[29] Most importantly, the military did not keep the Suez Canal open. The Egyptian blockship *Akka*, bombed by British aircraft, conveniently sank in the middle of the waterway. Within days, the Egyptians sank forty-eight more blockships, and Britain faced drastic fuel rationing and the heavy cost of oil purchases from the Western Hemisphere. The problem was compounded on 3 November when Syrian army troops, probably on Nasser's orders, demolished an Iraqi Petroleum Company pumping station.[30]

Meanwhile, the US Sixth Fleet hindered the Anglo-French carrier group. Aircraft repeatedly buzzed the ships, twice almost battling with British planes, and submarines shadowed the convoy. On 3 November, the Sixth Fleet's Commander assured the British that American submarines would remain on the surface and 'his aircraft [would] be more careful', but as late as the 5th, the British Chiefs of Staff feared that the Sixth Fleet would block access to Port Said.[31]

Finally, British commanders were plagued by Eden's failure to tell them of collusion. On 31 October, the French asked Admiral Grantham, the British Commander-in-Chief in the Mediterranean, to allow the French destroyer *Gazelle* to resupply Israeli troops and to transport Israeli wounded to hospitals in Israel. Curiously, Grantham, who had no executive responsibility in REVISE, approved the proposal without referring it to Keightley.[32] In Tel Aviv, REVISE's deputy air commander, General Brohon, supervised French collaboration with Israel, as French planes dropped jeeps, guns and ammunition, cigarettes, and jerricans of water to Israeli paratroopers. Mystère and F-84 fighters with French pilots operated from Israel with the markings of the Anglo-French force.[33] The cruiser *Georges Leygues* supported the Israeli advance by shelling Rafah on Sinai's northern coast. Another warship, *Kersaint*, damaged the Egyptian ship *Ibrahim el-Awal*, later captured by Israeli forces.[34]

Keightley belatedly discovered on 31 October that 'the French have established an effective liaison with the Israelis'. He informed the Chiefs of Staff, 'I would welcome direction at what stage or in what degree it is visualised we fight as the Allies of the Israelis.' Instructed by the Chiefs to warn the French against open co-operation with Israel, Keightley was surprised to learn from a French liaison officer 'that an agreement was made for certain help between governments and, if it is not honoured, the Israelis will publicise and exaggerate the agreement made'. After Keightley's political adviser, Ralph Murray, discovered that two Israeli officers had 'arrived at this headquarters in uniform under French auspices', Keightley ordered French officers not to allow further Israeli visits.[35]

Eden cabled Mollet on 1 November that the French actions were 'extremely embarrassing. . . . Nothing could do more harm to our role as peacemakers than to be identified in this way with one of the two parties.' Mollet told Ambassador Jebb that he would end the open Franco-Israeli co-operation, but problems remained. The British commanders probably were not told of Sèvres until Minister of Defence Head flew to Cyprus on 3 November. Moreover, French F-84s, operating from Israel on 4 November, destroyed eighteen Il-28 bombers, which had been moved to Luxor in central Egypt. On 8 November, two French squadrons were still with the Israeli air force.[36]

The downfall of REVISE, however, was its failure to implement Phase II, which was supposed 'to bring the Egyptians to the verge of surrender in a further six days'. Eden's failure to keep his military informed about the political situation and the subsequent limitations on operations was disastrous. From REVISE's headquarters, Air Chief Marshal E. C. Hudleston cabled the Air Ministry:

What a madhouse . . . Would help if we could be given [the] reason for apparently inexplicable decisions, for example, [the retraction of orders to bomb] Radio Cairo. . . . It would be interesting to have copy of ultimatum, our knowledge of which is still confined to BBC [broadcasts].[37]

The only aspect of Phase II that was fully implemented was the broadcasting of 'black' radio stations into Egypt. A typical item claimed:

Gamal Abdel Nasser promised a secret canal; he has brought war to the Canal. He promised the Egyptian people property and security; he has built a military machine at your expense and on your poverty; he promised the Egyptian people equality; he has given you dictatorship. He promised the Egyptian people peace; by provocation and defiance he has given you war.[38]

Even this tactic soon failed. The BBC Arabic Service station at Sharq el-Adna in Cyprus, requisitioned for government use on 30 October and renamed 'Voice of Britain', was rendered ineffective when its Arab staff left. Subsequently, three Arab employees were placed under house arrest after four attempts to sabotage the station and one attempt to make an unauthorised broadcast.[39]

The rest of the campaign was a non-starter. Bombing of oil tanks, telephone and telegraph systems, and railway lines, the precondition for the psychological campaign, was suspended by the Egypt Committee on 1

November. Ministers feared Arab retaliation against oil pipelines and long-term damage to the Egyptian economy as well as the effect on world opinion of heavy casualties. Cairo Radio was belatedly reclassified as a 'military' target, but it was not attacked until 2 November and was able to resume broadcasting within seventy-two hours. Canberra aircraft proved technically unable to drop leaflets and Air Force Headquarters would not risk 'losing valuable transport aircraft which were needed to mount the airborne assault'. Only one load of 500,000 leaflets was released, and two 'voice' aircraft were never used.[40]

Nasser's position was never threatened. Colonel Hassan Siyam, one of the dissident officers supported by MI6, allegedly asked his civilian conspirators to demand a meeting with Nasser, but they would not act until the military deposed Nasser. An MI6 officer later explained:

Some young Egyptian officers, who were strongly opposed to Nasser, had been scared and . . . special weapons had been buried at a convenient spot near Cairo. They were never used because certain circumstances essential to the operation did not materialise.

Just before the British bombed Egypt, a former member of the Revolutionary Command Council asked Nasser to surrender to the British Ambassador, but the President refused. The Chief of the General Staff, General Abdel Hakim Amer, called for a cease-fire, but Nasser, supported by the Minister of the Interior, Zacharia Mohieddin, and Wing Commander Hassan Latim Boghdadi, directed that all Egyptian units be withdrawn from the Sinai to defend against an Anglo-French invasion.[41]

On 2 November, the Egyptian President drove in an open-topped car to Friday prayers at Al-Azhar Mosque in Cairo and told the crowd, 'In Cairo I shall fight with you against any invasion. We shall fight to the last drop of our blood. We shall never surrender.' Messages on mobile transmitters announced that the US and sixty-four other nations had supported Egypt in the UN and urged, 'Take your arms and fight, kill your enemy wherever and whenever he appears.' Suleiman Hafez, a civilian leader who was not involved in the British-backed plots, finally contacted Amer and Boghdadi to ask that Nasser be replaced by his predecessor, General Mohammed Neguib, but Nasser resolved, over Amer's objections, to fight for Cairo until open resistance was useless and then to carry out a guerrilla war.[42]

Press Secretary Clark reported a 'curious peace' at 10 Downing Street, but others were not as complacent. At an informal meeting on 1 November, Kirkpatrick bleakly projected that Britain would have to leave the UN unless a quick remedy was found. Clark suggested that Britain accept a UN commander, and Lloyd agreed that UN troops might join the Anglo-French force. The meeting decided, however, that the UN could not act immediately, and Head reminded Ministers that the organisation was unlikely to adopt Britain's objective of overthrowing Nasser.[43]

The Minister of Fuel and Power, Aubrey Jones, told the Egypt Committee that oil consumption would have to be reduced by ten per cent in the next week to prepare for rationing. The Attorney-General, Reginald Manningham-Buller, reopened the issue of the invasion's legality, writing to Lloyd:

On what is known to me, I am unable to devise any argument which could purport to justify in international law either our demand that [Egypt], who had in no way threatened our nationals, should withdraw her forces from a part of her own territory which she is engaged in defending or the threat to occupy her territory by armed forces should she fail to accede to that demand.[44]

In the Foreign Office, junior officials considered mass resignation, and Assistant Undersecretary Beeley told his predecessor, Shuckburgh, that everyone except Kirkpatrick was 'equally depressed and astonished' by Anglo-French operations. Assistant Undersecretary of State Paul Gore-Booth informed Kirkpatrick, 'People are doing their duty but with a heavy heart and a feeling that, whatever our motives, we have terribly damaged our reputation.' Mountbatten said that 'he had spoken out against [the operations] up to the limit of what is possible and [he] was surprised that he was still in the job'.[45]

Most ominous was Macmillan's changing attitude. On 29 October, he told Treasury officials and the Bank of England that he was 'to remain firm and see the affair through', but $50 million in reserves was lost in the next forty-eight hours and the Suez Canal was blocked. 'The young Macmillan of the 1930s . . . , hat thrown in the air' gave way to a pessimist who told a colleague that the chances of success were '51 to 49'. He fretted about domestic support, complaining that people thought oil came out of taps and worrying that the US reaction 'was much worse than he had expected'.[46]

In the Commons, tension rose to breaking-point when Eden balked at answering Labour's question whether Britain was at war. Tempers flared, and the sitting was suspended for the first time since 1924. Clarissa Eden complained to Gaitskell's wife, 'Can you stand it?' Mrs Gaitskell replied coolly, 'The boys must express themselves.' Eden finally said that Britain was 'neither at war nor at peace', but he made a notable concession. Despite the doubts of the informal meeting that morning, he invited the UN to send a peace-keeping force to Egypt:

The first and urgent task is to separate [Egyptian and Israeli troops] and to stabilise the position. . . . If the UN were then willing to take over the physical task of maintaining peace in that area, no one would be better pleased than we.

Eden gambled that it would take days, if not weeks, to organise a force, and Britain and France could proceed with the invasion in the interim. The Opposition, awaiting UN developments, did not press its challenge, and the Government defeated a censure motion with a comfortable majority.[47]

After the Suez War ended on 6 November, British military commanders and Ministers who favoured the war claimed that Anglo-French forces needed no more than seventy-two hours to occupy the rest of the Suez Canal Zone. In fact, Britain had squandered her opportunity by 1 November. The Prime Minister firmly told the Cabinet on 24 October:

If . . . a military operation were undertaken against Egypt, its effect in other Arab countries would be serious. Unless it led to the early collapse of Colonel Nasser's regime. Both for this reason, and also because of the international pressures which would develop against our continuation of the operation, it must be quick and successful.[48]

However, to maintain the façade of 'peace-keeping', Eden ensured failure. He told his military nothing of collusion and prevented the launch of REVISE's main assault force, a minimum of nine days' sailing time from Egypt, until 27 October. Once the campaign of psychological warfare collapsed, ensuring that Nasser would not be overthrown, Britain's military action would be at the diplomatic mercy of the US and the UN. Keightley wrote ominously:

The devastation of Port Said is the price we must pay for changing our plans by elimination of Phase 11. Psychological warfare is now also most complicated as Nasser has cleverly bound up our attack with the Jews – and that is the only rallying point on which, probably, the whole nation and the whole Arab world are solidly behind him.[49]

24

Alliance Broken
1–4 November 1956

A t the National Security Council meeting on 1 November, the Americans had plenty of cause for anger at the British. Not only had the Administration concluded that Britain and France, failing to occupy the Canal Zone immediately, would continue to antagonise world opinion, but the attack upon Egypt was undermining American objectives in the Middle East, notably in Syria, and in Eastern Europe.

When the Council had met previously on 26 October, members thought that they were witnessing the long-awaited dissolution of the Soviet Empire and 'liberation' of Eastern European peoples. Polish leaders, despite Soviet opposition, had embarked upon a programme of political and economic reforms, and street demonstrations in Hungary had forced the withdrawal of Soviet troops.[1] However, when the protesters, encouraged by broadcasts from the CIA's Radio Free Europe, made new demands, including Hungary's withdrawal from the Warsaw Pact, the Soviet leadership ordered Soviet tanks to crush the uprising in Budapest. Robert Amory, the CIA's Deputy Director for Intelligence, called for tactical nuclear strikes in the Soviet Union, Poland and Romania, and Frank Wisner, head of the CIA's Directorate of Plans, sought the mobilisation of CIA-trained *émigrés*, supported by American forces. In the face of Anglo-French 'intervention' in Egypt, Allen Dulles vetoed action against the Soviet 'intervention'. He asked Foster Dulles, 'How can anything be done about the Russians, even if they suppress the revolt, when our own allies are guilty of exactly similar acts of aggression?'[2]

Anglo-French action also doomed implementation of OMEGA against Nasser. After months of planning, the CIA-backed coup in Syria, scheduled for 29 October, was foiled by the Israeli invasion of Egypt. Some American officials even suspected that Michel Ilyan, the chief CIA contact, postponed the coup from 25 to 29 October at the instigation of the British and the Iraqis, who would use the disorder created by the Israeli invasion of Egypt to control the coup and foster Iraqi-Syrian union. It was later alleged at the trial of the Anglo-Iraqi plotters that Ilyan had 'intervened with the Iraqis and had taken their word that there would be no assassinations, nor any cold murder, but that certain military and civilian personalities would simply be arrested'. A high-ranking American official summarised, 'We didn't know any of it, and we suspected that the British had betrayed us.'[3]

The following day, Foster Dulles told his brother, 'The conditions are such [that] it would be a mistake to try to pull [the coup] off.' Allen Dulles was not as conclusive: 'If the assets can be held together for a few days more without taking action, [the CIA] would much prefer it.'[4] Worse followed, however. While the American-backed conspiracy was not detected, the Anglo-Iraqi plot was discovered when the Syrian internal police intercepted two Druze leaders with hundreds of rifles and machine-guns, allegedly given to them by Iraq. Conspirators and leaders of the Partie Populaire Syrienne were arrested. Ilyan, taking no chances, fled to Lebanon with conspirators connected with Anglo-Iraqi planning. Eventually five defendants were sentenced to death. Eight were condemned *in absentia*, including Ilyan, PPS leader Ghassan Jedid, and the Iraqi Military Attaché in Damascus. The former dictator Adib Shishakli received a life sentence *in absentia*.[5]

Ilyan finally reached Turkey and told the British Ambassador, Sir James Bowker, in May 1957:

While the internal situation [in Syria] is very bad and full of danger for the whole area, it could be effectively changed and saved by an intervention from Iraq, and . . . the British could bring that intervention about if only they would let Nuri and certain key figures in Syria know in no uncertain terms they were in favour of it.

He was subsequently granted a visa to visit Britain.[6]

The most important consideration for the National Security Council was the General Assembly debate. The session could not be postponed until 2 November, as Foster Dulles hoped, because the United for Peace Resolution required that the Assembly debate occur within twenty-four hours of the Security Council meeting of 31 October. To protect American interests, Foster Dulles had to seize the initiative when the Assembly met at 5 p.m. He summarised:

For many years now, the US has been walking a tightrope between the effort to maintain our old and valued relations with our British and French allies on the one hand, and on the other try to assure ourselves of the friendship and understanding of the newly independent countries who have escaped from colonialism. . . . Unless we now assert and maintain this leadership, all of these newly independent countries will turn from us to the USSR. . . . We will be looked as for ever tied to British and French colonialist policies. In short, the US would survive or go down on the basis of the fate of colonialism if the US supports the French and British on the colonial issue. . . .

[Britain and France] have acted deliberately contrary to the clearest advice we could possibly give them. They have acted contrary both to principle and to what was expedient from the point of view of their own interests. . . . It is nothing less than tragic, at this very time, when we are on the point of winning an immense and long-hoped-for victory over Soviet colonialism in the Eastern Europe, [that] we should be forced to choose between following in the footsteps of Anglo-French colonialism in Asia and Africa or split our course away from theirs.

The Council divided on the methods to implement this policy. Foster Dulles tabled the State Department's agreed policy of limited sanctions against Israel. Eisenhower thought this 'was generally correct, though the sanctions . . . seemed a little mild'. Secretary of the Treasury Humphrey preferred no action until the UN formally identified aggressors, although he believed any steps against Israel should be accompanied by measures against Britain and France. Secretary of Defence Wilson echoed the sympathy of the Joint Chiefs of Staff for the use of force against Egypt.

Harold Stassen, the President's special representative for mutual aid, also accepted Anglo-French action, since 'the Suez Canal [was] an absolutely vital lifeline for the British'. Desperate to preserve the American position in the UN, Foster Dulles reminded Stassen 'with great warmth' that Britain and France would agree to a cease-fire only 'when they were thoroughly lodged in Egypt'. Unruffled, Stassen asked whether this type of cease-fire was not in the best interests of the US. Foster Dulles gave an 'emphatic negative', alleging, 'What the British and French had done was nothing but the straightforward old-fashioned variety of colonialism of the most obvious sort.'

The debate also raged over action in the UN, with Humphrey, Wilson and Stassen wanting only to ask the Assembly for a cease-fire and Foster Dulles protesting that a 'moderate' resolution by the US would produce a more extreme Soviet proposal. Eisenhower appeared indecisive, expressing at one moment his 'emphatic belief that these powers were going downhill with the kind of policy that they were . . . carrying out', then wondering what the argument was all about and asking Foster Dulles if the US needed 'to do anything beyond' a mild UN resolution. He even suggested that the US should 'continue to assist Britain [with military supplies] in order that she meet her NATO requirements', although he quickly added, 'If the British actually diverted these supplies to other purposes, we would have to consider such an action to represent another case of perfidious Albion.' Finally, the President proposed a draft 'of the mildest things we could do in an effort to block the introduction of a really mean and arbitrary resolution' while arms supplies to the Middle East were suspended.

Eisenhower's intervention did not resolve the issue. Foster Dulles argued, 'It is important that we suspend our economic assistance program to Israel,' but Humphrey and the Attorney-General, Herbert Brownell, continued to oppose economic sanctions against Tel Aviv alone. When Stassen insisted upon a resolution with no punitive measures, Foster Dulles, 'in some irritation', asked if Stassen meant to leave aggressors in possession of their gains. Stassen bluntly affirmed this view, 'for which there seemed to be some support among other members of the NSC'. Frustrated, Foster Dulles left to draft the American resolution. Eisenhower concluded ambiguously:

Of course, no one in the whole world really expected us to break off our long alliance with Great Britain and France. We must not permit ourselves to be blinded by the thought that *anything* we are going to do will result in our fighting with Great Britain and France. Such a course of action is simply unthinkable, and no one can possibly believe that we will do it.[7]

Ultimately, the Council's failure to agree strengthened Foster Dulles's hand. After the meeting, he obtained Eisenhower's consent to the suspension of military supplies and aid 'to the countries of the area of hostilities'. The US, to block any Soviet manoeuvre, would introduce a resolution in the UN General Assembly urging 'an immediate cease-fire' and withdrawal behind armistice lines and recommending that all UN members refrain 'from any acts which would delay or prevent the implementation of the present resolution'. Realising that State Department officials 'would like to go stronger', Foster Dulles told Secretary of Commerce Sinclair Weeks, 'We have other pressures for [Britain and France] but we don't want it publicly announced at the moment.'[8]

Just after midnight that evening, more than five hours into the Assembly debate, Foster Dulles took the podium. He began, 'No delegate could have spoken with a heavier heart than I speak with tonight', for the US had to act against 'three nations with whom it has ties, deep friendship, admiration, and respect'. However, failure 'to stop the fighting as rapidly as possible' would condemn the UN to 'apparent impotence'. He concluded, 'If, whenever a nation feels that it has been subjected to injustice, it should have the right to resort to force, . . . then I fear we should be tearing the Charter into shreds.'[9]

Sixty-four countries voted for the US resolution for an immediate cease-fire, and only five (Britain, France, Israel, Australia and New Zealand) voted against. Britain's last hope came from the Canadian Foreign Minister, Pearson, who had developed the idea of a UN Emergency Force (UNEF) even before the British and French bombed Egypt. Seizing upon Eden's statement of 1 November in the Commons that 'if the UN were . . . willing to take over the physical task of maintaining peace in the area, no one would be better pleased than we', he and Foster Dulles agreed that the Secretary would welcome the idea when moving the adjournment of the Assembly.[10]

The French, realising that US and UN pressure would soon halt REVISE, sought an immediate invasion of Egypt. On 31 October, Anglo-French planners had drafted Operation OMELETTE for the occupation of Port Said by paratroopers as early as 3 November. REVISE's commanders argued about the plan for two days until French pressure prevailed, and Pineau, supported by Generals Ely and Challe, obtained the British Cabinet's agreement. At the same time, the Cabinet agreed to notify the UN that Britain and France would transfer 'police responsibility' to the UNEF when it arrived in Egypt. Butler cited domestic political reasons, while Lloyd warned of American oil sanctions which might force Britain 'to occupy Kuwait and Qatar, the only suppliers of oil who were not members of the UN'. He concluded, 'We could not hope to avoid serious difficulties with the Arab states for more than a very short time longer, certainly not for as long as it would take us to complete an opposed occupation of Egypt.'[11]

Pineau, distressed with the façade of co-operation with the UN, proposed that, simultaneously with OMELETTE, Israeli troops advance to the Suez Canal's east bank. The British responded, with 'outraged indignation', that Israel would violate the provisions of the Anglo-French ultimatum, collusion would be exposed, and the pretext for the landing of British and French 'peace-keepers' would be ruined. Pineau complained:

The Prime Minister is no Churchill. He has neither the tenacity nor the steel nerves. The test, instead of strengthening him, exhausts him. It is not yet a 'breakdown', but we are not far from it.[12]

The Cabinet, in a later meeting on 2 November, rejected overt co-operation with Israel and snubbed Pineau by suspending British arms exports to Tel Aviv, but they agreed with France's essential condition that formation of UNEF should not halt an Anglo-French landing. Britain would stop military action 'as soon as . . . it was agreed that, until the UN force was constituted, detachments of Anglo-French troops should be stationed on Egyptian territory between the two combatants'. The Chiefs of Staff cabled Keightley: '[It] has become of great political importance in relation to activities in the UN Assembly to carry out such a drop before midday November 4.'[13]

OMELETTE collapsed almost immediately. British photo-reconnaissance on 2 November confirmed the withdrawal of Egyptian armour from Sinai to the Canal Zone and the reinforcement of Port Said's defences. An intelligence summary noted: 'Anti-aircraft and coastal artillery positions can be expected to stand firm and continue fighting except after intense direct air attack or accurate bombardment.' Keightley, who had always feared the resistance of Egyptian armour, sent no less than four cables to London, concluding, 'Any chances of an easy entry into Port Said are removed. . . . The probing operation will be pointless and impossible to carry out and we shall have to stick to our full assault operation on 6th November.'[14]

The Chiefs of Staff were divided. General Templer believed that the Egyptians would not fight, especially if they were told that Britain would attack with 'all possible weapons'. Mountbatten was concerned, however, that OMELETTE could not be implemented without considerable damage and loss of life. Keightley's anxiety finally prevailed, and OMELETTE was replaced by Operation SIMPLEX, in which paratroopers would drop on Gamil airfield outside Port Said and then advance upon the town. If there was strong Egyptian opposition, the paratroopers would hold Gamil and wait for relief by the amphibious landing. The operation was put at nine hours' notice from 5 a.m. on 4 November.[15]

Tired of waiting for the landing, Eisenhower complained to close friends about Anglo-French folly, writing:

If one has to have a fight, then that is that, but I don't see the point in getting into a fight to which there can be no satisfactory end and in which the whole world believes you are playing the part of the bully, and you do not even have the firm backing of your entire people.[16]

Pineau, seeking American support, told the story of collusion to Ambassador Dillon and spoke of 'French intelligence that the Soviets plan military intervention through a Syrian base'.[17] Neither ploy worked. Admiral Radford, Allen Dulles and the State Department 'strongly discounted the credibility' of Soviet intervention, and Foster Dulles was angered by Pineau's revelations. When Lodge told the Secretary that the British and French said 'there [would] be a bad impression at home if we [were] in a hurry to get them on the dock [in the UN], and drag on Russia' over the crushing of the Hungarian revolution, Foster Dulles snapped, 'It is a mockery for them to come in with bombs falling over Egypt and denounce the Soviet Union for perhaps doing something that is not quite as bad.'[18]

A cruel twist of fate finally doomed British hopes of American sympathy. Early on 3 November, Foster Dulles was taken to hospital. Tests revealed that he was suffering from cancer of the colon, and he had no part in American policy-making for the rest of the Suez War. Although Foster Dulles had taken the lead in condemning the British in the UN, primarily to prevent the Soviets seizing the initiative, he refrained from private measures against London. In his absence, pro-British officials like Wilson or Stassen were ineffective or had little influence, while Humphrey, who was unwilling to help Britain, was increasingly important because of his personal friendship with Eisenhower. More importantly, the Acting Secretary of State, Herbert Hoover Jr, had no love for the British after battles over Saudi Arabian oil concessions, Iran and Buraimi, and his opinion was shared by officials such as Assistant Secretary William Rountree, who was responsible for Middle Eastern affairs. Their sentiments were reflected by Vice-President Richard Nixon in a campaign speech on 2 November:

In the past the nations of Asia and Africa have always felt we would, when the pressure was on, side with the policies of the British and French Governments in relation to the once colonial areas. For the first time in history we have shown independence of Anglo-French policies towards Asia and Africa.[19]

On 3 November, Chester Cooper, the CIA liaison with Britain's Joint Intelligence Committee, was telephoned from Washington by Robert Amory, the Deputy Director of Intelligence, who said:

Tell your friends to comply with the God-damn ceasefire or go ahead with the God-damn invasion. Either way, we'll back them up if they do it fast. What we can't stand is their God-damn hesitation, waltzing while Hungary is burning.

Cooper told the Joint Intelligence Committee to cease fire or proceed with an immediate landing, adding, 'I'm not speaking without instructions.'[20]

By 9 a.m., London time, Amory's words were superseded by Foster Dulles's illness. Eden later received an account of the American attitude from the State Department's Legal Adviser, Herman Phleger:

They knew well enough that we intended in the last resort to take direct action. They were pained that we did not take them into our confidence about the meeting that took place in secret with the French and Israelis in Paris, but they assumed that once we had decided on action it would be swift and decisive. They foresaw that there would be a good deal of vociferous comment in the UN and elsewhere, but they calculated that this would not come to a head until our action had been effective.

In the event our military plan took far more time to carry through than they had allowed for and public opinion had got highly worked up not only in the UN but also elsewhere, including the US with an Election in progress. Consequently it no longer seemed practical for the US to stand aside until we had finished the job and then use their influence in the tidying-up operation.[21]

The Egypt Committee tried to delay the Americans by promising that Britain would cease military action when Egypt *and* Israel accepted the UNEF *if* the UN promised to maintain the force until the Suez Canal and Arab-Israeli disputes were settled. Dixon warned, however, that Lodge was 'quite clear' that Eisenhower was 'very cool' about these conditions.[22]

Moreover, General Keightley now opposed even a limited paratroop drop. After the Egypt Committee dismissed a proposal to drop paratroops at Haifa, Israel, with an advance through Israeli-held Sinai upon the Canal, some Ministers argued that SIMPLEX should proceed, as there was little more than one Egyptian brigade at Port Said and no reason to think that the Egyptians would fight any better than they had against the Israelis. Others emphasised the necessity of limiting civilian casualties. It was finally agreed that Minister of Defence Head and General Templer should consult Keightley in Cyprus while the drop on Gamil airfield was postponed.[23]

That afternoon, in a rare Saturday sitting of the Commons, the Opposition, buoyed by the UN call for a cease-fire, shouted Lloyd down. Eden accepted the UNEF *in principle*, but refused to halt the invasion, prompting Gaitskell to charge, 'What [Britain] did was to go in and help the burglar and shoot the householder.' As the Prime Minister left the chamber, the entire Labour front bench rose and called for his resignation. Accusations of 'murderers' were launched, and MPs nearly came to blows.[24]

Undaunted, Eden broadcast to the nation that evening. He portrayed Anglo-French operations as a 'police action' *in support* of UN objectives and recalled his career as 'a man of peace, a League of Nations man, a United Nations man'. The following morning, he noted that the newspapers were not unfavourable and that more than a hundred telegrams supported his speech. After photo-reconnaissance revealed that Egyptian defences around Port Said were not as extensive as Keightley feared, the Commander-in-Chief agreed with Head on an assault by Anglo-French paratroopers upon Port Said and the nearby town of Port Fuad on the morning of 5 November. The Egypt Committee accepted the plan, codenamed TELESCOPE, at 12.30 p.m. on 4 November.[25]

The Government, however, was now pressed by its own constituents. While the *Daily Express*, *Daily Mail* and *Daily Telegraph* supported Eden, 'centrist' publications such as the *Economist* turned against the war. The editor of *The Times*, William Haley, who knew of collusion from his political editor, Iveragh Macdonald, quoted Churchill in a leader of 2 November:

I hold it perfectly justifiable to deceive the enemy, even if, at the same time, your own people are for a while misled. There is one thing, however, which all must never do, and that is mislead your ally.

Haley concluded, 'On Britain and America's ability to trust each other, even in disagreement, the peace of the world depends.' The *Observer* threw down the gauntlet to the Prime Minister: 'We had not realised that our Government was capable of such folly and such crookedness. . . . In our view, there is one essential: Anthony Eden must go.'[26]

Asked by a Gallup poll of 1–2 November, 'Do you think we were right or wrong to take military action against Egypt?', thirty-seven per cent replied yes, forty-four per cent replied no, and nineteen per cent had no opinion. The Conservative Party Chairman, Oliver Poole, asserted that, while a majority of Conservatives backed the Government, a 'liberal' element of the country was strongly opposed and mobilising itself under the slogan, 'Law, not War'.[27]

More than thirty thousand anti-Government protesters gathered in Trafalgar Square on 4 November to hear Labour's Aneurin Bevan charge, 'Either Mr Eden is lying or he is too stupid to be Prime Minister', and Downing Street was 'closed to the public because of the riotous meeting'.[28] Clarissa Eden, who was present, incognito, at the rally, recalled the presence of counter-demonstrators for the Government, but Chester Cooper, monitoring events for the CIA, later wrote: 'Lady Eden was right about the presence of people carrying pro-Eden signs and hecklers, but the police removed them from the square when they appeared to be in danger of being drawn and quartered by the angry crowd.'[29] The Prime Minister, recalling the event, relied upon a letter from a London bus driver for support:

[You have] done the only thing possible – my opinion and also that of a great number of fellow bus employees – only a small proportion of London's multitudes – but if a bus driver agrees – he must be right – I personally thank God we've got one man who is not afraid to do the right thing. As regards the rioting of the other evening – as I was on a bus (driving) right in the middle of it – I saw possibly more than most people – 80 per cent of the crowd were of foreign extraction so there was no true consensus of opinion and can be ignored.[30]

Ironically, the Cabinet convened in emergency session as the rally was in full cry. Adverse developments at the UN had jeopardised the Anglo-French airdrops, approved only six hours earlier. Dixon cabled the previous evening, before yet another Assembly debate:

As things now stand, we have no chance of getting a fair hearing for our ideas unless my French colleague and I are in a position to announce . . . that Anglo-French forces are suspending all further military activities until we know whether the UN are prepared to deal with the whole situation effectively.

Early on the morning of 4 November, the Assembly adopted an Afro-Asian resolution asking the Secretary-General to arrange a cease-fire within twelve hours. The Egypt Committee, at 12.30 p.m., agreed 'to go as far as possible' towards accepting the purpose of a Canadian resolution which asked Hammarskjøld to prepare the plans for the UNEF within forty-eight hours.[31]

Distressing news then came from an unexpected source: Israel. Ben-Gurion always suspected that the British might renege on the Sèvres Protocol, and London's insistence on acting as a 'peace-keeper' of the Suez Canal, rather than as a co-belligerent with Israel, added to Israeli fears. Eden's statement to the Commons on 1 November that Britain and France would ensure Israeli withdrawal from the Sinai after Egypt's *fedayeen* bases were destroyed incensed Ben-Gurion, as did Lloyd's comments to Ambassador Elath that Britain could not be identified with collusion because of her relationships with Arab states.

Shortly after midnight in the Assembly debate of 3/4 November, the Israeli delegate, Abba Eban, said that 'Israel agreed to a cease-fire, provided a similar announcement was forthcoming from Egypt'. The Israeli army had occupied almost all of the Sinai Peninsula and would take its last objective, Sharm el-Sheikh, within hours. The Egyptian threat from the Gaza Strip had been cleared, the Egyptian army overwhelmed and most of its Soviet equipment destroyed, and the Gulf of Aqaba and Straits of Tiran opened to Israeli shipping. Ideally, the Israelis would have liked Britain and France to open the Suez Canal to Israeli ships, but they were frustrated by repeated delays in the Anglo-French landing.[32]

Having approved Operation TELESCOPE, the Egypt Committee met again at 3.30 p.m. to consider the Israeli news and other developments. Ambassador Wright again cabled that Britain's position in Iraq was untenable unless Britain overtly condemned Israeli aggression. When Lloyd added that oil sanctions against Britain, France and Israel were being discussed in New York, Macmillan allegedly exclaimed, 'Oil sanctions! That finishes it.' The meeting divided between Ministers who wished to delay TELESCOPE and the main landing for at least twenty-four hours and those who felt that a further delay 'would make it politically more difficult to resume military operations'. Finally, the Committee agreed to refer the matter to an emergency Cabinet.[33]

Eden gave the Cabinet three options: proceeding with the occupation of Port Said, delaying the airdrops for twenty-four hours, or deferring action indefinitely. Twelve Ministers wanted to proceed. Four – Butler, Kilmuir, Heathcoat-Amory and possibly Macmillan – voted for the delay, while Salisbury, probably swayed by the UN attitude, Buchan-Hepburn and Monckton, who had remained in the Cabinet as Paymaster-General, favoured an indefinite deferral. The three Service Ministers, asked for their views, also divided: the First Lord of the Admiralty, Lord Hailsham, wanted to continue operations, but the Secretary of State for Air, Nigel Birch, favoured a delay and the Secretary of State for War, John Hare, preferred indefinite postponement.

All Ministers except Monckton agreed to support the majority decision, but Eden was disconcerted by the significant vote against immediate operations. Unwilling to proceed without a clearer mandate, Eden took Butler, Macmillan and Salisbury aside and allegedly said that 'if they wouldn't go on, then he would have to resign'. Butler replied that 'no one else could form a Government', a statement endorsed by Macmillan and Salisbury. Eden temporarily adjourned the Cabinet and despatched an emergency cable to General Keightley, asking if a twenty-four-hour delay in TELESCOPE could be arranged. Keightley replied that this was possible, but it would shatter troop morale, allow Egypt to build up her defences and horrify the French.[34]

Eden was waiting for the Israelis to retract their agreement to a cease-fire. Bombarded by British and French messages, the Israeli Foreign Ministry finally instructed Eban that Israel would cease fire if Egypt halted her *fedayeen* attacks, ended her economic boycott against Israel and the ban on Israeli transit through the Suez Canal, and terminated the 'state of war' that existed since 1948, i.e. signed a peace settlement. The Israelis realised that Egypt would not accept these conditions, since they implied that the Israeli invasion was justified and allowed Israel to maintain her occupation of the Sinai. When Eden informed the Cabinet, 'Everyone laughed & banged the table with relief – except Birch and Monckton, who looked glum.'[35]

Meanwhile, Gaitskell broadcast in response to Eden's speech of 3 November. Labelling British troops as aggressors, Gaitskell called for the Prime Minister's resignation and offered to support any Conservative successor who complied with the UN resolutions. The broadcast aroused controversy at home and in the Mediterranean, where servicemen listened on the BBC World Service. Eden thought that the BBC should never have broadcast the speech, and the Government renewed its pressure upon the Corporation. An ad hoc committee on overseas broadcasting, with Lord Privy Seal Butler as Chairman, had already recommended that a Foreign Office liaison officer should work with the BBC because 'the views of HMG on specific issues of major importance often receive insufficient emphasis in broadcasts to other countries'. While Press Secretary Clark's claim that Eden 'instructed the Lord Chancellor to prepare an instrument which would take over the BBC [Overseas Services] altogether and subject it wholly to the will of the Government' cannot be verified, P. F. Grey, the supervising official for the Foreign Office's Information Research Department, told the BBC that it was 'not in the national interest to include in the Arabic Services news bulletins virtually identical with those now appearing in the Home Service'. The Corporation was instructed not to broadcast news bulletins on the Arabic Service for the near future.[36]

Despite the furor, Gaitskell's speech failed to mobilise a rebellion against Eden, as only eight Conservative MPs declined to support the Government and few Tory voters turned against the Prime Minister. The greatest threat to the Prime Minister was still the US. Desperate for American support, Eden prepared Eisenhower for the British airdrops:

If we had allowed things to drift, everything would have gone from bad to worse. Nasser would have become a kind of Moslem Mussolini, and our friends in Iraq, Jordan, Saudi Arabia, and even Iran would gradually have been brought down. His efforts would have spread westwards, and Libya and North Africa would have been brought under his control.

He concluded with the plea:

The future of all of us depends on the closest Anglo-American co-operation. It has of course been a grief to me to have had to make a temporary breach into it which I cannot disguise, but I know that you are a man of big enough heart and vision to take up things again on the basis of fact.[37]

The appeal was futile. When the President asked on 3 November if he should contact Eden 'to keep the channel open', Hoover, Rountree and Phleger insisted that the President wait for the UNEF's establishment. Eisenhower drafted a reply which indicated that he would accept Anglo-French entry into the Canal Zone, but he never sent the message.[38]

Having passed the resolution on 2 November for a cease-fire and Israeli withdrawal and repeated the demand on the early morning of 4 November, the General Assembly was scheduled to discuss the Canadian initiative for the UNEF on the evening of the 4th. The Foreign Office instructed Dixon that he should welcome the UNEF, but

Britain could not delay a landing because 'the Israeli forces and the Egyptians may be in close conflict at any point'. Dixon desperately asked Secretary-General Hammarskjøld to delay the Assembly's debate of the Canadian resolution, but Hammarskjøld merely extended the time limit for a cease-fire to 5 a.m., London time, 5 November.[39]

Kirkpatrick finally confirmed to Dixon after the long Cabinet meeting of 4 November that his reply 'will NOT make your task easier' as the landing would proceed. The cable was not deciphered quickly enough to reach Dixon before the Assembly debate, and the British delegate endured the discussion with no idea of Britain's position. At 12.15 a.m., the General Assembly voted 57–0, with Britain, France, Israel and sixteen other countries abstaining, to reaffirm its call for a cease-fire and to authorise the UNEF's creation.[40]

Britain and France were now alone.

25

Victory and Defeat
5–6 November 1956

A s the General Assembly voted on the Canadian resolution, 780
British paratroops landed at Gamil airfield and 487 French
paratroops occupied two bridges on the Canal at Raswa. Egyptian
resistance was stiff. Moreover, because the British, with no tail-loading
aircraft, had to use side-loading planes, no artillery could be dropped and
the paratroops were overloaded with supplies. Casualties were minimal,
however, because of close and intense air support, the high standards of
tactics and leadership, poor shooting by the Egyptians, and the sandy
ground, which reduced the force of explosions. Gamil was taken in two
hours and the edge of Port Said was reached in early afternoon. After a
second drop of 500 men, the French captured Port Fuad.[1]

Negotiations for Port Said's surrender began at 5 p.m. To isolate Port
Said from Cairo, British troops cut telephone wires, but they did not know
that there was an underwater cable to Cairo via Alexandria. Nasser
instructed the Governor of Port Said to refuse surrender, but Eden
believed, because of a mistranslation in communications, that Port Said
had surrendered. He announced this to the Commons, only to be
embarrassed a few hours later when Nasser issued a denial.[2]

The airdrops were a clear military success, but they were ultimately
judged on political grounds. Dixon cabled: 'We are inevitably being
placed in the same low category as the Russians in their bombing of
Budapest.' Eisenhower noted impending oil shortages in Britain and
France and told Hoover and Phleger, 'The purposes of peace and stability
would be served by not being too quick in attempting to render extraordinary assistance.'[3]

In London, Cabinet Secretary Brook allegedly told Press Secretary

Clark 'that no intelligent man could support the [British] policy'. Clark stated his intention to resign when the crisis eased, while Edward Boyle, junior Minister at the Treasury, joined Nutting in leaving the Government. On 5 November, senior Foreign Office members gathered for an 'explanation' of events in which, according to Assistant Undersecretary Gore-Booth, 'Kirkpatrick did his best to answer questions to which there was no answer.'[4] Assistant Undersecretary Ross recalled:

Kirkpatrick had only two things to say. One was that there was a complaint about lack of information: the fact was that there had not been any. The other was that the Foreign Office had not been consulted. Kirkpatrick said that Ministers were not obliged to consult their departments. . . . They expect the best advice, but to assume that Ministers have to rush to their departments for advice, we must get that out of our heads. That was the end of the meeting.[5]

Britain also contended with a new threat of Soviet action. Preoccupied with events in Hungary, the Soviets had previously limited involvement in Suez to support for Egypt in the UN. Syrian President Quwwatli, visiting Moscow when Israel invaded Egypt, asked Khrushchev to send aircraft and 'volunteer' aircrews to Egypt, but was refused. Soviet technicians were withdrawn from Egypt.[6]

On 5 November, the Soviets launched a three-pronged 'diplomatic' offensive. Firstly, Soviet Premier Bulganin sent notes to Britain, France and Israel hinting at military action. The message to Eden pondered:

In what position would Britain have found herself if she herself had been attacked by more powerful states possessing every kind of modern destructive weapon? And there are countries now which need not have sent a navy or air force to the coasts of Britain but could have used other means, such as rocket technique. . . . We are fully determined to crush the aggressors and restore peace in the East through the use of force. We hope at this critical moment you will display due prudence and draw the correct conclusions from this.

Secondly, Bulganin asked Eisenhower 'to join their forces in the UN for the adoption of decisive measures to put an end to the aggression'. Thirdly, Foreign Minister Shepilov submitted a draft resolution to the Security Council demanding that Britain, France and Israel cease fire within twelve hours and withdraw from Egypt within three days.[7]

No one, with the possible exception of Israeli leaders, believed that the Soviets would defend Egypt with nuclear weapons. The Air Ministry was assured by military intelligence that Soviet rockets could not reach Britain since the Soviets did not have launch sites in East Germany or Poland. It was feared, however, that the Soviets would land equipment and 'volunteers' in Egypt via Syria. Bulganin's note arrived in London at

2 a.m. on 6 November, hindering Eden's sleep and causing 'a bad night' for the Prime Minister's Office.[8]

In Washington, Eisenhower consulted Hoover, Phleger and his Chief of Staff, Sherman Adams. The US Ambassador in Moscow, Charles Bohlen, believed that the Soviets would not deliberately start a Third World War, but he thought that some form of Soviet assistance to Egypt was likely and that the Soviets might invade Iran. Although the Joint Chiefs of Staff believed 'that the Soviets could not immediately mount a major military operation in the Middle East', Hoover also expressed 'great concern' that the Soviets might send troops into Syria. The President, warning that 'the Soviets are scared and furious, and there is nothing more dangerous than a dictatorship in this state of mind', rejected Bulganin's suggestion of Soviet-American military intervention: 'In other words, we should give the Soviets a clear warning [to stay out of Egypt].' An observer added that Eisenhower hinted at the use of atomic weapons: 'If those fellows start something, we may have to hit them, and if necessary, with *everything* in the bucket.'[9]

For the British, the Soviet threat at least restored a modicum of Anglo-American co-operation between the intelligence services. Chester Cooper told the CIA that he would not discuss the Soviet threat with the Joint Intelligence Committee on 6 November unless the American embargo on intelligence to Britain was lifted. Last-minute instructions from Washington satisfied Cooper's demand.[10]

The main Anglo-French landing by amphibious craft and helicopter proceeded at dawn on 6 November. The French, fearing an imminent cease-fire, also planned a parachute assault on Qantara, thirty miles down the Canal, but British commanders, fearing Egyptian resistance, withdrew their consent shortly before the landings. At 11 a.m., it was again reported that Port Said had surrendered, and the British commanders, Stockwell, Durnford-Slater and Barnett, and the French land commander, General Beaufre, set out for shore in a small boat. A sniper's bullet, which passed between Stockwell and Durnford-Slater, convinced the commanders that perhaps the report of surrender was premature, and the town did not capitulate until late afternoon. By the time Anglo-French forces prepared to 'break out' of Port Said and Port Fuad, proceeding along the causeway to Suez at the southern end of the Canal, the British Cabinet had agreed to a cease-fire, to take effect at 5 p.m., London time.[11]

When the Cabinet gathered at 9.45 a.m., Lloyd set out three considerations for Ministers. Firstly, 'it was now urgently necessary that [Britain] should regain the initiative in bringing hostilities to an end while there was an opportunity to carry with us the more moderate sections of opinion in the General Assembly'. Secondly, 'it was equally important that we should shape our policy in such a way as to enlist the maximum sympathy and support from the US Government'. Finally, Britain had to 'maintain [her] position against the Soviet Union' and 'not appear to be yielding in face of Soviet threats'. Ministers favouring a cease-fire added:

[We] must reckon with the possibility of a Soviet invasion of Syria or some other area in the Middle East, and possibly a direct Soviet attack on the Anglo-French forces in the Canal area. It was also probable that the other Arab States in the Middle East would come actively to the aid of Egypt and that the United Nations would be alienated to the point of imposing collective measures, including oil sanctions, against the French and ourselves.

Ministers against a cease-fire, notably Head, Colonial Secretary Lennox-Boyd, and the President of the Board of Trade, Thorneycroft, noted the 'risk that an effective international force would never be established in the Canal area and . . . we should appear to have fallen short of that effective occupation of the Canal area which we had publicly declared to be one of our objectives'. It was finally agreed, however, that

in order to regain the initiative and to re-establish relations with those members of the United Nations who were fundamentally in sympathy with our aims, [Britain] should agree, subject to the concurrence of the French Government, to stop further military operations.[12]

The official reason for the cease-fire was that Britain and France brought peace through their operations, as Israel, after the capture of Sharm el-Sheikh on 5 November, informed the UN that she would stop fighting.[13] In fact, the stated goal of restoring peace between Egypt and Israel was always a mask for the Anglo-French goals of seizing control of the Canal and removing Nasser from power. Britain spectacularly failed to do this, suffering a week of humiliation at the UN and division at home.

Three factors were significant in the decision to cease fire. The first was American pressure upon the weak pound. In the first week of November, $85 million of the foreign reserves, almost five per cent of the total, was lost. The estimated annual bill for Western Hemisphere oil, replacing that lost from the Suez Canal's blockage and the demolition of the pipeline in Syria, was more than $800 million. At the present rate of depletion, the reserves would be exhausted in early 1957. Eden later summarised:

The fall of sterling . . . , apart from Indian and Chinese operations intended to weaken the pound, came mainly from New York. Harold [Macmillan] told me he had no doubt that this was encouraged by Washington. I would also think this so. We were therefore faced with the alternatives, a run on sterling and the loss of our gold and dollar reserves till they fell way below the safety margin . . . or make the best we could of UN 'takeover' and salvage what we could.[14]

No available evidence confirms that the US sponsored the run against the pound, although Foster Dulles and Eisenhower both considered economic measures to stop Anglo-French action. The Americans did not have to sabotage the pound to influence Britain, however; they merely had to refuse to support it. If Secretary of the Treasury Humphrey did not press American banks and investors to trade pounds for dollars, he certainly did not encourage them to hold sterling. When Macmillan belatedly tried to obtain finance from the International Monetary Fund, Humphrey refused to endorse the request. Even a German plan for accelerated repayment of debts to Britain was opposed by the US Treasury.[15]

Moreover, the Americans refused to implement the plan to divert oil supplies to Britain. As early as 31 October, the Foreign Office cabled the British Embassy in Washington that it was 'extremely urgent' that talks with the US on oil supplies 'be taken up again as soon as possible', but the Americans refused to consider activation of the Middle East Emergency Committee. The British Minister in Washington, Coulson, was refused a meeting on the subject until the morning of 6 November and Assistant Secretary Rountree then said that the Americans were still considering the matter.[16]

By 6 November, Macmillan was near panic. Humphrey told him 'that only a cease-fire by midnight would secure US support' of British financial measures. The Chancellor told Lloyd before the Cabinet 'that, in view of the financial and economic pressures, we must stop' and then informed Ministers that, without a cease-fire, '[He] could not be responsible for Her Majesty's Exchequer. . . . If sanctions were imposed on us, the country was finished.'[17] A calmer Macmillan later told William Haley, the editor of *The Times*, 'All politics, especially international politics, was a game of poker, but the golden rule of the good poker player was [that] the moment he knew he had no more chips, he gave up the game.'[18]

Eden, Macmillan and Lloyd denied, with hindsight, that the Soviet threat influenced their decision, but Moscow's possible intervention in Syria was prominent in the Cabinet's discussion. The British Ambassador, William Hayter, reported that the Soviets might take 'some violent independent action' and that it was 'vitally necessary to get into step with the US again immediately' to keep Moscow 'from committing dangerous acts of folly'. Eden allegedly read the telegram at 6.30 a.m. and said, 'Those [Soviet] threats, they're just twaddle,' but others were not so sure. The Iraqi royal family told Wright that three Soviet warships had entered the Mediterranean from Romania and eighty Soviet bombers had flown into Syria. Keightley was concerned about an air attack upon Cyprus, ordering 'all airfields . . . at the maximum state of preparedness' and 'the greatest possible dispersion of aircraft'. Allen Dulles reported to Eisenhower that the Soviets had told Egypt that 'they [would] "do something"', and a Special National Intelligence Estimate concluded that, although Soviet forces would not be employed 'on a large scale in the Eastern Mediterranean', the Soviets would furnish military aid and probably send volunteers. The President authorised 'high-reconnaissance in the area', with U-2 'flights over Syria and Israel'.[19]

According to MI6 official Peter Wright, the Soviets used the Egyptian Embassy in London to convince Britain of their intention of intervening. In mid-1956, MI5 'tapped' the Egyptian Embassy's cypher machine, and GCHQ in Cheltenham broke the cypher. Throughout the Suez crisis, British intelligence services read the Embassy's traffic, including an account of 'a meeting between the Soviet Foreign Minister and the Egyptian Ambassador in which the Russians outlined their intentions to mobilise aircraft in preparation for a confrontation with Britain'. Wright claimed that this information 'convinced the Joint Intelligence Committee that the Soviet Union were indeed serious in their threat . . . [and] did as much as anything to prompt Eden into withdrawal'.

Wright believed that the Soviets discovered the British 'tap' on the Egyptian cypher machine, but left it in place to feed information to the British that Moscow was serious about intervening. Nasser later told the US Ambassador, Raymond Hare, that Bulganin sent him a message offering aid, but he claimed that he decided it was preferable for Egypt to suffer further losses rather than risk a Third World War through Soviet intervention. Alternatively, the Soviets might have been feeding 'disinformation' to indicate to London that they would act, when, in fact, they had no intention of doing so.[20]

Ironically, the possibility of Soviet intervention was dismissed by Whitehall *after* the decision to cease fire. Although the Americans still refused to release their detailed estimate of Soviet intentions to the British, Cooper told the Joint Intelligence Committee at 10 a.m. on 6 November, as the Cabinet was meeting, that American intelligence indicated that the Soviets would not act. A general alert was not ordered for US forces, although Eisenhower authorised precautionary measures, including increased readiness of the Strategic Air Command, reinforcement of American fleets in the Atlantic, the Far East and the Persian Gulf, and the stationing of an air task force at the US base at Adana, Turkey.[21] The Chiefs of Staff informed Keightley at 4.42 p.m., '[We] do not consider Russian intervention likely.' The Foreign Office concluded that the Soviets would not unilaterally send forces to Syria, although they might do so under UN cover.[22]

Finally, the Cabinet faced continuing UN pressure. Dixon protested throughout 5 November that 'bombing' in support of the landings was upsetting the Assembly. The Royal Navy had technically refrained from bombardment, but fighter aircraft were strafing the Egyptians and the Navy's use of ground support fire may have differed little in effect from bombing.[23] When Eden called New York at 8.30 the next morning, Dixon said that he 'thought that he could hold on at the UN until the end of the week'. However, in Cabinet discussion, Lloyd and other Ministers cited UN opposition as a reason to cease fire.[24]

Eden wrote in January 1957: 'We and the French have been compelled by a combination of the US and the Soviet Union, acting inside and outside the UN, to withdraw from Port Said before we could ensure the clearance of the Canal.' In the end, however, the American position was the dominant influence, for US support would have removed all obstacles to continued Anglo-French action. Britain's economy would have been sustained by loans from the International Monetary Fund and the World Bank and by Western Hemisphere oil supplies. The Soviets would have been deterred by an American warning against intervention, and the US, with her UN allies, could have delayed, if not prevented, the passage of Assembly resolutions. The day after the cease-fire, Eden summarised:

It is clear we cannot now carry this through alone with France. We *must* now get US support. . . . Our aim would be to get them to tackle an Anglo-US policy for a long-term settlement in the Middle East.[25]

After the Cabinet, Eden phoned Mollet, who was in a meeting with the West German Chancellor, Konrad Adenauer. The French Prime Minister begged for two more days to seize the rest of the Canal, but Eden said that Britain could not withstand American pressure on the pound. When Mollet presented Eden's call to halt operations, the French Cabinet was far from united. Pineau and Bourges-Maunoury were ready to proceed with the Israelis, arguing that, with the British withdrawal from the operation, Israel had been released from her pledge not to cross the Suez Canal. Meanwhile, the French military discussed measures 'for liquidating Nasser', and General Gilles, the commander of the French paratroops, suggested seizure of the Canal by Israeli troops in French uniform.

Other French Ministers argued that continued operations meant shooting at the British, the 'peace-keepers' of the Canal Zone. After an hour of discussion, only Pineau, Bourges-Maunoury and one other Minister voted to continue military action. Notifying Eden of the French decision, Mollet obtained an extension of the cease-fire to midnight, London time, but the British refused further extensions.[26]

The only option for REVISE's commanders, who learned of the

cease-fire from a BBC bulletin, was to occupy as much of the Canal Zone as possible before the deadline. A hasty march by the main force ended at El Cap, twenty-five miles south of Port Said. Advance patrols at Fayid, twenty-five miles short of Suez, were recalled. The campaign cost twenty-three British and ten French lives, while Anglo-French forces killed 400 Egyptian soldiers. British estimates of Egyptian civilian deaths, initially set at 100 by General Stockwell, were revised, after much controversy, to between 650 and 1,000.[27]

The British military, constantly assured by Ministers that operations would not be halted by political considerations, were furious. A British commander complained that Eden had 'obstinately decided like a girl to scratch out the eyes of his opponent but hadn't quite thought of what would happen afterwards'.[28] Stockwell was reprimanded by Minister of Defence Head for telling reporters that the Anglo-French force could have taken Suez in forty-eight hours if the cease-fire had not been issued. Templer wrote to Stockwell: 'Thank you [for the gift of] the Russian rifle. If I could use it, I'd give my first attention to certain politicians in New York and London, and I'd have run out of ammunition before I could spare a round, even for Nasser.'[29]

In contrast, Eisenhower called London to express his pleasure at the cease-fire. He assured Eden that if the Soviet Union attacked the UNEF, Britain was 'not alone' and promised, 'Now that we know connections are so good, you can call me anytime you please.' Eden cabled Mollet:

The President of the US telephoned me on his own account. There is no doubt at all that the friendship between us all is restored and even strengthened. . . . I feel that, as a result of all our efforts, we have laid bare the reality of Soviet plans in the Middle East and are physically holding a position which can be decisive for the future.[30]

Perhaps all was not lost. Occupation of the area from Port Said to El Cap could be used as a 'bargaining counter' in negotiations with Egypt. The cut in oil consumption could be limited to ten per cent over the next fortnight while supplies were arranged with the US. The Americans had restored the intelligence link with Britain and could offer the protection of the 'nuclear umbrella' against Moscow. Resolutions for the UNEF would have to be respected, but Anglo-French forces could be maintained in the Canal Zone until the UNEF arrived and then be integrated into the force. Meanwhile, Britain and France would maintain economic and financial pressure upon Nasser, and the OMEGA programme with the US might be renewed. In Egypt, British military broadcasters desperately appealed to the population:

Believe the man [Nasser] whose lies are choking Egypt like weeds, who promised you greatness and is bringing you ruin. Believe him if you like, but you know in your heart of hearts that we, the voices of the Allies, are not lying. Listen to the Truth.[31]

26

Aftermath
7–17 November 1956

The morning after the cease-fire, the British Cabinet pondered how to turn a tenuous presence in the Canal Zone into victory over Nasser. Some Ministers preferred to form the UNEF without contingents from Security Council members, as this 'was probably an essential preliminary to re-establishing close relations with the US'. Other Ministers demanded a British presence in Egypt through representation in the UNEF, even if this brought further conflict with the Americans:

It was not clear that the US were yet seized of the gravity of the Middle Eastern situation, and there were grounds for believing that they were more immediately concerned to secure the removal of British and French troops from Egypt than to take an active part in seeking a comprehensive and lasting settlement of the problems of the area.

After heated discussion, a compromise was reached. Britain would 'devote [her] efforts to inducing [the Americans] to acknowledge the existence in the Middle East of the dangerous situation which they had consistently refused to recognise since the end of [the Second World War]'. Political and economic measures against Nasser could then be pursued as part of an Anglo-American policy. Meanwhile, Eden would

endeavour to convince [the US] that a final decision by the UN on the composition and functions of the international force in the Suez Canal area should, if possible, be deferred until the Governments of the UK and the US had reached a clearer understanding on their common objectives in the Middle East.[1]

Eden called Eisenhower, ostensibly to congratulate the President on his re-election the previous evening, and suggested a meeting with the French on the Middle Eastern situation and the Soviet threat. Eisenhower was receptive, since, 'after all, [this] is like a family spat', and he called Acting Secretary of State Hoover with the news. Believing that any concession to Britain would jeopardise American policy in the UN and the Arab world, Hoover, through Eisenhower's Chief of Staff, Sherman Adams, and Staff Secretary, Colonel Andrew Goodpaster, asked the President to confirm that Britain was committed to the UNEF. Eisenhower finally called Eden to warn, 'If we are going to discuss this plan [for the UNEF] and your people would find it necessary to disagree with us, then the resulting divided communiqué would be unfortunate.' When Eden assured that he and Mollet understood this, Eisenhower replied, 'Then I think my fears are groundless. . . . If we are going to talk about the future [in the Middle East] and about the Bear – okay.' The announcement of the summit would be made by Eden in the Commons and by a White House spokesman at 4 p.m., London time.[2]

Hoover, who entered Eisenhower's office during the call, was not satisfied. Noting British claims to the State Department that the Soviets had offered 250,000 'volunteers' to Egypt, he asserted that Eisenhower's welcome of Eden and Mollet risked the 'danger of a complete turnabout by the Arabs', with Egypt accepting the Soviet offer and the Arab world rejecting the UNEF. After a half-hour of discussion with Hoover, Adams, Goodpaster and Humphrey, Eisenhower called Eden to postpone the meeting. Firstly, the President noted:

You have given us something on the military side I didn't know [about the 250,000 Soviet 'volunteers']. . . . I have just had a partial Cabinet meeting on this thing and they think our timing is very, very bad. . . . We have got to get a coordinated military intelligence view.

Secondly, Eisenhower would meet Congressional leaders on 9–10 November to discuss the new Congress, in which the opposition Democratic Party had a majority in both houses. Finally, the UN was demanding that Egypt and Israel accept the UNEF, and 'any meeting until that gets done would exacerbate the situation'.

Eden pleaded for the President to reconsider, but Eisenhower would not defy his officials:

I just don't see how we could do it now with so much on our plate – we just can't handle this at the same time. I am really sorry because, as I told you this morning, I want to talk to you.

Desperate, the Prime Minister protested that nothing should prevent friends discussing matters, but Eisenhower replied, 'I am not talking about not meeting and talking with our friends, but I have had opposition about the timing.' The President then cut off further conversation, as he had to leave for a Cabinet meeting.³ He told Adams with regret, 'Turning down Eden's request for a personal talk did not seem to him the right thing to do. . . . This was not the time to be so concerned about appearance and propriety.'⁴

In fact, the President and Hoover visited Foster Dulles in hospital. Fearing Soviet intervention, Foster Dulles supported Hoover: 'It was extremely important to get the British and French troops out of Egypt as soon as possible. . . . If this is not done – at least within a week's time – the fire will go on burning.' Foster Dulles favoured 'an embargo on all funds going to Israel', including remittances by American citizens, but he and Eisenhower disagreed sharply over American treatment of Britain and France. According to William Macomber, Foster Dulles's Staff Secretary:

Eisenhower explained his invitation to Eden at length, referring to old friendships and the wartime alliance. Foster Dulles said he understood this, but the President persisted in his apologia to the point where the Secretary interrupted, 'I see!'

Macomber later told Foster Dulles that he was 'kind of mean to have been so stern on the morning after [Eisenhower] had been elected President of the US'. Eisenhower had promoted Eden's case that 'the important thing to remember in this present situation is that "the Bear is still the central enemy"', but Foster Dulles insisted that 'the British and the French going into Egypt was a "crazy act"'. He 'did not exclude the usefulness of a meeting between the President and Eden and Mollet', but 'the meeting [would] be contingent on the British and French having previously gotten their troops out of Egypt'. Foster Dulles's only concession was to agree to Eisenhower's recommendation of a special assistant in the White House to oversee the Middle East.⁵

Two important trends were set. Firstly, the US Government imposed a virtual 'blackout' on communications with Eden. Apart from an exchange of short letters on 11 November about a possible summit, the Americans did not contact Eden between 7 November and Eden's departure on the 23rd for a three-week vacation in Jamaica.⁶ Secondly, the President, deprived of his working relationship with Foster Dulles, was an unhappy spectator of the policy set by the State Department, led by Hoover, and the Treasury.

Despite Suez, Eisenhower thought that the British had a role to play in the Middle East as well as in NATO. When the new British Ambassador to the US, Harold Caccia, presented his credentials on 9 November, he found that the President 'could not personally have been more friendly or indeed more forgiving'. Eisenhower said, 'Just because Britain and the US had had a sharp difference over the attack on Egypt, there was no thought that we would not keep our friendship over the long term.' In contrast, Humphrey told the British Embassy's Economic Minister, Lord Harcourt, 'For the US to offer financial aid to the UK and France in the light of actions of the last 10 days would be totally unacceptable politically in the US for some considerable time', although he added, 'This opinion would not hold if the Russians were to make any major move in the Middle East.'[7] Foster Dulles, in an extended letter of 11 November to Eisenhower, reiterated his support of Hoover:

It seems unlikely that . . . British and French policies would be changed by a Big Three meeting. . . . Even a coverup of disagreement, by an outward appearance of agreement, would gravely prejudice our own position in the world and would seem to tie us to policies which would be doomed to failure and would expose the Middle East and Africa to almost certain Soviet penetration and dominance.[8]

The National Security Council defined American policy on 8 November. The Middle East Emergency Committee was ready to ship Western Hemisphere oil to Europe, but Humphrey's attitude that 'for the time being . . . he would oppose programming oil shipments to Europe' prevailed. Hoover informed the British Embassy, 'The question of supply could best be left to the oil companies to thrash out between themselves.' When Coulson interjected, correctly, that the Committee was set up for co-ordination between the US Government and the oil companies, Hoover replied that this was not 'in any way necessary'.[9]

The British were isolated. The other Baghdad Pact members stopped short of expelling Britain or condemning Anglo-French aggression, but they called upon Britain and France 'to stop hostilities, withdraw their forces, . . . and fully observe and respect the sovereignty, integrity and independence of Egypt'. The French, embittered by the cease-fire, were uninterested in negotiations over the UNEF or concessions to the Americans. The Israelis, after Ben-Gurion exultantly told the Knesset on 7 November that Israel would keep her military gains, were checked by an urgent message from Eisenhower: 'It is obvious to us that the Soviets are taking advantage of this situation for disastrous purposes. If that should happen, Israel would be the first to be swallowed up.'

Hoover not only reinforced Eisenhower's words in a meeting with Israeli Minister Reuven Shiloah, but also threatened to suspend all American aid, public and private, to Israel and to support UN sanctions and Israel's expulsion from the organisation. The warning was reinforced by the President of the World Jewish Congress, who told Ben-Gurion that American Jews would not support Israel if she kept the conquered territory. Besides the ban on private remittances to Israel, the US Government might persuade West Germany to stop paying reparations to Israel.[10]

The Americans also 'made it quite clear that they would not intervene on Israel's behalf in the event of an attack by Soviet "volunteers"'. The CIA may also have issued 'disinformation' that the Soviets intended to 'flatten the Israelis'. Pineau told the Israelis, 'France is ready to share with you whatever she has – but . . . we have no means of defence against missiles.' After extensive consultation with Eban, and a seven-hour Cabinet meeting, Ben-Gurion agreed to conditional withdrawal from the Sinai.[11]

On 7 November, the General Assembly considered two resolutions. An Argentine resolution, drafted by Canada, excluded Anglo-French troops from the UNEF, but allowed them to remain at Port Said until the international force was in place. In contrast, an Afro-Asian resolution demanded the withdrawal of foreign troops from Egypt within twenty-four hours. The Assembly easily passed the Argentine resolution, and the Afro-Asian resolution was approved after it was amended to allow withdrawal 'in accordance with earlier resolutions'. Lloyd repeated to the Cabinet, 'It was important that we should re-establish close relations with the US Government and secure their support for our policy in the Suez Canal area and the Middle East.'[12]

General Keightley was increasingly agitated about possible Soviet intervention, despite the Chiefs of Staff's assessment that this was unlikely and photo-reconnaissance indicating that there were no Soviet planes in Syria. On the afternoon of 6 November, NATO's Supreme Allied Commander informed London that 'Turkey [was] being overflown by jet aircraft', presumably Soviet, and that the 'Turkish Air Force [was] being alerted'. The report was not only exaggerated, but suspicious. The US Military Attaché in Ankara soon reported that the only aircraft detected on Turkish radar were two to nine aircraft over the Black Sea, not Turkey, for ten minutes. The incident was not unusual, and the Turkish air force did not go on special alert. Six hours after his initial message to London, the Supreme Allied Commander told Washington that his report was 'tenuous'. One can only speculate whether the report was deliberate 'disinformation', possibly spread by the CIA to scare the British into a cease-fire or by the Turks to push the US into intervention against Egypt or Syria.[13]

However, Keightley already had other reasons to worry. Late on the evening of 6 November, he informed London that a MIG-15 fighter, possibly one of eleven flown into Egypt in recent days, had strafed the

British position at Gamil airfield and that the Egyptians had repaired ten runways. It was later established that the MIG-15 was not Soviet but belonged to the Egyptian air force, but Keightley also reported that two Canberra B-6s on photo-reconnaissance over Syria were fired upon by fighters. One Canberra escaped with superficial damage, but the wreckage of the other was later found in Lebanon. One crew member was killed; the other two were flown to a military hospital in Cyprus, and RAF markings on the aircraft's rudder were obscured to prevent the Lebanese discovering the incident.[14]

Canberras normally flew at more than 48,000 feet, a height matched only by fighters like the MIG-15, and Keightley feared that a Soviet pilot was flying the 'enemy' plane. REVISE's Headquarters later learned that the two Canberras had descended to 15,000 feet because of cloud cover, where they were intercepted by two Meteor fighters of the Syrian air force. Keightley was not pacified, for a large unidentified jet flew over Cyprus at 54,000 feet at 3 a.m. on 7 November, the height indicating that the aircraft was superior to a MIG-15 or an Il-28 bomber. The British may have detected an American U-2 flight from Turkey, but Keightley, verging on panic, warned London that up to fifty MiGs could be flown into Egypt from Syria in one night.[15]

The US was also concerned about the Soviet threat. After reports from the American delegation at the UN that the Soviets were advising the Arab states to 'hold out until Soviet volunteers arrive', Hoover told Eisenhower on 9 November that he would see Foster Dulles about 'the Syrian thing. . . . If they [the Soviet Union] built it up past a certain point, then it will be hard to handle.' To persuade Moscow of American vigilance, the State Department publicly spread the disinformation that a large number of Soviet aircraft were present in Syria. Foster Dulles told Hoover that he would revive OMEGA, as Allen Dulles thought 'Operation STRAGGLE [to overthrow the Syrian Government] might be carried forward but when the British and French troops are out.'[16]

The State Department, however, rendered Eisenhower powerless to restore Anglo-American co-operation before full British withdrawal. Lloyd again denied collusion to Ambassador Aldrich: 'The British had no advance knowledge that the Israelis were going to attack Egypt . . . HMG had made no commitments whatever to Israel in anticipation of such a move.' More significantly, he tried to intimidate the Ambassador, citing Egyptian plans, with Soviet backing, to attack Israel in April 1957 and the imminent danger of a Syrian assault upon Tel Aviv. Unruffled, Aldrich said that the Americans had no evidence of Syrian plans to attack, and Dixon cabled from the UN that 'the US delegation continues to ignore us'.[17]

With Hoover, acting with Foster Dulles's acquiescence, in close contact with Eisenhower's Chief of Staff, Adams, the State Department covered the President's every move. The idea of inviting Saudi Arabia's King Saud 'as an offset' to any Eden–Mollet trip to Washington, passed to Foster Dulles by Adams, 'had merit', but when Eisenhower suggested visits by Ben-Gurion and Nuri Sa'id, Foster Dulles argued that it was 'a dangerous game inviting all these people over'.[18] On 10 November, a press release announced the appointment of Walter Bedell Smith, former Director of the CIA and Undersecretary of State, as 'special assistant to the President on foreign policy matters'. In the afternoon, however, an official statement insisted that no appointment had been made. Instead, State Department Counsellor Douglas MacArthur II acted as the liaison on Middle Eastern matters. White House officials blamed the change upon State Department opposition to a special assistant, and Bedell Smith later told Lloyd:

The trouble about the President was that he delegated responsibility and things had come up to him through the person in charge, in other words, through Hoover, as acting Secretary of State. Hoover was no good and had no influence over Lodge. Lodge was irresponsible and the best we could hope for was a speedy recovery by Dulles, because he at least thought about things in terms of what was practical.[19]

By 12 November, the Egypt Committee wavered in its determination to maintain an Anglo-French force on the Canal. A meeting between Treasury and Bank of England officials concluded that Britain could not continue to lose reserves without devaluation of the pound. Only with a 'friendly and compliant attitude' from the US could Britain take necessary economic steps, including a withdrawal of up to $1 billion from the International Monetary Fund, a waiver of the annual repayment of the 1946 loan from the US, and an Export-Import Bank loan for oil purchases. The meeting suggested that Lloyd, travelling to the UN, conduct face-to-face negotiations with Administration officials, and the Egypt Committee, in a tactical retreat, agreed in principle to a phased withdrawal of troops.[20]

The State Department remained intransigent. Aldrich reported that the British were disturbed 'more than anything else' by the impression that Eden's visit to Washington might be indefinitely delayed because of 'a protracted negotiation between Nasser and [the] UN'. The State Department was unmoved. Eisenhower thought 'it would be wrong if [Lloyd] were coming for a long conference but just as an old friend, it would be all right for him to call and pay his respects,' but Hoover vetoed the idea, as 'it [would] be almost as bad as Eden coming'. Eisenhower's secretary recorded that the President thought 'the State Department had a completely exaggerated view of the meaning that could be attached to seeing old friends'.[21]

Lloyd, refused a meeting with Hoover, settled for a talk with Lodge and tried to frighten the Americans into a high-level meeting. He indicated that Britain intended to topple the Syrian Government, possibly with Iraqi and Turkish co-operation, while Jordan would be partitioned between Iraq and Israel. Shaken, Lodge said that Hoover was coming to New York on 15 November and suggested that Lloyd also see Foster Dulles. He reported to the State Department, '[Lloyd's] attitude struck me as reckless and full of contradictions. . . . He is in a dangerous state of mind which could touch off a war.'[22]

Lloyd's desperate approach had a slight chance of success. British commanders adopted a plan, MUSKETEER RENEWED, to resume hostilities if their forces were attacked by the Egyptians or the Soviets. Keightley's reports of possible Soviet intervention were passed to the Americans, and Turkey again warned the US and Britain of 'alleged overflying by Russian military aircraft, the Russian build-up in Syria, and the exposed position of Iran'. Eisenhower eventually agreed to U-2 missions in the Middle East along the border of 'friendly countries' and to missions over the Soviet Union if they avoided the most sensitive areas.[23]

The CIA and the US military were more amenable than the State Department to reconciliation with Britain and France. British military representatives in Washington reported a 'cooling off at [the] top' with Secretary of Defense Wilson and the Joint Chiefs of Staff, but found no deterioration below the top level, where dinner parties had been 'even more cordial than usual'.[24] At a White House meeting on 16 November, Admiral Radford and Allen Dulles said that they had been invited to meet Lloyd when he came 'incognito' to Washington 'in the next day or two'. Hoover, noting the Soviet threat and Lloyd's comments to Lodge, accepted the private talks. Allen Dulles later met Pineau for two hours at the French Embassy, where the French Foreign Secretary suggested an 'autonomous Syria under [former dictator Adib] Shishakli (now in Switzerland) . . . UK and France [are] already in touch with him'.[25]

The Soviet threat was diminishing each day, however. Even the Joint Intelligence Committee in London had concluded, 'Although the Soviet Union will probably seek to win Arab sympathies by propaganda, economic assistance, strong diplomatic support, offers of arms, and possible volunteers, they themselves will not wish to become involved in fighting outside the UN framework.'[26] British photo-reconnaissance over Syria on 14 November finally confirmed that no build-up was occurring, and the flights were suspended from the 17th because their discovery might prompt Egypt to block the UNEF. U-2 flights of 15 November detected no Soviet presence in Syria,[27] and Allen Dulles refused Pineau's suggestion of action against the Syrian Government. Pineau tried to win Allen Dulles's confidence with a semi-accurate account of the collusion against Egypt, but the CIA Director concluded:

We found ourselves in agreement only on the following points: the importance of Franco-American understanding; that the Communist menace was our greatest danger; that Syria was a potential weak point from the viewpoint of Communist penetration, and that Egypt and the Arab world could well dispense with the services of Nasser. There was some degree of difference between us as to the degree of his rascality, and also as to the type of measures which were justifiable to effect a change.[28]

On 14 November, Albert Gazier told Eden of Pineau's 'master plan' for the Iraqi take-over of Syria and the partition of Jordan.[29] The next day, Gazier told Kirkpatrick that France wanted a new Egyptian Government 'based on progressive elements'. Kirkpatrick argued:

We did not believe that there was anyone in the progressive camp who could weld the heterogeneous Opposition and lead a successful coup against Nasser. Only the Wafd could do this.[30]

Undeterred, the SDECE plotted the assassination of Nasser, but the British could not even incite a coup. Keightley's headquarters had neither 'the resources and experience nor the time to give' to a psychological warfare campaign. On 15 November, the Chiefs of Staff agreed that the campaign should be given to the Foreign Office to be 'pursued more vigorously'. However, the Foreign Office was soon preoccupied with counter-propaganda to refute Egyptian claims of extensive civilian casualties and damage from the Anglo-French invasion. The psychological warfare unit in Cairo, under the command of General Bernard Fergusson, was instructed 'to produce photographs of street scenes in Port Said showing "happy" Egyptians fraternising with the troops with the normal life of a busy city as a background'. Unfortunately, 'initial efforts to achieve this were not oversuccessful', and the military was burdened with surveillance of Egyptians and Soviet diplomats. Keightley's political adviser, Ralph Murray, cabled London:

[The Soviet Consul in Port Said] is apparently being very active and has run up an an enormous electricity bill in recent months which suggests midnight goings on. Have you any ideas on how we might restrict his movements or eventually get rid of him? . . . Would imposition of Military Government in Port Said give us a status on basis which we could declare him *persona non grata* and get any other wild men under control as well?[31]

Furthermore, the British had no more luck than Pineau in winning American support. While Eden repeated his concern about the lack of Anglo-American co-operation to the Egypt Committee on 15 November, he refused to withdraw British troops until a satisfactory agreement to clear the Suez Canal had been implemented. The National Security Council reaffirmed the same day that no Western Hemisphere oil would be diverted to Britain.[32]

Lloyd cabled Eden that he was 'rather depressed' by his discussions with Radford and Allen Dulles. He concluded:

The plain fact is that, as Bedell [Smith] said, the President is the only man who matters and there is no one around him to give him advice who is of the slightest use. That the future of the Middle East should be at the mercy of Hoover and Lodge is a tragedy.[33]

Lloyd's last chance was the meeting with Foster Dulles in Walter Reed Hospital on 17 November, the legendary occasion when Foster Dulles asked, 'Selwyn, why did you stop?' The remark was not simply a joke at the expense of the British. Five days earlier, Foster Dulles had told Eisenhower:

The British, having gone in, should not have stopped until they had toppled Nasser. As it was, they now had the worst of both possible worlds. They had received all the onus of making the move and, at the same time, had not accomplished their major purpose.[34]

Just before Foster Dulles died in 1959, he said, 'Perhaps I made a mistake at Suez,' and Dean Rusk, later Secretary of State, claimed that Foster Dulles had told him, 'I would not have made some of the decisions which I made about Suez had I not been sick at the time.'[35]

Ambassador Caccia, who accompanied Lloyd to the hospital, told journalist Joseph Alsop that 'he was so angry that literally it required a physical effort not to leap up and swarm over the desk',[36] and British Ministers were incensed. However, Foster Dulles's words were consistent with his position throughout Suez. Like Eisenhower, he believed that Britain and France would not attack Egypt unless they were sure of a quick occupation of the Canal Zone and the overthrow of Nasser. The occupation did not occur, and the US, fearing that the Soviets would seize the diplomatic initiative with a resolution in the General Assembly condemning the invasion of Egypt, was forced to protect her position with the resolution of 1 November.

Foster Dulles did not act outside the UN to halt the Anglo-French operations, and American policy only forced British consideration of a cease-fire after his departure for hospital on 3 November. Lloyd concluded, after the visit in Walter Reed Hospital:

Foster Dulles was most friendly and intelligent but seemed to want to evade personal responsibility during the coming phase. Hoover was quite negative; I am afraid the same applies to Lodge. . . . Allen Dulles could not have been more cordial, but said that he did not influence policy. . . . It is clear that the most antagonistic elements are the second rank in the State Department (e.g., people like Rountree).[37]

The State Department had effectively ostracised the Eden Government, exposing the fragility of the Anglo-American 'alliance'. The long-term consequences of the American policy, especially for NATO and Britain's standing as a 'great power', were ominous, but even they were overshadowed by immediate danger for the British. In the first half of November, the drain on reserves was nearly $200 million with an anticipated deficit of $300 million for the entire month. Unable to transport oil through the blocked Suez Canal and the damaged Iraqi Petroleum Company pipeline, Britain would have to provide millions of dollars to pay for oil from the Western Hemisphere. At the current rate of depletion, the dollar and gold reserves would be exhausted by mid-1957, and Britain would not be able to pay for oil and other imports. The result would be a crippling recession.

At a meeting of the Organisation of European Economic Co-operation on 15 November, US observers bluntly refused Macmillan's request for help with oil supplies until British troops withdrew from Egypt. Eden, however, insisted that the Cabinet link withdrawal to the clearance of the Canal. The Prime Minister, to salvage his pride and British prestige, was now ready to choose economic catastrophe.[38]

27

Alliance Restored, or the Overthrow of Anthony Eden 18 November 1956–7 January 1957

With formal contacts doomed to failure, the only hope for the Anglo-American 'alliance' and the security of the Eden Government and the British economy lay in informal exchanges. As early as 8 November, the Lord Privy Seal, Butler, told Ambassador Aldrich 'with great earnestness how deeply he deplored the existence of what he termed mutual misunderstandings of policy which had arisen'. He confided to the Ambassador, 'You are the only man who is in a position to explain to your government in detail the various attitudes of the members of our government.' Within three days, Macmillan and Lord Salisbury also approached Aldrich.[1]

The Cabinet member with the most interest in American co-operation was Macmillan. Not only was he responsible for the pound, but he had shifted from being the most vocal proponent of military action against Egypt to the strongest advocate for a cease-fire. At any point, he could be branded a foolish warmonger by the left wing of the Conservative Party or a faint-hearted warrior by the right.

Fortunately for Macmillan, Eden unwittingly provided an opening to present to the Americans. Since August, Eden's doctors had recommended a holiday to ease the Prime Minister's pain from his 1953 operation.[2] On 16 November, Macmillan told Aldrich that he could visit Washington as 'Eden's deputy', since 'Eden was very tired and should have a rest' before attending a summit. Two days later, the Prime Minister's doctor, Horace Evans, told Macmillan that Eden must have a vacation, although he did not indicate that the Prime Minister would resign. Macmillan, fearing that the Americans would not negotiate if they thought Eden would return to office, was ready to disclose and even distort Evans's information.[3]

After meeting Evans, Macmillan visited Aldrich's residence. He told the Ambassador that Britain's foreign reserves would be exhausted within weeks and that the country would shut down from lack of oil. The Cabinet had two options: withdrawal from the Canal Zone or renewal of hostilities to occupy the entire Canal. Macmillan realised that Eisenhower was reluctant to meet British Ministers, but the Cabinet was 'completely to be reshuffled and . . . Eden [was] going out because of sickness'. The following afternoon, Macmillan reiterated that Eden had suffered 'a physical breakdown and [would] have to go on vacation immediately, first for one week and then for another, and this [would] lead to his retirement'. Butler, Macmillan and Salisbury would lead the new Government. The first action after Eden's departure would be a step towards withdrawal from Egypt 'if [the US could] give us a fig leaf to cover our nakedness'.[4]

The effect on the Americans was immediate. Aldrich called Eisenhower to tell him of Eden's departure and Macmillan's wish to visit Washington. Hoover was hesitant, saying, 'I think this is one time to sit tight, awaiting his further information.' Humphrey, however, indicated that he would support a Conservative Government without Eden, if only to keep the Labour Party from power: 'I hate to have a man [Macmillan] stick in there and go to a vote of confidence and get licked. If they throw him out, then we have these Socialists to lick.'[5]

On 20 November, Eisenhower, Hoover and Humphrey considered the response to Macmillan. Aldrich had cabled that Macmillan or Butler, considered by most Britons to be Eden's 'heir-apparent', would become Prime Minister. Humphrey thought Butler the 'stronger of the two men being mentioned', but Eisenhower said that he 'always thought most highly of Macmillan, who is a straight, fine man, and, so far as he is concerned, the outstanding one of the British he served with during the war'.

The question of collaboration with Butler and Macmillan remained. Apparently, Butler had not spoken to Aldrich, so the relationship between Butler and Macmillan was unknown. With Humphrey and Hoover present, Eisenhower called Aldrich:

EISENHOWER: You are dealing with at least one person – maybe two or three – on a very personal basis. Is it possible for you, without embarrassment, to get together the two that you mentioned in one of your messages?
ALDRICH: Yes. One of them [probably Macmillan] I have just been playing bridge with. Perhaps I can stop him.
EISENHOWER: I'd rather you talk to both together. You know who I mean? One

has same name as my predecessor at Columbia University Presidency [Butler]; the other was with me in the war [Macmillan].

ALDRICH: I know the one with you in the war. Oh yes, now I've got it.

EISENHOWER: Could you get them informally and say of course we are interested and sympathetic and, as soon as things happen that we anticipate, we can furnish 'a lot of fig leaves'?

ALDRICH: I can certainly say that. . . .

EISENHOWER: Herb [Hoover] probably will send you a cable later tonight. You see, we don't want to be in a position of interference between those two, but we want to have you personally tell them. They are both good friends. . . .

ALDRICH: That is wonderful. I will do this – tomorrow?

EISENHOWER: Yes, first thing in the morning.

ALDRICH: I shall certainly do it and will then communicate. Can do it without the slightest embarrassment.

EISENHOWER: Communicate through regular channels – through Herb.[6]

Aldrich was also in contact with Lord Salisbury, going to his residence, Hatfield House, 'for tea and talks'.[7]

Macmillan quickly exploited Eden's absence from the Cabinet. After Ministers were told on 20 November that Eden was cancelling his public engagements, Macmillan said that rationing would have to produce a twenty-five per cent reduction in oil consumption, even if Britain 'should receive from the US, without any considerable delay, the greater part of the supplies assigned to us under the emergency arrangements which had been agreed'. The Chancellor warned:

Cabinet might shortly face the grave choice of deciding whether to mobilise all our financial resources in order to maintain the sterling/dollar rate at its present level or to let the rate find its own level with the possible consequence that sterling might cease to be an international currency.

Macmillan did not reveal his contact with Aldrich, but he hinted that the solution to Britain's problems was discreet negotiation:

Although any formal approach to the US would be premature at the present time, we should endeavour to establish informal contact with them through the Treasury Delegation in Washington, in order gradually to enlist their support for the loans which we should have to raise. . . . If we were assured of the goodwill of the US in this respect, it might be possible for us to declare, simultaneously with the announcement of the loss of gold and dollars during November, our determination to maintain the existing sterling/dollar rate and to restore the economy by means of appropriate internal and external policies.[8]

The next morning, Butler and Macmillan assured Aldrich that the Cabinet would approve British withdrawal.[9] Meanwhile, Macmillan appealed by letter to Humphrey:

I know that there has been a deep division between our two countries in the action which we and the French took in Egypt. . . . I can only hope that time will show that we were not wrong. In the meantime, it would be tragic – and a major victory for the Communists – if we were to allow what has happened to result in an economic disaster for the Free World. We can surely prevent it – but only if we act speedily.[10]

Eden was oblivious to Macmillan's intrigues. Commenting on a CIA report about Nasser's internal position, he complained to Lloyd, 'It is only on that level [the intelligence services] that Americans co-operate nowadays.' He drafted a final plea to Eisenhower on 20 November, asking for US support of an 'effective' UNEF and British clearance of the Suez Canal:

I must tell you frankly that there is a body of opinion here which believes that we have been let down. For my part, I have steadfastly refused to say anything that will weaken what most matters in this world – the bond between our two countries.

For unknown reasons, the Prime Minister never sent the message.[11] On 23 November, he left Britain, still unaware of the discussions with the Americans, to recuperate in Jamaica at Golden Eye, the home of Ian Fleming, the creator of James Bond. The journalist Randolph Churchill compared Eden's resolve with Hitler's refusal to abandon Stalingrad, but added, 'Even Hitler did not winter in Jamaica.'[12]

The restoration of Anglo-American relations still had to overcome two obstacles. Firstly, Butler and Macmillan had to persuade the Cabinet to accept American conditions for aid. Colonial Secretary Lennox-Boyd, Commonwealth Secretary Home and Minister of Defence Head opposed concessions, and a larger number of Conservative backbenchers supported them. To defuse the opposition, Butler and Macmillan had to extract compensation, political as well as economic, in exchange for withdrawal. A cable to Lloyd in New York concluded: 'We have to persuade the Party and the country here that all this effort has gained something worthwhile, and we have to persuade the UN that they are really committed to carry out these tasks [in Egypt] in an honourable and effective way.'[13]

On 21 November, Macmillan and Butler suggested to Aldrich that, after British withdrawal, the US should join the Baghdad Pact. Eisenhower told Humphrey, 'Apparently "fig leaves" did not mean merely financial help. It may have been something else that we have not even guessed.' Humphrey, despite his worries about the Labour Party, refused any 'political' commitment to the British before complete withdrawal. Eisenhower noted: 'Between the British and ourselves there was a vagueness, not a frankness that I would like.' Humphrey concluded:

We have got to keep working with the Arabs. We are on their side until these fellows [Britain and France] get out [of Egypt]. After they get out, we ought to be in the position of neutral friend that both can trust to try to work out a fair deal.

Hoover accordingly instructed Aldrich to stall Butler and Macmillan:

We do not believe meeting with Butler and Macmillan [in Washington] would be feasible until possible week of December 3. . . . We remain firm in our conviction that withdrawal of troops is of prime urgency and must be moving toward accomplishment before other important questions can be considered.[14]

Butler and Macmillan's only option was to persuade the Cabinet to adopt gradual measures towards withdrawal while negotiations continued with the US. They told the Cabinet on 22 November:

If the US Government were prepared to guide the forthcoming debate in the General Assembly [on an Afro-Asian resolution for immediate withdrawal of foreign troops] on moderate lines and thereafter to state clearly that the problem of the Suez Canal would be firmly dealt with and that the Russians would not be allowed to exploit the situation in the Middle East to their advantage, we might hope to re-establish close political relations with the US and to secure a satisfactory and lasting settlement in the Middle East as a whole.

A token withdrawal of British forces should be undertaken while full withdrawal was linked to the Canal's clearance and the resumption of negotiations over the Canal.[15]

The second obstacle to Anglo-American reconciliation was the division in the US Administration. Eisenhower, needing an excuse to overcome the resistance of the State Department, finally found it when the US rebuffed the British over the Afro-Asian resolution for immediate withdrawal without conditions. The British delegation had sought amendments fulfilling the Cabinet's conditions of 22 November, and Lloyd was optimistic by the evening of the 23rd: the Belgians had sponsored the desired amendments, and he thought US delegate Lodge had no objections. Macmillan, telling Aldrich that the 'Cabinet changes which he previously forecast [would] take place within the next few days', warned that the Government's ability to carry through withdrawal depended on public support from Lodge and Eisenhower.[16]

In fact, the State Department and Lodge had no intention of supporting the Belgian amendments, Hoover telling Eisenhower that the US 'must stay four-square with the UN, so Britain must take some preliminary actions' on withdrawal. Lodge told Lloyd that the Afro-Asian resolution 'merely reiterated principles we had stood for' and advised the

State Department, 'If we abstain on Asian-African resolution, it may cause a distinct turn for the worse insofar as the withdrawal of troops is concerned.' When the vote was taken the next day, the US abstained on the Belgian measures, ensuring their defeat when other delegations followed the American lead. The Afro-Asian resolution subsequently passed easily.[17]

The US abstention occurred when the State Department decided that complete withdrawal superseded all other considerations. Deputy Undersecretary Murphy told Caccia and French Ambassador Herve Alphand 'that the US was now the prisoner of its own policy'. Lloyd proposed discussions on the Middle East's future, but failed to influence Hoover, who had cabled Aldrich that international control of the Suez Canal was no longer a practical objective.[18] Dixon complained to the Foreign Office that the Americans were 'temporarily beyond the bounds of reason', while Kirkpatrick wrote: 'What I did not expect was that they should become quite so irrational. Some of them are hoping that Russia will collar the Middle East – "serve the British right".'[19]

Throughout Britain, there was a furious backlash against the Americans. A motion 'deploring the attitude of the US, which is gravely endangering the Atlantic alliance', was signed by 130 Conservative MPs. Eisenhower's appearance on newsreels was hissed in cinemas, and petrol stations near US air force bases posted signs, 'No Americans Served Here'. The *Sunday Times* warned:

Only new actions and policies by the US can stem the swelling tide of distrust and ill-will. The danger to the Atlantic alliance, which we believe is of vital importance to both countries, is acute. . . . Not a day is to be lost if the breach is to be mended in time to withstand the dangers which beset both nations and their friends, not least in the Middle East.[20]

Butler told Aldrich:

The wave of anti-American feeling in Great Britain . . . could not possibly be exaggerated. . . . He did not think it beyond the bounds of possibility that, if the UN did not act with firmness to bring about immediate clearance of the Canal, Great Britain would withdraw from the UN and . . . the US would be asked to give up its bases in Great Britain.[21]

At last Eisenhower circumvented the State Department. He had been warned by Allen Dulles:

Britain's long-standing dominant position in Iraq has now become precarious as a result of the military action against Egypt. . . . [Prime Minister] Nuri Sa'id, long regarded in the Arab world as a British stooge, is being popularly indicted as having been involved in the British-French-Israeli action.[22]

Winston Churchill wrote to the President on 23 November:

Whatever the arguments adduced here and in the United States for or against Anthony's action in Egypt, to let events in the Middle East become a gulf between us would be an act of folly, on which our whole civilisation may founder.

Eisenhower replied, 'Nothing would please this country more nor, in fact, could help us more, than to see British prestige and strength renewed and rejuvenated in the Middle East.'[23]

The President avoided the risk of publicity attached to a special adviser's appointment. Instead, the White House, 'through discreet channels', suggested to Caccia 'discussing our major outstanding problems other than through the State Department'. The 'suggestion would have to be handled with the greatest care', since the attempt to appoint Bedell Smith 'had been torpedoed by the State Department'.[24]

Eisenhower confronted Hoover on 25 November. They agreed with Foster Dulles's suggestion that Britain definitively state her plans and immediate steps for withdrawal before the US offered aid, but they differed over the content of the statement. Hoover believed that 'it might be necessary to tell Britain that it looks as though they are through in the area and ask if they want us to pick up their commitments'. Eisenhower objected that Anglo-American partnership was still necessary and concluded, 'We should give the British every chance to work their way back into a position of influence and respect in the Middle East.'[25] He tried to stand up to Foster Dulles, despite the Secretary's reminder that 'it was they who double-crossed us and now try to put the blame on us', to draft a statement emphasising America's traditional friendship for Britain, although he delayed its release after pressure from Hoover.[26] The State Department finally cabled Lodge:

While we cannot deviate from basic principles that have guided us thus far *re* Middle East situation, . . . we must give urgent consideration to measures aimed at improvement [of] understanding of UK and France and Europeans generally regarding US attitude.[27]

Once the President committed himself, Humphrey, who had just returned from a short vacation, followed. The Treasury Secretary called Butler on 26 November to express Eisenhower's worry that the US 'were today opposed to [the] UK, whom they regarded as being disobedient to the UN commandments and in defiance of them'. Provided Britain withdrew from Egypt, the US, while supplying loans and oil, could press the Egyptians to make concessions over the powers of an international authority co-operating in the supervision of the waterway. Humphrey even held out the prospect of a visit to London, though this was 'difficult while the British attitude was uncertain'. He agreed with Butler that 'questions which could not be mentioned [over the phone] on the succession' to Eden would be addressed in the near future.[28]

Gradually, Butler and Macmillan, assisted by Salisbury, led the Government into accommodation with the US. Lloyd, unaware of the covert discussions, endorsed Butler and Macmillan's calls for withdrawal because of his distress at British difficulties in the UN. He reported from New York on 26 November that 4,000 UNEF troops would be in place by 5 December, negotiations on the Canal's status would start when the date of withdrawal had been fixed, and clearance of the Canal would begin when Anglo-French troops left Egypt. The Cabinet agreed to recall Lloyd immediately so that a decision could be reached, as Butler, 'considerably encouraged by his talk' with Humphrey, favoured an immediate decision on a date for withdrawal.[29]

Lloyd returned to London on 28 November. After his offer to resign over his role in Suez was declined, he informed the Cabinet:

If we withdrew the Anglo-French troops as rapidly as was practicable, we should regain the sympathy of the US Government; we should be better placed to ask for their support in any economic measure which we might need to take, and we should have removed, as far as lay in our power, all impediments to the further clearance of the Canal.[30]

Macmillan called for an immediate announcement of withdrawal, but the battle was not yet won. Dissenting Ministers argued that withdrawal was unacceptable to many Conservative backbenchers and obtained agreement that withdrawal would only occur with assurances of 1) a competent UN Emergency Force, 2) some action towards clearance of the Suez Canal, 3) suspension of the expulsion of British nationals from Egypt, and 4) immediate and tangible support from the US. Noting reports of internal political and economic deterioration in Egypt and a swing of public opinion towards the Government in Britain and the Commonwealth, some Ministers concluded that Britain should 'dig in'. Butler postponed a final decision on the pretext that Lloyd should consult the French.[31] Ministers told Aldrich, 'We have just had the most terrible meeting. We feel that we have come to the right conclusion, but we also feel that this may mean the fall of the Government.'[32]

The next morning Macmillan told the Cabinet of a loss of $450 million, more than twenty per cent of the reserves, since September, including a $270 million fall in November. The underlying situation was even worse. The actual fall in reserves in November was $401 million, but the Bank of England made up $130 million through 'forward' sales of sterling and the sale of short-term US bonds. The reserves stood at $1,965 million, and it was estimated that they would fall to $1,340 million by the end of the year.[33] Humphrey had again refused any concessions before Britain announced withdrawal, telling Caccia, 'The UK was an armed burglar who had climbed in through the window while Nasser was the householder in his nightshirt appealing to the world for protection.'[34]

Fears of a backbench revolt continued, but Lloyd obtained Secretary-General Hammarskjøld's promise that 'all available equipment' would be used to clear the Suez Canal and Egypt would be asked for a public statement guaranteeing free transit to British and French ships. Although some Ministers thought this inadequate, the Cabinet agreed on 30 November that Lloyd would inform the Commons about withdrawal on 3 December.[35] The Americans held out for the final concession of a definite date for withdrawal, and Butler, after some heated interchanges, agreed.

Butler and Cabinet Secretary Brook prevented Eden's intervention in the discussions. Told by Butler, 'Do not attempt to break your isolation. There is no major issue, i.e., Anglo-American policy at the moment,' Eden only cabled London for information on 29 November. When he received a summary, Eden, questioning the arrangements for withdrawal, clearance of the Canal and the UNEF, informed Ministers, 'I am better and shall be available for any consultation.' His generous offer was not accepted. Butler merely wrote: 'We shall continue our efforts in New York to obtain the best possible terms on clearance, future settlement, size of force, etc.'[36]

Eden was unhappy, since he 'never thought the Six Principles [for a Canal settlement] amounted to so much'. He wrote to his Private Secretary, Frederick Bishop:

I am sure that the only thing is to stand firm on the ground that we have chosen and I believe that [the UN] will come around. I quite understand that the financial position can meanwhile become quite difficult, but, after all, we have resources, which I would rather not put in a telegram.

Butler, aware that Eden might block withdrawal if he knew the details of its negotiation, replied on 2 December, after consulting Salisbury, Macmillan and Edward Heath, 'We believe that the policy on which we have decided is consistent with the course which you set for us. We hope you will feel that we have taken the right direction.' He added the next day, 'We of course considered very anxiously whether it was our duty to suggest to you that you should return. We concluded that you ought not to interrupt your rest.' Salisbury and Dr Evans agreed. The Prime Minister finally relented: 'I fully agree and will now pipe down.'[37]

Butler and Macmillan also instructed Eden not to make public statements from Jamaica and told the American television network NBC that he was unavailable for comment. Bishop and Robert Allan, Eden's Parliamentary Private Secretary, cabled the Prime Minister before his return to London:

You yourself are not giving interviews to the Press. You have been kept informed of the broad lines of policy, but might find difficulty over minor tricky questions. We all feel sure that a short statement on departure [from Heathrow for 10 Downing Street] . . . is the best course.[38]

When Eden, in his proposed statement, referred to 'the Moscow–Cairo Axis' and Nasser's dictatorial ambitions and criticised the UN, Butler, supported by Lloyd and Salisbury, responded that Eden's denunciation of the US, the Soviet Union, China and the UN 'would create a bad impression. . . . In particular there is a growing wish to end the breach with the US. It is important that your first pronouncement should be in tune with the changed atmosphere.' Criticism of Nasser should be deleted since it 'supported the contention that our real motive was to get rid of Nasser'. After further exchanges, Eden accepted Whitehall's draft.[39]

Once they knew of the intention to withdraw, the Americans eagerly fulfilled British requirements. Lodge told Dixon how much he admired Lloyd's 'skill and courage' in recent months and invited Dixon and his wife to dinner and the theatre. More significantly, an American statement pledged full support for the territorial integrity and sovereignty of the Baghdad Pact's members, and the President, modifying his draft announcement of 27 November, announced the activation of the Middle East Emergency Committee to prepare for oil shipments to Europe. 'A very relaxed and cheerful' Butler told Aldrich on 1 December that, as the American 'activation of [the emergency] oil committee and warning message regarding aggression against Turkey and other members of the Baghdad Pact had made [a] most favourable impression' in Britain, he 'thought he had turned the corner with the Suez rebels [in the Commons]'.[40]

On 3 December, Lloyd told the Commons that British troops would withdraw by mid-December if an effective UNEF was in place. The British would not insist on participation in the Canal's clearance and would not set preconditions on negotiations for a Canal settlement. The Americans could now implement their plan, agreed at the National Security Council meeting on 30 November, to shore up Butler. Macmillan was immediately assured that a loan from the Export-Import Bank was forthcoming, that Britain could borrow from the International Monetary Fund, and that the annual repayment of the interest due on the 1946

US loan would be waived. Within seventy-two hours of Lloyd's announcement, American oil supplies were sent to Europe, and Britain received almost $2 billion in US-backed loans and aid by 22 December.[41] Vice-President Nixon, who had previously condemned British 'colonialism', now publicly stated:

We are proud of our association with Britain and France and our common dedication to the principles of freedom and justice which joined us together as allies in both World War I and World War II.

We recognise that they were confronted with a series of aggressive acts short of the use of force; in addition to an ominous military build-up in a nation which they believed threatened their vital interests. In that no man's land between war and peace, it is difficult to decide which is the best course of action.

The British had survived the immediate crisis, but a new problem emerged. The Americans had negotiated on the assumption that Eden would not return to power, Humphrey telling Foster Dulles that 'nothing but a change of Government' would save the pound, but Eden, refreshed by his vacation, did not intend to resign as Prime Minister. Worse, Butler and Macmillan were quarrelling over the succession.[42]

Even though Macmillan was as responsible as Butler, if not more so, for the cease-fire and subsequent efforts for withdrawal, he placed the onus of 'retreat' upon his rival. As Acting Prime Minister, Butler took responsibility for withdrawal, while Macmillan's role was never revealed. The Chancellor only spoke once on economic matters in the Commons between 6 November and 9 January.[43] At a private meeting with Conservative MPs in late November, Butler indicated that Britain, for financial and economic reasons, had to withdraw her troops from Egypt. He later recalled:

The small private room became like a hornets' nest. They all hurried off to the Carlton Club to prepare representations to the government. Wherever I moved in the weeks that followed, I felt the party knives sticking into my back.[44]

The former Conservative Minister, Brendan Bracken, wrote to the newspaper baron, Lord Beaverbrook:

Macmillan is telling journalists that he intends to retire from politics and go to the morgue [the House of Lords]. He declares that he will never serve under Butler. His real intentions are to push his boss out of Number 10 and he has a fair following in the Tory Party. The so-called Canal die-hards think better of him than they do of Eden or Butler.[45]

At the meeting of the 1922 Committee of Conservative backbench MPs on 22 November, Butler gave a straightforward presentation of the situation and asked Macmillan for a few words on oil supplies. The

Chancellor turned the opportunity into a rousing thirty-five-minute speech. A Conservative Whip, Philip Goodhart, recalled:

Rab was not on his best form, whereas Harold was at his most ebullient and managed to win the day, not only on the merit of what he said . . . but also physically in that his expansive gestures nearly caused poor Rab to fall backwards from the adjacent seat.[46]

Douglas Dodds-Parker, the Parliamentary Undersecretary at the Foreign Office, claimed:

A document had been drawn up saying that, as Butler had dragged his feet over Suez, the signatories would not support him for the leadership; that this had been signed by some half of the Tory Party [MPs]; that he would therefore be unable to form an administration; and so there was no alternative to him but Macmillan. This document was sent on high through a Privy Councillor [Lord Scarborough].

Scarborough spent the evening of 3 January with Eden, but it cannot be determined if the Prime Minister's potential successors were discussed.[47]

At a NATO meeting in Paris on 12 December, Macmillan, distorting his role in Suez, tried to reassure Foster Dulles and win his support. The Secretary reported to Eisenhower:

[Macmillan] recognised that there had been a certain loss of confidence on the part of the President, myself, and others because of the Suez operation and the deception practiced upon us in that connection. . . . He, personally, was very unhappy with the way in which the matter was handled and the timing but . . . Eden had taken this entirely to himself and he, Macmillan, had had no real choice except to back Eden. Macmillan did not disguise the fact that he had always favored strong action but the point was that he did not like the manner and timing, particularly vis-à-vis the US.

Macmillan insisted that, even if Eden remained in office, he would not be in charge of British policy:

After Eden returned, there would be a question as to whether he would resign at once on account of ill-health. If not, he would probably hold on for six months, but he would be a constitutional Prime Minister.[48]

The Chancellor subsequently cabled Butler about a conversation with Humphrey, which indicated that the Americans would not lift their 'quarantine' on Eden:

It was like a business deal. They were putting a lot of money into the reorganisation of Britain and they would hope very much that the business would be successful. But, of course, when you were reconstructing a business that was in difficulties, the personal problems could not be ruled out.

I said: 'Don't you trust the board?' and he said: 'Well, since you ask me, I think it would be as well if we could deal as much as possible with the directors.' This rather cryptic observation he enlarged on to say that he would like to feel that he could always be on terms of private and, where necessary, telephonic, communication with you and me.[49]

Future US policy in the Middle East also had to be decided. Eisenhower foresaw renewed co-operation with Britain, but the State Department still assumed 'that [Britain's] position in the area has been seriously prejudiced by its action against Egypt and that the US must assume leadership in maintaining and restoring the Western position in the area'. In the short term, the US would use King Saud to 'moderate both extreme nationalist and pro-Soviet views among the Arabs'. If Jordan refused British subsidies, 'the US should offer to assist Jordan financially and perhaps militarily in the context of closer federation with Iraq'. In the long run, the US would fix Arab-Israeli boundaries through the UN, provide a unilateral assurance of aid to the Baghdad Pact, 'utilise all appropriate opportunities to isolate Egypt and reduce Nasser's prestige and influence', 'assist Iraq to expand its influence in Syria and Jordan', and 'further strengthen Saudi Arabia and reduce its ties with Egypt'.[50]

On 8 December, Foster Dulles outlined three alternatives to Eisenhower: accession to the Baghdad Pact, which was favoured by the Joint Chiefs of Staff; creation of a new regional organisation under the UN Charter; or bilateral arrangements with Middle Eastern countries. Foster Dulles favoured the bilateral approach, 'since you wouldn't get in trouble with the troublemakers [Britain and France]'. Eisenhower thought that, since 'Saudi Arabia and even Lebanon . . . might want to adhere to the Pact', the US 'would want to go in with them'; however, when Foster Dulles revived the objection that the US could not join the Pact without a guarantee of Israeli borders, the President gave way.[51]

Two general tenets of American policy emerged. First, King Saud would replace Nasser as the leader of the Arab world.[52] Second, the US would *unilaterally* guarantee the security of Middle Eastern states from Communist aggression inside or outside their borders. At a meeting on 20 December with Eisenhower, Hoover, Wilson and Radford, Foster Dulles said that the Senate's approval of American accession to the Baghdad Pact 'would be extremely difficult to obtain'. Furthermore, 'Nasser opposes [the Pact] and, more importantly, King Saud does also. . . . Saud is the only figure in the area . . . [who could] serve as a counterpoise to Nasser'. Instead, a Congressional resolution should authorise Presidential action to counter Communism in the Middle East, just as the Truman Doctrine of 1947 'defended' Greece and Turkey against Communism and the Formosa Doctrine of 1955 protected Taiwan.[53]

On 5 January, Eisenhower addressed Congress to request a resolution to 'authorise the US to cooperate with and assist any nation or group of nations in the general area of the Middle East in the development of economic strength dedicated to the maintenance of national independence'. Reasonable amounts of economic aid would be allocated, and the President could provide military assistance, including direct aid by American forces, 'against armed aggression from any nation controlled by international Communism'. The resolution was approved by Congress and signed by Eisenhower in March.[54]

It remained for Britain to accept the Americans' unilateral commitment, even though this implied British subservience to the US. Conveniently, Eden's fall from power was imminent. When the Prime Minister returned from Jamaica, a group led by Salisbury and Butler informed him that, 'while the Cabinet were willing to carry on under his leadership until Easter, if it was then clear that his health was not fully restored, they felt that a new head of Government would be necessary'.[55]

On 17 December, Eden returned to the House of Commons to silence, only a single Conservative MP rising to wave his order paper. The next day, he gave an unimpressive account of Suez to the 1922 Committee. Questioned about collusion, Eden replied that 'some [half-truths] – and if they existed at all, they were not serious or many in number – were necessary, and always are in this sort of operation which demands extreme secrecy'. He could not even answer a question about the relevance of the Tripartite Declaration. On the 20th, Eden, under close questioning from Gaitskell about collusion, resorted to outright deception of Parliament:

I want to say this on the question of foreknowledge and to say it quite bluntly to the House, that there was not foreknowledge that Israel would attack Egypt – there was not. But there was something else. There was – we knew it perfectly well – a risk of it, and, in the event of the risk of it, certain discussions and conversations took place as, I think, was absolutely right, and as, I think, anybody would do.[56]

Eden might have remained as Prime Minister for a few months, but he had effectively lost power. Labour's Aneurin Bevan had predicted, 'A cushion of time will be allowed to permit the amenities of political assassination. Even a minor Caesar is entitled to be despatched with due decorum.'[57]

Coincidentally, the pain of the Prime Minister's recurrent ailments undermined his confidence. Butler consulted Eden's Principal Private Secretary, Frederick Bishop, who warned that Eden's resignation 'might conceivably happen quite quickly'.[58] At the end of December, after a recurrence of his fevers, Eden began asking Ministers and prominent Conservative peers if he should continue.[59] From 1 January, Dr Evans saw Eden daily and, on 7 January, Eden was examined by Evans and two other specialists. Told that his health would be endangered if he stayed in office, Eden discussed the details of his resignation with Brook and Salisbury.[60]

On 9 January, Eden summoned Macmillan to Number 10 and told him that 'there was no way out'. Macmillan later recorded:

I could hardly believe that this was to be the end of the public life of a man so comparatively young, and with so much still to give.

We sat for some little time together. We spoke a few words about the First War, in which we had both served and suffered, and of how we had entered Parliament together at the same time. . . . I can see him now on that sad winter afternoon, still looking so youthful, so gay, so debonair – the representation of all that was best of the youth that had served in the 1914–18 War.

Given Macmillan's expectation since November of Eden's downfall, the entry is either extraordinarily sentimental or hypocritical.[61]

Two hours later, Eden told the Cabinet:

Since Nasser seized the Canal in July, I have been obliged to increase the drugs considerably and also increase the stimulants necessary to counteract the drugs. This has finally had an adverse effect on my rather precarious inside.[62]

Salisbury eulogised, 'The courage which [Eden] had shown during the events of the last six months had intensified the affection and admiration in which he was held throughout the country', and Butler claimed the resignation was 'not only a severe personal shock' but also 'a serious political blow for the Conservative Party'. It was Macmillan, the man who had planned for Eden's departure, who had the last word:

When the history of the Suez crisis came to be written, it would be recognised that the Prime Minister had been inspired by motives of the highest patriotism. His colleagues, if they followed his example, might be able to turn to good account the opportunities which his policy and action had created.[63]

Macmillan's succession was surprisingly easy, despite doubts by Salisbury. Four Cabinet supporters of the Chancellor discussed their strategy as soon as they learned that Eden intended to resign. Michael Adeane, the Queen's Private Secretary, not only consulted Salisbury but also Lord Waverly, Lord Chandos and Churchill, all of whom independently recommended Macmillan. When Salisbury, with his lisp, polled Ministers, 'Which is it to be: Hawold or Wab?', no more than three voted for Butler.[64]

Conclusion

Suez was a watershed for British influence, not only in the Middle East but throughout the world. After the Second World War, Britain granted independence to India, Burma and Ceylon and, under American pressure, relinquished her mandate for Palestine; however, she continued to maintain a global presence through the Commonwealth, African and Asian colonies, and political and military links with Arab states. In some cases, such as the campaign against insurgency in Malaya, Britain acted alone, but in others, such as the development of Middle Eastern policy after 1949, London recognised that it needed American support and assistance.

Eden's decision to act with France and Israel in late October 1956 was a final attempt to establish that Britain did not require Washington's endorsement to defend her interests. Financially and politically, that quest failed. Eden was ostracised by the Eisenhower Administration, and Butler and Macmillan had no choice but to accept American conditions for withdrawal from Egypt.

To restore the Anglo-American 'alliance', Britain paid the price of permanent subservience to American policy. The Eisenhower Doctrine of January 1957 established America's intention to act unilaterally to 'defend' the Middle East. When Macmillan, now Prime Minister, met Eisenhower in Bermuda in March, the symbolic reconciliation of Washington and London, he accepted US dominance. Britain would no longer base her position on the Iraqi-Jordanian axis and the Baghdad Pact, but, behind the American 'shield', concentrate on safeguarding her oil supplies from Arabian states on the Persian Gulf. While Britain sent paratroops into Jordan in July 1958 to support King Hussein against 'leftist' opponents, that operation was requested by Washington in support of American landings in Lebanon. Independent British operations between 1956 and Britain's withdrawal from east of Suez were limited to the rim on the Persian Gulf.

Yet there was nothing inevitable about the British downfall in Suez. The military operations were not foreordained: if French envoys had not approached Eden on 14 October with the plan for 'collusion' with Israel, Britain would have pursued negotiations with Egypt for a peaceful resolution of the crisis. Nor was American opposition predetermined: if

Anglo-French forces had occupied the Suez Canal Zone by 3 November, Foster Dulles and Eisenhower would have accepted the fait accompli. Why then did Britain fail?

The course of British policy was never 'irrational'. Eden may have had a personal hatred of Nasser, but the Cabinet decided in March 1956 to curb the Egyptian leader because of the perceived threat of Cairo to British influence in the Middle East. Military preparations, not only to take control of the Suez Canal Zone but also to overthrow Nasser, were considered a necessary riposte to the nationalisation of the Suez Canal Company. Most importantly, Eden agreed to action with France and Israel after the French raised the prospect of an Israeli-Jordanian war and the destruction of the Iraqi-Jordanian axis if 'collusion' against Egypt was not pursued.

Nor was British policy determined by the insistence of Cabinet 'hawks' for a war with Egypt. Macmillan's behaviour – his manoeuvring for military co-operation with Israel, his collaboration with Churchill to press Eden for not only an Anglo-Israeli operation but also a British attack from Libya upon Egypt, his deliberate misinterpretation of American policy to bolster the Prime Minister in early October – may have been a novel interpretation of his Ministerial authority, but it ultimately failed to prevent British acceptance of genuine negotiations with Egypt. Eden's resolve for conflict had been curbed; the Foreign Office, led by Lloyd, had seized the initiative; and the military was preparing to stand down operations until spring 1957.

Britain was finally undone by weaknesses in her system of policy-making. When Eden accepted 'collusion', he deceived not only the US, Parliament and the British public, but also his own officials. Few in the Treasury and the Foreign Office knew anything about the plans, and Britain's military commanders, preparing for a possible war to defend Israel against Jordan, never learned about the co-operation with Tel Aviv.

This near-absurd situation – the fighting of a war with no idea of the plans behind it – was far from an aberration. With no interdepartmental body to co-ordinate action, there was always the possibility that more than one British policy would be pursued in the Middle East. MI6 carried out operations without the knowledge of the Foreign Office or the approval of the Cabinet. With the dichotomy in British planning, it was always possible for Eden, weaned on MI6 'information' about Nasser, to work with the intelligence service even if this sabotaged the Foreign Office's efforts. The Ministerial decision of March 1956, supporting a long-term programme against Nasser, should have unified British policy, but the attempt was quickly undermined by MI6, with its three-phase programme, to overthrow the Syrian, Saudi and Egyptian Governments with the help of Turkey, Iraq and Israel. Meanwhile, the Prime Minister, leaked information to the American press about Britain's determination to topple Nasser, insisted on a show of strength in the Arabian Peninsula, and blocked Anglo-Saudi discussions on the Buraimi oasis.

During the Suez crisis, the 'official' British policy was paralleled by MI6's manoeuvres. The assassination of Nasser was considered, but shelved in favour of plans to replace him with an 'alternative' government. The Foreign Office and the military were not informed of MI6's operations, but the ill-fated Phase II of MUSKETEER REVISE, aerial and psychological warfare against Egypt, was based upon MI6's assurances that the plans would lead to Nasser's overthrow. REVISE was superseded in mid-October by the British negotiations with Egypt, but Eden easily revived it when the French mooted the idea of 'collusion'.

If Eden had reunified British policy by informing his officials of the co-operation with France and Israel, then the Treasury, Foreign Office and military could have prepared for the tribulations of war, but the Prime Minister now faced the conflict between MI6's plans and the Foreign Office's strategy. Exposure of 'collusion' with Israel would jeopardise the long-term policy of co-operation with Arab states, notably the Iraqi-Jordanian axis, as well as Britain's 'alliance' with Washington and her position in the UN. To minimise this danger, Eden maintained the division between his strategy and the 'official' British policy by keeping his officials in the dark and contriving the façade of the Anglo-French 'peace-keeping force'.

Eden's choice, supported by the 'inner circle' of Ministers who knew of the Sèvres Protocol, eventually ruined hopes of American acceptance of British action. Anglo-American relations were already strained, partly because of Foster Dulles's lack of diplomatic tact. His injudicious use of the phrase 'make Nasser disgorge what he had taken' gave the impression that the US would not accept control of the Suez Canal, but he was unable, because of opposition from the American Treasury, to back his promise with effective economic sanctions. Foster Dulles's only recourse, to avert Anglo-French military action, was to persist with plans for international operation of the Canal while stalling on their implementation.

Yet the recognition that Foster Dulles, either from duplicity or from lack of an alternative, used conference-making to prevent an attack upon Egypt exposes the myth, propagated by Eden and his defenders, that the American Secretary privately supported the use of force. From August to October, Foster Dulles repeatedly told Eden, Lloyd, Macmillan and Foreign Office officials that military action would have disastrous consequences for the West. Although he assuaged British sensibilities by referring to an assault as a 'last resort', Foster Dulles, as well as Eisenhower and State Department officials, never indicated that the point for military action had been reached.

Eden, despite his repetition of Foster Dulles's 'disgorge' statement, was not so obtuse that he failed to recognise the Secretary's aversion to force. Indeed, the American position was an important reason for British acceptance of negotiations with Egypt at the UN. On 14 October, however, the Prime Minister decided to disregard the American position. The US did not have to support an Anglo-French invasion, apart from deterring Soviet intervention; she merely had to refrain from opposition to London and Paris. Macmillan had already 'gingered' Eden with the misleading accounts of his trip to Washington, and the French were insisting that the Americans would only oppose the invasion of Egypt after the Presidential election on 6 November. On the basis of these reports, the Prime Minister and his 'inner circle' of Ministers risked the Anglo-American 'alliance'.

The gamble might have worked had Eden mobilised all of Britain's resources for the Suez operation, but this was precluded by the Prime Minister's decision to hide his plans from those implementing them. The Treasury was unprepared for speculation against the pound. British diplomats sincerely told the Eisenhower Administration that London would condemn the Israeli invasion of Egypt. When this did not occur, the Americans could only conclude that the British were lying. If British military commanders had known of the political co-operation with Israel, they might have agreed to the French request to accelerate the landings in the Canal Zone, but, unaware of the Sèvres Protocol, they could not assume that Israel would protect the Anglo-French flank.

From 3 November, London's 'window of opportunity', when it could have forced American acceptance of occupation of the Canal Zone, was gone. The UN General Assembly had begun the process of denouncing the Anglo-French intervention. Rationing of fuel and the depletion of Britain's foreign reserves were imminent. Foster Dulles's hospitalisation allowed anti-British sentiment to run unchecked within the Eisenhower Administration. Acting Secretary of State Hoover and Secretary of the Treasury Humphrey blocked any assistance to London until the growing political and economic pressure and the threat of Soviet intervention forced a cease-fire.

The immediate responsibility for British failure lay with a Prime Minister, encouraged by 'hawkish' Ministers and his foreign intelligence service, taking hasty action in a system which did not require the co-ordination of foreign policy and operations. This is insufficient, however, to explain the long-term causes of the disaster. Eden did not initiate 'collusion', but joined it long after France and Israel prepared for war with Egypt. Furthermore, the French persuaded the Prime Minister to act by placing 'collusion' within the context of Britain's Middle Eastern policy. Suez was merely one more setback, albeit the most visible and most significant, for a country which could no longer sustain herself without the consent and co-operation of others. The Attlee Government's strategy of 'partnership' with the Arab states had been shattered by 1948, and the dispute over Palestine and the creation of Israel further exposed British impotence in the face of nationalism, Jewish and Arab, and an uncertain American policy. Establishment of working co-operation with the US from 1949 to 1953 brought some stability to Britain's position, despite the Iranian and Egyptian crises, but deterioration of the position in the Suez Canal Zone and the 'independence' of the Eisenhower Administration finally forced London to replace Cairo with the Iraqi-Jordanian axis as the political and military centre of its position.

The formation and development of the Baghdad Pact in 1955 gave multi-national substance to the British strategy, and the US refusal to join was offset by her political, economic and military support for the organisation. At the same time, the seeds of Anglo-Egyptian conflict were sown, as Britain's pursuit of the axis clashed with Nasser's wish for an Arab organisation independent of the West. Every Arab country was embroiled in the struggle: the Saudis and Syrians, with their political and military agreement with Egypt, automatically became London's 'antagonists', while Jordan was torn between British attempts to bring her into the Baghdad Pact and Egyptian and Saudi manoeuvres to block the accession. In turn, 'local' developments, from the Anglo-Saudi dispute over Buraimi to Iraqi efforts at federation with Syria, were inevitably viewed through the Anglo-Egyptian prism.

The Glubb incident of March 1956 was a highly charged symbol of this clash. Without British leadership of her military, Jordan's support could not be assumed. Even if Nasser did not instigate Glubb's removal, the Egyptians might persuade Jordan to adopt a 'neutral' position or join Cairo's arrangements with Syria and Saudi Arabia. The threat could only be defused if Nasser's prestige was curtailed and his position in Egypt undermined, while Britain, with financial and military aid, would assure Jordan's dependence upon London.

Although the Suez crisis overshadowed the Iraqi-Jordanian issue, it re-emphasised the importance of a solid Arab foundation for Britain's position. By October 1956, the British military found itself in the unprecedented position of preparing, on the one hand, for a war with Egypt and, on the other, for a war with Israel in defence of Jordan.

To draw Britain into 'collusion', the French took advantage of

London's reliance upon the Iraqi-Jordanian axis. Even if the Israeli 'retaliation' against Qalqilya on 10 October was not contrived to frighten the British into co-operation, it raised the spectre of Israel, supported by France, overrunning Jordan. Action against Nasser would have to be abandoned as Britain's Middle Eastern position disintegrated.

When Eden chose 'collusion', he decided, in effect, to rely upon France and Israel rather than on the Anglo-American 'alliance' to defend Britain's long-term strategy. This illustrated that ties between London and Washington were never absolute but subject to two conditions: first, the convergence of British and American aims in the Middle East and, second, the actions of third countries. The US entered the Pentagon talks with Britain in 1947 and expanded those discussions in 1949 because she concluded that London's position in the Middle East was vital to Western strategy in a global Cold War with the Soviet Union. As the Truman Administration expanded its political and economic involvement in the region, ties with Britain were reinforced. Conversely, when the Eisenhower Administration concluded that Britain's deteriorating relations with Egypt and other Arab states were harming the American position and blocking a Middle Eastern defence organisation against the Soviet Union, Washington pursued 'independence'.

When the Americans decided in 1954 that an Arab-Israeli settlement was a prerequisite for their Middle East system and that Britain, having finally reached an agreement with Egypt over the Suez Canal Base, retained significant influence in Arab countries, the 'alliance' was renewed and maintained, in some form, until the Suez War. After ALPHA, the Anglo-American operation for Arab-Israeli peace, failed, Washington simply redirected its efforts to OMEGA, the Anglo-American effort to remove Nasser as the 'barrier' to a settlement.

This co-operation was persistently threatened, however, when British efforts to maintain her 'traditional' position challenged American interests in 'local' issues. Britain's dispute with Saudi Arabia over Buraimi, culminating in the occupation of the oasis by British-sponsored troops in October 1955, challenged a regime which not only was supported by the Americans, but was also perceived by Eisenhower as the key to long-term Western strategy. Washington also retained the suspicion that Britain was encouraging an Iraqi take-over of Syria, despite Israeli and Saudi fears of a 'Greater Iraq'.

The Anglo-American 'alliance' could also be jeopardised by differences over the methods to achieve a common goal. When Britain tried to obtain Jordanian accession to the Baghdad Pact in December 1955, she defied American warnings. Eden's whimsical forays into policy-making, notably the Guildhall speech, jeopardised ALPHA and detailed Anglo-

American plans. Most importantly, MI6, unchecked within the British system, tabled plans which were antithetical to fundamental tenets of American policy, notably support for King Saud and avoidance of co-operation with Israel against Arab states.

From the start of the Suez crisis, the Americans shared Britain's aim of toppling Nasser; however, the British reliance on military action always threatened to alienate Saudi Arabia and other Arab countries, endangering American interests and the priority of Middle Eastern unity against the Soviet Union. British Ministers had a choice: to suspend the Anglo-American 'alliance' and attack Egypt, or to suspend the use of force and preserve a common front with Washington against Nasser. As of 14 October, the latter course had been adopted and the 'alliance' was intact. The British entered negotiations with Egypt over the Suez Canal while OMEGA was covertly implemented. The Americans held out the prospect to Britain of a new Egyptian government within six months.

It was this co-operation that Eden rejected in favour of 'collusion'. The Prime Minister's disillusionment with Foster Dulles and his conference-making played a part in the decision, as did the misleading assurances of Macmillan about the American attitude. Eden's fundamental conclusion, however, was that deference to Washington and rejection of the French offer meant the end of the Iraqi-Jordanian axis. If Britain allowed her Middle Eastern position to self-destruct, the 'alliance' with Washington was worthless.

In 1957, Macmillan effectively promised Eisenhower that Britain no longer retained her right to defy the United States in the implementation of her foreign policy. 'Alliance' had been restored, but Britain was a junior partner dependent on American benevolence. The lion had left the Middle East, not with a roar, but with a whimper.

Notes

Preface

1 Avon Papers, AP23/60/171, Eden to Salisbury, 19 February 1970.
2 Robert Harris, *Sunday Times*, 12 August 1990.

Introduction

1 Lloyd, p. 221.
2 Hennessy, p. 8.

1: The Development of Anglo-American Relations in the Middle East, 1945–52

1 Bryson, pp. 175ff.
2 *Foreign Relations of the United States* (hereafter referred to as FRUS) 1950, Volume v, p. 124.
3 *Ibid.*
4 Devereux, p. 31.
5 Public Record Office (hereafter referred to as PRO), FO371/81907/E1023/3, Records of Anglo-American discussions, October 1949.
6 PRO, FO371/81907/E1023/12, Burrows to Wright, 6 April 1950; FRUS 1950 v, p. 1.
7 FRUS 1950, v, pp. 125ff.
8 PRO, FO371/E1023/10, Furlonge minute, 27 March 1950; FRUS 1950 v, p. 135; PRO, FO371/81907-81910/E1023/File.
9 PRO, FO371/81912/E1023/152G, Price to Furlonge, 20 September 1950; PRO, FO371/80382/JE1055/55G, Allen minute, 20 September 1950; PRO, FO371/81922/E10213/File; PRO, FO371/81967/E1195/4G, Ministry of Defence minute, 26 October 1950; FRUS 1951 v, p. 134; PRO, FO371/91185/E1024/24G, Franks to Morrison, 19 May 1951, and subsequent minutes.
10 Devereux, pp. 33ff.; PRO, FO371/81967/E1195/4G, Ministry of Defence minute, 26 October 1950.
11 FRUS 1951 v, p. 50; PRO, FO371/91219-91221/E1192/File.
12 FRUS 1951 v, p. 50 and p. 144; PRO, CAB128/26, C.M.36(51), 22 May 1951; PRO, FO371/91184/E1024/30G, Dudgeon minute, 31 May 1951.
13 PRO, FO371/90129-90151/JE1051/File.
14 Harry S. Truman Library (hereafter referred to as HST), Acheson Papers, Princeton Seminars, Box 80, 15–16 May 1954 Discussions.
15 PRO, FO371/91182/E1022/12, Washington to Foreign Office, Cable 1108 Saving, 27 October 1951, and E1022/14, Washington to Foreign Office, Cable 1146 Saving, 7 November 1951, and subsequent minutes; PRO, FO371/91200/E1057/8, Eastern Department memorandum, 29 October 1951.
16 *Ibid.*

17 FRUS 1950 V, p. 289; FRUS 1952–4 IX, pp. 585ff.; United States National Archives (hereafter referred to as USNA), Record Group 59, Central Decimal Files (CDF), 611.41 Series.

18 FRUS 1952–4 IX, p. 199. See also USNA, RG 59, Records of the Policy Planning Staff, Bonbright memorandum, 6 September 1951.

19 PRO, FO371/90150/JE1051/518, Foreign Office to Washington, Cable 6098, 14 December 1951; PRO, FO371/96920/JE1052/69, Cairo to Foreign Office, Cable 166, 26 January 1952; PRO, FO371/96921/JE1052/85, Foreign Office to *Queen Mary*, Cable 27, 27 January 1952; USNA, RG 59, CDF, 641.74/1-2752, Cairo to State Department, Cable 1158, 27 January 1952.

20 McGhee, pp. 329ff.; PRO, FO371/91184/E1024/15G, Boswall to Bowker, 29 March 1951; PRO, CAB128/19, C.M.51(51), 12 July 1951; HST, President's Standard File, Subject, Box 180, Iran, Paris to State Department, Cable 5189, 10 November 1951.

21 HST, Acheson Papers, Princeton Seminars, Box 80, 15–16 May 1954 Discussions.

22 USNA, RG 330 (Secretary of Defense), Office of the Administrative Secretary, Box 316, Lovett to Bruce, 16 August 1952, and Lovett to Acheson, 18 November 1952.

23 PRO, CAB129/55, C(52)354, 'Persia: US Ideas for a Settlement of the Oil Dispute', 23 October 1952.

24 Sayed-Ahmed, p. 59 and p. 69; FRUS 1949 V, p. 187.

25 Author's interviews with George McGhee, Sir John Wilton and Miles Copeland; Copeland, *The Game of Nations*, pp. 52ff.

26 Sayed-Ahmed, pp. 84ff.

27 Aronson, p. 51; USNA, RG 59, Records of the Policy Planning Staff, 1947–53, Box 14, National Security Council staff study, 18 January 1952.

28 Author's interviews with Lord Franks and George McGhee; HST, Acheson Papers, Memoranda of Conversations, Box 67, Acheson and Franks, 27 January 1952; FRUS 1952–4 IX, p. 1758.

29 Copeland, *The Game of Nations*, pp. 47ff.; Sayed-Ahmed, pp. 61ff.

30 Sayed-Ahmed, p. 74 and p. 80.

31 Copeland, *The Game of Nations*, pp. 52ff.

32 PRO, FO371/96876/JE1018/189, Strang minute, 2 July 1952; FRUS 1952–4 IX, pp. 1826ff.; USNA, RG 59, Central Decimal File, 641.74/7-1152, Cairo to State Department, Cable 64, 11 July 1952.

33 FRUS 1952–4 IX, p. 1838.

34 *Ibid.*, pp. 1826ff.; HST, HST Series, Naval Aide Files, State Department Briefs, Box 24, July–August 1952, 16 July 1952 Summary.

35 Author's interview with Julian Amery.

36 PRO, FO371/96877/JE1018/204, Cairo to Foreign Office, Cable 1060, 23 July 1952; PRO, FO371/96932/JE1052/398G, Eden minute, 5 August 1952.

37 USNA, RG 59, CDF, 774.00/7-2552, Cairo to State Department, Cable 182, 25 July 1952; Sayed-Ahmed, p. 95.

38 USNA, RG 59, CDF, 774.00/8-952, Cairo to State Department, Cable 315, 9 August 1952, and subsequent minutes; author's interview with Miles Copeland.

39 Dwight D. Eisenhower Library (hereafter referred to as DDE), James Hagerty Series, Diary Entries, Box 1, Hagerty diary, 25 January 1954.

40 PRO, FO371/96880/JE1018/33G, Cairo to Foreign Office, Cable 1279, 27 August 1952; HST, HST Series, Naval Aide Files, State Department Briefs, Box 24, September 1952, 9 September 1952 Summary; USNA, 774.00/9-752, Cairo to State Department, Cable 593, 7 September 1952, and 774.00/9-852, Washington to State

Department, Cable 1334, 8 September 1952; PRO, FO371/96896/JE10345/14, Washington to Foreign Office, Cable 1715, 8 September 1952, and JE10345/18, Cairo to Foreign Office, 9 September 1952, and subsequent minutes; FRUS 1952–4 IX, p. 1857.

41 PRO, FO371/96896/JE10345/27, Cairo to Foreign Office, Cable 1493, 9 October 1952; Eveland, p. 262; USNA, RG 84, Cairo Embassy Records, 1949–54, 320.1 Anglo-Egyptian Negotiations, Cairo to State Department, Cable 1990, 5 March 1953; *The Times*, 14 January 1953; USNA, RG 59, CDF, 641.74/1–1453, State Department to Cairo, Cable 1401, 14 January 1953; PRO, FO371/102731/JE10345/1, Strang minute, 29 January 1953, and JE10345/14, Hankey to Bowker, 23 June 1953; author's interview with Sir John Wilton.

42 FRUS 1952–4 IX, p. 222.

2: *Division and Reconciliation, 1953–4*

1 DDE, Ann Whitman Series, DDE Diaries, Box 8, DDE Diary, December 1954 (2), Eisenhower to Hazlett, 8 December 1954; DDE, Pre-Presidential Series, Princeton File, Box 72, Robert A. Lovett (1), Lovett to Eisenhower, 24 January 1952; PRO, PREM11/89, New York to Foreign Office, Cable 7, 6 January 1953; Ferrell, p. 222.

2 Ewald, p. 95; DDE, James Hagerty Series, Diary Entries, Box 1, Eisenhower–Muir meeting, 22 July 1954; DDE, Ann Whitman Series, DDE Diaries, Box 3, DDE Personal Diary, January–November 1954 (2), Eisenhower to Churchill, 22 July 1954; DDE, Ann Whitman Series, DDE Diaries, Box 8, DDE Diary, August 1954 (1), Churchill to Eisenhower, 8 August 1954.

3 DDE, C. D. Jackson Series, Papers, Box 37, General Robert Cutler, Jackson to Cutler, 11 May 1953.

4 DDE, C. D. Jackson Series, Records 1953–4, Box 2, Bermuda Conference Briefing Book (5), CIA, 'Political and Psychological Warfare Exploitation of Bermuda', undated.

5 *Ibid.*, Division of Near East and Africa Affairs, 'Communiqué of the Bermuda Conference', undated.

6 Hoopes, pp. 52ff.; Beal, pp. 13ff.; Gerson, pp. 15ff.

7 Gerson, p. 28 and p. 72.

8 Gerson, pp. 38ff. and 45ff.

9 John Foster Dulles Library, Princeton University, Robert Bowie oral history, 10 August 1964. See also Menzies, p. 159.

10 AP, AP23/5, Eden record, undated.

11 Eden, p. 63.

12 C.f. John Foster Dulles Library, Princeton University, Robert Bowie oral history, 10 August 1964.

13 Mosley, p. 329.

14 DDE, Oral History Collection, OH-205, Dillon Anderson, 30 December 1969; author's interview with General Andrew Goodpaster.

15 DDE, Oral History Collection, OH-188, John Hanes, 30 December 1970.

16 DDE, Ann Whitman Series, DDE Diaries, Box 12, January 1956 Diary, Eisenhower memorandum, 10 January 1956.

17 John Foster Dulles Library, Princeton University, George Humphrey oral history, 5 May 1964.

18 Adams, p. 90. See also DDE, John Foster Dulles Series, Telephone Calls, White House, Box 10, Eisenhower to Foster Dulles, 8 July 1953.

19 Neff, p. 143; Carlton, *Anthony Eden*, p. 323; Mosley, p. 292.

20 Neff, p. 145.

21 Author's interview with Lord Sherfield (Roger Makins).

22 Woodhouse, p. 123; Roosevelt, p. 120; West, p. 90; PRO, FO800/739, Foster Dulles–Eden and Foster Dulles–Eden–Eisenhower meetings, 6 March 1953; DDE, Ann Whitman Series, National Security Council, Box 4, 132nd NSC meeting, 18 February 1953, and 136th NSC meeting, 11 March 1953.

23 PRO, FO371/102795-102796/JE1192/File.

24 PRO, PREM11/486, Washington to Foreign Office, Cable 479, 6 March 1953, and Eisenhower to Churchill, 19 March 1953.

25 FRUS 1952–4 IX, p. 2032.

26 *Ibid.*, pp. 27ff.; Brands, p. 451.

27 FRUS 1952–4, IX, pp. 25 ff. and p. 379.

28 *Ibid.*, pp. 379ff.

29 USNA, RG 59, Records of the Policy Planning Staff, 1947–53, Foster Dulles memorandum, 1 June 1953.

30 PRO, FO371/104257/23, Washington to Foreign Office, Cable 1174, 2 June 1953. C.f. USNA, RG 59, Records of the Policy Planning Staff, 1947–53, Box 14.

31 Eisenhower, *Mandate for Change*, p. 155; PRO, FO371/102731-102732/JE10345/File.

32 FRUS 1952–4 IX, p. 2108 and p. 2124; USNA, RG 59, CDF, 641.74/7-2253, State Department to Cairo, Cable 96, 22 July 1953.

33 PRO, CAB128/26, C.C.42(53), 13 July 1953.

34 FRUS 1952–4 IX, p. 379 and p. 466.

35 PRO, FO371/102818/JE1192/568G, Eden–Foster Dulles meeting, 17 October 1953.

36 PRO, DEFE4/56, COS(52)121st meeting, 26 August 1952; author's interview with Julian Amery.

37 Gilbert, pp. 719ff. and pp. 795ff.

38 Author's interview with Julian Amery.

39 PRO, CAB128/26, C.C.60(53), 22 October 1953; PRO, FO371/102818/JE1192/560G, Cairo to Foreign Office, Cable 1449, 23 October 1953, and subsequent minutes.

40 PRO, FO800/774, Washington to Foreign Office, Cable 2373, 3 November 1953; DDE, John Foster Dulles Series, Chronological, Box 5, Foster Dulles memorandum, 3 November 1953.

41 Heikal, *Nasser*, pp. 45ff.; Heikal, *Cutting the Lion's Tail*, pp. 46ff.

42 FRUS 1952–4 IX, pp. 1958ff.; PRO, PREM11/395/File; PRO, PREM11/699/File; PRO, FO371/102843/JE11345/9G, Dixon minute, 16 December 1953; PRO, PREM11/484, Boothby minute, 18 December 1953.

43 PRO, PREM11/699, Foreign Office to Washington, Cable 5334, 19 December 1953.

44 PRO, PREM11/701, Washington to Foreign Office, Cable 86, 13 January 1954.

45 PRO, FO371/102766/JE1052/148, Amery to Churchill, 7 October 1953; PRO, CAB128/26, C.C.79(53), 14 December 1953, and subsequent meetings.

46 FRUS 1952–4 IX, pp. 416ff, and p. 433; DDE, Ann Whitman Series, Dulles–Herter, Box 1, Foster Dulles memorandum, 10 November 1953. See also Jalal, pp. 430ff.

47 PRO, FO371/106935-106936/FY1192/File; PRO, FO371/106937/FY1192/66, Eden minute, 4 December 1953, and subsequent minutes.

48 FRUS 1952–4 IX, pp. 439ff.; PRO, FO371/106937/FY1192/94, Washington to Foreign Office, Cable 2793, 29 December 1953, and subsequent minutes; DDE, John Foster Dulles, White House Memoranda, Chronological, Box 1, Meeting with the President 1954 (4), Foster Dulles memorandum, 5 January 1954; PRO, FO371/112315/DY1192/47, Eden to Foreign Office, Cable 7, 24 January 1954.

49 Louis in Louis and Owen, pp. 46ff. and p. 64.

50 USNA, RG 59, CDF, 787.5-MSP/11-2553, State Department to Baghdad, Cable 302, 25 November 1953; Jalal, p. 430; PRO, FO371/104676/EQ10345/3, Troutbeck to Eden, 1 December 1953.

51 PRO, FO371/104326/E1197/14, Eden minute on BMEO to Cairo, Cable F233, 27 March 1953; PRO, CAB128/27, C.C.62(53), 29 October 1953.

52 PRO, FO371/110819/V1193/8, Eden minute, 12 January 1954.

53 PRO, FO371/110819-110821/V1193/File.

54 PRO, FO371/108413-108445/JE1193/File.

55 PRO, FO371/112316/DY1192/62, Ankara to Foreign Office, Cable 57, 2 February 1954; PRO, FO371/112314-112322/DY1192/File.

56 DDE, Ann Whitman Series, DDE Diaries, Box 5, Telephone Calls, Eisenhower minute, 8 October 1953; DDE, Ann Whitman Series, Administration, Box 22, Eric Johnston (1), 'Report to the President on Middle Eastern Mission', 19 November 1953.

57 FRUS 1952–4 IX, p. 1406 and p. 1502; DDE, John Foster Dulles Series, Chronological, Box 7, April 1954 (2), Foster Dulles to Byroade, 10 April 1954; DDE, John Foster Dulles Series, Telephone Calls, Box 2, Foster Dulles to Nixon, 13 August 1954.

58 USNA, RG 84, Cairo Embassy Records, 1953–5, Box 1, 322.2 TVA-Jordan Valley Project, Johnston minute, 26 June 1954.

59 DDE, Ann Whitman Series, National Security Council, Box 7, 207th NSC meeting, 22 July 1954.

60 Ibid.; FRUS 1952–4 IX, p. 506.

61 PRO, FO371/104238/E1197/71G, War Office to Bruce, 13 October 1953, and E1197/83G, Scott-Fox to Hood, 16 December 1953; PRO, FO371/110826-110827/V1195/File.

62 PRO, FO371/110822/V1193/79G, COS(54)212, 'Co-ordination in Middle Eastern Defence Planning', 25 June 1954, and subseqent minutes; USNA, RG 218, Records of the JCS, Geographical Files, 1954–6, 381 EMMEA (11-19-47), S. 22, Joint Strategic Plans Committee report, 11 August 1955.

63 Shamir in Louis and Owen, p. 79. The Nasser–Yadin meeting was abandoned after Egypt's execution of two members of the Lavon spy ring in January 1955.

64 FRUS 1952–4 IX, p. 1662, p. 1683 and p. 1693.

65 Carlton, Anthony Eden, p. 338; DDE, Oral History Collection, OH-117, Livingston Merchant, 5 April 1967.

66 Hoopes, pp. 214ff.; Carlton, ibid., pp. 341ff.; Eden, p. 100.

67 Shuckburgh, p. 20; Mosley, pp. 356ff.

68 Shuckburgh, pp. 186ff.; DDE, Ann Whitman Series, Dulles–Herter, Box 2, Geneva to State Department, Cable DULTE 33, 30 April 1954.

69 PRO, FO800/742, Makins to Eden, 18 June 1954.

70 DDE, James Hagerty Series, Diary Entries, Box 1, 24 June 1954 entry.

71 DDE, John Foster Dulles Series, Telephone Calls, Box 2, Foster Dulles to Lodge,

25 June 1954; DDE, Ann Whitman Series, Ann Whitman Diary, Box 2, ACW Diary, Churchill–Eisenhower meeting, 26 June 1954; DDE, John Foster Dulles Series, Telephone Calls, White House, Box 10, Eisenhower to Foster Dulles, 26 June 1954; DDE, Ann Whitman Series, DDE Diaries, Box 7, DDE Diary, Eisenhower to Churchill, 7 July 1954.

72 Eden, p. 63; Mosley, p. 353.

73 DDE, John Foster Dulles Series, Telephone Calls, Box 2, Foster Dulles to Lodge, 25 June 1954.

74 PRO, FO371/104258/E10345/40, Pelham to Bowker, 5 July 1953; PRO, FO371/114874/ES1051/File; Mosley, p. 348.

75 USNA, RG 59, CDF, 774.5-MSP Series, State Department to Cairo, Cable 144, 28 July 1954, Eisenhower minute, 12 August 1954, and State Department to Cairo, Cable 382, 4 September 1954; Simpson, pp. 249ff.

76 USNA, RG 59, CDF, 774.5-MSP/9-2754, Cairo to State Department, Despatch 545, 27 September 1954, and subsequent minutes; DDE, John Foster Dulles Series, Telephone Calls, Box 3, Foster Dulles to Allen Dulles, 27 October 1954; Copeland, *The Game of Nations*, p. 123; Eveland, p. 91.

77 USNA, RG 59, CDF, 780.5/9-2754, London to State Department, Despatch 876, 27 September 1954; PRO, FO371/110788/V1073/57, Falla minute, 2 October 1954, and subsequent minutes; Shuckburgh, p. 237.

78 PRO, FO371/110787-110788/V1073/File.

79 *Ibid.*

80 USNA, RG 59, CDF, 641.74 Series, London to State Department, Cable 2506, 25 October 1954, and Cairo to State Department, Despatch 761, 21 October 1954.

81 PRO, FO371/108485/JE11932/5, BMEO to Foreign Office, Cable 614, 9 December 1954.

3: Seeds of Conflict, February–September 1955

1 Heikal, *Cutting the Lion's Tail*, pp. 73ff.; Carlton, *Anthony Eden*, p. 365; Nutting, *Nasser*, p. 89; Love, p. 199.

2 PRO, FO371/115492/V1073/289, Cairo to Foreign Office, Cable 269, 21 February 1955; Rhodes James, p. 398; FRUS 1955–7, XIV, p. 71.

3 PRO, FO371/115583/V1193/31G, Bangkok to Foreign Office, Cable 146, 23 February 1955; PRO, FO371/115866/VR1076/28G, Cairo to Foreign Office, Cable 278, 22 February 1955; PRO, FO371/115492/V1073/289, Cairo to Foreign Office, Cable 269, 21 February 1955; Love, p. 199; FRUS 1955–7 XIV, p. 71.

4 PRO, FO371/115484/V1073/11, Baghdad to Foreign Office, Cable 25, 11 January 1955; PRO, FO371/115485/V1073/56, Hooper to Shuckburgh, 12 January 1955; PRO, FO371/115484/V1073/2, Shuckburgh minute, 6 January 1955. See also Eilts in Louis and Owen, p. 350.

5 PRO, FO371/115484/V1073/26, Shuckburgh minute, 11 January 1955. See also Avon Papers (hereafter cited as AP), AP20/23, Bowker to Eden, 1 March 1956.

6 PRO, FO371/115484/V1073/33, Foreign Office to Baghdad, Cable 45, 14 January 1955; PRO, FO371/115488/V1073/175, Foreign Office to Baghdad, Cable 153, 5 February 1955; PRO, FO371/115490/V1073/229, Foreign Office to Ankara, Cable 199, 10 February 1955.

7 Shamir in Louis and Owen, pp. 73ff.; Oren, pp. 353ff.; Sayed-Ahmed, pp. 195ff. and pp. 206ff.; Green, pp. 101ff.; Nutting, *Nasser*, p. 93; USNA, RG 84, Cairo Embassy

Records, 1949−54, Box 5, To Department, Cairo to State Department, Cable 1819, 10 February 1953.

8 The following section on Israeli policy is based upon Shlaim, pp. 180ff.; Bar-Zohar, *Ben-Gurion*, pp. 217ff.; USNA, RG 59, CDF, 684A.86/5-2055, Tel Aviv to State Department, Despatch 728, 20 May 1955; Lucas, 'Israeli Foreign Policy and Civil-Military Relations, 1953−6'; Sharon and Chanoff, pp. 83ff.

9 See Melman and Raviv, pp. 64ff.

10 Shlaim, p. 188; Bar-Zohar, *Ben-Gurion*, p. 217; USNA, RG 59, CDF, 684A.86/5-2055, Tel Aviv to State Department, Despatch 728, 20 May 1955; USNA, RG 59, CDF, 674.84A/3-155, Cairo to State Department, Cable 1256, 1 March 1956.

11 Shlaim, p. 188; Bar-Zohar, *Ben-Gurion*, p. 218; USNA, RG 59, CDF, 674.84A/3-455, Tel Aviv to State Department, Cable 754, 4 March 1955.

12 Bar-Zohar, *ibid.*, p. 219; Neff, p. 33.

13 See Crosbie; Bar-Zohar, *Suez Ultra-Secret*, pp. 58ff.; Brecher, pp. 262ff.; Melman and Raviv, p. 99.

14 PRO, FO371/115495/V1073/399, Cairo to Foreign Office, Cable 350, 5 March 1955, and V1073/406, Damascus to Foreign Office, Cable 91, 7 March 1955; PRO, FO371/115496/V1073/407, Jedda to Foreign Office, Cable 56, 7 March 1955; USNA, RG 59, CDF, 774.00/3-1155, Cairo to State Department, Cable 1330, 11 March 1955.

15 PRO, FO371/115496/V1073/408, Amman to Foreign Office, Cable 95, 7 March 1955, and subsequent minutes.

16 PRO, CAB128/28, C.C.24(55), 15 March 1955; PRO, FO371/115751-115759/VO1051/File.

17 PRO, FO371/115484/V1073/2G, Shuckburgh minute, 11 January 1955.

18 PRO, FO371/115469/V1023/3G, Washington to Foreign Office, Cable 631 Saving, 28 January 1955.

19 PRO, FO371/115487/V1073/115, Baghdad to Foreign Office, Cable 68, 27 January 1955, and V1073/133, Ankara to Foreign Office, Cable 69, 31 January 1955; PRO, FO371/115488/V1073/161, Washington to Foreign Office, Cable 332, 4 February 1955; PRO, FO371/115489/V1073/176, Washington to Foreign Office, Cable 387, 9 February 1955; PRO, CAB128/28, C.C.24(55), 15 March 1955.

20 PRO, FO371/115502/V1073/568, Washington to Foreign Office, Cable 649, 24 March 1955, and subsequent minutes.

21 PRO, FO371/115964-115867/VR1076/File; FRUS 1955−7 XIV, pp. 24ff. and p. 90; DDE, John Foster Dulles Series, Special Assistants, Chronological, Box 7, February 1955 (3), Hanes to Russell, 15 February 1955.

22 FRUS 1955−7 XIV, p. 50 and p. 60.

23 *Ibid.*, p. 141, p. 169 and pp. 176ff.; PRO, FO800/678, Macmillan−Foster Dulles meeting, 12 May 1955; DDE, John Foster Dulles Series, White House Memoranda, Chronological, Box 3, Meeting with the President (4), MacArthur to Foster Dulles, 5 May 1955, and enclosed memoranda.

24 PRO, FO371/113591/JE1022/7, Cairo to Foreign Office, Cable 633, 17 May 1955, and JE1022/8, Cairo to Foreign Office, Cable 641, 19 May 1955; PRO, FO371/115868/VR1076/85G, Cairo to Foreign Office, Cable 609, 10 May 1955; PRO, FO371/115869/VR1076/105G, Washington to Foreign Office, Cable 1244, 31 May 1955; Aronson, p. 126.

25 PRO, FO371/115870/VR1076/112G, Cairo to Foreign Office, Cable 727, 9 June

1955; PRO, FO371/113680/JE1194/368. Trevelyan to Foreign Office, 24 October 1955. Foster Dulles tried, at the last minute, to delay Byroade's approach to Nasser, but the Ambassador had already acted (FRUS 1955–7, XIV, pp. 231ff.).

26 PRO, FO371/113669/JE1194/35, Shuckburgh minute, 10 March 1955, and subsequent minutes, and JE1194/36, Shuckburgh minute, 15 March 1955.

27 Heikal, *Nasser*, pp. 55ff.; *The End of Empire: Egypt*, interview with Ali Sabri; Hoopes, p. 324; Love, p. 90.

28 PRO, FO371/113675/JE1194/190, BBC Monitoring Report, 8 October 1955; Love, p. 90; Neff, p. 81; Hoopes, p. 324; USNA, RG 59, CDF, 780.5/6-955, Cairo to State Department, Cable 1881, 9 June 1955; USNA, RG 59, CDF, 674.84A/6-1755, Cairo to State Department, Cable 1928, 17 June 1955.

29 PRO, FO371/113608/JE1057/5, Bromley minute, 3 June 1955, and subsequent minutes.

30 PRO, FO371/113608/JE1057/7, de Zulueta minute, 22 June 1955, and subsequent minutes, and JE1057/8, de Zulueta to Graham, 8 July 1955, and subsequent minutes.

31 *Ibid.*, PRO, FO371/113608/JE1057/10G, Lloyd to Macmillan, 4 August 1955, and subsequent minutes.

32 FRUS 1955–7 XIV, p. 274.

33 PRO, FO371/113670/JE1194/File; Love, p. 90; Hoopes, p. 324; *The End of Empire: Egypt*, interview with Ali Sabri.

34 Copeland, *The Game of Nations*, p. 148; Neff, p. 81; Mosley, p. 386; DDE, John Foster Dulles Series, Chronological, Box 12, Foster Dulles memorandum, 5 August 1955.

35 Israeli State Archives, 2382/9, Elath to Foreign Ministry, February and April 1955.

36 USNA, RG 59, CDF, 684A.86/2-1455, State Department to Tel Aviv, Cable 456, 14 February 1955.

37 FRUS 1955–7 XIV, p. 209.

38 *Ibid.*, p. 222; USNA, RG 59, CDF, 684A.86/5-2855, State Department to Cairo, Cable 2069, 28 May 1955.

39 USNA, RG 59, CDF, 684A.86/5-3055, London to State Department, Cable 5222, 30 May 1955.

40 PRO, FO371/115871/VR1076/131G, Shuckburgh to Kirkpatrick, 8 July 1955, and subsequent minutes, and VR1076/128G, Macmillan to Eden, 12 July 1955; PRO, CAB128/29, C.M.23(55), 14 July 1955; FRUS 1955–7 XIV, pp. 295ff.

41 PRO, FO371/115871/VR1076/134G, Foreign Office to Washington, Cable 3338, 19 July 1955; CAB128/29, C.M.27(55), 28 July 1955; DDE, John Foster Dulles Series, White House Memoranda, Chronological, Box 3, Meetings with the President (2), Foster Dulles memorandum, 11 August 1955; PRO, FO371/115586/V1193/97G, Washington to Foreign Office, Cable 1902, 16 August 1956.

42 PRO, FO371/115873/VR1076/177G, Washington to Foreign Office, Cable 1938, 19 August 1955, and subsequent minutes; *US Declassified Document Reference System* (hereafter cited as US DDRS), US83 001051; PRO, FO371/115874/VR1076/200G, Graham to Macmillan, 25 August 1955.

43 US DDRS, US86 000218; DDE, Ann Whitman Series, Dulles–Herter, Box 4, September 1955 (2), Foster Dulles to Eisenhower, 1 September 1955; CAB129/77, C.P.(55)127, 'Palestine', 20 September 1955; PRO, FO371/115875/VR1076/208, Tel Aviv to Foreign Office, Cable 291, 28 August 1955; PRO, FO371/115879/VR1076/306G, Cairo to Foreign Office, Cable 1286, 20 September 1955; PRO, FO371/115876/VR1076/218G, Arthur minute, 30 August 1955.

44 Shlaim, pp. 191ff.

45 DDE, John Foster Dulles Series, Telephone Calls, Box 4, Foster Dulles to Lawson, 31 August 1955, and Foster Dulles to Allen, 1 September 1955.

46 Love, p. 98 and p. 142; Abel Thomas, pp. 19ff.; Bar-Zohar, *Ben-Gurion*, pp. 227ff.; Childers, p. 133; Hoopes, p. 136; Copeland, *The Game of Nations*, p. 132.

47 USNA, RG 59, CDF, 611.74/8-1155, Cairo to State Department, Despatch 164, 11 August 1955.

48 USNA, RG 59, CDF, 774.56/8-1555, Cairo to State Department, Cable 234, 15 August 1955; DDE, John Foster Dulles Series, Telephone Calls, Box 4, Foster Dulles to Allen Dulles, 17 August 1955, and Foster Dulles to Cabell, 29 August 1955; US DDRS, US76 224G.

49 US DDRS, US76 182E.

50 USNA, RG 59, CDF, 684A.86 Series, State Department to Cairo, Cable 515, 15 September 1955, Cairo to State Department, Cable 485, 16 September 1955, and State Department to Cairo, Cable 537, 20 September 1955.

51 USNA, RG 59, CDF, 774.56/9-1955, State Department to New York, Cable TEDUL 2, 19 September 1955; Heikal, *Nasser*, p. 57.

52 Neff, p. 89; PRO, FO800/669, Macmillan to Eden, 22 September 1955; PRO, FO371/113674/JE1194/149, Cairo to Foreign Office, Cable 1315, 25 September 1955, and JE1194/151, Shuckburgh minute, 22 September 1955.

53 PRO, FO371/115518/V1073/998, Washington to Foreign Office, Cable 1945, 19 August 1955; PRO, FO371/115521/V1073/1066G, Morris to Hadow, 29 September 1955; PRO, FO371/115585/V1193/94G, Washington to Foreign Office, Cable 456 Saving, 13 August 1955; PRO, FO371/115586/V1193/97G, Eden to Macmillan, 19 August 1955; PRO, FO371/115877/VR1076/272G, Graham minute, 29 August 1955; PRO, FO371/115876/VR1076/218G, Eden minute, 31 August 1955. See also AP, AP20/1, Eden diary entry, 30 August 1955.

54 Private information; Shuckburgh, p. 12.

55 Pimlott, p. 582; William Clark Papers (hereafter cited as WCP), Clark Diary, 24 October 1955.

56 AP, AP3/2/7, unnamed draft for Clarissa Eden, 19 January 1955.

57 Clark, pp. 156ff.; Shuckburgh, p. 66 and p. 70; Horne, p. 375.

58 Neff, p. 148.

59 Colville, pp. 673ff.; Shuckburgh, p. 14.

60 Shuckburgh, p. 14.

61 Shuckburgh, p. 14 and p. 48; Clark, p. 159; Rhodes James, p. 366.

62 Author's interview with Sir Andrew Stark.

63 Author's interview with Sir Harold Beeley.

64 Rhodes James, p. 406; Shuckburgh, p. 42; Williams, p. 421; Clark, p. 164.

65 Pimlott, p. 367; Horne, p. 374.

66 Eden, p. 269; Horne, p. 371; Shuckburgh, p. 277.

67 Shuckburgh, p. 14.

68 WCP, Clark diary, 24–25 October 1955.

69 Shuckburgh, p. 42; Williams, p. 421 and p. 450; USNA, RG 59, CDF, 741.00/3-2156, London to State Department, Despatch 2271, 21 March 1956; author's interview with Julian Amery.

70 Neff, p. 187; 'Political Commentary' by Henry Fairlie, *Spectator*, 7 October 1955, p. 436.

4: The Search for an Egyptian Policy, September–October 1955

1 DDE, John Foster Dulles Series, Telephone Calls, Box 4, Foster Dulles to Allen Dulles and Foster Dulles to Hoover, 20 September 1955; USNA, RG 59, CDF, 774.56/9-2755, State Department to New York, Cable TEDUL 3, 27 September 1955.

2 Copeland, *The Game of Nations*, pp. 132ff.

3 DDE, John Foster Dulles Series, Telephone Calls, White House, Box 10, Foster Dulles to Eisenhower, 23 September 1955.

4 Adams, pp. 182ff.; author's interview with General Andrew Goodpaster; PRO, FO800/669, Washington to Foreign Office, Cable 2582, 25 October 1955; USNA, RG 59, CDF, 774.56/9-2755, State Department to New York, Cable TEDUL 4, 27 September 1955.

5 See PRO, FO371/119009/JE1223/62, New York to Foreign Office, Cable 780, 20 September 1955.

6 AP, AP20/22, Washington to Foreign Office, Cable 2582, 25 October 1956; PRO, FO371/113674/JE1194/151G, Shuckburgh minute, 22 September 1955, and subsequent minutes.

7 PRO, FO371/113674/JE1194/152G, Caccia minute, 23 September 1955, and JE1194/156G, Macmillan minute, 23 September 1955; Horne, p. 368.

8 Copeland, *The Game of Nations*, pp. 134ff.; USNA, RG 59, CDF, 774.56/9-2755, State Department to New York, Cable TEDUL 2, 27 September 1955.

9 Copeland, *ibid.* Roosevelt's suggestion may have been superfluous. The Soviet Ambassador to Egypt, Daniel Solod, had told Nasser that 'the transaction could be disguised as a deal between Egypt and Czechoslovakia' (PRO, FO371/113673/JE1194/134, Trevelyan to Shuckburgh, 23 August 1955).

10 Copeland, *ibid.*; PRO, FO371/113674/JE1194/163, Cairo to Foreign Office, Cable 1330, 26 September 1955, and JE1194/182, Cairo to Foreign Office, Cable 1340, 28 September 1955.

11 Neff, p. 91; Copeland, *ibid.*, pp. 136ff.; Heikal, *Nasser*, p. 56; PRO, FO371/113675/JE1194/190, Cairo to Foreign Office, Cable 1350, 27 September 1955; USNA, RG 59, CDF, 611.74/8-1156, Cairo to State Department, Despatch 164, 11 August 1955; author's interview with Miles Copeland.

12 Neff, p. 92; Copeland, *The Game of Nations*, p. 138; Eveland, p. 148; USNA, RG 59, CDF, 684A.86/9-2855, Cairo to State Department, Cable 590, 28 September 1955.

13 Shuckburgh, p. 281.

14 FRUS 1955–7 XIV, pp. 516ff.

15 PRO, FO371/113674/JE1194/180, New York to Foreign Office, Cable 844, 27 September 1955, and JE1194/178, New York to Foreign Office, Cable 847, 27 September 1955; DDE, John Foster Dulles Series, Telephone Calls, Box 4, Foster Dulles to Hoover, 27 September 1955.

16 DDE, John Foster Dulles Series, Chronological, Box 12, Foster Dulles letter to Nasser, 27 September 1955.

17 USNA, RG 59, CDF, 684A.86/9-2755, New York to State Department, Cable DULTE 4, 27 September 1955; Trevelyan, p. 90; Copeland, *The Game of Nations*, pp. 140ff.; USNA, RG 59, CDF, 774.56/11-655.

18 DDE, John Foster Dulles Series, Telephone Calls, Box 4, Hoover to Foster Dulles and Foster Dulles to Allen, 28 September 1955.

19 Neff, p. 94; Heikal, *Nasser*, pp. 59ff.; DDE, John Foster Dulles Series, Telephone Calls, Box 4, Foster Dulles to Allen Dulles, 29 September 1955.

20 Neff, p. 95; author's interview with Miles Copeland.
21 USNA, RG 59, CDF, 774.56/10-155, Cairo to State Department, Cable 632, 1 October 1955, and 774.56/10-355, Cairo to State Department, Cable 654, 3 October 1955.
22 Shuckburgh, p. 281; PRO, FO371/113676/JE1194/248, Bromley minute, 27 September 1955, and subsequent minutes.
23 PRO, FO371/113678/JE1194/289G, Shuckburgh record, 29 September 1955.
24 PRO, FO371/113678/JE1194/286G, Washington to Foreign Office, Cables 2339 and 2340, 30 September 1955, and subsequent minutes.
25 Author's interview with Sir John Wilton; USNA, RG 84, Cairo Embassy General Records, 050 Prominent Persons, Cairo to State Department, Despatch 1957, 13 April 1955.
26 Horne, p. 369.
27 PRO, FO800/678, Washington to Foreign Office, Cable 2340, 30 September 1955.
28 PRO, FO371/113676/JE1194/260G, Record of Anglo-American meeting, 3 October 1955; USNA, RG 59, 774.56/10-355, Wilkins memorandum, 3 October 1955. See also Horne, p. 369.
29 Neff, p. 103; Love, p. 109; PRO, FO371/113675/JE1194/206, Cairo to Foreign Office, Cable 1368, 2 October 1955, and JE1194/207, Cairo to Foreign Office, Cable 1369, 3 October 1955; PRO, FO371/113676/JE1194/251, Paris to Foreign Office, Cable 391 Saving, 5 October 1955.
30 AP, AP20/20, Eden to Macmillan, 12 October 1955.
31 PRO, FO371/113608/JE1057/11, Cairo to Foreign Office, Cable 1326, 26 September 1955; PRO, FO371/113674/JE1194/161, Cairo to Foreign Office, Cable 1325, 26 September 1955, and JE1194/162, Cairo to Foreign Office, Cable 1326, 26 September 1955; PRO, FO800/669, Foreign Office to New York, Cable 1283, 27 September 1955; Shuckburgh, p. 284.
32 AP, AP20/22, Foreign Office to New York, Cable 1304, 28 September 1955, and subsequent minutes.
33 WCP, Clark Diary, 3 October 1955.
34 PRO, CAB128/29, C.M.34(55), 4 October 1955.
35 *Ibid.*
36 PRO, FO800/678, Washington to Foreign Office, Cable 2433, 9 October 1955.
37 See AP, AP20/23, Foreign Office to Washington, Cable 4074, 3 September 1955, and AP20/22, Eden minute on Tehran to Foreign Office, Cable 589, 23 August 1955, and Eden minute on New York to Foreign Office, Cable 865, 28 September 1955.
38 USNA, RG 59, CDF, 774.56/9-2755, New York to State Department, Cable DULTE 2, 27 September 1955; AP, AP20/23, Washington to Foreign Office, Cable 2365, 3 October 1955, and GEN507/1st meeting, 5 October 1955.
39 DDE, John Foster Dulles Series, Telephone Calls, Box 4, Foster Dulles to Allen Dulles and Wilson to Foster Dulles, 6 October 1955.
40 PRO, FO371/115522/V1073/1089, Hadow minute, 24 September 1955, and subsequent minutes; PRO, FO371/115523/V1073/1108, Washington to Foreign Office, Cable 2473, 13 October 1955.
41 DDE, Ann Whitman Series, National Security Council, Box 1, Record of Actions by NSC 1954, Action 1421, 27 October 1955.
42 CAB129/78, C.P.(55)152, 'Middle East Oil', 14 October 1955; CAB128/29, C.M.35(55), 18 October 1955, and C.M.36(55), 20 October 1955.
43 Nutting, *Nasser*, pp. 129ff.

44 DDE, Ann Whitman, Dulles–Herter, Box 1, Eisenhower to Matthews, 23 April 1953; USNA, RG 59, Records of the Policy Planning Staff, 1947–53, Eisenhower to Foster Dulles, 23 April 1953; FRUS 1952–4 IX, p. 1908; USNA, RG 59, CDF, 774.5-MSP/4-2853, Byroade to Smith, 28 April 1953, and subsequent minutes.

45 FRUS 1955–7 XIV, p. 632.

46 Shuckburgh, p. 293; PRO, FO371/115469/V1023/14G, Paris to Foreign Office, Cable 419 Saving, 26 October 1955, and V1023/15G, Paris to Foreign Office, Cable 421 Saving, 26 October 1955; PRO, FO371/115387/V1193/149, Paris to Foreign Office, Cable 420 Saving, 26 October 1955; Macmillan, *Tides of Fortune*, p. 642; FRUS 1955–7 XIV, pp. 650ff.

47 USNA, RG 59, CDF, 684A.86/10-2955, State Department to Geneva, Cable TEDUL 36, 29 October 1955.

5: An Uneasy Partnership, October–December 1955

1 USNA, RG 59, CDF, 780.022 Series.

2 *Ibid.*; Mosley, p. 348.

3 USNA, RG 59, CDF, 780.001 Series, Geneva to State Department, Cable 737, 17 September 1955, and Newsom memorandum, 10 October 1955; DDE, John Foster Dulles Series, White House Memoranda, Box 8, Conversation with Allen Dulles, undated.

4 Shuckburgh, p. 289; PRO, CAB128/29, C.M.35(55), 18 October 1955; PRO, FO800/678, Kirkpatrick to Eden, 25 October 1955.

5 FRUS 1955–7 XIV, p. 656; AP, AP20/1, Geneva to Foreign Office, Cable 3, 26 October 1955.

6 PRO, FO371/115954/VY10393/10G, Hoover–Makins meeting, 27 October 1955. See also USNA, RG 59, CDF, 780.022/11-455, State Department to Jedda, Cable 223, 4 November 1955.

7 FRUS 1955–7 XIV, p. 671; DDE, Ann Whitman Series, Dulles–Herter, Box 5, Goodpaster to Adams, 1 November 1955.

8 USNA, RG 59, CDF, 784A.56/10-2855, Tel Aviv to State Department, Cable 426, 28 October 1955; DDE, Ann Whitman Series, Dulles–Herter, Box 4, October 1955, Goodpaster to Adams, 31 October 1955; Shlaim, p. 193; DDE, Ann Whitman Series, National Security Council, Box 7, 264th NSC meeting, 3 November 1955.

9 DDE, Ann Whitman Series, Dulles–Herter, Box 5, Goodpaster to Whitman, 4 November 1955, and Minnich to Goodpaster, 7 November 1955; Shlaim, p. 194; Bar-Zohar, *Ben-Gurion*, p. 223.

10 Shuckburgh, p. 296.

11 Lamb, pp. 174ff.

12 PRO, FO371/115880/VR1076/331G, Arthur minute, 4 November 1955.

13 PRO, FO371/115881/VR1976/350G, Cairo to Foreign Office, Cable 1706, 12 November 1955, and VR1076/383, Tel Aviv to Foreign Office, Cable 475, 16 November 1955; USNA, RG 59, CDF, 684A.86 Series, Tel Aviv to State Department, Cable 501, 14 November 1955, and Cable 508, 16 November 1955; USNA, RG 59, CDF, 774.56/11-1755, Tel Aviv to State Department, Cable 515, 17 November 1955. See also Israeli State Archives, Eytan to Nicholls, November 1955.

14 FRUS 1955–7 XIV, p. 720; AP, AP20/22, Geneva to Foreign Office, Cable 124, 9 November 1955.

15 DDE, Ann Whitman Series, National Security Council, Box 7, 267th NSC meeting, 21 November 1955.

16 DDE, Ann Whitman Series, Dulles–Herter, Box 5, State Department to Adams, Cable TODEN 18, 8 November 1955, and Eisenhower statement, 9 November 1955.

17 PRO, FO371/115881/VR1076/357, Foreign Office to Geneva, Cable 392, 11 November 1955; Shuckburgh, p. 299; Israeli State Archives, Shuckburgh–Elath meeting, November 1955; DDE, White House Office, Office of the Staff Secretary, Subject, State Department, Box 70, Hoover to White House (Gettysburg), 18 November 1955.

18 AP, AP20/23, Eden minute on Ankara to Foreign Office, Cable 734, 14 October 1955; PRO, FO371/115954/VY10393/10G, Makins–Hoover meeting, 28 October 1955; DDE, Ann Whitman Series, Dulles–Herter, Box 5, Goodpaster to Adams, 31 October 1955.

19 USNA, RG 59, CDF, 684A.86/10-2955, State Department to Geneva, Cable TEDUL 36, 29 October 1955; PRO, FO371/115527/V1073/1220, Hadow minute, 1 November 1955, and subsequent minutes; PRO, FO371/115527/V1073/1222, Washington to Foreign Office, Cable 2675, 3 November 1955.

20 PRO, FO371/115527/V1073/1224, Amman to Foreign Office, Cable 460, 6 November 1955, and subsequent minutes; PRO, FO371/115528/V1073/1246, Amman to Foreign Office, Cable 480, 9 November 1955.

21 PRO, FO371/115649/V1023/20, Cairo to Foreign Office, Cable 1609, 2 November 1955, and V1023/24, Macmillan–Dulles meeting, 9 November 1955; PRO, FO371/115533/V1073/1370, Morris to Hadow, 2 December 1955; FRUS 1955–7 XIV, p. 722.

22 PRO, FO371/115529/V1073/1222, Stark minute, 11 November 1955; AP, AP20/23, DC(55)14th meeting, 8 November 1955, Amman to Foreign Office, Cable 507, 18 November 1955, and Foreign Office to Amman, Cable 778, 19 November 1955.

23 PRO, FO800/678, Macmillan–Menderes meeting, 22 November 1955; PRO, FO371/115532/V1073/1342, Hooper to Rose, 24 November 1955.

24 PRO, FO371/115532/V1073/1336G, Shuckburgh draft, 24 November 1955, and subsequent minutes.

25 PRO, FO371/115656-115658/VJ1051/File; FRUS 1955–7 XIII, p. 1; USNA, RG 84, Cairo Embassy General Records 1955, 350 Other Countries A–Z, Amman to State Department, Cable 26, 1 September 1955, and Cable 285, 18 December 1955; Mosley, p. 350.

26 PRO, FO371/115469/V1023/28G, Aldrich to Macmillan, 6 December 1955; DDE, Ann Whitman Series, Ann Whitman Diary, Box 7, Eisenhower minute, 16 December 1955.

27 PRO, FO371/115469/V1023/23G, Shuckburgh minute, 10 November 1955, and subsequent minutes; PRO, FO371/115531/V1073/1317, Washington to Foreign Office, Cable 669 Saving, 23 November 1955.

28 PRO, FO371/115882/VR1076/391G, Cairo to Foreign Office, Cable 174 Saving, 17 November 1955; PRO, FO371/115884/VR1076/456G, Cairo to Foreign Office, Cable 1813, 28 November 1955.

29 PRO, FO371/115883/VR1073/421G, Washington to Foreign Office, Cable 2839, 21 November 1955, and subsequent minutes, and VR1076/422G, Washington to Foreign Office, Cable 2840, 21 November 1955; FRUS 1955–7 XIV, p. 793.

30 USNA, RG 59, CDF, 684A.86 Series, State Department to Paris, Cable TEDUL 12, 25 October 1955, and Paris to State Department, Cable DULTE 11, 26 October

1955, and State Department to Geneva, Cable TEDUL 30, 29 October 1955; DDE, John Foster Dulles Series, Telephone Calls, White House, Box 10, Hoover memorandum, 28 November 1955; PRO, FO371/115885/VR1076/485G, Washington to Foreign Office, Cable 2983, 6 December 1955; DDE, John Foster Dulles Series, Telephone Calls, Box 4, Allen Dulles to Foster Dulles and Foster Dulles to Allen, 6 December 1955.

31 USNA, RG 59, CDF, 674.84A/1-656, State Department to Tel Aviv, Cable 466, 6 January 1956; FRUS 1955–7 XV, p. 35; Copeland, *The Game of Nations*, p. 136.

32 USNA, RG 59, CDF, 784A.56/1-1056, Tel Aviv to State Department, Cable 693, 10 January 1956; FRUS 1955–7 XIV, pp. 24ff., p. 727 and p. 734; USNA, RG 59, CDF, 674.84A/11-1255, Tel Aviv to State Department, Cable 496, 12 November 1955.

33 PRO, FO371/115887/VR1076/504G, Arthur minute, 8 December 1955, and VR1076/524G, Shuckburgh minute, 16 December 1955; DDE, John Foster Dulles Series, Telephone Calls, Box 4, Foster Dulles to Allen Dulles, 23 December 1955; FRUS 1955–7 XV, p. 9; DDE 130.

34 FRUS 1955–7 XIV, p. 672.

35 PRO, FO371/113739/JE1423/269G, Foreign Office to Washington, Cable 5631, 26 November 1955.

36 DDE, John Foster Dulles Series, Telephone Calls, White House, Box 10, Eisenhower to Foster Dulles, 29 November 1955; PRO, FO371/113739/JE1423/275G, Washington to Foreign Office, Cable 2907, 30 November 1955.

37 DDE, Ann Whitman Series, National Security Council, Box 7, 268th NSC meeting, 1 December 1955; PRO, FO371/113740/JE1423/File.

38 PRO, FO371/113739/JE1423/269G, Foreign Office to Washington, Cable 5631, 26 November 1955; DDE, John Foster Dulles Series, Telephone Calls, White House, Box 10, Eisenhower to Foster Dulles, 28 and 29 November 1955.

39 AP, AP20/22, Geneva to Foreign Office, Cable 3, 26 October 1956.

40 PRO, FO800/678, Macmillan–Nuri Sa'id meeting, 20 November 1955; PRO, FO371/115532/V1073/1342, Hooper to Rose, 24 November 1955.

41 AP, AP20/23, Macmillan to Eden, 25 November 1956.

42 PRO, FO371/115469/V1023/26G, Macmillan to Foster Dulles, 25 November 1955, and V1023/28G, Aldrich to Macmillan, 6 December 1955, and subsequent minutes; Shuckburgh, p. 308.

43 Shuckburgh, pp. 311ff.

44 *Ibid.*; PRO, FO800/678, Macmillan–Foster Dulles meeting, 15 December 1955.

45 Rhodes James, p. 410; Shuckburgh, p. 313; author's interview with Sir John Wilton; AP, AP20/1, Eden diary, 17 September and 3 October 1955.

46 Shuckburgh, p. 131 and pp. 312ff.

47 Author's interview with Sir Donald Logan.

48 Author's interview with Sir Harold Beeley.

49 Horne, p. 372; DDE, John Foster Dulles Papers, Subject, Alphabetical, Box 11, Eden–Macmillan–Lloyd Correspondence (2), Foster Dulles to Macmillan, 20 December 1955, and Macmillan to Foster Dulles, 21 December 1955.

6: Towards a Summit, January–March 1956

1 PRO, FO371/121762/VJ1051/19G, Amman to Foreign Office, Cable 57, 9 January 1956; PRO, CAB128/30, C.M.3(56), 11 January 1956; PRO, FO371/121463/

VJ1015/44G, Amman to Foreign Office, Cable 72, 10 January 1956, and subsequent cables and minutes.

2 PRO, FO371/121462/VJ1015/36G, Foreign Office to Washington, Cable 199, 12 January 1956, and VJ1015/57G, Jedda to Foreign Office, Cable 6, 11 January 1956; PRO, FO371/121241/V1071/19, Cairo to Foreign Office, Cable 53, 11 January 1956.

3 PRO, DEFE4/82, JP(55)100(F), 22 December 1955; PRO, DEFE4/83, COS(56)11th meeting, 24 January 1956, COS(56)12th meeting, 26 January 1956, and COS(56)22nd meeting, 21 February 1956.

4 PRO, FO371/115532/V1073/1353, Amman to Foreign Office, Cable 558, 4 December 1955, and subsequent minutes.

5 PRO, FO371/115659/VJ1051/149G, Baghdad to Foreign Office, Cable 1083, 30 December 1955; PRO, FO371/121462/VJ1015/27G, Amman to Foreign Office, Cable 59, 9 January 1956, and subsequent minutes; PRO, FO371/121484/VJ10393/1G, Baghdad to Foreign Office, Cable 81, 18 January 1956; PRO, FO371/121237/V1071/120, Amman to Foreign Office, Cable 84, 11 January 1956.

6 PRO, FO371/121648/VQ1022/File; PRO, FO371/121870/VY10393/File.

7 PRO, FO371/121491/VJ1051/41, Arthur minute, 14 January 1956; Shuckburgh, p. 327.

8 PRO, FO371/121280/V1077/1G, Bishop to Resident Clerk, 15 January 1956.

9 FRUS 1955–7 XIII, pp. 223ff.; PRO, FO371/120525/E1021/2, Samuel minute, 10 January 1956.

10 PRO, FO371/121270/V1075/5G, Shuckburgh minute, 19 January 1956; PRO, CAB129/79, C.P.(56)9, 'Buraimi', 9 January 1956; FRUS 1955–7 XIII, p. 318; PRO, FO115/4548, Washington to Foreign Office, Cable 33 Saving, 14 January 1956.

11 Eveland, p. 160.

12 Shuckburgh, p. 323.

13 PRO, FO115/4548, Commonwealth Relations Office to UK High Commissioners, Circular Cable W15, 23 January 1956; PRO, FO371/121271/V1075/39, Arthur memoranda, 7 January 1956. See also PRO, FO371//118832/JE1015/1G, Trevelyan to Shuckburgh, 2 December 1955, and subsequent minutes.

14 PRO, FO371/121270/V1075/5G, Shuckburgh minute, 19 January 1956.

15 Daily Telegraph, 3 January 1956.

16 Nutting, No End of a Lesson, pp. 257ff.

17 WCP, File 7, Clark diary, 2 January and 5 January 1956.

18 HST, President's Personal File, Name, Box 26, Anthony Eden, Bradford Speech, 18 January 1956; Howard, p. 222.

19 Shuckburgh, p. 325, p. 327 and p. 330.

20 FRUS 1955–7 XIII, p. 324; Shuckburgh, p. 327.

21 FRUS 1955–7 XV, pp. 29ff.

22 Neff, pp. 135ff.; Heikal, Cutting the Lion's Tail, p. 105; Nutting, Nasser, p. 128; FRUS 1955–7 XV, p. 62.

23 FRUS 1955–7 XV, p. 36.

24 Ibid., p. 60.

25 Ibid., p. 69, p. 88 and p. 93.

26 The account of the summit meetings is based upon the records in DDE, Ann Whitman Series, International, Box 20, Eden Visit; AP, AP20/29/2, Records of Washington Summit; PRO, FO115/4548, Washington to Foreign Office, Cable 241, 30 January 1956; DDE, James Hagerty, Diary Entries, Box 5, Sir Anthony Eden, 31 January 1956 meeting.

27 See also PRO, FO371/121722/VR1073/45G, Whiteley to Dickson, Cable JW 11, 1 February 1956, and VR1073/46G, Whiteley to Dickson, Cable JW 14, 1 February 1956.
28 Eden, p. 336.
29 DDE, Ann Whitman Series, International Subseries, Box 20, Eden Visit, Foster Dulles–Eden meeting (ETW MC-1), 30 January 1956.
30 DDE, Ann Whitman Series, Dulles–Herter, Box 5, February 1956 (2), Washington Declaration, 1 February 1956.
31 Shuckburgh, p. 324; DDE, Ann Whitman Series, International, Box 20, Eden Visit, Foster Dulles–Eisenhower–Eden meeting (ETW MC-5), 31 January 1956.
32 *Ibid.*
33 *Ibid.*
34 AP, AP 20/24, Washington to Foreign Office, Cable 286, 1 February 1956.
35 USNA, RG 218, Records of the JCS, Geographical File 1954–6, Box 12, 381 EMMEA (11-19-47), S.26, JCS memorandum, 8 February 1956; PRO, FO371/121761/VR1076/54G, Rose minute, 18 February 1956, and VR1076/51G, Rose minute, 1 March 1956; PRO, FO371/121759/VR1076/9G, Washington to Foreign Office, Cable 351, 11 February 1956, and subsequent minutes; PRO, CAB134/1298, Middle East (Official) Committee Papers.
36 PRO, FO371/121484/VJ10393/2G, Amman to Foreign Office, Cable 185, 6 February 1956; PRO, DEFE4/83, COS(56)21st meeting, 17 February 1956, and COS(56)22nd meeting, 21 February 1956.
37 PRO, FO371/121650/VQ10316/21, Eden minute on Cairo to Foreign Office, Cable 209, 2 February 1956.
38 Horne, pp. 210ff.
39 Horne, p. 377 and p. 379.
40 Kilmuir, p. 255; WCP, File 7, Clark diary, 20 December 1955 and 6–9 April 1956; Rhodes James, pp. 423ff.; PRO, CAB128/30, C.M.6–7(56) and 11–15(56), January–February 1956; Horne, p. 380.
41 Shuckburgh, p. 332, p. 334 and pp. 337ff.
42 PRO, CAB128/30, C.M.16(56), 22 February 1956.

7: The Turning-point: London, March 1956

1 PRO, FO800/724, Amman to Foreign Office, Cable 276, 1 March 1956, and subsequent minutes; PRO, FO371/121540/VJ1201/8G, Amman to Foreign Office, Cable 280, 1 March 1956, and subsequent minutes, and VJ1201/11G, Amman to Foreign Office, Cable 280, 1 March 1956, and subsequent minutes.
2 Lamb, pp. 186ff.
3 *The End of Empire: Egypt*, interview with King Hussein; Hoopes, p. 335; Heikal, *Cutting the Lion's Tail*, p. 109; USNA, RG 59, CDF, 741.5274/3-1356, Amman to State Department, Despatch 311, 13 March 1956.
4 PRO, FO371/124020/RK1051/31, Lloyd–Menderes discussion, 11 March 1956; USNA, RG 59, CDF, 641.85/3-956, London to State Department, Cable 3834, 9 March 1956, and 780.00/4-1256, London to State Department, Cable 4604, 12 April 1956; Eden, pp. 347ff.; Joseph Alsop Papers, Joseph Alsop to Stuart Alsop, 5 April 1956, and Joseph Alsop to Felicite and Tony Rumbold, 12 July 1956. See also PRO, FO371/127876/VJ1011/1, Johnston to Lloyd, 19 March 1957.
5 PRO, FO371/118861/JE1053/7G, Shuckburgh minute, 22 February 1956, and

subsequent minutes; PRO, FO371/121270/V1075/22, Arthur to Rose, 20 January 1956.

6 AP, AP20/24, Bahrain to Foreign Office, Cable 155A, 2 March 1956; Lloyd, pp. 44ff.; Heikal, *Nasser*, pp. 84ff.; Love, pp. 210ff.; Trevelyan, pp. 64ff.; PRO, FO371/121243/V1071/85, Cairo to Foreign Office, Cable 413, 2 March 1956.

7 PRO, FO371/121243/V1071/85, Cairo to Foreign Office, Cable 413, 2 March 1956; Lloyd, p. 47; Heikal, *Cutting the Lion's Tail*, p. 110; PRO, FO371/121540/VJ1201/24G, Bahrain to Foreign Office, Cable 156, 2 March 1956; Calvocoressi, p. 34.

8 Lloyd, pp. 49ff.; Nutting, *No End of a Lesson*, p. 28; PRO, FO800/734, Delhi to Commonwealth Relations Office, Cable 361, 4 March 1956; AP, AP20/24, Bahrain to Foreign Office, Cable 155A, 2 March 1956.

9 Nutting, *No End of a Lesson*, p. 17.

10 Shuckburgh, pp. 339ff.

11 *Ibid.*, p. 341.

12 *Ibid.*, p. 342; PRO, FO371/121541/VJ1201/41G, Foreign Office to Amman, Cable 403, 5 March 1956.

13 Shuckburgh, p. 342; Nutting, *No End of a Lesson*, p. 30; PRO, FO371/121541/VJ1201/37G, Amman to Foreign Office, Cable 335, 4 March 1956.

14 Shuckburgh, p. 343; Eden, p. 350; PRO, CAB128/30, C.M.18(56), 5 March 1956.

15 Shuckburgh, p. 343; PRO, FO800/734, Nutting to Eden, 5 March 1956.

16 Shuckburgh, p. 343; PRO, CAB128/30, C.M.19(56), 6 March 1956. Present were Eden, Salisbury, Macmillan, Butler, Alan Lennox-Boyd, Edward Heath, Norman Brook, Templer, Edward Boyle, Kirkpatrick, Nutting and Shuckburgh.

17 PRO, CAB128/30, C.M.19(56), 6 March 1956.

18 PRO, FO800/734, Foreign Office to Karachi, Cable 651, 7 March 1956.

19 Shuckburgh, p. 344.

20 Eden, p. 352; *Hansard*, 7 March 1956.

21 Carlton, *Anthony Eden*, pp. 398ff.; WCP, File 7, Clark diary, 7 March 1956; Howard, p. 228; Rhodes James, p. 432.

22 USNA, 741.00/3-2156, London to State Department, Despatch 2271, 21 March 1956.

23 PRO, FO371/121235/V1054/70G, Shuckburgh to Kirkpatrick, 10 March 1956, and subsequent minutes; Shuckburgh, p. 346.

24 *Ibid.*

25 The Nutting minute is missing from PRO, FO371/121235/V1054/70G and retained in PRO, FO800/734, but its contents can be deduced by tracing the Foreign Office minutes between Shuckburgh's inquiry of 10 March and Lloyd's presentation to Cabinet on 21 March.

26 Nutting later claimed that Eden's original words were, 'I want him *murdered*, can't you understand?' (*The end of Empire: Egypt*, interview with Anthony Nutting.)

27 Nutting, *No End of a Lesson*, pp. 34ff.

28 *Ibid.*; PRO, CAB128/30, C.M.21(56), 9 March 1956; Shuckburgh, p. 345.

29 PRO, CAB128/30, C.M.21(56), 9 March 1956; PRO, FO371/121243/V1071/102, Foreign Office draft, 13 March 1956.

30 Shuckburgh, p. 346; PRO, FO800/734, Amman to Foreign Office, Cable 422, 15 March 1956; PRO, FO371/121484/VJ10393/15, Amman to Foreign Office, Cable 427, 15 March 1956; PRO, CAB131/17, D.C.(56)7, 'Review of UK Position in Jordan', 22 March 1956.

31 AP, AP20/21, Eden to Monckton, 3 March 1956; Shuckburgh, p. 345; Clark, p. 162; PRO, FO800/734, Nutting to Eden, 9 March 1956; PRO, FO371/120571/EA1055/1, Shuckburgh to Templer, 14 March 1956.

32 AP, AP20/21, Eden to Monckton, 10 March 1956. See also AP, AP20/21, Eden to Lloyd, 17 March 1956.

33 Shuckburgh, pp. 346ff.

34 PRO, CAB21/2866, Starkey to Warren, 15 March 1956.

35 PRO, CAB128/30, C.M.24(56), 21 March 1956.

36 Wright, p. 160; PRO, FO371/125423/JE1019/File; author's interviews with Julian Amery and Miles Copeland.

37 *Ibid.*

38 See West, pp. 79ff., for a full account of the mission.

39 AP, AP20/21, Eden to Head, 22 December 1956; Horne, pp. 384ff.

40 Wright, pp. 73 and 160; West, pp. 83ff.; Macdermott, p. 129.

41 USNA, RG 59, CDF, 741.13/2-757, London to State Department, Despatch 1912, 7 February 1957. I am grateful to Tracy Steele for bringing this document to my attention.

42 Quoted in Cavendish, p. xi.

8: The Turning-point: Washington, March 1956

1 FRUS 1955–7 XV, pp. 138ff.

2 PRO, FO371/121271/V1075, Bailey to Shuckburgh, 24 February 1956.

3 USNA, RG 59, CDF, 684A.86/2-2456, Foster Dulles statement, 24 February 1956.

4 USNA, RG 59, CDF, 684A.86/2-2956, Tel Aviv to State Department, Cable 861, 29 February 1956.

5 FRUS, 1955–7 XV, p. 255.

6 US DDRS, US84 002554.

7 DDE, Ann Whitman Series, DDE Diaries, Box 14, March 1956 Miscellaneous (6), US Cabinet meeting, 2 March 1956.

8 PRO, FO371/121271/V1075/55, Washington to Foreign Office, Cable 582, 3 March 1956; PRO, FO800/734, Foreign Office to Washington, Cable 1246, 5 March 1956.

9 PRO, FO800/734, Foreign Office to Karachi, Cable 531, 5 March 1956, and Nutting to Eden, 6 March 1956; Lloyd, p. 53; PRO, FO371/121271/V1075/61G, Karachi to Foreign Office, Cable DORAN 29, 7 March 1956.

10 FRUS 1955–7 XV, pp. 302ff.

11 PRO, FO371/121271/V1075/64, Baghdad to Foreign Office, Cable 292, 9 March 1956; PRO, FO371/118842/JE1022/11G, Karachi to Foreign Office, Cable DORAN 33, 7 March 1956.

12 Shuckburgh, p. 345; DDE, Ann Whitman Series, Dulles–Herter, Box 5, Foster Dulles to Hoover, 8 March 1956.

13 DDE, Ann Whitman Series, DDE Diaries, Box 13, March 1956 Diary, Eisenhower diary entry, 8 March 1956. See also DDE, Ann Whitman Series, Dulles–Herter, Box 5, Eisenhower to Foster Dulles, 10 March 1956.

14 PRO, PREM11/1177, Eisenhower to Eden, 10 March 1956.

15 DDE, John Foster Dulles Papers, White House Memoranda, Chronological, Box 4, Hoover to Foster Dulles, 12 March 1956.

16 Heikal, *Cutting the Lion's Tail*, p. 107.

17 FRUS 1955–7 XV, pp. 28ff.

18 DDE, John Foster Dulles Papers, Subject, Alphabetical, Box 10, Israeli Relations, 1951–7 (4), Foster Dulles memorandum, 11 January 1956.

19 DDE, Ann Whitman Series, DDE Diaries, Box 13, March 1956 Diary, Eisenhower diary entry, 13 March 1956.

20 PRO, PREM11/1177, Eden to Eisenhower, 15 March 1956.

21 USNA, RG 59, CDF, 641.74/3-2256, Wilson memorandum, 21 March 1956.

22 PRO, FO371/121726/VR1073/118G, Trevelyan to Shuckburgh, 8 March 1956.

23 PRO, FO371/121761/VR1076/64, Dickson to Whiteley, 15 March 1956, and VR1076/64A, Whiteley to Dickson, 16 March 1956.

24 PRO, FO371/121726/VR1073/119G, Trevelyan to Shuckburgh, 15 March 1956, and VR1073/128G, Washington to Foreign Office, Cable 801, 28 March 1956.

25 DDE, Ann Whitman Series, Dulles–Herter, Box 5, Eisenhower to Eden, 20 March 1956.

26 USNA, RG 59, CDF, 511.74/4-1056, Damon to MacArthur, 10 April 1956.

27 DDE, Ann Whitman Series, DDE Diaries, Box 13, March 1956 Goodpaster, Goodpaster memorandum, 15 March 1956.

28 DDE, John Foster Dulles Papers, White House Memoranda, Chronological, Box 4, Meetings with the President, January–July 1956 (4), Hoover to Foster Dulles, 16 March 1956.

29 FRUS 1955–7 XV, p. 352.

30 British Embassy *aide-mémoire*, March 1956 (copy in author's possession); FRUS 1955–7 XV, p. 383; DDE, John Foster Dulles Papers, Telephone Calls, Box 5, Memoranda of Telephone Conversations, General, 3 January–30 April 1956 (4), Foster Dulles to Allen Dulles, 23 March 1956; DDE, John Foster Dulles Papers, Subject, Alphabetical, Box 10, Israeli Relations 1951–7 (4), State Department memorandum, 24 March 1956.

31 DDE, Ann Whitman Series, DDE Diaries, Box 13, March 1956 Diary, Foster Dulles memorandum, 28 March 1956; DDE, John Foster Dulles Papers, Subject, Alphabetical, Box 10, Israeli Relations 1951–7 (4), Foster Dulles's long-hand notes, 27 March 1956; FRUS 1955–7 XV, p. 409.

32 DDE, Ann Whitman Series, DDE Diaries, Box 13, March 1956 Diary, White House meeting, 28 March 1956.

33 DDE, Ann Whitman Series, DDE Diaries, Box 13, March 1956 Diary, Eisenhower diary entry, 28 March 1956.

34 FRUS 1955–7 XV, pp. 461ff.; Eveland, p. 180.

35 PRO, FO371/119047/JE1422/28, Foreign Office to Washington, Cable 257, 17 January 1956; PRO, FO371/119051/JE1422/File; Love, p. 311; FRUS 1955–7 XV, pp. 90ff.

36 DDE, Ann Whitman Series, DDE Diaries, Box 14, March 1956 Miscellaneous (6), Eisenhower to Thornton, 8 March 1956.

37 See PRO, FO371/119054/JE1422/File.

38 See Gorst and Lucas, *Intelligence and National Security*, pp. 576ff.

39 PRO, FO371/115946/VY1015/File; Heikal, *Nasser*, p. 87.

40 USNA, RG 84, Cairo Embassy Records 1949–54, 350 Other Countries, Beirut to State Department, Cable 221, 30 August 1955, and 350 Syria, Damascus to State Department, Cable 167, 26 August 1955, and subsequent cables; PRO, FO371/115954/VY10393/2G, Foreign Office to Baghdad, Cable 1394, 8 October 1955; PRO, FO371/115947/V1015/94G, Stewart to Rose, 6 December 1955; FRUS 1955–7 XIII, pp. 543ff.

41 USNA, RG 84, Cairo Embassy Records 1949–54, 350 Syria, Damascus to State Department, Cable 400, 24 October 1956.

42 PRO, FO371/115954/VY10393/7G, Arthur minute, 10 October 1955, and subsequent minutes.

43 Shuckburgh, pp. 289ff.

44 PRO, FO371/115954/VY10393/3G, Washington to Foreign Office, Cable 2414, 6 October 1955, and VY10393/9G, Washington to Foreign Office, Cable 2616, 27 October 1955, VY10393/10G, Record of Anglo-American meeting, 28 October 1955, and VY10393/14G, Baghdad to Foreign Office, Cable 855, 3 November 1955.

45 FRUS 1955–7 XIII, pp. 563ff.; DDE, John Foster Dulles, Telephone Calls, Box 5, Allen Dulles to Foster Dulles, 13 January 1956.

46 PRO, FO371/121858/VY1015/13G, Tehran to Foreign Office, Cable 187, 10 March 1956.

9: *The OMEGA Discussions, April 1956*

1 CIA London Station to Director CIA, Cable LOND 7064, 1 April 1956 (copy in author's possession).

2 Eveland, p. 168 and p. 171; Heikal, *Nasser*, p. 117; Neff, p. 217; FRUS 1955–7 XV, pp. 504ff.

3 FRUS 1955–7 XV, p. 435; PRO, FO371/121250/V1073/108G, Washington to Foreign Office, Cable 819, 1 April 1956.

4 PRO, FO371/121272/V1075/89G, Dean minute, 6 April 1956; PRO, FO371/118869/JE1071/4, Monckton to Lloyd, 10 April 1956; DDE, Ann Whitman Series, DDE Diaries, Box 15, April 1956 Goodpaster, Record of Eisenhower–Dickson meeting, 3 April 1956.

5 FRUS 1955–7 XV, p. 458.

6 USNA, RG 59, CDF, 684A.86/4-656, Cairo to State Department, Cable 4467, 6 April 1956.

7 FRUS 1955–7 XV, p. 435.

8 PRO, FO371/118861/JE1053/12, *Observer* and *Sunday Times*, 25 March 1956, and JE1053/16, Foreign Office to Cairo, Cable 911, 25 March 1956; Trevelyan, p. 69.

9 See USNA, RG 59, CDF, 780.00/4-356, London to State Department, Cable 2379, 3 April 1956; WCP, File 7, Clark diary, 6–9 April 1956.

10 PRO, FO371/118861/JE1053/13, Foreign Office to Cairo, Cable 988, 3 April 1956; PRO, FO115/4549, Foreign Office to Washington, Cables 1890 and 1891, 4 April 1956.

11 PRO, FO371/118861/JE1053/17G, Trevelyan to Shuckburgh, 5 April 1956, and JE1053/5G, Wilton minute, 14 April 1956; USNA, RG 59, CDF, 611.74/4-656, Cairo to State Department, Cable 1996, 6 April 1956.

12 PRO, FO371/121662/VQ1051/29, *The Times*, 14 April 1956.

13 USNA, RG 59, CDF, 684A.86 Series, London to US Information Agency, Cable TOUSI 394, 3 April 1956, and London to State Department, Cable 4467, 6 April 1956.

14 DDE, Ann Whitman, Ann Whitman Diary, Box 8, April 1956 Diary, 10 April 1956; DDE, John Foster Dulles Series, Telephone Calls, White House, Box 10, Eisenhower to Foster Dulles, 10 April 1956.

15 USNA, RG 59, CDF, 774.13 Series.

16 PRO, FO371/120765/ES1051/14, Jedda to Foreign Office, Cable 23, 26 March

1956, and subsequent minutes, and ES1051/18, Riches minute, 5 April 1956; FRUS 1955–7 XV, pp. 436ff.

17 DDE, John Foster Dulles Series, Telephone Calls, Box 5, MacArthur to Foster Dulles, 31 March 1956; DDE, Ann Whitman Series, DDE Diaries, Box 15, April 1956 Telephone Calls, Eisenhower to Foster Dulles, 7 April 1956; DDE, John Foster Dulles Series, Telephone Calls, Box 5, Hill to Foster Dulles, 16 April 1956, and Foster Dulles to Allen Dulles, 17 April 1956.

18 Neff, p. 225; PRO, FO800/735, Eden to Lloyd, 12 April 1956, and Lloyd to Eden, 14 April 1956; PRO, CAB128/30, C.M.30(56), 19 April 1956.

19 See PRO, FO371/118862/JE1053/19G, Watson minute, 11 April 1956; PRO, FO371/121762/VR1076/100G, Bailey to Rose, 14 April 1956.

20 USNA, RG 218, Records of the JCS, Geographical File 1954–6, Box 12, 381 EMMEA (11-19-47), S. 29, Picher to Currie, 4 April 1956; PRO, FO371/121272/V1075/100G, COS(56)150, 18 April 1956; PRO, FO371/121273/V1075/101G-105G, COS(56)151-5, 18 April 1956.

21 DDE, Ann Whitman Series, DDE Diaries, Box 14, April 1956 Miscellaneous (5), Eisenhower to Eden, 5 April 1956.

22 DDE, John Foster Dulles Series, White House Memoranda, Chronological, Box 4, Meetings with President, MacArthur memorandum, 13 April 1956.

23 PRO, PREM11/1177, Eden to Eisenhower, 18 and 30 April 1956.

24 Brecher, p. 263; Golan, p. 38.

25 Pineau, p. 33.

26 Nutting, *Nasser*, pp. 125ff.

27 Neff, p. 234; Abel Thomas, p. 55, pp. 73ff. and pp. 94ff.; Bar-Zohar, *Ben-Gurion*, pp. 227ff.

28 Shlaim, pp. 193ff.; Dayan, *Diary of the Sinai Campaign*, pp. 20ff.; Eban, pp. 198ff.

29 PRO, FO371/121773/VR1091/File.

30 See DDE, John Foster Dulles Series, White House Memoranda, Chronological, Box 4, Meetings with the President, Foster Dulles memorandum, 6 April 1956.

31 US DDRS, US84 002128.

32 PRO, FO371/121762/VR1076/86, Washington to Foreign Office, Cable 926, 11 April 1956, and VR1076/87, Hancock to Lloyd, 9 April 1956; DDE, John Foster Dulles Series, Telephone Calls, Box 5, Foster Dulles to O'Connor, Foster Dulles to Wilkins, Foster Dulles to Allen Dulles, and Foster Dulles to Radford, 9 April 1956, and Foster Dulles to Radford, 10 April 1956.

33 FRUS 1955–7 XV, p. 481.

34 US DDRS, US81 192D and US84 000623; DDE, John Foster Dulles Series, Telephone Calls, White House, Box 10, Foster Dulles to Eisenhower, 11–13 April 1956.

35 PRO, FO371/80381/JE1054/57, Stewart minute, 25 November 1950, and subsequent minutes; PRO, FO371/96918/JE1052/22, Allen minute, 28 December 1951. See also PRO, FO371/121759/VR1076/9G, Washington to Foreign Office, Cable 351, 11 February 1956, and subsequent minutes, and VR1076/16, Bailey to Rose, 10 February 1956, and subsequent minutes; PRO, FO371/121760/VR1076/48, Jebb to Pink, 22 February 1956, and subsequent minutes; PRO, FO371/121761/VR1076/54G, Rose minute, 18 February 1956.

36 PRO, FO371/121762/VR1076/100G, Bailey to Rose, 14 April 1956, and subsequent minutes, and VR1076/108G, Watson minute, 19 April 1956, and subsequent minutes.

37 PRO, PREM11/1690, Eden to Churchill, 21 April 1956.

38 PRO, FO371/120765/ES1051/19, Lloyd minute, 13 April 1956.

39 PRO, FO371/120765/ES1021/20G, Washington to Foreign Office, Cable 964, 17 April 1956, and subsequent minutes.

40 PRO, CAB129/80, C.P.(56)80, 'Bahrain', 14 April 1956; PRO, PREM11/1440, Record of ad hoc Ministerial meeting, 13 April 1956; PRO, PREM11/1457, Brook to Eden, 14 April 1956.

41 PRO, PREM11/1457, Bishop to Brook, 15 April 1956; PRO, PREM11/1440, Monckton to Eden, 25 April 1956, and Eden to Monckton, 29 April 1956.

42 PRO, PREM11/1440, D.C.(56)5th meeting, 1 May 1956, and subsequent minutes; PRO, CAB128/30, C.M.36(56), 15 May 1956. See also AP, AP20/21/File.

43 PRO, FO371/118862/JE1053/26G, Watson minute, 25 April 1956.

44 PRO, FO800/735, Bishop to Logan, 18 April 1956; PRO, PREM11/1690, Eden to Churchill, 21 April 1956.

10: OMEGA – The First Steps, May–July 1956

1 See Shuckburgh, p. 355.

2 PRO, FO371/121273/V1075/117G, Foster Dulles–Lloyd meeting, 3 May 1956.

3 *Ibid.*; FRUS 1955–7 XV, pp. 604ff.

4 Shuckburgh, p. 355; PRO, FO371/120755/ES1021/30G, Shuckburgh minute, 4 May 1956; FRUS 1955–7 XIII, p. 377, p. 388 and pp. 392ff.; PRO, FO371/120770/ES1051/File.

5 PRO, FO115/4549, Kirkpatrick to Dixon, 18 May 1956; DDE, Ann Whitman Series, Dulles–Herter, Box 5, May 1956, Paris to State Department, Cable DULTE 12, 6 May 1956.

6 PRO, FO371/121273/V1075/117G, Foster Dulles–Lloyd meeting, 3 May 1956; DDE, John Foster Dulles Series, Subject, Alphabetical, Box 10, Israeli Relations, 1951–7 (2), Foster Dulles–Lloyd meeting, 6 May 1956 (classified); FRUS 1955–7 XV, p. 667; PRO, FO800/723, Shuckburgh minute, 29 May 1956; Eveland, p. 181.

7 PRO, FO371/121485/VJ10393/File; PRO, CAB129/81, C.P.(56)106, 'Jordan', 1 May 1956; PRO, CAB128/30, C.M.32(56), 3 May 1956; PRO, FO371/121273/V1075/117G, Foster Dulles–Lloyd meeting, 3 May 1956.

8 Nutting, *Nasser*, p. 138; PRO, FO371/118843/JE1022/28, Trevelyan to Shuckburgh, 26 May 1956.

9 Hoopes, p. 336; Neff, p. 253. See also DDE, John Foster Dulles Series, Telephone Calls, Box 5, Foster Dulles to Allen Dulles, 18 May 1956; PRO, FO371/118843/JE1022/28, Trevelyan to Shuckburgh, 26 May 1956.

10 DDE, John Foster Dulles Series, Telephone Calls, Box 10, Foster Dulles to Snyder, 23 May 1956; Neff, p. 255.

11 PRO, FO371/119054/JE1422/186G, Kirkpatrick minute, 1 June 1956.

12 PRO, FO371/119054/JE1422/167G, Millard to Graham, 7 May 1956.

13 PRO, FO371/119055/JE1422/198G, Washington to Foreign Office, Cable 1344, 13 June 1956; FRUS 1955–7 XV, p. 725.

14 PRO, CAB134/1298, ME(O)C(56)35, 'High Aswan Dam', 12 June 1956.

15 PRO, FO371/119055/JE1422/206G, Cairo to Foreign Office, 21 June 1956, and JE1422/219, Bailey to Watson, 30 June 1956. See also Eisenhower, p. 32; Lloyd, p. 69; Love, p. 325; DDE, Oral History Collection, OH-341, Eugene Black oral history, 13 May 1975.

16 USNA, RG 59, CDF, 661.74/6-2756, Allen Dulles to Foster Dulles, 27 June 1956; FRUS 1955–7 XV, p. 865.

17 See USNA, RG 59, CDF, 684A.86/4-1956, Cairo to State Department, Cable 2020, 19 April 1956, and 611.74/7-1256, Byroade to State Department, 12 July 1956.

18 USNA, RG 59, CDF, 874.2614/7-1056, Cairo to State Department, Cable 45, 10 July 1956.

19 DDE, John Foster Dulles Papers, White House Memoranda, Chronological, Box 4, Foster Dulles–Eisenhower meeting, 13 July 1956.

20 Adams, pp. 182ff.; Records in Eisenhower Library.

21 PRO, FO371/119056/JE1422/229G, Washington to Foreign Office, Cable 1508, 13 July 1956; USNA, RG 59, CDF, 874.2614/7-1356, Burdett memorandum, 13 July 1956.

22 Eveland, pp. 181ff.; PRO, FO371/121858/VY1015/File.

23 PRO, *ibid.*

24 PRO, FO371/121858/VY1015/37, Damascus to Foreign Office, Cable 311, 20 June 1956.

25 Eveland, p. 189.

26 PRO, FO371/121858/VY1015/File; Joseph Alsop Papers, Eveland to Stewart Alsop, 24 July 1956.

27 PRO, FO371/121495/VJ1051/126, Baghdad to Foreign Office, Cable 567, 17 May 1956; AP, AP20/21, Eden to Lloyd, 15 April 1956.

28 PRO, FO371/121495/VJ1051/127, Foreign Office to Baghdad, Cable 1166, 4 June 1956, and VJ1051/132G, Baghdad to Foreign Office, Cable 655, 11 June 1956.

29 PRO, FO371/121484-121485/File; PRO, FO371/121485/VJ10393/45G, Baghdad to Foreign Office, Cable 676, 17 June 1956, and subsequent minutes; PRO, FO371/121554/VJ1203/File.

30 PRO, FO371/121728/VR1073/195, Amman to Foreign Office, Cable 935, 3 July 1956; USNA, RG 59, CDF, 684A.85 Series, Tel Aviv to State Department, Cable 1, 2 July 1956, and Amman to State Department, Cable 8, 5 July 1956. See also PRO, FO371/121728/VR1073/195, Laurence minute, 4 July 1956.

31 USNA, RG 59, CDF, 684A.85/7-1356, Tel Aviv to State Department, Cable 39, 13 July 1956; PRO, FO371/121729/VR1073/243, Washington to Foreign Office, Cable 1512, 14 July 1956. See also PRO, FO371/121730/VR1073/253, Chancery (Tel Aviv) to Levant Department, Despatch 10310/56, 16 July 1956, and VR1073/265, Duke to Rose, 4 August 1956.

32 PRO, FO371/121496/VJ1051/154G, Chiefs of Staff brief, 27 June 1956; PRO, FO371/121730/VR1073/266G, British Defence Co-ordinating Committee (Middle East) to COS, Cable MECOS 162, 9 August 1956.

33 PRO, FO953/1650/PB1041/30, Hebblethwaite minute, 27 March 1956.

34 PRO, FO953/1658/PB1045/File; PRO, FO953/1659/PB1045/109, Baghdad to Foreign Office, Cable 974, 3 September 1956, and subsequent minutes. See also AP, AP20/21, Eden to Lloyd, 4 May, 15 May and 3 June 1956.

35 WCP, File 7, Clark diary, 2 May 1956.

36 PRO, FO953/1641/PB1011/20, Dodds-Parker minute, 11 July 1956.

37 PRO, CAB134/1298, ME(O)C(56)33, 'Working Paper on Middle Eastern Expenditure', 11 June 1956; PRO, FO371/120812/UEE10062/9G, Dodds-Parker minute, 19 July 1956.

38 PRO, FO371/118862/JE1053/37G, Shuckburgh to Middle Eastern posts, 28 May 1956.

39 Love, p. 218.
40 PRO, FO371/118864/JE1053/67G, Wilton minute, 5 July 1956, and JE1053/74G, Lloyd memorandum, 20 July 1956.
41 FRUS 1955–7 XV, p. 797.

11: Western Attack, Egyptian Counter-attack, 19–26 July 1956

1 Eisenhower, p. 32; Murphy, p. 459.
2 FRUS 1955–7 XV, pp. 859ff.
3 DDE, John Foster Dulles Papers, Telephone Calls, Box 5, Foster Dulles to Allen Dulles, 19 July 1956.
4 *Ibid.*; PRO, FO371/119056/JE1422/247G, Washington to Foreign Office, Cable 1552, 19 July 1956; USNA, RG 59, CDF, 874.2614/7-1956, Rountree memorandum, 19 July 1956; Mosley, p. 402; Love, p. 316.
5 USNA, RG 59, CDF, 874.2614/6-656, Rountree to Foster Dulles, 6 June 1956.
6 PRO, FO371/119056/JE1422/232G, Washington to Foreign Office, Cable 1528, 17 July 1956; DDE, Ann Whitman Series, Dulles–Herter, Box 5, Foster Dulles to Eisenhower, 16 July 1956; Neff, p. 260.
7 See Eden, p. 422; Macmillan, *Riding the Storm*, p. 98.
8 PRO, FO371/119056/229G, Washington to Foreign Office, Cable 1508, 13 July 1956; PRO, CAB128/30, C.M.50(56), 17 July 1956.
9 PRO, FO371/119056/JE1422/230G, Washington to Foreign Office, Cable 1541, 18 July 1956, and Foreign Office to Washington, Cable 3256, 19 July 1956.
10 PRO, FO371/119056/JE1422/245, Washington to Foreign Office, Cable 1545, 19 July 1956; USNA, RG 59, CDF, 874.2614/7-1956, Allen memorandum, 19 July 1956. See also PRO, FO371/119058/JE1422/297G, Wright minute, 27 November 1956, and subsequent minutes.
11 Neff, p. 260. See also DDE, Oral History Collection, OH-14, Dwight Eisenhower oral history, 28 July 1964.
12 PRO, FO371/118864/JE1053/74G, Lloyd memorandum, 20 July 1956; PRO, CAB128/30, C.M.52(56), 24 July 1956, and C.M.53(56), 26 July 1956; Carlton, *Britain and the Suez Crisis*, p. 33. For a full review of the events leading to the withdrawal of aid for the Dam, see PRO, FO371/119058/JE1422/297G, Wright minute, 27 November 1956, and subsequent minutes.
13 Calvocoressi, p. 41; Heikal, *Cutting the Lion's Tail*, p. 130.
14 Mosley, p. 404.
15 See Calvocoressi, p. 43.
16 USNA, RG 59, CDF, 974.7301/7-3056, Cairo to State Department, Cable 176, 30 July 1956.
17 Heikal, *Nasser*, pp. 87ff., and *Cutting the Lion's Tail*, pp. 133ff.; Love, p. 335; Nutting, *Nasser*, p. 147.
18 PRO, FO371/119056/JE1422/248, Moscow to Foreign Office, Cable 1002, 21 July 1956; PRO, FO371/119087/JE14211/291, Cairo to Foreign Office, Cable 1430, 5 August 1956.
19 Hoopes, p. 345.
20 USNA, RG 59, CDF, 974.7301 Series, Cairo to State Department, Cable 146, 26 July 1956, and Alexandria to State Department, Cable 20, 28 July 1956, and 774.11/7-2856, Alexandria to State Department, Despatch 1, 28 July 1956. See also PRO, FO371/118844/JE1022/46, Cairo to Foreign Office, Cable 1283, 27 July 1956.

21 USNA, RG 59, CDF, 774.11/7-2856, Alexandria to State Department, Despatch 1, 28 July 1956.
22 PRO, PREM11/1100, Trevelyan to Lloyd, 1 September 1956; Calvocoressi, p. 39; USNA, RG 59, CDF, 611.74/7-2556, Cairo to State Department, Cable 133, 25 July 1956; Love, p. 217; FRUS 1955–7 XV, p. 852 and p. 901; John Foster Dulles Library, Oral History Collection, Couve de Murville transcript, 19 June 1964.
23 See FRUS 1955–7 XIII, pp. 582ff.
24 Eveland, pp. 192ff.; private information.
25 Ibid.

12: Britain's Quest to 'Hit, Hit Now, and Hit Hard', 26–31 July 1956

1 Heikal, Nasser, p. 94; Hugh Thomas, p. 38.
2 WCP, File 7, Clark diary, 26–27 July 1956.
3 DDE, Ann Whitman Series, Dulles–Herter, Box 5, London to State Department, Cable 481, 27 July 1956.
4 Neither War nor Peace at 10 Downing Street, interview with William Clark.
5 PRO, CAB131/17, D.C.(56)17, 'UK Requirements in the Middle East', 3 July 1956; PRO, CAB134/1315, P.R.(56)11, 3 July 1956.
6 Ziegler, p. 538; Lamb, p. 199; Hugh Thomas, pp. 50ff.
7 Ziegler, p. 538.
8 AP, AP23/37/24B, Head to Eden, 3 May 1962, and AP33/2, Templer to Eden, 21 August 1976.
9 Author's interview with Brigadier David Hunt.
10 Neither War nor Peace at 10 Downing Street, interview with William Clark.
11 DDE, Ann Whitman Series, Dulles–Herter, Box 5, London to State Department, Cable 481, 27 July 1956.
12 PRO, CAB128/30, C.M.54(56), 27 July 1956; PRO, ADM205/117, First Sea Lord to Vice Chief Naval Staff, 27 July 1956.
13 DDE, Ann Whitman Series, DDE Diaries, Box 16, July 1956 Diary, Staff Memoranda, Goodpaster memorandum, 27 July 1956. See also DDE, Oral History Collection, Dwight Eisenhower oral history, 28 July 1964.
14 DDE, Ann Whitman Series, DDE Diaries, Box 16, July 1956 Diary, Staff Memoranda, Goodpaster memorandum, 27 July 1956.
15 USNA, RG 59, CDF, 974.7301/7-2856, State Department to Lima, Cable TEDUL 20, 28 July 1956.
16 USNA, RG 59, CDF, 974.7301/7-2756, State Department to London, Cable 545, 27 July 1956 (classified); PRO, FO371/119092/JE14211/421G, Lloyd–Chauvel–Foster meeting, 27 July 1956.
17 DDE, Anne Whitman Series, International, Box 19, Eden, Eden to Eisenhower, 27 July 1956.
18 USNA, RG 59, CDF, 974.7301/7-2856, State Department to Lima, Cable 20, 28 July 1956; DDE, Ann Whitman Series, DDE Diaries, Box 16, July 1956 Diary, Staff Memoranda, Goodpaster memoranda, 27–28 July 1956.
19 USNA, RG 218, Records of the JCS, Geographical File 1954–6, Box 15, 092 Egypt (7-28-56), S. 1, JCS draft to Secretary of Defense, undated.
20 US DDRS, US81 384B; DDE, Ann Whitman Series, International, Box 19, Eden, Eisenhower to Eden, 28 July 1956.
21 PRO, CAB134/126, E.C.(56)1st and 2nd meetings, 27–28 July 1956.

22 PRO, FO371/118863/JE1053/57G, Foreign Office to Tel Aviv, Cable 568, 19 June 1956.

23 PRO, FO371/121706/VR1052/23G, Ross minute, 28 July 1956; USNA, RG 59, CDF, 974.7301/7-2756, London to State Department, Cable 510, 27 July 1956.

24 PRO, CAB134/1216, E.C.(56)2nd meeting, 28 July 1956.

25 DDE, Ann Whitman Series, Dulles-Herter, Box 5, Goodpaster memorandum, 28 July 1956; PRO, PREM11/1098, Washington to Foreign Office, Cable 1609, 28 July 1956.

26 PRO, FO371/124441/WF1051/19, Mollet–Eden meeting, 11 March 1956.

27 DDE, Ann Whitman Series, Dulles–Herter, Box 5, Paris to State Department, Cable 469, 27 July 1956.

28 DDE, Ann Whitman Series, Dulles–Herter, Box 5, Paris to State Department, Cable 549, 31 July 1956.

29 PRO, ADM205/117, First Sea Lord to Vice Chief of Naval Staff, 30 July 1956; PRO, CAB134/1216, E.C.(56)3rd meeting, 29 July 1956.

30 DDE, Ann Whitman Series, Dulles–Herter, Box 5, July 1956, London to State Department, Cable 517, 29 July 1956 (italics added).

31 USNA, RG 59, CDF, 974.7301/7-2956, London to State Department, Cable 521, 29 July 1956; PRO, FO371/119081/JE14211/124G, Lloyd–Pineau meeting, 29 July 1956, and JE14211/121G–122G, 1st-2nd Lloyd–Pineau–Murphy meetings, 29 July 1956.

32 Rhodes James, p. 470; PRO, PREM11/1098, Lloyd minute, 31 July 1956.

33 PRO, FO371/119081/JE14211/125G, Eden–Lloyd–Pineau meeting, 31 July 1956; PRO, CAB134/1216, E.C.(56)4th meeting, 30 July 1956.

34 Murphy, pp. 462ff.; USNA, RG 59, CDF, 674.84A/7-3156, London to State Department, Cable 550, 31 July 1956.

35 Lloyd, pp. 91ff.; Horne, p. 398.

36 FRUS 1955–7 XVI, p. 37; DDE, John Foster Dulles Series, Telephone Calls, White House, Box 10, Foster Dulles to Eisenhower, 30 July 1956; USNA, RG 59, CDF, 674.84A/7-3156, London to State Department, Cable 550, 31 July 1956.

37 PRO, FO371/119080/JE14211/87G, Washington to Foreign Office, Cable 1613, 30 July 1956.

38 DDE, Ann Whitman Series, DDE Diaries, Box 16, July 1956 Diary, Staff Memoranda, Goodpaster memorandum, 31 July 1956.

39 DDE, Ann Whitman Series, International, Box 19, Eden, Eisenhower to Eden, 31 July 1956; DDE, Ann Whitman Series, DDE Diaries, Box 15, July 1956 Miscellaneous (1), Eisenhower to Foster Dulles, 31 July 1956; DDE, John Foster Dulles Series, Subject, Alphabetical, Box 11, Miscellaneous Papers – UK (4), Foster Dulles to Eden, 1 August 1956.

40 PRO, CAB134/1216, E.C.(56)5th and 6th meetings, 31 July 1956; PRO, FO371/119083/JE14211/212G, Lloyd–Pineau meeting, 31 July 1956.

13: *The Dance of Diplomacy, 1–14 August 1956*

1 PRO, FO371/119088/JE14211/307G, Caccia minute, 1 August 1956.

2 PRO, PREM11/1098, Lloyd–Foster Dulles meeting, 1 August 1956; USNA, RG 59, CDF, 974.7301/7-3156, Murphy memorandum, 1 August 1956; Lloyd, p. 99.

3 Lloyd, p. 99.

4 MacDonald, p. 265.

5 Murphy, p. 467; Mosley, p. 410.

6 Eden, p. 437; USNA, RG 59, CDF, 974.7301/8-156, Foster Dulles memorandum, 1 August 1956.

7 Eden, p. 437; USNA, RG 59, CDF, 974.7301/8-156, Foster Dulles memorandum, 1 August 1956; Lloyd, pp. 99ff.; Carlton, *Anthony Eden*, p. 414. See also Vaisse in Louis and Owen, p. 140.

8 Carlton, *ibid.*, pp. 410 and 413.

9 PRO, FO371/119092/JE14211/422G, Lloyd–Pineau–Foster Dulles meeting, 1 August 1956.

10 PRO, FO371/119092/JE14211/423G and 424G, Lloyd–Pineau–Foster Dulles meetings, 2 August 1956; FRUS 1955–7 XVI, p. 125 and pp. 142ff.

11 USNA, RG 59, CDF, 974.7301/8-156, Murphy and Aldrich memoranda, 1 August 1956.

12 PRO, CAB128/30, C.M.57(56), 2 August 1956; PRO, CAB134/1216, E.C.(56)9th, 2 August 1956; WCP, File 7, Clark Diary, 2 August 1956.

13 PRO, FO371/119083/JE14211/209, Paris to Foreign Office, Cable 196, 2 August 1956; PRO, FO371/119085/JE14211/249, Paris to Foreign Office, Cable 303 Saving, 3 August 1956.

14 PRO, FO371/119080/JE14211/69, San Francisco to Foreign Office, Cable 2, 28 July 1956; PRO, FO371/119081/JE14211/132G, Washington to Foreign Office, Cable 1624, 31 July 1956, and Cable 1633, 2 August 1956.

15 PRO, FO371/121662/VQ1051/43G, Wright minute, 30 July 1956, and VQ1051/45G, Lloyd–Nuri–Abdul Illah meeting, 3 August 1956.

16 PRO, FO371/119083/JE14211/193, Moscow to Foreign Office, Cable 1054, 2 August 1956.

17 *The Times*, 1 August 1956.

18 Williams, p. 552 and pp. 561ff.; *Hansard*, 27 July 1956.

19 *Hansard*, 2 August 1956.

20 Jay, p. 254.

21 *Ibid.*, PRO, PREM11/1159, Gaitskell to Eden, 3 August 1956.

22 Israeli State Archives, 193/1, Israeli Ministry of Foreign Affairs to Washington, 2 February 1956.

23 PRO, CAB134/1216, E.C.(56)9th meeting, 2 August 1956; Horne, p. 401.

24 PRO, CAB134/1217, E.G.(56)9, 'France and the Middle East', 7 August 1956.

25 PRO, CAB134/1216, E.C.(56)10th meeting, 3 August 1956; PRO, FO371/119090/JE14211/368G, Lloyd–Elath meeting, 3 August 1956.

26 Abel Thomas, p. 58; Brecher, pp. 264ff.; Dayan, *The Story of My Life*, p. 149; Bar-Zohar, *Ben-Gurion*, pp. 228ff.; Golan, pp. 45ff.

27 Golan, p. 48; Dayan, *ibid.*, pp. 149ff.; 'Ben-Gurion's Diary', 3 August 1956, in Troen and Shemesh, p. 292.

28 Brecher, p. 264; Golan, p. 48; Abel Thomas, p. 94; USNA, RG 59, CDF, 784A.5622/9-2056, Rountree to Hoover, 20 September 1956. See also PRO, FO371/118871/JE1073/6G, Paris to Foreign Office, Cable 227, 11 August 1956; PRO, PREM11/1100, Lloyd–Pineau meeting, 24 August 1956.

29 PRO, PREM11/1098, Foreign Office to Washington, Cable 3568, 5 August 1956.

30 PRO, PREM11/1099, E.C.(56)8, 'Action Against Egypt', 7 August 1956.

31 Gilbert, pp. 1203ff.; Horne, p. 403.

32 Horne, p. 404; PRO, CAB134/1216, E.C.(56)11th meeting, 7 August 1956.

33 PRO, CAB134/1216, E.C.(56)13th meeting, 9 August 1956.

34 PRO, DEFE32/5, COS(56)78 C.A., 'Operation MUSKETEER – Force Commanders' Outline Plan', 9 August 1956.

35 PRO, CAB134/1216, E.C.(56)14th meeting, 10 August 1956; Hugh Thomas, p. 72.

36 PRO, CAB134/1216, E.C.(56)14th meeting, 10 August 1956; PRO, FO371/118864/JE1053/79, Briefs for Pineau visit, 26 July 1956.

37 USNA, RG 59, CDF, 974.7301/7-3056, Cairo to State Department, Cable 176, 30 July 1956; PRO, FO371/119080/JE14211/89, Cairo to Foreign Office, Cable 1330, 30 July 1956.

38 PRO, FO371/119086/JE14211/281, Cairo to Foreign Office, Cable 1414, 4 August 1956. See also USNA, RG 59, CDF, 974.7301/8-656, Cairo to State Department, Cable 272, 6 August 1956.

39 USNA, RG 59, CDF, 974.7301/8-756, Elbrick memorandum, 7 August 1956.

40 DDE, John Foster Dulles Series, Telephone Calls, White House, Box 10, Anderson to Foster Dulles, 8 August 1956; DDE, Ann Whitman Series, DDE Diaries, Box 17, August 1956 Diary, Eisenhower diary entry, 8 August 1956; DDE, Ann Whitman Series, National Security Council, Box 8, 292nd NSC meeting, 9 August 1956, and 295th NSC meeting, 30 August 1956.

41 PRO, PREM11/1099, Washington to Foreign Office, Cable 1691, 10 August 1956.

42 PRO, FO371/119260/JE15310/3, Washington to Foreign Office, Cable 1693, 10 August 1956.

43 See DDE, Ann Whitman Series, Ann Whitman Diary, Box 8, August 1956 Diary, Ann Whitman diary entry, 12 August 1956; Neff, p. 292.

44 DDE, Ann Whitman Series, DDE Diaries, Box 16, August 1956 Press Conferences, Foster Dulles to Eisenhower, 8 August 1956. See also DDE, John Foster Dulles Series, White House Memoranda, Chronological, Box 5, Foster Dulles memorandum, 14 August 1956.

45 Wyndham-Goldie, pp. 176ff.; *Television and Number 10*, interview with William Clark; WCP, File 7, Clark diary, 11 July 1956; AP, AP3/2/1, Clarissa Eden to Clark, 9 August 1956.

46 Rhodes James, p. 492; Love, p. 395; Eden, p. 444.

47 PRO, PREM11/1099, Washington to Foreign Office, Cable 1691, 10 August 1956; PRO, PREM11/1126, Jebb to Eden, 10 August 1956; PRO, PREM11/1123, *News Chronicle* Gallup poll, 10 August 1956.

48 PRO, FO371/119094/JE14211/613, Washington to Foreign Office, Cable 569 Saving, 9 August 1956; PRO, PREM11/1159, Gaitskell to Eden, 10 August 1956; Jay, pp. 254ff.; PRO, PREM11/1123, *News Chronicle* Gallup poll, 10 August 1956. See also USNA, RG 59, CDF, 974.7301/8-1456, London to State Department, Cable 870, 14 August 1956.

49 PRO, FO371/119100/JE14211/667, Cairo to Foreign Office, Cable 1536, 12 August 1956; PRO, FO371/119093/JE14211/450, Cairo to Foreign Office, Cable 1478, 8 August 1956.

50 PRO, FO371/118871/JE1073/File.

51 PRO, PREM11/1099, E.C.(56)18, Staff Conference of 11 August, 13 August 1956, and Record of Anglo-French discussions, undated. See also PRO, PREM11/1126, Jebb to Eden, 14 August 1956.

52 PRO, CAB128/30, C.M.59(56), 14 August 1956.

53 PRO, CAB134/1216, E.C.(56)15th meeting, 14 August 1956.

54 AP, AP20/1, Eden diary, August 1956; WCP, File 7, Clark diary, 8 and 22 August 1956.

55 WCP, File 7, Clark diary, 8 August 1956; *A Canal Too Far*, interview with Lord Home.
56 PRO, CAB134/1215, P.R.(56)9th meeting, 25 July 1956.
57 WCP, File 7, Clark diary, 7 August and 15 August 1956; Wyndham-Goldie, p. 178.
58 PRO, PREM11/1089A/File; Partner, pp. 101ff. See also Gilbert, p. 1208.
59 DDE, John Foster Dulles Series, White House Memoranda, Chronological, Box 5, Foster Dulles memorandum, 14 August 1956; USNA, RG 59, CDF, 974.7301/8-356, Bowie memorandum, 3 August 1956.

14: Washington's Leash upon London, 15 August–3 September 1956

1 Rhodes James, p. 501; USNA, RG 59, CDF, 974.7301/8-1656, London to State Department, Cable SECTO 5, 16 August 1956.
2 PRO, CAB134/1216, E.C.(56)16th meeting, 16 August 1956.
3 DDE, Ann Whitman Series, Dulles–Herter, Box 5, London to State Department, Cable DULTE 1, 16 August 1956.
4 Lloyd, pp. 115ff.; Rhodes James, p. 501; Macmillan, *Riding the Storm*, p. 107; DDE, Ann Whitman Series, Dulles–Herter, Box 5, London to State Department, Cable DULTE 4, 16 August 1956.
5 DDE, Ann Whitman Series, Dulles–Herter, Box 5, London to State Department, Cable DULTE 10, 18 August 1956. See also Horne, p. 393.
6 USNA, RG 59, Lot 62 D 11, Suez Conference Files, Box 1, Foster Dulles–Eden meeting, 19 August 1956.
7 Horne, p. 408; DDE, Ann Whitman Series, Dulles–Herter, Box 5, London to State Department, Cable DULTE 12, 19 August 1956.
8 USNA, RG 59, CDF, 974.7301/8-1556, Cairo to State Department, Cable 382, 15 August 1956; DDE, Ann Whitman Series, Dulles-Herter, Box 5, Eisenhower to Foster Dulles, 19 August 1956.
9 DDE, Ann Whitman Series, Dulles–Herter, Box 5, London to State Department, Cable DULTE 17, 20 August 1956; USNA, RG 59, CDF, 974.7301/8-2056, Washington to London, Cable TEDUL 15, 20 August 1956.
10 DDE, Ann Whitman Series, Dulles–Herter, Box 5, London to State Department, Cable DULTE 22, 22 August 1956.
11 DDE 56; FRUS 1955–7 XVI, p. 235 and pp. 256ff.; DDE, John Foster Dulles Papers, General Memoranda of Conversations, Box 1, L-M (1), Foster Dulles–Macmillan meeting, 21 August 1956.
12 PRO, CAB134/126, E.C.(56)18th meeting, 20 August 1956; USNA, Lot 62 D 11, Suez Conference Files, Foster Dulles memorandum, 19 August 1956.
13 PRO, T236/4625, Macmillan memorandum, 17 August 1956; PRO, CAB134/1216, E.C.(56)18th meeting, 20 August 1956.
14 PRO, CAB128/30, C.M.60(56), 21 August 1956; PRO, PREM11/1099, Lloyd–Foster Dulles meeting, 21 August 1956.
15 PRO, PREM11/1099, Lloyd–Foster Dulles–Pineau meeting, 23 August 1956.
16 PRO, PREM11/1100, E.C.(56)28, 'Egypt: Military Planning', 20 August 1956; WCP, File 7, Clark diary, 21 August 1956.
17 Nutting, *Nasser*, p. 152; PRO, FO953/1659/PB1045/100, Dodds-Parker minute, 3 August 1956, and PB1045/99, Tel Aviv to Foreign Office, Cable 343, 3 August 1956, and subsequent minutes; PRO, FO371/118865/JE1053/87, Cairo to Foreign Office, Cable 2480, 17 October 1956. See also USNA, RG 59, CDF, 974.7301/8-2256, State Department to London, Cable TOSEC 45, 22 August 1956.

18 Author's interview with Norman Reddaway.

19 USNA, RG 59, CDF, 774.00(W)/9-656, SANA to State Department, Despatch 189, 6 September 1956.

20 Horne, p. 427; PRO, WO32/16709, Key to Head, 21 August 1956; PRO, CAB134/1216, E.C.(56)19th meeting, 22 August 1956.

21 WCP, File 7, Clark diary, 22 August 1956; PRO, FO371/121237/V1054/125G, Macmillan to Eden, 24 August 1956.

22 WCP, File 7, Clark diary, 23 August 1956.

23 PRO, PREM11/1152, Home to Eden and Eden to Sandys, 22 August 1956.

24 PRO, CAB134/1216, E.C.(56)21st meeting, 24 August 1956.

25 DDE, John Foster Dulles Papers, Subject, Alphabetical, Box 11, Miscellaneous Paper–UK(4), Foster Dulles memorandum, 24 August 1956. I am grateful to Samantha Badham for her interpretation of this document.

26 PRO, CAB134/1216, E.C.(56)21st meeting, 24 August 1956.

27 WCP, File 7, Clark diary, 27 August 1956; PRO, CAB134/1216, E.C.(56)21st meeting, 24 August 1956.

28 WCP, File 7, Clark diary, 27 August 1956; PRO, PREM11/1152, Lennox-Boyd to Eden, 24 August 1956.

29 PRO, PREM11/1152, Home to Eden, 24 August 1956.

30 Ibid., Salisbury to Eden, 24 August 1956. See also AP, AP20/33, Salisbury to Eden, 24 August 1956.

31 PRO, PREM11/1152, Brook to Eden, 25 August 1956.

32 PRO, PREM11/1100, Lloyd minute, 'The UN and Suez', undated, and Eden to Lloyd, 26 August 1956; PRO, CAB134/1216, E.C.(56)22nd meeting, 27 August 1956.

33 PRO, CAB128/30, C.M.62(56), 28 August 1956.

34 PRO, CAB134/1216, E.C.(56)23rd meeting, 28 August 1956.

35 USNA, RG 59, CDF, 974.7301/8-1756, State Department to London, Cable TEDUL 8, 17 August 1956.

36 US DDRS, US87 000570; DDE, Ann Whitman Series, International, Box 42, Saudi Arabia, King Saud 1952–6 (3), Eisenhower to Saud, 20 August 1956; Eveland, pp. 209ff.; USNA, RG 59, CDF, 974.7301/8-2356, Dhahran to State Department, Cable 77, 23 August 1956; Copeland, The Real Spy World, p. 192.

37 FRUS 1955–7 XVI, pp. 288ff. and pp. 301ff.

38 Ibid., p. 349; USNA, RG 59, CDF, 974.7301 Series, Saud to Eisenhower, 24 August 1956, Jedda to State Department, Cable 97, 24 August 1956, Cairo to State Department, Cable 508, 29 August 1956, State Department to Jedda, Cable 180, 10 September 1956, Jedda to State Department, Cable 292, 15 September 1956, and State Department to Jedda, Cable 199, 19 September 1956.

39 PRO, PREM11/1177, Eden to Eisenhower, 27 August 1956.

40 US DDRS, US85 000276.

41 DDE, Ann Whitman Series, National Security Council, Box 7, 295th NSC meeting, 30 August 1956.

42 PRO, PREM11/1177, Eisenhower to Eden, 3 September 1956.

43 WCP, File 7, Clark diary, 5 September 1956; Horne, p. 412; Hugh Thomas, p. 77; PRO, PREM11/1100, Washington to Foreign Office, Cable 1761, 29 August 1956, and de Zulueta minute, 28 August 1956; USNA, RG 59, CDF, 974.7301/8-2856, London to State Department, Cable 1131, 28 August 1956; PRO, FO800/739, Foreign Office to Cairo, Cable 2611, 30 August 1956.

44 PRO, PREM11/1123, Poole to Eden, 29 August 1956, and *News Chronicle* Gallup poll, 31 August 1956.
45 PRO, FO371/11996/JE11924/366, Commonwealth Relations Office minute, 9 August 1956.
46 PRO, FO371/118857/JE10393/2G, Baghdad to Foreign Office, Cable 914, 20 August 1956, and subsequent cables and minutes.
47 DDE, John Foster Dulles Series, Telephone Calls, Box 5, Foster Dulles to Wisner, 30 August 1956.
48 PRO, FO371/119128/JE14211/1390G, Beeley minute, 18 August 1956, and subsequent minutes.
49 PRO, FO371/119154/JE14211/2127, Kirkpatrick to Lloyd, 4 September 1956.
50 PRO, FO800/740, Kirkpatrick to Makins, 10 September 1956.
51 PRO, PREM11/1177, Eden to Eisenhower, 6 September 1956.
52 PRO, FO371/119133/JE14211/1492, Kirkpatrick minute, 17 September 1956.
53 PRO, FO371/119107/JE14211/812, Baghdad to Foreign Office, Cable 892, 15 August 1956. See also USNA, RG 59, CDF, 974.7301/9-656, Baghdad to State Department, Cable 374, 6 September 1956.
54 PRO, FO371/119100/JE14211/651, Tehran to Foreign Office, Cable 651, 11 August 1956; USNA, RG 59, CDF, 974.7301/8-2356, Tehran to State Department, Cable 306, 23 August 1956.
55 Lloyd, p. 109 and p. 123; PREM11/1148/File.
56 PRO, FO371/120756/ES1021/55G, Baghdad to Foreign Office, Cable 954, 30 August 1956.
57 PRO, WO32/16709, Troopers to Middle East Main, Cable 05718/DMO, 1 October 1956, and subsequent minutes; PRO, DEFE32/5, COS(56)100(4) C.A., 12 October 1956.
58 USNA, RG 59, CDF, 684A.86/11-2456, State Department to Damascus, Cable 973, 24 November 1956.
59 DDE, John Foster Dulles Series, Telephone Calls, White House, Box 10, Foster Dulles to Eisenhower, 7 September 1956.
60 PRO, PREM11/1177, Eisenhower to Eden, 8 September 1956.

15: Force Revised, 4–11 September 1956

1 Love, p. 417; Hoopes, p. 356.
2 PRO, PREM11/1100, Cairo to State Department, Cable 1885, 4 September 1956; USNA, RG 59, CDF, 974.7301/9-356, Cairo to State Department, Cable 575, 3 September 1956; Heikal, *Cutting the Lion's Tail*, pp. 164ff. See also Menzies, p. 164.
3 Heikal, *ibid.*, p. 166; DDE, Ann Whitman Series, International, Box 43, Suez Summaries, 5 September 1956; USNA, RG 59, CDF, 974.7301/9-556, Cairo to State Department, Cable 596, 5 September 1956.
4 PRO, PREM11/1100, Cairo to Foreign Office, Cable 1919, 5 September 1956.
5 PRO, FO371/119126/JE14211/1339, Washington to Foreign Office, Cable 1808, 5 September 1956; *Public Papers of the President of the United States, Dwight D. Eisenhower, 1956*, p. 737.
6 PRO, PREM11/1101, Menzies to Eden, 9 September 1956.
7 Trevelyan, p. 98; USNA, RG 59, CDF, 974.7301/9-556, Cairo to State Department, Cable 613, 5 September 1956; PRO, PREM11/1100, Cairo to Foreign Office, Cable 1919, 5 September 1956. See also PRO, PREM11/1101, Menzies to Eden,

9 September 1956; USNA, RG 59, CDF, 974.7301/9-956, Cairo to State Department, Cable 674, and State Department to Cairo, Cable 722, 9 September 1956.

8 PRO, PREM11/1100, Cairo to Foreign Office, Cables 1936 and 1942, 6 September 1956, and Cable 1980, 7 September 1956; DDE, Ann Whitman Series, International, Box 43, Suez Summaries, 6 September 1956; PRO, FO800/740, Foreign Office to Cairo, Cable 2745, 6 September 1956; USNA, RG 59, CDF, 974.7301/9-756, Cairo to State Department, Cable 643, 7 September 1956.

9 PRO, PREM11/1100, Cairo to Foreign Office, Cable 2010, 9 September 1956; Menzies, p. 169.

10 PRO, PREM11/1101, Menzies to Eden, 9 September 1956; Menzies, p. 164.

11 Thorpe, p. 222; DDE, Ann Whitman Series, Dulles–Herter, Box 5, September 1956 (2), London to State Department, Cable 1249, 1 September 1956, and Paris to State Department, Cable 1050, 2 September 1956; DDE, John Foster Dulles Papers, White House Memoranda, Chronological, Box 5, Meetings with the President, August–December 1956 (7), Foster Dulles memorandum, 29 August 1956. See also WCP, File 7, Clark diary, 20 September 1956.

12 DDE, John Foster Dulles Series, White House, Box 4, Meetings with the President, Foster Dulles memorandum, 2 September 1956.

13 PRO, PREM11/1100, Washington to Foreign Office, Cable 1804, 4 September 1956, and Foreign Office to Washington, Cable 4032, 5 September 1956, and Cables 4062 and 4069, 6 September 1956.

14 Bernard Levin, *The Times*, 5 November 1980.

15 PRO, PREM11/1104, E.C.(56)43, 'Operation MUSKETEER: Implications of Postponement', 6 September 1956.

16 *Ibid.*; Levin, *The Times*, 5 November 1980.

17 Rhodes James, p. 501; AP, AP20/1, Eden diary, 7 September 1956.

18 AP, AP20/1, Eden diary, 7 September 1956; PRO, CAB134/1216, E.C.(56)25th meeting, 7 September 1956.

19 PRO, CAB134/1216, E.C.(56)25th meeting, 7 September 1956; PRO, FO371/119134/JE14211/1549, Foreign Office to Paris, Cable 1623, 8 September 1956; PRO, FO371/119135/JE14211/1590G, Anglo-French meeting, 8 September 1956.

20 PRO, FO371/119141/JE14211/1784G, Watkinson minute, 10 September 1956.

21 DDE, John Foster Dulles Papers, Telephone Calls, White House, Box 10, Eisenhower to Foster Dulles, 7 September 1956.

22 PRO, PREM11/1100, Washington to Foreign Office, Cable 1823, 7 September 1956.

23 *Ibid.*, Cables 1827–1832, 7 September 1956.

24 *Ibid.*, Foreign Office to Washington, Cable 4102, 8 September 1956.

25 *Ibid.*, Washington to Foreign Office, Cable 1838, 8 September 1956.

26 PRO, PREM11/1101, Washington to State Department, Cables 1845–1847, 9 September 1956; USNA, RG 59, CDF, 974.7301/9-956, Rountree memorandum, 9 September 1956.

27 DDE, Ann Whitman Series, International, Box 43, Suez Summaries, 11 September 1956; USNA, RG 59, CDF, 684A.86/9-1156, London to State Department, Cable 1410, 11 September 1956.

28 PRO, CAB134/1216, E.C.(56)26th meeting, 10 September 1956.

29 PRO, DEFE4/89, COS(56)77th meeting, 2 August 1956; AP, AP20/28, E.C.(56)9th meeting, 2 August 1956.

30 PRO, AIR20/10128, Birch to Lloyd, 3 August 1956; PRO, WO288/38/File.

31 PRO, PREM11/1104, COS(56)360, 'Alternative to MUSKETEER', 18 September 1956.
32 PRO, PREM11/1149/File; West, p. 96; Partner, pp. 100ff.
33 FRUS 1955–7 XV, p. 726.
34 Wright, p. 81; PRO, AIR20/10216/File; PRO, AIR20/10621, Lloyd to Jones, 20 September 1956.
35 Wright, p. 160; *The Times*, 19 June 1975, p. 1; author's interview with Miles Copeland.
36 PRO, FO371/118304-118307/JE1693/File.
37 PRO, FO371/125423/JE1019/File; PRO, FO371/125612-125621/JE1691/File; West, pp. 113ff. See also PRO, FO371/125423/JE1019/1, Brenchley minute, 26 July 1957, and subsequent minutes.
38 Author's interview with Julian Amery.
39 *Ibid.* See also PRO, FO371/125423/JE1019/7, Brenchley minute, 24 December 1957, and subsequent minutes.
40 PRO, FO371/118864/JE1053/79, Ross minute, 28 July 1956.
41 PRO, FO371/118832/JE1015/45, Cairo to Foreign Office, Cable 1788, 30 August 1956; PRO, FO371/118996/JE11924/64G, Shattock to Murray, 28 August 1956.
42 Author's interview with Julian Amery; PRO, WO288/38, Maguire to Phillips, 1 September 1956; PRO, AIR20/9570, Doughty-Wylie report, 3 September 1956.
43 PRO, CAB134/1225, EOC(56)1, 5 September 1956.
44 PRO, FO371/118897/JE11924/61G, Murray minute, 4 September 1956, and subsequent minutes; PRO, FO371/118832/JE1015/50, Flux minute, 29 September 1956.
45 Macdermott, p. 137; author's interview with Sir Archibald Ross.
46 Author's interview with Brigadier David Hunt.
47 Beaufre, p. 49; PRO, WO288/77, Stockwell report on MUSKETEER, 1 February 1957; *A Canal Too Far*, interview with Air Chief Marshal Denis Barnett.
48 Kyle in Louis and Owen, p. 120.
49 Robertson, p. 111. See also USNA, RG 59, CDF, 974.7301/9-1056, Paris to State Department, Cable 1158, 10 September 1956.
50 PRO, PREM11/1101, draft Declaration of Anglo-French Union, undated.
51 Clark, p. 185.
52 Beaufre, p. 76.
53 PRO, CAB128/30, C.M.64(56), 11 September 1956.
54 PRO, PREM11/1101, Foreign Office to Washington, Cable 4136, 10 September 1956.

16: Impaled on a SCUA, 12–18 September 1956

1 PRO, CAB134/1216, E.C.(56)26th meeting, 10 September 1956; DDE, John Foster Dulles Papers, Subject, Alphabetical, Box 4, Miscellaneous Paper – UK (1), Foster Dulles memorandum, 8 September 1956.
2 PRO, PREM11/1101, Washington to Foreign Office, Cable 1865, 10 September 1956, and Foreign Office to Washington, Cable 4155, 11 September 1956; PRO, FO800/740, Kirkpatrick to Makins, 10 September 1956.
3 PRO, PREM11/1101, Washington to Foreign Office, Cables 1869, 1873, 1875 and 1879, 11 September 1956.
4 See PRO, PREM11/1101, Washington to Foreign Office, Cable 1896, 11 September 1956.

5 DDE, Ann Whitman Series, International, Box 43, Suez Summaries, Number 7, 13 September 1956.

6 PRO, PREM11/1101, Washington to Foreign Office, Cable 1891, 11 September 1956.

7 PRO, CAB134/1216, E.C.(56)27th meeting, 12 September 1956.

8 *Hansard*, 12 September 1956. See also USNA, RG 59, CDF, 974.7301/9-1356, London to State Department, Cable 1442, 13 September 1956.

9 WCP, File 7, Clark diary, 12 September 1956; USNA, RG 59, CDF, 974.7301/9-1356, London to State Department, Cable 1442, 13 September 1956.

10 DDE, John Foster Dulles Papers, Telephone Calls, Box 5, Foster Dulles to Makins, 11 September 1956, and Flemming to Foster Dulles, 12 September 1956.

11 PRO, PREM11/1101, Washington to Foreign Office, Cable 1916, 13 September 1956.

12 Eden, p. 484.

13 *Hansard*, 13 September 1956.

14 Clark, p. 188; USNA, RG 59, CDF, 974.7301/9-1756, London to State Department, Cable 1520, 17 September 1956.

15 Clark, p. 188.

16 DDE, John Foster Dulles Papers, Telephone Calls, Box 5, Foster Dulles to Humphrey, 13 September 1956; DDE, John Foster Dulles Papers, White House, Box 10, Eisenhower to Foster Dulles, 13 September 1956. See also DDE, John Foster Dulles Papers, Telephone Calls, Box 5, Foster Dulles to Smith, 14 September 1956.

17 Eden, p. 484; DDE, Ann Whitman Series, International, Box 43, Suez Summaries, 11 September 1956.

18 USNA, RG 59, CDF, 774.00/9-2156, Port Said to State Department, Cable 39, 21 September 1956, and 774.00(W)/10-1156, SANA (Cairo) to State Department, 11 October 1956; PRO, CAB134/1216, E.C.(56)29th meeting, 17 September 1956; PRO, FO371/119140/JE14211/1757, Giles to Logan, 18 September 1956.

19 Pearson, pp. 231ff.; Canadian National Archives, DEA 50372-40, Vol. 4, London to Department of External Affairs, Cable 1200, 3 September 1956. I am grateful to Brian Hearndon for bringing the Canadian document to my attention.

20 PRO, CAB134/1225, EOC(56)1, 5 September 1956.

21 Henriques, *Spectator*, 6 November 1959, p. 623, and 4 December 1959, p. 823; Bar-Zohar, *The Armed Prophet*, p. 222.

22 DDE, John Foster Dulles Papers, White House Memoranda, Chronological, Box 4, Foster Dulles–Eisenhower meeting, 17 September 1956.

17: Sliding towards a Settlement, 19 September–4 October 1956

1 DDE, Ann Whitman Series, Dulles–Herter, Box 5, London to State Department, Cable DULTE 2, 19 September 1956.

2 DDE, Ann Whitman Series, Dulles–Herter, Box 5, Cable DULTE 6, 20 September 1956; USNA, RG 59, CDF, 974.7301 Series, London to State Department, Cables SECTO 11, 19 September 1956, and SECTO 12, 20 September 1956.

3 Lloyd, p. 144; USNA, RG 59, CEDF, 974.7301/9-2256, London to State Department, Cable SECTO 24, 22 September 1956; DDE, John Foster Dulles Papers, Subject, Alphabetical, Box 11, Miscellaneous Paper – UK (4), Foster Dulles–Eden meeting, 21 September 1956.

4 Hugh Thomas, p. 88; USNA, RG 59, CDF, 974.7301/9-2056, London to State Department, Cable SECTO 20, 20 September 1956.

5 WCP, File 7, Clark diary, 20 September 1956; Lloyd, p. 145; USNA, RG 59, CDF, 974.7301/9-2256, London to State Department, Cable SECTO 24, 22 September 1956.

6 USNA, RG 59, CDF, 974.7301 Series, London to State Department, Cable SECTO 15, 20 September 1956, and Cables DULTE 8 and SECTO 25, 21 September 1956.

7 FRUS 1955–7 XVI, p. 550; WCP, File 7, Clark diary, 21 September 1956. See also AP, AP14/4, Jebb to Eden, 14 September 1956.

8 Gilbert, p. 1210; Rhodes James, p. 514.

9 USNA, RG 59, CDF, 974.7301/9-2156, Foster Dulles memorandum, 21 September 1956.

10 PRO, PREM11/1102, Eden to Lloyd and Foster Dulles–Lloyd meeting, 21 September 1956; USNA, RG 59, CDF, 974.7301/9-2156, Foster Dulles memorandum, 21 September 1956.

11 PRO, PREM11/1102, Foreign Office to Washington, Cable 4389, Washington to Foreign Office, Cables 1974 and 1975, and Foreign Office to Washington, Cable 4403, 22 September 1956.

12 PRO, PREM11/1102, Washington to Foreign Office, 22 September 1956, and Brook minute, 23 September 1956; USNA, RG 59, CDF, 974.7301/9-2256, Wilcox memorandum, 22 September 1956.

13 PRO, FO371/119141/JE14211/1791, Washington to Foreign Office. Cable 1980, 23 September 1956; DDE, John Foster Dulles Papers, Telephone Calls, Box 5, Spender to Foster Dulles, 24 September 1956.

14 Dayan, *The Story of My Life*, pp. 151ff.

15 Golan, p. 49; Bar-Zohar, *Ben-Gurion*, pp. 230ff.; Abel Thomas, p. 145; Dayan, *ibid.*, pp. 152ff.; 'Ben-Gurion's Diary', 25 September 1956, in Troen and Shemesh, p. 299; PRO, FO371/121696/VR1022/18, Tel Aviv to Foreign Office, Cable 429, 24 September 1956.

16 Robertson, pp. 134ff.

17 Brecher, p. 265; Dayan, *Diary of the Sinai Campaign*, p. 30; 'Ben-Gurion's Diary', 25 September 1956, in Troen and Shemesh, p. 299.

18 PRO, T236/4188, Bridges to Macmillan, 8 August 1956, and Rowan to Macmillan, 21 September 1956, and subsequent minutes; PRO, T234/78, 'Suez: The Economic Effects of the Long Haul', 21 September 1956.

19 PRO, PREM11/1102, Washington to Foreign Office, Cable 2004, 25 September 1956; Horne, p. 420.

20 DDE, Ann Whitman Series, DDE Diaries, Box 18, September 1956 Telephone Calls, Foster Dulles to Eisenhower, 25 September 1956; AP, AP23/52/65, Middleton manuscript, 'Where Has Last July Gone?'; Horne, p. 421; author's interview with Lord Sherfield.

21 Horne, p. 422; PRO, PREM11/1102, Washington to Foreign Office, Cables 2000 and 2001, 25 September 1956; USNA, RG 59, CDF, 974.7301/9-2556, Elbrick memorandum, 25 September 1956; DDE, John Foster Dulles Papers, General Memoranda of Conversations, Box 1, Foster Dulles–Macmillan meeting, 25 September 1956.

22 PRO, PREM11/1102, Washington to Foreign Office, Cable 2002, 25 September 1956.

23 *Ibid.*, Macmillan to Eden, 25 and 26 September 1956.

24 PRO, FO800/740, Washington to Foreign Office, Cable 1942, 17 September 1956.

25 PRO, FO371/120342/AU1057/1, Makins memorandum, 29 September 1956; Horne, p. 422.

26 *Neither War nor Peace at 10 Downing Street*, interview with William Clark.

27 Shuckburgh, p. 360.

28 Pearson, p. 240.

29 PRO, CAB134/1216, E.C.(56)31st meeting, 25 September 1956.

30 PRO, PREM11/1102, Bishop minute and Eden revisions, 25 September 1956; PRO, CAB128/30, C.M.(56)67, 26 September 1956.

31 PRO, PREM11/1102, Paris to Foreign Office, Cable 337, 26 September 1956.

32 USNA, RG 59, CDF, 974.7301/9-2756, Paris to State Department, Cable 1485, 27 September 1956.

33 DDE, Ann Whitman Series, International, Box 43, Suez Summaries, 28 September 1956; Gilbert, p. 1214.

34 PRO, CAB134/1216, E.C.(56)32nd meeting, 1 October 1956.

35 DDE, Ann Whitman Series, Dulles–Herter, Box 5, London to State Department, Cable 1932, 9 October 1956.

36 PRO, PREM11/1177, Eden to Eisenhower, 1 October 1956.

37 Dayan, *The Story of My Life*, pp. 157ff.; Bar-Zohar, *Ben-Gurion*, pp. 231ff.; Golan, pp. 50ff.; Abel Thomas, pp. 145ff.

38 *Ibid.*; Neff, p. 324.

39 DDE, John Foster Dulles Papers, Telephone Calls, Box 5, Foster Dulles to Lodge, 2 October 1956.

40 PRO, PREM11/1174, Washington to Foreign Office, Cable 2046, 2 October 1956.

41 *Ibid.*, Washington to Foreign Office, Cable 2052, 3 October 1956, and Makins to Eden, 4 October 1956.

42 WCP, File 7, Clark diary, 2 October 1956; PRO, PREM11/1174, *The Times*, 3 October 1956.

43 Nutting, *No End of a Lesson*, p. 70; PRO, PREM11/1174, Foreign Office to Washington, Cable 4592, 4 October 1956.

44 DDE, Ann Whitman Series, National Security Council, Box 7, 299th NSC meeting, 4 October 1956; DDE, Ann Whitman Series, International, Box 43, Suez Summaries, 1 October 1956, and Number 21, 2 October 1956.

45 MacDonald, *The History of the Times*, p. 268.

46 PRO, CAB128/30, C.M.(56)68, 3 October 1956; Macdermott, p. 143; Hugh Thomas, p. 96.

47 DDE, John Foster Dulles Papers, Subject, Alphabetical, Box 11, Miscellaneous Paper – UK (4), Foster Dulles Memorandum, 21 September 1956; FRUS 1955–7 XVI, p. 549.

48 DDE, John Foster Dulles Papers, White House Memoranda, Chronological, Box 4, Foster Dulles–Eisenhower meeting, 2 October 1956; DDE, Ann Whitman Series, DDE Diaries, Box 19, October 1956 Diary, Staff Memoranda, Goodpaster memorandum, 6 October 1956.

49 Private information; author's interview with Sir Harold Beeley; AP, AP20/34/4, Eden memorandum, undated; FRUS 1955–7 XVI, p. 1270; Eveland, p. 217.

50 Private information; PRO, FO371/121858-121859/VY1015/File; PRO, FO371/128220/VY1015/File; FRUS 1955–7 XVI, pp. 579ff.

51 PRO/FO371/128220/VY1015/File.

18: Force Dismissed, 5–14 October 1956

1 PRO, PREM11/1102, Foster Dulles–Lloyd–Pineau meeting, 5 October 1956; USNA, RG 59, CDF, 974.7301/10-556, Lodge memorandum, 5 October 1956. See also USNA, RG 59, CDF, 974.7301/10-656, New York to State Department, Cable DULTE 1, 5 October 1956.

2 Love, p. 444.

3 PRO, PREM11/1102, Foreign Office to New York, Cable 1070, 7 October 1956.

4 *Ibid.*, New York to Foreign Office, Cable 798, 7 October 1956, and Cable 801, 8 October 1956.

5 *Ibid.*, Record of SCUA 1st plenary meeting, 1 October 1956; Love, p. 438; Hugh Thomas, pp. 87ff. See also USNA, RG 59, CDF, 974.7301/10-356, State Department to London, Cable 2426, 3 October 1956.

6 PRO, CAB134/1216, E.C.(56)33rd meeting, 8 October 1956.

7 FRUS 1952–4 XIV, Part 1, p. 1017. I am grateful to Tracy Steele for bringing this quote to my attention.

8 AP, AP20/49/File.

9 PRO, PREM11/1102, Foreign Office to New York, Cable 1075, 8 October 1956.

10 *Ibid.*, Foreign Office to New York, Cable 1086, 9 October 1956, and Cable 1106, 10 October 1956.

11 *Ibid.*, New York to Foreign Office, Cable 814, 9 October 1956.

12 PRO, CAB134/1216, E.C.(56)34th meeting, 10 October 1956.

13 PRO, PREM11/1102, New York to Foreign Office, Cable 819, 10 October 1956, and Cable 821, 11 October 1956.

14 *Ibid.*, Ministerial meeting, 11 October 1956, and Foreign Office to New York, Cable 1125, 11 October 1956.

15 *Ibid.*, New York to Foreign Office, Cable 829, 11 October 1956.

16 *Ibid.*, New York to Foreign Office, Cable 830, 11 October 1956, and Cable 835, 12 October 1956.

17 Lloyd, p. 159.

18 PRO, PREM11/1102, New York to Foreign Office, Cables 835 and 845, 12 October 1956; PRO, FO371/119184/JE14214/269G, New York to Foreign Office, Cable 839, 12 October 1956.

19 DDE, Ann Whitman Series, National Security Council, Box 8, 300th NSC meeting, 12 October 1956.

20 Lloyd, p. 160.

21 DDE, Ann Whitman Series, DDE Diaries, Box 18, October 1956 Miscellaneous (4), Eisenhower to Foster Dulles, 13 October 1956.

22 PRO, PREM11/1102, New York to Foreign Office, Cable 852, 13 October 1956.

23 Lloyd, p. 160; PRO, PREM11/1102, New York to Foreign Office, Cable 854, 14 October 1956.

24 Eden, p. 507; Rhodes James, pp. 526ff.; USNA, RG 59, CDF, 741.00/10-1856, London to State Department, Cable 2134, 18 October 1956.

25 PRO, PREM11/1102, Foreign Office to New York, Cable 1198, 14 October 1956.

26 Eden, pp. 505ff.

27 Nutting, *No End of a Lesson*, p. 90; Lloyd, pp. 162ff.

28 PRO, WO32/16709, Middle East Rear Command to War Office, Cable 78719/PSZ, 3 October 1956, and Troopers to Forces, Cable 06161/AG, 10 October 1956.

29 PRO, PREM11/1104, COS(56)380, 'Operation MUSKETEER: Winter Plan', 12 October 1956.

19: Force Resurrected, 14 October 1956

1 Nutting, *No End of a Lesson*, pp. 90ff.

2 PRO, FO371/121780/VR1091/278, Laurence minute, 26 September 1956.

3 PRO, FO371/119079/JE14211/53, Amman to Foreign Office, Cable 1034, 28 July 1956.

4 PRO, FO371/121486/VJ10393/60, Baghdad to Foreign Office, Cable 1048, 15 September 1956; USNA, RG 59, CDF, 685.87/9-1556, Baghdad to State Department, Cable 446, 15 September 1956.

5 PRO, FO371/121587/VJ10393/106G, Extract from Lloyd minute, 17 September 1956; PRO, DEFE4/90, COS(56)94th meeting, 18 September 1956; PRO, FO371/121486/VJ10393/60, Foreign Office to Baghdad, Cable 1872, 20 September 1956.

6 PRO, FO371/121780/VR1091/278, Laurence minute, 26 September 1956; PRO, FO371/121486/VJ10393/69G, Baghdad to Foreign Office, Cable 1097, 27 September 1956.

7 USNA, RG 59, CDF, 685.87/9-2756, Tel Aviv to State Department, Cable 295, 27 September 1956; PRO, FO371/121486/VJ10393/69G, Foreign Office to Baghdad, Cable 1947, 28 September 1956.

8 PRO, FO371/121486/VJ10393/69G, Foreign Office to Baghdad, Cables 1947–9, 28 September 1956, and VJ10393/72G, Baghdad to Foreign Office, Cable 1110, 29 September 1956.

9 PRO, CAB134/1216, E.C.(56)32nd meeting, 1 October 1956; PRO, CAB131/17, D.C.(56)7th meeting, 2 October 1956; PRO, FO371/121487/VJ10393/82, Washington to Foreign Office, Cable 2053, 3 October 1956; USNA, RG 59, CDF, 684A.85 Series, Tel Aviv to State Department, Cable 310, 3 October 1956, and State Department to Tel Aviv, Cable 268, 4 October 1956; USNA, RG 59, CDF, 974.7301/10-756, Ludlow memorandum, 7 October 1956.

10 PRO, FO371/121487/VJ10393/102, Tel Aviv to Foreign Office, Cable 467, 6 October 1956, and Holmer minute, 8 October 1956; USNA, RG 59, CDF, 684A.85/10-656, Tel Aviv to State Department, Cable 330, 6 October 1956; Israeli State Archives, Israeli Foreign Ministry to Eban, 10 October 1956.

11 USNA, RG 59, CDF, 684A.85/10-856, State Department to Tel Aviv, Cable 278, 8 October 1956; PRO, FO371/121487/VJ10393/109, Tel Aviv to Foreign Office, Cable 471, 9 October 1956, and Foreign Office to Baghdad, Cable 2077, 10 October 1956.

12 USNA, RG 59, CDF, 684A.85/7-756, Tel Aviv to State Department, Cable 348, 7 July 1956.

13 PRO, FO371/121780/VR1091/297, Makins to Foreign Office, Cable 2096, 10 October 1956; USNA, RG 59, CDF, 684A.85 Series, Tel Aviv to State Department, Cable 340, 9 October 1956, and Cable 346, 10 October 1956. See also PRO, FO371/121782/VR1091/350, Tel Aviv to Foreign Office, Cable 528, 18 October 1956.

14 USNA, RG 218, Records of the Joint Chiefs of Staff, Geographical File, 1954–6, Box 14, S. 42, Collins to Radford, 11 October 1956; USNA, RG 59, CDF, 684A.85/10-1856, Tel Aviv to State Department, Cable 220, 18 October 1956.

15 Dayan, *The Story of My Life*, p. 172; PRO, FO371/121782/VR1091/359, Chancery (Tel Aviv) to Levant Department, 18 October 1956; PRO, FO371/121780/VR1091/301, Tel Aviv to Foreign Office, Cable 480, 11 October 1956; PRO, FO371/121781/VR1091/319, Amman to Foreign Office, Cable 1462, 15 October

1956; USNA, RG 59, CDF, 684A.85/10-1056, Tel Aviv to State Department, Cable 348, 10 October 1956.

16 PRO, FO371/121780/VR1091/334A, Higgins to Levant Department, 25 October 1956; PRO, FO371/121781/VR1091/316G, Amman to Foreign Office, Cable 1459, 13 October 1956; Abel Thomas, p. 164.

17 PRO, FO371/121780/VR1091/310, Tel Aviv to Foreign Office, Cable 491, 12 October 1956.

18 PRO, FO371/121488/VJ10393/126G, Westlake to Foreign Office, Cable 488, 12 October 1956. See also USNA, RG 59, CDF, 684A.85/10-1256, Tel Aviv to State Department, Cable 365, 12 October 1956.

19 PRO, FO371/121780/VR1091/311, Tel Aviv to Foreign Office, Cable 494, 14 October 1956, and VR1091/323, Tel Aviv to Foreign Office, Cable 506, 15 October 1956.

20 PRO, FO371/121488/VJ10393/113, Washington to Foreign Office, Cable 2085, 9 October 1956; PRO, FO371/121781/VR1091/321, Tel Aviv to Foreign Office, Cable 497, 14 October 1956, and VR1091/320, Jerusalem to Foreign Office, Cable 385, 15 October 1956; PRO, FO371/121781/VR1091/332, Jerusalem to Foreign Office, Cable 390, 16 October 1956; DDE, John Foster Dulles Series, Telephone Calls, Box 5, Foster Dulles to Allen Dulles, 15 October 1956; DDE, Ann Whitman Series, Dulles-Herter, Box 6, 'US Opportunities in the Middle East', updated memorandum; DDE, Ann Whitman Series, DDE Diaries, Box 18, October 1956 Telephone Calls, Eisenhower to Foster Dulles, 15 October 1956; FRUS 1955-7 XVI, pp. 727ff.

21 PRO, DEFE4/90, COS(56)97th meeting, 9 October 1956; PRO, DEFE4/91, COS(56)98th meeting, 10 October 1956.

22 PRO, FO371/121728/VR1073/185, Chancery (Tel Aviv) to Levant Department, 21 June 1956; Bar-Zohar, *The Armed Prophet*, p. 222; Ben-Gurion Archives, Sde Boker, Israel, Ben-Gurion diary entry, 6 October 1956.

23 General Staff/Operations Branch, 'Esau Planning', 21 October 1956, in *Study of the Sinai Campaign File*, Appendix J, Archive of Israeli Defence Force Military History, cited in Sheffy, pp. 33ff.

24 Sheffy, pp. 35ff.; Love, p. 443.

25 Beaufre, p. 69 and p. 77; Dayan, *Diary of the Sinai Campaign*, pp. 42ff.

26 USNA, RG 59, CDF, 684A.86/10-856, Tel Aviv to State Department, Cable 334, 8 October 1956.

27 Dayan, *The Story of My Life*, pp. 166ff.; Bar-Zohar, *Ben-Gurion*, p. 233.

28 Abel Thomas, p. 150; Ben-Gurion Archives, Ben-Gurion diary entry, 3 October 1956.

29 Beaufre, p. 77; Nutting, *No End of a Lesson*, pp. 88ff.; PRO, FO371/121782/VR1091/363, Nicholls to Rose, 17 October 1956.

30 See Israeli State Archives, 2595/6, Elath to Israeli Foreign Ministry, 10 October 1956.

31 PRO, FO371/121780/VR1091/297, Washington to Foreign Office, Cable 2096, 10 October 1956, and Laurence minute, 11 October 1956; 'Ben-Gurion's Diary', 9 October 1956, in Troen and Shemesh, p. 301.

32 Challe, pp. 26ff.; Brecher, p. 278; PRO, FO800/725, Lloyd minute, 'M. Pineau and Mr. Dulles in New York', 18 October 1956; Abel Thomas, p. 162; 'Ben-Gurion's Diary', 15 October 1956, in Troen and Shemesh, p. 302.

33 Nutting, *No End of a Lesson*, pp. 90ff.; PRO, FO371/121488/VJ10393/134, Foreign Office to Baghdad, Cable 2152, 14 October 1956.

20: *Collusion, 15–24 October 1956*

1 PRO, FO371/121781/VR1091/316G, Amman to Foreign Office, Cable 1459, 13 October 1956, and subsequent minutes and VR1091/315G, Foreign Office to Amman, Cable 2008, 14 October 1956; Nutting, *No End of a Lesson*, p. 89.

2 Nutting, *ibid.*, p. 95; PRO, FO371/121488/VJ10393/131G, Foreign Office to Baghdad, Cable 2164, 15 October 1956; PRO, FO371/121781/VR1091/315G, Foreign Office to Amman, Cable 2008, 14 October 1956; PRO, FO371/121489/VJ10393/166, Cairncross to Cloake, 19 October 1956.

3 PRO, FO371/121780/VR1091/303, Amman to Foreign Office, Cables 1948–50, 11 October 1956, and subsequent minutes and cables; PRO, AIR8/2093, ACAS (Ops) to SASO (MEAF), Cable 2147/ACAS, 12 October 1956; PRO, FO371/121488/VJ10393/1G, COS(56)96th meeting, 2 October 1956; PRO, DEFE4/91, COS(56)101st meeting, 15 October 1956.

4 PRO, DEFE4/91, COS(56)102nd meeting, 16 October 1956; PRO, FO371/121535/VJ1192/116G, BDCC (ME) to COS, Cable MECOS 186, 16 October 1956.

5 Nutting, *No End of a Lesson*, pp. 95ff.

6 Lamb, pp. 231ff.; Hugh Thomas, p. 113.

7 Nutting, *No End of a Lesson*, pp. 97ff.

8 PRO, FO800/725, Lloyd minute, 18 October 1956; PRO, PREM11/1126, Jebb to Lloyd, 17 October 1956; Bar-On in Louis and Owen, p. 150.

9 Nutting, *No End of a Lesson*, pp. 98ff.

10 See MacDonald, *The History of the Times*.

11 PRO, CAB134/1216, E.C.(56)35th meeting, 17 October 1956.

12 PRO, CAB128/30, C.M.71(56), 18 October 1956; Lloyd, p. 177; Butler, p. 192.

13 PRO, PREM11/1102, Dixon to Foreign Office, Cables 846 and 847, 13 October 1956; PRO, PREM11/1103, Lloyd to Foster Dulles and Foster Dulles to Lloyd, 15 October 1956; DDE, John Foster Dulles Series, Telephone Calls, Box 5, Foster Dulles to Rountree, 15 October 1956.

14 USNA, RG 59, CDF, 974.7301 Series, Rountree–Niazi meeting and Foster Dulles to Lloyd, 19 October 1956.

15 DDE, John Foster Dulles Series, Telephone Calls, Box 5, Lodge to Foster Dulles, 17 October 1956, and Foster Dulles to Allen Dulles, 18 October 1956.

16 PRO, FO371/121781/VR1091/327, Tel Aviv to Foreign Office, Cable 511, 15 October 1956; Brecher, p. 248.

17 Golan, p. 53; Bar-Zohar, *Ben-Gurion*, p. 234; Bar-On in Louis and Owen, pp. 149ff; Troen and Shemesh, pp. 302ff.

18 PRO, FO371/121745/VR1074/412, Dixon to Foreign Office, Cable 876, 17 October 1956, and de Zulueta to Graham, 19 October 1956; PRO, FO371/121746/VR1074/436, Eden to Lloyd, 20 October 1956.

19 PRO, DEFE4/91, COS(56)103rd meeting, 18 October 1956; PRO, ADM205/137, Mountbatten to Durnford-Slater, 18 October 1956.

20 PRO, AIR20/9965/File.

21 PRO, FO371/121535/VJ1192/118G, COS to BDCC (ME), COSME 150, and Rose to Ross, 18 October 1956.

22 PRO, FO371/121536/VJ1192/122 (missing from PRO): PRO, PREM11/1508, Hailsham to Eden, 22 October 1956, and Eden to Hailsham, 23 October 1956.

23 Dayan, *The Story of My Life*, pp. 175ff.; Bar-Zohar, *Ben-Gurion*, pp. 234ff.; 'Ben-Gurion's Diary', 22 October 1956, in Troen and Shemesh, pp. 305ff.

24 Shlaim, p. 186; Israeli State Archives, Ben-Gurion–Gilbert meeting, 19 October

1956; 'Ben-Gurion's Diary', 22 October 1956, in Troen and Shemesh, pp. 305ff.

25 Bar-Zohar, *Ben-Gurion*, pp. 236ff.; Dayan, *The Story of My Life*, pp. 177ff.; Brecher, p. 271.

26 Author's interview with Sir Richard Powell; Thorpe, p. 236; AP, AP20/30/2, Chequers Book, 21 October 1956, and AP23/44/83A–B, Hill to Lloyd, 26 April 1967.

27 *The Times*, 2 January 1987; Lloyd, p. 181; *Secrets of Suez*, interview with Maurice Bourges-Maunoury; Bar-On, in Louis and Owen, p. 157.

28 Dayan, *The Story of My Life*, pp. 179ff.; Bar-Zohar, *Ben-Gurion*, pp. 238ff.; 'Ben-Gurion's Diary', 22 October 1956, in Troen and Shemesh, pp. 308ff.

29 Dayan, *ibid.*, p. 182.

30 PRO, CAB128/30, C.M.72(56), 23 October 1956; PRO, FO800/728, Lloyd notes, undated.

31 Nutting, *No End of a Lesson*, p. 102.

32 Bar-Zohar, *Ben-Gurion*, p. 240; Dayan, *The Story of My Life*, p. 184; 'Ben-Gurion's Diary', 22–25 October 1956, in Troen and Shemesh, pp. 305ff.

33 PRO, FO800/725, Lloyd minute, 24 October 1956.

34 PRO, CAB128/30, C.M.73(56), 24 October 1956.

35 Lloyd, pp. 186ff.; author's interview with Donald Logan.

36 Bar-Zohar, *Ben-Gurion*, p. 241; Dayan, *The Story of My Life*, pp. 189ff.

37 Bar-Zohar, *ibid.*, pp. 242ff.; Dayan, *ibid.*, pp. 191ff.; author's interview with Donald Logan.

21: *Preparing for 'Peace-keeping', 24–29 October 1956*

1 Lloyd, p. 188; *The Times*, 2 January 1987; author's interview with Donald Logan.

2 PRO, CAB128/30, C.M.74(56), 25 October 1956.

3 Rhodes James, p. 535; Walter Monckton Papers, File 7, Monckton to Eden drafts, September 1956; Astor, 'The *Observer* and Suez'.

4 Thorpe, p. 246.

5 Hugh Thomas, p. 182.

6 Astor, 'The *Observer* and Suez'.

7 AP, AP33/7, Eden record, October 1972.

8 Horne, p. 402 and p. 417; author's interview with Lord Sherfield.

9 Author's interview with Lord Sherfield; Horne, p. 434.

10 Horne, p. 444.

11 *Ibid.*, pp. 402ff. and p. 430.

12 *Ibid.*, p. 430 and p. 447.

13 *Ibid.*, p. 388.

14 *Ibid.*, p. 429.

15 PRO, CAB128/30, C.M.85(56), 26 October 1956.

16 PRO, PREM11/1103, E.C.(56)63, 'Military Implications of Mounting Operation MUSKETEER', 25 October 1956; Stockwell Papers, Liddell Hart Centre for Military Archives, King's College, London, 8/2/2, Stockwell report on MUSKETEER, p. 38; PRO, ADM205/118, unsigned note to Prime Minister, 26 October 1956.

17 Bernard Levin, *The Times*, 11 November 1980; Ziegler, p. 544.

18 Stockwell Papers, 8/2/2, Stockwell report on MUSKETEER, p. 39, and handwritten notes at beginning of report.

19 *A Canal Too Far*, interview with Kenneth Darling.

20 Stockwell Papers, 8/2/2, Stockwell report on MUSKETEER, pp. 39ff.; PRO, ADM205/161, CTF 345 report, 22 December 1956. The original naval report was removed from circulation because it was too explicit about Britain's 'advance' planning and a revised report distributed.

21 PRO, AIR20/9965, CINCMEAF to CAS, Cable CINC190, 25 October 1956, and CAS to CINCMEAF, Cable A2988/CAS, 27 October 1956; *A Canal Too Far*, interview with Denis Barnett.

22 Stockwell Papers, 8/2/2, Stockwell report on MUSKETEER, p. 39.

23 Dayan, *The Story of My Life*, p. 193; Bar-Zohar, *The Armed Prophet*, p. 234; USNA, RG 59, CDF, 684A.86/12-1056, Tel Aviv to State Department, Cable 317, 10 December 1956.

24 Nutting, *No End of a Lesson*, p. 103; PRO, FO371/121469/V1015/274, Duke to Foreign Office, Cable 1522, 23 October 1956.

25 PRO, FO371/119156/JE14211/2180, Coulson to Foreign Office, Cable 2136, 18 October 1956, and Foreign Office to Washington, Cable 5875, 21 October 1956; USNA, RG 59, CDF, 974.7301/10-1956, Paris to State Department, Cable 1839, 19 October 1956; US DDRS, US85 000227.

26 Hugh Thomas, p. 115.

27 USNA, RG 59, CDF, 974.7301/10-2456, London to State Department, Cable 2215, 23 October 1956.

28 USNA, RG 218, Records of the Joint Chiefs of Staff, Geographical File, 1954-6, Box 14, S. 42, JCS to Posts, Cable 912329, 26 October 1956; Mosley, p. 411.

29 DDE, Ann Whitman Series, DDE Diaries, Box 19, October 1956 Diary, Staff Memoranda, Goodpaster record, 27 October 1956; DDE, Ann Whitman Series, International, Box 29, Israel (5), Eisenhower to Ben-Gurion, 27 October 1956.

30 DDE, Ann Whitman Series, DDE Diaries, Box 19, October 1956 Diary, Staff Memoranda, Goodpaster record, 27 October 1956; Bar-Zohar, *Ben-Gurion*, p. 244; USNA, RG 59, CDF, 974.7301/10-2656, London to State Department, Cable 2295, 26 October 1956; DDE, John Foster Dulles Series, Telephone Calls, White House, Box 10, Foster Dulles memorandum, 28 October 1956; Eban, p. 210.

31 USNA, RG 59, CDF, 684A.86/10-2956, London to State Department, Cable 2322, 29 October 1956; Aldrich, pp. 541ff. See also Hetherington, p. 19.

32 Cooper, p. 159.

33 DDE, Ann Whitman Series, International, Box 28, Israel (5), Eisenhower to Ben-Gurion, 28 October 1956; DDE, John Foster Dulles Papers, Telephone Calls, Box 5, Foster Dulles to McCloy, 28 October 1956.

34 FRUS 1955-7 XVI, pp. 798ff.; USNA, RG 218, Records of the Joint Chiefs of Staff, Geographical File, 1954-6, Box 14, S. 42, JCS to Commands, Cable 912389, 29 October 1956.

35 DDE, Ann Whitman Series, DDE Diaries, Box 18, October 1956 Telephone Calls, Foster Dulles to Eisenhower, 29 October 1956.

36 USNA, 684A.86/10-2956, Wilkins memorandum, 29 October 1956; Neff, p. 362.

37 DDE, John Foster Dulles Papers, Telephone Calls, Box 5, Foster Dulles to Lodge, 29 October 1956.

22: *Alliance Endangered, 29–31 October 1956*

1 PRO, FO371/121782/VR1091/368, Foreign Office to Tel Aviv, Cable 1025, 27 October 1956; author's interview with Sir Harold Beeley.

2 PRO, FO371/121763/VR1076/122, Washington to Foreign Office, Cable 2190, 28 October 1956, and subsequent minutes; PRO, FO371/121782/VR1091/377, Tel Aviv to Foreign Office, Cable 575, 29 October 1956.

3 PRO, FO371/121763/VR1076/122, Millard and Ross minutes and Foreign Office to Washington, Cable 4987, 29 October 1956.

4 PRO, FO371/121476/VR1074/429, Washington to Foreign Office, Cable 2197, 29 October 1956.

5 DDE, John Foster Dulles Papers, Telephone Calls, Box 5, Foster Dulles to Knowland, 29 October 1956.

6 DDE, Ann Whitman Series, DDE Diaries, Box 19, October 1956, Staff Memoranda, Goodpaster memorandum, 29 October 1956.

7 PRO, FO800/741, Washington to Foreign Office, Cable 2200, 29 October 1956; DDE, Ann Whitman Series, DDE Diaries, Box 19, October 1956, Staff Memoranda, Foster Dulles–Eisenhower–Coulson meeting, 29 October 1956.

8 PRO, PREM11/1103, New York to Foreign Office, Cable 967, 30 October 1956; DDE, John Foster Dulles Papers, Telephone Calls, Box 5, Foster Dulles to Lodge, 29 October 1956; DDE, Ann Whitman Series, DDE Diaries, Box 18, October 1956 Telephone Calls, Eisenhower to Foster Dulles, 30 October 1956; USNA, RG 59, CDF, 684A.86/10-3056, New York to State Department, Cable 443, 30 October 1956.

9 Aldrich, pp. 541ff.; PRO, FO371/121783/VR1091/418; Lloyd minute, 30 October 1956; USNA, RG 59, CDF, 974.7301/10-3056, London to State Department, Cable 2343, 30 October 1956.

10 PRO, CAB128/30, C.M.75(56), 30 October 1956.

11 PRO, PREM11/1177, Foreign Office to Washington, Cable 5010, 30 October 1956.

12 DDE, White House Office, Office of the Staff Secretary, Subject, State Department, Box 1, State Department to London, Cable 3080, 30 October 1956.

13 DDE, Ann Whitman Series, DDE Diaries, Box 19, October 1956 Diary, Staff Memoranda, Goodpaster memorandum, 30 October 1956; DDE, John Foster Dulles Papers, Telephone Calls, Box 5, Foster Dulles to Lodge, 30 October 1956.

14 PRO, FO371/121784/VR1091/431, Foreign Office to Amman, Cable 2215, 30 October 1956.

15 PRO, PREM11/1105, New York to Foreign Office, Cable 989, 30 October 1956; USNA, RG 59, CDF, 684A.86/10-3056, New York to State Department, Cables 443, 445, and 452, 30 October 1956; DDE, Ann Whitman, DDE Diaries, Box 19, October 1956 Diary, Staff Memoranda, Goodpaster memorandum, 30 October 1956.

16 DDE, John Foster Dulles Papers, Telephone Calls, White House, Box 10, Foster Dulles to Eisenhower, 30 October 1956.

17 Hansard, 30 October 1956.

18 USNA, RG 59, CDF, 684A.86/12-556, London to State Department, Despatch 1363, 5 December 1956.

19 Hayter, p. 142.

20 Author's interview with Lord Jay.

21 Hansard, 30 October 1956; Rhodes James, p. 544.

22 Aldrich, 541ff.; PRO, FO371/118902/JE1094/4, Kirkpatrick minute, 30 October 1956.

23 PRO, PREM11/1177, Foreign Office to Washington, Cable 5025, 30 October 1956; DDE, John Foster Dulles Papers, Telephone Calls, White House, Box 10, Eisenhower to Foster Dulles, 30 October 1956.

24 PRO, PREM11/1177, Foreign Office to Washington, Cable 5180, 5 November 1956; DDE, John Foster Dulles Papers, Telephone Calls, Box 5, Knowland to Foster Dulles and Foster Dulles to George, 30 October 1956; DDE, John Foster Dulles Papers, Telephone Calls, White House, Box 10, Foster Dulles to Eisenhower, 30 October 1956.

25 PRO, FO800/741, Washington to Foreign Office, Cable 2206, 30 October 1956; USNA, RG 59, CDF, 684A.86/10-3056, Elbrick memorandum, 30 October 1956.

26 DDE, John Foster Dulles Papers, Telephone Calls, White House, Box 10, Foster Dulles to Eisenhower, 30 October 1956; DDE, White House Office, Office of the Staff Secretary, Subject, State Department, Box 1, State Department to London, Cable 3083, 30 October 1956.

27 Clark, p. 200.

28 *Neither War nor Peace at 10 Downing Street*, interview with William Clark; Clark, p. 200.

29 PRO, PREM11/1105, New York to Foreign Office, Cables 975–7 and 989, 30 October 1956; USNA, RG 59, CDF, 684A.86/10-3056, New York to State Department, Cable 452, 30 October 1956.

30 PRO, PREM11/1105, New York to Foreign Office, Cable 989, 30 October 1956.

31 PRO, FO371/121783/VR1091/406, Cairo to Foreign Office, Cable 2590, 30 October 1956; PRO, CAB128/30, C.M.76(56), 31 October 1956.

32 DDE, John Foster Dulles Papers, Telephone Calls, Box 5, Nixon to Foster Dulles, 31 October 1956.

23: *Britain's Last Chance, 31 October–1 November 1956*

1 DDE, John Foster Dulles Papers, Telephone Calls, Box 5, Knowland to Foster Dulles and Lawrence to Foster Dulles, 31 October 1956.

2 DDE, Ann Whitman Series, Dulles–Herter, Box 5, October 1956 (1), Eisenhower to Eden draft, 30 October 1956; DDE, John Foster Dulles Papers, Telephone Calls, Box 5, Lodge to Foster Dulles, 31 October 1956.

3 PRO, FO371/121746/VR1074/451, New York to Foreign Office, Cable 993, 31 October 1956; DDE, John Foster Dulles Papers, Telephone Calls, Box 5, Lodge to Foster Dulles, 31 October 1956; FRUS 1955–7 XVI, p. 889.

4 DDE, John Foster Dulles Papers, Telephone Calls, Box 5, Lodge to Foster Dulles, 31 October 1956.

5 Mosley, pp. 417ff.

6 *Ibid.;* DDE, Oral History Collection, OH-284, Admiral Arleigh Burke, 14 November 1972.

7 Eisenhower, *Waging Peace*, p. 81.

8 Nutting, *No End of a Lesson*, pp. 122ff.

9 WCP, File 7, Clark diary, 3 November 1956.

10 PRO, FO371/121748/VR1074/527, Ross minute, 30 October 1956.

11 AP, AP33/7, Eden record, 21 May 1976; PRO, PREM11/1090/File.

12 *Hansard*, 31 October 1956; USNA, RG 59, CDF, 641.74/10-3156, London to State Department, Cable 2402, 31 October 1956.

13 *Hansard*, 31 October 1956.

14 Lloyd, pp. 246ff.; Pineau, p. 134; Thorpe, p. 241.

15 Thorpe, p. 249.

16 FRUS 1955–7 XVI, pp. 1266ff.

17 PRO, FO371/121783/VR1091/4071, Baghdad to Foreign Office, Cable 1230, and

Foreign Office to Baghdad, Cable 2343, 31 October 1956, and VR1091/416, Baghdad to Foreign Office, Cable 1234, and Foreign Office to Baghdad, Cable 2353, 31 October 1956; PRO, FO371/121489/VJ10393/176, Baghdad to Foreign Office, Cable 1238, 1 November 1956, and Foreign Office to Baghdad, Cable 2361, 1 November 1956.

18 Rhodes James, pp. 55off.; PRO, FO371/121748/VR1074/550, Karachi to Commonwealth Relations Office, Cable 1777, 1 November 1956; Pearson, p. 244; AP. AP20/25, Canberra to Commonwealth Relations Office, Cable 2545, 1 November 1956, Ottawa to Commonwealth Relations Office, Cable 1040, 1 November 1956, and Suhrawardy to Eden, 4 November 1956.

19 FRUS 1955–7 XVI, pp. 891ff.

20 PRO, FO371/118902/JE1094/14, Washington to Foreign Office, Cable 2223, 1 November 1956.

21 DDE, Ann Whitman Series, International, Box 19, Eden, Eisenhower to Eden draft, 1 November 1956.

22 DDE, Oral History Collection, OH-14, Eisenhower oral history, 28 July 1964.

23 Author's interview with General Andrew Goodpaster.

24 DDE, John Foster Dulles Papers, Telephone Calls, Box 5, Foster Dulles to Allen Dulles, 1 November 1956.

25 DDE, John Foster Dulles Papers, Telephone Calls, White House, Box 10, Eisenhower to Foster Dulles, 30 October 1956; Hughes, p. 216.

26 USNA, RG 218, Records of the Joint Chiefs of Staff, Geographical File, 1954–6, EMMEA (11-19-47), Box 14, S. 46, CINCLANT to Commanders, Cable 5959, 1 November 1956. See also USNA, RG 59, CDF, 684A.86/10-3056, US Army Attaché (Paris) to State Department, Cable CX 195, 30 October 1956.

27 USNA, RG 59, CDF, 684A.86/11-256, US Army Attaché (Cairo) to State Department, Cable CX 238-56, 2 November 1956.

28 PRO, AIR24/2426/File, including Air Task Force Directive, Cable AO 476, 1 November 1956.

29 PRO, AIR24/2426, General Summary of Events, 31 October 1956, and AFHQ to SASO, ATF, 31 October 1956.

30 PRO, ADM205/150, 'A Short Account of Operation MUSKETEER and Its Aftermath, 31 Oct. 1956–Nov. 1956', undated; PRO, AIR24/2426, Summary of FOA Carriers, 20 November 1956; PRO, WO288/99, Mideast Intelligence Summary No. 201, 28 October–10 November 1956.

31 PRO, ADM205/139-140/File; PRO, AIR8/2097, MUSKETEER Naval Situation Report 3, 3 November 1956; PRO, DEFE4/91, COS(56)111th meeting, 5 November 1956.

32 Abel Thomas, p. 110; Bar-Zohar, *The Armed Prophet*, p. 240; PRO, ADM205/139, CINCMED to HMS *Newfoundland*, 31 October 1956.

33 See PRO, AIR8/2097, HQATF to HQ Bomber Malta, Cable AG611, 1 November 1956.

34 PRO, ADM205/150, 'A Short Account of Operation MUSKETEER', undated; Lamb, p. 247.

35 PRO, AIR8/1940, Keightley to COS, KEYCOS 2, 31 October 1956, and KEYCOS 16, 2 November 1956; PRO, DEFE4/91, COS(56)108th meeting, 1 November 1956; Lamb, p. 248.

36 PRO, PREM11/1132, Foreign Office to Paris, Cable 2863, 1 November 1956, and Paris to Foreign Office, Cable 397, 2 November 1956; Fullick and Powell, p. 119;

author's interview with Richard Powell; PRO, AIR20/10127, Keightley to Chiefs of Staff, KEYCOS 60, 8 November 1956.

37 PRO, AIR8/2097, AFHQ to Air Ministry, Cable COSAIR/1, 1 November 1956.

38 PRO, AIR20/10369, Memorandum for Director of Psychological Warfare, 3 November 1956.

39 PRO, ADM205/150, 'A Short Account of Operation MUSKETEER', undated; PRO, AIR20/10369, Keightley to Ministry of Defence, Cable CIC/560, 16 November 1956; PRO, AIR20/10369/File.

40 PRO, CAB134/1216, E.C.(56)36th meeting, 1 November 1956; PRO, AIR8/2097, 3rd Summary of Operations, 2 November 1956; PRO, FO953/1786/PB1045/13, James minute, 13 June 1957; PRO, AIR20/10369/File.

41 Pincher, p. 90; PRO, FO371/125423/JE1019/1, Brenchley minute, 26 July 1957; 'Abd Al-Latif Al-Bughdadi's Memoirs', in Troen and Shemesh, pp. 336ff.

42 Heikal, *Cutting the Lion's Tail*, pp. 196ff.; Nutting, *Nasser*, p. 166.

43 WCP, File 7, Clark diary, 12 November 1956.

44 PRO, CAB134/1216, E.C.(56)36th meeting, 1 November 1956; PRO, PREM11/1129, Manningham-Buller to Lloyd, 1 November 1956.

45 Shuckburgh, pp. 363ff.; Lamb, p. 261.

46 PRO, T236/4188, Rowan memorandum, 31 October 1956, and Ricketts memorandum, 2 November 1956; Clark, p. 203; Hugh Thomas, p. 138.

47 *Hansard*, 1 November 1956; Hugh Thomas, p. 115; PRO, CAB134/1216, E.C.(56)37th meeting, 1 November 1956.

48 PRO, CAB128/30, C.M.73(56), 24 October 1956.

49 PRO, AIR8/1940, Keightley to Chiefs of Staff, Cable KEYCOS 17, 2 November 1956.

24: Alliance Broken, 1–4 November 1956

1 DDE, Ann Whitman Series, National Security Council, Box 8, 301st NSC meeting, 26 October 1956; Ranelagh, pp. 287ff.

2 Ranelagh, pp. 287ff.; Mosley, p. 420.

3 Private information; PRO, FO371/128221/VY1015/23, Chancery (Beirut) to Levant Department, 22 February 1957.

4 DDE, John Foster Dulles Papers, Telephone Calls, Box 5, Foster Dulles to Allen Dulles, 30 October 1956.

5 Seale, pp. 268ff.; PRO, FO371/128220/File; USNA, RG 59, CDF, 641.86/11-1956, Damascus to State Department, Cable 1208, 19 November 1956.

6 PRO, FO371/128236/VY1022/9, Bowker to Ross, 23 May 1957.

7 DDE, Ann Whitman Series, National Security Council, Box 8, 302nd NSC meeting, 1 November 1956.

8 DDE, John Foster Dulles Papers, Telephone Calls, Box 5, Foster Dulles to Weeks, 1 November 1956.

9 Hoopes, p. 379; Carlton, *Anthony Eden*, p. 447.

10 PRO, PREM11/1105, New York to Foreign Office, Cable 1009, 2 November 1956; Pearson, pp. 243ff.; Fry in Louis and Owen, pp. 308ff.

11 PRO, AIR24/2426, 'Operation OMELETTE', 31 October 1956; Stockwell Papers, 8/2/2, Stockwell report on MUSKETEER, p. 40; PRO, AIR8/1940, COS(56)109th meeting, 2 November 1956; PRO, CAB134/1216, C.M.77(56), 2 November 1956.

12 Neff, p. 397.

13 PRO, CAB134/1216, C.M.78(56), 2 November 1956; PRO, AIR8/1940, COS to Keightley, Cable COSKEY 23, 2 November 1956.

14 PRO, AIR8/1940, Keightley to COS, Cable KEYSEC 5, 2 November 1956, and KEYCOS 17, 2 November 1956; PRO, WO288/98, HQ to 2(BR) Corps, Cable PERINTERP 1, 3 November 1956. See also PRO, WO288/1, Butler to Darling, 16 October 1956.

15 PRO, AIR8/1940/File; Stockwell Papers, 8/2/2, Stockwell report on MUSKETEER, p. 40.

16 DDE, Ann Whitman Papers, DDE Diaries, Box 20, Eisenhower to Gruenther, 2 November 1956.

17 USNA, RG 59, CDF, 651.74/11-156, Paris to State Department, Cables 2120, 2123, and 2129, 1 November 1956; FRUS 1955–7 XVI, p. 931.

18 USNA, RG 59, CDF, 684A.86/11-156, State Department to New York, Cable TEDUL 2, 1 November 1956; DDE, Ann Whitman, DDE Diaries, Box 19, November 1956 Telephone Calls, Foster Dulles to Rountree, 2 November 1956; DDE, John Foster Dulles Papers, Telephone Calls, Box 5, Foster Dulles to Lodge, 2 November 1956.

19 Finer, p. 397.

20 Cooper, pp. 181ff.

21 AP, AP33/7, unsigned record, undated.

22 PRO, CAB134/1216, E.C.(56)38th meeting, 3 November 1956; PRO, FO371/121747/VR1074/491, New York to Foreign Office, Cable 1035, 3 November 1956.

23 PRO, CAB134/1216, E.C.(56)38th, 3 November 1956.

24 Hansard, 3 November 1956; Jay, p. 259.

25 Rhodes James, p. 569; Clark, p. 208; PRO, AIR8/1940, Keightley to COS, Cable KEYCOS 24, 3 November 1956; PRO, CAB134/1216, E.C.(56)39th meeting, 4 November 1956.

26 The Times, 2 November 1956; Observer, 4 November 1956.

27 Rhodes James, p. 557; PRO, PREM11/1123, Poole to Eden, 2 November 1956.

28 AP, AP20/30/1, Downing Street diary, 4 November 1956.

29 Cooper, p. 187.

30 Eden, p. 546.

31 PRO, PREM11/1105, New York to Foreign Office, Cable 1035, 3 November 1956; PRO, CAB134/1216, E.C.(56)39th meeting, 4 November 1956.

32 PRO, FO371/121747/VR1074/477, New York to Foreign Office, Cable 1047, 4 November 1956.

33 PRO, CAB134/1216, E.C.(56)40th meeting, 4 November 1956; Carlton, Anthony Eden, p. 451.

34 PRO, CAB128/30, C.M.79(56), 4 November 1956; Rhodes James, pp. 566ff.; PRO, AIR8/1940, COS to Keightley, Cable COSKEY 32, 4 November 1956; AP, AP20/1, Eden diary, 1957, and AP33/7, Eden record, undated.

35 PRO, FO371/121748/VR1074/545, New York to Foreign Office, Cable 1065, 5 November 1956; Rhodes James, p. 567; AP, AP23/13/24, Butler to Eden, 19 June 1969.

36 Rhodes James, pp. 569ff.; Wyndham-Goldie, p. 184; PRO, PREM11/1149, draft report by Committee on Overseas Broadcasting, 7 November 1956, and Grey to Acting Director-General, BBC, 3 November 1956; AP, AP20/51/1 and AP20/51/8; WCP, File 7, Clark diary, 12 November 1956.

37 PRO, PREM11/1177, Foreign Office to Washington, Cable 5180, 5 November 1956.
38 DDE, Ann Whitman Series, DDE Diaries, Box 19, November 1956 Diary, Staff Memoranda, Goodpaster memorandum, 3 November 1956; DDE, Ann Whitman Series, International, Box 17, Eden, Eisenhower to Eden draft, 5 November 1956.
39 PRO, FO371/121747/VR1074/495, Foreign Office to New York, Cable 1235 Saving, 4 November 1956, and VR1074/503, New York to Foreign Office, Cable 1053, 4 November 1956.
40 PRO, FO371/121747/VR1074/503, Foreign Office to New York, Cable 1563, 5 November 1956, and FO371/121748/VR1074/512, New York to Foreign Office, Cable 1064, 5 November 1956.

25: Victory and Defeat, 5–6 November 1956

1 PRO, WO288/152, HQ 2(BR) Corps War Diary, 5 November 1956; PRO, WO288/74, 16th Independent Paratroop Brigade report, 17 December 1956.
2 PRO, AIR8/1940, Keightley to COS, Cables KEYCOS 33, 37 and 38, 5 November 1956, and Stockwell to Templer, 17 November 1956; *Hansard*, 5 November 1956.
3 PRO, PREM11/1105, New York to Foreign Office, Cable 1071, 5 November 1956.
4 WCP, File 7, Clark diary, 5 November 1956; Gore-Booth, p. 230.
5 Author's interview with Sir Archibald Ross.
6 PRO, AIR8/2097, 3rd Summary of Operations, 2 November 1956; Heikal, *Nasser*, p. 108.
7 *Middle East Affairs*, January 1957, p. 11; Love, p. 614.
8 Liddell Hart Papers, 'Notes for History', 31 August 1957; WCP, File 7, Clark diary, 12 November 1956; author's interview with Sir William Hayter.
9 DDE, Ann Whitman Series, DDE Diaries, Box 19, November 1956 Diary, Staff Memoranda, Goodpaster memorandum, 5 November 1956; FRUS 1955–7 XVI, pp. 968ff.; Hughes, p. 223.
10 Cooper, p. 197.
11 PRO, WO288/152, HQ 2(BR) Corps War Diary, 6 November 1956.
12 PRO, CAB128/30, C.M.80(56), 6 November 1956. See also Horne, p. 441; Hugh Thomas, p. 146 and pp. 163ff.; WCP, File 7, Clark Diary, 6 November 1956.
13 Eden, p. 557; Macmillan, *Riding the Storm*, p. 166; Lloyd, p. 210.
14 PRO, T236/4188, Record of Treasury meeting, 7 November 1956; AP, AP20/1, Eden diary, 1957.
15 PRO, FO371/120832/UES1171/123, Washington to Foreign Office, Cable 2218, 30 October 1956, and UES1171/130, Washington to Foreign Office, Cable 2257, 6 November 1956; Macmillan, *Riding the Storm*, p. 164; USNA, RG 59, CDF, 974.7301/11-656, Summary of State Department meeting, 6 November 1956.
16 PRO, FO371/120832/UES1171/126, Foreign Office to Washington, Cables 5052–3, 31 October 1956, and UES1171/130, Washington to Foreign Office, Cable 2257, 6 November 1956.
17 Lloyd, p. 209; Hugh Thomas, pp. 146ff. Macmillan's account in his memoirs appears to be a convenient revision of history (Macmillan, *Riding the Storm*, p. 164).
18 MacDonald, *The History of The Times*, p. 272.
19 PRO, FO371/121867/VY10338/15, Moscow to Foreign Office, Cable 1557, 5 November 1956; Hayter, p. 147; Clark, p. 211; PRO, AIR8/1940, AFHQ to CINCMED and others, Cable CINC 145, 6 November 1956; DDE, Ann Whitman Series, DDE Diaries, Box 19, November 1956 Diary, Staff Memoranda, Goodpaster

memorandum, 6 November 1956; USNA, Department of State, INR-NIE Files, SNIE 11-9-56, 6 November 1956.

20 Wright, pp. 84ff.

21 Cooper, p. 200; FRUS 1955–7 XVI, p. 1018; USNA, RG 218, Records of the Joint Chiefs of Staff, *The Joint Chiefs of Staff and National Policy*, Volume VI, 1955–6, Chapter X, 'The Suez Canal Crisis'.

22 PRO, AIR28/9890, COS to Keightley, Cable COSKEY 48, 6 November 1956; PRO, 121689/VR1022/21G, Foreign Office to Tel Aviv, Cable 1173, 6 November 1956.

23 PRO, FO371/121747/VR1074/516, New York to Foreign Office, Cable 1070, 5 November 1956, VR1074/517, New York to Foreign Office, Cable 1071, 5 November 1956, and VR1074/518, New York to Foreign Office, Cable 1072, 5 November 1956.

24 PRO, FO371/121748/VR1074/525, Foreign Office to New York, Cable 1565, 5 November 1956; Lloyd, p. 209.

25 PRO, PREM11/1826, Eden minute, 5 January 1957; PRO, PREM11/1105, Eden minute, 7 November 1956. See also Colville, p. 724; Stockwell Papers, 8/4/1, Templer to Stockwell, 14 November 1956.

26 Love, p. 626; AP, AP20/1, Eden diary, 1957; Baeyens, p. 109; Massu, p. 215.

27 PRO, WO288/152, HQ 2(BR)Corps War Diary, 6 November 1956; Stockwell Papers, 8/2/2, Stockwell report on MUSKETEER, p. 49; *Damage and Casualties in Port Said*, Cmd. 47, HMSO, December 1956; *A Canal Too Far*, interview with General Sir Kenneth Darling.

28 Hugh Thomas, p. 178.

29 Stockwell Papers, 8/4/1, Templer to Stockwell, 14 November 1956.

30 PRO, PREM11/1105, Foreign Office to Paris, Cable 2498, 6 November 1956; DDE, Ann Whitman Series, Ann Whitman Diary, Box 8, November 1956 Diary (2), Eisenhower to Eden, 6 November 1956.

31 PRO, AIR20/10371, Records of British military broadcasts, November 1956.

26: Aftermath, 7–17 November 1956

1 PRO, CAB128/30, C.M.81(56), 7 November 1956.

2 DDE, Ann Whitman Series, Ann Whitman Diary, Box 8, November 1956 Diary (2), Eden to Eisenhower and Eisenhower to Eden, 7 November 1956.

3 DDE, Ann Whitman Series, DDE Diaries, Box 19, November 1956 Diary, Staff Memoranda, Goodpaster memorandum, 7 November 1956; DDE, Ann Whitman Series, Ann Whitman Diary, Box 8, November 1956 Diary (2), Eisenhower to Eden, 7 November 1956; AP, AP20/1, Eden diary, 1957.

4 Adams, p. 260.

5 DDE, John Foster Dulles Papers, White House Memoranda, Chronological, Box 4, Meetings with the President, Macomber memorandum, 7 November 1956.

6 PRO, PREM11/1177, Eden to Eisenhower and Eisenhower to Eden, 7 November 1956.

7 PRO, PREM11/1106, Washington to Foreign Office, Cable 2277, 9 November 1956; DDE, Ann Whitman Series, DDE Diaries, Box 19, November 1956 Diary, Staff Memoranda, Goodpaster memorandum, 9 November 1956; PRO, FO371/120832/UES1171/132, Washington to Foreign Office, Cable 2272, 8 November 1956.

8 DDE, John Foster Dulles Papers, Subject, Alphabetical, Box 7, Suez Problem, Foster Dulles memorandum, 11 November 1956.

9 DDE, Ann Whitman Series, National Security Council, Box 8, 303rd NSC meeting, 8

November 1956; PRO, FO371/120832/UES1171/137, Washington to Foreign Office, Cable 2278, 9 November 1956.

10 USNA, RG 59, CDF, 684A.86 Series, Tehran to State Department, Cable 727, 8 November 1956, and State Department to Tel Aviv, Cable 483, 7 November 1956; Bar-Zohar, *The Armed Prophet*, p. 243; Eban, p. 230.

11 Bar-Zohar, *Ben-Gurion*, pp. 251ff.; Brecher, pp. 284ff.; Eban, pp. 228ff.

12 PRO, CAB128/30, C.M.82(56), 8 November 1956.

13 PRO, AIR20/10757, AFHQ to HMS *Tyne*, Cable CIC/155, 6 November 1956; USNA, RG 59, CDF, 684A.86/11-656, ALUSNA (Ankara) to State Department, Cable 062240Z, 6 November 1956.

14 PRO, AIR20/9890, Keightley to COS, Cable KEYCOS 52, 6 November 1956; PRO, AIR24/2426, General Summary of Events, 6 November 1956; PRO, AIR8/2111, AFHQ to Air Ministry, 6 November 1956.

15 PRO, AIR20/9890, Keightley to COS, Cables KEYCOS 55, 7 November 1956, and KEYCOS 57, 8 November 1956.

16 USNA, RG 59, CDF, 684A.86/11-756, State Department to Posts, Depcirtel 372, 7 November 1956; DDE, Ann Whitman, DDE Diaries, Box 19, November 1956 Telephone Calls, Eisenhower to Hoover, 9 November 1956; PRO, AIR20/9890, Keightley to COS, KEYCOS, Cable KEYCOS 65, 10 November 1956; DDE, John Foster Dulles Papers, Telephone Calls, Box 5, Foster Dulles to Hoover, 9 November 1956.

17 PRO, PREM11/1106, Lloyd to Caccia and New York to Foreign Office, Cable 1163, 9 November 1956; USNA, RG 59, CDF, 684A.86/11-1056, London to State Department, Cable 2639, 10 November 1956.

18 DDE, John Foster Dulles Papers, Subject, Alphabetical, Box 6, Personnel Matters 1955-7 (5), Foster Dulles memorandum, 9 November 1956; DDE, Ann Whitman Series, DDE Diaries, Box 19, November 1956 Telephone Calls, Foster Dulles to Eisenhower, 9 November 1956.

19 PRO, FO371/120320/AU1017/21, Washington to Foreign Office, Cable 2285, and AU1017/22, Washington to Foreign Office, Cable 2286, 10 November 1956; FRUS 1955-7 XVI, pp. 1120ff.; PRO, PREM11/1176, Lloyd–Smith meeting, 18 November 1956.

20 PRO, T236/4189, Treasury–Bank of England meeting, 12 November 1956; PRO, CAB134/1216, E.C.(56)43rd meeting, 12 November 1956.

21 DDE, Ann Whitman Series, Dulles–Herter, Box 5, November 1956 (2), London to State Department, Cable 2648, 12 November 1956; DDE, Ann Whitman Series, DDE Diaries, Box 19, November 1956 Telephone Calls, Hoover to Eisenhower, 13 November 1956; DDE, Ann Whitman Series, Ann Whitman Diary, Box 8, November 1956 Diary (1), Ann Whitman diary entry, 15 November 1956.

22 PRO, PREM11/1137, New York to Foreign Office, Cable 1216, 14 November 1956; DDE, Ann Whitman Series, DDE Diaries, Box 19, November 1956 Staff Memoranda, Goodpaster memorandum, 16 November 1956; USNA, RG 59, CDF, 684A.86/11-1456, New York to State Department, Cable DELGA 87, 14 November 1956.

23 PRO, AIR24/2426, 'Operation MUSKETEER RENEWED', 11 November 1956, DDE, White House Office, Office of the Staff Secretary, Subject, Alphabetical, Box 14, Intelligence Matters (2), Goodpaster memorandum, 15 November 1956.

24 PRO, FO115/4545, Denny to Caccia, 16 November 1956.

25 DDE, Ann Whitman Series, DDE Diaries, Box 19, November 1956 Staff Mem-

oranda, Goodpaster memorandum, 16 November 1956; USNA, RG 59, CDF, 611.84A/11-1556, New York to State Department, Cable DELGA 99, 15 November 1956.

26 PRO, DEFE4/92, JP(56)176(F), 14 November 1956.

27 PRO, AIR20/9630, JIC Intelligence Summary Number 16, 16 November 1956; PRO, AIR20/9890, Keightley to COS, Cable KEYCOS 81, 16 November 1956.

28 USNA, RG 59, CDF, 611.51/11-1756, Tyler memorandum, 17 November 1956; DDE, White House Office, Office of the Staff Secretary, Subject, Alphabetical, Box 7, CIA, Volume I (4), Allen Dulles to Goodpaster, 17 November 1956.

29 PRO, FO371/118872, Record of Eden–Gazier conversation, 14 November 1956.

30 PRO, FO371/118833/JE1015/72, Kirkpatrick minute, 15 November 1956.

31 PRO, AIR20/10369, AFHQ to Ministry of Defence, Cable KEYCOS 74, 13 November 1956, and COS to Keightley, Cable COSKEY 69, 15 November 1956; PRO, AIR20/10371/File; PRO, ADM205/150, 'A Short Account of MUSKETEER', undated; PRO, AIR20/10757, Murray to Foreign Office, Cables PA/285, 9 November 1956, and PA/482, 14 November 1956. See also Walter Monckton Papers, Box 8, Monckton record, 22 November 1956.

32 USNA, RG 59, CDF, 611.84A/11-1656, London to State Department, Cable 2770, 16 November 1956; PRO, CAB134/1216, E.C.(56)44th meeting, 15 November 1956; DDE, Ann Whitman Series, National Security Council, Box 8, 304th NSC meeting, 15 November 1956.

33 PRO, PREM11/1106, New York to Foreign Office, Cable 1282, 18 November 1956.

34 DDE, John Foster Dulles Papers, White House Memoranda, Chronological, Box 4, Meetings with the President, August–December 1956 (3), Macomber memorandum, 12 November 1956.

35 AP, AP33/2, Heaton to Wheeler-Bennett, 4 September 1973, and Rusk to Wheeler-Bennett, 26 July 1974.

36 Joseph Alsop Papers, Alsop oral history, 4 March 1966.

37 AP, AP20/25, Washington to Foreign Office, Cable 2307, 17 November 1956.

38 Macmillan, *Riding the Storm*, p. 169; PRO, CAB128/30, C.M.84(56), 16 November 1956.

27: *Alliance Restored, or the Overthrow of Anthony Eden, 18 November 1956–7 January 1957*

1 USNA, RG 59, CDF, 974.7301/11-1256, London to State Department, Cable 2648, 12 November 1956.

2 AP, AP20/1, Eden diary, 21 August 1956.

3 USNA, RG 59, CDF, 974.7301/11-1956, London to State Department, Cable 2791, 19 November 1956; Macmillan, *Riding the Storm*, p. 174. See also Winthrop Aldrich Papers, Harvard University, Boston, Massachusetts, USA, Aldrich appointments diary, 18 November 1956. I am grateful to Dr David Carlton for this reference.

4 USNA, RG 59, CDF, 974.7301/11-1956, London to State Department, Cables 2791 and 2814, 19 November 1956; DDE, Ann Whitman Series, DDE Diaries, Box 19, November 1956 Telephone Calls, Aldrich to Eisenhower, 19 November 1956.

5 DDE, Ann Whitman Series, DDE Diaries, Box 19, November 1956 Telephone Calls, Eisenhower to Hoover and Eisenhower to Humphrey, 19 November 1956.

6 DDE, Ann Whitman Series, DDE Diaries, Box 19, November 1956 Diary, Staff

Memoranda, Goodpaster memorandum, 21 November 1956, and November 1956 Telephone Calls, Eisenhower to Aldrich, 20 November 1956.

7 Carlton, *Anthony Eden*, p. 456; Joseph Alsop Papers, Van Patten to Joseph Alsop, 24 November 1956.

8 PRO, CAB128/30, C.M.85(56), 20 November 1956.

9 USNA, RG 59, CDF, 974.7301/11-2156, London to State Department, Cable 2841, 21 November 1956.

10 PRO, FO371/120816/UEE10073/16, Foreign Office to Washington, Cables 5488–5489, 22 November 1956.

11 PRO, FO800/742, Foreign Office to New York, unnumbered, 20 November 1956.

12 Carlton, *The Suez Crisis*, pp. 86ff.

13 PRO, FO371/118873/JE1074/45, Foreign Office to New York, Cable 2086, 21 November 1956.

14 USNA, RG 59, CDF, 974.7301/11-2156, London to State Department, Cable 2841, and State Department to London, Cable 3665, 21 November 1956; DDE, Ann Whitman Series, DDE Diaries, Box 19, November 1956 Telephone Calls, Eisenhower to Humphrey, 21 November 1956.

15 PRO, CAB128/30, C.M.87(56), 22 November 1956.

16 USNA, RG 59, CDF, 684A.86/11-2256, State Department to London, Cable 2871, 22 November 1956.

17 DDE, Ann Whitman Series, DDE Diaries, Box 19, November 1956 Diary, Staff Memoranda, Goodpaster memorandum, 23 November 1956; USNA, RG 59, CDF, 684A.86/11-2356, New York to State Department, Cable DELGA 178, 23 November 1956; PRO, PREM11/1106, New York to Foreign Office, Cable 1401, 24 November 1956.

18 PRO, PREM11/1106, Washington to Foreign Office, Cable 2342, 24 November 1956, Cable 2330, 21 November 1956, and Cable 2334, 23 November 1956; DDE, White House Office, Office of the Staff Secretary, Subject, Alphabetical, Box 82, Suez Canal Crisis (2), State Department to London, Cable 3666, 21 November 1956, and Cable 3702, 23 November 1956.

19 PRO, FO115/4550, New York to Foreign Office, Cable 524, 27 November 1956; PRO, FO371/118855/JE10345/4, Kirkpatrick minute, 28 November 1956.

20 Joseph Alsop Papers, Van Patten to Joseph Alsop, 27 November 1956, and *Sunday Times* article, 25 November 1956.

21 USNA, RG 59, CDF, 974.7301/11-2656, London to State Department, Cable 2917, 26 November 1956.

22 DDE, White House Office, Office of the Staff Secretary, Subject, Alphabetical, Box 7, CIA, Volume 1 (4), Allen Dulles to Hoover, 22 November 1956.

23 DDE, Ann Whitman Series, International, Box 18, Winston Churchill, Churchill to Eisenhower, 23 November 1956, and Eisenhower to Churchill, 27 November 1956.

24 PRO, PREM11/1137, Washington to Foreign Office, Cable 2343, 24 November 1956.

25 DDE, Ann Whitman Series, DDE Diaries, Box 19, November 1956, Staff Memoranda, Goodpaster memorandum, 26 November 1956.

26 DDE, Ann Whitman Series, DDE Diaries, Box 19, November 1956 Telephone Calls, Foster Dulles to Eisenhower, 27 November 1956; DDE, Ann Whitman Series, National Security Council, Box 7, 305th NSC meeting, 30 November 1956.

27 USNA, RG 59, CDF, 684A.86/11-2756, State Department to New York, Cable GADEL 32, 27 November 1956.

28 PRO, PREM11/1106, Humphrey to Butler, 26 November 1956; PRO, FO371/120816, Washington to Foreign Office, Cable 2347, 26 November 1956.

29 Joseph Alsop Papers, Van Patten to Alsop, 24 November 1956; PRO, FO115/4550, New York to Foreign Office, Cable 524, 27 November 1956; PRO, CAB128/30, C.M.88(56), 26 November 1956; DDE, White House Office, Office of the Staff Secretary, Subject, Alphabetical, Box 82, Suez Canal Crisis (2), London to State Department, Cable 2948, 27 November 1956.

30 PRO, CAB128/30, C.M.90(56), 28 November 1956; Thorpe, p. 254; PRO, FO800/728, Lloyd–Eden meeting, 30 May 1958. See also USNA, RG 59, CDF, 974.7301/11-3056, London to State Department, Cable 3036, 30 November 1956.

31 PRO, CAB128/30, C.M.90(56), 28 November 1956.

32 USNA, RG 59, CDF, 684A.86/11-2956, London to State Department, Cable 3017, 29 November 1956.

33 PRO, CAB128/30, C.M.91(56), 29 November 1956; PRO, T236/4190, Rowan to Makins and Makins to Macmillan, 30 November 1956.

34 Carlton, *The Suez Crisis*, p. 90.

35 PRO, CAB128/30, C.M.91(56), 29 November 1956.

36 Rhodes James, pp. 587ff.; AP, AP20/25, Brook to Eden, 30 November 1956, and Butler to Eden, undated.

37 AP, AP20/25, Jamaica to Colonial Office, Cables PERS 102 and 103, 1 December 1956, Colonial Office to Jamaica, Cable PERS 70, 2 December 1956, Cable PERS 72, 3 December 1956, and Cable PERS 75, 4 December 1956, and Jamaica to Colonial Office, Cable PERS 117, 4 December 1956.

38 Rhodes James, pp. 589ff.

39 AP, AP20/25, Jamaica to Colonial Office, Cables PERS 141 and 145, 11 December 1956, Colonial Office to Jamaica, Cable PERS 105, 12 December 1956, Jamaica to Colonial Office, Cable PERS 147, 13 December 1956, and Colonial Office to Jamaica, Cable PERS 107, 13 December 1956; Rhodes James, p. 590.

40 PRO, FO115/4545, Dixon to Lloyd, 30 November 1956; USNA, RG 59, CDF, 974.7301/12-156, London to State Department, Cable 2915, 1 December 1956.

41 *Hansard*, 3 December 1956; DDE, Ann Whitman Series, National Security Council, Box 8, 305th NSC meeting, 30 November 1956; PRO, FO115/4551, Washington to Foreign Office, Cable 2436, 7 December 1956; PRO, FO371/120329/AU1021/43, Nixon speech, 6 December 1956.

42 Horne, p. 452.

43 *Ibid.*, p. 455.

44 Butler, p. 194.

45 Lysaght, p. 302.

46 Horne, p. 455. See also Howard, p. 241.

47 Dodds-Parker, p. 117; author's interview with Douglas Dodds-Parker; AP, AP20/30/1, Prime Minister's appointments diary, 3 January 1957.

48 DDE, John Foster Dulles Papers, General Correspondence and Memoranda, Box 1, L-M (2), Macmillan–Foster Dulles meeting, 12 December 1956.

49 Horne, p. 452.

50 US DDRS, US81 555A.

51 DDE, Ann Whitman Series, DDE Diaries, Box 20, December 1956 Telephone Calls, Eisenhower to Foster Dulles, 8 December 1956.

52 See DDE, Ann Whitman Series, Dulles–Herter, Box 6, December 1956, Eisenhower to Foster Dulles, 12 December 1956.

53 DDE, Ann Whitman Series, DDE Diaries, Box 20, December 1956, Staff Memoranda, Goodpaster memorandum, 20 December 1956.

54 Eisenhower, *Waging Peace*, p. 180.

55 Hugh Thomas, pp. 225ff.; Carlton, *Anthony Eden*, pp. 463ff.

56 *Hansard*, 20 December 1956.

57 Foot, p. 521.

58 Author's interview with Frederick Bishop.

59 See AP20/33/7, Buchan-Hepburn to Eden, 28 December 1956, and AP20/33/19, Coleraine to Eden, 5 January 1957.

60 AP, AP20/30/1, Prime Minister's appointments diary, January 1957, AP33/8, Brook to Eden, 8 January 1957, and AP33/10A, draft Eden to Churchill, 8 January 1957.

61 Horne, pp. 458ff.

62 Rhodes James, p. 597.

63 PRO, CAB128/30, C.M.4(57), 9 January 1957.

64 Colville, p. 722; Gilbert, p. 1227. See also Horne, p. 458; Howard, p. 247.

Bibliography

ARCHIVES

Dwight D. Eisenhower Presidential Library, Abilene, Kansas, USA
Harry S. Truman Presidential Library, Independence, Missouri, USA
John Foster Dulles Library, Princeton University, Princeton, New Jersey, USA
Public Record Office, Kew, Surrey, United Kingdom

ADM205	First Sea Lord Papers
AIR8	Chief of Air Staff Papers
AIR20	Air Ministry, Unregistered Papers
AIR24	Operations Record Book
CAB21	Cabinet Office Registered Papers
CAB128	Cabinet Meetings
CAB129	Cabinet Memoranda
CAB130	Cabinet Committee (AD Hoc) Files
CAB131	Defence Committee
CAB134	Cabinet Committee (Standing) Files
DEFE4	Chiefs of Staff Committee Meetings
DEFE5	Chiefs of Staff Memoranda
DEFE32	Chiefs of Staff, Secretary's Standard File
FO115	Records of the British Embassy in Washington
FO371	Foreign Office, General Political Correspondence
FO800	Foreign Secretary's Papers
FO953	Foreign Office, Information Departments
PREM8	Prime Minister's Correspondence
PREM11	Prime Minister's Correspondence
T234	Home and Overseas Planning Staff Division
T236	Treasury Overseas Finance Division Files
WO32	Registered Files, General Series
WO288	War Office Intelligence Summaries

US National Archives, Washington, DC, USA

Lot 62 D 11, Suez Conference Files	
RG 59	State Department Central Decimal Files
RG 84	Embassy and Consular Files
RG 218	Records of the Joint Chiefs of Staff
RG 319	Secretary of Army Files
RG 330	Secretary of Defense Files
State Department Policy Planning Staff Files	

PRIVATE PAPERS

Alsop Papers, Library of Congress, Washington, DC, USA
Avon Papers, University of Birmingham, Birmingham, United Kingdom
Bracken Papers, Churchill College, University of Cambridge, Cambridge, United Kingdom
Butler Papers, Trinity College, University of Cambridge, Cambridge, United Kingdom
Clark Papers, Bodleian Library, University of Oxford, Oxford, United Kingdom
Kilmuir Papers, Churchill College, University of Cambridge, Cambridge, United Kingdom
Liddell Hart Papers, Liddell Hart Centre for Military Archives, King's College, University of London, London, United Kingdom
Monckton Papers, Bodleian Library, University of Oxford, Oxford, United Kingdom
Stockwell Papers, Liddell Hart Centre for Military Archives, King's College, University of London, London, United Kingdom

PUBLISHED DOCUMENTS AND RECORDS

Foreign Relations of the United States (Washington, DC, 1979–90)
    1950, Volume V: The Near East
    1951, Volume V: The Near East
    1952–4, Volume IX: The Near East
    1955–7, Volume XIII: The Near East, Jordan-Yemen
    1955–7, Volume XIV: The Arab-Israeli Dispute, 1955
    1955–7, Volume XV: The Arab-Israeli Dispute, 1 January–26 July 1956
    1955–7, Volume XVI: The Suez Crisis, 26 July–31 December 1956
Hansard, House of Commons Debates, 1950–7
The Presidential Papers of Dwight D. Eisenhower (Washington, DC, 1958–61)
US Declassified Document Reference System (Washington, DC, 1976–90)

DIARIES AND MEMOIRS

Acheson, Dean, *Present at the Creation* (New York, 1969)
Adams, Sherman, *First-Hand Report* (London, 1962)
Baeyens, Jacques, *Un Coup d'Epee dans l'Eau du Canal* (Paris, 1976)
Beaufre, André, *The Suez Expedition* (London, 1969)
Bohlen, Charles, *Witness to History* (New York, 1973)
Butler, R. A., *The Art of the Possible* (London, 1971)
Cavendish, Anthony, *Inside Intelligence* (London, 1990)
Challe, Maurice, *Notre Revolte* (Paris, 1968)
Clark, William, *From Three Worlds* (London, 1986)
Colville, John, *The Fringes of Power: Downing Street Diaries, 1939–55* (London, 1985)
Cooper, Chester, *The Lion's Last Roar* (London, 1978)

Copeland, Miles, *The Game of Nations* (London, 1969)
Dayan, Moshe, *Diary of the Sinai Campaign* (London, 1967)
Dayan, Moshe, *The Story of My Life* (London, 1976)
Dodds-Parker, Douglas, *Political Eunuch* (Springwood, Berkshire, 1986)
Eban, Abba, *An Autobiography* (New York, 1977)
Eden, Anthony, *Full Circle* (London, 1960)
Eisenhower, Dwight, *The White House Years: Mandate for Change, 1953–6* (London, 1963)
Eisenhower, Dwight, *The White House Years: Waging Peace, 1956–61* (London, 1966)
Eveland, Wilbur, *Ropes of Sand* (London, 1980)
Ferrell, Robert (ed.), *The Eisenhower Diaries* (London, 1982)
Gladwyn, Lord, *The Memoirs of Lord Gladwyn* (London, 1972)
Glubb, General John Bagot, *Changing Scenes of Life* (London, 1983)
Gore-Booth, Paul, *With Great Truth and Respect* (London, 1974)
Hailsham, Lord, *The Door Wherein I Went* (London, 1975)
Hayter, William, *The Kremlin and the Embassy* (London, 1966)
Hetherington, Alistair, *Guardian Years* (London, 1981)
Hughes, Emmet, *The Ordeal of Power: The Inside Story of the Eisenhower Administration* (London, 1963)
Jay, Douglas, *Change and Fortune* (London, 1980)
Kilmuir, Lord, *Political Adventure* (London, 1964)
Kirkpatrick, Ivone, *The Inner Circle* (London, 1959)
Lloyd, Selwyn, *Suez 1956* (New York, 1978)
MacDonald, Iveragh, *A Man of the Times* (London, 1976)
Macmillan, Harold, *Tides of Fortune, 1945–55* (London, 1969)
Macmillan, Harold, *Riding the Storm, 1956–9* (London, 1971)
Massu, Jacques, *Vérité sur Suez* (Paris, 1978)
McGhee, George, *Envoy to the Middle World* (New York, 1983)
Meir, Golda, *My Life* (London, 1975)
Menzies, Robert, *Afternoon Light* (London, 1967)
Murphy, Robert, *Diplomat Among Warriors* (London, 1964)
Nutting, Anthony, *No End of a Lesson* (London, 1967)
Pearson, Lester, *Memoirs, Volume II, 1948–57: The International Years* (London, 1974)
Pimlott, Ben (ed.), *The Political Diary of Hugh Dalton, 1918–40, 1945–60* (London, 1986)
Pineau, Christian, *Suez 1956* (Paris, 1978)
Raphael, Gideon, *Destination Peace: Three Decades of Israeli Foreign Policy* (London, 1981)
Roosevelt, Kermit, *Countercoup* (New York, 1979)
Sharon, Ariel, *Warrior: An Autobiography* (London, 1989)
Shuckburgh, Evelyn, *Descent to Suez* (London, 1986)
Thomas, Abel, *Comment Israel Fut Sauve* (Paris, 1978)
Trevelyan, Humphrey, *The Middle East in Revolution* (London, 1970)

Truman, Harry S., *Memoirs, Volume II: Years of Trial and Hope, 1946–53* (London, 1956)

Williams, Philip (ed.), *The Diary of Hugh Gaitskell, 1945–56* (London, 1983)

Woodhouse, Christopher, *Something Ventured* (London, 1982)

Wright, Peter, *Spycatcher* (New York, 1987)

Wyndham-Goldie, Grace, *Facing the Nation: Television and Politics, 1936–76* (London, 1977)

Young, Kenneth (ed.), *The Diaries of Sir Robert Bruce Lockhart, 1939–65* (London, 1980)

BIOGRAPHIES

Ambrose, Stephen, *Eisenhower the President* (London, 1982)

Aster, Sidney, *Anthony Eden* (London, 1976)

Bar-Zohar, Michael, *The Armed Prophet: A Biography of Ben-Gurion* (London, 1967)

Beal, J. R., *John Foster Dulles* (New York, 1959)

Bullock, Alan, *Ernest Bevin: Foreign Secretary, 1945–51* (Oxford, 1985)

Campbell, John, *Nye Bevan and the Mirage of British Socialism* (London, 1987)

Carlton, David, *Anthony Eden* (London, 1981)

Childs, Marquis, *Eisenhower: Captive Hero* (London, 1959)

Dixon, Piers, *Double Diploma* (London, 1968)

Donovan, Robert, *Tumultuous Years* (New York, 1982)

Ewald, William, *Eisenhower the President* (Englewood Cliffs, New Jersey, 1981)

Foot, Michael, *Aneurin Bevan, Volume II, 1945–60* (London, 1973)

Gerson, Louis, *John Foster Dulles* (New York, 1967)

Gilbert, Martin, *Winston S. Churchill, Volume VIII: Never Despair, 1945–65* (London, 1988)

Golan, Matti, *Shimon Peres* (London, 1982)

Guhin, Michael, *John Foster Dulles: A Statesman and His Times* (New York, 1972)

Heikal, Mohammed, *Nasser: The Cairo Documents* (London, 1972)

Hoopes, Townsend, *The Devil and John Foster Dulles* (Boston, 1973)

Horne, Alistair, *Harold Macmillan: Volume I, 1894–1956* (London, 1988)

Howard, Anthony, *Rab* (London, 1987)

Lacouture, Jean (translated by Daniel Hofstadter), *Nasser* (London, 1973)

Lyon, Peter, *Eisenhower: Portrait of a Hero* (Boston, 1974)

Lysaght, Charles, *Brendan Bracken* (London, 1979)

Moran, Lord, *Winston Churchill* (London, 1966)

Mosley, Leonard, *Dulles* (New York, 1978)

Nutting, Anthony, *Nasser* (London, 1972)

Rhodes James, Robert, *Anthony Eden* (London, 1986)

Smith, Gaddis, *Dean Acheson* (New York, 1972)

Thorpe, D. R., *Selwyn Lloyd* (London, 1989)

Ziegler, Philip, *Mountbatten* (London, 1985)

BOOKS AND MONOGRAPHS

Abadi, Jacob, *Britain's Withdrawal from the Middle East, 1947–71: The Economic and Strategic Imperatives* (Princeton, New Jersey, 1983)

Allen, H. C., and Thompson, Roger (eds), *Contrast and Connection: Bicentennial Essays in Anglo-American History* (London, 1976)

Ambrose, Stephen, and Immerman, Richard, *Eisenhower's Spies* (Garden City, New York, 1981)

Aronson, Geoffrey, *From Sideshow to Centre Stage: US Policy Towards Egypt, 1946–56* (Boulder, Colorado, 1986)

Bar-Zohar, Michael, *Suez Ultra-Secret* (Paris, 1964)

Barker, A. J., *Suez: The Seven-Day War* (London, 1964)

Bell, Coral, *The Debatable Alliance* (London, 1964)

Braddon, Russell, *Suez: Splitting of a Nation* (Glasgow, 1973)

Brecher, Michael, *Decisions in Israeli Foreign Policy* (Oxford, 1974)

Bromberger, Merry, and Bromberger, Serry (translated by James Cameron), *The Secrets of Suez* (London, 1957)

Bryson, Thomas, *Seeds of Mideast Crisis* (Jefferson, North Carolina, 1981)

Calvocoressi, Peter, *Suez: Ten Years After* (London, 1967)

Carlton, David, *Britain and the Suez Crisis* (London, 1988)

Caroz, Yaacov, *The Arab Secret Services* (London, 1978)

Childers, Erskine, *The Road to Suez* (London, 1962)

Cook, Blanche, *The Declassified Eisenhower* (Garden City, New York, 1981)

Copeland, Miles, *The Real Spy World* (London, 1978)

Crosbie, Sylvia, *A Tacit Alliance* (Princeton, 1974)

Divine, Robert, *Eisenhower and the Cold War* (Oxford, 1981)

Drummond, Roscoe, and Coblenz, Gaston, *Duel at the Brink* (London, 1961)

Eayrs, James, *The Commonwealth and Suez* (London, 1964)

Epstein, Leon, *Britain – Uneasy Ally* (Chicago, 1954)

Epstein, Leon, *British Policy in the Suez Crisis* (London, 1964)

Faligot, Roger, and Koop, Pascal, *La Piscine* (London, 1989)

Finer, Herman, *Dulles over Suez* (London, 1964)

Fullick, Roy, and Powell, Geoffrey, *Suez: The Double War* (London, 1979)

Green, Stephen, *Taking Sides: America's Secret Relations with a Militant Israel, 1948–67* (London, 1984)

Greenstein, Fred, *The Hidden-Hand Presidency* (New York, 1982)

Heikal, Mohammed, *Cutting the Lion's Tail* (London, 1986)

Kuniholm, Bruce, *The Cold War in the Near East* (Princeton, New Jersey, 1980)

Lamb, Richard, *The Failure of the Eden Government* (London, 1987)

Louis, W. R., *The British Empire in the Middle East, 1945–51* (Oxford, 1984)

Louis, W. R., and Owen, Roger (eds), *Suez 1956: The Crisis and its Consequences* (Oxford, 1989)

Love, Kennett, *Suez: The Twice-Fought War* (London, 1970)

MacDermott, Geoffrey, *The Eden Legacy* (London, 1969)

MacDonald, Iveragh, *The History of the Times: Volume V, Struggles in War and Peace, 1939–66* (London, 1984)

Melman, Yossi, and Raviv, Dan, *Imperfect Spies: The History of Israeli Intelligence* (London, 1989)

Monroe, Elizabeth, *Britain's Moment in the Middle East, 1914–71* (London, 1981)

Neff, Donald, *Warriors at Suez* (New York, 1981)

Neustadt, Richard, *Alliance Politics* (New York, 1970)

Nicholas, H. G., *Britain and the United States* (London, 1963)

Northedge, F. S., *Descent from Power* (London, 1974)

Parmet, Herbert, *Eisenhower and the American Crusade* (London, 1972)

Partner, Peter, *Arab Voices: The BBC Arabic Service, 1938–88* (London, 1988)

Peri, Yoram, *Between Bullets and Ballots: The Israeli Military in Politics* (Cambridge, 1983)

Ranelagh, John, *The Rise and Fall of the CIA* (New York, 1987)

Robertson, Terence, *Crisis: The Inside Story of the Suez Conspiracy* (London, 1965)

Rovere, Robert, *Affairs of State: The Eisenhower Years* (New York, 1956)

Rubin, Barry, *The Great Powers in the Middle East, 1941–7* (London, 1980)

Seale, Patrick, *The Struggle for Syria* (Oxford, 1965)

Simpson, Christopher, *Blowback: America's Recruitment of Nazis and its Effects on the Cold War* (London, 1988)

Thomas, Hugh, *The Suez Affair* (London, 1966)

Troen, Selwyn Ilan, and Shemesh, Moshe (eds), *The Suez-Sinai Crisis of 1956: Retrospective and Reappraisal* (London, 1990)

Verrier, Anthony, *Through the Looking Glass: British Foreign Policy in an Age of Illusions* (London, 1983)

Watt, D. Cameron, *Succeeding John Bull: America in Britain's Place, 1900–75* (Cambridge, 1984)

West, Nigel, *The Friends: Britain's Post-War Secret Intelligence Operations* (London, 1988)

ARTICLES

Aldrich, Winthrop, 'The Suez Crisis: A Footnote to History', *Foreign Affairs* (April 1967)

Bernard, Jean-Yves, 'Politique Interieure et Decisions Britannique dans la Crise de Suez, 1956', *Relations Internationales* (Autumn 1988)

Brands, H. W., 'The Cairo-Tehran Connection in Anglo-American Rivalry in the Middle East', *International History Review* (August 1989)

Cohen, Raymond, 'Israeli Military Intelligence before the 1956 Sinai Campaign', *Intelligence and National Security* (January 1988)

Dooley, Howard J., 'Great Britain's "Last Battle" in the Middle East: Notes on Cabinet Planning During the Suez Crisis of 1956', *International History Review* (August 1989)

Gorst, A., and Lucas, W. S., 'The Other Collusion: Operation *Straggle* and Anglo-American Intervention in Syria, 1955–6', *Intelligence and National Security* (July 1988)

Gorst, A., and Lucas, W. S., 'Suez 1956: Strategy and the Diplomatic Process', *Journal of Strategic Studies* (December 1988)

Hahn, Peter, 'Containment and Egyptian Nationalism: The Unsuccessful Effort to Establish the Middle East Command, 1950–3', *Diplomatic History* (Winter 1987)

Hennessy, Peter, 'The Secrets Which Will Stay Secret for Ever', *The Listener* (11 September 1986)

Henriques, Robert, 'The Ultimatum: A Dissenting View', *Spectator* (6 November 1959)

Henriques, Robert, 'The Ultimatum', *Spectator* (4 December 1959)

Jalal, Ayesha, 'Towards the Baghdad Pact: South Asia and Middle Eastern Defence in the Cold War, 1947–55', *International History Review* (August 1989)

Johnman, Lewis, 'Defending the Pound: The Economics of the Suez Crisis, 1956', in Gorst, A., Johnman, L., and Lucas, W. S. (eds), *Post-War Britain: Themes and Perspectives, 1945–64* (London, 1989)

Little, Douglas, 'Cold War and Covert Action: The United States and Syria, 1945–58', *Middle East Journal* (Winter 1990)

Lucas, W. S., 'NATO, Alliance, and the Suez Crisis', in Heuser, Beatrice (ed.), *NATO and the Cold War* (London, 1991)

Lucas, W. S., 'Neustadt Revisited: The Suez Crisis and the Anglo-American "Alliance"', in Gorst, A., Johnman, L., and Lucas, W. S. (eds), *Post-War Britain: Themes and Perspectives 1945–64* (London, 1989)

Lucas, W. S., 'The Path to Suez: Britain and the Struggle for the Middle East, 1953–6', in Anne Deighton (ed.), *Britain and the First Cold War* (London, 1990).

Lucas, W. S., 'Redefining the Suez "Collusion": A Regional Approach', *Middle Eastern Studies* (January, 1990)

Lucas, W. S., 'Suez, the Americans, and the Overthrow of Anthony Eden', *LSE Quarterly* (September 1987)

Oren, Michael, 'Secret Egyptian-Israeli Peace Initiatives Prior to the Suez Campaign', *Middle East Journal* (July 1990)

RAF Historical Society, 'Suez 1956 – Air Aspects', *Proceedings of the RAF Historical Society* (January 1988)

Reynolds, David, 'Eden the Diplomatist, 1931–56: Suezide of a Statesman', *History* (February 1989)

Sheffy, Yigal, 'Unconcern at Dawn, Surprise at Sunset: Egyptian Intelligence Appreciations before the Sinai Campaign, 1956', *Intelligence and National Security* (July 1990)

Shlaim, Avi, 'Conflicting Approaches to Israel's Relations with the Arabs: Ben-Gurion and Sharett, 1953–6', *Middle East Journal* (Spring 1983)

Warner, Geoffrey, 'Collusion and the Suez Crisis', *International Affairs* (April 1979)

RADIO AND TELEVISION DOCUMENTARIES

British Broadcasting Corporation Radio Four, *A Canal Too Far* (1987)
British Broadcasting Corporation Radio Four, *Neither War nor Peace at 10 Downing Street* (1979)
British Broadcasting Corporation Television, *Television and Number 10* (1988)
Channel Four, *The End of Empire: Egypt* (1985)
Channel Four, *The End of Empire: Iran* (1985)
Thames Television, *The Day Before Yesterday* (1971)

THESES AND CONFERENCE PAPERS

Astor, David, 'The *Observer* and Suez' (Institute of Contemporary British History/London School of Economics Summer School, 1989)
Devereux, David, *Between Friend and Foe: The Formulation of British Defence Policy Towards the Middle East, 1948–56* (PhD, University of London, 1988)
Lucas, W. S., 'Israeli Foreign Policy and Civil-Military Relations, 1953–6' (Political Studies Association Conference, 1990)
Sayed-Ahmed, M. A. W., *Nasser and American Foreign Policy, 1952–6* (PhD, University of London, 1987)

Index